U0093553

高分單字╳關鍵搭配詞╳萬用例句

三步驟掌握新制多益高分祕訣

本書使用方式

step1

高分單字一網打盡

本書精選多益測驗常見單字，不只基礎單字要熟練，高分單字也要一網打盡！有效攻略新制多益就從單字開始準備，不管是聽力還是閱讀能力都能因單字量提升，而快速進步！

step2

關鍵搭配詞練就英文語感

搭配詞是英文母語者平時「常說、常寫、常用」的樣貌，學會關鍵搭配詞，就能掌握單字的生活化用法，遇到強調生活化的新制多益題目也難不倒你！

step3

萬用例句掌握應用方法

背誦單字不等於學會單字，只有學會如何實際運用單字才能真正提升英文能力。萬用例句搭配外師親錄音檔，讓你學會單字的同時提升英文聽力能力！

Preface 前言

「多益證書」在臺灣被眾多公司行號與學校當作英文能力的重要參考準據，不論是在職場應徵還是在入學申請、英文學分抵免上，有好的多益測驗成績都可以帶來程度不一的優勢，也因此每年都吸引許多人報名考取。

多益測驗「TOEIC」為Test of English for International Communication（國際溝通英語測驗）的簡稱，從這個名稱中我們不難看出，多益考試強調的是實務性、生活性的英文應用能力。而在2018年三月，臺灣的多益考試題目正式改制，加入了現代化生活的內容如：通訊、社群軟體的閱讀，並且展現出靈活性，於聽力部分新增了多人對話的題型。這些改變與舊制相比，雖然考題內容看似更難，但也更加確立了考試的準備方向，只要將較生活、實用與職場的英文準備妥當，基本上成績就不會考得太差，同時分數也會直接表現在你的日常英文應用上，確實達到英語溝通能力測驗的目的。

要在多益考試前做足準備，單字是最不能遺漏的基礎。單字若準備得當，不管是聽力試題亦或是閱讀試題，都能讓你的答題速度與信心大幅提升。那麼要如何打好單字基礎、備戰多益呢？

本書有鑒於新制多益考試採生活實務導向，嚴選了多益最常考的單字，並將其按主題分門別類，讓你以直覺的方式聯想單字，有效累積單字儲備量。另外也提供了大量的搭配詞補充，讓你熟悉英文母語人士的溝通習慣，遇到慣用語也能快速反應。單字與例句更附上外師親錄MP3音檔，讓你眼耳並用高效記憶單字，還能同步提升聽力能力，只要拿起手機掃描書上的QR code，就能隨掃隨聽全書音檔。

衷心希望本書能幫助各位考生在繁忙的生活中，以最有效的方式準備多益測驗，掌握必勝英文關鍵能力，並於多益測驗取得佳績！

寫在本書之前

新制多益考什麼？

翻開本書的你，想必是希望能夠在多益測驗拿到高分，為自己增添一份亮眼的語言能力證明的。如同求學過程中遇到的所有測驗，要想在多益測驗拿高分，我們首先須要了解多益測驗的考試範圍及測驗題型。

● 新制多益考試範疇

自2018年三月，臺灣的多益考試題目正式改制，加入了現代化生活的內容如：通訊、社群軟體的閱讀等，並且展現出靈活性，於聽力部分新增了多人對話的題型。這些改變與舊制相比，更加生活化，也更能反映出時下英語使用的狀況。

依據多益測驗官網公布的測驗內容，測驗可分為以下生活情境：

一般商務	契約、談判、行銷、銷售、商業企劃、會議
製造業	工廠管理、生產線、品管
金融／預算	銀行業務、投資、税務、會計、帳單
企業發展	研究、產品研發
辦公室	董事會、委員會、信件、備忘錄、電話、傳真、電子郵件、辦公室器材與傢俱、辦公室流程
人事	招考、雇用、退休、薪資、升遷、應徵與廣告
採購	比價、訂貨、送貨、發票
技術層面	電子、科技、電腦、實驗室與相關器材、技術規格
房屋／公司地產	建築、規格、購買租賃、電力瓦斯服務
旅遊	火車、飛機、計程車、巴士、船隻、渡輪、票務、時刻表、車站、機場廣播、租車、飯店、預訂、脱班與取消
外食	商務／非正式午餐、宴會、招待會、餐廳訂位
娛樂	電影、劇場、音樂、藝術、媒體
保健	醫藥保險、看醫生、牙醫、診所、醫院

本書依不同生活情境，分為17個主題單元，緊扣新制多益命題走向。掌握多益單字，讀者只須按本書內容準備即可！

● 新制多益題型

多益測驗分為「聽力」與「閱讀」兩部分，各100題，共200題，皆為單選題。

配分為「聽力」與「閱讀」各495分，滿分共990分。

	聽力測驗	閱讀測驗
測驗時間	測驗時間約為45分鐘	測驗時間為75分鐘
測驗題型	照片描述	句子填空
	應答問題	段落填空
	簡短對話	單篇閱讀
	簡短獨白	多篇閱讀

● 多益考生考前請務必注意！

不管是聽力還是閱讀部分，都不可以越區作答。在聽力考試時間不得先作答閱讀部分；同樣地在閱讀考試時間亦不可回頭作答聽力部分，否則以違規論，成績不予計分。因此，在作答聽力題時，即使碰到不會寫的題目，也要在進入下一題之前把握時間劃記一個選項（答錯不倒扣）。

多益考試時不得在題本上作任何記號。若是在試題本上做上任何記號（畫線、筆記、簽名等等皆是），將以違規論，成績不予計分。

多益答案卡上僅限填上考生的基本資料及劃記答案，不可再加註任何記號，否則一樣以違規論，成績不予計分。

考生選好答案後，要在與題目卷分開的答案卷上劃卡。雖然答題時間為兩小時，但考試時考生尚須在答案卷上填寫個人資料，並簡短的回答關於教育與工作經歷的問卷，因此真正待在考場內時間會較長。

Contents 目錄

Unit 01 和食有關的單字

多益測驗的命題強調生活化與實用性，學會這些與「食」有關的單字，不僅能讓你在多益考場上所向披靡，在日常生活上也可以靈活運用喔！

點餐時可以這麼說

- **What can I get for you today? I recommend our signature grilled cheese sandwich.** 今天想吃什麼呢？我推薦我們的招牌烤起司三明治。
- **I'd like a beef sandwich without crust and a coffee with two sugar.**
  我要一份牛肉三明治，吐司去邊，還有一杯咖啡加兩塊方糖。
- **I'd like a small popcorn and a large coke, thank you.**
  我要一個小的爆米花和大杯可樂，謝謝。

減肥餐可以這麼說

- **Since I'm on a diet, I'll have some tofu salad for lunch.**
  因為我正在節食，所以我午餐吃豆腐沙拉就好。
- **Instant oatmeal and fresh fruit is the perfect combination for breakfast.**
  即食燕麥和新鮮水果是早餐的最佳組合。

形容餐點美味可以這麼說

- **This is the most delicious BBQ ribs I have ever had.**
  這是我吃過最美味的燒烤肋排。
- **The sauce has a hint of smoke flavor, and the meat is perfectly cooked that it falls off the bone easily.**
  醬汁帶有一點煙燻風味，而且肉烹調得恰到好處，讓肉跟骨頭可以輕易地分離。

描述烘焙步驟可以這麼說

- **Today, we are going to bake an apple pie. Make sure you have every ingredient you need.**
  今天，我們要烤一個蘋果派。請確認你是否有所有需用食材。
- **First, mix four tablespoons of all-purpose flour with four tablespoons of sugar and two tablespoons of cocoa powder.**
  首先，混合四匙中筋麵粉、四匙糖和兩匙可可粉。

吃到不合口味的食物可以這麼說

- **This chicken curry is way too spicy for me. I need some cold milk.**
  這個雞肉咖哩對我來說太辣了。我需要一些冰牛奶。
- **The yolk pastry is too greasy for my taste, and the red bean paste inside is also too sweet.**
  這個蛋黃酥對我來說太油了，而且裡面的豆沙餡也太甜。

Unit 01 和食有關的單字

alcohol [ˋælkə͵hɔl] n. 酒精 Track 0001

例句 When you drink too much alcohol everyday, your liver will gradually become unable to metabolize it, leading to alcohol poisoning. 當你每日過度飲酒，你的肝變得逐漸無法代謝酒精，導致酒精中毒。

搭配詞 alcohol poisoning 酒精中毒

---

appetite [ˋæpə͵taɪt] n. 食慾 Track 0002

例句 Constant lack of appetite might indicate that something is wrong with your body. 經常性的食慾不佳，可能表示你的身體出了問題。

搭配詞 lack of appetite 沒有食慾

---

apron [ˋeprən] n. 圍裙 Track 0003

例句 Even though he's 50, he is still tied to his mother's apron strings. 儘管他已經50歲了，他還是事事唯母是從。

搭配詞 tied to one's mother's apron strings 綁在媽媽的圍裙帶上＝媽寶

---

bacon [ˋbekən] n. 培根、燻肉 Track 0004

例句 You should try my grandmother's bacon sandwhich recipe. Boy does it taste good!
你應該參考我祖母的培根三明治食譜。好吃到爆！

搭配詞 bacon sandwich 培根三明治

---

bake [bek] v. 烘、烤 Track 0005

例句 My wife can make perfect baked potato—crispy on the outside and fluffy on the inside.
我太太可以做出風味絕佳的烤馬鈴薯，外皮酥脆，內裡鬆軟。

搭配詞 baked potato 烤馬鈴薯

---

bakery [ˋbekərɪ] n. 烘焙坊、麵包店 Track 0006

例句 To make delicious bread, you need good baking skills and high quality bakery equipment.
要做出可口的麵包，你需要有好的烘焙手藝和高品質的烘焙器具。

搭配詞 bakery equipment 烘焙用具

---

banquet [ˋbæŋkwɪt] n. 宴會 Track 0007

例句 The new couple invited their families and friends to join their wedding banquet.
這對新婚夫妻邀請他們的親朋好友，參加他們的結婚宴會。

搭配詞 wedding banquet 結婚宴會

---

barbecue/BBQ [ˋbɑrbɪkju] n. 烤肉 Track 0008

例句 My mother's homemade barbecue sauce is incredibly easy to make but tastes amazingly good!
我媽媽自製的烤肉醬很容易做，但好吃極了！

搭配詞 barbecue sauce 烤肉醬

bean [bin] n. 豆子 Track 0009

例句 For vegetarians, bean curd is a good source of protein.
對素食者來說，豆腐是攝取蛋白質的好來源。

搭配詞 bean curd 豆腐

beef [bif] n. 牛肉 Track 0010

例句 I still remember the first time I made beef stew. It was a disaster.
我還記得我第一次煮牛肉濃湯，煮得很糟糕。

搭配詞 beef stew 牛肉濃湯

beer [bɪr] n. 啤酒 Track 0011

例句 Binge drinking can definitely give you a bigger beer belly.
酗酒絕對會讓你的啤酒肚變得更大。

搭配詞 beer belly 啤酒肚

biscuit [ˋbɪskɪt] n. 餅乾、小甜麵包 Track 0012

例句 Inside this biscuit box are oatcakes and chocolates.
這個餅乾盒裡裝有燕麥餅和巧克力。

搭配詞 biscuit box 餅乾盒

bread [brɛd] n. 麵包 Track 0013

例句 She is a software engineer, and writing computer codes is her bread and butter.
她是軟體工程師，寫電腦程式是她的麵包來源（即工作）。

搭配詞 bread and butter 謀生之道

breakfast [ˋbrɛkfəst] n. 早餐 Track 0014

例句 The Queen usually has breakfast tea every morning.
女王每天早上通常都要喝點早餐茶。

搭配詞 breakfast tea 早餐茶

broil [brɔɪl] v. 烤、炙 Track 0015

例句 I'd like to have some brioled duck breast as my main dish.
我的主菜想點烤鴨胸肉。

搭配詞 broiled duck 烤鴨

broth [brɔθ] n. 湯、清湯 Track 0016

例句 Nothing beats the chicken broth my mom makes.
我媽媽熬的雞湯無人能敵。

搭配詞 chicken broth 雞湯

brunch [brʌntʃ] n. 早午餐 Track 0017

例句 I'm having brunch with some high school friends today.
我今天會跟一些高中朋友去吃早午餐。

搭配詞 have brunch 吃早午餐

buffet [bəˋfe] n. 自助餐 Track 0018

例句 I'm starving! Give me a list of good buffet and grill restaurants.
我好餓！幫我列一些好的自助與燒烤餐廳。

搭配詞 buffet and grill 自助與燒烤餐廳

bun/roll [bʌn]/[rol] **n.** 小麵包圈、麵包捲 ◀Track 0019

例句 Are you hungry? Shall I bring you some honey buns?
你餓了嗎？要不要我幫你帶一點蜂蜜小麵包？

搭配詞 honey bun 蜂蜜小麵包

butter [ˋbʌtɚ] **n.** 奶油 ◀Track 0020

例句 With this butter knife, you can spread butter with ease.
使用這個奶油刀，你能輕輕鬆鬆地抹奶油。

搭配詞 butter knife 抹奶油的刀

cabbage [ˋkæbɪdʒ] **n.** 包心菜 ◀Track 0021

例句 One of my favorite dishes in this restaurant is cabbage roll casserole.
我最喜歡這家餐廳的菜餚之一就是焗烤包心菜捲。

搭配詞 cabbage roll 包心菜捲

cafe/café [kəˋfe] **n.** 咖啡館 ◀Track 0022

例句 I feel invigorated after having a cup of cafe au lait.
喝完一杯咖啡牛奶以後，我覺得精力充沛。

易混淆字 cafe au lait 咖啡加牛奶（一般稱為「咖啡歐蕾」）

cafeteria [ˏkæfəˋtɪrɪə] **n.** 自助餐館 ◀Track 0023

例句 The young man is a cafeteria worker, who gives free food to kids when they can't afford it. 這位年輕人是自助餐館的員工，若有小朋友買不起食物，他就免費送他們。

搭配詞 cafeteria worker 自助餐館工作人員

cake [kek] **n.** 蛋糕 ◀Track 0024

例句 He smashed the cake into his classmate's face.
他把蛋糕砸在同學的臉上。

搭配詞 birthday cake 生日蛋糕

candy/sweet [ˋkændɪ]/[swit] **n.** 糖果 ◀Track 0025

例句 George proposed to his girlfriend with a ring hidden in a candy wrapper. 喬治把戒指藏在糖果包裝紙裡，向女友求婚。

搭配詞 candy wrapper 糖果包裝紙

carbohydrate [ˏkɑrboˋhaɪdret] **n.** 碳水化合物、醣 ◀Track 0026

例句 With carbohydrate counting, you can plan your meals and manage your blood glucose.
透過計算碳水化合物的攝取量，你能做好規劃飲食，控制血糖。

搭配詞 carbohydrate counting 計算攝取的碳水化合物

carrot [ˋkærət] **n.** 胡蘿蔔 ◀Track 0027

例句 I will bring some carrot cakes for the birthday party.
我會帶一些胡蘿蔔蛋糕到生日派對。

搭配詞 carrot cake 胡蘿蔔蛋糕

cereal [ˋsɪrɪəl] **n.** 穀片 ◀Track 0028

例句 The design of the cereal box aims to attract children.
這個穀片盒的設計主要是為了吸引孩子們的目光。

搭配詞 cereal box 穀片盒

champagne [ʃæm`pen] n. 白葡萄酒、香檳 Track 0029

例句 You can easily open sparkling wines with this champagne opener.
使用這個香檳開瓶器，你能輕易地打開氣泡酒。

搭配詞 champagne opener 香檳開瓶器

cheese [tʃiz] n. 乾酪、乳酪 Track 0030

例句 Have you had the cheese cake from that bakery? It's very famous.
你吃過那家烘焙坊賣的乳酪蛋糕嗎？很有名的。

搭配詞 cheese cake 乳酪蛋糕

chestnut [`tʃɛsnət] n. 栗子 Track 0031

例句 Her chestnut hair looks gorgeous with strawberry-blonde hightlights.
她的栗色頭髮帶有金紅色挑染，看起來美極了。

搭配詞 chestnut hair 栗子色的頭髮

chew [tʃu] v. 咀嚼、啃 Track 0032

例句 A mouse chewed through the aircraft wiring, causing the flight to delay. 一隻小老鼠把飛機上的線路啃斷了，導致班機延誤起飛。

搭配詞 chew through 啃破

chocolate [`tʃɔkəlɪt] n. 巧克力 Track 0033

例句 I will bring a box of chocolate chip cookies as her birthday present.
我會帶一盒巧克力碎片餅乾當她的生日禮物。

搭配詞 chocolate chip cookie 巧克力碎片餅乾

chopstick(s) [`tʃɑp͵stɪk(s)] n. 筷子 Track 0034

例句 The chopstick rest is aesthetically appealing and highly functoinal.
這個筷子座既美觀又實用。

搭配詞 chopstick rest 筷子座

cigar [sɪ`gɑr] n. 雪茄 Track 0035

例句 His name is Hans not Hunt. Close, but no cigar.
他名叫韓斯，不是韓特。很接近了，但還是差一點。

搭配詞 close, but no cigar 很接近了，但還是差一點（來源：大約19世紀時，美國有一種園遊會以雪茄作為獎品，當遊客差一點得獎時，攤販就會說close, but no cigar）

cigarette [`sɪgə͵rɛt] n. 香菸 Track 0036

例句 The vintage cigarette lighter was recently sold for US$100.
這款經典的點菸器最近賣到了美金100元。

搭配詞 cigarette lighter 點菸器

cocktail [`kɑk͵tel] n. 雞尾酒 Track 0037

例句 You look fetching in this cocktail dress.
你穿這件酒會晚禮服，看起來很迷人。

搭配詞 cocktail dress 酒會晚禮服（正式場合穿的晚禮服）

cocoa [`koko] n. 可可粉、可可飲料 Track 0038

例句 Chocolate is made from the processed seed of cocoa tree.
可可樹的種籽經過加工後，便成了巧克力。

搭配詞 cocoa tree 可可樹

coconut [ˋkokənət] **n.** 椰子 Track 0039

例句 It's swelteringly hot. Let's have some coconut juice.
今天爆熱了，我們來喝點椰子汁吧。

搭配詞 coconut juice 椰子汁

coffee [ˋkɔfɪ] **n.** 咖啡 Track 0040

例句 For coffee lovers, a smart coffee machine is a necessity.
對於愛喝咖啡的人來說，智慧型咖啡機是生活必備品。

搭配詞 coffee machine 咖啡機

cola/Coke [ˋkolə]/[kok] **n.** 可樂 Track 0041

例句 I'd like a hamburger and a diet coke.
我要點一個漢堡和一杯低熱量可樂。

搭配詞 diet coke 低熱量可樂

consume [kənˋsjum] **v.** 消耗、消費、吃 Track 0042

例句 Translating Lord of the Rings is a hugely time-consuming task.
翻譯《魔戒》這部鉅著是十分耗時的工作。

搭配詞 time-consuming 耗費時間的

cook [kʊk] **v.** 烹調 Track 0043

例句 A good cook book features nutritious and delicious recipes that are easy to read and follow. 一本好的烹飪書主要特點是提供營養而可口的食譜，且易讀易做。

搭配詞 cook book 食譜（烹飪書）

cooker [kʊkɚ] **n.** 炊具、鍋 Track 0044

例句 This pressure cooker is a great kitchen appliance to cook beef stew.
這個壓力鍋是烹飪牛肉濃湯的好廚房用具。

搭配詞 pressure cooker 壓力鍋

cookie/cooky [ˋkʊkɪ] **n.** 餅乾 Track 0045

例句 Who stole the cookie from the cookie jar?
是誰從餅乾罐裡偷拿了一塊餅乾？

搭配詞 cookie jar 餅乾罐

cracker [ˋkrækɚ] **n.** 薄脆餅乾 Track 0045-1

例句 I ripped open a box of wheat crackers and dove straight in.
我撕開小麥餅乾盒，大吃起來。

搭配詞 wheat cracker 小麥薄餅

cream [krim] **n.** 奶油、乳製品 Track 0046

例句 The Michelin star chef makes perfect cream puff that wows every customer.
這位米其林主廚做的奶油泡芙超讚的，令每位顧客驚豔不已。

搭配詞 cream puff 奶油泡芙

crisp/crispy [krɪsp]/[ˋkrɪspɪ] **adj.** 脆的 Track 0047

例句 Mandy usually has a crispy waffle for her breakfast.
曼蒂的早餐通常是脆鬆餅。

搭配詞 crispy waffle 脆鬆餅

crunchy [ˋkrʌntʃɪ] adj. 鬆脆的、易裂的 Track 0048
＊字尾-y有轉變為形容詞之意
例句 Crunchy fried chicken is a comfort food that many people choose to eat at a fast food restaurant.
酥脆炸雞是很多人到速食餐廳會點來慰勞自己的食物。
搭配詞 crunchy fried chicken 酥脆炸雞

crust [krʌst] n. 麵包皮、派皮 Track 0049
例句 Actually, bread crust is not any healthier than the inside.
事實上，麵包皮的營養並沒有比麵包本身多。
搭配詞 bread crust 麵包皮

cucumber [ˋkjukʌmbɚ] n. 小黃瓜、黃瓜 Track 0050
例句 Cucumber roll-ups are perfect as a party starter.
小黃瓜壽司捲是完美的派對前菜。
搭配詞 cucumber roll-up 小黃瓜壽司捲

cuisine [kwɪˋzin] n. 菜餚 Track 0051
例句 Come home with me and try my mom's authentic Chinese cuisine.
跟我回家，吃吃看我媽的道地中國菜。
搭配詞 Chinese cuisine 中國菜

curry [ˋkɝɪ] n. 咖哩 Track 0052
例句 Though popular, Japanese curry rice can be somewhat pricy.
雖然日式咖哩飯很受歡迎，但是有點貴。
搭配詞 curry rice 咖哩飯

delicious [dɪˋlɪʃəs] adj. 美味的 Track 0053
例句 It's delicious! I'd like some more.
真好吃！我還想要一點。
同義字 tasty; savory

dessert [dɪˋzɝt] n. 餐後點心、甜點 Track 0054
例句 Don't eat too much dessert, or you will get fat.
別吃太多點心，不然你會變胖。
易混淆字 desert 沙漠

diet [ˋdaɪət] n. 飲食、節食 Track 0055
例句 She went on a diet due to her health problem.
因為健康因素，她開始節食。
搭配詞 go on a diet 節食

dine [daɪn] v. 用餐 Track 0056
例句 I don't feel like dining in tonight. Let's go to a restaurant.
我今晚不想在家吃飯，我們去餐廳用餐吧。
搭配詞 dine in 在家用餐

dinner [ˋdɪnɚ] n. 晚餐、晚宴 Track 0057
例句 She was totally surprised when her crush invited her to a dinner date. 她暗戀的對象邀她赴晚餐約會，令她十分驚訝。
搭配詞 dinner date 晚餐約會

dish [dɪʃ] **n.** （盛食物的）盤、碟 Track 0058

例句 My dad installed a satellite dish so we could watch our favorite television channels from all over the world. 我爸爸裝了一個衛星碟形天線，讓我們可以在全球電視台中，觀賞我們最愛的幾台。

搭配詞 satellite dish 衛星碟形天線

dizzy [ˋdɪzɪ] **adj.** 暈眩的 Track 0059

例句 He suffered from a dizzy spell and was sent to a hospital.
他覺得一陣暈眩，於是被送到醫院。

搭配詞 dizzy spell 一陣暈眩

dough [do] **n.** 生麵團 Track 0060

例句 Dough figurine is a traditional Chinese handicraft that requires highly artistic skills.
捏麵人是一項需要高度藝術技巧的中國傳統手工藝。

搭配詞 dough figurine 捏麵人

doughnut [ˋdo͵nʌt] **n.** 甜甜圈 Track 0061

例句 The restaurant introduced a doughnut burger last year, which has become widely popular.
這家餐廳去年引進甜甜圈漢堡，並大受歡迎。

搭配詞 doughnut burger 甜甜圈漢堡

drink [drɪŋk] **n.** 飲料 Track 0062

例句 Can you get me some energy drink? I'm too thirsty to get it myself.
你可以幫我弄點運動飲料來嗎？我太渴了，自己去不了。

搭配詞 energy drink 運動飲料

drunk [drʌŋk] **adj.** 酒醉的 Track 0063

例句 He finally plucked up enough courage to confess his love for Amber, but he sent a drunk text to his mom instead of Amber.
他終於鼓起勇氣要向安柏告白，結果在醉醺醺時發了簡訊給他的媽媽，而不是安柏。

搭配詞 drunk text 喝醉時發的簡訊

dumpling [ˋdʌmplɪŋ] **n.** 麵團、餃子 Track 0064

例句 You need to dust each dumpling wrapper with flour so they won't stick to each other.
你必須在每張餃子皮上灑些麵粉，這樣它們才不會黏在一起。

搭配詞 dumpling wrapper 餃子皮

eat [it] **v.** 吃 Track 0065

例句 People nowadays usually eat out.
現代人常外食。

搭配詞 eat out 在外面吃飯

edible [ˋɛdəbl̩] **adj.** 可食用的 Track 0066

＊字尾-ible有「可……、能夠……」之意

例句 The company was involved in an edible oil scandal.
這家公司涉及食用油醜聞。

搭配詞 edible oil 食用油

egg [ɛg] **n.** 蛋 Track 0067

例句 Use an egg beater for whipping cream.
使用打蛋器來把奶油打發。

搭配詞 egg beater 打蛋器

empty [ˋɛmptɪ] adj. 空的 ◀ Track 0068

例句 It would be impolite to visit our grandparents empty-handed.
我們若兩手空空去看祖父母，這樣很失禮。

搭配詞 empty-handed 兩手空空

enjoy [ɪnˋdʒɔɪ] v. 享受、欣賞 ◀ Track 0069

例句 The new Model 3 released by the car company features its autopilot, which allows car owners to better enjoy their ride.
這家汽車公司的新車款Model 3推出自動駕駛，讓車主更能盡情享受乘車的愉悅感。

搭配詞 enjoy the ride 享受整個過程

feast [fist] v. 宴請、使享受 ◀ Track 0070

例句 They feasted on caviar and champagne in the banquet.
他們在晚宴中大快朵頤，享受魚子醬和香檳。

搭配詞 feast on 大肆享受某物

feed [fid] v. 餵 ◀ Track 0071

例句 My boss fed me a line about our company's poor performance that led to a massive layoff.
我的老闆謊稱公司績效不佳，導致大規模裁員。

搭配詞 feed sb a line 餵給某人謊言

fin [fɪn] n. 鰭、魚翅 ◀ Track 0072

例句 Shark fin soup is banned in some states because of animal cruelty legislation. 因為有停止虐待動物的明文規定，食用鯊魚鰭湯（魚翅湯）在有些州是被禁止的。

搭配詞 shark fin 鯊魚鰭（即魚翅）

flavor [ˋflevɚ] n. 味道、風味 ◀ Track 0072-1

例句 Some people prefer flavored water to pure water.
有些人喜歡喝調味水勝於純水。

搭配詞 flavored water 調味水

flour [flaʊr] n. 麵粉 ◀ Track 0073

例句 Some people used flour sack to make clothes during the Great Depression.
在1930年代經濟大蕭條時期，有些人將麵粉袋做成衣服。

搭配詞 flour sack 麵粉袋

food [fud] n. 食物 ◀ Track 0074

例句 Would you like some junk food, like potato chips?
你想吃點零食，像是洋芋片之類的嗎？

搭配詞 junk food 零食

fork [fɔrk] n. 叉 ◀ Track 0075

例句 There is a fork in the road. Do I turn right or left?
前方有岔路，我該轉右或轉左？

搭配詞 fork in the road 岔路

fry [ˋfraɪ] v. 油炸、炸 ◀ Track 0076

例句 I love fried chicken, even though it is very unhealthy.
我喜歡吃炸雞，就算很不健康也一樣。

搭配詞 fried chicken 炸雞

garlic [ˋgɑrlɪk] n. 蒜 ◀Track 0077

例句 I don't like garlic bread because it gives me bad breath.
我不喜歡大蒜麵包，因為它會讓我有口臭。

搭配詞 garlic bread 大蒜麵包

glass [ˋglæs] n. 玻璃、玻璃杯 ◀Track 0078

例句 Hillary Clinton tried to break the "highest, hardest glass ceiling" by running the US presidential election. 希拉蕊・柯林頓藉由競選美國總統，試圖打破美國政壇的玻璃天花板。

搭配詞 glass ceiling 玻璃天花板

grain [gren] n. 穀類、穀粒 ◀Track 0079

例句 In the fashion industry, sometimes you need to take criticism with a grain of salt. 在時尚界，有時你必須別把批評放在心上。

搭配詞 take it with a grain of salt 把它當作穀粒大小的鹽＝完全不在意

grease [gris] n. 油脂 ◀Track 0080

例句 If you want to establish a company here, you need to grease someone's palm. 你如果要在這裡成立公司，就必須賄賂某人。

搭配詞 grease one's palm 在某人的掌心抹油（即賄賂）

greasy [ˋgrizɪ] adj. 油膩的 ◀Track 0081

例句 I need an herbal shampoo that can manage my greasy hair.
我需要一罐能控制我的大油頭的草本洗髮精。

搭配詞 greasy hair 油膩的頭髮

greedy [ˋgridɪ] adj. 貪婪的 ◀Track 0082

＊字尾-y有轉變為形容詞之意

例句 She is a greedy person who loves money above all else.
她人很貪婪，把錢看得比什麼都重。

同義字 grabby; coveting

grill [grɪl] n. 烤架 ◀Track 0083

例句 With this grill pan, you'll find how easy it is to make the most tender and juicy meat at home.
有了這個燒烤煎鍋，你將發現在家也能輕鬆料理出香嫩多汁的肉。

搭配詞 grill pan 燒烤煎鍋

gum [gʌm] n. 膠、口香糖 ◀Track 0084

例句 Chewing gum is environmentally unfriendly because it is basically plastic. 口香糖並不環保，因為它基本上是由塑膠組成。

搭配詞 chewing gum 口香糖

ham [hæm] n. 火腿 ◀Track 0085

例句 I eat Parma ham sandwiches for breakfast sometimes.
我有時吃帕爾瑪火腿三明治當早餐。

搭配詞 Parma ham 帕爾瑪火腿

hamburger/burger [ˋhæmbɝgɚ]/[ˋbɝgɚ] ◀Track 0086

n. 漢堡

例句 What wouldn't I give for a cheese hamburger right now!
我現在想吃起士漢堡想到什麼都可以不要了！

搭配詞 cheese burger 起士漢堡

hunger [ˋhʌŋgɚ] n. 餓、飢餓 Track 0087

＊字尾-er有轉變為名詞的意思

例句 Some employees have gone on a hunger strike to protest about the wage discrepancy.
有些員工絕食抗議，以表達對於工資差異的不滿。

搭配詞 hunger strike 絕食抗議

hungry [ˋhʌŋgrɪ] adj. 飢餓的 Track 0088

＊字尾-y有轉變為形容詞之意

例句 The starlet was so hungry for success that she tried to do her very best in every audition she could get. 這個小明星如此渴望成功，以致於她在每個試鏡機會都盡最大的努力表現。

搭配詞 hungry for... 渴望某事

ingredient [ɪnˋgridɪənt] n. 成分、原料 Track 0089

例句 I never read the ingredient labels before buying any food products.
我買食物，都沒看成分標籤。

搭配詞 ingredient label 成分標籤

instant [ˋɪnstənt] adj. 立即的、瞬間的 Track 0090

例句 I like instant noodles very much, but they are unhealthy.
我很喜歡吃即食泡麵，但是泡麵不健康。

搭配詞 instant noodles 即食泡麵

jam [dʒæm] n. 果醬 Track 0091

例句 I can't eat toast without strawberry jam.
沒有草莓果醬，我沒辦法吃吐司。

搭配詞 strawberry jam 草莓果醬

jelly [ˋdʒɛlɪ] n. 果凍 Track 0092

例句 Before the interview, he was so nervous that he got jelly legs.
他在面試前太過緊張，以致腳軟。

搭配詞 jelly legs 像果凍一樣軟掉的雙腿（即腿軟）

jug [dʒʌg] n. 帶柄的水壺 Track 0093

例句 She smashed the milk jug on the floor in anger.
她氣到把牛奶壺摔在地上了。

搭配詞 milk jug 牛奶壺

juice [dʒus] n. 果汁 Track 0094

例句 I would like a glass of orange juice.
我想來一杯柳橙汁。

搭配詞 orange juice 柳橙汁

juicy [ˋdʒusɪ] adj. 多汁的 Track 0095

＊字尾-y有轉變為形容詞之意

例句 The tabloids spread a lot of juicy gossip about the split of one of Holleywood's golden couples.
多家小報寫了許多有關好萊塢的一對金童玉女離婚的勁爆八卦。

搭配詞 juicy gossip 多汁的（勁爆的）八卦

ketchup [ˋkɛtʃəp] n. 蕃茄醬 Track 0096

例句 I never eat fries with tomato ketchup.
我吃薯條都不配蕃茄醬的。

搭配詞 tomato ketchup 蕃茄醬

kettle [ˋkɛtḷ] n. 水壺 ◀Track 0097

例句 Mary accused us of being immature. Talk about the pot calling the kettle black! 瑪莉責備我們很幼稚。真是「五十步笑百步」。

搭配詞 pot calling the kettle black 鍋子説水壺黑＝五十步笑百步

lemonade [ˏlɛmənˋed] n. 檸檬水 ◀Track 0098

＊字尾-ade有「由……製成的飲料」之意

例句 Elizabeth and her brother run a lemonade stand to help Syrian refugees. 伊麗莎白和她弟弟擺了一個賣檸檬水的攤子，來籌錢幫助敘利亞難民。

搭配詞 lemonade stand 賣檸檬水的攤子

lick [lɪk] v. 舔 ◀Track 0099

例句 The little boy was licking his lips when he saw his birthday cake. 小男孩看到他的生日蛋糕，忍不住舔起嘴唇來了。

搭配詞 lick one's lips 舔嘴唇

liquor [ˋlɪkɚ] n. 烈酒、酒 ◀Track 0100

例句 The owner of the liquor store couldn't believe that I was old enough to buy alcohol.
賣酒的店主人無法相信我已經成年，可以買酒了。

搭配詞 liquor store 賣酒的店

loaf [lof] n. 一條（麵包） ◀Track 0101

例句 The lady gives a loaf of bread to the little girl so that she will go away. 女士給了小女孩一條麵包，這樣她才不會一直在這邊不走。

搭配詞 a loaf of bread 一條麵包

lobster [ˋlɑbstɚ] n. 龍蝦 ◀Track 0102

例句 Dad was completely at a loss when he received a box of live lobsters.
當爸爸收到一箱活跳跳的龍蝦時，他完全不知道是怎麼一回事。

搭配詞 lobster bar 龍蝦酒吧

lollipop [ˋlɑlɪˏpɑp] n. 棒棒糖 ◀Track 0103

例句 Carrie gave everyone lollipops on Valentine's day.
在情人節那天，凱莉給每個人棒棒糖。

簡稱 lolly

lunch/luncheon [lʌntʃ]/[ˋlʌntʃən] n. 午餐 ◀Track 0104

例句 Francis always brings his lunch box when he goes to school.
法蘭西斯上學時，總是帶著他的午餐盒。

搭配詞 lunch box 午餐盒

mayonnaise [ˏmeəˋnez] n. 蛋黃醬、美乃滋 ◀Track 0105

例句 Johnny's favorite food is mayonnaise pasta.
強尼最喜歡的食物是蛋黃醬義大利麵。

搭配詞 mayonnaise pasta 蛋黃醬義大利麵

meal [mil] n. 一餐、餐 ◀Track 0106

例句 To celebrate its 70th anniversary, the fast food restaurant provides buy-one-get-one free meal coupons during this month.
這家速食店為慶祝70週年，本月提供買一送一的用餐折扣券。

搭配詞 meal coupon 用餐折扣券

a b c d e f g h i j k l m n o p q r s t u v w x y z

meat [mit] n. （食用）肉 Track 0107

例句 Brock doesn't like meat balls and avoids them if possible.
布洛克不喜歡吃肉球，都會盡量避免。

搭配詞 meat ball 肉球

menu [ˋmɛnju] n. 菜單 Track 0108

例句 Where's the breakfast menu? I'm hungry.
早餐菜單呢？我餓了。

搭配詞 breakfast menu 早餐菜單

microwave [ˋmaɪkrə͵wev] n. 微波爐 Track 0109

例句 Making microwave popcorn at home is easy. Simply push the button and voila. 在家做微波爆米花很簡單，按個鈕就好了。

搭配詞 microwave popcorn 微波爆米花

milk [mɪlk] n. 牛奶 Track 0110

例句 Chocolate milk upsets my stomach if I have it in the morning.
如果我早上喝巧克力牛奶，我的肚子會不舒服。

搭配詞 chocolate milk 巧克力牛奶

mustard [ˋmʌstəd] n. 芥末 Track 0111

例句 Jesus said, "The kingdom of Heaven is like a grain of mustard seed that a man took and sowed in his field."
耶穌打個比喻說：「天國好像一粒芥菜種，有人拿去種在田裏。」

搭配詞 mustard seed 芥菜種子

mutton [ˋmʌtn̩] n. 羊肉 Track 0112

例句 What? What I just ate was mutton curry?
什麼？我剛吃的是羊肉咖哩嗎？

搭配詞 mutton curry 羊肉咖哩

napkin [ˋnæpkɪn] n. 餐巾紙 Track 0113

例句 Would you please give me some paper napkins to wipe the desk with? 可以請你給我一些紙巾讓我擦書桌嗎？

搭配詞 paper napkin 紙巾

noodle [ˋnudl̩] n. 麵條 Track 0114

例句 Would you like some chicken noodles to go with it?
要不要配一點雞肉麵？

搭配詞 chicken noodles 雞肉麵

nourish [ˋnɝɪʃ] v. 滋養 Track 0115

例句 This nourishing cream can reduce wrinkles.
這罐滋養霜能減少皺紋。

搭配詞 nourishing cream 滋養霜

nourishment [ˋnɝɪʃmənt] n. 營養 Track 0116

＊字尾-ment有轉變為名詞之意

例句 The government has just launched a project of beach nourishment.
政府最近才推動一項養灘計畫。

搭配詞 beach nourishment 養灘

nutrient [ˋnjutrɪənt] n. 營養素 ◀Track 0117

例句 My dietitian suggested that I consider a healthy diet so I can absorb as many nutrients as possible.
我的營養師建議我考慮健康的飲食，盡可能地攝取多元的營養素。

---

nutrition [njuˋtrɪʃən] n. 營養物、營養 ◀Track 0118

＊字尾-tion有轉變為名詞的意思

例句 A lot of people don't realize how important nutrition is in our lives.
許多人不知道營養在我們的生活中有多重要。

反義字
malnutrition 營養不良

---

nutritious [njuˋtrɪʃəs] adj. 有養分的、營養的 ◀Track 0119

＊字尾-ious有轉變為形容詞之意

例句 The nutritious bar tastes absolutely delicious.
這個牌子的營養糧食棒可口極了。

搭配詞
nutritious bar 營養糧食棒

---

oatmeal [ˋotˏmil] n. 燕麥片 ◀Track 0120

例句 I'd like to have oatmeal cookies and bread as my breakfast.
我早餐想吃燕麥餅乾和麵包。

搭配詞
oatmeal cookie 燕麥餅乾

---

oven [ˋʌvən] n. 爐子、烤箱 ◀Track 0121

例句 Do you know how to make oven-baked salmon?
你知道怎麼用烤箱烤鮭魚嗎？

搭配詞
oven-baked 用烤箱烤的

---

pan [pæn] n. 平底鍋 ◀Track 0122

例句 How do you cook pancakes without a frying pan?
你沒煎鍋，怎麼做薄煎餅？

搭配詞
frying pan 煎鍋

---

pancake [ˋpænˏkek] n. 薄煎餅 ◀Track 0123

例句 Would you like some breakfast pancakes made by my mother?
你想吃一點我媽做的早餐薄煎餅嗎？

搭配詞
breakfast pancake 早餐薄煎餅

---

pasta [ˋpɑstə] n. 義大利麵 ◀Track 0124

例句 What's for dinner? Pasta again?
晚餐吃什麼？又是義大利麵喔？

易混淆字
past 過去的

---

pastry [ˋpestrɪ] n. 糕餅 ◀Track 0125

例句 My mom's hobby is making green-been pastry.
我媽的嗜好是做綠豆糕。

搭配詞
green-been pastry 綠豆糕

---

pea [pi] n. 豌豆 ◀Track 0126

例句 Cranberry and pea shoot salad is packed with flavors.
蔓越莓和豌豆苗沙拉味道很豐富。

搭配詞
pea shoot 豌豆苗

peel [pil] n. 果皮 Track 0127

例句 Add some lemon peels to the punch.
加一點檸檬皮到水果酒裡調味。

搭配詞 lemon peel 檸檬皮

pickle [ˋpɪkḷ] n. 醃菜 Track 0128

例句 Pickled cabbage is my grandma's favorite food.
我奶奶最愛泡菜。

搭配詞 pickled cabbage 泡菜

picnic [ˋpɪknɪk] n. 野餐 Track 0129

例句 Shall we bring a picnic blanket to the park?
要帶野餐墊去公園嗎？

搭配詞 picnic blanket 野餐墊

pie [paɪ] n. 派 Track 0130

例句 I'd like a slice of pie, please.
請給我一片派。

搭配詞 a slice of pie 一片派

pizza [ˋpitsə] n. 披薩 Track 0131

例句 There is a pizza parlor near our school.
我們學校附近有家披薩店。

搭配詞 pizza parlor 披薩店

plate [plet] n. 盤子 Track 0132

例句 Would you please wash these plates as soon as possible?
你可不可以盡快洗這些盤子？

同義字 dish

plum [plʌm] n. 李子、梅子 Track 0133

例句 After the plum blossom season, the hill was full of garbage left by visitors. 梅花季過後，小山丘充滿遊客留下來的垃圾。

搭配詞 plum blossom 梅花

poach [potʃ] v. 水煮 Track 0134

例句 I have a poached egg for my breakfast every day.
我每天都用水煮一顆蛋當早餐。

搭配詞 poached egg 水煮蛋

popcorn [ˋpɑp͵kɔrn] n. 爆米花 Track 0135

例句 Lucy loves movie popcorn even though she has a lot of pimples.
露西長了很多痘痘，但還是愛吃電影院爆米花。

搭配詞 movie popcorn 電影院爆米花

pork [pork] n. 豬肉 Track 0136

例句 She can't eat pork chop because she is a Muslim.
她是穆斯林，所以不可以吃豬排。

搭配詞 pork chop 豬排

pot [pɑt] n. 鍋、壺 Track 0137

例句 I can't find any of the pots because grandma hid them again.
我找不到鍋子，因為奶奶又把它們藏起來了。

搭配詞 hot pot 火鍋

pour [por] v. 澆、倒 Track 0138

例句 He poured out the hot tea carefully.
他小心翼翼地把熱茶倒出來。

搭配詞 pour out 傾倒

prune [prun] n. 乾梅子 Track 0139

例句 She worked as a prune picker during summer vacation.
她放暑假時去當果園工人。

搭配詞 prune picker 果園工人

pub [pʌb] n. 酒館 Track 0140

例句 Peter went on a pub crawl with his friends on Friday night.
彼德和朋友星期五晚上去好幾間酒館喝酒。

搭配詞 pub crawl 去好幾間酒館喝酒

pudding [ˋpudɪŋ] n. 布丁 Track 0141

例句 He ate the rice pudding and didn't leave anything for his little sister.
他把米布丁吃掉了，完全沒留任何東西給他的妹妹吃。

搭配詞 rice pudding 米布丁

quench [kwɛntʃ] v. 弄熄、解渴 Track 0142

例句 A small sip of water is enough to quench my thirst.
啜飲一小口水就夠讓我解渴了。

同義字 extinguish

raisin [ˋrezn̩] n. 葡萄乾 Track 0143

例句 We were caught eating raisins in math class.
我們被逮到在數學課吃葡萄乾。

易混淆字 raising 提高

recipe [ˋrɛsəpɪ] n. 食譜 Track 0144

例句 I stole Aunt Jenna's cookie recipe.
我偷了珍娜舅媽的餅乾食譜。

易混淆字 receipt 收據

refreshment(s) [rɪˋfrɛʃmənt(s)] Track 0145

n. 清爽、提神之物　＊字尾-ment有轉變為名詞之意

例句 A little refreshment in the afternoon helps me work more efficiently.
午後來點提神的食物幫助我工作更有效率。

同義字 pick-me-up 提神飲料

relish [ˋrɛlɪʃ] v. 細細品味 n. 滋味、風味 Track 0146

例句 Ginger gives relish to the beer.
薑汁給啤酒添加風味。

搭配詞 give relish to　給……添加風味

remove [rɪˋmuv] v. 去除 ◀Track 0147

＊字首re-有「回、再」之意

例句 You can use the bleach to remove a blot on your shirt.
你可以用漂白水去除襯衫上的污點。

搭配詞 remove a blot 去除污點

require [rɪˋkwaɪr] v. 需要 ◀Track 0148

例句 Making a good stew requires patience.
要做一鍋好吃的燉菜需要耐心。

同義字 need

restaurant [ˋrɛstərənt] n. 餐廳 ◀Track 0149

例句 There's a beautiful restaurant near our house.
我們家附近有一間很漂亮的餐廳。

同義字 diner

rice [raɪs] n. 稻米、米飯 ◀Track 0150

例句 The rice paddy field didn't produce any harvest due to serious drought. 這片稻米田因為嚴重乾旱，導致沒有收成。

搭配詞 rice paddy 稻米田

roast [rost] v. 烘烤 ◀Track 0151

例句 My favorite sandwich flavor is roast beef.
我最喜歡的三明治口味是烤牛肉。

同義字 broil

sack [sæk] n. 大包、袋子 ◀Track 0152

例句 Cassie lugged a giant sack of rice home.
凱西拖了一大袋米回家。

易混淆字 sake 原因

salad [ˋsæləd] n. 生菜食品、沙拉 ◀Track 0153

例句 I start the day with a good Caesar salad.
我吃美味的凱撒沙拉，作為一天的開始。

搭配詞 Caesar salad 凱撒沙拉

salt [sɔlt] n. 鹽 ◀Track 0154

例句 Sprinkle a little sea salt on the fish.
在魚上灑一點海鹽。

搭配詞 sea salt 海鹽

salty [ˋsɔltɪ] adj. 鹹的 ◀Track 0155

＊字尾-y有轉變為形容詞之意

例句 The dish is too salty; I'm going to puke.
這道菜太鹹了，我要吐了。

同義字 saline

sandwich [ˋsændwɪtʃ] n. 三明治 ◀Track 0156

例句 I got you a sandwich and some soup.
我幫你買了一個三明治和一點湯。

sauce [sɔs] n. 醬料 ◀Track 0157

例句 My favorite salad dressing is salsa sauce.
我最喜歡的沙拉醬是莎莎醬。

搭配詞
tomato sauce 番茄醬

saucer [ˋsɔsɚ] n. 茶碟 ◀Track 0158

例句 People still debate on whether Roswell flying saucer crash was real or fake.
人們至今仍在討論羅斯威爾飛碟墜毀事件是真的還是假的。

搭配詞
flying saucer 飛碟

sausage [ˋsɔsɪdʒ] n. 臘腸、香腸 ◀Track 0159

例句 The puppy stared at the sausage with wild love and adoration in its eyes. 小狗用瘋狂愛慕的眼神盯著臘腸。

同義字
banger【俚】香腸，臘腸

scarce [skɛrs] adj. 稀少的 ◀Track 0160

例句 People starved to death because the food was scarce in this area.
人們餓死了，因為這一區食物很少。

反義字
plentiful 充足的

serve [sɝv] v. 服務 ◀Track 0161

例句 Dr. Roland Brown established the Mennonite Christian Hospital to serve the needs of the underprivileged.
薄柔纜醫師設立花蓮門諾醫院，服務需要幫助的人。

搭配詞
serve the needs of 滿足……的需要

shred [ʃrɛd] n. 細長的片段 ◀Track 0162

例句 Joanie carefully cut the carrot into shreds.
鍾妮小心地把紅蘿蔔切成細長的片段。

同義字
fragment

sip [sɪp] v. 啜飲、小口地喝 ◀Track 0163

例句 You can take a sip of the wine before sleeping.
你睡前可以小小啜飲一口酒。

搭配詞
a sip of 一小口

slice [slaɪs] n. 片、薄的切片 ◀Track 0164

例句 Naomi sautéed some fish slices for us.
娜歐咪煎了一些魚片給我們。

搭配詞
fish slice 魚片

snack [snæk] n. 小吃、點心 ◀Track 0165

例句 She likes eating snacks after dinner every day.
她喜歡每天吃完晚餐後吃點點心。

反義字
meal 正餐

soda [ˋsodə] n. 汽水、蘇打 ◀Track 0166

例句 Aaron turned up at the doorstep holding two bottles of soda pop.
亞倫在門口出現，拿著兩瓶汽水。

搭配詞
soda pop 汽水

a b c d e f g h i j k l m n o p q r s t u v w x y z

soup [sup] n. 湯 Track 0167

例句 The pumpkin soup is thick and creamy.
這道南瓜湯味道濃郁且具有奶油口感。

搭配詞 pumpkin soup 南瓜湯

sour [ˋsaʊr] adj. 酸的 Track 0168

例句 Alice dislikes Jessica because of her sour grape mindset.
艾莉絲因為酸葡萄心理，而討厭潔西卡。

搭配詞 sour grapes 酸葡萄心理

spaghetti [spəˋgɛtɪ] n. 義大利麵 Track 0169

例句 I want to have some spaghetti Bolognese for dinner.
我晚餐想吃肉醬義大利麵。

搭配詞 Spaghetti Bolognese 肉醬義大利麵

spice [spaɪs] n. 香料 Track 0170

例句 You can get different kinds of spices from the Mexican supermarket.
你可以從墨西哥超市買到各種不同的香料。

同義字 seasoning 調味

spicy [ˋspaɪsɪ] adj. 辛辣的、加香料的 Track 0171

＊字尾-y有轉變為形容詞之意

例句 The dish is too spicy for me.
這道菜對我來說太辣了。

反義字 light 清淡的

spill [spɪl] v. 濺出 Track 0172

例句 Milly tried not to spill over her discontent into her family life outside the office.
米莉努力不讓內心的不滿影響到辦公室以外的家庭生活。

搭配詞 spill over 從某個東西溢出

spoon [spun] n. 湯匙、調羹 Track 0173

例句 Oops, I forgot to bring my tea spoon.
糟糕，我忘記帶自己的茶匙了。

搭配詞 tea spoon 茶匙

sprinkle [ˋsprɪŋkl] v. 撒、灑、噴淋 Track 0174

例句 She sprinkled the pepper all over the steak.
她把牛排整個撒滿胡椒粉。

同義字 dredge（用麵粉、砂糖等）撒

stale [stel] adj. 不新鮮的、陳舊的 Track 0175

例句 This restaurant is terrible. Even the coffee tastes stale.
這餐廳真糟，連咖啡都可以喝起來不新鮮。

反義字 fresh 新鮮的

starch [stɑrtʃ] n. 澱粉 Track 0176

例句 Starch syrup is not as sweet as sugar.
澱粉糖漿不像蔗糖那麼甜。

搭配詞 starch syrup 澱粉糖漿

starvation [stɑrˋveʃən] **n.** 飢餓、餓死 ◀ Track 0177

＊字尾-tion有轉變為名詞的意思

例句 There are still many people living on the verge of starvation in our society. 我們的社會中還有不少人在飢餓邊緣求生存。

同義字 famine 饑荒

---

starve [stɑrv] **v.** 餓、飢餓 ◀ Track 0178

例句 Go out and eat something, or you will starve to death.
出去吃點東西，不然你會餓死。

搭配詞 starve to death 餓死

---

steak [stek] **n.** 牛排 ◀ Track 0179

例句 How do you like your pork steak?
你喜歡多熟的豬排？

搭配詞 pork steak 豬排

---

stew [stju] **n.** 燉菜 ◀ Track 0180

例句 I will never forget the lovely beef stew I had in Swansea.
我永遠忘不了我在史旺西吃的那道美味燉牛肉。

搭配詞 beef stew 燉牛肉

---

stir [stɝ] **v.** 攪拌 ◀ Track 0181

例句 Squeeze a lemon to get some juice, then stir it into the sauce.
把一顆檸檬擠出些汁，然後把檸檬汁攪拌入醬汁裡。

搭配詞 stir into 攪入

---

suck [sʌk] **v.** 吸、吸取 ◀ Track 0182

例句 Elon is a bright kid. He can suck up as much knowledge as he can simply by reading.
伊隆是個聰明的孩子，他從閱讀就能吸收很多的知識。

搭配詞 suck up 吸收

---

sugar [ˋʃugɚ] **n.** 糖 ◀ Track 0183

例句 Sugar is made from sugar canes.
糖是從甘蔗提煉出來的。

搭配詞 cane sugar 蔗糖

---

supper [ˋsʌpɚ] **n.** 晚餐 ◀ Track 0184

例句 I want to play tennis after supper.
吃完晚餐後，我想打網球。

同義字 dinner

---

sweet [swit] **adj.** 甜的、甜味的 ◀ Track 0185

例句 Melody has a sweet tooth, so she always carries candy with her.
美樂蒂喜歡吃甜食，總是隨身帶著糖果。

搭配詞 sweet tooth 喜歡吃甜食

---

syrup [ˋsɪrəp] **n.** 糖漿 ◀ Track 0186

例句 Maple syrup is my favorite doughnut flavor.
我最喜歡楓糖漿口味的甜甜圈。

搭配詞 maple syrup 楓糖漿

a b c d e f g h i j k l m n o p q r **s t** u **v** w x y z

tart [ˋtɑrt] n. 酥皮塔 ◀Track 0187

例句 Jenny from next door brought us some egg tarts.
住隔壁的珍妮帶了一些蛋塔來給我們。

搭配詞
egg tart 蛋塔

---

taste [test] n. 口味 ◀Track 0188

例句 This tiramisu can tickle your taste buds.
這個提拉米蘇能挑動你的味蕾。

搭配詞
taste bud 味蕾

---

tasty [ˋtestɪ] adj. 好吃的 ◀Track 0189

＊字尾-y有轉變為形容詞之意

例句 The food in that restaurant is very tasty, but the decorations are falling apart. 那家餐廳裡的食物很好吃，但擺飾都很舊了。

同義字
yummy【口】好吃的

---

tea [ti] n. 茶 ◀Track 0190

例句 Would you like some tea cake?
你要一些茶點嗎？

搭配詞
tea cake 茶點

---

thirsty [ˋθɝstɪ] adj. 口渴的 ◀Track 0191

＊字尾-y有轉變為形容詞之意

例句 Left as an orphan at the age of two, he has been thirsty for love ever since. 他在2歲成為孤兒，從此十分渴望愛。

搭配詞
thirsty for 渴望

---

toast [tost] n. 吐司麵包 ◀Track 0192

例句 Terry walked out of the kitchen chewing on French toast.
泰瑞邊走出廚房邊咬法式吐司。

搭配詞
Frech toast 法式吐司

---

tofu/bean curd [ˋtofu]/[bin kɝd] n. 豆腐 ◀Track 0193

例句 Many foreigners can't stand the smell of stinky tofu.
許多外國人無法忍受臭豆腐的味道。

搭配詞
stinky tofu 臭豆腐

---

tomato [təˋmeto] n. 蕃茄 ◀Track 0194

例句 I've never met anyone who likes tomato paste as much as you do.
我沒見過哪個人像你這麼喜歡蕃茄泥的。

搭配詞
tomato paste 蕃茄泥

---

turkey [ˋtɝkɪ] n. 火雞 ◀Track 0195

例句 Tom played a turkey cock in the ganster movie.
湯姆在這部幫派電影中，飾演一個傲慢自大的人。

搭配詞
turkey cock 雄火雞＝傲慢自大的人

---

vanilla [vəˋnɪlə] n. 香草 ◀Track 0196

例句 Vanilla ice cream is my favorite flavor.
香草冰淇淋是我最喜歡的口味。

搭配詞
vanilla ice cream 香草冰淇淋

vegetable [ˋvɛdʒətəbl̩] n. 蔬菜 Track 0197

例句 I'm going to the supermarket to buy some vegetables.
我要去超級市場買一些蔬菜。

搭配詞
vegetarian 素食者

vinegar [ˋvɪnɪgɚ] n. 醋 Track 0198

例句 Please pass me the wine vinegar.
請把酒醋傳給我。

搭配詞
wine vinegar 酒醋

whiskey/whisky [ˋwɪskɪ] n. 威士忌 Track 0199

例句 Which one do you like better, Whiskey or Brandy?
你喜歡哪一種，威士忌還是白蘭地？

wine [waɪn] n. 葡萄酒 Track 0200

例句 We like to relax with some good wine after dinner.
我們喜歡在晚餐後喝杯好葡萄酒好好休息

搭配詞
white wine 白葡萄酒

yogurt [ˋjogɚt] n. 優格 Track 0201

例句 I need three cups of yogurt and two bottles of milk.
我需要三杯優格、兩瓶牛奶。

搭配詞
low-fat yogurt 低脂優格

yolk [jok] n. 蛋黃 Track 0202

例句 Yolk pastry and sun cakes are popular souvenirs for foreign tourists.
蛋黃酥和太陽餅是很受外國觀光客歡迎的伴手禮。

搭配詞
yolk pastry 蛋黃酥

食

a b c d e f g h i j k l m n o p q r s t u **v** **w** x **y** z

NOTE

Test 01 關鍵英單總測驗第1回

以下測驗題皆出自書中第一回「**和食有關的單字**」，快來檢視自己的學習成果吧！

一、選擇題

1. Muslims don't eat ____ for religious reasons.
   (A) meat
   (B) pork
   (C) fish
   (D) lobsters

2. The doctor suggested that she go on a ____ to prevent obesity.
   (A) date
   (B) day
   (C) diet
   (D) dream

3. My father usually has some ___ after dinner.
   (A) desert
   (B) depth
   (C) dough
   (D) dessert

4. Let's go to the cafeteria. I'm ____.
   (A) starving
   (B) starvation
   (C) hunger
   (D) toast

5. To make the salad taste better, you can sprinkle some _____ to add flavors in it.
   (A) powder
   (B) spices
   (C) herbal
   (D) spicy

6. People who are underage are not allowed to buy ___.
   (A) liquor
   (B) soda
   (C) juice
   (D) yogurt

7. He always buys a ____ of bread and some milk in that bakery.
   (A) load
   (B) leaf
   (C) loaf
   (D) life

8. Artificial _____ are not considered healthy.
   (A) ingredients
   (B) input
   (C) instant
   (D) ingress

9. She used a _____ oven to cook dinner.
   (A) microwave
   (B) mustard
   (C) meal
   (D) menu

10. I'd like my ____ medium well.
   (A) snack
   (B) suck
   (C) steak
   (D) doughnut

二、克漏字測驗

Some people think cooking is taxing, especially after a tiring day. But, let me show you how to make things easier. To make a quick __1__ for dinner, simply chop off the tough ends of most vegetables and scrub them well. Tear up the cabbage into bite-sized bits and put them in a big bowl. Add a little grated carrot and cucumber. Drizzle the greens with some extra virgin olive oil. Finally, garnish the pile of greens with some pepper, nuts, cheese, and __2__.

Then, let's cook chicken breasts. To make them tender, you need to pound the chicken breasts with the bottom of a wide glass. Season them with a pinch of salt. Heat the pan and add some __3__. Sauté the chicken breasts and flip them over.

At the same time, bring a pot of water to boil. Cook potatoes until they're tender. Mash them with a beater and slowly blend milk and spices into the mixture until smooth and creamy. Voila, the __4__ dinner is ready to __5__.

1. (A) cooker
   (B) gum
   (C) spoon
   (D) salad

2. (A) raisins
   (B) bakery
   (C) glass
   (D) jug

3. (A) sweet
   (B) butter
   (C) starch
   (D) crispy

4. (A) awful
   (B) yuck
   (C) nutritious
   (D) disgusting

5. (A) serve
   (B) serious
   (C) severe
   (D) shred

關鍵英單總測驗第 1 回 中譯與解答

一、選擇題

1. 穆斯林教徒因為宗教因素不吃豬肉。
   (A) 肉類
   (B) 豬肉
   (C) 魚肉
   (D) 龍蝦

2. 醫師建議她應該節食，以預防肥胖問題。
   (A) 約會
   (B) 日子
   (C) 飲食
   (D) 作夢

3. 我爸爸通常在晚飯後會吃一些點心。
   (A) 沙漠
   (B) 深度
   (C) 麵團
   (D) 點心

4. 我們一起去自助餐廳吧，我快餓死了。
   (A) 飢餓的
   (B) 飢餓（名詞）
   (C) 飢餓（名詞）
   (D) 土司

5. 為讓沙拉好吃一點，你可以灑一點辛香料增加風味。
   (A) 粉末
   (B) 辛香料
   (C) 草藥的
   (D) 辣的

6. 未成年人不准買酒精飲品。
   (A) 酒精飲品
   (B) 汽水
   (C) 果汁
   (D) 優格

7. 他向來都到那家烘焙坊買條吐司和一些牛奶。
   (A) 工作量
   (B) 葉子
   (C) 一條（麵包的單位）
   (D) 生活

8. 人工調味料被視為不健康的。
   (A) 成份
   (B) 輸入
   (C) 立即的
   (D) 進入

9. 她用微波爐煮晚餐。
   (A) 微波爐
   (B) 芥末
   (C) 餐點
   (D) 菜單

10. 我想要七分熟的牛排。
   (A) 零食
   (B) 吸東西
   (C) 牛排
   (D) 甜圈圈

二、克漏字測驗

有些人覺得烹飪是件挺累人的事，尤其是經過一天的疲憊，不過讓我告訴你怎麼簡化烹飪這件事。要快速做晚餐的沙拉，只要把蔬菜的梗切掉，並把菜本身洗乾淨就好。把包心菜撕成可以入口的大小，放進一個大碗裡，加進一點刨絲的紅蘿蔔和小黃瓜，淋上特級初榨冷壓橄欖油，最後在這堆蔬菜上加一點胡椒、堅果、起士、葡萄乾來點綴。

接著來煮雞胸肉，為了讓肉質口感鮮嫩，你得先用一個大玻璃杯的底盤來拍打雞胸肉，用一小撮鹽調味，把平底鍋熱鍋後加上奶油，香煎肉片並翻過來再煎一次。

在此同時，煮滾一鍋水後，把馬鈴薯煮到軟，用攪拌器把它打成泥狀並慢慢拌入牛奶和辛香料，直到馬鈴薯泥很滑順、濃郁。好了，營養的晚餐準備上桌了。

1.
A. 電鍋
B. 口香糖
C. 湯匙
D. 沙拉

2.
(A) 葡萄乾
(B) 烘焙坊
(C) 玻璃杯
(D) 水壺

3.
(A) 甜的
(B) 奶油
(C) 澱粉
(D) 酥脆的

4.
(A) 糟糕的
(B) 噁心
(C) 營養的
(D) 噁心的

5.
(A) 上菜
(B) 嚴肅的
(C) 嚴重的
(D) 撕碎

一、選擇題

1.(B) 2.(C) 3.(D) 4.(A) 5.(B)
6.(A) 7.(C) 8.(A) 9.(A) 10. (C)

二、克漏字測驗

1.(D) 2.(A) 3.(B)
4.(C) 5.(A)

Unit 02 和衣有關的單字

多益測驗的命題強調生活化與實用性，學會這些與「衣」有關的單字，不僅能讓你在多益考場上所向披靡，在日常生活上也可以靈活運用喔！

形容身著婚紗的美麗新娘可以這麼說

- **The bride looks stunning in that beaded fishtail wedding dress.**
  新娘身著一襲帶珠繡的魚尾婚紗，美得令人驚嘆。
- **Grandma brought her antique lace veil to complete the bride's look.**
  奶奶把她的古董蕾絲面紗帶來，作為新娘裝扮的完美點綴。

在挑選衣服時可以這麼說

- **This dress doesn't go well with my heels.**
  這件裙子跟我的高跟鞋不搭。
- **I'm looking for an appropriate outfit to attend a black tie wedding.**
  我正在尋找適合參加正式禮服婚禮的服裝。
- **Does this sweater come in a bigger size?**
  這件毛衣有更大的尺寸嗎？

根據天氣穿搭可以這麼說

- **It's raining outside. Don't forget to put on your trench coat.**
  外面在下雨了。別忘了穿上風衣。
- **I need to go buy some extra blankets to survive this freezing weather.**
  我需要多買幾張毛毯才能抵擋這嚴寒的氣候。

首飾配件搭配可以這麼說

- **That emerald brooch on her collar really enhanced her green eyes.**
  她衣領上的祖母綠胸針和她的綠色眼睛相得益彰。
- **The leather necklace she wears is a gift from her friend.**
  她配戴的皮革項鍊是朋友送她的禮物。

描述妝髮造型可以這麼說

- **He spent an hour in the morning to style his mustache.**
  他早上花了一小時來刮鬍子和造型他的鬍鬚。
- **I like my hair braided during summer.**
  在夏天，我喜歡將我的頭髮編成辮子。

Unit 02 和衣有關的單字

appearance [ə`pɪrəns] n. 外表 Track 0203
＊字尾-ance有轉變為名詞之意
例句 The politician avoids making an appearance after the money laundry scandal. 這位政客在洗錢醜聞爆發後，就避免露面了。

搭配詞 make an appearance 露面

appropriate [ə`proprɪ͵et] adj. 適當的、適切的 Track 0204
＊字尾-ate有轉變為形容詞之意
例句 This tie is not appropriate for the occasion.
在這個場合打這條領帶不適當。

搭配詞 be appropriate for 適用於

armor [`ɑrmɚ] n. 盔甲 Track 0205
例句 I tried on the armor my mom bought me for Halloween.
我試穿了媽媽為了萬聖節替我買的盔甲。

bare [bɛr] adj. 裸露的 Track 0206
例句 He arrived at the warzone bare-handed and was seriously injured by rebels there. 他手無寸鐵地抵達戰區，並遭到當地反叛軍重傷。

搭配詞 bare-handed 赤手空拳的、手無寸鐵的

bead [bid] n. 珠子、串珠 Track 0207
例句 I'm trying to make my own necklace with colorful beads I got from the market.
我正在試著用在市場買到的彩色珠子做一條自己的項鍊。

易混淆字 bean 豆子

beard [bɪrd] n. 鬍子 Track 0208
例句 You'd better shave your beard before the interview today.
你今天去面試前最好刮個鬍子吧。

同義字 goatee

belt [bɛlt] n. 皮帶 Track 0209
例句 Please fasten your seat belt before you drive.
開車前請繫好安全帶。

搭配詞 fasten your seat belt 繫上安全帶

blanket [`blæŋkɪt] n. 毯子 Track 0210
例句 Would you like me to bring you an extra blanket?
你要我幫你多帶一條毯子嗎？

易混淆字 basket 籃子

a b c d e f g h i j k l m n o p q r s t u v w x y z

blond/blonde [blɑnd] n. 金髮的人 Track 0211

例句 Gemma Ward is famous for her doll face and blonde hair.
潔瑪・沃德以她洋娃娃般的臉孔和金髮聞名。

搭配詞 blonde hair 金髮

blot/stain [blɑt] n. 污痕、污漬 Track 0212

例句 I used vinegar to remove the ink stain on my shirt.
我用醋把衣服上的墨水污痕去除。

搭配詞 ink stain 墨水污漬

blouse [blaus] n. 短衫、女襯衫 Track 0213

例句 I picked up a blouse to match my trousers for the interview.
我為了面試買了一件搭配長褲的短衫。

boot [but] n. 長靴 Track 0214

例句 I wore a pair of snow boots during the snowstorm.
我在暴風雪天穿了一雙雪靴。

搭配詞 snow boots 雪靴

bracelet [ˋbreslɪt] n. 手鐲（鍊） Track 0215

＊字尾-let有「小」的意思

例句 My parents bought me a bracelet as a gift on my 21st birthday.
我父母在我21歲生日時買了一個手鍊給我當禮物。

同義字 bangle 手環

braid [bred] n. 髮辮、辮子 Track 0216

例句 The superstar showed up on the red carpet with her hair in braids.
這位超級巨星綁著辮子在紅毯星光大道上亮相。

搭配詞 in braids （綁著）辮子

brassiere [brəˋzɪr] n. 胸罩、內衣 Track 0217

例句 There are support brassiere you can wear when doing exercise.
現在有一些你在運動時可以穿的支撐型胸罩。

brooch [brotʃ] n. 別針、胸針 Track 0218

例句 She wears a beautiful brooch on the shirt.
她在襯衫上戴了一個很美的胸針。

同義字 breastpin

buckle [ˋbʌkḷ] n. 皮帶扣環 Track 0219

例句 The design of the shoe buckle is exquisite.
這個鞋扣的設計很精緻。

搭配詞 shoe buckle 鞋扣

button [ˋbʌtn̩] n. 鈕子 Track 0220

例句 He went back to his office and undid the top button of his shirt.
他回到自己的辦公室，並解開襯衫最上面的一顆鈕子。

搭配詞 undo a button 解開扣子

change [tʃendʒ] v. 改變、兌換 Track 0221

例句 We've fridged some tiramisu for you in case you change your mind.
我們幫你把一些提拉米蘇冰起來，以免你改變心意，突然想吃了。

搭配詞 change one's mind 改變心意

charm [tʃɑrm] n. 魅力 Track 0222

例句 Her gentle, droopy eyes are her greatest charm.
她溫和而下垂的雙眼是她最大的魅力所在。

同義字 glamour 光彩

cloth [klɔθ] n. 布料 Track 0223

例句 She made the apron from the tea cloth she found in the market.
她用在市場找到的茶布做了這條圍裙。

搭配詞 tea cloth 茶布

clothe [kloð] v. 穿衣、給……穿衣 Track 0224

例句 The old lady clothed the little baby in the cradle.
老太太幫搖籃裡的小寶寶穿了衣服。

反義字 unclothe 脫去……衣服

clothes [kloz] n. 衣服 Track 0225

例句 I bought some new clothes for my little daughter, and I needed more clothes hangers. 我替小女兒買了一些新衣，我需要更多的衣架。

搭配詞 clothes hanger 衣架

clothing [ˋkloðɪŋ] n. 衣服、衣著 Track 0226

例句 This antique clothing looks elegant.
古董衣衫看起來很雅緻。

搭配詞 antique clothing 古董衣衫

coarse [kors] adj. 粗糙的 Track 0227

例句 The inside of this shirt is pretty coarse; I get itchy when wearing it.
這件襯衫裡面很粗糙，我穿時會覺得很癢。

反義字 delicate 精細的

coat [kot] n. 外套 Track 0228

例句 I bought a heavy coat for this new season.
我為了這一季買了一件厚重的外套。

搭配詞 heavy coat 厚重外套

collar [ˋkɑlɚ] n. 領帶、領結 Track 0229

例句 My father is a white-collar worker.
我爸是個白領階級工作人員。

易混淆字 color 顏色

comb [kom] n. 梳子 Track 0230

例句 The little boy combs his hair every morning.
小男孩每天早上都會梳頭髮。

同義字 hairbrush

a b c d e f g h i j k l m n o p q r s t u v w x y z

conventional [kən`vɛnʃənl] adj. 傳統的 Track 0231
＊字尾-al有轉變為形容詞之意
例句 It's better to wear conventional clothes for a situation like this.
這樣的場合還是穿傳統的衣服比較好。
同義字 traditional

cosmetic [kɑz`mɛtɪk] adj. 化妝用的、美容的 Track 0232
例句 Her fans are curious about what she puts inside her cosmetic bag.
她的粉絲很好奇她的化妝包裡放些什麼。
搭配詞 cosmetic bag 化妝包

cosmetics [kɑz`mɛtɪks] n. 化妝品 Track 0233
＊字尾-s有轉變為複數之意
例句 My sisters linger at the cosmetics section whenever we go shopping. 我們去逛街時，我的姊妹們總是在化妝品區待很久。
同義字 make-up

costume [`kɑstjum] n. 服裝、服飾、劇裝 Track 0234
例句 Kids will put on special costumes for Halloween.
孩子們會為了萬聖節穿上特別的服裝。
易混淆字 custom 習俗

cotton [`kɑtn̩] n. 棉花 Track 0235
例句 Do you like a pineapple cotton candy or a grape one?
你要鳳梨口味的棉花糖還是葡萄口味？
搭配詞 cotton candy 棉花糖

dandruff [`dændrəf] n. 頭皮屑 Track 0236
例句 My dandruff problem gets more serious when I'm under pressure.
我的壓力一大，頭皮屑問題就更嚴重。

discount [`dɪskaunt] n. 折扣 Track 0237
＊字首dis-有「不、無」的意思
例句 If you are our VIP, you'll get cash discount.
如果你是本店的VIP，就可以享受現金折扣。
搭配詞 cash discount 現金折扣

dress [drɛs] n. 洋裝 Track 0238
例句 The dress code for the banquet is formal.
參加這場晚宴的衣著要很正式。
搭配詞 dress code 穿衣標準

durable [`djurəbl̩] adj. 耐穿的、耐磨的 Track 0239
＊字尾-able有「可以、能」的意思
例句 I got you a canvas bag; it's much more durable than the one you have. 我幫你買了一個帆布包，比你現在那個耐用多了。
反義字 fragile 脆弱的

dye [daɪ] n. 染料 Track 0240
例句 We used organic dye to beautify our bedsheets.
我們用有機染料讓床單更漂亮。
同義字 color

elegant [ˋɛləgənt] adj. 優雅的 ◀Track 0241
＊字尾-ant有轉變為形容詞的意思
例句 I love your new gown; it's really elegant.
我很喜歡你的新禮服，超優雅的。

同義字 graceful

exquisite [ˋɛkskwɪzɪt] adj. 精緻的 ◀Track 0242
＊字尾-ite有轉變為形容詞的意思
例句 I buy clothes from Sandra's shop because the stuff here is exquisite.
我都在珊卓的店買衣服，因為這裡的東西很精緻。

反義字 harsh 粗糙的

fabric [ˋfæbrɪk] n. 紡織品、布料 ◀Track 0243
例句 What kind of fabric is this? It feels pretty smooth.
這是什麼布料？摸起來挺順的。

同義字 textile

fashion [ˋfæʃən] n. 時尚 ◀Track 0244
例句 This attire is out of fashion now.
這件衣服已經不流行了。

搭配詞 out of fashion 不流行

fashionable [ˋfæʃənəbl̩] adj. 流行的、時髦的 ◀Track 0245
＊字尾-able有「可以、能」的意思
例句 Only the most fashionable items make their ways into her closet.
只有最時髦的單品才會出現在她的衣櫃。

同義字 stylish

feather [ˋfɛðɚ] n. 羽毛 ◀Track 0246
例句 A feather jacket will keep you warm through this winter.
一件羽毛外套可以讓你在冬天保持溫暖。

搭配詞 feather duster 羽毛撢子

fold [fold] v. 折疊 ◀Track 0247
例句 I don't want to fold a page on this book because it's very precious.
我不想在這本書折頁，因為它很珍貴。

搭配詞 fold a page 折頁

garment [ˋgɑrmənt] n. 衣服 ◀Track 0248
例句 His curious choice of garments makes me wonder if he's really all there. 他穿的衣服有夠奇怪，讓我懷疑他是否腦袋正常。

同義字 apparel

glamour [ˋglæmɚ] n. 魅力 ◀Track 0249
例句 Lisa walked in wearing sunglasses and giving an aura of absolute glamour.
莉莎戴著太陽眼鏡走進來，整個人散發出一種超有魅力的氛圍。

同義字 charm

glove(s) [glʌv(z)] n. 手套 ◀Track 0250
例句 My dad always wears a pair of leather gloves when riding his Harley-Davidson. 爸爸在騎哈雷重機車時，總是戴著一雙皮手套。

搭配詞 leather gloves 皮手套

gown [gaʊn] n. 長袍、長上衣 Track 0251

例句 Lucy looked gorgeous in her bridal gown.
露西穿新娘禮袍美極了。

搭配詞 bridal gown 新娘禮袍

hairstyle/hairdo [ˋhɛr͵staɪl]/[ˋhɛr͵du] n. 髮型 Track 0252

例句 Audrey Hepburn wore beehive hairstyle in the award ceremony.
奧黛麗・赫本梳了蜂巢式髮型出席頒獎典禮。

搭配詞 beehive hairstyle 蜂巢式髮型

handkerchief [ˋhæŋkɚtʃɪf] n. 手帕 Track 0253

例句 I always keep a handkerchief in the pocket with me.
我總是在口袋裡攜帶手帕。

同義字 bandanna

handsome [ˋhænsəm] adj. 英俊的 Track 0254

例句 He sure is a handsome boy.
他確實是個帥哥。

搭配詞 handsome boy 帥哥

hat [hæt] n. 帽子 Track 0255

例句 She is good at doing tricks with her fur hat.
她擅長用毛皮帽變把戲。

搭配詞 fur hat 毛皮帽

heel [hil] n. 腳後跟 Track 0256

例句 I wear high heels when I go to work.
我去上班時都穿高跟鞋。

搭配詞 high heels 高跟鞋

helmet [ˋhɛlmɪt] n. 安全帽 Track 0257

例句 Bicycle helmets can be cute too. I saw a pink one earlier.
腳踏車安全帽也可以很可愛啊，我之前就看過一頂粉紅色的。

同義字 hard hat 工地用安全帽

hook [hʊk] n. 鉤子 Track 0257-1

例句 Mum helped me hang my raincoat on the hook.
媽媽幫我把雨衣掛在鉤子上。

搭配詞 hook up 鉤住

jacket [ˋdʒækɪt] n. 夾克、外套 Track 0258

例句 I left my basketball jacket in the restaurant.
我把棒球夾克留在餐廳了。

搭配詞 baseball jacket 棒球夾克

jeans [dʒinz] n. 牛仔褲 Track 0259

＊字尾-s有轉變為複數之意

例句 I like my skinny jeans. It makes me look slim.
我喜歡我的貼身牛仔褲。它讓我看起來很苗條。

搭配詞 skinny jeans 貼身牛仔褲

jewelry [ˋdʒuəlrɪ] n. 珠寶 ◀Track 0260

＊字尾-ry有轉變為名詞之意

例句 I don't wear junk jewelry because it looks tacky.
我不戴廉價珠寶，因為看起來很俗氣。

搭配詞
junk jewelry 廉價珠寶

knit [nɪt] v. 編織 ◀Track 0261

例句 The scarf is expensive because it was hand-knit.
這條圍巾很貴，因為它是純手工編織的。

搭配詞
hand-knit 用手編織的

lace [les] n. 花邊、緞帶、蕾絲 ◀Track 0262

例句 My favorite part about this dress is the intricate lace pattern.
這件洋裝最讓我喜歡的地方就是細緻的花邊圖案。

搭配詞
lace pattern 花邊圖案

laundry [ˋlɔndrɪ] n. 洗衣店、送洗的衣服 ◀Track 0263

例句 I do my laundry twice a week.
我一個禮拜洗兩次衣服。

搭配詞
do the laundry 洗衣服

leather [ˋlɛðɚ] n. 皮革 ◀Track 0264

例句 I gave my brother a leather wallet on his birthday.
我在哥哥生日時給了他一個皮的錢包。

搭配詞
leather product 皮製品

linen [ˋlɪnɪn] n. 亞麻製品 ◀Track 0265

例句 Linen clothes are comfortable to wear in summer.
亞麻的衣服在夏天穿很舒服。

易混淆字
line 線條

lipstick [ˋlɪp͵stɪk] n. 口紅、唇膏 ◀Track 0266

例句 I wear red lipstick for important events.
參加重要活動時，我會擦紅色口紅。

搭配詞
red lipstick 紅色口紅

loose [lus] adj. 寬鬆的 ◀Track 0267

例句 I like to wear loose shirts so that my bulging belly doesn't look obvious.
我喜歡穿寬鬆的衣服，這樣我的大肚子才不會看起來很明顯。

反義字
tight 緊的

mask [mæsk] n. 面具、口罩 ◀Track 0268

例句 You have to wear a mask in the masquerade.
參加這場化妝舞會時，你必須戴上面具。

搭配詞
wear a mask 戴面具／口罩

mend [mɛnd] v. 修補、修改 ◀Track 0269

例句 Would you please mend these trousers for me?
可以請你幫我修補這條長褲嗎？

易混淆字
mind 心、想法

modern [ˋmɑdɚn] adj. 現代的 ◀Track 0270

例句 The shop is designed in a modern style, but the clothes it sells are old-fashioned. 這家店設計很現代，但賣的衣服卻很老式。

反義字 old 陳舊的

mustache [ˋmʌstæʃ] n. 鬍鬚 ◀Track 0271

例句 He has a handlebar mustache, dark skin, and gray hair. 他留著翹八字鬍鬚、膚色黝黑、頭髮灰白。

搭配詞 handlebar mustache 翹八字鬍

necklace [ˋnɛklɪs] n. 項圈、項鍊 ◀Track 0272

例句 I wore a necklace to match my dress. 我戴了一條項鍊來配我的洋裝。

同義字 choker

necktie [ˋnɛk͵taɪ] n. 領帶 ◀Track 0273

例句 I bought a necktie for my father on his birthday. 我在爸爸生日時為他買了一條領帶。

同義字 tie

needle [ˋnidl̩] n. 針、縫衣針 ◀Track 0274

例句 Don't leave your sewing needles lying around; the cat might eat them. 別把縫衣針到處放，貓可能會吃下去。

易混淆字 needless 不需要的

normal [ˋnɔrml̩] adj. 標準的、正常的 ◀Track 0275

例句 Is it normal for a bride to wear green? 新娘穿綠色正常嗎？

反義字 abnormal 不正常的

nylon [ˋnaɪlɑn] n. 尼龍 ◀Track 0276

例句 I don't wear clothes made of nylon. 我不穿尼龍製的衣服。

搭配詞 nylon fabric 尼龍織物

overcoat [ˋovɚ͵kot] n. 大衣、外套 ◀Track 0277

＊字首over-有「覆蓋、上面的」之意

例句 My dad left his overcoat at the office again. 我爸又把大衣留在辦公室了。

同義字 topcoat

pajamas [pəˋdʒæməz] n. 睡衣 ◀Track 0278

＊字尾-s有轉變為複數之意

例句 Judy invited me to her pajama party. 茱蒂邀請我去參加她的睡衣派對。

搭配詞 pajama party 睡衣派對

pants [pænts] n. 褲子 ＊字尾-s有轉變為複數之意 ◀Track 0279

例句 You shouldn't leave your pants in the bathtub. 你不該把褲子丟在浴缸裡。

patch [pætʃ] n. 補丁、碎片 Track 0280

例句 My grandma made several beautiful patch quilts.
我祖母做了好幾件漂亮的拼布床單。

搭配詞
patch quilt 拼布床單

perfume [ˋpɝfjum] n. 香水 Track 0281

例句 My dad brought me a bottle of limited edition perfume from overseas.
我爸幫我從海外帶了一瓶限量的香水。

易混淆字 perform 表演

pocket [ˋpɑkɪt] n. 口袋 Track 0282

例句 The politician lined his own pocket when brokering the transactions.
這名政客仲介這筆交易時，中飽私囊。

搭配詞
line one's own pocket 中飽私囊

powder [ˋpaʊəq] n. 粉 Track 0283

例句 Make sure to clean your powder puff regularly.
一定要定期清理你的粉撲。

搭配詞
powder puff 粉撲

purse [pɝs] n. 錢包 Track 0284

例句 Helen left her change purse behind in the cinema.
海倫把錢包留在電影院了。

搭配詞
change purse 小錢包

rag [ræg] n. 破布、碎布 Track 0285

例句 The teenager created an app and went from rags to riches.
這個青少年寫了一個行動應用程式，從此由貧致富。

搭配詞
from rags to riches 由貧致富

razor [ˋrezɚ] n. 剃刀、刮鬍刀 Track 0286

例句 I'm running out of razor blades.
我的剃刀快用完了。

搭配詞
razor blade 刮鬍刀片

ribbon [ˋrɪbən] n. 絲帶、蝴蝶結 Track 0287

例句 She won the Blue Ribbon Award for Best Supporting Actress.
她贏得藍絲帶獎的最佳女配角。

搭配詞
blue ribbon 藍絲帶（意指最佳）

robe [rob] n. 長袍 Track 0288

例句 The wizard trudged towards us in a robe.
巫師穿著長袍沉重地朝著我們走來。

易混淆字
rope 繩子

sandal [ˋsændl̩] n. 涼鞋、便鞋 Track 0289

例句 I wore a pair of sandals to the beach.
我穿了一雙涼鞋去海邊。

易混淆字
scandal 醜聞

scarf [skɑrf] n. 圍巾 Track 0290

例句 Mom bought a red and green silk scarf for me.
媽媽買了一條紅綠相間的絲質圍巾給我。

搭配詞 silk scarf 絲質圍巾

sew [so] v. 縫、縫上 Track 0291

例句 The surgeon sew up the patient's wound.
外科醫生把病人的傷口縫合了。

搭配詞 sew up 縫合

shave [ʃev] v. 刮鬍子、剃 Track 0292

例句 My dad shaves his face every morning in the shower.
我爸每天早上在淋浴時都刮鬍子。

搭配詞 shave one's face 剃鬍

shirt [ʃɝt] n. 襯衫 Track 0293

例句 I need the right necklace to match my dress shirt.
我需要一條對的項鍊來搭配我的正式襯衫。

搭配詞 dress shirt 正式襯衫

shoe(s) [ʃu(z)] n. 鞋 Track 0294

例句 I bought a new pair of loafer shoes in a basement sale.
我趁百貨公司地下室特價活動，買了一雙新的樂福鞋。

搭配詞 loafer shoes 樂福鞋

shorts [ʃɔrts] n. 短褲 ＊字尾-s有轉變為複數之意 Track 0295

例句 I wear shorts in the summer because it's too hot for jeans.
我夏天都穿短褲，因為穿牛仔褲太熱了。

易混淆字 shirt 襯衫

silk [sɪlk] n. 絲、綢 Track 0296

例句 Your scarf is lovely. Is it silk?
你的圍巾真美，是絲的嗎？

搭配詞 silky 絲緞般柔軟的

skirt [skɝt] n. 裙子 Track 0297

例句 Amy took off her mini skirt and flung it across the room.
愛咪脫下迷你裙，將它甩到房間另一頭。

搭配詞 mini skirt 迷你裙

sleeve [sliv] n. 衣袖、袖子 Track 0298

例句 He rolled up his shirt sleeves to show his scars.
他捲起襯衫袖子以露出他的疤痕。

搭配詞 shirt sleeves 襯衫袖子

slipper(s) [ˋslɪpɚ(z)] n. 拖鞋 Track 0298-1

例句 Please take off your shoes before entering the house and put on the plastic slippers instead.
請在進入房子裡前脫掉鞋子，改穿塑膠拖鞋。

搭配詞 plastic slippers 塑膠拖鞋

sneaker(s) [ˋsnikɚ(s)] n. 慢跑鞋 Track 0299

例句 She wears sneakers on the way to work, and changes to high heels in the office. 她穿著慢跑鞋去上班，到了辦公室再換成高跟鞋。

易混淆字 snicker 竊笑

soak [sok] v. 浸泡 Track 0300

例句 Soak your jeans in vinegar to prevent the dye from fading out. 把牛仔褲浸泡在醋中，以防染劑褪色。

反義字 dehydrate 脫水

sock(s) [sɑk(s)] n. 短襪 Track 0301

例句 Toe socks are popular because they help prevent your toes from getting blisters. 五指襪很受歡迎，因為它能保護腳指不起水泡。

搭配詞 toe socks 五指襪

stocking(s) [ˋstɑkɪŋ(z)] n. 長襪 Track 0302

例句 Melanie pulled off her knee stockings and sighed in relief. 梅拉妮拉下過膝襪，放鬆地長嘆一聲。

搭配詞 knee stockings 過膝襪

stylish [ˋstaɪlɪʃ] adj. 時髦的、漂亮的 Track 0303

＊字尾-ish有轉變為形容詞的意思

例句 He is very stylish; others copy his style. 他很時髦，其他人都模仿他的風格。

同義字 fashionable

suit [sut] n. 西裝 Track 0304

例句 I need to rent a black suit because I'll be giving a speech next week. 我得租一套黑西裝，因為我下禮拜要演講。

易混淆字 suite 套

suitcase [ˋsutˌkes] n. 手提箱 Track 0305

例句 I lost my carry-on suitcase during the flight. 我在飛行途中，遺失了可帶到機上的手提箱。

搭配詞 carry-on suitcase 可帶到機上的手提箱

sweater [ˋswɛtɚ] n. 毛衣、厚運動衫 Track 0306

例句 It is snowy in Beijing now; you should bring some sweaters with you. 現在北京在下雪，你該帶幾件毛衣。

搭配詞 woolly 羊毛衫

tag [tæg] n. 標籤 Track 0307

例句 I always check the price tag before I pay at the cashier. 我到收銀台付錢時，一定會先看價格標籤。

搭配詞 dog tag 狗牌

textile [ˋtɛkstaɪl] n. 布料 Track 0308

例句 Norman's parents work in a textile factory. 諾曼的父母在布工廠工作。

同義字 fabric

thick [θɪk] adj. 厚的、密的 Track 0309

例句 The fabric is thick and warm.
這個布料又厚又暖。

反義字 thin 細的、稀疏的

thin [θɪn] adj. 薄的、稀疏的 Track 0310

例句 His hair began thinning out due to stress.
他因為壓力，頭髮變稀疏了。

搭配詞 thin out 變稀薄

thread [θrɛd] n. 線 Track 0311

例句 She licked the end of the thread so as to make it go through the needle eye easier. 她舔了線的末端，以讓它更容易穿過針孔。

搭配詞 needle 針

tie [taɪ] n. 領帶、領結 Track 0312

例句 He tied the knot with his high school sweetheart.
他和在中學結識的女友結婚了。

搭配詞 tie the knot 結婚

tight [taɪt] adj. 緊的、緊密的 Track 0313

例句 Ivanka has been tight-lipped about what she and the Japanese prime minister talked during the meeting.
伊凡卡對於她和日本首相在會面時談論的內容，三緘其口。

搭配詞 tight-lipped 緊閉嘴巴的

trousers [ˋtrauzəz] n. 褲子 Track 0314

＊字尾-s有轉變為複數之意

例句 Pete had a dream that he went to school without wearing trousers.
彼特夢到他沒穿褲子就去上學了。

同義字 pants

T-shirt [ˋtiʃɜt] n. 運動衫、T恤 Track 0315

例句 His company manufactures custom T-shirts.
他的公司生產客製T恤。

搭配詞 custom T-shirt 客製T恤

tuck [tʌk] n. 縫摺 v. 塞進 Track 0316

例句 There are two tucks at the back of your pants.
你的長褲後面有兩個縫摺。

反義字 untuck 拆開

ugly [ˋʌglɪ] adj. 醜的、難看的 Track 0317

例句 When she was young, she was really an ugly duckling.
她小時候真的是醜小鴨。

搭配詞 ugly duckling 醜小鴨

underwear [ˋʌndɚ,wɛr] v. 內衣 Track 0318

＊字首under-有「下方的」之意

例句 She marched out to the hotel lobby in her underwear.
她只穿著內衣就走到旅館大廳去了。

同義字 underclothes

uniform [ˋjunə͵fɔrm] n. 制服、校服 Track 0319

＊字首uni-有「單一的」之意

例句 We wear school uniforms at school.
我們上學時穿制服。

搭配詞 school uniform 學校制服

veil [vel] n. 面紗 Track 0320

例句 Prince Harry lifted the wedding veil of his bride, Meghan Markle.
哈利王子掀開他的新娘梅根・馬克爾的婚紗。

搭配詞 wedding veil 婚禮面紗

velvet [ˋvɛlvɪt] n. 天鵝絨 Track 0321

例句 She decorated the living room with velvet curtains.
她用天鵝絨窗簾裝飾客廳。

搭配詞 velvet curtains 天鵝絨窗簾

vest [vɛst] n. 背心、馬甲 Track 0322

例句 The SWAT team must wear bullet-proof vests when on duty.
美國特種警察部隊出任務時，必定會穿上防彈背心。

搭配詞 bullet-proof vest 防彈背心

waist [west] n. 腰部 Track 0323

例句 They got a lady to measure my waist.
他們找了一個女士來量我的腰圍。

搭配詞 thigh 大腿

wallet [ˋwalɪt] n. 錢包、錢袋 Track 0324

例句 Paypal has totally revolutionized the banking industry by promoting digital wallet usage.
Paypal透過推廣使用電子錢包，澈底改革了銀行業的運作模式。

搭配詞 digital wallet 電子錢包

wardrobe [ˋwɔrd͵rob] n. 衣櫃、衣櫥 Track 0325

例句 I need a bigger wardrobe for my dresses.
我需要一個更大的衣櫃來放我的洋裝。

同義字 closet

warm [wɔrm] adj. 暖和的、溫暖的 Track 0326

例句 I got warm greetings from my college classmates.
我收到大學同學捎來的溫暖問候。

搭配詞 warm greetings 溫暖的問候

wear [wɛr] v. 穿、戴、耐久 Track 0327

例句 I wear perfume at the office.
我在辨公室，會擦香水。

搭配詞 wear perfume 擦香水

wet [wɛt] adj. 潮濕的 Track 0328

例句 I forgot to bring my umbrella and got wet.
我忘了帶傘，結果弄得濕答答的。

搭配詞 get wet 弄濕

wool [wul] n. 羊毛 ◀ *Track 0329*

例句 I can't afford this woolen scarf.
我買不起這條羊毛圍巾。

同義字
woolen 羊毛的

zipper [ˋzɪpɚ] n. 拉鍊 ◀ *Track 0330*

＊字尾-er有轉變為名詞的意思

例句 My jacket zipper is stuck.
我的外套拉鍊卡住了。

搭配詞
jacket zipper 外套拉鍊

關鍵英單總測驗第2回

以下測驗題皆出自書中第二回「**和衣著有關的單字**」，快來檢視自己的學習成果吧！

一、選擇題

1. The beehive ________ was made famous by Audrey Hepburn in the movie "Breakfast in Tiffany."
   (A) hairstyle
   (B) handkerchief
   (C) helmet
   (D) mustache

2. Would you like to come to my _____ party this Saturday night?
   (A) suitcase
   (B) rag
   (C) pajama
   (D) loose

3. She was ___ about whether her company was going to merge with another company.
   (A) durable
   (B) thin
   (C) fashion
   (D) tight-lipped

4. The dress is so beautiful, but look at the price ___. It's too expensive.
   (A) suit (B) tag
   (C) scarf (D) tie

5. Eton College requires that each student wear _____ at school.
   (A) threads
   (B) uniforms
   (C) wardrobes
   (D) zippers

6. After the accident, he was paralyzed from the ___ down.
   (A) vest
   (B) waist
   (C) sandal
   (D) wool

7. The supermodel started the trend of mini ____ recently.
   (A) robes
   (B) razors
   (C) modern
   (D) skirts

8. The boy wore a Donald Trump _____ on Halloween night.
   (A) lace
   (B) cotton
   (C) discount
   (D) mask

9. She bought Chanel ______ as a birthday gift for her mother.
   (A) pocket
   (B) nylon
   (C) perfume
   (D) glamour

10. Princess Diana's wedding gown was definitely _____.
    (A) exquisite
    (B) handsome
    (C) coarse
    (D) sloppy

二、克漏字測驗

An Australian supermodel, Gemma Ward appeared on the __1__ magazine, Vogue, at the age of only 16. Her ethereal look and beautiful __2__ hair have made her one of the most gorgeous and __3__ models on the catwalk.

Due to work, she sometimes needs to wear stunningly high __4__ and haute couture __5__ when taking photographs or attending fashion shows. As exhausting as it might be, she enjoys her work and doesn't really tire out. A fashion crew still remembered her lack of any complaints after shooting on a set until 3:30 am.

Gemma took a break for a few runway seasons after the death of a good friend. Now 31, she's a mother of two children and is staging her official comeback. Her fans are all very happy to see her shine again in the modelling industry.

1.
(A) fashion
(B) gloves
(C) fold
(D) dye

2.
(A) blonde
(B) cosmetic
(C) comb
(D) mend

3.
(A) costume
(B) durable
(C) charming
(D) glamour

4.
(A) slippers
(B) heels
(C) jeans
(D) hooks

5.
(A) dandruffs
(B) armors
(C) garments
(D) blankets

關鍵英單總測驗第2回
中譯與解答

一、選擇題

1. 奧黛麗赫本在《第凡內早餐》這部電影讓蜂窩頭髮造型風靡一時。
   (A) 髮型
   (B) 手帕
   (C) 鋼盔
   (D) 鬍鬚

2. 你星期六晚上要來參加我的睡衣派對嗎?
   (A) 皮箱
   (B) 破布
   (C) 睡衣
   (D) 寬鬆

3. 她對於公司是否要和另一家公司合併一事，三緘其口。
   (A) 持久的
   (B) 瘦的
   (C) 時尚
   (D) 口風很緊

4. 這件洋裝真美，不過看看標價，太貴了吧。
   (A) 西裝
   (B) 標籤
   (C) 圍巾
   (D) 領帶

5. 伊頓學院要求每位學生上學都要穿制服。
   (A) 線
   (B) 制服
   (C) 衣櫥
   (D) 拉鏈

6. 他發生意外後，腰部以下癱瘓。
   (A) 背心
   (B) 腰部
   (C) 涼鞋
   (D) 羊毛

7. 這名超模最近引領了迷你裙的潮流。
   (A) 長袍
   (B) 刮鬍刀
   (C) 現代化的
   (D) 裙子

8. 這名小男孩在萬聖節晚上戴了唐納川普的面具。
   (A) 花邊緞帶
   (B) 棉花
   (C) 折扣
   (D) 面具

9. 她買了香奈兒的香水當生日禮物送給媽媽。
   (A) 口袋
   (B) 尼龍
   (C) 香水
   (D) 魅力

10. 黛安娜王妃的婚紗真是精緻極了。
   (A) 精緻的
   (B) 英俊的
   (C) 粗糙的
   (D) 邋遢的

二、克漏字測驗

潔瑪沃德是來自澳洲的超模，在年僅16歲時就登上時尚雜誌Vogue。她仙氣般的外表和美麗的金髮使她成為伸展台上最耀眼、迷人的模特兒之一。

由於工作要拍照或參加時尚秀，她經常必須穿上高得嚇人的高跟鞋和名貴服飾。雖然行程很累，她卻很享受工作，且不覺得疲累。有個時尚團隊仍記得她拍照拍到凌晨3點半才收工，卻一點抱怨都沒有。

潔瑪在一位好友離世後，曾在時尚季消失了一陣子。現在她31歲，是2個小孩的媽媽，且已正式展開復出，她的粉絲都很高興看到她在模特兒界再度發光。

1.
(A) 時尚
(B) 手套
(C) 折疊
(D) 染色

2.
(A) 金髮
(B) 化妝品的
(C) 梳子
(D) 修補

3.
(A) 劇裝
(B) 持久的
(C) 迷人的
(D) 魅力

4.
(A) 拖鞋
(B) 鞋跟
(C) 牛仔褲
(D) 鉤子

5.
(A) 頭皮屑
(B) 盔甲
(C) 服飾
(D) 毯子

一、選擇題

1.(A) 2.(C) 3.(D) 4.(B) 5.(B)
6.(B) 7.(D) 8.(D) 9.(C) 10.(A)

二、克漏字測驗

1.(A) 2.(A) 3.(C)
4.(B) 5.(C)

Unit 03 和住有關的單字

多益測驗的命題強調生活化與實用性，學會這些與「住」有關的單字，不僅能讓你在多益考場上所向披靡，在日常生活上也可以靈活運用喔！

描述周遭環境可以這麼說

- **There's a shopping mall near this neighborhood.**
  這附近有一間購物中心。
- **He stayed at a suburban hostel for a week.**
  他在郊區的一家青年旅社待了一個星期。

預約賞屋可以這麼說

- **I'm looking for a spacious apartment near the MRT station.**
  我正在找鄰近捷運站，且空間寬敞的公寓。
- **There are some properties for sale near the station, but the housing prices are higher than expected.**
  捷運站附近有幾處房產正待出售，但房價比預期的還高。
- **The layout of this flat is not good. A lot of space is wasted.**
  這間公寓的格局不是很好。有很多空間被浪費了。

規劃裝潢可以這麼說

- **I want to paint my bedroom pink, and replace the shutters with blackout curtains.** 我想把我的臥室漆成粉色，然後把百葉窗換成遮光窗簾。
- **I'll design a build-in book shelf to save some space in the bedroom.**
  我會設計一款嵌入式的書櫃來節省臥室的空間。

選購傢俱可以這麼說

- **I want my furniture to have a consistent style.**
  我想讓我的傢俱有統一的風格。
- **I'm looking for a rug to pair with my armchair.**
  我正在找一個地毯好搭配我的扶手椅。

家居布置可以這麼說

- **The stockings will be hanged above the fireplace during Christmas.**
  長襪在聖誕節期間會掛在壁爐上。
- **To decorate the living room, she put a Turkish candle lamp on the side table.**
  為了裝飾客廳，她將一個土耳其蠟燭燈放在茶几上。

Unit 03 和住有關的單字

account [ə`kaunt] n. 帳戶、記錄 Track 0331

例句 He gave me all the money in his bank account.
他把銀行帳戶裡的錢都給我了。

搭配詞
bank account 銀行帳戶

---

adequate [`ædəkwɪt] adj. 適當的、足夠的 Track 0332

例句 The house was a mess but of adequate size.
那棟房子裡面很亂，但大小適當。

同義字
sufficient

---

apartment [ə`pɑrtmənt] n. 公寓 Track 0333

例句 This apartment is for rent.
這間公寓出租中。

搭配詞
apartment for rent
出租公寓

---

appliance [ə`plaɪəns] n. 器具、家電用品 Track 0334

＊字尾-ance有轉變為名詞之意

例句 Lucy said she's gone to buy some household appliances.
露西說她去買一些家電用品了。

易混淆字
applicant 申請人

---

architecture [`ɑrkə͵tɛktʃɚ] n. Track 0335

建築、建築學、建築物　＊字尾-ure有轉變為名詞之意

例句 My brother studies architecture in university.
我哥哥在大學念建築學。

同義字
building

---

armchair [`ɑrm͵tʃɛr] n. 扶椅 Track 0336

例句 The armchair in the living room belongs to the cat.
客廳的扶椅是給貓坐的。

同義字
recliner 躺椅

---

arrangement [ə`rendʒmənt] n. 佈置、準備 Track 0337

＊字尾-ment有轉變為名詞之意

例句 Our manager will make arrangements for your accommodations.
我們的經理會為您的住宿事宜做好安排。

搭配詞
make an arrangement
做安排

---

ash [æʃ] n. 灰燼、灰 Track 0338

例句 Ashes to ashes, dust to dust
塵歸塵，土歸土。（聖經）

搭配詞
volcano ash 火山灰

---

asleep [əˋslip] adj. 睡著的 Track 0339
例句 It was almost two hours before I fell asleep last night.
我昨晚花了快兩個小時才睡著。
搭配詞 fall asleep 睡著

attic [ˋætɪk] n. 閣樓、頂樓 Track 0340
例句 Would you please put the books in the attic?
可以請你把書放到閣樓嗎？
同義字 loft

bag [bæg] n. 袋子 Track 0341
例句 I just bought a hand bag from a flea market.
我剛從跳蚤市場買了一個手拿包。
搭配詞 hand bag 手拿包

balcony [ˋbælkənɪ] n. 陽臺 Track 0342
例句 I swept the back balcony up just now.
我剛剛才掃了後陽臺。
搭配詞 back balcony 後陽臺

barely [ˋbɛrlɪ] adv. 簡直沒有、幾乎不能 Track 0343
＊字尾-ly有轉變為副詞之意
例句 The room is barely furnished. 這房間幾乎沒有擺家具。
同義字 scarcely

barn [bɑrn] n. 穀倉 Track 0344
例句 Turn off the barn light when you leave.
離開時，記得要把穀倉燈關掉。
搭配詞 barn light 穀倉燈

basement [ˋbesmənt] n. 地下室、地窖 Track 0345
＊字尾-ment有轉變為名詞之意
例句 In the bargain basement, you can get the best deals.
百貨公司特價品活動時，你能買到最划算的東西。
搭配詞 bargain basement 百貨公司特價品（百貨公司地下室商品通常較1樓以上商品便宜）

bath [bæθ] n. 洗澡 Track 0346
例句 Taking a warm bath before going to bed is good for our health.
睡前洗個熱熱的澡對我們的健康有益。
搭配詞 take a bath 洗澡

bathroom [ˋbæθˏrum] n. 浴室 Track 0347
例句 All I've wanted in life is to own a luxurious bathroom.
我人生的夢想就是擁有一間豪華浴室。
搭配詞 toilet 廁所

bay [be] n. 海灣、月桂樹、小房間 Track 0348
例句 The bay resort is famed for its views.
這個海灣景點以美景聞名。
搭配詞 bay resort 海灣景點

bed [bɛd] **n.** 床 Track 0349

例句 I need to go to bed early because I have a meeting at 7:00 am tomorrow. 我明天早上7點要開會，所以必須早點上床睡覺。

搭配詞 go to bed 去床上睡覺

bedroom [ˋbɛd͵rum] **n.** 臥房 Track 0350

例句 Here is the master bedroom. 這間是主臥室。

搭配詞 master bedroom 主臥室

bench [bɛntʃ] **n.** 長凳 Track 0351

例句 My mother often takes a rest on the bench when she is tired. 我媽媽累的時候常會在長凳上休息。

易混淆字 beach 沙灘

bleach [blitʃ] **n.** 漂白劑 Track 0352

例句 She used bleach to clean her dirty shirt. 她用漂白劑來洗淨她的髒襯衫。

搭配詞 bleaching powder 漂白粉

bolt [bolt] **n.** 門閂 Track 0353

例句 Remember to slide the bolt in before you go to bed. 睡前記得把門閂拴好。

易混淆字 bold 大膽的

bookcase [ˋbuk͵kes] **n.** 書櫃、書架 Track 0354

例句 I will put all the books into the bookcase. 我會把書都放到書櫃裡。

bottle [ˋbɑtl̩] **n.** 瓶 Track 0355

例句 The milk is stored in a glass bottle. 牛奶裝在玻璃瓶。

搭配詞 glass bottle 玻璃瓶

bowl [bol] **n.** 碗 Track 0356

例句 I poured some milk into the soup bowl and left it on the ground for the cat. 我倒了一些牛奶到湯碗裡，放在地上給貓喝。

搭配詞 soup bowl 湯碗

box [bɑks] **n.** 盒子、箱 Track 0357

例句 The chocolates are contained in a cardboard box. 這些巧克力放在紙箱裡。

搭配詞 cardboard box 紙箱

broom [brum] **n.** 掃帚 Track 0358

例句 Grandpa chased the boy out with a broom. 爺爺拿著掃帚把男孩趕出去了。

搭配詞 dust pan 畚斗

bubble [ˋbʌbl̩] n. 泡沫、氣泡 Track 0359

例句 Bubble milk tea is one of Taiwan's delicacies.
珍珠奶茶是台灣的美食之一。

搭配詞 bubble milk tea 珍珠奶茶

---

build [bɪld] v. 建立、建築 Track 0360

例句 It takes two months to build a house.
蓋好一棟房子要兩個月。

搭配詞 build a fire 生火

---

building [ˋbɪldɪŋ] n. 建築物 Track 0361

例句 The building is big enough to hold two hundred people.
這棟建築夠大，可以容納兩百人。

同義字 architecture 建築學

---

buy [baɪ] v. 買 Track 0362

例句 Could you buy some batteries for me on the way?
你在來的路上可以幫我買些電池嗎？

易混淆字 buyer 買家

---

cabin [ˋkæbɪn] n. 小屋、茅屋、艙 Track 0363

例句 The cabin crew sacrificed their lives during the hijacking.
機艙人員在劫機事件中， 犧牲了性命。

搭配詞 cabin crew 機艙人員

---

cage [kedʒ] n. 籠子、獸籠、鳥籠 Track 0364

例句 Who let the hamster out of the cage?
誰把黃金鼠從籠子裡放出來的？

搭配詞 prison 監獄

---

candle [ˋkændl̩] n. 蠟燭、燭光 Track 0365

例句 I would like to buy some scented candles.
我想買一些香氛蠟燭。

搭配詞 scented candle 香氛蠟燭

---

carpet [ˋkɑrpɪt] n. 地毯 Track 0366

例句 The story of Aladdin and his magic carpet was adapted and made into a Disney motion picture.
阿拉丁和魔毯的故事被改拍成迪士尼動畫片。

搭配詞 magic carpet 魔毯

---

cassette [kæˋsɛt] n. 卡帶、盒子 Track 0367

＊字尾-ette有「小」之意

例句 People rarely use cassette players now.
現在人們不太用卡帶播放機了。

搭配詞 cassette player 卡帶播放機

---

castle [ˋkæsl̩] n. 城堡 Track 0368

例句 Mark made a sand castle at the beach.
馬克在沙灘上做了一個沙堡。

搭配詞 sand castle 沙堡

cave [kev] **n.** 洞穴 Track 0369

例句 Israel has one of the most impressive stalactite caves in the world.
以色列擁有全世界最著名的鍾乳石洞之一。

搭配詞 stalactite cave 鍾乳石洞

ceiling [ˋsilɪŋ] **n.** 天花板 Track 0370

例句 We have a ceiling fan in the living room.
我們的客廳有一座天花板吊扇。

搭配詞 ceiling fan 天花板吊扇

cellar [ˋsɛlɚ] **n.** 地窖、地下室 Track 0371

例句 The wine cellar is used for storing wine.
地窖是我們儲放酒的地方。

搭配詞 wine cellar 藏酒窖

chair [tʃɛr] **n.** 椅子、主席席位 Track 0372

例句 I like to sit on the office chair by the window.
我喜歡坐在窗邊的辦公椅。

搭配詞 office chair 辦公椅

chamber [ˋtʃembɚ] **n.** 房間、寢室 Track 0373

例句 Would you like to go to the chamber concert tonight?
你今晚想去看室內音樂會嗎？

搭配詞 chamber concert 室內音樂會

chimney [ˋtʃɪmnɪ] **n.** 煙囱 Track 0374

例句 On Christmas Eve, Santa Claus sends lots of gifts through the chimneys. 聖誕前夕，聖誕老公公會從煙囱送很多禮物。

搭配詞 fireplace 火爐

chore [tʃor] **n.** 雜事、打雜 Track 0375

例句 Household chores should be split evenly between all family members.
家中的雜事應該由全部的家人平分。

易混淆字 core 核心

circulate [ˋsɝkjə͵let] **v.** 傳佈、循環 Track 0376

＊字尾-ate有轉變為動詞的意思

例句 Several newsletters are still circulating rumors about his death.
許多電子報仍在散播他死亡的謠言。

搭配詞 circulate rumor 散播謠言

clean [klin] **adj.** 乾淨的 Track 0377

例句 You would need to make sure the bedsheets are clean before sleeping on them. 你得先確認床單是乾淨的，才能睡在上面。

反義字 dirty 骯髒的

closet [ˋklɑzɪt] **n.** 櫥櫃 Track 0378

例句 Could you please help me clean up the closet?
你可以幫我整理櫥櫃嗎？

易混淆字 closed 關閉的

comfort [ˋkʌmfɚt] n./v. 舒適 ◀Track 0379

例句 I prefer to live a boring life of comfort instead of a dangerous and exciting life.
我寧可過無聊又舒適的生活，也不要過危險又刺激的生活。

反義字 discomfort 不舒適

community [kəˋmjunətɪ] n. 社區 ◀Track 0380

例句 We'll have a community meeting tomorrow morning.
我們明天早上要舉辦社區會議。

搭配詞 community meeting 社區會議

concrete [ˋkɑnkrit] n. 水泥、混凝土 ◀Track 0381

例句 The pavement is made of concrete.
走道是水泥做的。

搭配詞 steel 鋼筋

costly [ˋkɔstlɪ] adj. 價格高的 ◀Track 0382

例句 The antique armchair is too costly for me.
這古董扶椅對我來說太貴了。

同義字 expensive

couch [kautʃ] n. 長沙發、睡椅 ◀Track 0383

例句 He is a couch potato after work.
他下班後習慣坐在沙發上看電視。

搭配詞 couch potato 整天坐在沙發上看電視的人

courtyard [ˋkort͵jɑrd] n. 庭院、天井 ◀Track 0384

例句 My mother often sweeps the courtyard.
媽媽常會掃庭院。

crib [krɪb] n. 嬰兒床 ◀Track 0385

例句 We'll have to get a crib for little Tommy.
我們得幫小湯米買張嬰兒床。

同義字 cradle 搖籃

cup [kʌp] n. 杯子 ◀Track 0386

例句 Would you like a cup of coffee?
你要來杯咖啡嗎？

搭配詞 mug 馬克杯

cupboard [ˋkʌbɚd] n. 食櫥、餐具廚 ◀Track 0387

例句 I will get some sugar from the cupboard for you.
我會從食櫥拿點糖來給你。

curtain/drape [ˋkɝtn̩]/[drep] n. 窗簾 ◀Track 0388

例句 I need thicker curtains to block out the ridiculous neon lights of the store below.
我需要厚一點的窗簾來擋住樓下店家那扯到不行的霓虹燈。

搭配詞 shutters 百葉窗

cushion [ˋkuʃən] n. 墊子 ◀Track 0389

例句 I think the cushion matches the sofa.
我覺得墊子跟沙發蠻搭的。

搭配詞
couch surfing 沙發旅行、沙發客

---

decorate [ˋdɛkə͵ret] v. 裝飾、佈置 ◀Track 0390

例句 He decorated the house with colorful light bulbs.
他用色彩豐富的燈裝飾房子。

搭配詞
decorate sth wtih
以……為裝飾

---

decoration [͵dɛkəˋreʃən] n. 裝飾 ◀Track 0390-1

＊字尾-tion有轉變為名詞的意思

例句 The interior decorations in this room are stunning.
這個房間的室內裝潢美極了。

搭配詞
interior decoration
室內裝潢

---

desk [dɛsk] n. 書桌 ◀Track 0391

例句 She left all the important documents on the desk.
她把重要文件都放在書桌上了。

易混淆字
deck 甲板

---

detergent [dɪˋtɝdʒənt] n. 清潔劑 ◀Track 0392

例句 Wear gloves when washing dishes, or the detergent might do damage to your hands.
洗碗時要戴手套，不然清潔劑可能會傷害你的手。

搭配詞
laundry detergent 洗衣精

---

dirty [ˋdɝtɪ] adj. 髒的 ◀Track 0393

＊字尾-y有轉變為形容詞之意

例句 I can't stand how dirty your room is.
你房間太髒了，我受不了。

搭配詞
dirty work 骯髒不法行為

---

disconnect [͵dɪskəˋnɛkt] v. 斷絕、打斷 ◀Track 0394

＊字首dis-有「不」之意

例句 Did the Internet disconnect yet again?
網路又斷了喔？

反義字
connect 連接

---

disorder [dɪsˋɔrdɚ] n. 無秩序 ◀Track 0395

＊字首dis-有「不」之意

例句 The model is suffering from eating disorder.
這位模特兒飽受飲食失調之苦。

搭配詞
eating disorder 飲食失調

---

district [ˋdɪstrɪkt] n. 區域 ◀Track 0396

例句 If you live here, you should be familiar with the district.
如果你住在這裡，你應該會對這個區域很熟才對。

搭配詞
Da-an district 大安區

---

dome [dom] n. 拱形圓屋頂 ◀Track 0397

例句 The farewell concert was held in the dome.
再見演唱會在拱形會場裡舉辦。

易混淆字
done 已完成的

door [dor] n. 門 Track 0398

例句 The scout tried to sell his homemade cookies door to door.
這名男童軍挨家挨戶賣自製餅乾。

搭配詞 door to door 挨家挨戶

drag [dræg] v. 拖曳 Track 0399

例句 She wouldn't wake up, so her mom had to drag her out of bed.
她不肯起床，媽媽只好硬把她從床上拖下來。

易混淆字 drug 藥物

dresser [ˋdrɛsɚ] n. 梳妝台、鏡台 Track 0400

＊字尾-er有轉變為名詞的意思

例句 I found my watch in the dresser drawer.
我在梳妝台抽屜找到了我的手錶。

搭配詞 dresser drawer 梳妝台抽屜

dressing [ˋdrɛsɪŋ] n. 梳理、服飾、裝飾、醬 Track 0401

例句 This book contains several recipes of salad dressing.
這本書中包含好幾種沙拉醬的做法。

搭配詞 salad dressing 沙拉醬

dryer [draɪɚ] n. 烘乾機、吹風機 Track 0402

＊字尾-er有轉變為名詞的意思

例句 My hair dryer is not working. 我的吹風機壞了。

搭配詞 hair dryer 吹風機

dust [dʌst] n. 灰塵、灰 Track 0403

例句 A large dust storm is approaching Arizona.
一場大沙塵暴正逐漸接近亞利桑那州。

搭配詞 dust storm 沙塵暴

dwell [dwɛl] v. 住、居住、詳述 Track 0404

例句 I had dwelled in Paris for ten years.
我之前在巴黎住了十年。

同義字 inhabit

echo [ˋɛko] n. 回音 Track 0405

例句 The room is so large you can actually hear echoes when you speak.
這房間之大，你甚至可以在說話時聽到回音。

搭配詞 echo back 回響

electric/electrical [ɪˋlɛktrɪk]/[ɪˋlɛktrɪkḷ] Track 0406

adj. 電的 ＊字尾-al有轉變為形容詞的意思

例句 Tesla manufactures high-quality elecric cars.
特斯拉製造高品質的電動汽車。

搭配詞 electric car 電動汽車

electricity [ˌɪlɛkˋtrɪsətɪ] n. 電 Track 0407

＊字尾-ity有轉變為名詞的意思

例句 A factory needs high electricity power to maintain its operation.
這間工廠需要高電力來維持運作。

搭配詞 electricity power 電力

environment [ɪnˋvaɪrənmənt] **n.** 環境 ◀Track 0408

＊字尾-ment有轉變為名詞之意

例句 I like the environment of this university.
我喜歡這個大學的環境。

搭配詞 natural environment 自然環境

faucet/tap [ˋfɔsɪt]/[tæp] **n.** 水龍頭 ◀Track 0409

例句 Sensor faucets are environmentally friendly.
感應式水龍頭很環保。

搭配詞 sensor faucet 感應式水龍頭

fax [fæx] **n.** 傳真 ◀Track 0410

例句 What is your company's fax number?
你們公司的傳真號碼多少？

易混淆字 fox 狐狸

fence [fɛns] **n.** 籬笆、圍牆 ◀Track 0411

例句 I want to have a house and a picket fence around the garden.
我想要有一棟房子，花園旁邊要有尖木籬笆。

搭配詞 picket fence 尖木籬笆

fireplace [ˋfaɪr͵ples] **n.** 壁爐、火爐 ◀Track 0412

例句 Please hang the portrait above the fireplace.
請把畫像掛在壁爐上方。

flat [flæt] **n.** 平的東西、公寓 ◀Track 0413

例句 She decided to move to a new flat.
她決定要搬到新的公寓。

易混淆字 flap 拍打

floor [flor] **n.** 地板、樓層 ◀Track 0414

例句 The hair salon is on the ground floor.
美髮沙龍店位在一樓。

搭配詞 ground floor 第一層樓

freezer [ˋfrizɚ] **n.** 冰庫、冷凍庫 ◀Track 0415

＊字尾-er有轉變為名詞的意思

例句 The door to the freezer compartment is broken, so the foods are all rotten. 冷凍庫的門壞了，所以裡面的食物都壞了。

搭配詞 freezer compartment 冷凍庫

furnish [ˋfɝnɪʃ] **v.** 供給、裝備、佈置 ◀Track 0416

例句 My tutor furnished me with all the information I need to score high in SAT. 我的家教提供我很多如何在美國學測得到高分的資訊。

搭配詞 furnish with 給……裝備、提供

furniture [ˋfɝnɪtʃɚ] **n.** 傢俱、設備 ◀Track 0417

＊字尾-ure有轉變為名詞之意

例句 I want to buy some period furniture for the new house.
我想為新房子買點仿古家具。

搭配詞 period furniture 仿古傢俱

garage [gəˋrɑdʒ] **n.** 車庫 Track 0418

例句 You can park your car in our neighbors' garage. They're out today.
你的車可以停在我們鄰居的車庫，他們今天不在。

易混淆字 garbage 垃圾

---

garbage [ˋgɑrbɪdʒ] **n.** 垃圾 Track 0419

例句 The garbage can is full.
垃圾桶滿了。

搭配詞 garbage can 垃圾桶

---

gas [gæs] **n.** 汽油、瓦斯 Track 0420

例句 Using natural gas helps to reduce carbon emissions.
使用天然氣有助降低排碳量。

搭配詞 natural gas 天然氣

---

gate [get] **n.** 門、閘門 Track 0421

例句 We'd better arrive at the boarding gate 30 minutes earlier.
我們最好提早30分鐘抵達登機門。

搭配詞 boarding gate 登機門

---

glassware [ˋglæs͵wɛr] **n.** 玻璃製品、玻璃器皿 Track 0422

例句 We were extra careful when opening her glassware cabinet.
我們在開她的玻璃櫥櫃時，可是加倍地小心。

搭配詞 glassware cabinet 玻璃櫥櫃

---

hall [hɔl] **n.** 廳、堂 Track 0423

例句 Mayor Ko is fielding questions from journalists at the Taipei City Hall. 柯市長在台北市政府大廳回應記者的問題。

搭配詞 city hall 市政廳

---

hang [hæŋ] **v.** 吊、掛 Track 0424

例句 Hang in there. It will be alright!
堅持下去，事情會好轉的。

搭配詞 hang in there 堅持下去

---

heap [hip] **n.** 積累、一堆 Track 0425

例句 Olivia got heaps of clothes to wash.
奧莉薇雅有一大堆衣服要洗。

搭配詞 heaps of 一大堆

---

hive [haɪv] **n.** 蜂巢、鬧區 Track 0426

例句 There's a bee hive in the backyard. Steer clear of it and you'll be fine. 後院有個蜂巢，離它遠一點就沒事。

易混淆字 have 擁有

---

hometown [ˋhomˋtaʊn] **n.** 家鄉 Track 0427

例句 I would love to show you around my beautiful hometown.
我很樂意帶你參觀我美麗的家鄉。

同義字 homeland

hostel [ˋhɑstl̩] n. 青年旅社 ◀Track 0428

例句 I must find a hostel for the night.
我得找個青年旅社晚上住。

易混淆字
hostile 有敵意的

---

hotel [hoˋtɛl] n. 旅館 ◀Track 0429

例句 The luxury hotel was built by Donald Trump.
這間五星級酒店是唐納・川普蓋的。

搭配詞
luxury hotel 五星級酒店

---

house [haʊs] n. 房子、住宅 ◀Track 0430

例句 The agreement between the two companies is like a house of cards, for it's not legally-binding.
這兩家公司之間的協定就像紙牌屋，因為該協定並無法律約束力。

搭配詞
house of cards 紙牌屋（極易出問題的計劃）

---

housing [ˋhaʊzɪŋ] n. 住宅的供給、住宅 ◀Track 0431

例句 Housing prices have kept rising over the past 30 years.
過去30年來，房價一直在上漲。

搭配詞
housing price 房價

---

hut [hʌt] n. 小屋、茅舍 ◀Track 0432

例句 There is a little wooden hut in the forest.
樹林裡有個小木屋。

易混淆字
nut 核桃

---

immigrate [ˋɪməˏgret] v. 遷移、移入 ◀Track 0433

例句 My brother wants to immigrate to France.
我哥哥想移民到法國去。

反義字
emmigrate 移出

---

indoor [ˋɪnˏdor] adj. 屋內的、室內的 ◀Track 0434

例句 I like indoor activities, such as playing Monopoly and Legos.
我喜歡室內活動，例如玩大富翁、樂高。

搭配詞
indoor activity 室內活動

---

indoors [ˏɪnˋdorz] adv. 在室內 ◀Track 0435

例句 A patient should stay indoors.
病人該待在室內才對。

反義字
outdoors 在戶外

---

inhabit [ɪnˋhæbɪt] v. 居住 ◀Track 0436

例句 Only a few people inhabit this district.
只有一點點人居住在這一區。

同義字
dwell

---

inhabitant [ɪnˋhæbətənt] n. 居民 ◀Track 0437

例句 They are the indigenous inhabitants of this town.
他們是這個城鎮的原生居民。

搭配詞
indigenous inhabitant 原生居民

island [ˋaɪlənd] n. 島、安全島 Track 0438

例句 You can't park a bike on the traffic island.
你不能把腳踏車停在安全島上。

搭配詞 traffic island 安全島

item [ˋaɪtəm] n. 項目、物品 Track 0439

例句 My mom keeps her jewelry and other luxury items in a safe.
我媽媽把她的珠寶和其它奢華的物品放在保險箱。

搭配詞 luxury item 奢華的物品

junk [dʒʌŋk] n. 垃圾 Track 0440

例句 My mom doesn't allow me to eat junk food.
我媽媽不准我吃垃圾食物。

搭配詞 junk food 垃圾食物

kitchen [ˋkɪtʃɪn] n. 廚房 Track 0441

例句 The company produces smart kitchen appliances.
這家公司生產智慧型廚房電器。

搭配詞 kitchen appliance 廚房電器

ladder [ˋlædɚ] n. 梯子 Track 0442

例句 He fell down when climbing a ladder.
他爬梯子時摔下來了。

搭配詞 climb a ladder 爬梯子

lamp [læmp] n. 燈 Track 0443

例句 The street lamp is not working.
街燈壞了。

易混淆字 lame 跛的

layout [ˋle͵aut] n. 規劃、佈局 Track 0444

例句 What is the layout of this building?
這棟大樓的佈局是什麼樣子？

同義字 blueprint

length [lɛŋθ] n. 長度 Track 0445

例句 The desk is about three feet in length.
這張書桌大約三尺長。

搭配詞 in length 長度

light [laɪt] n. 光、燈 Track 0446

例句 It's peach-dark. Turn on the light.
這裡一片漆黑，把燈打開。

搭配詞 turn on the light 把燈打開

lobby [ˋlɑbɪ] n. 休息室、大廳 Track 0447

例句 The departure lobby is on the second floor of Terminal 1.
出境大廳在第一航廈的2樓。

搭配詞 departure lobby 出境大廳

local [ˋlokḷ] adj. 當地的 Track 0448

例句 Jim is the editor-in-chief of a local paper.
吉姆是地方小報的主編。

搭配詞
local paper 地方小報

locate [ˋloket] v. 位於、定位 Track 0449

例句 I can't locate their secret hideout on the map.
我無法在地圖上找到他們祕密基地的位置。

反義字
displace 移開

lock [lɑk] n. 鎖 Track 0450

例句 Go and buy a new electronic lock; yours is broken.
去買個新的電子鎖啊，你的壞了。

搭配詞
electronic lock 電子鎖

lodge [lɑdʒ] n. 小屋 Track 0451

例句 Where is the ski lodge we're going to stay in?
我們要住的滑雪小屋在哪？

搭配詞
ski lodge 滑雪小屋

lofty [ˋlɔftɪ] adj. 非常高的、高聳的 Track 0452

＊字尾-y有轉變為形容詞之意

例句 Unfortunately, his lofty ideals don't work in reality.
可惜的是，他的崇高理想無法在現實生活中實現。

搭配詞
lofty ideals 崇高理想

lotion [ˋloʃən] n. 藥膏、乳液 Track 0453

例句 Remember to apply some suntan lotion when you go to the beach.
去海邊玩時，記得要擦防曬乳液。

搭配詞
suntan lotion 防曬乳液

mansion [ˋmænʃən] n. 宅邸、大廈 Track 0454

例句 Our executive mansion is located on the Downing Street.
我們的行政大樓位在唐寧街。

搭配詞
executive mansion
行政大樓

marble [ˋmɑrbḷ] n. 大理石 Track 0455

例句 I saw a huge marble statue on the way here.
我在來的路上看到一座巨大的大理石雕像。

易混淆字
marvel 令人驚奇的事

mat [ˋmæt] n. 墊子 Track 0456

例句 She asked for a mat because the floor is too cold.
因為地上太冷了，她去要了一個墊子。

易混淆字
mate 同伴

match [mætʃ] v./n. 搭配 Track 0457

例句 Keith believed he had found his perfect match—a 30-year-old secretary working in the White House. 凱斯相信他已找到理想的另一伴了——一位年約30歲在白宮擔任秘書的小姐。

搭配詞
perfect match
絕配、完美情人

mattress [ˋmætrɪs] n. 床墊 Track 0458

例句 Could you please give me a new foam mattress? This one is terrible.
可以再給我一個新的乳膠床墊嗎？這個好糟。

搭配詞 foam mattress 乳膠床墊

mental [ˋmɛntḷ] adj. 心理的、心智的 Track 0459

例句 Parents should pay attention to the children's mental health.
父母應該要關心孩子的心理健康才對。

搭配詞 mental health 心理健康

mess [mɛs] n. 雜亂 Track 0460

例句 After his girlfriend left, his life has been in a mess.
他的女朋友跟他分手後，他的生活就陷入一團混亂。

搭配詞 in a mess 一團雜亂

messy [ˋmɛsɪ] adj. 凌亂的 Track 0461

＊字尾-y有轉變為形容詞之意

例句 Your bedroom is messy, but mine is no better.
你的臥室很亂，但我的也沒好到哪去。

反義字 orderly 井然有序的

migrate [ˋmaɪgret] v. 遷徙、移居 Track 0462

例句 Why do the birds migrate to the south?
鳥兒們為什麼要遷徙到南方呢？

反義字 remain 逗留

migration [maɪˋgreʃən] n. 遷移 Track 0463

＊字尾-tion有轉變為名詞的意思

例句 She is interested in the pattern of animal migration.
她對動物遷徙的方式很有興趣。

搭配詞 migrant bird 候鳥

mop [mɑp] n. 拖把 v. 拖地 Track 0464

例句 My mother mops the floor every day.
我媽天天拖地。

搭配詞 mop the floor 拖地

motel [moˋtɛl] n. 汽車旅館 Track 0465

例句 Would you please tell me where the nearest villa motel is?
你可以告訴我最近的渡假汽車旅館在哪嗎？

搭配詞 villa motel 渡假汽車旅館

mug [mʌg] n. 帶柄的大杯子、馬克杯 Track 0466

例句 I can't find my mug. Please tell me you didn't break it!
我找不到我的馬克杯。你可沒打破它對吧！

易混淆字 mud 泥土

narrow [ˋnæro] adj. 窄的、狹長的 Track 0467

例句 Alice doesn't have any friends because she is very narrow-minded.
艾莉絲沒有朋友，因為她心胸太狹窄了。

搭配詞 narrow-minded 心胸狹窄的

neat [nit] adj. 整潔的 Track 0468

例句 Her handwriting is always neat.
她寫的字總是很整齊。

同義字
tidy

neighbor [ˋnebɚ] n. 鄰居 Track 0469

例句 People rarely talk to their neighbors now.
現在的人很少和鄰居交談了。

neighborhood [ˋnebɚ͵hʊd] n. 社區 Track 0470

例句 There is a supermarket in this neighborhood.
這個社區有家超市。

搭配詞
in the neighborhood
在附近

ornament [ˋɔrnəmənt] n. 裝飾（品） Track 0471

＊字尾-ment有轉變為名詞之意

例句 The ornaments on my grandma's kitchen wall were stolen.
外婆家廚房牆上的裝飾品被偷了。

同義字
decoration

owner [ˋonɚ] n. 物主、所有者 Track 0472

＊字尾-er有轉變為名詞的意思

例句 Do you know the owner of this key?
你知道這鑰匙的主人是誰嗎？

同義字
possessor

pad [pæd] n. 墊子、印臺 Track 0473

例句 Wow, look! Her swimsuit bra pads are floating in the sea!
哇，快看！她的泳衣胸墊在海上漂呢！

paint [pent] n./v. 顏料、油漆 Track 0474

例句 If you use the right paint brush, you can get the job done faster.
如果你用對油漆刷，很快就漆完了。

搭配詞
paint brush 油漆刷

parlor [ˋpɑrlɚ] n. 客廳、起居室 Track 0475

例句 Emma went to a beauty parlor to have a facial.
艾瑪去美容院做臉。

搭配詞
beauty parlor 美容院

pillar [ˋpɪlɚ] n. 樑柱、棟樑 Track 0476

例句 The memorial pillar was built to commemorate soldiers who died during the war.
這個紀念柱是為了紀念在戰爭失去性命的軍人所建的。

搭配詞
memorial pillar 紀念柱

pillow [ˋpɪlo] n. 枕頭 Track 0477

例句 I threw a pillow at his head.
我拿一個枕頭丟向他的頭。

易混淆字
willow 柳樹

populate [ˋpɑpjəˏlet] v. 居住 Track 0478

例句 The city is heavily populated by immigrants.
這個城市裡居住著許多移民人口。

同義字 inhabit

porcelain/china [ˋpɔrslɪn]/[ˋtʃaɪnə] n. 瓷器 Track 0479

例句 The antique porcelain doll is my grandpa's favorite.
這個古董瓷器娃娃是我爺爺的最愛。

搭配詞 antique porcelain 古董瓷器

porch [portʃ] n. 玄關、入口處、門廊 Track 0480

例句 Don't sit in the porch; it's too cold.
別在玄關坐著，太冷了。

搭配詞 front porch 前門玄關

pottery/ceramics [ˋpɑtərɪ]/[səˋræmɪks] Track 0481

n. 陶器 ＊字尾-s有轉變為複數之意

例句 I brought this pottery bowl from a handicraft shop.
我在一家手工藝店買了這個陶碗。

property [ˋprɑpətɪ] n. 財產 Track 0482

例句 Real estate properties in the center of Beijing is becoming more expensive. 北京中心的房產已經越來越貴了。

易混淆字 properly 恰當地

proposal [prəˋpozḷ] n. 提議、求婚 Track 0483

例句 Dan was devastated when his girlfriend rejected his proposal.
丹向女友求婚卻被拒絕，感到傷心欲絕。

搭配詞 reject a proposal 拒絕求婚

quilt [kwɪlt] n. 棉被 Track 0484

例句 The wool quilt is thick enough for me.
這羊毛被對我來說夠厚了。

搭配詞 wool quilt 羊毛被

refrigerator/icebox [rɪˋfrɪdʒəˏretə]/[ˋaɪsˏbɑks] Track 0485

n. 冰箱

例句 I want a refrigerator like yours.
我想要一台像你一樣的冰箱。

縮寫 fridge

rent [rɛnt] n. 租金 Track 0486

例句 I think the rent is too expensive.
我覺得房租太貴了。

易混淆字 rant 大聲嚷嚷

residential [ˏrɛzəˋdɛnʃəl] adj. 居住的 Track 0487

＊字尾-ial有轉變為形容詞之意

例句 This is a residential area. 這是個住宅區。

搭配詞 residential building 住宅用建築

reside [rɪˋzaɪd] v. 居住 Track 0488

例句 Our family has resided in France for 10 years.
我們家已經在法國住十年了。

同義字 live

---

residence [ˋrɛzədəns] n. 住家 Track 0489

＊字尾-ence有轉變為名詞之意

例句 The professor rarely invites people to his residence.
這位教授很少邀請人去他家。

---

resident [ˋrɛzədənt] n. 居民 Track 0490

＊字尾-ent有轉變為名詞之意

例句 There are many local residents attending his party.
有很多當地居民參加他的派對。

搭配詞 local resident 當地居民

---

restroom [ˋrɛstˌrum] n. 洗手間、廁所 Track 0491

例句 Would you tell me where the restroom is?
你可以跟我說廁所在哪嗎？

同義字 bathroom

---

rid [rɪd] v. 擺脫、除去 Track 0492

例句 Let's get rid of the old books.
我們把舊書丟掉吧。

搭配詞 get rid of 除去

---

roof [ruf] n. 屋頂、車頂 Track 0493

例句 Let's have a picnic on top of the roof.
我們在屋頂上野餐吧。

---

room [rum] n. 房間、室 Track 0494

例句 Melania explained what her husband said was just a locker room banter. 梅蘭妮亞解釋，她先生所說的話只是更衣室裡的插科打諢。

搭配詞 locker room 更衣室

---

rug [rʌg] n. 地毯 Track 0495

例句 She spilled grape juice all over the bath rug.
她把葡萄汁倒得整個浴室地毯都是。

搭配詞 bath rug 浴室地毯

---

scrub [skrʌb] v. 擦拭、擦洗 Track 0496

例句 Some people have hyper sensitive skin, and can't use any scrub creams. 有些人是超敏感肌膚，不能用任何的磨砂膏。

搭配詞 scrub cream 磨砂膏

---

separate [ˋsɛpəˌret] adj. 分開的 Track 0497

例句 Would you please give us separate bedrooms?
你可以提供我們個別的臥室嗎？

反義字 unite 聯合的

a b c d e f g h i j k l m n o p q r s t u v w x y z

settle [ˋsɛtḷ] v. 安排、解決、穩定 Track 0498

例句 Jack considers settling down. After all, he's 35.
傑克想要定下來，畢竟他已經35歲了。

搭配詞 settle down 穩定下來

shampoo [ʃæmˋpu] n. 洗髮精 Track 0499

例句 Which kind of anti-dandruff shampoo do you prefer?
你喜歡哪種的去頭皮屑洗髮精？

搭配詞 anti-dandruff shampoo 去頭皮屑洗髮精

sheet [ʃit] n. 床單、紙 Track 0500

例句 His face was white as a sheet when he learned his mom was diagnosed with cancer. 他得知他媽媽罹癌時，臉色變得慘白。

搭配詞 white as a sheet 蒼白如紙

shelf [ʃɛlf] n. 棚架、架子 Track 0501

例句 She puts a photo on the book shelf.
她在書架上放一張照片。

搭配詞 book shelf 書架

shelter [ˋʃɛltɚ] n. 避難所、庇護所 Track 0502

例句 Civilians ran to hide in a bomb shelter when the Code Red alert siren sounded across a number of communities. 民眾聽到防空警報在多個社區間響起時，便紛紛跑到防空避難所躲起來。

搭配詞 bomb shelter 防空避難所

shutter [ˋʃʌtɚ] n. 百葉窗 Track 0503

＊字尾-er有轉變為名詞的意思

例句 Can you open the wooden shutters for me?
你可以幫我開一下木製百葉窗嗎？

搭配詞 wooden shutter 木製百葉窗

sit [sɪt] v. 坐 Track 0504

例句 Sit down, please.
請坐下。

搭配詞 sit down 坐下

skyscraper [ˋskaɪˏskrepɚ] n. 摩天大樓 Track 0505

＊字尾-er有轉變為名詞的意思

例句 The skyscraper ad is very attention-grabbing.
摩天大樓上的廣告很醒目。

搭配詞 skyscraper ad 登在摩天大樓上的廣告

sleep [slip] v. 睡 Track 0506

例句 I slept over at my friend's house last night.
我昨晚在朋友家過夜。

搭配詞 sleep over 在別人家過夜

soap [sop] n. 肥皂 Track 0507

例句 I usually watch Korean soap opera after work.
我下班後通常會看韓劇。

搭配詞 soap opera 肥皂劇

sofa [ˋsofə] n. 沙發 ◀ Track 0508

例句 My wife wants to put a sofa bed in the room.
我太太想在房間裡放一張沙發床。

搭配詞
sofa bed 沙發床

solitude [ˋsɑlə͵tjud] n. 獨處、獨居 ◀ Track 0509

例句 Do you like living in solitude?
你喜歡獨居嗎？

搭配詞
in solitude

spacious [ˋspeʃəs] adj. 寬敞的、寬廣的 ◀ Track 0510

＊字尾-ious有轉變為形容詞之意

例句 The room that I found is not only spacious but also comfortable.
我找到的房間不但寬敞又舒服。

同義字
roomy

spit [spɪt] v. 吐口水 ◀ Track 0511

例句 Don't spit on the street.
別在大街上吐口水。

易混淆字
spot 污漬

spotlight [ˋspɑt͵laɪt] n. 聚光燈、焦點 ◀ Track 0512

例句 Betty complained that her brother stole the spotlight from her at her birthday party.
貝蒂抱怨弟弟在她的生日派對，搶走了焦點。

搭配詞
steal the spotlight 搶走焦點

stair [stɛr] n. 樓梯 ◀ Track 0513

例句 She was out of breath after climbing up the spiral stairs.
她爬上螺旋式樓梯後喘不過氣來。

搭配詞
spiral stair 螺旋式樓梯

steady [ˋstɛdɪ] adj. 穩固的、穩定的 ◀ Track 0514

例句 Please hold the ladder steady for him.
請幫他把梯子抓穩。

反義字
unsteady 不穩定的

stiff [stɪf] n. 僵硬的 ◀ Track 0515

例句 Sitting for too long can lead to a stiff back.
坐太久可能導致背脊僵硬。

搭配詞
stiff back 僵硬背脊

stink [stɪŋk] v. 發出惡臭、臭 ◀ Track 0516

例句 There's a stink bug in my house. No wonder it stinks!
我的房子有臭蟲，難怪這麼臭。

搭配詞
stink bug 臭蟲

stool [stul] n. 凳子 ◀ Track 0517

例句 The little girl sat waiting for her mother on the stool.
小女孩坐在凳子上等她媽媽。

易混淆字
tool 工具

suburb [ˋsʌbɝb] n. 市郊、郊區 Track 0518
＊字首sub-有「下層的、次要的」之意
例句 My wife wants to move to the suburbs.
我太太想搬去郊區。

反義字
center 中心

suburban [səˋbɝbən] adj. 郊外的、市郊的 Track 0519
＊字首sub-有「下層的、次要的」之意
例句 I like to live in a suburban area. 我喜歡住在郊區。

搭配詞
suburban area 郊區

suite [swit] n. 套房 Track 0520
例句 Would you please book a suite for me?
你可以幫我訂一間套房嗎？

易混淆字
suit 套裝

surroundings [səˋraʊndɪŋz] n. 環境、周圍 Track 0521
例句 Can you adapt to new surroundings quickly?
你能很快地習慣新環境嗎？

sweep [swip] v. 掃、打掃 Track 0522
例句 Can you sweep away the dead cockroach?
你可以把死蟑螂掃走嗎？

搭配詞
sweep away 掃走

switch [swɪtʃ] n./v. 開關 Track 0523
例句 He switched on a light and looked around.
他開燈，並環視四周。

搭配詞
switch on 開關打開

table [ˋtebl̩] n. 桌子 Track 0524
例句 There is a cup of tea on the lunch table.
午餐餐桌上有一杯茶。

搭配詞
lunch table 午餐餐桌

terrace [ˋtɛrəs] n. 房屋的平頂、陽臺、梯田 Track 0525
例句 We have a terrace house in the suburban area.
我們家在郊區有間有陽台的房子

搭配詞
terrace house
有陽台的房子

tidy [ˋtaɪdɪ] adj. 整潔的 Track 0526
例句 Keep your room tidy and put everything in order.
請保持你的房間整潔，把所有東西放整齊。

同義字
neat

tile [taɪl] n. 磚瓦 Track 0527
例句 These ceramic tiles look sleek and stylish.
這些瓷磚看起來很光亮、時尚。

搭配詞
ceramic tile 瓷磚

tissue [ˋtɪʃʊ] **n.** 面紙 ◀Track 0528

例句 She cried so hard that she used up all the tissues.
她哭得太厲害，衛生紙都用光了。

toilet [ˋtɔɪlɪt] **n.** 洗手間、馬桶 ◀Track 0529

例句 Please flush the toilet after you use it.
用完馬桶請沖水。

同義字 loo 廁所（英國）

towel [taʊl] **n.** 毛巾 ◀Track 0530

例句 Don't forget to bring a towel with you to the swimming pool.
去游泳池可別忘了帶一條毛巾。

易混淆字 tower 塔

trash [træʃ] **n.** 垃圾 ◀Track 0531

例句 Can you take out the trash for me?
幫我把垃圾拿出去倒好不好？

同義字 rubbish

tray [tre] **n.** 托盤 ◀Track 0532

例句 Put the cup on the tea tray.
把茶杯放在茶盤上。

搭配詞 tea tray 茶盤

trim [trɪm] **v.** 使整齊、修整 ◀Track 0533

例句 He should get his hair trimmed.
他該去把頭髮修一修了。

unlock [ʌnˋlɑk] **v.** 開鎖、揭開 ◀Track 0534

＊字首un-有「不、反」之意

例句 Can you unlock the door for me? I forgot my keys.
你可以幫我開鎖嗎？我忘記帶鑰匙了。

反義字 lock 上鎖

unpack [ʌnˋpæk] **v.** 卸下、打開行李 ◀Track 0535

＊字首un-有「不、反」之意

例句 Let's unpack after we get home.
我們回家再打開行李吧。

同義字 unload

vase [ves] **n.** 花瓶 ◀Track 0536

例句 Put the flowers in the porcelain vase.
把花放進陶瓷花瓶吧。

搭配詞 porcelain vase 陶瓷花瓶

villa [ˋvɪlə] **n.** 別墅 ◀Track 0537

例句 The villa is famous for its beautiful surroundings.
這別墅因周遭環境很美而出名。

village [ˋvɪlɪdʒ] n. 村莊 ◀Track 0538

例句 As a member of the global village, we should try to protect our environment. 身為地球村的一員，我們應善盡保護環境之責。

搭配詞 global village 地球村

wall [wɔl] n. 牆壁 ◀Track 0539

例句 I want to hang the painting on the wall.
我想在牆上掛上這幅畫。

wash [wɑʃ] v. 洗、洗滌 ◀Track 0540

例句 Would you help me wash the dishes, honey?
親愛的，幫我洗碗好嗎？

搭配詞 wash dishes 洗碗

wide [waɪd] adj. 寬廣的 ◀Track 0541

例句 The road isn't wide enough for the car to go through.
路不夠寬，車子過不去。

同義字 broad

width [wɪdθ] n. 寬、廣 ◀Track 0542

例句 Do you know the width of the street?
你知道這條街多寬嗎？

反義字 depth 縱、深

window [ˋwɪndo] n. 窗戶 ◀Track 0543

例句 You can see a park from the window.
你可以從窗戶那邊看到一個公園。

易混淆字 widow 寡婦

wipe [waɪp] v. 擦、消除、拭去 ◀Track 0544

例句 He wiped away Jenny's tears, telling her it wasn't her fault.
他擦掉珍妮的眼淚，並告訴她這不是她的錯。

搭配詞 wipe one's tears away 擦拭某人的眼淚

yard [jɑrd] n. 庭院、院子 ◀Track 0545

例句 My mother planted lots of cabbages in our back yard.
我媽媽在後院裡種了很多包心菜。

搭配詞 back yard 後院

Test 03 關鍵英單總測驗第3回

以下測驗題皆出自書中第三回「**和住有關的單字**」，快來檢視自己的學習成果吧！

一、選擇題

1. Alan sat in the ____ and smoked.
   (A) porch
   (B) quilt
   (C) vase
   (D) table

2. Your room ________. Take out the garbage right now.
   (A) stiff
   (B) neat
   (C) stinks
   (D) comfortable

3. The Neuschwanstein ____ is a beautiful tourist destination.
   (A) dust
   (B) cassette
   (C) Castle
   (D) match

4. The billionaire owns three ____ in New York.
   (A) tissues
   (B) mansions
   (C) separate
   (D) roofs

5. My mother goes to a beauty _____ to have a facial every Saturday.
   (A) pillow
   (B) lotion
   (C) hall
   (D) parlor

6. They like the ____ of the house.
   (A) hut
   (B) immigrate
   (C) lofty
   (D) layout

7. He found a chest in the ____ that contained his grandmother's jewelry.
   (A) bay
   (B) chore
   (C) faucet
   (D) attic

8. It's important that we should protect our _____ from being polluted.
   (A) gate
   (B) fireplace
   (C) shampoo
   (D) environment

9. He offered the refugees a _____ from the oppression of their fascist leader.
   (A) skyscraper
   (B) lock
   (C) shelter
   (D) dome

10. She _____ her room with Millet's paintings.
    (A) decorated
    (B) echoed
    (C) hanged
    (D) dwelled

二、克漏字測驗

Due to high housing prices, many people cannot afford a __1__. As a result, they can only rent a suite or an __2__ and live in cramped conditions.

Some people claim that the problem is caused mainly by low wages and speculative investors. In fact, when you walk around at night, you'll find that many expensive __3__ almost disappear in the dark, with only a handful of windows lit by people __4__ within.

So why don't __5__ developers build affordable houses to meet the market demand? The answer is simple—profits. Unless stronger regulations are introduced, young people will only be left with little hope that they will ever have a home of their own.

1. (A) island
   (B) house
   (C) ladder
   (D) neighborhood

2. (A) mansion
   (B) apartment
   (C) balcony
   (D) restroom

3. (A) hostels
   (B) shelves
   (C) marble
   (D) buildings

4. (A) residing
   (B) costly
   (C) painting
   (D) asleep

5. (A) environment
   (B) property
   (C) cushion
   (D) fence

關鍵英單總測驗第3回
中譯與解答

一、選擇題

1. 艾倫坐在門廊前抽烟。
   (A) 門廊
   (B) 棉被
   (C) 花瓶
   (D) 餐桌

2. 你的房間發臭了，現在就把垃圾拿去丟掉。
   (A) 僵硬
   (B) 乾淨的
   (C) 發臭
   (D) 舒服的

3. 新天鵝堡是美麗的觀光景點。
   (A) 灰塵
   (B) 卡帶
   (C) 城堡
   (D) 搭配

4. 這個億萬富翁在紐約有3間豪宅。
   (A) 衛生紙
   (B) 豪宅
   (C) 分開的
   (D) 屋頂

5. 我媽媽每週六都會去美容院做臉。
   (A) 枕頭
   (B) 乳液
   (C) 大廳
   (D) 店鋪

6. 他們很喜歡房子的格局。
   (A) 小木屋
   (B) 移民
   (C) 崇高的
   (D) 格局

7. 他在閣樓發現一只木盒，裡面裝著祖母留下來的珠寶。
   (A) 海灣
   (B) 雜事
   (C) 水籠頭
   (D) 閣樓

8. 保護環境不受污染，人人有責。
   (A) 閘門
   (B) 火爐
   (C) 洗髮精
   (D) 環境

9. 他提供難民庇護所，以躲避法西斯主義領袖的壓迫。
   (A) 摩天大樓
   (B) 鎖
   (C) 庇護所
   (D) 拱圓形屋頂

10. 她用米勒的畫來裝飾她的房間。
   (A) 裝飾
   (B) 回音
   (C) 懸掛
   (D) 居住

二、克漏字測驗

由於高房價，許多人買不起房子。他們因此只能租間小套房或公寓，住在狹小的空間裡。

有些人認為居住問題的主因是低薪和投資客。事實上，當你晚上走一圈，並稍加觀察，便會發現許多高價的建築物幾乎消失在夜色中，只有少數幾戶人家的窗戶是有光透出來的。

所以，為何建商不蓋人們買得起的房子來因應市場需求呢?答案很簡單，利潤使然。除非引用更嚴格的法規，否則年輕人想擁有自己房子的希望非常渺茫。

1.
(1) 島嶼
(2) 房子
(3) 階梯
(4) 社區

2.
(A) 豪宅
(B) 公寓
(C) 陽台
(D) 廁所

3.
(A) 青年旅舍
(B) 架子
(C) 大理石
(D) 建築物

4.
(A) 住在
(B) 昂貴的
(C) 上油漆
(D) 睡著的

5.
(A) 環境
(B) 房產
(C) 墊子
(D) 籬笆

一、選擇題

1.(A) 2. (C) 3.(C) 4.(B) 5.(D)
6.(D) 7. (D) 8.(D) 9.(C) 10. (A)

二、克漏字測驗

1.(B) 2.(B) 3.(D)
4.(A) 5.(B)

Unit 04 和行有關的單字

多益測驗的命題強調生活化與實用性，學會這些與「行」有關的單字，不僅能讓你在多益考場上所向披靡，在日常生活上也可以靈活運用喔！

描述旅行的目的地可以這麼說

- **I always want to go to Barcelona to see the magnificent Sagrada Família.**
  我一直都很想去巴塞隆納參觀壯觀的聖家堂。
- **We booked the famous Nile River Cruise to explore the land of Pharaohs.**
  我們訂了有名的尼羅河遊輪行程探索法老的國度。
- **Napa Valley is known for vineyard and wine production.**
  納帕山谷以酒莊與紅酒製造而聞名。

交通安全注意事項可以這麼說

- **Please fasten your seat belt.**
  請繫好安全帶。
- **Please remain calm when emergency event occurs.**
  當緊急情況發生時，請勿驚慌。

到了機場可以這麼說

- **Budget airlines' check-in counters are at terminal 2.**
  廉價航空的報到櫃台在第二航廈。
- **Please check your luggage before you leave the baggage claim area.**
  請在離開行李領取區之前確認好您的行李。

跟團出遊可以這麼說

- **We wlll assemble at the train station, and then go to the airport by bus.**
  我們會先在火車站集合，然後搭巴士到機場。
- **I just confirmed with the travel agency that our trip would be postponed due to new COVID restriction.**
  我剛才和旅行社確認過了，我們的行程因為新的疫情出入境限制延期了。

旅行途中可以這麼說

- **I'll send you a postcard when I arrive.**
  等我抵達目的地，我會寄一張明信片給你。
- **Since we are here, we must visit the ocean park.**
  既然我們都已經在這裡了，我們一定要去參觀海洋公園。

Unit 04 和行有關的單字

aboard [əˋbord] adv. 在船（飛機、火車）上 Track 0546

例句 Passengers with small children are allowed to come aboard first.
帶著小朋友的乘客，可以先登機。

易混淆字 abroad 在國外

---

access [ˋæksɛs] Track 0547

n./v. 接近、通道、入口、連接權、使用權

例句 I have full access to the company's database.
我有公司資料庫的完整使用權。

搭配詞 internet access 連接網路

---

accident [ˋæksədənt] n. 事故、偶發事件 Track 0548

例句 She got in a car accident this morning and couldn't come to the meeting. 她早上遇到了一點車禍事故，無法來參加會議。

搭配詞 car accident 車禍事故

---

accompany [əˋkʌmpənɪ] v. 隨行、陪伴、伴隨 Track 0549

例句 Can you accompany grandma to the park?
你能陪奶奶去公園嗎？

易混淆字 company 公司

---

across [əˋkrɔs] prep. 橫過、在……對面 Track 0550

例句 She waved at the man across the street.
她和對街的男子揮手。

搭配詞 across the street 對街

---

address [əˋdrɛs] n. 住址 Track 0551

例句 You can send your request to this email address.
你可以把你的需求寄到這個電子郵件地址給我們。

搭配詞 mail address 郵件地址

---

admission [ədˋmɪʃən] Track 0552

adv./prep. 准許進入、入場費　＊字尾-sion有轉變為名詞的意思

例句 Law school admission requirements vary from school to school.
法學院入學要求的標準，各校不同。

搭配詞 school admission 入學許可

---

advance [ədˋvæns] n. 前進、先前 Track 0553

例句 You need to book seats at the restaurant for Valentine's Day in advance. 你得預先為了情人節在那家餐廳訂位。

搭配詞 in advance 事先

---

adventure [əd`vɛntʃɚ] n. 冒險 Track 0554

例句 How I miss the adventure stories my grandfather told me.
我真懷念阿公以前跟我說的冒險故事。

搭配詞 adventure story 冒險故事

aircraft [`ɛr͵kræft] n. 飛機、飛行器 Track 0555

例句 What model of aircraft is this? 這是哪種機型的飛機？

同義字 airplane

airline [`ɛr͵laɪn] n. （飛機）航線、航空公司 Track 0556

例句 There are several budget airlines that fly from Auckland to London every day. 有很多廉價航空公司天天從奧克蘭飛到倫敦。

搭配詞 budget airline 廉價航空

airmail [`ɛr͵mel] n. 航空郵件 Track 0557

例句 How much does this parcel cost if I send it by airmail?
如果我用航空郵件寄這個包裹，要多少錢？

airplane/plane [`ɛr͵plen]/[plen] n. 飛機 Track 0558

例句 We went to Kaohsiung by airplane.
我們搭飛機去高雄。

搭配詞 by airplane 搭飛機

airport [`ɛr͵port] n. 機場 Track 0559

例句 It takes about one hour to drive from the international airport to our city. 從國際機場開車到我們的城市，要大概一個小時。

相關字 concourse 機場中央大廳

airtight [`ɛr͵taɪt] adj. 密閉的、氣密的 Track 0560

例句 Mom keeps food in the airtight container to keep it fresh.
媽媽把食物放在密閉保鮮盒以維持新鮮。

搭配詞 airtight container 保鮮盒

airway [`ɛr͵we] n. 空中航線、航空公司、呼吸道 Track 0561

例句 Thank you for traveling with British Airways.
謝謝您搭乘英國航空。

aisle [aɪl] n. 教堂的側廊、通道 Track 0562

例句 I prefer the aisle seat as I go to the restroom often.
我經常上廁所，所以我比較想要走道的位子。

搭配詞 aisle seat 靠走道位

alley [`ælɪ] n. 巷、小徑 Track 0563

例句 The cat lives in the alley.
那隻貓就住在這條巷子裡。

易混淆字 ally 同盟國

along [ə`lɔŋ] adv. 向前、沿著 Track 0564

例句 Walk along the street then turn left. You'll see that KFC is on your right-hand side.
沿著這條路直走，接著左轉，你就會看到肯德基在你的右手邊。

搭配詞 walk along 沿著……走路

altitude [`æltə,tjud] n. 高度、海拔 Track 0565

例句 The current altitude we're at is around 14,000 meters.
我們現在所在的海拔是大約14,000公尺。

易混淆字 attitude 態度

ample [`æmp!] adj. 充分的、廣闊的 Track 0566

例句 You'll have ample opportunities to ask questions after the talk.
演講完後，你們會有充分的機會可以問問題。

搭配詞 ample reason 充分的理由

anchor [`æŋkɚ] n. 錨狀物 Track 0567

例句 He tossed the boat anchor into the water; they were here to stay for the night. 他把船錨扔進水裡；他們今晚要在這裡過夜了。

搭配詞 boat anchor 船錨

Antarctic/antarctic [æn`tɑrktɪk] Track 0568
adj. 南極洲的

例句 I can't imagine what life must be like in the Antarctic circle.
我真難想像南極圈裡的生活會是什麼樣子。

搭配詞 Antarctic circle 南極圈

anywhere/anyplace [`ɛnɪ,hwɛr]/[`ɛnɪ,ples] Track 0569
adv. 任何地方

例句 It is raining outside; we cannot go anywhere.
外面在下雨，我們哪裡也不能去。

搭配詞 go anywhere 去任何地方

apart [ə`pɑrt] adv. 分散地、遠離地 Track 0570

例句 No one can tear the lovers apart.
沒有人能拆散這對情人。

搭配詞 tear apart 拆開

approach [ə`protʃ] v. 接近 Track 0571

例句 Our bus is approaching the beautiful Stonehenge.
我們的遊覽車接近美麗的巨石陣了。

反義字 withdraw 拉開

aquarium [ə`kwɛrɪəm] n. 水族館 Track 0572
＊字首aqua-有「水」之意

例句 We visit the tropical aquarium every summer.
我們每年夏天都到這座熱帶水族館參觀。

搭配詞 tropical aquarium 熱帶水族館

Arctic/arctic [`ɑrktɪk] adj. 北極地區 Track 0573

例句 The icebergs in the Arctic circle are melting due to global warming.
北極圈的冰山因地球暖化而融化。

around [əˋraʊnd] prep./adv. 大約、在周圍、轉 Track 0574

例句 He turned around to make sure that his daughter was around.
他轉身看，以確認女兒還在附近。

搭配詞 turn around 轉身

arrival [əˋraɪvḷ] n. 到達 Track 0575

例句 I'm waiting in the arrival lobby to pick up my brother.
我在入境大廳等著接我弟。

搭配詞 arrival lobby 入境大廳

arrive [əˋraɪv] v. 到達、來臨 Track 0576

例句 After a 10-hour flight, we finally arrived at Hawaii.
飛行十個小時後，我們終於抵達夏威夷。

搭配詞 arrive at 到達

artery [ˋɑrtərɪ] n. 動脈、主要道路 Track 0577

例句 An unhealthy diet may lead to coronary artery diseases.
不健康的飲食會導致冠狀動脈疾病。

搭配詞 coronary artery 冠狀動脈

assemble [əˋsɛmbḷ] v. 聚集、集合 Track 0578

例句 In case of an emergency, students should assemble at the front door. 如果發生意外，學生們須在前門集合。

反義字 disperse 分散

at [æt] prep. 在 Track 0579

例句 The party will be held at noon.
派對將在中午舉辦。

搭配詞 at noon 在中午

attach [əˋtætʃ] v. 連接、附屬、附加 Track 0580

例句 The boy is very attached to his mother.
這個小男孩很黏媽媽。

搭配詞 attach to 附加

auditorium [ˌɔdəˋtorɪəm] n. 禮堂、演講廳 Track 0581

例句 Our school will have a new auditorium next year.
我們學校明年會有新的禮堂。

同義字 hall

automobile [ˋɔtəməˌbil] n. 汽車 Track 0582

＊字首auto-有「自動」之意

例句 The new generation of automobiles is environmentally friendly.
新一代的汽車很環保。

縮寫 auto

avenue [ˋævəˌnju] n. 大道、大街 Track 0583

例句 There are a lot of boutiques on the Fifth Avenue.
第五大道有很多精品店。

搭配詞 Fifth Avenue 第五大道

aviation [͵evɪˋeʃən] n. 航空、飛行 ◀Track 0584
＊字尾-tion有轉變為名詞的意思
例句 Many airlines have tightened their aviation security due to the threat from terrorists.
許多航空公司因為恐怖份子發出威脅，而加強飛航安全。
搭配詞 aviation security 飛航安全

away [əˋwe] adv. 遠離、離開、走開 ◀Track 0585
例句 Could you take away your garbage?
你可以把垃圾帶走嗎？
搭配詞 take away 帶走

baggage [ˋbægɪdʒ] n. 行李 ◀Track 0586
例句 Passengers check in their baggages before boarding the plane.
上飛機前，乘客會先托運行李。
搭配詞 baggage room 行李寄放處

ban [bæn] n. 禁止 ◀Track 0587
例句 Our boss put a ban on smoking in the factory.
我們老闆禁止員工在工廠裡吸煙。
搭配詞 ban on smoking 禁止吸菸

bank [bæŋk] n. 銀行、堤、岸 ◀Track 0588
例句 I just opened a bank account online.
我剛在網路上開了一個銀行帳戶。
搭配詞 bank account 銀行帳戶

beg [bɛg] v. 乞討、懇求 ◀Track 0589
例句 He is begging for her forgiveness.
他在懇求她的原諒。
易混淆字 bag 袋子

besides [bɪˋsaɪdz] adv. 除了……之外 ◀Track 0590
例句 Besides the cake, we need to buy some wine for the party.
除了蛋糕之外，我們還要為派對買點酒。
易混淆字 beside 旁邊

beyond [bɪˋjɑnd] adv. 在遠處、超過 ◀Track 0591
例句 The beauty of the town is beyond our imagination.
這個城鎮的美，超乎我們的想像。
搭配詞 beyond imagination 超乎想像

bicycle/bike [ˋbaɪsɪkḷ]/[baɪk] n. 自行車 ◀Track 0592
＊字首bi-有「兩、雙」之意
例句 I bought a shiny mountain bike for my son.
我為兒子買了台閃亮亮的越野腳踏車。
搭配詞 mountain bike 越野自行車

bill [bɪl] n. 帳單 ◀Track 0593
例句 Let me pay the bill. My treat.
我來付帳單，我請客。
搭配詞 pay a bill 付帳單

block [blɑk] n. 街區、木塊、石塊 Track 0594

例句 The pharmacy is just a block away.
藥房離這裡只有一個街區遠。

易混淆字
black 黑色的

board [bord] n. 板、佈告欄 Track 0595

例句 We have a black board at the community center.
在我們的社區中心有個黑板。

搭配詞
black board 黑板

boat [bot] n. 船 Track 0596

例句 She rowed a boat in a rainy day.
她在下雨天划船。

搭配詞
row a boat 划船

booth [buθ] n. 棚子、攤子 Track 0597

例句 She opened a lemonade stand next to a phone booth.
她在電話亭旁邊開了一個賣檸檬汁的攤子。

搭配詞
phone booth 電話亭

bother [ˋbɑðɚ] v. 打擾、麻煩 Track 0598

例句 It is getting dark, so don't bother to drive me home.
有點晚了，別麻煩了，不用載我回家。

易混淆字
brother 兄弟

boulevard [ˋbuləˏvɑrd] n. 林蔭大道 Track 0599

例句 He lived on the boulevard where most rich people live.
他住在那個很多有錢人住的林蔭大道上。

bow [bau] n. 彎腰、鞠躬 Track 0600

例句 The actors took their bows and left the stage.
演員們鞠躬後就下台了。

搭配詞
take a bow 鞠躬

brake [brek] v. 煞車 Track 0601

例句 It was reported that the emergency brake didn't work, which caused the accident.
根據報導，由於緊急煞車失靈，導致發生意外。

搭配詞
emergency brake 緊急煞車

bridge [brɪdʒ] n. 橋 Track 0602

例句 Sydney Harbour Bridge is one of the longest bridges in the world.
雪梨港大橋是全世界最長的橋之一。

搭配詞
iron bridge 鐵橋

broad [brɔd] adj. 寬闊的 Track 0603

例句 The new mayor is broad-minded and open to all opinions.
新的市長心胸開闊，接受各種意見。

搭配詞
broad-minded 心胸開闊的

brook [bruk] n. 川、小河、溪流 ◀ Track 0604

例句 There is a brook winding through the forest.
有條溪流從森林中蜿蜒而過。

同義字 stream

bump [bʌmp] v. 碰、撞 ◀ Track 0605

例句 We bumped into the car in front of us because it stopped suddenly.
我們撞到前面的車，因為它忽然停下來。

搭配詞 bump into 碰撞上

bundle [ˋbʌndḷ] n. 捆、包裹 ◀ Track 0606

例句 He came in carrying a bundle of clothes.
他抱著一大包衣服走進來。

搭配詞 a bundle of 一大包

bus [bʌs] n. 公車 ◀ Track 0607

例句 With a smart phone, you can find the nearest bus stop in just a few seconds.
運用智慧型手機，你在幾秒內就能找到離你最近的公車站。

搭配詞 bus stop 公車站

call [kɔl] n./v. 呼叫、打電話 ◀ Track 0608

例句 Please give me a phone call if you need any help.
你需要幫忙的話，請打通電話給我。

搭配詞 phone call 一通電話

campus [ˋkæmpəs] n. 校區、校園 ◀ Track 0609

例句 We'd better follow the campus rules in order to stay away from trouble. 我們最好遵守校規，以免惹麻煩。

搭配詞 campus rules 校規

canal [kəˋnæl] n. 運河、人工渠道 ◀ Track 0610

例句 The Panama Canal was built a long time ago.
巴拿馬運河是很久前蓋的。

搭配詞 Panama Canal 巴拿馬運河

canyon [ˋkænjən] n. 峽谷 ◀ Track 0611

例句 The Grand Canyon in America is one of the most magnificent scenic spots in the world. 美國大峽谷是全世界最壯觀的景點之一。

搭配詞 Grand Canyon 美國大峽谷

cape [kep] n. 岬、海角 ◀ Track 0612

例句 I've always wanted to go to Cape Cod.
我一直很想去鱈魚角。

易混淆字 cap 帽子

car [kɑr] n. 汽車 ◀ Track 0613

例句 We just bought a larger car so the whole family can fit in.
我們剛買了一台大一點的車，這樣全家人才能塞得進去。

同義字 vehicle

card [kɑrd] n. 卡片 Track 0614

例句 He left his businesss card and contact info.
他有留下名片和聯絡方式。

搭配詞 business card 名片

---

cargo [ˋkɑrgo] n. 貨物、船貨 Track 0615

例句 DHL is one of the biggest airline cargo carriers in the world.
DHL是全世界最大的航空貨櫃運輸公司之一。

搭配詞 cargo carriers 貨櫃

---

carry [ˋkærɪ] v. 攜帶、搬運、拿 Track 0616

例句 Workers are carrying the bags up the mountain.
工人們正在把袋子搬上山。

搭配詞 carry on 持續進行

---

cart [kɑrt] n. 手拉車、拖車 Track 0617

例句 The couple bought a baby cart for their newborn baby.
那對夫妻為了新生兒，買了一座嬰兒車。

搭配詞 baby cart 嬰兒車

---

cash [kæʃ] n. 現金 Track 0618

例句 The way you manage your cash flow is the key to your business' success. 如何管理現金流，是決定你事業成功的重要關鍵。

搭配詞 cash flow 現金流

---

center [ˋsɛntɚ] n. 中心、中央 Track 0619

例句 At 60, she is still very self-centered.
她已60歲了，仍然很自我中心。

搭配詞 self-centered 自我中心的

---

central [ˋsɛntrəl] adj. 中央的 Track 0620

＊字尾-al有轉變為形容詞之意

例句 The central government is in charge of major policies in a country.
中央政府主管國家的施政方針。

搭配詞 central government 中央政府

---

channel [ˋtʃænl̩] n. 通道、頻道 Track 0621

例句 If you pay NT$500 per month, you can enjoy 100 TV channels.
如果你每個月付台幣500元，就能看到100個電視頻道。

搭配詞 TV channel 電視頻道

---

charge [tʃɑrdʒ] v. 索價、命令 Track 0622

例句 Lawyers charge by minutes.
律師是根據雇用時間索價的。

---

cheap [tʃip] adj. 低價的、易取得的 Track 0623

例句 Backpackers travel on cheap budget.
背包客用低價的方式旅行。

反義字 expensive 昂貴的

church [tʃɝtʃ] n. 教堂、教會 Track 0624

例句 The couple had a church wedding on a beautiful Sunday morning.
那對夫妻在美麗的星期天早上舉辦他們的教堂婚禮。

搭配詞
church wedding 教堂婚禮

city [ˋsɪtɪ] n. 城市 Track 0625

例句 Taipei and Houston became sister cities in 1961.
台北市和休士頓在1961年成為姐妹城市。

搭配詞
sister city 姐妹城市

coastline [ˋkostˌlaɪn] n. 海岸線 Track 0626

例句 We drive along the coastline on weekends for the view.
我們週末常沿著海岸線開車賞風景。

coin [kɔɪn] n. 硬幣 Track 0627

例句 Let's toss a coin to see which team goes first.
咱們丟擲硬幣來決定哪一隊先開球。

搭配詞
toss a coin 丟擲硬幣

come [kʌm] v. 來 Track 0628

例句 Here comes the train. Get your baggages ready.
火車來了，快把行李準備好。

反義字
go 去

commonplace [ˋkɑmənˌples] adj. 平凡的 Track 0629

例句 Having two cellphones is commonplace for young people now.
對年輕人來說有兩支手機是很平凡的事。

同義字
ordinary

commuter [kəˋmjutɚ] n. 通勤者 Track 0630

＊字尾-er有轉變為名詞的意思

例句 Most of my colleagues are bike commuters.
我們大部分的同事都是腳踏車通勤者。

搭配詞
bike commuter
以腳踏車通勤者

confirm [kənˋfɝm] v. 證實、確認 Track 0631

例句 I'm calling to confirm my booking on this Saturday night.
我打來是要確認這禮拜六晚上的訂位。

易混淆字
conform 符合

construct [kənˋstrʌkt] v. 建造、構築 Track 0632

例句 It took the Chinese two thousand years to construct the Great Wall. 中國人們花了兩千年來建造長城。

反義字
deconstruct 解構

construction [kənˋstrʌkʃən] n. 建築、結構 Track 0633

例句 The new hotel is still under construction.
新旅館仍在建造中。

搭配詞
under construction
在建造中

contact [ˋkɑntækt] n./v. 接觸、親近、聯絡 Track 0634

例句 Let's keep in contact.
我們繼續保持聯絡吧。

搭配詞
keep in contact 保持聯絡

convenience [kənˋvinjəns] n. 便利 Track 0635

例句 There is a convenience store around the corner.
街角就有一家便利商店。

搭配詞
convenience store
便利商店

convey [kənˋve] v. 傳達、運送 Track 0636

例句 The spokesperson conveyed a message to Jesse on behalf of his boss. 公司發言人代表老闆，向傑西傳達消息。

搭配詞
convey a message
傳達消息

corner [ˋkɔrnɚ] n. 角落 Track 0637

例句 There is a Chinese noodle restaurant just around the corner.
在街角有一家中式麵店。

搭配詞
around the corner 在角落

corridor [ˋkɔrədɚ] n. 走廊、通道 Track 0638

例句 The air corridor between Yemen and Saudi Arabia was inaugurated to boost trade between the two nations.
葉門和沙烏地阿拉伯之間的空中通道啟用，以促進兩國貿易。

搭配詞
air corridor 空中通道

countryside [ˋkʌntrɪˏsaɪd] n. 鄉間 Track 0639

例句 My parents plan to move to the countryside after they both retire.
我父母打算在退休後搬去鄉間。

同義字
rural area 農村地區

crash [kræʃ] n. 撞擊 Track 0640

例句 The car crash killed 5 people, the driver included.
車禍撞擊造成5人身亡，包含駕駛。

搭配詞
car crash 車禍撞擊

crawl [krɔl] v. 爬 Track 0641

例句 I watched a snail crawl across the edge of a sharp kitchen knife.
我看到一隻鍋牛爬過一把鋭利的廚房刀鋒。

搭配詞
crawl across 爬過

crossing [ˋkrɔsɪŋ] n. 橫越、橫渡 Track 0642

例句 Slow down before you reach the pedestrian crossing.
接近行人穿越道時要開慢一點。

搭配詞
level crossing 平交道

cruise [kruz] n. 航行、巡航 Track 0643

例句 The Viking Adventure was selected as the best cruise ship for families. 維京探險被評選為最適合全家共遊的遊輪。

搭配詞
cruise ship 遊輪

cruiser [ˋkruzɚ] n. 遊艇 Track 0644

例句 The cruiser tour will take you around the beautiful lake.
這次遊艇旅遊會帶著你環繞這座美麗的湖泊。

搭配詞 cruiser tour 遊艇旅遊

dairy [ˋdɛrɪ] n. 酪農場、奶製品 Track 0645

例句 Dairy is important in your everyday diet.
在你每天的飲食中，奶製品是很重要的。

易混淆字 diary 日記

dam [dæm] n. 水壩 Track 0646

例句 Building a dam is a huge undertaking.
建造水壩是個大工程。

搭配詞 build a dam 建造水壩

debt [dɛt] n. 債、欠款 Track 0647

例句 You need to pay off your debts before you leave the country.
離開這個國家前，你得先還清欠款。

搭配詞 owe a debt 欠下債款

deck [dɛk] n. 甲板 Track 0648

例句 Let's go onto the deck and enjoy the breeze.
我們到甲板上享受海風吧。

搭配詞 on deck 在甲板上

delay [dɪˋle] v. 延緩 Track 0649

例句 We deliverd the goods without delay.
我們準時交貨，並無延遲。

搭配詞 without delay 毫不延遲地

deliver [dɪˋlɪvɚ] v. 傳送、遞送 Track 0650

例句 Former US Vice President Al Gore delivered a speech on global warming. 美國前副總統高爾發表有關全球暖化的演講。

搭配詞 deliver a speech 演講

delivery [dɪˋlɪvərɪ] n. 傳送、傳遞 Track 0651

＊字尾-y有轉變為形容詞之意

例句 We need an urgent delivery; can you please arrange that?
我們有急件要送，你可以幫我們處理嗎？

搭配詞 delivery of goods 交貨

depart [dɪˋpɑrt] v. 離開、走開 Track 0652

例句 He departed from the world after a long life without leaving any legacy for his family.
他很長壽才離開人世，不過沒留給家人任何遺產。

搭配詞 depart from the world 離開人世

departure [dɪˋpɑrtʃɚ] n. 離去、出發 Track 0653

例句 We will see her off at the departure lobby.
我們會在出境大廳送她。

搭配詞 departure lobby 出境大廳

desert [ˋdɛzɚt] n. 沙漠、荒地 Track 0654

例句 I used to live in a desert. We barely had rain every year.
我以前住在沙漠中，每年幾乎都沒下雨。

易混淆字
dessert 甜點

direction [dəˋrɛkʃən] n. 指導、方向 Track 0655

＊字尾-tion有轉變為名詞的意思

例句 To install the driver, please follow the direction in the manual.
在安裝驅動程式時，請遵守手冊裡的指引。

搭配詞
follow the direction
遵從指引

disappear [ˏdɪsəˋpɪr] v. 消失、不見 Track 0656

＊字首dis-有「不」之意

例句 The car was speeding and finally disappeared over the cliff.
這台車超速開得很快，結果終於從懸崖邊消失了。

反義字
appear 出現

distance [ˋdɪstəns] n. 距離 Track 0657

例句 On a foggy day, you can barely see the green mountain in the distance.
天氣霧茫茫時，你很難在一段距離外看到那座綠油油的山。

搭配詞
in the distance
在一段距離外

distant [ˋdɪstənt] adj. 疏遠的、有距離的 Track 0658

例句 Neighbors are dearer than distant relatives.
鄰居比疏遠的親戚更親。

搭配詞
distant relative 遠房親戚

ditch [dɪtʃ] n. 排水溝、水道 Track 0659

例句 The farmer dugged a ditch to prevent the fields from flooding.
農夫挖了一條水溝，以防止田野淹水。

搭配詞
dig a ditch 挖水溝

dock [dɑk] n. 船塢、碼頭 Track 0660

例句 The ship was in dock, waiting to be restocked.
輪船正停在碼頭，要重新裝貨。

易混淆字
duck 鴨子

doorway [ˋdorˏwe] n. 門口、出入口 Track 0661

例句 Why are you standing in the doorway and not coming in?
你怎麼站在門口不進來呢？

搭配詞
in the doorway 在門口

down [daʊn] adv. 向下的 Track 0662

例句 We slowly drove down the mountain.
我們慢慢地從山上往下開。

反義字
up 向上的

downstairs [ˏdaʊnˋstɛrz] adv. 在樓下、往樓下 Track 0663

例句 We went downstairs to have dinner.
我們下樓吃晚餐。

搭配詞
go downstairs 下樓

downtown [ˋdaʊnˋtaʊn] adv. 往鬧區的 ◀ Track 0664

例句 We went downtown for dinner last night. The food was amazing!
我們昨晚到市中心吃晚餐，食物太棒了！

搭配詞 go downtown 到市中心去

doze [doz] v. 打瞌睡 ◀ Track 0665

例句 It is very dangerous if you doze off while driving.
開車打瞌睡是很危險的。

搭配詞 doze off 打起瞌睡來

drift [drɪft] v. 漂移 ◀ Track 0666

例句 Angela and Betty are drifting apart after some misunderstanding.
安琪拉和貝蒂因為誤會，逐漸疏遠了。

搭配詞 drift apart 逐漸疏遠

drive [draɪv] v. 駕車、車道 ◀ Track 0667

例句 He drove a car to the supermarket.
他開車去超級市場。

搭配詞 drive a car 開車

driveway [ˋdraɪv͵we] n. 私用車道、車道 ◀ Track 0668

例句 You can park the car on the driveway.
你可以把車停在車道上。

搭配詞 park on driveway 在車道上停車

drugstore [ˋdrʌg͵stor] n. 藥房 ◀ Track 0669

例句 There is a famous chain drugstore in the shopping mall.
購物中心有家有名的連鎖藥房。

搭配詞 chain drugstore 連鎖藥房

earn [ɝn] v. 賺取、得到 ◀ Track 0670

例句 The scientist earned worldwide respect because of his great contribution to humanity.
這位科學家因為對人類做出卓越貢獻，而獲得世人尊敬。

搭配詞 earn respect 得到尊敬

earth [ɝθ] n. 地球、陸地、地面 ◀ Track 0671

例句 This is the tallest building on earth.
這是全地球最高的大樓。

搭配詞 on earth 在地球上

east [ist] adj. 東方的 ◀ Track 0672

例句 The sun comes up from the east.
太陽從東邊升起。

搭配詞 to the east 朝向東方

eastern [ˋistɚn] adj. 東方的 ◀ Track 0673

例句 Kenny can make authentic Middle Eastern food.
肯尼能做道地的中東食物。

搭配詞 Middle Eastern 中東的

economical [ˌikəˋnɑmɪkḷ] Track 0674
adj. 節儉的、節省的、經濟實惠的　＊字尾-al有轉變為形容詞之意
例句 It is economical to ride the bike to work rather than drive.
騎腳踏車而不開車去上班是很經濟實惠的。
同義字 prudent

elderly [ˋɛldəlɪ] adj. 上了年紀的 Track 0675
例句 Social welfare is supposed to take care of the elderly.
社會福利理應要照顧長者。
搭配詞 the elderly 長者

elevator [ˋɛləˌvetə] n. 升降機、電梯 Track 0676
例句 The elevator is for the disabled and the elderly.
這個電梯是給行動不便與年長的人使用的。
搭配詞 take an elevator 搭電梯

e-mail/email [ˋimel] n. 電子郵件 Track 0677
例句 I need to send an e-mail to my client before 5 pm.
我必須在下午五點前寄電子郵件給我的客戶。
搭配詞 send an e-mail 寄電子郵件

emergency [ɪˋmɝdʒənsɪ] n. 緊急情況 Track 0678
例句 The seriously-injured patient was sent to an emergency room.
那位重傷病患被送到急診室。
搭配詞 emergency room 急診室

enclose [ɪnˋkloz] v. 包圍、附上 Track 0679
例句 Please enclose your bank statement.
請把銀行帳單附上。
反義字 disclose 露出

engine [ˋɛndʒən] n. 引擎 Track 0680
例句 I can't get the engine to start.
我沒辦法把引擎發動。
搭配詞 car engine 汽車引擎

entrance [ˋɛntrəns] n. 入口 Track 0681
＊字尾-ance有轉變為名詞之意
例句 This is the main entrance to the Building. 這是大樓的主要入口。
反義字 exit 出口

entry [ˋɛntrɪ] n. 入口 Track 0682
例句 The entry of the tunnel was sealed due to the falling rocks.
山洞的入口因為落石被封起來了。
同義字 entrance

envelope [ˋɛnvəˌlop] n. 信封 Track 0683
例句 It's a Chinese tradition to give children red envelopes during the Chinese New Year. 中國傳統習俗中，會在農曆新年給小孩紅包。
搭配詞 red envelope 紅包

escalator [ˋɛskə͵letɚ] **n.** 手扶梯 Track 0684

例句 Please stand on the right side of the escalator, so other passengers may pass through on the left side.
請站在手扶梯右側，其他乘客才能從左邊通過。

---

escape [əˋskep] **v.** 逃走 Track 0685

例句 Thank God, Judy escaped her violent boyfriend's cluthes.
感謝老天，茱蒂從暴力男友手中逃走了。

搭配詞 escape sb's clutches 從某人手中逃走

---

evacuate [ɪˋvækjʊ͵et] **v.** 撤離 Track 0686

例句 We need to evacuate before the tsunami strikes.
我們必須在海嘯來襲前撤離。

---

exit [ˋɛgzɪt] **n.** 出口 Track 0687

例句 I can't find the exit to the building.
我找不到大樓出口。

易混淆字 exist 生存、存在

---

expedition [͵ɛkspɪˋdɪʃən] **n.** 探險、遠征 Track 0688

例句 If I were younger, I would join you in the expedition trips to Antarctica.
如果我更年輕一點，我就會跟著你去南極探險旅遊。

搭配詞 expedition trips 探險旅遊

---

expensive [ɪkˋspɛnsɪv] **adj.** 昂貴的 Track 0689

例句 I can't afford this expensive racing car.
我買不起這台昂貴的賽車。

同義字 costly

---

famous [ˋfeməs] **adj.** 有名的、出名的 Track 0690

例句 The singer was famous a few years ago, but nobody knows her today. 這個歌手幾年前很有名，但現在沒人認識她了。

同義字 well-known

---

far [fɑr] **adj.** 遙遠的、遠（方）的 Track 0691

例句 Mars is far from the Earth.
火星離地球很遠。

搭配詞 far from 遠離

---

fare [fɛr] **n.** 費用、運費 Track 0692

例句 Mum gave me some bus fare before I went to school.
我上學前，媽媽給了我一些公車費。

---

farm [fɑrm] **n.** 農場、農田 Track 0693

例句 Would you like to work on our farm? We need extra hands to help out in the harvest season.
你想在我們的農場工作嗎？我們在收穫季需要更多幫手。

同義字 ranch

farther [ˋfɑrðɚ] adv. 更遠地 Track 0694
＊字尾-er有「更」之意
例句 I can't run any farther; let's take a rest.
我不能再跑更遠了，我們休息一下吧。
易混淆字
father 父親

fast [fæst] adj. 快速的 Track 0695
例句 If you can finish your job faster, you can leave earlier.
你如果工作可以更快做完，就可以更早走了。
搭配詞
fast food 速食

fasten [ˋfæsn̩et] v. 緊固、繫緊 Track 0696
例句 His dad is showing him how to fasten down the anchors with a bolt.
他爸爸正在教他怎麼用螺栓固定船錨。
搭配詞
fasten down 繫牢

fee [fi] n. 費用 Track 0697
例句 The hotel adds an extra fee when clients pay with a Mastercard.
若房客使用萬事達信用卡付費，這家旅館將增收額外的費用。
搭配詞
extra fee 額外費用

ferry [ˋfɛrɪ] n. 渡口、渡船 Track 0698
例句 The ferry pier is currently under major construction.
渡船碼頭正在進行重大維修工程。
搭配詞
ferry pier 渡船碼頭

flight [flaɪt] n. 飛行 Track 0699
例句 She is a flight attendant of British Airways.
她是個英國航空的空服員。
搭配詞
flight attendant 空服員

forth [forθ] adv. 向外、向前、在前方 Track 0700
例句 When we asked for helpers, many students came forth.
我們找人幫忙時，許多學生都前來幫忙。
搭配詞
back and forth 來來回回地

forward [ˋfɔrwɚd] adv. 向前地 Track 0701
例句 We look forward to hearing from you again.
我們期待再次聽到你的消息。
搭配詞
look forward to 期待

fountain [ˋfauntn̩] n. 噴泉、噴水池 Track 0702
例句 We built a stone fountain in the center of the park.
我們在公園中央建造了一個石頭噴水池。
易混淆字
fortune 運氣

freeway [ˋfriˌwe] n. 高速公路 Track 0703
例句 The speed limit on the freeway is 100km/h.
在高速公路上的速限是100公里。
同義字
expressway

freight [fret] n. 貨物、貨運 Track 0704

例句 We provide the best freight services in the logistics industry.
我們在物流業提供最佳的貨運服務。

搭配詞
freight service 貨運服務

---

frequency [ˋfrikwənsɪ] n. 時常發生、頻率 Track 0705

例句 Radio frequency ID (RFID) is a commonly used technology in libraries. 無線射頻辯識系統很常運用在圖書館。

搭配詞
radio frequency 收音機頻率

---

gallon [ˋgælən] n. 加侖 Track 0706

例句 I wonder how many miles your car can run with a gallon of gas.
我很好奇你的車用一加侖的汽油可以跑幾哩。

---

gallop [ˋgæləp] v. 疾馳、飛奔 Track 0707

例句 The young horse galloped around the field.
那匹小馬在原野中奔跑。

易混淆字
gallon 加崙

---

gap [gæp] n. 差距、缺口 Track 0708

例句 Communication and empathy help bridge the gap between parents and children. 溝通和同理心有助填補親子間的缺口。

搭配詞
bridge the gap 填補缺口

---

gasoline [ˋgæsl̩in] n. 汽油 Track 0709

例句 We ran out of gas on the way and had to push the car to the side of the road. 我們在路上沒汽油了，只好把車推到路邊。

縮寫
gas

---

global [ˋglobl̩] adj. 球狀的、全球的 Track 0710

＊字尾-al有轉變為形容詞之意

例句 Global warming is getting more and more serious.
全球暖化越來越嚴重了。

搭配詞
global warming
全球暖化現象

---

globe [glob] n. 地球、球 Track 0711

例句 Our product is sold everywhere around the globe.
我們的產品在全球都有販售。

同義字
earth

---

go [go] v. 去、走 Track 0712

例句 Go away. Stop pestering me.
走開，不要來煩我。

搭配詞
go away 走開

---

good-bye [gudˋbaɪ] n. 再見 Track 0713

例句 It's time to say good-bye to my friends.
該和我的朋友們說再見了。

縮寫
bye

goods [gʊdz] n. 商品、貨物 Track 0714
＊字尾-s有轉變為複數之意
例句 Consumer goods companies are facing big challenges as trade wars ramp up.
隨著貿易戰越趨白熱化，使得消費性商品公司面臨巨大挑戰。

搭配詞
consumer goods
消費性商品

gorge [gɔrdʒ] n. 峽谷、山峽 Track 0715
例句 The Taroko Gorge on the east Coast of Taiwan is worth visiting.
在台灣東岸的太魯閣峽谷非常值得一去。

greet [grit] v. 迎接、問候 Track 0716
例句 We greet each other on the first day of the year.
一年的第一天，我們彼此問候。

搭配詞
greeting card 問候卡

grocer [ˋgrosɚ] n. 雜貨店 Track 0717
例句 I met her at the green grocer at the corner of the street.
我在街角的蔬果雜貨店遇到她。

搭配詞
green grocer 蔬果雜貨店

grocery [ˋgrosərɪ] n. 雜貨 Track 0718
例句 I need to go to a grocery store to buy some milk.
我得去雜貨店買點牛奶。

搭配詞
grocery store 雜貨店

handy [ˋhændɪ] adj. 方便的、隨手可得的 Track 0719
例句 The bicycle is really handy in the city area; you never get stuck in the traffic. 腳踏車在城市中很方便，你永遠不會塞在車陣中。

harbor [ˋhɑrbɚ] n. 碼頭 Track 0720
例句 Pearl Harbor was attacked during the Second World War.
珍珠港在第二次世界大戰被攻擊。

同義字
port

haste [hest] n. 急忙、急速 Track 0721
例句 Make haste, or we'll miss the train.
趕快，不然我們要錯過火車了。

搭配詞
make haste 趕快

hasten [ˋhesn̩] v. 趕緊、趕快 Track 0722
例句 I have to hasten to explain the situation to my manager, or he will be upset with me.
我得趕快把情況解釋給主管聽，不然他一定會生氣。

hasty [ˋhestɪ] adj. 快速的 Track 0723
＊字尾-y有轉變為形容詞之意
例句 We had a hasty breakfast and then left for work.
我們快速地吃了早餐，就去上班了。

同義字
swift

haunt [hɔnt] n. 常到的場所 ◀ Track 0724

例句 This coffee shop is our favorite haunt during the weekend.
這咖啡店是我們週末常到的場所。

搭配詞
a favorite haunt 常到的場所

---

height [haɪt] n. 高度 ◀ Track 0725

例句 She has acrophobia. She just can't overcome her fear of height.
她有懼高症，她就是不能克服對高度的恐懼。

搭配詞
fear of height 懼高症

---

helicopter [ˋhɛlɪ͵kɑptɚ] n. 直升機 ◀ Track 0726

例句 We have medical helicopters for emergency purposes.
我們有醫療直升機，發生意外時使用。

搭配詞
helicopter pad
直升機停機坪

---

here [hɪr] n./adv. 這裡 ◀ Track 0727

例句 There are magazines here and there on the desk.
書桌上到處都是雜誌。

搭配詞
here and there
這裡與那裡；到處

---

highly [ˋhaɪlɪ] adv. 大大地、高高地 ◀ Track 0728

＊字尾-ly有轉變為副詞之意

例句 The cough syrup is highly recommended by doctors.
這個咳嗽糖漿被醫生大力推薦。

搭配詞
highly recommended
大力推薦的

---

highway [ˋhaɪ͵we] n. 公路、大路 ◀ Track 0729

例句 It took them two years to finish constructing the highway.
他們花了兩年完成這條公路。

同義字
road

---

hike [haɪk] v. 徒步旅行、健行 ◀ Track 0730

例句 Every spring, we go mountain hiking with family.
每年春天，我們都和家人一起去山上健行。

搭配詞
go hiking 去健行

---

hill [hɪl] n. 小山 ◀ Track 0731

例句 What can you see from up the hill?
你在小山上可以看到什麼？

---

horror [ˋhɑrɚ] n. 恐怖、畏懼 ◀ Track 0732

例句 What is your favorite horror movie?
你最喜歡哪部恐怖片？

搭配詞
horror movie 恐怖片

---

hurry [ˋhɝɪ] v. （使）趕緊 ◀ Track 0733

例句 Hurry up! Or we will miss the train.
快點！不然我們會錯過火車。

搭配詞
hurry up 趕快

icy [ˋaɪsɪ] adj. 冰的 ＊字尾-y有轉變為形容詞之意 Track 0734

例句 I felt the icy wind on my face when a strong cold air mass came into Taiwan. 強勁的冷氣團籠罩台灣，我的臉感覺冰冰的。

搭配詞 icy wind 寒風

imposing [ɪmˋpozɪŋ] adj. 顯眼的、宏偉壯麗的 Track 0735

例句 The hospital was a rather imposing building. 那家醫院是個很宏偉的建築。

同義字 majestic

income [ˋɪn͵kʌm] n. 所得、收入 Track 0736

例句 One third of his monthly income is used to pay rent. 他三分之一的月收入都拿去付房租了。

搭配詞 monthly income 每月所得

inspection [ɪnˋspɛkʃən] n. 檢查、調查 Track 0737

＊字尾-tion有轉變為名詞的意思

例句 We called in two professionals to do a thorough inspection for damage in the house. 我們找了兩個專業的人來檢查房子損壞的地方。

搭配詞 thorough inspection 澈底檢查

intersection [͵ɪntɚˋsɛkʃən] n. 橫斷、交叉口 Track 0738

＊字尾-tion有轉變為名詞的意思

例句 A new fast food restaurant opened at the intersection. 在交叉路口開了一家新的速食餐廳。

易混淆字 interruption 阻礙

isle [aɪl] n. 島 Track 0739

例句 This beautiful isle is formed by volcanic lava. 這個美麗的島是火山熔岩形成的。

搭配詞 British Isles 不列顛群島

jam [dʒæm] n. 阻塞 Track 0740

例句 It is normal for traffic jams to happen at this hour. 這個時間發生塞車是很正常的。

搭配詞 traffic jam 塞車

jaywalk [ˋdʒe͵wɔk] v. 不守交通規則穿越街道 Track 0741

例句 Jaywalking is very dangerous. 不守規則穿越街道是很危險的。

jet [dʒɛt] n. 噴射機、噴嘴 Track 0742

例句 The army has developed a new jet plane which can fly even faster. 軍隊發展了一種新的噴射機，可以飛得更快。

搭配詞 jet plane 噴射機

journey [ˋdʒɝnɪ] n. 旅程 Track 0743

例句 The reality show offers US$10,000 for the champion to make a journey of a lifetime. 這個實境節目提供冠軍一萬美元，體驗生平獨一無二的旅行。

搭配詞 make a journey 旅行

lake [lek] n. 湖 ◀Track 0744

例句 Sun Moon Lake is a famed scenic spot in Taiwan.
日月潭是台灣著名的景點。

搭配詞 Sun Moon Lake 日月潭

land [lænd] n. 陸地、土地 v. 降落 ◀Track 0745

例句 Alexander landed a job in NASA.
亞歷山大在美國太空總署找到工作。

搭配詞 land a job 找到工作

landmark [ˋlændˏmɑrk] n. 路標、地標 ◀Track 0746

例句 The Statue of Liberty is regarded as New York's landmark.
自由女神像被當作是紐約的地標。

landscape [ˋlænskep] n. 風景名勝 ◀Track 0747

例句 I collect landscape postcards from around the world.
我收集世界各地風景名勝的明信片。

landslide [ˋlændˏslaɪd] n. 山崩 ◀Track 0748

例句 The village suffered from a serious landslide last year.
這個村莊去年被一場嚴重的山崩摧殘。

同義字 landslip

lane [len] n. 小路、巷 ◀Track 0749

例句 Once the four-lane highway is completed, it will boost the region's economy. 這個四車道公路一旦完工以後，將帶動區域經濟。

搭配詞 four-lane highway 四車道公路

language [ˋlæŋgwɪdʒ] n. 語言 ◀Track 0750

例句 French is one of the most beautiful foreign languages, but it is very diffucult to learn. 法文是最美麗的外國語言之一，但卻很難學。

搭配詞 foreign language 外語

leave [liv] v. 離開 ◀Track 0751

例句 We will leave for New York next week.
我們下禮拜就前往紐約了。

搭配詞 leave for 前往（某地）

left [lɛft] n. 左邊 ◀Track 0752

例句 My brother is left-handed.
我弟弟是左撇子。

搭配詞 left-handed 左撇子

lend [lɛnd] v. 借出 ◀Track 0753

例句 We will lend you a car while yours is under maintenance.
你的車還在維修時，我們會借你一台。

易混淆字 land 土地

lighthouse [ˋlaɪt͵haʊs] n. 燈塔 Track 0754

例句 There is a tall lighthouse there on the hill.
在山丘上有個高高的燈塔。

---

limousine [lɪmə͵zin] n. 大型豪華轎車、小型巴士 Track 0755

例句 Can you please arrange a limo service when we arrive at the airport? 我們到機場時，你可以安排豪華轎車服務嗎？

縮寫 limo

---

location [loˋkeʃən] n. 位置 Track 0756

例句 Can you please tell him the location of the nearest police station?
可以請你告訴他最近的警察局的位置嗎？

同義字 site

---

locker [ˋlɑkɚ] n. 有鎖的收納櫃、寄物櫃 Track 0757

例句 I rented a locker to keep valuables.
我租了一個寄物櫃，存放寶貴物品。

搭配詞 rent a locker 租寄物櫃

---

lounge [laʊndʒ] n. 交誼廳、音樂酒吧 Track 0758

例句 Please wait in the lounge bar before we arrive.
我們抵達前，請你在交誼廳內等候。

搭配詞 lounge bar 音樂酒吧

---

luggage [ˋlʌgɪdʒ] n. 行李 Track 0759

例句 I will leave you now so that you can unpack your luggage.
我現在就離開，好讓你可以把行李打開。

同義字 baggage

---

magnificent [mægˋnɪfəsənt] Track 0760

adj. 壯觀的、華麗的

例句 It is a maganificent church built in 1890.
這是個在1890年蓋好的壯觀教堂。

同義字 splendid

---

mail [mel] n. 郵件 Track 0761

例句 Two bent mail boxes became a tourist attraction in Taipei after a huge typhoon. 強颱過後，有兩個彎腰郵筒變成了台北觀光景點。

搭配詞 mail box 郵筒

---

maintain [menˋten] v. 維持 Track 0762

例句 Jack tried to maintain a long-distance relationship with his girlfriend, but he didn't work it out.
傑克試著和女友維持遠距關係，但他失敗了。

搭配詞 maintain a relationship 維持關係

---

market [ˋmɑrkɪt] n. 市場 Track 0763

例句 We went to the night market for local gourmet food.
我們去夜市品嘗當地美食。

搭配詞 night market 夜市

marvelous [ˋmɑrvələs] adj. 令人驚訝的、極好的 Track 0764

＊字尾-ous有轉變為形容詞之意

例句 The restaurant was in a marvelous location.
這家餐廳在一個極好的位置。

同義字 fabulous

---

massive [ˋmæsɪv] adj. 笨重的、大量的 Track 0765

例句 The city has had a few massive changes after the war.
這個城市在戰爭後有許多巨大的改變。

反義字 tiny 微小的

---

message [ˋmɛsɪdʒ] n. 訊息 Track 0766

例句 He will reply to your message as soon as he gets back to the office. 他一回到辦公室，就會回覆你的訊息了。

搭配詞 text message 簡訊

---

middle [ˋmɪdḷ] adj. 中部、中間的、在……中間 Track 0767

例句 The supermodel felt panic when she was in her middle age.
這位名模因屆齡中年，而感到恐慌。

搭配詞 middle age 中年

---

milestone [ˋmaɪlˏston] n. 里程碑 Track 0768

例句 Marriage is considered a milestone in my life.
在我的人生中，結婚算是個里程碑了。

搭配詞 milestone in life
生命中的里程碑

---

monument [ˋmɑnjəmənt] n. 紀念碑 Track 0769

例句 They erected a historical monument to commemorate the victory in war. 他們蓋了一座歷史紀念碑以紀念戰爭勝利。

搭配詞 historical monument
歷史紀念碑

---

motorcycle [ˋmotɚˏsaɪkḷ] n. 摩托車 Track 0770

例句 You need a license to ride a motorcycle.
要騎機車得先有執照。

搭配詞 ride a motorcycle 騎摩托車

---

mound [maʊnd] n. 丘陵、堆 Track 0771

例句 There is a mound of new books on my desk to read.
我桌上有一堆新書要讀。

易混淆字 mount 坐騎、山

---

mount [maʊnt] n. 山 Track 0772

例句 Mount Jade is the highest mountain in Taiwan.
玉山是台灣最高的山。

搭配詞 Mount Jade 玉山

---

mountain [ˋmaʊntṇ] n. 高山 Track 0773

例句 Mountain climbing is a challenging sport.
登山健行是很有挑戰的運動。

搭配詞 mountain climbing
登山健行

mountainous [ˋmaʊntṇəs] ◀ Track 0774
adj. 多山的、有山的　＊字尾-ous有轉變為形容詞之意
例句 Taiwan is a mountainous island. 台灣是個多山的島嶼。

搭配詞
mountainous region
多山地帶

museum [mjuˋziəm] n. 博物館 ◀ Track 0775
例句 Students are visiting the National Palace Museum for a school project. 學生們為了學校的報告在故宮博物院參觀。

搭配詞
National Palace Museum
國立故宮博物院

navigation [ˏnævəˋgeʃən] n. 航海、航空、導航 ◀ Track 0776
＊字尾-tion有轉變為名詞的意思
例句 Knowledge navigation is instrumental in digital libraries.
在數位圖書館，知識導航能力很重要。

搭配詞
knowledge navigation
知識導航能力

neon [ˋniˏɑn] n. 霓虹、氖 ◀ Track 0777
例句 You will see the colorful neon lights on the skyscrapers in Tokyo.
你會在東京的摩天大樓上看到多彩的霓虹燈。

搭配詞
neon color 霓虹色

nearby [ˋnɪrˋbaɪ] adj. 短距離內的、附近 ◀ Track 0778
例句 I live nearby, so I walk to the school every day.
我就住附近，所以我天天走路上學。

搭配詞
a place nearby 很近的地方

north [nɔrθ] n. 北、北方 ◀ Track 0779
例句 She is staying in a room facing north.
她住在一間朝北的房間。

搭配詞
north pole 北極

northern [ˋnɔrðən] adj. 北方的 ◀ Track 0780
例句 The storm is coming from the northern coast.
暴風雨是從北海岸那裡來的。

反義字
southern 南方的

oasis [oˋesɪs] n. 綠洲 ◀ Track 0781
例句 This is the only oasis in this great desert.
這是整個大沙漠中唯一的綠洲。

ocean [ˋoʃən] n. 海洋 ◀ Track 0782
例句 We can arrange a trip to the ocean park when we visit Japan.
我們去日本觀光，可以安排順便去海洋公園。

搭配詞
ocean park 海洋公園

onto [ˋɑntu] prep. 在……之上 ◀ Track 0783
例句 The dog jumped onto my sofa.
狗跳到了我的沙發上。

搭配詞
jump onto 跳上

out [aut] prep. 離開、向外 ◀Track 0784

例句 Chris has been in and out of prison since he was a teenager.
克里斯自從青少年起，就一直進進出出監獄。

搭配詞
in and out 裡裡外外

---

outdoor [ˋautˏdor] adj. 戶外的 ◀Track 0785

＊字首out-有「外」之意

例句 I enjoy outdoor sports, such as hiking and bungee jumping.
我喜歡戶外運動，比如健走和高空彈跳。

搭配詞
outdoor sport 戶外運動

---

outside [ˋautˏsaɪd] adv. 在……外面 ◀Track 0786

＊字首out-有「外」之意

例句 I forgot to bring my key, and I was locked outside.
我忘記帶鑰匙，就被鎖在外面了。

反義字
inside 在……裡面

---

outskirts [ˋautˏskɜts] n. 郊區 ◀Track 0787

＊字首out-有「外」之意

例句 We can't afford a house in central London, so we live in the ouskirts of London.
我們買不起倫敦市區的房子，所以我們住在倫敦郊區。

搭配詞
in the outskirts of
在……的郊區

---

outward(s) [ˋautwɚd(z)] adj. 向外的、外面的 ◀Track 0788

＊字首out-有「外」之意

例句 The outward appearance of the church is magnificent.
這間教堂的外觀非常壯麗。

搭配詞
outward appearance 外觀

---

overpass [ˏovɚˋpæs] n. 天橋、高架橋 ◀Track 0789

＊字首over-有「越過、超過」之意

例句 Please use the pedestrian overpass to cross the street.
請使用行人天橋過馬路。

反義字
underpass 地下道

---

overtake [ˏovɚˋtek] n./v. 趕上、突擊 ◀Track 0790

＊字首over-有「越過、超過」之意

例句 We want to overtake the slow bus in front of us, but how far is it to the overtaking lane?
我們想超過前面那輛很慢的公車，但超車道還要多遠才會到？

搭配詞
overtaking lane 超車道

---

pacific [pəˋsɪfɪk] adj. 太平洋的、平靜的 ◀Track 0791

例句 There are several islands located in the Pacific Ocean.
在太平洋中有許多島。

同義字
calm

---

package [ˋpækɪdʒ] n. 包裹 ◀Track 0792

例句 We bought a package tour to Thailand for our honeymoon.
我們去泰國渡蜜月是參加套裝行程的。

搭配詞
package tour 套裝行程

---

packet [ˋpækɪt] n. 小包裹 ◀Track 0793

例句 Can you please get me a packet of cigarettes?
可以請你幫我買一小包菸嗎？

易混淆字
pocket 口袋

parachute [ˋpærə͵ʃut] n. 降落傘 Track 0794

例句 He did a parachute jump for charity.
他為了慈善活動，去做高空跳傘。

搭配詞 parachute jump 高空跳傘

parcel [ˋpɑrsḷ] n. 包裹 Track 0795

例句 This parcel post arrived at the front desk this morning.
這個包裹郵件今天早上抵達櫃臺。

搭配詞 parcel post 包裹郵件

park [pɑrk] n. 公園 Track 0796

例句 The kindergarten arranged a trip for the children to play at an amusement park. 這所幼稚園為孩子安排一次遊樂園之旅。

搭配詞 amusement park 遊樂園

passage [ˋpæsɪdʒ] n. 通道 Track 0797

例句 You will find the bathroom at the end of the passage.
你會在通道盡頭找到廁所。

易混淆字 massage 按摩

passenger [ˋpæsṇdʒɚ] n. 乘客 Track 0798

例句 There are 245 passenger seats on the airbus.
這台空中巴士有245個乘客座。

搭配詞 passenger seat 乘客座

path [pæθ] n. 路徑 Track 0799

例句 I hope we'll cross our paths in the not-so-distant future.
但願我們在不久的未來，可以再度相遇。

搭配詞 cross one's path 再度相遇

pavement [ˋpevmənt] n. 人行道 Track 0800

例句 Food stalls are not allowed on the pavement.
人行道上不允許擺小吃攤。

peak [pik] n. 山頂、頂點 Track 0801

例句 Christmas is the peak time for tourism.
聖誕節是觀光季節的頂峰。

反義字 nadir 最低點

pedal [ˋpɛdḷ] n. 踏板 Track 0802

例句 She put her foot on the brake pedal and stopped the car in time.
她把腳踩上煞車踏板，及時把車子停了下來。

易混淆字 peddle 叫賣

peddle [ˋpɛdḷ] v. 叫賣、兜售 Track 0803

例句 The drug dealers peddle drugs in the dark alley.
藥頭在暗巷兜售毒品。

搭配詞 peddle drugs 販賣毒品

pedestrian [pəˋdɛstrɪən] n. 行人 ◀Track 0804

＊字尾-ian有「……的人」的意思

例句 Sarah walked over the pedestrian crossing with her umbrella on a big sunny day. 莎拉在豔陽下，撐著洋傘走過行人穿越道。

搭配詞 pedestrian crossing 行人穿越道

peninsula [pəˋnɪnsələ] n. 半島 ◀Track 0805

例句 Spain is located at the Iberian Península.
西班牙位於伊比利半島。

搭配詞 Arabian Peninsula 阿拉伯半島

per [pɚ] prep. 每、經由 ◀Track 0806

例句 We provide one bottle of water per traveler.
我們提供每一名旅客一瓶水。

同義字 for each

pier [pɪr] n. 碼頭 ◀Track 0807

例句 We walked along the pier and enjoyed the quiet night.
我們沿著碼頭走，享受寧靜的夜晚。

同義字 wharf

pilgrim [ˋpɪlgrɪm] n. 朝聖者；旅行者 ◀Track 0808

例句 The pilgrims finally reached their temple.
朝聖者終於來到他們的廟。

place [ples] n. 地方、地區、地位 ◀Track 0809

例句 Where is this place? I have never been here before.
這是什麼地方？我從來沒來過。

易混淆字 pace 步伐

platform [ˋplæt͵fɔrm] n. 平台、月台 ◀Track 0810

例句 She will be waiting for you on platform number two.
她會在二號月台等你。

polar [ˋpolɚ] adj. 極地的 ◀Track 0811

例句 Polar bears are endangered species due to global warming.
由於全球暖化，北極熊成為瀕臨絕種的動物。

搭配詞 polar bear 北極熊

pond [pɑnd] n. 池塘 ◀Track 0812

例句 There's a fish pond in front of the house.
房子前面有個魚池。

搭配詞 fish pond 魚池

pool [pul] n. 水池 ◀Track 0813

例句 The swimming pool is closed every Monday.
游泳池每週一是關閉的。

搭配詞 swimming pool 游泳池

port [port] n. 港口 Track 0814

例句 We must reach the port by tomorrow evening.
我們明天晚上前要到達港口。

易混淆字 pork 豬肉

post [post] n. 郵件 Track 0815

例句 You can also pay for your utility bills in the post office.
你也可以在郵局繳水電費。

搭配詞 post office 郵局

postage [ˋpostɪdʒ] n. 郵資 Track 0816

例句 The return envelope is postage included.
這個回信信封是包含郵資的。

搭配詞 postage and packing 郵資及包裹費

postcard [ˋpostˏkɑrd] n. 明信片 Track 0817

例句 He sent his son a hand-made postcard whenever he travelled to a new country.
他每次到一個新的國家旅行，就會寄一張手作明信片給兒子。

搭配詞 hand-made postcard 手作明信片

postpone [postˋpon] v. 延緩、延遲 Track 0818

例句 Our flight will be postponed for one day because of the hurricane.
我們的班機將會因颶風而延遲一日。

同義字 delay

quick [kwɪk] adj. 快的 Track 0819

例句 Which is the quickest way to get there, bus or taxi?
去那裡最快的方法是哪一個，公車還是計程車？

反義字 slow 慢的

raft [ræft] n. 木筏 Track 0820

例句 The survivors drifted on a raft for 5 days before they were rescued.
倖存者在木筏上漂了五天才被救起。

易混淆字 craft 工藝

rail [rel] n. 橫桿、鐵軌 Track 0821

例句 Grip the hand rails tightly; it's gonna be a bumpy ride.
抓緊扶桿，這次旅程會很晃。

搭配詞 hand rail 扶桿

railroad [ˋrelˏrod] n. 鐵路 Track 0822

例句 A new railroad is under construction.
新的鐵路已經在蓋了。

同義字 railway

ranch [ræntʃ] n. 大農場 Track 0823

例句 He operates a dude ranch in Colorado and accepts guests to stay at his hand-built cabins.
他經營渡假農場，並接受遊客在他親手建築的小木屋過夜。

搭配詞 dude ranch 渡假農場

rapid [ˋræpɪd] adj. 迅速的 ◀Track 0824

例句 Taipei MRT is one of the best metro rapid transit systems in the world. 台北捷運是世界上最好的都會高速運輸系統之一。

搭配詞 rapid transit system 高速運輸系統

reef [rif] n. 暗礁 ◀Track 0825

例句 There are beautiful coral reefs in Kenting.
在墾丁有很美的珊瑚礁。

搭配詞 coral reef 珊瑚礁

region [ˋridʒən] n. 區域 ◀Track 0826

例句 We live in the tropical region.
我們住在熱帶區域。

同義字 area

reservoir [ˋrɛzɚ͵vɔr] n. 水庫、倉庫 ◀Track 0827

例句 The reservoir supplied the entire city with clean water.
這個水庫提供整個城市乾淨的水。

ridge [rɪdʒ] n. 背脊、山脊、山脈 ◀Track 0828

例句 The view is magnificent from the top of the ridge.
從山脊頂上看下去的景色很壯觀。

易混淆字 fridge 冰箱

right [raɪt] adj. 正確的、右邊的 ◀Track 0829

例句 The tall man standing on her right side is her husband.
站在她右邊那個高高的男人是她的丈夫。

同義字 correct

ring [rɪŋ] v. 按鈴、打電話 ◀Track 0830

例句 Please ring the bell when you arrive.
你到時，請按我家門鈴。

搭配詞 ring the bell 按鈴

road [rod] n. 路、道路、街道、路線 ◀Track 0831

例句 There is no royal road to learning.
學習無捷徑。

搭配詞 royal road 捷徑、坦途

rock [rɑk] n. 岩石 ◀Track 0832

例句 He is as stubborn as a rock.
他跟岩石一樣固執。

rocky [ˋrɑkɪ] adj. 岩石的、搖擺的 ◀Track 0833

＊字尾-y有轉變為形容詞之意

例句 This is a rocky road, so drive carefully.
這是條岩石很多的路，請小心開車。

搭配詞 rocky road 岩石很多的路

rough [rʌf] adj. 粗糙的 Track 0834

例句 His fingers are rough from playing guitar.
他因為彈吉他，手指很粗糙。

反義字
delicate 精細的

route [rut] n. 路線 Track 0835

例句 This is the only bike route from Auckland to Hamilton.
這是從奧克蘭去漢米爾頓唯一的一條自行車路線。

搭配詞
bike route 自行車路線

rural [ˋrurəl] adj. 農村的 Track 0836

例句 My parents live a rural life, but I prefer a city life.
我的父母過著農村生活，但我比較喜歡城市生活。

搭配詞
rural life 農村生活

rush [rʌʃ] v. 突擊、匆忙地送 Track 0837

例句 The injured passenger was rushed to the nearest hospital.
受傷的乘客被匆忙地送到了最近的醫院。

sail [sel] n./v. 帆、篷、航行、船隻 Track 0838

例句 Our ship will sail to Shanghai tomorrow.
我們的船明天會航行前往上海。

send [sɛnd] v. 派遣、寄出 Track 0839

例句 The event coordinator will send out invitations by Friday.
活動籌辦者在星期五以前將把邀請函全部寄發出去。

搭配詞
send out 寄出

shade [ʃed] n. 蔭涼處、樹蔭 Track 0840

例句 We rested in the shade and had lunch.
我們在樹蔭下休息、吃午餐。

易混淆字
shake 搖晃

ship [ʃɪp] n. 大船、海船 Track 0841

例句 Two battle ships recently cruised across the Taiwan Strait.
兩艘戰艦最近在台灣海峽航行。

搭配詞
battle ship 戰艦

shop/store [ʃɑp]/[stor] n. 商店、店鋪 Track 0842

例句 Toys "R" Us is one of the most popular toy stores in the world.
玩具反斗城是全球最受歡迎的玩具店之一。

搭配詞
toy store 玩具店

sidewalk [ˋsaɪd͵wɔk] n. 人行道 Track 0843

例句 She slipped on the sidewalk and was very embarrassed.
她在人行道上滑倒，非常尷尬。

同義字
pavement

signal [ˋsɪgnḷ] v./n. 打信號、號誌 Track 0844

例句 The teacher signaled for them to come forward.
老師打信號要他們過來。

sink [sɪŋk] v. 沉沒 Track 0845

例句 The Titanic sank into the North Atlantic Ocean during its maiden voyage. 鐵達尼於首航時沉沒到北大西洋海裡。

搭配詞 sink into 沉沒入

slippery [ˋslɪpərɪ] adj. 滑溜的 Track 0846

例句 Alice is a slippery customer. She always brings trouble to people.
艾莉絲是狡猾的人。她總是給別人惹麻煩。

搭配詞 slippery customer 狡猾的人

slum [slʌm] n. 貧民區 Track 0847

例句 The children came from the slums in Chicago.
這些孩子們是從芝加哥的貧民區來的。

易混淆字 slam 猛推

source [sors] n. 來源、水源地 Track 0848

例句 Linux is one of the most widely used open source software.
Linux是最為廣用的自由軟體之一。

搭配詞 open source software 自由軟體

south [saʊθ] n. 南、南方 Track 0849

例句 The doctor advised him to nurse his own health in the south.
醫師建議他到南方去休養。

反義字 north 北、北方

southern [ˋsʌðən] adj. 南方的 Track 0850

例句 Australia is in the Southern Hemisphere.
澳洲位於南半球。

搭配詞 Southern Hemisphere 南半球

specific [spɪˋsɪfɪk] adj. 具體的、特殊的、明確的 Track 0851

例句 Where are we having dinner? Anything specific in mind?
我們要在哪裡吃晚餐？你有什麼特定的想法嗎？

speed [spid] n. 速度、急速 Track 0852

例句 Speed cameras are installed across Taiwan for safety purposes.
為了安全起見，全台都設置了測速照相機。

搭配詞 speed camera 測速照相機

splash [splæʃ] v. 濺起來 Track 0853

例句 The baby enjoyed the bath and splashed in his tub.
小寶寶很享受洗澡，在澡盆裡濺水花。

同義字 dash

squash [skwɑʃ] v. 壓擠 Track 0854

例句 Ripe strawberries get squashed easily; we should keep them in a container.
成熟的草莓很容易壓擠到；我們該把它們找個容器裝著。

反義字 release 鬆開

squeeze [skwiz] v. 壓擠、擠壓 Track 0855

例句 I hope I'll be able to squeeze out some time to join your birthday party. 我希望能挪出一些時間，去參加你的生日派對。

搭配詞 squeeze out 榨出

station [ˋsteʃən] n. 車站 Track 0856

例句 Taipei Train Station is well connected to public transport.
台北火車站和大眾運輸連結很完整。

搭配詞 train station 火車站

stay [ste] v. 逗留、停留 Track 0857

例句 Stay here, and let's make some custard tarts.
留下來，我們一起做葡式蛋塔吧。

搭配詞 stay here 留在這裡

steamer [stimɚ] n. 汽船、輪船 Track 0858

例句 We rarely see steamers like this these days.
這些年很少看到這樣的汽船了。

steep [stip] adj. 險峻的 Track 0859

例句 Without training, it's very dangerous to climb this steep slope.
沒有訓練的話，爬這個險坡是很危險的。

搭配詞 steep slope 險坡

step [stɛp] n. 腳步、步驟 Track 0860

例句 A foreign language must be learned step by step.
學外語必須按部就班來。

搭配詞 step by step 按步驟來

strait [stret] n. 海峽 Track 0861

例句 Two destroyers were sent by the US navy through the Taiwan Strait earlier in July. 美國海軍在7月初派遣兩艘軍艦通過台灣海峽。

搭配詞 Taiwan Strait 台灣海峽

stream [strim] n. 小溪 Track 0862

例句 There is a lovely stream behind my home.
我家後面有條可愛的小溪。

易混淆字 steam 蒸氣

street [strit] n. 街、街道 Track 0863

例句 His street art is very creative.
他的街頭藝術非常有創意。

搭配詞 street art 街頭藝術

stroll [strol] n. 漫步、閒逛 ◀ Track 0864

例句 We took a stroll in the park after dinner.
我們吃完晚餐後在公園裡閒逛。

搭配詞
take a stroll 散步

---

submarine [ˋsʌbmə͵rin] n. 潛水艇 ◀ Track 0865

＊字首sub-有「次級的、下方的」之意

例句 I'd like a submarine sandwich for dinner. 我晚餐想吃潛艇堡。

搭配詞
submarine sandwich
潛艇堡

---

subway [ˋsʌb͵we] n. 地下鐵 ◀ Track 0866

例句 We'll have to take the subway there.
我們得到那裡搭地下鐵。

同義字
metro

---

supermarket [ˋsupɚ͵mɑrkɪt] n. 超級市場 ◀ Track 0867

例句 There are some special deals in the supermarket this week.
這個禮拜超市有一些特價活動。

---

surpass [sɚˋpæs] v. 超過、超越 ◀ Track 0868

例句 Steve Jobs always strived to surpass himself.
賈伯斯總是努力自我超越。

搭配詞
surpass oneself 自我超越

---

surround [səˋraund] v. 圍繞 ◀ Track 0869

例句 The princess was surrounded by paparazzi when she showed up for the charity. 那位公主出席慈善活動時，被狗仔隊包圍。

搭配詞
be surrounded by
被……圍繞

---

survivor [sɚˋvaɪvɚ] n. 生還者 ◀ Track 0870

例句 She is the sole survivor from the train accident.
她是那場火車意外中的唯一生還者。

搭配詞
sole survivor 唯一生還者

---

tavern [ˋtævɚn] n. 酒店、酒館 ◀ Track 0871

例句 Let's go to the new tavern downtown to have a drink.
我們到城裡的新酒館喝點酒吧。

同義字
bar

---

tax [tæks] n. 稅 ◀ Track 0872

例句 Which income tax bracket are you in?
你的所得稅等級是哪一層？

搭配詞
income tax 所得稅

---

taxi/cab [ˋtæksɪ]/[kæb] n. 計程車 ◀ Track 0873

例句 This taxi stand is known for its excellent service.
這個計程車招呼站以服務優良聞名。

搭配詞
taxi stand 計程車招呼站

telegram [ˋtɛlə͵græm] n. 電報 Track 0874
＊字首tele-有「電信的」之意
例句 My mom sent an urgent telegram to me last night.
我媽媽昨晚發了一封緊急電報給我。

搭配詞 send a telegram 發電報

temple [ˋtɛmp!] n. 寺院、神殿 Track 0875
例句 There are many famous Buddist temples in China.
中國有許多知名佛寺。

搭配詞 buddhist temple 禪寺

tempo [ˋtɛmpo] n. 速度、拍子 Track 0876
例句 I like the fast tempo of the song.
我喜歡這首歌的快節奏。

terminate [ˋtɝmə͵net] v. 終止、中斷 Track 0877
例句 We have to terminate the contract with the dishonest company.
我們得終止與那家不誠實的公司的合約。

反義字 continue 繼續

there [ðɛr] adv. 在那裡、往那裡 Track 0878
例句 The children are playing hide-and-seek over there.
孩子們在那裡玩躲貓貓。

搭配詞 over there 在那裡

through [θru] prep. 穿過、通過 Track 0879
例句 Let's run through the park and see who gets home first.
我們穿過公園跑，看誰先到家。

易混淆字 though 然而

ticket [ˋtɪkɪt] n. 車票、入場券 Track 0880
例句 You have to pay for the movie tickets first before entering the theater. 進戲院之前必須先付電影票錢。

搭配詞 movie ticket 電影票

tip [tɪp] n. 小費、暗示 Track 0881
例句 We should give the waiter a tip; he has been serving us well tonight.
我們應該要給服務生小費；他今天晚上對我們服務得挺好的。

同義字 gratuity

toll [tol] n. 傷亡、通行費 Track 0882
例句 After being robbed, Amber made a toll call to her dad for help.
安柏遇到搶劫後，打長途付費電話給她爸爸求救。

搭配詞 toll call長途付費電話

tour [tur] n. 旅行、導覽、旅遊 Track 0883
例句 She works as a tour guide.
她的工作是導遊。

搭配詞 tour guide 導遊

tourism [ˋturɪzəm] n. 觀光、遊覽 ◀Track 0884
＊字尾-ism有「主義」之意
例句 Taiwan's tourism industry is suffering as Chinese tourists stay away.
台灣的觀光業正處於蕭條期，因為陸客不來。

搭配詞
tourism industry 觀光產業

---

tourist [ˋturɪst] n. 觀光客 ◀Track 0885
例句 Alishan is a great tourist attraction.
阿里山是很棒的觀光勝地。

搭配詞
tourist attraction 觀光勝地

---

tow [to] v. 拖曳 ◀Track 0886
例句 The police towed the stolen vehicle away.
警察把被偷的車拖走了。

易混淆字
two 二

---

tower [ˋtauɚ] n. 塔 ◀Track 0887
例句 There is a tall tower standing on the top of the castle.
在城堡頂上有個高塔。

---

town [taun] n. 城鎮、鎮 ◀Track 0888
例句 The FBI agents were in town to investigate in a homicide.
美國聯邦調查局探員到鎮上調查一起殺人案。

搭配詞
in town 在鎮上

---

traffic [ˋtræfɪk] n. 交通 ◀Track 0889
例句 The traffic light is out of order.
紅綠燈故障了。

搭配詞
traffic light 紅綠燈

---

trail [trel] n. 痕跡、小徑 ◀Track 0890
例句 Many trails you see here are generally used by people out for a short hike.
你在這裡看到的許多小徑通常都是給要短暫健走的人用的。

易混淆字
trial 試練

---

train [tren] n. 火車 ◀Track 0891
例句 Taking an express train can save us a lot of time.
搭特快火車可以省去我們很多時間。

搭配詞
express train 特快火車

---

trample [ˋtræmpḷ] v. 踐踏、踩踏 ◀Track 0892
例句 The small child was nearly trampled alive at the movie theater.
那個小孩在電影院差點活生生被一堆人踩踏。

---

transmit [trænsˋmɪt] v. 寄送、傳播 ◀Track 0893
＊字首trans-有「穿越、轉變」之意
例句 Nikola Tesla was a great electrical engineer, who completely changed the way we transmit electricity. 尼古拉・特斯拉是位偉大的機械工程師，他澈底改變人類傳送電力的方式。

搭配詞
transmit electricity
傳送電力

a b c d e f g h i j k l m n o p q r s t u v w x y z

transport [ˋtrænsport] v. 輸送、運輸 ◀Track 0894

＊字首trans-有「穿越、轉變」之意

例句 The sample will be transported to New York by air.
這個樣本會用空運運送到紐約。

易混淆字 transpose 顛倒

transportation [ˏtrænspɚˋteʃən] ◀Track 0895

n. 輸送、運輸工具 ＊字首trans-有「穿越、轉變」之意

例句 Our city has a good public transportation system.
我們的城市有個很好的大眾運輸系統。

搭配詞 public transportation 大眾運輸工具

travel [ˋtrævl] v. 旅行 ◀Track 0896

例句 Globetrotter is a family-owned travel agency.
環球觀光是由家族經營的旅行社。

搭配詞 travel agency 旅行社

traveler [ˋtrævlɚ] n. 旅行者、旅客 ◀Track 0897

＊字尾-er有轉變為名詞的意思

例句 Young travelers prefer to stay at the hostel.
年輕的旅行者偏好住在青年旅館。

搭配詞 individual traveler 獨自旅行者

tread [trɛd] n./v. 腳步、踩 ◀Track 0898

例句 Tread carefully, or you might step on one of Tommy's tennis balls.
小心腳步，不然可能會踩到湯米的網球。

易混淆字 thread 線

trench [trɛntʃ] n. 溝、渠 ◀Track 0899

例句 The trench coat is well-designed and sells pretty well.
這款軍用雨衣設計得很漂亮，銷售成績亮眼。

搭配詞 trench coat 軍用雨衣

trip [trɪp] n. 旅行 ◀Track 0900

例句 He took a trip to Egypt for a week.
他到埃及旅行一週。

搭配詞 take a trip 去旅行

truck [trʌk] n. 卡車 ◀Track 0901

例句 I need to rent a truck to move my furniture.
我得租一台卡車幫我搬運傢俱。

易混淆字 track 足跡

tunnel [ˋtʌnl] n. 隧道、地道 ◀Track 0902

例句 The 1927 Holland Tunnel was the first underwater tunnel designed for automobiles.
1927年的荷蘭隧道是第一條為車子所設計的水底隧道。

搭配詞 underwater tunnel 水底隧道

underpass [ˋʌndɚpæs] n. 地下道 ◀Track 0903

＊字首under-有「下方的」之意

例句 I can never figure out which exit to take when going through the underpass. 走地下道的時候，我每次都搞不清楚走哪一個出口。

反義字 overpass 天橋

upstairs [ˋʌpˏstɛrz] adv. 往（在）樓上 Track 0904

例句 She ran upstairs and shut the window before the rain came.
下雨前，她跑上樓，把窗戶關起來。

反義字
downstairs 往（在）樓下

urgency [ˋɝdʒənsɪ] n. 迫切、急迫 Track 0905

例句 This is a matter of utmost urgency. Please call your supervisor immediately. 這件事極為急迫，請立刻打給你的主管。

valley [ˋvælɪ] n. 溪谷、山谷 Track 0906

例句 She lives in a little farm at the bottom of the valley.
她住在山谷底下一個小農場中。

van [væn] n. 貨車 Track 0907

例句 We need to rent a camper van, for our whole family will go camping in Colorado.
我們全家都要去科羅拉多州露營，所以需要租一台露營車。

搭配詞
camper van 露營車

vehicle [ˋviɪkl̩] n. 交通工具、車輛 Track 0908

例句 This motor vehicle doesn't use fossil fuel. Instead, it uses batteries. 這部汽車不用汽油，而是用電池。

搭配詞
motor vehicle 汽車

via [ˋvaɪə] prep. 經由 Track 0909

例句 You can contact me via email.
你可以經由電郵聯絡我。

搭配詞
via email 經由電子郵件

volcano [vɑlˋkeno] n. 火山 Track 0910

例句 California's Shasta is a dormant volcano.
加州的沙斯塔山是休眠火山。

搭配詞
dormant volcano 休眠火山

voyage [ˋvɔɪɪdʒ] n. 旅行、航海 Track 0911

例句 She came to the airport to see us off and wished us bon voyage.
她來機場替我們送行，而且祝我們一路順風。

搭配詞
bon voyage 一路順風

wade [wed] v. 涉水、跋涉 Track 0912

例句 We need to wade through legal documents before signing an agreement. 在簽協定之前，我們必須費力讀完法律文件。

搭配詞
wade through 費力進行

walk [wɔk] v. 走、步行 Track 0913

例句 He walked around the house to see where the ants came from.
他在房裡到處走動，想找出螞蟻從哪裡來的。

搭配詞
walk around 到處走動

warehouse [ˋwɛr͵haus] n. 倉庫、貨棧 Track 0914

例句 The furniture are stacked in a warehouse by the shop.
家具被堆在店旁邊的倉庫中。

同義字 storehouse

waterfall [ˋwɔtɚ͵fɔl] n. 瀑布 Track 0915

例句 These are the loveliest waterfalls I've ever seen.
這些是我見過最漂亮的瀑布了。

同義字 cascade

way [we] n. 路、道路 Track 0916

例句 I'm on my way to the Buckingham Palace.
我正在前往白金漢宮的路上。

搭配詞 on one's way to 去……的路上

wharf [wɔrf] n. 碼頭 Track 0917

例句 She is waiting for her lover to return on the wharf.
她在碼頭等著她的愛人歸來。

同義字 pier

wheel [wil] n. 輪子、輪 Track 0918

例句 The company is manufacturing mini four-wheeled vehicles for those who only have limited budget.
這家公司製造迷你四輪轎車，提供預算有限的人們購買。

搭配詞 four-wheeled vehicle 四輪轎車

where [wɛr] adv. 在哪裡 Track 0919

例句 I will follow you no matter where you go.
無論你去哪裡，我都會跟著你。

搭配詞 no matter where 不管在哪裡

wherever [wɛrˋɛvɚ] adv. 無論何處 Track 0920

例句 I will follow you wherever you go.
無論你去哪裡，我都會跟著你。

world [wɝld] n. 地球、世界 Track 0921

例句 My dream is to travel around the world.
我的夢想是環遊世界。

搭配詞 travel around the world 環遊世界

yacht [jɑt] n. 遊艇 Track 0922

例句 He invited us to his yacht club.
他邀請我們到他的遊艇俱樂部。

搭配詞 yacht club 遊艇俱樂部

ZIP [zɪp] n. 郵遞區號 Track 0923

例句 Writing the ZIP code on the envelope will help it get delivered faster. 在信封上寫郵遞區號，會讓你的信比較快送達。

搭配詞 ZIP code 郵遞區號

Test 04 關鍵英單總測驗第4回

以下測驗題皆出自書中第四回「**和行有關的單字**」，快來檢視自己的學習成果吧！

一、選擇題

1. The breaking news was _____ via the Internet.
   (A) squeezed
   (B) transmitted
   (C) greeted
   (D) trampled

2. Traffic____ usually occur during rush hours.
   (A) heights
   (B) jams
   (C) hasty
   (D) gallop

3. She aspires to be a ___ attendant so she can travel around the world.
   (A) gorge
   (B) flight
   (C) harbor
   (D) commuter

4. Tesla Motor is an electric ________ company.
   (A) volcano
   (B) trail
   (C) submarine
   (D) vehicle

5. The seminar serves as a _____ for students to exchange their research findings.
   (A) pool
   (B) lighthouse
   (C) grocery
   (D) platform

6. _____ warming will jeopardize the survival of mankind.
   (A) Eastern
   (B) Pacific
   (C) Global
   (D) Parachuting

7. More than 1 million ____ visit Mecca every year.
   (A) luggage
   (B) expeditions
   (C) journey
   (D) pilgrims

8. Residents in the area were _____ before the hurricane arrived.
   (A) evacuated
   (B) waded
   (C) arrived
   (D) traveled

9. Please _____ your seatbelt before the airplane takes off.
   (A) enclose
   (B) fasten
   (C) maintain
   (D) earn

10. They bought a mansion in the ____ of London.
    (A) post
    (B) source
    (C) outskirts
    (D) slum

二、克漏字測驗

In the Mission: Impossible franchise, Tom Cruise plays a senior field operations agent named Ethan Hunt, who __1__ around the world to handle highly dangerous international missions. Ethan is fluent in fifteen __2__ and is capable of lip-reading.

One of his most death-defying experiences is battling against an IMF traitor on a moving TGV bullet __3__. To stop the traitor from getting on a __4__ , Ethan placed an explosive chewing gum on the windshield of the chopper. It then exploded and hurled Ethan onto the back of the train.

This year, Ethan is assigned with a new task. His __5__ will surely give you an adrenaline rush like his previous ones did before.

1. (A) accesses
   (B) begs
   (C) departs
   (D) travels

2. (A) languages
   (B) fees
   (C) entrances
   (D) highways

3. (A) jam
   (B) mountains
   (C) train
   (D) limousines

4. (A) platform
   (B) helicopter
   (C) overpass
   (D) passage

5. (A) adventure
   (B) tavern
   (C) ship
   (D) tourism

關鍵英單總測驗第4回
中譯與解答

一、選擇題

1. 這則即時重大新聞是透過網路傳送的。
   (A) 擠壓
   (B) 傳送
   (C) 問候
   (D) 踐踏

2. 交通阻塞通常發生在尖峰時刻。
   (A) 高度
   (B) 阻塞
   (C) 快速的
   (D) 疾馳

3. 她立志要當空服員，這樣她就可以環遊世界了。
   (A) 峽谷
   (B) 飛行
   (C) 碼頭
   (D) 通勤族

4. 特斯拉是一家電動車公司。
   (A) 火山
   (B) 小徑
   (C) 潛艇
   (D) 車輛

5. 這場研討會扮演讓學生交流研究發現的平台。
   (A) 水池
   (B) 燈塔
   (C) 雜貨店
   (D) 平台

6. 全球暖化將危及人類生存。
   (A) 東部的
   (B) 太平洋的
   (C) 全球的
   (D) 跳降落傘

7. 每年有超過上百萬的朝聖者前往麥加。
   (A) 行李
   (B) 探險
   (C) 旅程
   (D) 朝聖者

8. 颶風來臨前，這區的居民都被撤離了。
   (A) 撤離
   (B) 涉水
   (C) 到達
   (D) 旅行

9. 飛機起飛前，請繫緊你的安全帶。
   (A) 包圍
   (B) 繫緊
   (C) 維持
   (D) 賺取

10. 他們在倫敦的郊區買了一間豪宅。
   (A) 郵局
   (B) 來源
   (C) 郊區
   (D) 貧民區

二、克漏字測驗

在《不可能的任務》系列電影中，湯姆克魯斯扮演資深特務伊森韓特這個角色。伊森周遊世界各國，專門處理高度危險的國際任務，他精通15國語言，並能讀唇語。

他最出生入死的經驗之一，包括在法國高速列車（Train à Grande Vitesse, TGV）上與IMF情報組織的叛徒搏鬥。為了阻止那位叛徒搭上直升機逃走，伊森把一個有引爆作用的口香糖黏在直升機的擋風玻璃上，隨後直升機爆炸的力道把伊森彈到火車的車尾。

今年伊森又被指派一項新任務，他的冒險肯定會像以前一樣讓你的腎上腺素隨之飆升。

1.
(A) 近用
(B) 乞求
(C) 離開
(D) 旅行

2.
(A) 語言
(B) 費用
(C) 入口
(D) 公路

3.
(A) 阻塞
(B) 山脈
(C) 火車
(D) 大型豪華轎車

4.
(A) 月台
(B) 直升機
(C) 天橋
(D) 通道

5.
(A) 冒險
(B) 酒館
(C) 船隻
(D) 觀光

一、選擇題

1.(B) 2. (B) 3.(B) 4.(D) 5.(D)
6.(C) 7. (D) 8.(A) 9.(B) 10.(C)

二、克漏字測驗

1.(D) 2.(A) 3.(C)
4.(B) 5.(A)

Unit 05 和育有關的單字

多益測驗的命題強調生活化與實用性，學會這些與「育」有關的單字，不僅能讓你在多益考場上所向披靡，在日常生活上也可以靈活運用喔！

誇讚人非常有智慧可以這麼說

- **Her words of wisdom really inspired me to keep on my research.**
  她充滿智慧的話語啟發我繼續我的研究。
- **His cutting edge technology hit the headline.**
  他的領先科技登上了頭條新聞。
- **She is such a genius. You wouldn't believe she is only six if you didn't see it yourself.**
  她真是個天才。如果你沒有親眼看見，你不會相信她只有六歲。

不同學科可以這麼說

- **Mathematics is my favorite subject.**
  數學是我最喜歡的科目。
- **I major in accounting in college.**
  我大學主修會計。

上台報告可以這麼說

- **The diagram presents a rapid sales growth in the first season.**
  這個圖表呈現出了第一季銷售額的快速成長。
- **If you have any question, please feel free to ask.**
  如果你有任何疑問，請不吝提出。

勤奮好學可以這麼說

- **I have been taking extra curriculum since last semester.**
  我從上個學期就開始上額外課程。

- **Given your extraordinary performance at school, you can totally apply for full scholarship.**
  考量你在學校的優異表現，你完全可以申請全額獎學金。

準備考試可以這麼說

- **Prayers won't help, if you don't start preparing for your examination.**
  如果你不開始為考試做準備的話，祈禱也不會有任何幫助的。

- **I'm afraid I will fail the chemistry test. I don't understand a single word Mr. Chen said in class.**
  我擔心我的化學考試會不及格。陳老師上課講的話我一個字都聽不懂。

Unit 05 和育有關的單字

able [ˋebḷ] adj. 能幹的、有能力的 Track 0924

例句 How much are you able to finish in one day?
你一天有能力完成多少？

搭配詞 be able to 能夠……

academic [ˏækəˋdɛmɪk] Track 0925

adj. 學院的、大學的、學術的

例句 Academic freedom should be protected. 學術自由應該被保障。

搭配詞 academic freedom 學術自由

academy [əˋkædəmɪ] n. 學院、專科院校 Track 0926

例句 Emma Stone won the Academy Award for Best Leading Actress.
艾瑪·史東獲得奧斯卡最佳女主獎。

搭配詞 Academy Award 學院獎＝奧斯卡金像獎

accounting [əˋkaʊntɪŋ] n. 會計、會計學 Track 0927

例句 Financial accounting is his favorite subject at school.
財務會計是他在學校最喜歡的課。

搭配詞 financial accounting 財務會計

accurate [ˋækjərɪt] adj. 正確的、準確的 Track 0928

例句 No one knew the accurate answer to his question.
沒有人知道他這個問題的正確答案。

同義字 exact

addition [əˋdɪʃən] n. 加、加法 Track 0929

＊字尾-tion有轉變為名詞的意思

例句 The student is trying to solve these addition and subtraction math questions. 這個學生正試著要解決這些加法與減法的數學問題。

adjective [ˋædʒɪktɪv] n. 形容詞 Track 0930

例句 We can use adjective phrases to describe or add extra meanings to a noun.
我們能使用形容詞片語來形容一個名詞或對它加上更多意義。

搭配詞 adjective phrase 形容詞片語

admiration [ˏædməˋreʃən] n. 欽佩、讚賞 Track 0931

＊字尾-tion有轉變為名詞的意思

例句 Her self-admiration blinded her to see her own shortcomings.
她自我欣賞的程度，使她無法看見自己的缺點。

搭配詞 self-admiration 自我欣賞

a b c d e f g h i j k l m n o p q r s t u v w x y z

adverb [əd`vɝb] n. 副詞 Track 0932

例句 We learned that relative adverbs are used to start a description for a noun.
我們學習到：關係副詞是用來引出對名詞的描述。

搭配詞 relative adverb 關係副詞

agriculture [`ægrɪˌkʌltʃɚ] n. 農業、農藝、農學 Track 0933

＊字首agri-有「農田的」之意

例句 The development of agriculture is very important to a country.
農業發展對一個國家來說很重要。

aim [em] n./v. 瞄準、目標 Track 0934

例句 The project aims at helping the poor.
這項計畫目標在於幫助貧困人士。

搭配詞 aim at 以……為目標

alphabet [`ælfəˌbɛt] n. 字母、字母表 Track 0935

例句 My 2-year-old son can sing alphabet song.
我的兩歲兒子會唱字母歌。

搭配詞 alphabet song 字母歌

ambition [æm`bɪʃən] n. 雄心壯志、志向 Track 0936

＊字尾-tion有轉變為名詞的意思

例句 His daughter's ambition is to become a president in the future.
他女兒的志向是未來成為總統。

搭配詞 ambition to 有……的志向

ancient [`enʃənt] adj. 古老的、古代的 Track 0937

例句 It took archaeologists centuries to study the Ancient Egypt.
考古學家花了數百年研究古埃及。

搭配詞 Ancient Egypt 古埃及

angel [`endʒəl] n. 天使 Track 0938

例句 She's practically an angel. 她簡直是個天使。

易混淆字 angle 角度

angle [`æŋg!] n. 角度、立場 Track 0939

例句 We should sometimes look at things from a different angle.
我們有時得換個角度看事情。

answer [`ænsɚ] n./v. 回答、答案 Track 0940

例句 The naughty boy quickly answered back with a punchline.
這個調皮的小男孩很快回嘴了很有笑點的一句話。

搭配詞 answer back 回嘴

antonym [`æntəˌnɪm] n. 反義字 Track 0941

例句 It is quite clear that "fat" is the antonym of "thin."
很明顯地，「胖」是「瘦」的反義字。

反義字 synonym 同義字

anything [ˋɛnɪ͵θɪŋ] pro. 任何事物 Track 0942

例句 She is anything but nice. 她根本就不好相處。

搭配詞 anything but 根本不……

---

apply [əˋplaɪ] v. 請求、應用 Track 0943

例句 We have to apply for a visa before going to the States.
我們去美國前得申請簽證。

搭配詞 apply for 申請

---

area [ˋɛrɪə] n. 地區、領域、面積、方面 Track 0944

例句 How many convenience stores are there in this rural area?
這個鄉下地區有幾家便利商店？

搭配詞 rural area 鄉下地區

---

argue [ˋɑrgjʊ] v. 爭辯、辯論 Track 0945

例句 My son argued with me this morning. 我兒子早上和我爭辯。

搭配詞 argue with 與……爭辯

---

argument [ˋɑrgjəmənt] n. 爭論、議論 Track 0946

＊字尾-ment有轉變為名詞之意

例句 They had an argument when I was out.
我不在時，他們進行了一場爭論。

搭配詞 have an argument 產生爭論

---

arithmetic [əˋrɪθmə͵tɪk] n. 算術 Track 0947

例句 She is good at mental arithmetic. 她心算很強。

搭配詞 mental arithmetic 心算

---

article/essay [ˋɑrtɪkḷ]/[ˋɛse] n. 文章、論文 Track 0948

例句 He writes articles on his blog everyday. 他在部落格每天發表文章。

搭配詞 write an article 寫文章

---

ask [æsk] v. 問、要求 Track 0949

例句 You asked for it. 你活該。

搭配詞 ask for 要求、活該

---

astronomy [əsˋtrɑnəmɪ] n. 天文學 Track 0950

例句 I am very interested in astrology and astronomy.
我對星象學和天文學很有興趣。

---

attention [əˋtɛnʃən] n. 注意、專心 Track 0951

＊字尾-tion有轉變為名詞的意思

例句 We should pay attention when the flight attendants are talking.
空服員在說話時，我們應該專心聽。

搭配詞 pay attention 專心

a b c d e f g h i j k l m n o p q r s t u v w x y z

attitude [ˋætə,tjud] n. 態度、心態 Track 0952

例句 It's not professional to have an attitude in the office.
在辦公室耍脾氣很不專業。

搭配詞 have an attitude 耍脾氣

autobiography [,ɔtəbaɪˋɑgrəfɪ] n. 自傳 Track 0953

＊字首auto-有「自動的、自我的」之意

例句 I am reading Obama's autobiography. 我在讀歐巴馬的自傳。

搭配詞 biography 傳記

avoid [əˋvɔɪd] v. 避開、避免 Track 0954

例句 Learn from a mistake, and avoid making it again.
從錯誤中學習，並避免再發生一樣的錯誤。

搭配詞 avoid doing sth 避免做某事

bachelor [ˋbætʃələ] n. 單身漢、學士 Track 0955

例句 We are having a bachelor party tonight. 我們今晚要開單身派對。

backward [ˋbækwəd] Track 0956

adj./adv. 向後方的、面對後方的

例句 Driving your car backwards isn't very safe.
倒退著開車不是很安全。

反義字 forward 向前

basic [ˋbesɪk] adj. 基本、要素 Track 0957

例句 These are very basic rules that we need to follow.
我們必須遵守這些很基本的規則。

搭配詞 basic rule 基本規則

beginner [bɪˋgɪnə] n. 初學者 Track 0958

＊字尾-er有「者」之意

例句 It's all right for a beginner to know nothing.
初學者什麼都不知道也沒關係。

同義字 newcomer

behave [bɪˋhev] v. 行動、舉止 Track 0959

例句 The child impressed his teacher because he was so well-behaved.
這孩子讓老師印象深刻，因為他彬彬有禮。

搭配詞 well-behaved 行為良好的

belief [bɪˋlif] n. 相信、信念 Track 0960

例句 I don't think we should argue about religious beliefs.
我覺得我們不應該吵宗教信念的事。

反義字 disbelief 不相信

believe [bɪˋliv] v. 認為、相信 Track 0961

例句 Do you believe in superstitions? 你相信迷信嗎？

搭配詞 believe in 相信……

biological [ˌbaɪoˋlɑdʒɪkḷ] Track 0962
adj. 生物學的、有關生物學的
例句 His biological clock was thrown completely out of kilter.
他的生理時鐘被弄得很混亂。

搭配詞 biological clock 生理時鐘

---

bible [ˋbaɪbḷ] n. 聖經 Track 0963
例句 I read the Holy Bible before going to bed every night.
我在每晚睡前都會讀聖經。

搭配詞 Holy Bible 聖經

---

biography [baɪˋɑgrəfɪ] n. 傳記 Track 0964
例句 Have you read any biographies of Lincoln? 你讀過林肯的傳記嗎？

搭配詞 autobiography 自傳

---

biology [baɪˋɑlədʒɪ] n. 生物學 Track 0965
例句 Biology is Jenny's favorite subject because she could dissect frogs.
珍妮最喜歡生物課，因為她可以解剖青蛙。

---

blackboard [ˋblækˌbord] n. 黑板 Track 0966
例句 The teacher drew a big circle on the blackboard.
老師在黑板上畫了一個大圓圈。

搭配詞 on the blackboard 在黑板上

---

blank [blæŋk] adj./n. 空白的、空格 Track 0967
例句 Please write your name and address in the blanks.
請把名字和地址寫在空白處。

反義字 full 填滿的

---

book [bʊk] n. 書 Track 0968
例句 I am writing a reference book about my hometown.
我在寫一本和我的家鄉有關的參考書。

搭配詞 reference book 參考書

---

borrow [ˋbɑro] v. 借來、採用 Track 0969
例句 Please return the pen that you borrowed from me yesterday.
請把你昨天跟我借的那枝筆還我。

搭配詞 borrow from 向……借來

---

botany [ˋbɑtənɪ] n. 植物學 Track 0970
例句 We learnt at school today that zoology and botany are the two main branches of biology.
我們今天在學校學到：動物學和植物學是生物學的兩大分支。

易混淆字 baton 權杖

---

brilliant [ˋbrɪljənt] adj. 有才氣的、出色的 Track 0971
例句 The pianist gave a brilliant performance to the audience.
這位鋼琴家為聽眾帶來出色的表演。

搭配詞 brilliant performance 出色表現

capable [ˋkepəbl̩] adj. 有能力的 Track 0972
＊字尾-able有「可以、能」的意思
例句 No one is capable of living alone in their entire life.
沒有人有能力可以一生都一個人住。
搭配詞 capable of 有……的能力

celebrate [ˋsɛlə͵bret] v. 慶祝、慶賀 Track 0973
例句 The event will be held in celebration of the company's 80th anniversary. 這個活動是為慶祝公司成立80週年。
搭配詞 in celebration of 為……慶祝

chalk [tʃɔk] n. 粉筆 Track 0974
例句 Would you please bring three boxes of chalk for our teacher?
你可以幫我們的老師帶三盒粉筆來嗎？
易混淆字 choke 嗆到

chapter [ˋtʃæptɚ] n. 章、章節 Track 0975
例句 It took me only one hour to finish chapter one of this novel.
我只花了一個小時就看完這本小說的第一章了。
搭配詞 chapter one 第一章

chart [tʃɑrt] n. 圖表 Track 0976
例句 Should we use a pie chart to show the growth of our new product?
我們該用一個圓餅圖來表示我們新產品的成長嗎？
搭配詞 pie chart 圓餅圖

cheat [tʃit] v. 欺騙、作弊 Track 0977
例句 He cheated on his wife. 他對妻子不忠。
搭配詞 cheat on sb 對某人不忠

chemical [ˋkɛmɪkl̩] adj. 化學的 Track 0978
例句 The chemical weapons are lethal, and they should be banned.
這些化學武器是致命的，應該被禁止。
搭配詞 chemical weapon 化學武器

chemistry [ˋkɛmɪstrɪ] n. 化學 Track 0979
例句 I scored higher in organic chemistry than in math.
我有機化學考得比數學高。
搭配詞 organic chemistry 有機化學

choice [tʃɔɪs] n. 選擇 Track 0980
例句 He was admitted by MIT and Harvard, so he needed to make a choice. 他被麻省理工學院和哈佛大學錄取，所以他得做個選擇。
搭配詞 make a choice 做選擇

choose [tʃuz] v. 選擇 Track 0981
例句 We choose the best products for our customers.
我們選最好的產品，提供給消費者。
搭配詞 choose the best 選最好的

claim [klem] n./v. 主張、要求 Track 0982

例句 The thief claimed that he didn't steal anything.
這個竊賊主張他什麼也沒偷。

搭配詞 claim that... 主張

class [klæs] n. 班級、階級、種類 Track 0983

例句 The CEO can fly first-class for free wherever he travels.
這位執行長無論到哪裡，都能免費搭頭等艙。

搭配詞 first-class 頭等的

clever [ˋklɛvɚ] adj. 聰明的、伶俐的 Track 0984

例句 I think my daughter is clever enough to work out the math problem.
我想我的女兒夠聰明，可以解開這題數學題。

同義字 intelligent

collect [kəˋlɛkt] v. 收集 Track 0985

例句 What do you think of the stamps I have collected since I was eight years old? 你覺得我從八歲開始收集的郵票如何呢？

搭配詞 collect stamps 收藏郵票

college [ˋkɑlɪdʒ] n. 學院、大學 Track 0986

例句 My son is going to the Royal College of Art in England.
我兒子要去英國上皇家藝術大學。

搭配詞 college of art 藝術學院

comma [ˋkɑmə] n. 逗號 Track 0987

例句 Using a comma in a sentence can help the reader understand you better. 在句子中使用逗號可以幫助讀者更瞭解你的意思。

易混淆字 coma 昏迷

commentary [ˋkɑmənˏtɛrɪ] n. 注釋、評論 Track 0988

例句 The anchor is giving a running commentary on the sport event.
主播正在連續報導這場賽事。

搭配詞 running commentary 連續報導

competence [ˋkɑmpətəns] n. 能力、才能 Track 0989

例句 I admire her competence in language.
我很欣賞她語言的才能。

competent [ˋkɑmpətənt] adj. 能幹的、有能力的 Track 0990

＊字尾-ent有轉變為形容詞的意思

例句 She is competent enough for the marketing manager's position.
她夠能幹，有能力勝任行銷主管的位置。

搭配詞 be competent for 勝任

Confucius [kənˋfjuʃəs] n. 孔子 Track 0991

例句 The Confucius Institute was established in China.
孔子學院是在中國成立的。

搭配詞 Confucius Institute 孔子學院

a b c d e f g h i j k l m n o p q r s t u v w x y z

congratulations [kən͵grætʃə`leʃənz] Track 0992

n. 祝賀、恭喜　＊字尾-s有轉變為複數之意

例句 Congratulations on your graduation. We are very proud of you.
恭喜你畢業。我們很為你驕傲。

搭配詞 congratulations on 對……祝賀

conjunction [kən`dʒʌŋkʃən] n. 連接、關聯 Track 0993

＊字尾-tion有轉變為名詞的意思

例句 This novel should be read in conjunction with the author's biography.
這本小說應該要和作者的傳記一起連接著讀。

conservative [kən`sɝvətɪv] Track 0994

n./adj. 保守主義者、保守的

例句 I come from a very conservative family.
我來自一個很保守的家庭。

反義字 progressive 革新主義者、進步的

consider [kən`sɪdɚ] v. 仔細考慮、認為 Track 0995

例句 The proposal was ill-considered and caused a backlash from many employees. 這項提案欠缺思慮，造成許多員工的反彈。

搭配詞 ill-considered 欠缺考慮的

consonant [`kɑnsənənt] n. 子音、輔音 Track 0996

例句 This voiceless consonant is very hard to pronounce.
這個無聲子音很難發音。

搭配詞 voiceless consonant 無聲子音

contest [`kɑntɛst] n. 比賽 Track 0997

例句 There will be a singing contest in our neighborhood.
我們的社區會辦一場歌唱比賽。

同義字 competition

correct [kə`rɛkt] adj. 正確的 Track 0998

例句 Your answer is correct. 你的答案是正確的。

反義字 incorrect 不正確的

course [kors] n. 課程、講座、過程、路線 Track 0999

例句 This is the toughest online course in school.
這是學校最難的線上課程。

搭配詞 online course 線上課程

crayon [`kreən] n. 蠟筆 Track 1000

例句 My daughter is drawing with crayons.
我女兒正在用蠟筆畫畫。

同義字 pastel

create [krɪ`et] v. 創造 Track 1001

例句 You can create an account on this website.
你可以在這個網站創立帳號。

搭配詞 create an account 創立帳號

creation [krɪ`eʃən] n. 創造 Track 1002

＊字尾-tion有轉變為名詞的意思

例句 The eccentric scientist's latest creation is a pill that makes you glow in the dark. 那個古怪科學家的最新創造物是一個可以讓你在黑暗中發光的藥丸。

搭配詞 latest creations 最新創造物

creativity [ˌkrie`tɪvətɪ] n. 創造力 Track 1003

例句 Creativity is the most important thing for fashion design. 時尚設計最重要的就是創造力。

criticism [`krɪtəˌsɪzəm] n. 評論、批評的論文 Track 1004

例句 Her blog is full of constructive criticisms on politics. 她的部落格滿滿都是富有建設性的政治評論。

搭配詞 constructive criticism 建設性評論

criticize [`krɪtəˌsaɪz] v. 批評、批判 Track 1005

例句 She criticized him for cheating on his wife. 她批評他對妻子不忠。

搭配詞 criticize sb for 為……批評某人

curriculum [kə`rɪkjələm] n. 課程 Track 1006

例句 He takes part in extra curriculum activities. 他參加很多課外活動。

搭配詞 extra curriculum 額外課程

dangerous [`dendʒərəs] adj. 危險的 Track 1007

＊字尾-ous有轉變為形容詞之意

例句 It is dangerous to drink before driving. 開車前喝酒是很危險的。

搭配詞 dangerous area 危險區域

data [`detə] n. 資料、事實、材料 Track 1008

例句 The online data is very convenient. 這個線上資料庫很方便。

搭配詞 data base 數據資料庫

depict [dɪ`pɪkt] v. 描述、敘述 Track 1009

例句 She depicted the love between brothers beautifully in her new novel. 她在她的新小説中優美地描述了兄弟愛。

同義字 describe

descend [dɪ`sɛnd] v. 下降、突襲 Track 1010

＊字首de-有「下、反」之意

例句 The elevator is descending to the first floor. 電梯要下降到一樓去。

反義字 ascend 上升

debate [dɪ`bet] n./v. 討論、辯論 Track 1011

例句 They're having a fierce debate on human nature. 他們在進行一場和人的天性有關的激烈辯論。

搭配詞 fierce debate 激烈辯論

decision [dɪˋsɪʒən] n. 決定、決斷力 Track 1012

例句 Marrying my best friend is the best decision I have ever made.
和我最好的朋友結婚是我做過最好的決定。

搭配詞 make a decision 下決定

define [dɪˋfaɪn] v. 下定義 Track 1013

例句 Can you tell me how you define “a lot”?
你可以跟我說你對「很多」的定義是多少嗎？

definition [ˏdɛfəˋnɪʃən] n. 定義 Track 1014

＊字尾-tion有轉變為名詞的意思

例句 What's the clear definition of love? 愛的明確定義是什麼？

搭配詞 clear definition 清楚定義

degree [dɪˋgri] n. 學位、程度 Track 1015

例句 She has a bachelor's degree in arts. 她有大學藝術學位。

搭配詞 bachelor's degree 大學學位

description [dɪˋskrɪpʃən] n. 敘述、說明 Track 1016

＊字尾-tion有轉變為名詞的意思

例句 It's hard for me to give a description of the color of the dress.
我很難說明那件洋裝的顏色是什麼樣子。

design [dɪˋzaɪn] n./v. 設計 Track 1017

例句 This cellphone is well-designed; no wonder it sold out quickly.
這支手機的設計精良，難怪很快就賣完。

搭配詞 well-designed 設計良好的

devil [ˋdɛvḷ] n. 魔鬼、惡魔 Track 1018

例句 Children sometimes are like little devils.
孩子們有時候像小惡魔似的。

反義字 angel 天使

diagram [ˋdaɪəˏgræm] n. 圖表、圖樣 Track 1019

例句 I have to make a tree diagram for my presentation.
我為了報告要做一個樹狀圖。

搭配詞 tree diagram 樹狀圖

dictation [dɪkˋteʃən] n. 口述、口授 Track 1020

＊字尾-tion有轉變為名詞的意思

例句 The secretary took dictation for her boss.
那名秘書為老闆打出他口述的內容。

搭配詞 take dictation 做聽寫

dictate [ˋdɪktet] v. 口授、聽寫、命令 Track 1021

例句 He dictated me to leave the bookstore. 他命令我離開書店。

搭配詞 dictate sb to do sth 命令某人做某事

differentiate [dɪfəˋrɛnʃɪ͵et] v. 辨別、區分 Track 1022

例句 I don't know how to differentiate between the twin brothers.
這對雙胞胎兄弟之間怎麼分辨，我還真不知道。

difference [ˋdɪfərəns] n. 差異、差別 Track 1023

例句 Young people can make a difference with their innovative ideas and execution skills.
年輕人運用他們的創新點子和良好的執行力，也能有所作為。

搭配詞 make a difference 有所作為

diploma [dɪˋplomə] n. 文憑、畢業證書

例句 I hope I'll get my college diploma this year.
我希望今年可以拿到大學文憑。

搭配詞 college diploma 大學文憑

disagreement [͵dɪsəˋgrimənt] Track 1024

n. 意見不合、不同意 ＊字尾-ment有轉變為名詞之意

例句 They are in disagreement on where to spend their Christmas holiday. 他們對於在哪度過聖誕假期這件事意見不合。

反義字 agreement 同意

discipline [ˋdɪsəplɪn] n. 紀律、訓練 Track 1025

例句 Good discipline is very important when training military students.
紀律嚴明對於訓練軍校生來說，是很重要的。

搭配詞 good discipline 紀律嚴明

discover [dɪˋskʌvɚ] v. 發現 Track 1026

＊字首dis-有「不」之意

例句 She discovered a lovely stream in the forest.
她在樹林中發現了一條可愛的小溪。

同義字 find

discuss [dɪˋskʌs] v. 討論、商議 Track 1027

例句 They discuss everything with their teacher.
他們和老師討論所有的事情。

搭配詞 discuss with 與……討論

discussion [dɪˋskʌʃən] n. 討論、商議 Track 1028

例句 The legislation of same-sex marriage is still under discussion.
同性婚姻的立法仍在討論中。

搭配詞 under discussion 討論中

dishonest [dɪsˋɑnɪst] adj. 不誠實的 Track 1029

＊字首dis-有「不」之意

例句 It was very dishonest of you to cheat in the exam.
你考試作弊真是不誠實。

反義字 honest 誠實的

division [dəˋvɪʒən] n. 分割、除去 Track 1030

例句 Not all the people agree upon a division of the team into male and female.
並不是大家都同意把團隊分成男女兩邊。

doubt [daʊt] n. 疑問 Track 1031

例句 There is no doubt that he's guilty. Just look at his face.
他毫無疑問地有罪。看他的臉就知道了。

搭配詞 no doubt 沒有疑問

draft [dræft] n. 草稿 Track 1032

例句 I spent too much time writing a draft.
我花太多時間打草稿了。

易混淆字 draff 殘渣

ecology [ɪˋkɑlədʒɪ] n. 生態學 Track 1033

例句 I am glad I took wildlife ecology at college.
我很高興我在大學時有上野生動物生態學。

搭配詞 wildlife ecology 野生動物生態學

economics [ˏikəˋnɑmɪks] n. 經濟學 Track 1034

例句 She might major in macro economics in college.
她大學可能會主修總體經濟學。

搭配詞 macro economics 總體經濟學

educate [ˋɛdʒəˏket] v. 教育 Track 1035

例句 She educates her son at home by herself.
她自己在家裡教育兒子。

同義字 instruct

education [ˏɛdʒəˋkeʃən] n. 教育 Track 1036

＊字尾-tion有轉變為名詞的意思

例句 Most children in the area don't have the opportunity to take physical education. 這一區大部分的孩子都沒有機會上到體育課程。

搭配詞 physical education 體育課程

educational [ˏɛdʒəˋkeʃənl] adj. 教育性的 Track 1037

＊字尾-al有轉變為形容詞之意

例句 This educational institution is reputated for its English courses.
這所教育機構以英文課程著稱。

搭配詞 educational institution 教育機構

effort [ˋɛfɚt] n. 努力 Track 1038

例句 I made a lot of effort to make sure that my PowerPoint slides look pretty.
我花很大的努力讓我的投影片看起來漂亮。

搭配詞 make effort 努力

electronics [ɪlɛkˋtrɑnɪks] n. 電機工程學、電子 Track 1039

例句 Taiwan is famous for its electronics industry.
台灣的電子工業很有名。

搭配詞 electronics industry 電子工業

elementary [ˏɛləˋmɛntərɪ] adj. 基本的 Track 1040

例句 Jimmy studies at this elementary school.
吉米在這所小學就讀。

搭配詞 elementary school 小學

eliminate [ɪˋlɪmə͵net] v. 消除、淘汰 Track 1041

例句 The pesticide can effectively eliminate pests.
這罐殺蟲劑能有效消滅害蟲。

搭配詞
eliminate pests 消滅害蟲

eloquence [ˋɛləkwəns] n. 雄辯、口才 Track 1042

例句 She wins people over with her eloquence.
她利用口才贏得人心。

eloquent [ˋɛləkwənt] adj. 辯才無礙的 Track 1043

*字尾-ent有轉變為形容詞之意

例句 She is not only eloquent but also diligent.
她不但辯才無礙，也很努力工作。

同義字
well-spoken

encyclopedia/encyclopaedia Track 1044

[ɪn͵saɪkləˋpidɪə] n. 百科全書

例句 The child is dubbed as a walking encyclopedia.
這孩子被大家封為行動百科全書。

搭配詞
walking encyclopedia
活動百科全書

engineering [͵ɛndʒəˋnɪrɪŋ] n. 工程學 Track 1045

例句 He gave up studying genetic engineering and worked as a veterinarian. 他放棄讀基因工程學，成為獸醫。

搭配詞
genetic engineering
基因工程

enlighten [ɪnˋlaɪtn̩] v. 啟發 Track 1046

*字首en-有「使」之意

例句 After reading the book, I felt kind of enlightened.
讀完那本書，我感覺好像被啟發了。

同義字
illuminate

equation [ɪˋkweʃən] n. 相等 Track 1047

例句 The chemical equation is difficult to understand.
這個化學相等式很難懂。

搭配詞
chemical equation
化學相等式

equivalent [ɪˋkwɪvələnt] n./adj. 相等物、相等的 Track 1048

*字尾-tion有轉變為名詞的意思

例句 We know that 50/100 is equivalent to 1/2.
我們知道50/100相當於1/2。

搭配詞
be equivalent to
與……相當

erase [ɪˋres] v. 擦掉 Track 1049

例句 He wants to invent something that can erase horrible momeries.
他想要發明能抹去可怕回憶的東西。

搭配詞
erase memory 抹去記憶

eraser [ɪˋresɚ] n. 橡皮擦 Track 1050

*字尾-er有轉變為名詞的意思

例句 Why do I lose my eraser all the time?
我為什麼老是把橡皮擦弄丟呢？

a b c d e f g h i j k l m n o p q r s t u v w x y z

error [ˋɛrɚ] n. 錯誤 Track 1051

例句 You need to correct the errors in the letter.
你必須把信裡面的錯誤改正。

同義字 mistake

especially [əˋspɛʃəlɪ] adv. 特別地 Track 1052

＊字尾-ly有轉變為副詞之意

例句 Please pay attention to these kids, especially Joanna.
請看著這些小孩，尤其特別要注意喬安娜。

同義字 particularly

essay [ˋɛse] n. 短文、隨筆、論說文 Track 1053

例句 Could you help me proofread my essay? I need to present it tomorrow. 你可以幫我校對論文嗎？我明天要發表。

搭配詞 present an essay 發表論文

ethical [ˋɛθɪkl] adj. 道德的 Track 1054

＊字尾-al有轉變為形容詞之意

例句 He is unethical and unscrupulous. 他既不道德又厚顏無恥。

反義字 unethical 不道德的

ethics [ˋɛθɪks] n. 倫理（學） Track 1055

例句 You can accomplish anything if you have strong work ethics.
如果你有強烈的職業道德，必能成就任何事。

搭配詞 work ethics 職業道德

examination [ɪg͵zæməˋneʃən] n. 考試 Track 1056

＊字尾-tion有轉變為名詞的意思

例句 All these students are going to take the same examination at the end of the year. 這些學生在年底都要考同一場考試。

縮寫 exam

examine [ɪgˋzæmɪn] v. 檢查、考試 Track 1057

例句 The doctor examined his ears. 醫師檢查了他的耳朵。

example [ɪgˋzæmpl] n. 榜樣、例子 Track 1058

例句 For example, an apple is a kind of fruit.
舉例來說，蘋果是一種水果。

搭配詞 for example 舉例來說

excerpt [ˋɛksɝpt] n. 摘錄 Track 1059

例句 Our English teacher printed out the excerpt of the book for us to read.
我們的英文老師把書中摘錄的部分印出來給我們讀。

易混淆字 except 除了

exhibition [͵ɛksəˋbɪʃən] n. 展覽 Track 1060

＊字尾-tion有轉變為名詞的意思

例句 The exhibition hall displays Van Gogh's paintings.
這個展場展示梵谷的畫。

搭配詞 exhibition hall 展場

expertise [ˏɛkspɚˋtiz] n./v. 專門知識 Track 1061

例句 His business expertise helps our company a lot.
他的商業專門知識對我們的公司很有幫助。

搭配詞
the expertise in sth. 專精於

explain [ɪkˋsplen] v. 解釋 Track 1062

例句 Could you please explain this equation in detail? I still don't get it.
你可以詳細解釋這個數學方程式嗎？我還是不懂。

搭配詞
explain in detail 詳細解釋

explanation [ˏɛkspləˋneʃən] n. 說明、解釋 Track 1063

＊字尾-tion有轉變為名詞的意思

例句 The fact is so obvious that it needs no explanation.
這個事實顯而易見，無需解釋。

搭配詞
need no explanation
無需解釋

express [ɪkˋsprɛs] v. 表達、說明 Track 1064

例句 You need to express yourself when needed.
你在必要時，應表達自己的立場。

搭配詞
express oneself 表達立場

expression [ɪkˋsprɛʃən] n. 表達、表情 Track 1065

例句 His facial expression said it all.
他臉上的表情就說得一清二楚了。

搭配詞
facial expression 臉部表情

extension [ɪkˋstɛnʃən] n. 擴大、延長、分支 Track 1066

＊字首ex-有「外」的意思

例句 She coiled the extension cord and then put it in a drawer.
她把延長線捲起來，收到抽屜裡。

搭配詞
extension cord 延長線

extensive [ɪkˋstɛnsɪv] adj. 廣泛的、廣大的 Track 1067

＊字首ex-有「外」的意思

例句 I will do extensive reading during my long vacation.
我會在長假中廣泛閱讀。

反義字
intensive 密集的

extract [ˋɛkstrækt] n. 摘錄 Track 1068

＊字首ex-有「外」的意思

例句 The ingredients of this shampoo include yeast extract.
這個洗髮精的成分包含酵母萃取物。

搭配詞
yeast extract 酵母萃取物

extracurricular [ˏɛkstrəkəˋrɪkjələ] adj. 課外的 Track 1069

例句 Extracurricular activities are important for all students.
課外活動對所有學生都很重要。

搭配詞
extracurricular activity
課外活動

fable [ˋfebḷ] n. 寓言 Track 1070

例句 I read Aesop's Fables when I was a child.
我在孩提時期就讀過伊索寓言。

搭配詞
Aesop's Fables 伊索寓言

a b c d e f g h i j k l m n o p q r s t u v w x y z

faculty [ˋfækḷtɪ] n. 全體教員、系所 Track 1071

例句 It's hard to persuade all the faculty members to agree on the plan.
很難說服所有教職員同意這個計畫。

搭配詞 faculty member 教員

fact [fækt] n. 事實 Track 1072

例句 In fact, he has been broke for some time.
事實是他已經破產一陣子了。

搭配詞 in fact 事實上

fail [fel] n./v. 失敗、不及格 Track 1073

例句 I failed to make up with him.
我想跟他和好的努力失敗了。

搭配詞 fail to 失敗

fairy [ˋfɛrɪ] n. 仙子 Track 1074

例句 She looked like a princess from the fairy tale.
她像個從童話故事走出來的公主似的。

搭配詞 fairy tale 童話

false [fɔls] adj. 錯誤的、假的、虛偽的 Track 1075

例句 A kitten is a young cat. True or false?
「kitten」指的是小貓。對還是錯？

反義字 true 真實的

fancy [ˋfænsɪ] adj./n./v. 想像力、愛好、豪華的 Track 1076

例句 She stayed in a fancy hotel. 她在豪華的旅館下榻。

搭配詞 fancy hotel 豪華旅館

fiction [ˋfɪkʃən] n. 小說、虛構 Track 1077

例句 I am fond of reading science fictions. 我喜歡讀科幻小說。

搭配詞 science fiction 科幻小說

fill [fɪl] v. 填空、填滿 Track 1078

例句 Would you please fill in all the blanks on this application form?
你可以把這張申請單上的空格都填好嗎？

搭配詞 fill in 填寫

find [faɪnd] v. 找到、發現 Track 1079

例句 The police found the criminal's whereabouts.
警方找到罪犯的下落了。

搭配詞 find out 找到

flunk [flʌŋk] v. 失敗、不及格 Track 1080

例句 I can't believe that he flunked the test.
我真難想像他居然會考不及格。

易混淆字 fluent 流暢的

folklore [ˋfok͵lor] n. 民間傳說、民俗 Track 1081

例句 This painting is inspired by the Chinese folklore.
這幅畫的靈感來自於中國民間傳說。

搭配詞 Chinese folklore 中國民間故事

foolish [ˋfulɪʃ] adj. 愚笨的、愚蠢的 Track 1082

＊字尾-ish有「像、類似」的意思

例句 He is so foolish that he came to school without his backpack.
他笨到連包包都沒帶就來上學了。

同義字 stupid

form [fɔrm] n. 形式、表格 Track 1083

例句 Would you please fill out the form at the reception desk first?
可以請你先在接待櫃臺填好這張表格嗎？

搭配詞 fill out a form 填寫表格

formula [ˋfɔrmjələ] n. 公式、法則 Track 1084

例句 Formula One is a kind of motorsport.
一級方程式是一種賽車競賽。

搭配詞 Formula One 一級方程式賽車

freshman [ˋfrɛʃmən] n. 新生、大一生 Track 1085

例句 I lived in the dormitory in my freshman year at college.
我大一時住在宿舍。

gain [gen] n./v. 得到、獲得 Track 1086

例句 He gained her trust by showing her his ID card.
他把身分證明給她看，以得到她的信任。

反義字 loss 失去

genetic [dʒəˋnɛtɪk] adj. 遺傳性 Track 1087

例句 His father specializes in genetic diseases.
他父親專攻遺傳性疾病。

搭配詞 genetic disease 遺傳性疾病

genius [ˋdʒinjəs] n. 天才 Track 1088

例句 I don't think that he is a music genius.
我不覺得他是音樂天才。

反義字 idiot 傻瓜

geographical [͵dʒiəˋgræfɪkl̩] Track 1089

adj. 地理學的、地理的

例句 He made a geographical discovery and changed the history of native Americans. 他的地理發現改變了美國原住民的歷史。

搭配詞 geographical discovery 地理發現

geography [dʒiˋɑgrəfɪ] n. 地理（學） Track 1090

例句 I love physcial geography classes because I like learning about other countries.
我喜歡自然地理課，因為我喜歡學習有關其他國家的事。

搭配詞 physical geography 自然地理學

geometry [dʒɪ`ɑmətrɪ] n. 幾何學 Track 1091

例句 Plane geometry was fun for me, but I'm hopeless at calculus.
我覺得平面幾何學很好玩，但微積分我就沒指望了。

搭配詞 plane geometry 平面幾何學

giant [`dʒaɪənt] n./adj. 巨人、巨大的 Track 1092

例句 Wow, that's a giant-sized snake. 哇，那真是條特大號的蛇。

搭配詞 giant-sized 特大號的

gifted [`gɪftɪd] adj. 有天賦的、有才能的 Track 1093

例句 That pianist is very gifted. 那個鋼琴家非常有天賦。

同義字 talented

goal [gol] n. 目標 Track 1094

例句 He pursues his life goal with all his effort.
他全心全力地追求人生目標。

搭配詞 life goal 人生目標

grade [gred] n. 年級、等級 Track 1095

例句 He is only 4, but he studies in the fifth grade.
他才4歲，但已讀五年級了。

搭配詞 fifth grade 五年級

graduate [`grædʒʊ͵et] v. 畢業 Track 1096

例句 My sister graduated from college last year.
我姊姊去年從大學畢業了。

搭配詞 graduate from 從……畢業

graduation [͵grædʒʊ`eʃən] n. 畢業 Track 1097

＊字尾-tion有轉變為名詞的意思

例句 My dad attended my graduation ceremony.
我爸有來參加我的畢業典禮。

搭配詞 graduation ceremony 畢業典禮

grammar [`græmɚ] n. 文法 Track 1098

例句 I worry about my English grammar a lot.
我常擔心我的英文文法。

搭配詞 English grammar 英文文法

grammatical [grə`mætɪkl] adj. 文法上的 Track 1099

例句 There are several grammatical errors in the composition.
這篇作文中有好幾個文法上的錯誤。

搭配詞 grammatical error 文法上的錯誤

graph [græf] n. 曲線圖、圖表 Track 1100

例句 You can make a bar graph easily with this app.
用這個應用程式，很容易就可以做好一張長條圖。

搭配詞 bar graph 長條圖

graphic [ˋgræfɪk] adj. 圖解的、生動的 Track 1101

例句 The movie was adapted from its graphic novel version.
這部電影是由同名圖像小說改編而成。

搭配詞 graphic novel 圖像小說

grasp [græsp] v. 掌握、領悟、抓牢 Track 1102

例句 The meaning of abstract concepts is hard to grasp.
抽象概念的意思很難掌握。

guide [gaɪd] n./v. 引導者、指南 Track 1103

例句 With this travel guide, you won't get lost in Berlin.
有了這本旅遊指南，你就不會在柏林迷路了。

搭配詞 travel guide 旅遊指南

headline [ˋhɛd͵laɪn] n. 標題 Track 1104

例句 What's the headline news in the newspaper today?
今天報紙的頭版標題是什麼？

搭配詞 headline news 頭條新聞

help [hɛlp] v. 幫助 Track 1105

例句 He helped Jenny out when she had no money to raise her kids.
珍妮沒錢養孩子時，他幫助她擺脫困境。

搭配詞 help out 幫助……擺脫困難

helpful [ˋhɛlpfəl] adj. 有用的 Track 1106

＊字尾-ful有「充滿」的意思

例句 The books might be helpful to them. 這些書對他們可能會有用。

反義字 helpless 無用的

hero/heroine [ˋhɪro]/[ˋhɛro͵ɪn] Track 1107

n. 英雄、勇士／女傑、女英雄

例句 He loves to read stories about heroes.
他喜歡讀和英雄有關的故事。

反義字 coward 懦夫

hint [hɪnt] n. 暗示 Track 1108

例句 I've given him a lot of hints, but he still can't guess the answer.
我已經給他很多暗示了，可是他還是猜不到答案。

搭配詞 give a hint 給暗示

history [ˋhɪstərɪ] n. 歷史 Track 1109

例句 I like learning about modern history of different countries.
我喜歡學習不同國家的近代史。

搭配詞 modern history 近代史

hobby [ˋhɑbɪ] n. 興趣、嗜好 Track 1110

例句 It is my hobby to collect earrings. 我的興趣是收集耳環。

homework [ˋhom͵wɝk] n. 家庭作業 Track 1111

例句 There is so much homework to do today; I have to start immediately.
今天好多功課要做，我得馬上開始了。

搭配詞 do homework 寫作業

honest [ˋɑnɪst] adj. 誠實的、耿直的 Track 1112

例句 He is an honest broker, so we all count on him to resolve our problems. 他是調解人，我們仰賴他解決問題。

搭配詞 honest broker 調解人

humble [ˋhʌmbḷ] adj. 身份卑微的、謙虛的 Track 1113

例句 Never look down on a man just because of his humble beginning.
別只因為一個人出身卑微就輕視他。

搭配詞 humble beginning 出身卑微

hygiene [ˋhaɪdʒin] n. 衛生學、衛生 Track 1114

例句 I studied public hygiene for my master's degree.
我讀研究所時專攻公眾衛生。

搭配詞 public hygiene 公眾衛生

idea [aɪˋdiə] n. 主意、想法、觀念 Track 1115

例句 The main idea of this article is about national security.
這篇文章的主旨是關於國家安全。

搭配詞 main idea 主旨

ignorance [ˋɪgnərəns] n. 無知、不學無術 Track 1116

＊字尾-ance有轉變為名詞之意

例句 Please forgive his ignorance. 請原諒他的無知。

反義詞 knowledge

ignorant [ˋɪgnərənt] adj. 缺乏教育的、無知的 Track 1117

＊字尾-ant有轉變為形容詞之意

例句 He is ignorant of what happened in his class.
他不知道他班上發生了什麼事。

搭配詞 be ignorant of 不知道……

illustrate [ˋɪləstret] v. 舉例說明、畫插圖 Track 1118

例句 Children's books are usually well-illustrated.
童書通常有很多插圖。

搭配詞 well-illustrated 插圖很多的

illustration [ɪ͵lʌsˋtreʃən] n. 說明、插圖 Track 1119

＊字尾-tion有轉變為名詞的意思

例句 I like books with colorful illustrations. 我喜歡有彩色插圖的書。

搭配詞 colorful illustration 彩色插圖

importance [ɪmˋpɔrtṇs] n. 重要性 Track 1120

＊字尾-ance有轉變為名詞之意

例句 Not everyone knows the importance of being on time.
不是每個人都知道準時的重要性。

同義字 significance

include [ɪnˋklud] v. 包含、包括、含有 Track 1121

例句 There are 29 people in our office, including 7 males and 22 females. 我們的辦公室有29個人，包括7名男性與22名女性。

反義字 exclude 不包含

individual [ˏɪndəˋvɪdʒuəl] adj. 個別的 Track 1122

例句 This travel agency specializes in individual travel packages. 這家旅行社擅長安排個人旅遊行程。

搭配詞 individual travel 個人旅遊

inference [ˋɪnfərəns] n. 推理 Track 1123

例句 The species' existence is only known by inference. 我們只能根據推斷，這個物種曾經存在過。

搭配詞 by inference 根據推斷

influence [ˋɪnfluəns] n. 影響 Track 1124

例句 Peter's father has a great influence on him. 彼得的爸爸對他影響很大。

搭配詞 have an influence on 對……有影響

information [ˏɪnfɚˋmeʃən] n. 知識、資訊 Track 1125

＊字尾-tion有轉變為名詞的意思

例句 The information desk is over there. 資訊台在那邊。

搭配詞 information desk 資訊台

ingenious [ɪnˋdʒinjəs] adj. 巧妙的、有獨創性的 Track 1126

＊字尾-ous有轉變為形容詞之意

例句 Ocean's Eleven is about a group of con artists who devised a ingenious plan to steal money. 《瞞天過海》這部電影是關於一群詐騙份子設計巧妙的計畫來偷錢。

搭配詞 ingenious plan 巧妙的

ingenuity [ˏɪndʒəˋnuətɪ] n. 發明才能、聰明才智 Track 1127

例句 Human ingenuity is instrumental to technological development. 人類智慧是科技進步的重要關鍵。

搭配詞 human ingenuity 人類智慧

inherent [ɪnˋhɪrənt] adj. 天生的、固有的 Track 1128

例句 There is an inherent weakness in the structure of his house. 他家的建築架構有個固有的弱點。

insist [ɪnˋsɪst] v. 堅持、強調 Track 1129

例句 We insist that you stay with us tonight. 我們堅持要你今晚在我們這裡過夜。

搭配詞 insist in 堅持

instance [ˋɪnstəns] n. 實例 Track 1130

例句 There are jobs more dangerous than truck driving; for instance, miner. 有些工作比開卡車更危險，舉例來說，礦工就是。

搭配詞 for instance 例如

instruct [ɪn`strʌkt] v. 教導、指令 Track 1131

例句 My manager instructed me to forward this email to our boss.
我的經理指使我把這封電子郵件轉寄給老闆。

搭配詞 instruct sb to do sth 指使某人去做某事

instruction [ɪn`strʌkʃən] n. 指令、教導 Track 1132

＊字尾-tion有轉變為名詞的意思

例句 To installing a driver, please follow the instructions in the manual.
安裝驅動程式時，請遵從手冊裡的指引。

搭配詞 follow the instruction 遵從指令

integrity [ɪn`tɛgrətɪ] n. 正直、誠實、完整 Track 1133

例句 She is a lady of integrity. 她是個正直的女士。

同義字 uprightness

intellect [`ɪntl̩ɛkt] n. 理解力、才智 Track 1134

例句 Elon is a man of intellect. 伊隆是個才智出眾的人。

搭配詞 man of intellect 才智出眾的人

interpret [ɪn`tɝprɪt] v. 說明、解讀、翻譯 Track 1135

＊字首inter-有「互相」之意

例句 Would you please interpret for me? I don't understand the language. 你可以替我翻譯嗎？我不懂這個語言。

易混淆字 interest 興趣

intelligence quotient Track 1136
[ɪn`tɛlədʒəns `kwoʃənt] n. 智商

例句 Even though his IQ is high, his EQ is quite low.
雖然他的智商很高，他的EQ倒是很低。

縮寫 IQ

journal [`dʒɝnl] n. 期刊 Track 1137

例句 It's a great idea to subscribe to this medical journal.
訂閱這份醫學期刊是個好主意。

搭配詞 medical journal 醫學期刊

journalism [`dʒɝnl̩ɪzəm] n. 新聞學、新聞業 Track 1138

＊字尾-ism有「主義、學問」的意思

例句 Citizen journalism has been everywhere since smart phones became a daily necessity.
自從智慧型手機變成日用品以後，公民新聞就充斥各處。

搭配詞 citizen journalism 公民新聞

joyful [`dʒɔɪfəl] adj. 愉快的、喜悅的 Track 1139

＊字尾-ful有「充滿」的意思

例句 Her wedding is such a joyful event. 她的婚禮真是件愉快的活動。

同義字 pleased

judgement/judgment [`dʒʌdʒmənt] Track 1140

n. 判斷、判斷力　＊字尾-ment有轉變為名詞之意

例句 I don't trust my own judgment. 我自己不相信自己的判斷力。

kindergarten [ˋkɪndɚ͵gartn̩] n. 幼稚園 ◀Track 1141

例句 I went to pick up my daughter at the kindergarten.
我到幼稚園去接我的女兒。

know [no] v. 知道、瞭解、認識 ◀Track 1142

例句 The book provides a lot of know-hows on how to write a good resume.
這本書提供很多有關如何寫好履歷表的訣竅。

搭配詞 know-how 訣竅

knowledge [ˋnalɪdʒ] n. 知識 ◀Track 1143

例句 The old professor loves to share his knowledge with us.
這位老教授喜歡和我們分享知識。

knowledgeable [ˋnalɪdʒəbl̩] adj. 博學的 ◀Track 1144

＊字尾-able有「可以、能」的意思

例句 My teacher is very knowledgeable about Chinese history.
我老師在中國歷史方面很博學。

反義字 unknowledgeable 無知的

laboratory [ˋlæbrə͵torɪ] n. 實驗室 ◀Track 1145

例句 I had to work until very late in the laboratory.
我得在實驗室工作到很晚。

縮寫 lab

lazy [ˋlezɪ] adj. 懶惰的 ◀Track 1146

例句 My husband is too lazy to help me with the housework.
我老公太懶了，都不幫我做家事。

反義字 diligent 勤奮的

learn [lɝn] v. 學習、知悉、瞭解 ◀Track 1147

例句 She is a devout Christian, and learns the Bible by heart.
她是虔誠的基督徒，能熟記聖經。

搭配詞 learn by heart 熟記

lecture [ˋlɛktʃɚ] n. 對……演講 ◀Track 1148

例句 Will you give a lecture to the class on Friday, Mr. White?
白先生，禮拜五可以請你對全班演講嗎？

搭配詞 give lecture 對……演講

legend [ˋlɛdʒənd] n. 傳奇 ◀Track 1149

例句 The story is about a scary urban legend.
這個故事是關於一個恐怖的都市傳說。

搭配詞 urban legend 都市傳說

lesson [ˋlɛsn̩] n. 課 ◀Track 1150

例句 I learned a lesson from the horrible experience.
我從這次可怕的經驗學到教訓。

搭配詞 learn a lesson 得到教訓

a b c d e f g h i j k l m n o p q r s t u v w x y z

letter [ˋlɛtɚ] n. 字母、信 ◀Track 1151

例句 He sent me a love letter with beautiful handwriting.
他寄給我一封字很漂亮的情書。

搭配詞 love letter 情書

---

level [ˋlɛvl̩] n. 水準、標準 ◀Track 1152

例句 Sea level is rising due to global warming.
由於全球暖化，海平面持續上升。

搭配詞 sea level 海平面

---

liberal [ˋlɪbərəl] adj. 自由主義的、慷慨的 ◀Track 1153

例句 Many educators are advocating a liberal education.
許多教育家主張要自由主義的教育。

反義字 authoritarian 獨裁的

---

library [ˋlaɪˏbrɛrɪ] n. 圖書館 ◀Track 1154

例句 Would you show him around the public library? He is a new student.
你可以帶他到市立圖書館看看嗎？他是新來的學生。

搭配詞 public library 市立圖書館

---

link [lɪŋk] n./v. 關聯、連結 ◀Track 1155

例句 Click the link, and you will reach their homepage.
按一下連結，就會到他們的官方網站了。

相關字 hyperlink 超連結

---

literacy [ˋlɪtərəsɪ] n. 讀寫能力 ◀Track 1156

例句 To eliminate poverty, a government must boost mass literacy.
為消滅貧窮，一國政府必須提升公民識字率。

搭配詞 mass literacy 公民識字率

---

literal [ˋlɪtərəl] adj. 文字的、照字面的、原義的 ◀Track 1157

例句 What's the literal meaning of this word?
這個字的字面意義是什麼？

搭配詞 literal meaning 字面意義

---

literary [ˋlɪtəˏrɛrɪ] adj. 文學的 ◀Track 1158

例句 I don't like literary films. They are too gushy.
我不喜歡文藝片，太矯情了。

搭配詞 literary film 文藝片

---

literature [ˋlɪtərətʃɚ] n. 文學 ◀Track 1159

＊字尾-ure有轉變為名詞之意

例句 Twilight is categorized as popular literature.
《暮光之城》被歸類為大眾文學。

搭配詞 popular literature 大眾文學

---

logic [ˋlɑdʒɪk] n. 邏輯、道理 ◀Track 1160

例句 Your complicated logic totally confused me.
你複雜的邏輯讓我很困惑。

logical [ˋlɑdʒɪkḷ] adj. 合邏輯的 ◀Track 1161
＊字尾-al有轉變為形容詞之意
例句 I don't think that's a logical argument.
我不覺得那個論點在邏輯上說得通。

反義字 illogical 不合邏輯的

lyric [ˋlɪrɪk] n. 抒情詩、歌詞 ◀Track 1162
例句 The melody of the song is great, but the lyrics are terrible.
這首歌的曲很棒，但歌詞很糟。

搭配詞 song lyrics 歌詞

main [men] adj. 主要的 ◀Track 1163
例句 The main point of the essay is that we should not believe in love at first sight. 這篇文章的主要論點是我們不能相信一見鍾情。

搭配詞 main point 主要論點

manner [ˋmænɚ] n. 方法、禮貌 ◀Track 1164
例句 Tom! Mind your manners! 湯姆！注意禮貌！

搭配詞 table manners 餐桌禮儀

manuscript [ˋmænjə͵skrɪpt] n. 手稿、原稿 ◀Track 1165
例句 I guess that the manuscript requires an expert to understand it.
我想這個手稿需要專家才看得懂。

map [mæp] n. 地圖 ◀Track 1166
例句 I bought a map before I visited the city.
我在拜訪這個城市之前買了一張地圖。

易混淆字 mop 拖把

mark [mɑrk] n. 標記 ◀Track 1167
例句 The calf has a birth mark that shapes like a heart.
這隻小牛有一個心型胎記。

搭配詞 birth mark 胎記

material(ism) [məˋtɪrɪəl]/[məˋtɪrɪə͵lɪzṃ] ◀Track 1168
n. 材質、材料、唯物論
例句 It seems that this kind of raw material is popular on the market.
看來這種原料在市場上很受歡迎。

搭配詞 raw material 原料

mathematical [͵mæθəˋmætɪkḷ] adj. 數學的 ◀Track 1169
例句 Will you teach me how to comprehend this mathematical formula?
你願意教我理解這道數學公式嗎？

搭配詞 mathematical formula 數學公式

mathematics [͵mæθəˋmætɪks] n. 數學 ◀Track 1170
例句 My brother does well in mathematics, and so do I.
我哥哥數學很好，我也是。

縮寫 math

a b c d e f g h i j k l m n o p q r s t u v w x y z

matter [ˋmætɚ] n. 事情、問題、關係 Track 1171

例句 Whatever the outcome is, it doesn't matter.
無論結局如何，都沒關係。

搭配詞 it doesn't matter 沒關係

meaning [ˋminɪŋ] n. 意義 Track 1172

例句 Will you explain the meanings of these Spanish words?
你可以解釋這些西班牙文字的意義嗎？

反義字 meaningless 不具意義的

means [minz] n. 方法 Track 1173

例句 She achieved her goal by means of brlbing.
她透過賄賂的方式達到目的。

搭配詞 by means of 透過……的方法

mechanics [məˋkænɪks] n. 機械學、力學 Track 1174

例句 For the first time, he failed in his fluid mechanics exam.
他第一次流體力學考試不及格。

搭配詞 fluid mechanics 流體力學

meditate [ˋmɛdə͵tet] v. 沉思 Track 1175

例句 She meditates on the issue early in the morning.
她一早就在沉思問題。

同義字 ponder

meditation [͵mɛdəˋteʃən] n. 熟慮、冥想、沉思 Track 1176

＊字尾-tion有轉變為名詞的意思

例句 He made the decision after much meditation.
他在沉思許久後下了決定。

易混淆字 mediation 調解

memorize [ˋmɛmə͵raɪz] v. 記憶 Track 1177

＊字尾-ize有「使」的意思

例句 It is not possible for him to memorize all the lyrics the teacher has taught. 他不可能記憶老師所教的所有歌詞。

搭配詞 memorize lyrics 記歌詞

mind [maɪnd] n. 頭腦、思想 Track 1178

例句 Are you out of your mind? 你精神失常了嗎？

搭配詞 out of mind 精神失常

monthly [ˋmʌnθlɪ] n. 月刊 Track 1179

例句 This magazine is a free monthly publication.
這雜誌是免費的月刊。

搭配詞 free monthly 免費月刊

morality [mɔˋrælətɪ] n. 道德、德行 Track 1180

＊字尾-ity有轉變為名詞之意

例句 My brother is a man of strict morality. 我哥哥是個道德嚴謹的人。

同義字 moral

motto [ˋmɑto] n. 座右銘 ◀Track 1181

例句 His motto is, "eat now, regret later".
他的座右銘是「現在先吃，待會再來後悔」。

---

myth [mɪθ] n. 神話、傳說 ◀Track 1182

例句 The idea that saliva can cure bee stings is an urban myth.
用口水可以治好蜜蜂螫過的傷口只是都市傳說。

搭配詞 urban myth 都市傳說

---

mythology [mɪˋθɑlədʒɪ] n. 神話 ◀Track 1183

＊字尾-ology有「學問、學科」之意

例句 We studied Greek and Roman mythology in college.
我們在大學時讀了希臘和羅馬神話。

搭配詞 Greek mythology 希臘神話

---

narrate [næˋret] v. 敘述、講故事 ◀Track 1184

例句 The writer narrated the story in a humorous tone.
這個作家以詼諧的語調敘述故事。

搭配詞 narrate a story 講故事

---

note [not] n. 筆記 ◀Track 1185

例句 I always take notes in class.
我上課時總是做筆記。

搭配詞 take notes 做筆記

---

notebook [ˋnot͵bʊk] n. 筆記本 ◀Track 1186

例句 The students bought new notebooks.
這些學生買了新的筆記本。

搭配詞 notebook computer 筆記型電腦

---

noun [naʊn] n. 名詞 ◀Track 1187

例句 Please pay attention to the single and the uncountable nouns.
請注意單數和不可數名詞。

搭配詞 uncountable noun 不可數名詞

---

nursery [ˋnɝsərɪ] n. 托兒所 ◀Track 1188

例句 I always send my child to a nursery school on Wednesdays.
我每個星期三總是把我的孩子送到托兒所。

搭配詞 nursery school 托兒所

---

observation [͵ɑbzɝˋveʃən] n. 觀察力、觀察到的事 ◀Track 1189

＊字尾-tion有轉變為名詞的意思

例句 He has keen observations about the royal family.
他對皇室有很細膩的觀察。

搭配詞 keen observation 觀測細膩

---

opinion [əˋpɪnjən] n. 觀點、意見 ◀Track 1190

例句 In my opinion, he is not tough enough to be a salesman.
我個人意見是覺得他不夠堅強，不能當推銷員。

搭配詞 in my opinion 我個人觀點

a b c d e f g h i j k l m n o p q r s t u v w x y z

optimism [ˋɑptəmɪzəm] n. 樂觀主義 Track 1191
＊字尾-ism有「主義、學問」的意思
例句 I pride myself on my optimism. 我對我的樂觀主義很自豪。

反義字 pessimism 消極主義

outlook [ˋaʊt͵lʊk] n. 觀點、態度 Track 1192
＊字首out-有「外」之意
例句 She has a pessimistic outlook on life. 她對人生的態度很消極。

搭配詞 outlook on sth 對某事的觀點

page [pedʒ] n. （書上的）頁 Track 1193
例句 To visit ROC's official home page, please go to www.president.gov.tw.
要看中華民國的官網首頁，請上www.president.gov.tw。

搭配詞 home page （網站）首頁

participle [ˋpɑrtəsəpl̩] n. 分詞 Track 1194
例句 My teacher thinks that learning all about past participles is a must.
我老師認為一定要澈底瞭解過去分詞。

易混淆字 practical 實際的

pass [pæs] v. （考試）及格、通行證 Track 1195
例句 You need to practice more in order to pass the driving test.
你要多練習才能考駕照考及格。

搭配詞 pass an exam 通過考試

pen [pɛn] n. 鋼筆、原子筆 Track 1196
例句 Do you have any pen pals? 你有筆友嗎？

搭配詞 pen pal 筆友

pencil [ˋpɛnsl̩] n. 鉛筆 Track 1197
例句 I will buy my daughter a new pencial case as her birthday gift.
我會買一個新的鉛筆盒給我女兒當生日禮物。

搭配詞 pencil case 鉛筆盒

personality [͵pɝsn̩ˋælətɪ] n. 個性、人格 Track 1198
＊字尾-ity有轉變為名詞之意
例句 Her normally gentle personality turned rough after her divorce.
她平常溫順的性格在離婚後就變得粗魯了。

同義字 individuality

pessimism [ˋpɛsəmɪzəm] n. 悲觀、悲觀主義 Track 1199
＊字尾-ism有「主義、學問」的意思
例句 It is obvious that he has a tendency towards pessimism.
他很明顯地有悲觀傾向。

反義字 optimism 樂觀主義

philosophy [fəˋlɑsəfɪ] n. 哲學 Track 1200
例句 Would you share your philosophy of life with us?
你願意和我們分享你人生的哲學嗎？

photography [fəˋtɑgrəfɪ] n. 攝影學 Track 1201

例句 I spent a lot of money on photography books.
我花了很多錢買攝影書。

搭配詞 photography book 攝影書

phrase [frez] n. 片語 Track 1202

例句 Try to memorize as many English words and phrases as possible before the test. 考試前請試著記住越多英文單字與片語越好。

搭配詞 noun phrase 名詞片語

physics [ˋfɪzɪks] n. 物理學 Track 1203

例句 Tom does really well in nuclear physics in our class.
湯姆在我們班上算是核子物理學很好。

搭配詞 nuclear physics 核子物理學

plus [plʌs] v. 加 Track 1204

例句 Nine plus two equals eleven. 九加二是十一。

反義字 minus 減

poem [ˋpoɪm] n. 詩 Track 1205

例句 She wrote a lyric poem to describe her fantasy world.
她寫了一首抒情詩形容她的幻想世界。

搭配詞 lyric poem 抒情詩

politics [ˋpɑlə͵tɪks] n. 政治學 Track 1206

例句 Wars are all about party politics in this country.
這個國家戰爭都是政黨政治造成的。

搭配詞 party politics 政黨政治

positive [ˋpɑzətɪv] adj. 確信的、積極的、正面的 Track 1207

例句 Look on the positive side. At least you're still alive!
往正面想，至少你還活著啊！

搭配詞 positive attitude
積極的態度

possibility [͵pɑsəˋbɪlətɪ] n. 可能性 Track 1208

例句 He is aware of the possibility that he might have been lied to.
他知道他有可能被騙了。

同義字 probability

practice [ˋpræktɪs] n./v. 實踐、練習、熟練 Track 1209

例句 My son enjoys practicing the piano. 我兒子很喜歡練鋼琴。

搭配詞 practice the piano 練習鋼琴

prayer [prɛr] n. 禱告 Track 1210

例句 She said a pious prayer before going to bed.
她在睡前先虔誠禱告。

搭配詞 pious prayer 虔誠禱告

a b c d e f g h i j k l m n o p q r s t u v w x y z

preparation [ˌprɛpəˋreʃən] n. 準備 ◀Track 1211
＊字尾-tion有轉變為名詞的意思
例句 The family sold all their houses in preparation for emigrating to the US. 這家人把房子全賣了，以準備移民到美國。

搭配詞 in preparation 準備中

prepare [priˋpɛr] v. 預備、準備 ◀Track 1212
例句 Please prepare for the test. 請為考試好好準備。

搭配詞 prepare for a test 準備考試

preposition [ˌprɛpəˋzɪʃən] n. 介系詞 ◀Track 1213
＊字尾-tion有轉變為名詞的意思
例句 "Out" can be used as a preposition as well.
「out」這個字也能用來當介系詞。

presence [ˋprɛzn̩s] n. 出席 ◀Track 1214
例句 Your presence at our party will be a great honor for us.
若您能出席我們的晚會，我們會倍感榮耀。

反義字 absence 缺席

problem [ˋprɑbləm] n. 問題 ◀Track 1215
例句 I need to solve a math problem.
我要解一個數學問題。

搭配詞 solve a problem 解決問題

pronounce [prəˋnaʊns] v. 發音 ◀Track 1216
例句 How do you pronounce this word correctly?
這個字怎麼發音才對？

易混淆字 pronoun 代名詞

prose [proz] n. 散文 ◀Track 1217
例句 This novel is written in prose. 這本小說是以散文寫成的。

搭配詞 written in prose 以散文寫成

psychological [ˌsaɪkəˋlɑdʒɪkl̩] adj. 心理學的 ◀Track 1218
例句 The doctor said he had some psychological trauma, and asked him to stay in the hospital for further examination.
醫生說他有一些心理的創傷，請他待在醫院接受更多檢查。

搭配詞 psychological trauma
心理創傷

psychology [saɪˋkɑlədʒɪ] n. 心理學 ◀Track 1219
＊字尾-ology有「學問、學論」的意思
例句 He obtained a degree in clinical psychology this year.
他今年拿到了臨床心理學的學位。

搭配詞 clinical psychology
臨床心理學

puzzle [ˋpʌzl̩] n. 難題、謎 ◀Track 1220
例句 He is fond of Chinese puzzles. 他喜歡中式解謎拼圖。

搭配詞 Chinese puzzle
中式解謎拼圖

qualify [ˋkwɑlə͵faɪ] **v.** 使合格 Track 1221

例句 It took the company one year to find a qualified employee.
這間公司花了一年時間，才找到合格人選。

搭配詞 qualified person 合格人選

---

query [ˋkwɪrɪ] **n.** 問題、疑問 Track 1222

例句 If you have any further queries, do not hesitate to call me.
如果你有什麼其他的疑問，請不要猶豫，打給我。

反義字 reply 回應

---

question [ˋkwɛstʃən] **n.** 疑問、詢問 Track 1223

＊字尾-tion有轉變為名詞的意思

例句 Do you have any other questions? 還有什麼其他的問題嗎？

搭配詞 have a question 有疑問

---

questionnaire [͵kwɛstʃənˋɛr] **n.** 問卷、調查表 Track 1224

例句 The questionnaire format is badly-designed.
這份問卷格式設計不好。

搭配詞 questionnaire format 問卷格式

---

quiz [kwɪz] **n.** 測驗 Track 1225

例句 I'm quite nervous about the English quiz tomorrow morning.
我為明天早上的英文測驗很緊張。

搭配詞 English quiz 英文測驗

---

quote [kwot] **n./v.** 引用、引證 Track 1226

例句 Do you think it is appropriate to use these sentences quoted from this book? 你覺得引用這本書的這幾句是合宜的嗎？

同義字 cite

---

range [rendʒ] **n.** 範圍 Track 1227

例句 Is it possible for you to provide us with products within the price range? 你能提供我們這個價格範圍的產品嗎？

搭配詞 price range 價位

---

renaissance [ˋrɛnəsɑns] **n.** 再生、文藝復興 Track 1228

例句 He was a painter from the Renaissance era.
他是文藝復興時期的一名畫家。

搭配詞 The Renaissance era 文藝復興時期

---

read [rid] **v.** 讀、看（書、報等）、朗讀 Track 1229

例句 I read newspapers every morning. 我每天早上都看報紙。

搭配詞 read newspapers 看報紙

---

realize [ˋriə͵laɪz] **v.** 實現、瞭解 Track 1230

例句 He has worked very hard to realize dreams.
他為了實現夢想，工作很勤奮。

搭配詞 realize one's dream 實現夢想

recommendation [ˏrɛkəmɛnˋdeʃən] n. 推薦 Track 1231
＊字尾-tion有轉變為名詞的意思
例句 To apply for a good college, you need your professor's recommendation letters.
為了申請好的大學，你需要教授的推薦信。
搭配詞 recommendation letter 推薦信

recite [rɪˋsaɪt] v. 背誦 Track 1232
例句 Don't you think that children reciting poems look like creepy little robots? 你不覺得背誦詩的小朋友看起來很像恐怖的小機器人嗎？
搭配詞 recite a poem 背誦詩歌

remember [rɪˋmɛmbɚ] v. 記得 Track 1233
例句 Please remember to clean the dishes. 請記得要洗碗。
搭配詞 remember to do sth 記得做某事

report [rɪˋport] n. 報告、報導 Track 1234
例句 I am still working on the weather report.
我還在努力做氣象報告。
搭配詞 weather report 氣象報告

respect [rɪˋspɛkt] n./v. 尊重 Track 1235
例句 You need to show your respect to your boss.
你要尊重你的老闆。
搭配詞 show one's respect 表示尊重

result [rɪˋzʌlt] n. 結果 Track 1236
例句 He didn't study hard. As a result, he failed the exam.
他不用功，結果考試不及格。
搭配詞 as a result 結果

return [rɪˋtɝn] v. 歸還、送回 Track 1237
＊字首re-有「再次」之意
例句 Please help me return the book to the library by 5 pm.
請在下午五點前幫我把這本書歸還給圖書館。

review [rɪˋvju] n./v. 複習 Track 1238
＊字首re-有「再次」之意
例句 The report is under review. 這份報告正在審視中。
搭配詞 under review 檢查

rhyme [raɪm] n./v. 韻、韻文、押韻 Track 1239
例句 "Cat" and "fat" rhyme. 「cat」和「fat」兩字有押韻。

rust [rʌst] n./v. 鐵銹、生銹 Track 1240
例句 My grandmother reads extensively so that she can keep her mind from rusting. 我奶奶廣泛地閱讀，以免腦袋生鏽。

scholarship [ˋskɑlɚ͵ʃɪp] n. 獎學金 ◀ Track 1241

例句 They don't provide athletic scholarship in this university.
這所大學沒有提供體育獎學金。

搭配詞 athletic scholarship 體育獎學金

school [skul] n. 學校 ◀ Track 1242

例句 He takes piano lessons after school. 他放學就去學鋼琴。

搭配詞 after school 放學

scope [skop] n. 範圍、領域 ◀ Track 1243

例句 I'm afraid your question is beyond the scope of my understanding.
恐怕你的問題已經超出我的理解範圍了。

score [skor] n. 分數 ◀ Track 1244

例句 Can you tell me how to get a perfect score in the math examination?
你可告訴我數學考試怎麼拿高分嗎？

搭配詞 perfect score 滿分

scroll [skrol] n. 卷軸 ◀ Track 1245

例句 There are several scroll bars on your computer screen.
在你的電腦螢幕上有幾個長條卷軸。

搭配詞 scroll bar （電腦）長條卷軸

search [sɝtʃ] v. 搜索、搜尋 ◀ Track 1246

例句 You can search for anything you want on the Internet.
你在網路上搜尋什麼都可以。

搭配詞 search for 尋找

seat [sit] n. 座位 ◀ Track 1247

例句 There are only 10 priority seats on the bus.
巴士上只有10個博愛座。

搭配詞 priority seat 博愛座

secret [ˋsikrɪt] n. 祕密 ◀ Track 1248

例句 He promised me to keep it in secret. 他答應替我保守祕密。

搭配詞 in secret 祕密地

section [ˋsɛkʃən] n. 部分、區域 ◀ Track 1249

＊字尾-tion有轉變為名詞的意思

例句 The vegetables can be found in this section.
蔬菜可以在這個區域找到。

反義字 whole 整體

see [si] v. 看、理解 ◀ Track 1250

例句 Did you see the new English teacher?
你有看到新來的英文老師嗎？

搭配詞 I see 我懂了

seminar [ˋsɛmənɑr] n. 研討會 Track 1251

例句 The international seminar will be held in London.
這場國際研討會將在倫敦舉辦。

搭配詞 international seminar 國際研討會

sentence [ˋsɛntəns] n. 句子、判決 Track 1252

例句 Please make a sentence after learning each new word.
每學一個新字，請造句練習。

搭配詞 make a sentence 造句

serious [ˋsɪrɪəs] adj. 嚴肅的 Track 1253

＊字尾-ous有轉變為形容詞之意

例句 High housing prices is a serious problem.
高房價是個很嚴肅的問題。

搭配詞 serious problem 嚴肅的問題

shame [ʃem] n. 羞恥、羞愧 Track 1254

例句 You are very mean to her. Shame on you.
你對她態度很差，你真可恥。

搭配詞 shame on you 真丟臉

simple [ˋsɪmpḷ] adj. 簡單的、簡易的 Track 1255

例句 The questions are all about simple ideas; you should know the answers. 這些問題觀念都很簡單，你應該知道答案。

搭配詞 simple idea 簡單的想法

simplicity [sɪmˋplɪsətɪ] n. 簡單、單純 Track 1256

例句 The beauty of the design of the room is in its simplicity.
這個房間設計最棒的地方就是它很簡約。

skill [skɪl] n. 技能 Track 1257

例句 He went to a skill center to learn computer programming.
他到技能訓練中心學寫電腦程式。

搭配詞 skill center 技能訓練中心

slang [slæŋ] n. 俚語 Track 1258

例句 I love using Internet slang. 我喜歡用網路俚語。

易混淆字 slant 傾斜

smart [smɑrt] adj. 聰明的 Track 1259

例句 She was a smart child but very much misunderstood.
她是個聰明的孩子，卻常被誤解。

同義字 clever

sociology [͵soʃɪˋɑlədʒɪ] n. 社會學 Track 1260

＊字尾-ology有「學問、學論」之意

例句 We took sociology of education in the third year of university.
我們在大三的時候上了教育社會學。

搭配詞 sociology of education 教育社會學

sophomore [ˋsɑfm͵or] ◀ Track 1261

n. （大學、高中）二年級學生

例句 She went to Japan when she was a sophomore.
她在二年級時去了日本。

species [ˋspiʃɪz] n. 物種 ◀ Track 1262

例句 Polar bears are endangered species due to climate change.
由於氣候變遷，北極熊成為瀕臨滅絕的物種。

搭配詞 endangered species 瀕臨滅絕的物種

specify [ˋspɛsə͵faɪ] v. 詳述、詳載 ◀ Track 1263

＊字尾-ify有「使」之意

例句 Would you please specify your location?
你可以詳述你的所在地點嗎？

speculate [ˋspɛkjə͵let] v. 沉思、推測 ◀ Track 1264

例句 She speculated about her boyfriend's motives.
她推測她男朋友的動機。

搭配詞 speculate about 沉思

spell [spɛl] v. 用字母拼、拼寫 ◀ Track 1265

例句 How do you spell your family name? 你的姓怎麼拼？

搭配詞 spell a word 拼字

spelling [spɛlɪŋ] n. 拼讀、拼法 ◀ Track 1266

例句 The teacher asked her students to correct their wrong spelling in their compositions. 老師要求學生訂正作文裡的拼字錯誤。

搭配詞 wrong spelling 拼法錯誤

spoil [spɔɪl] v. 寵壞、損壞 ◀ Track 1267

例句 Never spoil your dogs. 別寵壞你的狗了。

squad [skwɑd] n. 小隊、班 ◀ Track 1268

例句 Don't you know that Mom was on the cheer squad at high school?
你不知道媽媽以前唸高中時是啦啦隊嗎？

搭配詞 cheer squad 啦啦隊

stamp [stæmp] v. 壓印 ◀ Track 1269

例句 He stamped on a turd when strolling on the sidewalk.
他在行人道上散步時踩到狗屎。

搭配詞 stamp on 踩踏

stationery [ˋsteʃən͵ɛrɪ] n. 文具 ◀ Track 1270

例句 Her favorite shopping place is that stationery store.
她最喜歡在那間文具店買東西。

易混淆字 stationary 不動的

stripe [straɪp] n. 條、臨時跑道、條紋 Track 1271
例句 He looks good in that striped shirt.
他穿那件條紋衣看起來很好看。
易混淆字 strip 脫去

structure [ˋstrʌktʃɚ] n. 構造、結構 Track 1272
＊字尾-ure有轉變為名詞之意
例句 The structure of the building is old and weak.
那棟建築的結構已經又老又脆弱了。

student [ˋstjudn̩t] n. 學生 Track 1273
例句 I am an exchange student at Harvard.
我是哈佛的交換學生。
搭配詞 exchange student 交換學生

study [ˋstʌdɪ] v. 學習、讀書 Track 1274
例句 I need a completely quiet place to study hard.
我需要一個完全安靜的地方來努力讀書。
搭配詞 study hard 努力學習

stupid [ˋstjupɪd] adj. 愚蠢的、笨的 Track 1275
例句 Are you stupid? Of course he's male!
你是笨蛋嗎？他當然是男的啊！
反義字 smart 聰明的

subject [ˋsʌbdʒɪkt] n. 主題、科目 Track 1276
例句 Don't change the subject! 別岔開話題！
搭配詞 change the subject 改變主題

subjective [səbˋdʒɛktɪv] adj. 主觀的 Track 1277
例句 A manager should not be subjective at work.
主管在工作時不該太主觀。
同義字 objective

subtract [səbˋtrækt] n. 扣除、減 Track 1278
例句 It is not easy for two-year-old kids to add and subtract.
要兩歲小朋友做加減太難了。
同義字 deduct

summarize [ˋsʌmə͵raɪz] v. 總結、概述 Track 1279
＊字尾-ize有「使」之意
例句 Let's summarize what you learned in this summer camp.
我們總結一下你在這次夏令營學到了什麼。

supplement [ˋsʌpləmənt] Track 1280
n. 副刊、補充 ＊字尾-ment有轉變為名詞之意
例句 I bought some dietary supplements for my parents.
我幫我父母買了一些營養補充品。
搭配詞 dietary supplement 膳食補充品

syllable [ˋsɪləbḷ] n. 音節 ◀Track 1281

例句 How many syllables are there in the word “irresistable”?
「irresistable」這個字裡有幾個音節？

搭配詞
single syllable 單音節

---

synonym [ˋsɪnə͵nɪm] n. 同義字 ◀Track 1282

例句 Please write down the synonym of these ten words.
請寫下這十個字的同義字。

反義字
antonym 反義字

---

talent [ˋtælənt] n. 天份、天賦 ◀Track 1283

例句 He stunned the audience in the talent show.
他在才藝演出中，表現讓觀眾驚艷。

搭配詞
talent show 才藝演出

---

teach [titʃ] v. 教、教書、教導 ◀Track 1284

例句 Can you teach the children English? 你可以教孩子們英文嗎？

搭配詞
teach English 教英文

---

technology [tɛkˋnɑlədʒɪ] n. 技術學、科技 ◀Track 1285

＊字尾-ology有「學問、學論」之意

例句 I find it hard to catch up with new technology.
我覺得要趕上新科技潮流太困難了。

---

tell [tɛl] v. 告訴、說明、分辨 ◀Track 1286

例句 Can you tell me the truth? 你可以告訴我實情嗎？

搭配詞
tell the truth 說實話

---

test [tɛst] n. 考試 ◀Track 1287

例句 They took a written test first thing in the morning.
他們一早就考筆試。

搭配詞
written test 筆試

---

text [tɛkst] n. 課文、本文 ◀Track 1288

例句 Can you send me a text message? 你可以發簡訊給我嗎？

搭配詞
text message 簡訊

---

textbook [ˋtɛkst͵buk] n. 教科書 ◀Track 1289

例句 I burned all my textbooks. 我把我的教科書都燒了。

---

theme [θim] n. 主題、題目 ◀Track 1290

例句 What's the theme song of your party?
你的派對主題曲是什麼？

搭配詞
theme song 主題曲

a b c d e f g h i j k l m n o p q r s t u v w x y z

theoretical [ˌθiəˋrɛtɪkḷ] ◀Track 1291
adj. 理論上的、好理論的、精於理論的
例句 From a theoretical perspective, they won't succeed.
理論上來講，他們不會成功。

反義字 concrete 具體的

think [θɪŋk] v. 想、思考 ◀Track 1292
例句 What do you think of my new dress?
你對我的新洋裝怎麼想呢？

thought [θɔt] n. 思考、思維 ◀Track 1293
例句 On second thought, maybe we should reconsider.
再思考一下後，我覺得我們可能要重新考慮了。

易混淆字 though 然而

title [ˋtaɪtḷ] n. 稱號、標題 ◀Track 1294
例句 Could you give this book a title? 你可以給這本書取個標題嗎？

搭配詞 book title 書名

topic [ˋtɑpɪk] n. 主題、談論 ◀Track 1295
例句 The topic of the speech today is about home schooling.
今天演講的主題是在家自學。

同義字 subject

trait [tret] n. 特色、特性 ◀Track 1296
例句 Her two most charming traits are her smile and her dimples.
她最迷人的兩個特色就是她的笑容與酒窩。

translate [trænsˋlet] v. 翻譯 ◀Track 1297
例句 I have to translate my dissertation into English.
我得把論文翻譯成英文。

搭配詞 translate into 翻譯成……文

translation [trænsˋleʃən] n. 譯文、翻譯 ◀Track 1298
*字首trans-有「穿越、轉變」之意
例句 The literal translation is not accurate. 這句的字面翻譯不精確。

搭配詞 literal translation 照字面上翻譯

tremor [ˋtrɛmɚ] n. 震動 ◀Track 1299
例句 There was a slight tremor in this building five minutes ago.
五分鐘前，這棟大樓震了一下。

truth [truθ] n. 真相、真理 ◀Track 1300
例句 The truth is, I have no idea. 說真的，我也不知道呢。

同義字 reality

tuition [tju`ɪʃən] n. 教學、講授、學費 ◀Track 1301

例句 The tuition of that school is too high for her.
那所學校的學費對她來說太高了。

---

undergraduate [ˌʌndə`grædʒuɪt] n. 大學生 ◀Track 1302

＊字首under-有「下方的」之意

例句 Not every undergraduate goes to graduate school.
不是每個大學生都會去念研究所。

反義字
graduate 研究生

---

understand [ˌʌndə`stænd] v. 瞭解、明白 ◀Track 1303

例句 Do you totally understand what he just said?
你全盤瞭解他剛講的話嗎？

搭配詞
totally understand 全盤瞭解

---

university [ˌjunə`vɝsətɪ] n. 大學 ◀Track 1304

＊字首uni-有「單一的」之意

例句 He went to university at the age of 12. 他12歲就讀大學了。

搭配詞
go to university 上大學

---

upbringing [`ʌpˌbrɪŋɪŋ] n. 養育、教養 ◀Track 1305

＊字首up-有「上」之意

例句 His misdemeanor can be attributed to poor upbringing.
他品行不端，可歸因於不良好的教養方式。

搭配詞
poor upbringing 沒教養

---

usage [`jusɪdʒ] n. 習慣、習俗、使用 ◀Track 1306

例句 I often get confused by the usage of English grammar.
我常對英文文法的用法感到困惑。

---

useful [`jusfəl] adj. 有用的、有益的、有幫助的 ◀Track 1307

＊字尾-ful有「充滿」的意思

例句 Alternate current is a useful invention. 交流電是有用的發明。

搭配詞
useful invention
有用的發明

---

versatile [`vɝsətl̩] adj. 多才多藝的、多用途的 ◀Track 1308

例句 He is always the most versatile actor among the group.
他一向都是這一群人中最多才多藝的演員。

反義字
dull 愚鈍的

---

version [`vɝʒən] n. 說法、版本 ◀Track 1309

例句 I bought the latest English version of this book online.
我在網路上買了這本書最新的英文版本。

搭配詞
the latest version 最新版本

---

verb [vɝb] n. 動詞 ◀Track 1310

例句 Could you tell me how to use this verb properly?
你可以告訴我怎麼正確使用這個動詞嗎？

---

a b c d e f g h i j k l m n o p q r s t u v w x y z

view [vju] n. 看見、景觀、見解 Track 1311

例句 How's the view from up there? 上面那裡景觀怎樣？

vocal [ˋvokḷ] adj./n. 發聲的、歌手 Track 1312

例句 She is a vocal in this band. 她是這個樂團裡的歌手之一。

vocabulary [vəˋkæbjəˏlɛrɪ] n. 單字、字彙 Track 1313

例句 To pass GRE, we need to memorize a lot of vocabulary.
要通過GRE，我們需要記很多單字。

搭配詞 memorize vocabulary 記單字

vowel [ˋvauəl] n. 母音 Track 1314

例句 Y can be a vowel or a consonant.
「Y」可以是母音也可以是子音。

搭配詞 short vowel 短母音

whatsoever [ˏhwɑtsoˋɛvɚ] adv. 任何的 Track 1315

例句 I have no opinion whatsoever. 我完全沒有任何意見。

搭配詞 no... whatsoever 沒有任何

wisdom [ˋwɪzdəm] n. 智慧 Track 1316

例句 The old lady told us words of wisdom.
那位老太太告訴我們一些有智慧的話語。

word [wɝd] n. 字、單字、話 Track 1317

例句 He is a man of his words. 他是個說話算話的人。

搭配詞 man of his words 說話算話的人

write [raɪt] v. 書寫、寫下、寫字 Track 1318

例句 Please write down your name here. 請在這裡寫下你的名字。

搭配詞 write down 寫下

Test 05 關鍵英單總測驗第5回

以下測驗題皆出自書中第五回「**和育有關的單字**」，快來檢視自己的學習成果吧！

一、選擇題

1. The students are learning how to solve ____ and subtraction equations.
   (A) article
   (B) addition
   (C) essay
   (D) chalk
2. ________ weapons can cause large-scale destruction.
   (A) Doubt
   (B) Dictation
   (C) Formula
   (D) Chemical
3. She is a language ______. She can speak six languages without accent.
   (A) ignorant
   (B) gifted
   (C) knowledge
   (D) genius
4. _________ makes perfect. So let's work harder.
   (A) Practice
   (B) Questions
   (C) Section
   (D) Literary
5. What a lame excuse! Your dog ate your _____?
   (A) think
   (B) slang
   (C) textbook
   (D) realize
6. Should you have further ______, please feel free to contact us.
   (A) questions
   (B) morality
   (C) presence
   (D) personality
7. Her _____ is, "silence is golden".
   (A) motto
   (B) lyrics
   (C) mind
   (D) journalism
8. He ______ his physics exam.
   (A) crayon
   (B) argued
   (C) extracted
   (D) flunked
9. She paid _______ to the teacher's lecture.
   (A) claim
   (B) book
   (C) attention
   (D) congratulations
10. He is a _____ scientist working for Google.
    (A) discipline
    (B) data
    (C) Confucius
    (D) effort

二、克漏字測驗

In 2016, a commemorative stamp was issued by the United States Postal Service in honor of Jaime Escalante, a fine educator known for teaching ___1___ to trouble students at Garfield High School and helping them ___2___ the Advanced Placement (AP) test in calculus.

When Escalante started his teaching career at Garfield High School, he found many of his students had serious problems with drugs and violence. But Escalante never gave up on them. He told them basic math was too easy and that they had the ability to excel. In 1982, eighteen of his students aced the AP test. Staff of the testing center suspected the students of ___3___. He urged his students to take the test again. Twelve repeated the test and aced it again. Five even earned top ___4___.

Some of Escalante's students later became engineers, scientists, and university ___5___. Because of his contributions, he received numerous teaching awards, including the Presidential Medal of Excellence in Education. In 1988, a movie about him, Stand and Deliver, was released. In 1989, Escalante passed away. He was 79 years old.

1.
(A) mathematics
(B) psychological
(C) renaissance
(D) prayer

2.
(A) meditate
(B) flunk
(C) pass
(D) find

3.
(A) erasing
(B) cheating
(C) failing
(D) designing

4.
(A) data
(B) criticism
(C) blank
(D) scores

5.
(A) professors
(B) beginners
(C) stationery
(D) accounting

關鍵英單總測驗第5回
中譯與解答

一、選擇題

1. 學生正在學習加減法。
   (A) 文章
   (B) 加法
   (C) 論説文
   (D) 粉筆

2. 化學武器可能導致大規模破壞。
   (A) 懷疑
   (B) 口述
   (C) 方程式
   (D) 化學的

3. 她是語言天才，能説6國語言而且沒有奇怪的口音。
   (A) 無知的
   (B) 有天份的
   (C) 知識
   (D) 天才

4. 熟能生巧，我們加把勁吧。
   (A) 練習
   (B) 問題
   (C) 區域
   (D) 文學的

5. 好爛的藉口！你的小狗把你的教科書吃掉了？
   (A) 思考
   (B) 俚語
   (C) 教科書
   (D) 瞭解

6. 若你有其他問題，請不要客氣、聯絡我們。
   (A) 問題
   (B) 道德
   (C) 存在
   (D) 人格

7. 她的座右銘是「沈默是金」。
   (A) 座右銘
   (B) 歌詞
   (C) 心思
   (D) 新聞業

8. 他的物理考試不及格。
   (A) 蠟筆
   (B) 爭辯
   (C) 萃取
   (D) 考不及格

9. 她專注聽老師的講授。
   (A) 堅稱
   (B) 書本
   (C) 專注
   (D) 恭喜

10. 他是Google的資料科學家。
    (A) 紀律
    (B) 資料
    (C) 孔子
    (D) 努力

二、克漏字測驗

2016年，美國郵政發行紀念郵票，以表達對Jaime Escalante的崇高敬意。Escalante是一位傑出的教育家，因教導加爾菲高中的問題學生數學，並幫助他們通過美國大學學分先修課程微積分考試而聲名遠播。

當Escalante開始在加爾菲高中教書時，他發現很多學生都有嗑藥和暴力的問題。但他沒有放棄他的學生，他告訴他們基礎數學對他們來說太簡單了，而且他們有能力能成為卓越的人。1982年，他的18名學生通過了美國大學學分先修課程微積分考試。測驗中心的人懷疑他的學生作弊，於是他鼓勵學生再考一次。有12名學生再度接受測驗，而且全都考得很好，其中5名學生分數達到高標。

Escalante的學生隨後成為工程師、科學家、大學教授。因為他的貢獻，他獲頒許多獎章，其中包括美國總統頒發的教育卓越獎。1988年，根據他的故事改編的電影《為人師表》發行了。1989年他離世，享年79歲。

1.
(A) 數學
(B) 心理學的
(C) 文藝復興
(D) 禱告

2.
(A) 冥想
(B) 考砸
(C) 通過
(D) 發現

3.
(A) 擦掉
(B) 作弊
(C) 失敗
(D) 設計

4
(A) 資料
(B) 批評
(C) 空白的
(D) 分數

5.
(A) 教授
(B) 初學者
(C) 文具
(D) 會計學

一、選擇題

1.(B) 2. (D) 3.(D) 4.(A) 5.(C)
6.(A) 7. (A) 8.(D) 9.(C) 10.(B)

二、克漏字測驗

1.(A) 2.(C) 3.(B)
4.(D) 5.(A)

Unit 06 和樂有關的單字

多益測驗的命題強調生活化與實用性，學會這些與「樂」有關的單字，不僅能讓你在多益考場上所向披靡，在日常生活上也可以靈活運用喔！

去聽音樂會可以這麼說

- **The City Symphony Orchestra will be performing at the Civic Square tomorrow.** 城市交響樂團明天將會在市民廣場演出。
- **Pipe organ is a huge instrument that creates very loud sound.**
  管風琴是一種聲音非常大聲的巨大樂器

介紹一部電影可以這麼說

- **The Silence Of The Lambs was a horror movie adapted from a novel of the same name.**
  《沉默的羔羊》是一部由同名小說改編的恐怖電影。
- **This is a documentary film about former Supreme Court justice, Ruth Bader Ginsburg.**
  這是一部有關前最高法院大法官露絲‧貝德‧金斯伯格的紀錄片。
- **The director shows his ambition to build a cinematic universe in this sequel.** 導演在這部續集電影展現了他想建立一個電影世界觀的野心。

和朋友出遊可以這麼說

- **We are going to go to the amusement park this weekend.**
  我們這個週末要去遊樂園。

- **There's a sculpture of a clown handing out balloons at the center of the park.**
  在園區的中心，有一個在發氣球的小丑雕像。

追星可以這麼說

- **I am a huge fan of this band. And I already bought every album they had released.**
  我是這個樂團的忠實粉絲。他們出的所有專輯我都有買。
- **I have subscribed to various fashion magazines to keep up with trends.**
  為了緊跟潮流，我已訂閱多家時尚雜誌。

在音樂課上可以這麼說

- **Can you read sheet music?**
  你看得懂樂譜嗎？
- **Your violin is out of tune.**
  你的小提琴走音了。

Unit 06 和樂有關的單字

album [ˋælbəm] n. 相簿、專輯 ◀ *Track 1319*

例句 The singer released a single album in July.
這名歌手在7月發行單曲專輯。

搭配詞 single album 單曲專輯

---

amuse [əˋmjuz] v. 娛樂、消遣 ◀ *Track 1320*

例句 I amused myself by playing guitar on weekends.
我在週末彈吉他來自我消遣。

同義字 entertain

---

amusement [əˋmjuzmənt] n. 娛樂、有趣 ◀ *Track 1321*

*字尾-ment有轉變為名詞之意

例句 Disneyland is an amusement park. 迪士尼樂園是一所遊樂園。

搭配詞 amusement park 遊樂園

---

antique [ænˋtik] n./adj. 古玩、古董 ◀ *Track 1322*

例句 There's an exhibition of antique clothing at the art gallery.
在藝術展覽館有一場古董衣服的展覽。

搭配詞 antique clothing 古董衣服

---

applaud [əˋplɔd] v. 鼓掌、喝采、誇讚 ◀ *Track 1323*

例句 Everyone stood up and applauded for the symphony orchestra for their performance. 交響樂團表演完後，大家都站起來鼓掌。

搭配詞 applaud sb for 為……喝采

---

applause [əˋplɔz] n. 喝采 ◀ *Track 1324*

例句 His speech was met with polite applause.
他的演講得到禮貌性鼓掌。

搭配詞 polite applause 禮貌性鼓掌

---

appreciate [əˋpriʃɪˌet] v. 欣賞、鑒賞 ◀ *Track 1325*

例句 He stood back and appreciated the painting.
他往後站，鑑賞這幅畫。

反義字 depreciate 輕視

---

art [ɑrt] n. 藝術 ◀ *Track 1326*

例句 He enjoys art class. 他喜歡藝術課。

搭配詞 art class 藝術課

---

artistic [ɑrˋtɪstɪk] **adj.** 藝術的、美術的 Track 1327

例句 You can see from her outfit that she's a very artistic person.
你可以從她的穿著看出她是個很藝術的人。

audience [ˋɔdɪəns] **n.** 聽眾、觀眾 Track 1328

例句 The audience enjoyed every minute of the concert.
這場演唱會讓觀眾們每分每秒都很享受。

ball [bɔl] **n.** 舞會、球 Track 1329

例句 Everyone should wear masks when attending the masked ball.
參加這場化妝舞會時，每個人都必須戴面具。

搭配詞 masked ball 化妝舞會

balloon [bəˋlun] **n.** 氣球 Track 1330

例句 There is a man giving away colorful balloons at the entrance of the park. 有個男人在公園門口分發彩色的氣球。

band [bænd] **n.** 帶子、隊、樂隊 Track 1331

例句 The rock band played several songs last night.
這個搖滾樂團昨晚表演了好幾首歌。

搭配詞 rock band 搖滾樂團

beach [bitʃ] **n.** 海灘 Track 1332

例句 There are a great number of people under the beach umbrella.
有許多人在海灘遮陽傘底下納涼。

搭配詞 beach umbrella 海灘遮陽傘

beautiful [ˋbjutəfəl] **adj.** 美麗的、漂亮的 Track 1333

＊字尾-ful有「充滿」的意思

例句 The actress is not only beautiful but also very talented.
這位女演員不但美麗，也很有天分。

同義字 pretty

beauty [ˋbjutɪ] **n.** 美、美人、美的東西 Track 1334

例句 Angela goes to beauty salon every Saturday.
安琪拉每週六去美容沙龍。

搭配詞 beauty salon 美容沙龍

bell [bɛl] **n.** 鐘、鈴 Track 1335

例句 Please ring the bell if you need my assistance.
如果需要我的幫忙，請搖鈴。

搭配詞 ring a bell 搖鈴

bingo [ˋbɪŋgo] **n.** 賓果遊戲 Track 1336

例句 We play bingo every Friday night with church friends.
我們每個禮拜五晚上都與教會的朋友玩賓果。

搭配詞 play bingo 玩賓果

blow [blo] v. 吹、打擊 Track 1337

例句 The storm blew down several large trees on the street.
暴風雨把街上許多大樹都吹倒了。

搭配詞 blow down 吹倒

---

blues [bluz] n. 憂鬱、藍調 Track 1338

例句 Rhythm and Blues is one of the most popular music genres in this century. 節奏藍調是這個世紀最受歡迎的一種音樂類型之一。

搭配詞 Rhythm and Blues 節奏藍調（R & B）

---

broadcast [ˋbrɔd͵kæst] n. 廣播、播出 Track 1339

例句 This is a live national broadcast from the president.
這是總統的實況全國廣播。

搭配詞 live broadcast 實況轉播

---

cancel [ˋkænsḷ] v. 取消 Track 1340

例句 The outing was cancelled because of the rain, and we will reschedule it. 這次外出因雨取消，我們會改期舉行。

同義字 call off

---

cartoon [kɑrˋtun] n. 卡通 Track 1341

例句 She didn't like it when her children watched cartoons.
她不喜歡她的小孩看卡通。

同義字 animation

---

cater [ˋketɚ] v. 提供食物、提供娛樂 Track 1342

例句 We cater for birthday parties, gatherings, and meetings.
我們會為生日派對、聚會與會議提供食物。

易混淆字 carter 卡車司機

CD/compact disk [ˋsiˋdi]/[ˋkɑmpækt dɪsk] Track 1343
n. 光碟

例句 I like to listen to CDs before I go to bed. 我喜歡在去睡覺前聽光碟。

---

cello [ˋtʃɛlo] n. 大提琴 Track 1344

例句 My elder sister plays the cello in the school orchestra.
我姊姊在學校樂隊裡拉大提琴。

搭配詞 play the cello 拉大提琴

---

chess [tʃɛs] n. 西洋棋 Track 1345

例句 Playing Chinese chess is a good hobby for elderly people.
玩象棋是適合老人的興趣。

搭配詞 Chinese chess 象棋

---

chord [kɔrd] n. 琴弦、和弦 Track 1346

例句 I can't find the right chord for this part of the song.
我找不到這首歌這個部分正確的和弦。

cinema [ˋsɪnəmə] n. 電影院、電影 Track 1347

例句 I prefer to watch movies at cinemas.
我比較喜歡在電影院看電影。

同義字
movie theater

circus [ˋsɝkəs] n. 馬戲團 Track 1348

例句 Grandma took the children to the circus on Easter day.
奶奶在復活節帶孩子們到馬戲團。

易混淆字
circuit 電路回圈

clap [klæp] v. 鼓（掌）、拍擊 Track 1349

例句 She clapped her hands and the puppy came running over.
她一拍手，小狗就跑過來了。

搭配詞
clap hands 拍手

classic [ˋklæsɪk] adj. 經典的 Track 1350

例句 Romeo and Juliet by Shakespeare is a literary classic.
莎士比亞的《羅密歐與茱麗葉》是個文學經典。

搭配詞
classic book 經典書籍

classical [ˋklæsɪkl] adj. 古典的 Track 1351

例句 She prefers pop music to classical music.
比起古典音樂，她比較喜歡流行音樂。

搭配詞
classical music 古典音樂

clay [kle] n. 黏土 Track 1352

例句 My children enjoy playing with clay.
我的小孩喜歡玩黏土。

搭配詞
clay court 紅土網球場

clown [klaun] n. 小丑、丑角 Track 1353

例句 Clowns bring laughter and happiness to children.
小丑給孩子們帶來笑聲與歡樂。

易混淆字
colon 冒號

club [klʌb] n. 俱樂部、社團 Track 1354

例句 Jane belongs to the table tennis club.
珍妮是桌球社的成員。

comedy [ˋkɑmədɪ] n. 喜劇 Track 1355

例句 Romantic comedy is my favorite type of movie.
浪漫喜劇是我最喜歡的一種電影。

反義字
tragedy 悲劇

comic [ˋkɑmɪk] adj. 滑稽的、漫畫的 Track 1356

例句 Garfield is a famous comic book character.
加菲貓是一個有名的漫畫角色。

搭配詞
comic book 漫畫書

compare [kəm`pɛr] **v.** 比較 ◀Track 1357
＊字首com-有「共同」之意
例句 My parents like to compare me with my brothers.
我的父母喜歡把我和我兄弟做比較。

搭配詞 compare to 與……相比

concert [`kɑnsɝt] **n.** 音樂會、演奏會 ◀Track 1358
例句 The program will present Justin Bieber's live concert.
這個節目將播出小賈斯汀的現場演唱會。

搭配詞 live concert 現場演唱會

creative [krɪ`etɪv] **adj.** 有創造力的 ◀Track 1359
＊字尾-ive有轉變為形容詞的意思
例句 Her creative ideas are what make her stand out from her peers.
她有創造力的點子是她和同儕所不同的地方。

搭配詞 creative ideas 創意思維

dance [dæns] **v./n.** 舞蹈 ◀Track 1360
例句 She teaches belly dance at the gym.
她在健身房教肚皮舞。

搭配詞 belly dance 肚皮舞

disco/discotheque [`dɪsko]/[ˏdɪskə`tɛk] ◀Track 1361
n. 迪斯可、酒吧、小舞廳
例句 My dad enjoys disco music. 我爸爸喜歡迪斯可音樂。

搭配詞 disco music 迪斯可音樂

disk/disc [dɪsk] **n.** 唱片、碟片、圓盤狀的東西 ◀Track 1362
例句 Please back up the files in the hard disk.
請把文件備份在硬碟中。

搭配詞 hard disk （電腦）硬碟

display [dɪ`sple] **v.** 展出 ◀Track 1363
例句 We need to show these new products in the display cabinet, so people can see them.
我們得把這些新產品放在展示櫃中，人們才看得到它們。

搭配詞 display cabinet 展示櫃

documentary [ˏdɑkjə`mɛntərɪ] **n.** 紀錄、紀錄片 ◀Track 1364
例句 We watched a documentary film about dolphins last night.
我們昨晚看了一齣和海豚有關的紀錄片。

搭配詞 documentary film 紀錄片

doll [dɑl] **n.** 玩具娃娃 ◀Track 1365
例句 My sister likes to collect Barbie Dolls.
我妹妹喜歡收集芭比娃娃。

搭配詞 Barbie Doll 芭比娃娃

download [`daunˏlod] **v.** 下載、往下傳送 ◀Track 1366
例句 You need to download the software to install this device on computers. 你得下載這個軟體，才能把這個裝置安裝在電腦上。

a b c d e f g h i j k l m n o p q r s t u v w x y z

drama [ˋdrɑmə] n. 劇本、戲劇 Track 1367

例句 She is a drama queen. 她是個很戲劇化的人。

dramatic [drəˋmætɪk] adj. 戲劇性的 Track 1368

例句 He made a dramatic change after quitting drugs.
他戒毒了以後，有了戲劇性的轉變。

搭配詞
dramatic change
戲劇性轉變

draw [drɔ] v. 拉、拖、提取、畫、繪製 Track 1369

例句 Can you draw a picture of me sitting in the garden?
你可以畫一張我坐在花園的圖嗎？

drum [drʌm] n. 鼓 Track 1370

例句 He plays bass drums in the band.
他在樂隊裡打大鼓。

搭配詞
bass drum 大鼓

DVD/digital video disk [ˋdɪdʒɪtḷ ˋvɪdɪˏo dɪsk] Track 1371
n. 影音光碟

例句 Do you know how to use a DVD-rom?
你知道如何使用DVD光碟機嗎？

搭配詞
DVD-rom DVD光碟機

earphone [ˋɪrˏfon] n. 耳機 Track 1372

例句 I need a pair of better earphones.
我需要更好的一副耳機。

搭配詞
wear earphones 戴耳機

enjoyable [ɪnˋdʒɔɪəbḷ] adj. 愉快的 Track 1373
＊字尾-able有「可以、能」的意思

例句 The music festival in the park last night was very enjoyable.
昨晚公園的音樂祭非常令人愉快。

同義字
pleasurable

enjoyment [ɪnˋdʒɔɪmənt] n. 享受、愉快 Track 1374
＊字尾-ment有轉變為名詞之意

例句 Reading classic novels gives me a lot of enjoyment.
讀古典小說讓我很享受。

entertain [ˏɛntəˋten] v. 招待、娛樂、接受 Track 1375

例句 We need to entertain our families and friends this weekend.
我們這週末得招待親戚朋友。

entertainment [ˏɛntəˋtenmənt] n. 款待、娛樂 Track 1376
＊字尾-ment有轉變為名詞之意

例句 What's your favorite form of entertainment? 你最喜歡哪種娛樂？

enthusiasm [ɪn`θjuzɪ͵æzəm] **n.** 熱衷、熱情 Track 1377
例句 He does his job with enthusiasm. 他總是熱情地工作。

搭配詞 with enthusiasm 熱情地

---

expressive [ɪk`sprɛsɪv] **adj.** 表達的 Track 1378
＊字尾-ive有轉變為形容詞之意
例句 I love expressive pieces of music. 我喜歡表達力強的音樂。

---

fabulous [`fæbjələs] **adj.** 傳說中的、極好的 Track 1379
例句 This is a fabulous show. I would recommend it to my friends. 這是個極好的表演。我會推薦給我朋友。

同義字 marvelous

---

fad [fæd] **n.** 一時的流行 Track 1380
例句 The latest fad is to mix and match. 混搭是最新的流行。

易混淆字 fade 褪去

---

fake [fek] **v./adj.** 仿造、假裝、假的 Track 1381
例句 The police found that he made a lot of fake notes at home. 警方發現他在家裡製造很多偽鈔。

搭配詞 fake note 偽鈔

---

fan/fanatic [fæn]/[fə`nætɪk] Track 1382
n. 狂熱者、迷（粉絲）
例句 My brother is a sudoku fan. 我弟弟是個數獨狂熱者。

---

fiddle [`fɪdḷ] **n.** 小提琴 Track 1383
例句 He played the fiddle to entertain the guests. 他拉小提琴以娛樂客人。

易混淆字 riddle 謎語

---

film [fɪlm] **n.** 電影、膠捲 Track 1384
例句 Have you heard about the new action film? 你聽說了最新的動作片的事了嗎？

搭配詞 action film 動作片

---

firework [`faɪr͵wɝk] **n.** 煙火 Track 1385
例句 Come over to my room. You can see firework display from my window. 來我房間，你可以從我的窗戶看到煙火。

搭配詞 firework display 煙火秀

---

flute [flut] **n.** 長笛 Track 1386
例句 You need to make use of your tongue and lips when playing the flute. 你必須要使用舌頭和嘴唇來吹長笛。

易混淆字 fluent 流暢的

full [fʊl] adj. 滿的、充滿的 Track 1387

例句 Within a year, the newcomer has become a full-fledged editor-in-chief. 在一年之內，這位新人已變為稱職的總編了。

搭配詞 full-fledged 成熟的

fun [fʌn] n. 樂趣、玩笑 Track 1388

例句 I had so much fun in the summer camp.
我在夏令營玩得很開心。

搭配詞 have fun 玩得愉快

funny [`fʌnɪ] adj. 滑稽的、有趣的 Track 1389

例句 This is not funny! Stop laughing at me.
這不好笑！不要笑我。

反義字 solemn 嚴肅的

gallery [`gælərɪ] n. 畫廊、美術館 Track 1390

例句 There is a new exhibition in the art gallery this month.
這個月美術館有新展覽。

搭配詞 art gallery 美術館

gamble [`gæmbḷ] v. 賭博 Track 1391

例句 He gambled away all his belongings.
他把所有財產都賭光了。

搭配詞 gamble away 賭博輸光

game [gem] n. 遊戲、比賽 Track 1392

例句 The children were playing a card game called Mafia.
孩子們在玩一個叫做殺手的紙牌遊戲。

搭配詞 card game 紙牌遊戲

garden [`gɑrdṇ] n. 花園 Track 1393

例句 We visited the botanical gardens. 我們去了植物園。

搭配詞 botanical garden 植物園

grab [græb] v. 急抓、逮捕 Track 1394

例句 I grabbed a sandwich for lunch.
我急急抓了一個三明治當午餐。

同義字 seize

group [grup] n. 團體、組、群 Track 1395

例句 Her group of friends are mostly tall girls.
她那一群朋友大部分都是比較高的女生。

guitar [gɪ`tɑr] n. 吉他 Track 1396

例句 The man is a guitar player in the band.
那個男人是樂團的吉他手。

搭配詞 guitar player 吉他手

haircut [ˋhɛr͵kʌt] n. 理髮 ◀Track 1397

例句 My hair is getting too long; I need to have a haircut.
我的頭髮太長了，我需要理髮。

搭配詞
have a haircut 去理髮

---

harmonica [hɑrˋmɑnɪkə] n. 口琴 ◀Track 1398

例句 She pretended to play the harmonica at the beginning of the song.
她在這首歌開始時假裝吹口琴。

易混淆字
harmonic 和聲的

---

horn [hɔrn] n. 喇叭 ◀Track 1399

例句 A car honked its horn at the old lady.
一輛車對那位老太太按喇叭。

---

humor [ˋhjumɚ] n. 詼諧、幽默 ◀Track 1400

例句 He has a good sense of humor and is a good conversationist.
他很有幽默感，也很好聊。

搭配詞
sense of humor 幽默感

---

humorous [ˋhjumərəs] adj. 幽默的、滑稽的 ◀Track 1401

＊字尾-ous有轉變為形容詞之意

例句 He deliverd a humorous speech in the seminar.
他在研討會發表了一個很幽默的演說。

搭配詞
humorous speech
幽默的演說

---

idol [ˋaɪdḷ] n. 偶像 ◀Track 1402

例句 I have idol posters all over my wall.
我牆上都是偶像海報。

---

illusion [ɪˋljuʒən] n. 錯覺、幻覺 ◀Track 1403

例句 He is under the illusion that someone is trying to poison him.
他一直有幻覺，認為有人想毒死他。

反義字
disillusion 醒悟

---

image [ˋɪmɪdʒ] n. 影像、形象 ◀Track 1404

例句 She is trying to maintain an innocent and cute image.
她試著維持一個無辜又可愛的形象。

---

imagination [ɪ͵mædʒəˋneʃən] n. 想像力、創作力 ◀Track 1405

＊字尾-tion有轉變為名詞的意思

例句 She likes to lie in bed and let her imagination run wild.
她喜歡躺在床上，讓想像力盡情揮灑。

---

imagine [ɪˋmædʒɪn] v. 想像、設想 ◀Track 1406

例句 Can you imagine dad baking a cake?
你可以想像老爸做蛋糕的樣子嗎？

搭配詞
imagine sb doing sth
想像某人做某事

impress [ɪmˋprɛs] v. 留下深刻印象、使感動 Track 1407

例句 I was deeply impressed by his generosity.
我被他的大方深深感動了。

搭配詞
be impressed by
被……感動

impressive [ɪmˋprɛsɪv] adj. 令人印象深刻的 Track 1408

＊字尾-ive有轉變為形容詞之意

例句 Her grades were impressive enough to get her into the best school.
她的成績夠令人印象深刻，所以她能進入最好的一所學校。

introduce [ˏɪntrəˋdjus] v. 介紹、引進 Track 1409

例句 Can you introduce yourself?
你可以自我介紹一下嗎？

搭配詞
introduce oneself 自我介紹

invitation [ˏɪnvəˋteʃən] n. 請帖、邀請 Track 1410

＊字尾-tion有轉變為名詞的意思

例句 We need to send out the wedding invitations at least one month earlier. 我們必須至少在一個月前就把婚禮請帖送出去。

搭配詞
wedding invitation 喜帖

invite [ɪnˋvaɪt] v. 邀請、招待 Track 1411

例句 We can invite our neighbors to the party.
我們可以邀請鄰居來參加派對。

搭配詞
invite sb to 邀請某人

instrument [ˋɪnstrəmənt] n. 樂器、器具 Track 1412

＊字尾-ment有轉變為名詞之意

例句 The only musical instrument I can play is the guitar.
我唯一會彈的樂器是吉他。

搭配詞
musical instrument 樂器

interest [ˋɪntərɪst] n. 興趣、利益 Track 1413

例句 Her article piqued my interest.
她的文章引起了我的興趣。

jazz [dʒæz] n. 爵士樂 Track 1414

例句 I went to a jazz concert on a lazy Sunday afternoon.
我在懶洋洋的一個星期天下午去聽爵士樂音樂會。

搭配詞
jazz concert 爵士音樂會

joke [dʒok] n. 笑話、玩笑 Track 1415

例句 He told a joke but no one laughed.
他說了一個笑話，但沒人有笑。

搭配詞
tell a joke 說笑話

lantern [ˋlæntən] n. 燈籠 Track 1416

例句 We eat sticky rice balls to celebrate the Lantern Festival.
我們吃湯圓慶祝元宵節。

搭配詞
Lantern Festival 元宵節

laugh [læf] v. 笑、笑聲 ◀Track 1417

例句 She simply laughed off their derisive remarks.
她對他們的嘲諷，只是一笑置之。

搭配詞 laugh off 一笑置之

laughter [ˋlæftɚ] n. 笑聲 ◀Track 1418

例句 She burst into laughter while watching the comedy.
她邊看喜劇邊放聲大笑。

搭配詞 burst into laughter 爆笑出聲

listener [ˋlɪsn̩ɚ] n. 聽眾、聽者 ◀Track 1419

＊字尾-er有「者」的意思

例句 Sometimes a good listener is all I need when I feel sad.
我心情不好時，有時只需要一個好的聆聽者。

搭配詞 good listener 好聽眾

loud [laʊd] adj. 大聲的、響亮的 ◀Track 1420

例句 You are too loud. The neighbors are complaining.
你太大聲了，隔壁的鄰居在抗議了。

low [lo] adj. 低聲的、低的 ◀Track 1421

例句 I've been feeling low all day; I need to go out to get some fresh air.
我整天都覺得很低潮，我得出去呼吸新鮮空氣。

反義字 high 高的

lullaby [ˋlʌlə͵baɪ] n. 搖籃曲 ◀Track 1422

例句 You can hum a lullaby and rock the baby to sleep.
你可以哼搖籃曲哄嬰兒入睡。

搭配詞 hum a lullaby 哼搖籃曲

magazine [͵mægəˋzin] n. 雜誌 ◀Track 1423

例句 Billboard is one of the best-selling magazines.
《告示牌》是最暢銷的雜誌之一。

搭配詞 best-selling magazine 暢銷雜誌

magic [ˋmædʒɪk] n. 魔術 ◀Track 1424

例句 The magic of her healing voice charmed the audience.
她魔術般的治癒系嗓音迷倒了所有聽眾。

mall [mɔl] n. 購物中心 ◀Track 1425

例句 I need to go to the shopping mall to do my Christmas shopping.
我得去購物中心買聖誕節禮物。

搭配詞 shopping mall 購物中心

medium/media [ˋmidɪəm]/[ˋmidɪə] n. 媒體 ◀Track 1426

例句 The mass media is partly responsible for the public having a bad impression of politicians.
大眾對政治家印象不好，媒體也有一部分的責任。

搭配詞 mass media 大眾傳播媒體

a b c d e f g h i j k l m n o p q r s t u v w x y z

melody [ˋmɛlədɪ] n. 旋律 Track 1427

例句 He hummed the cheerful melody all day.
他整天都哼著愉快的旋律。

搭配詞 cheerful melody 愉快的旋律

membership [ˋmɛmbɚ͵ʃɪp] n. 會員 Track 1428

例句 The membership of this club is limited to pregnant women only.
這個俱樂部的會員只限懷孕的女性。

memory [ˋmɛmərɪ] n. 記憶、回憶 Track 1429

例句 The memory card can store a huge amount of data.
這個記憶卡能儲存很多資料。

搭配詞 memory card 記憶卡

microphone [ˋmaɪkrə͵fon] n. 麥克風 Track 1430

例句 Please turn the microphone on so our audience can hear you properly. 請把麥克風打開，觀眾才聽得清楚你講話。

縮寫 mike

model [ˋmɑdḷ] n. 模型、模特兒 Track 1431

例句 She was a fashion model in her 20s.
她在20幾歲時，是個時裝模特兒。

搭配詞 fashion model 時裝模特兒

movie/film [ˋmuvɪ]/[fɪlm] n. （一部）電影 Track 1432

例句 Grace Kelly was one of the biggest movie stars in Hollywood.
葛麗絲・凱莉曾是好萊塢最大咖的電影明星之一。

搭配詞 movie star 電影明星

music [ˋmjuzɪk] n. 音樂 Track 1433

例句 Let's turn up the music and have some fun.
我們來把音樂打開，好好玩一場吧。

musical [ˋmjuzɪkḷ] adj. 音樂的 Track 1434

例句 She is a musical critic with her own website.
她是個音樂評論家，有自己的網站。

news [njuz] n. 新聞、消息 Track 1435

例句 The journalist got an exclusive news on the royal wedding.
這名記者取得有關皇室婚禮的獨家新聞。

搭配詞 exclusive news 獨家新聞

newspaper [ˋnjuz͵pepɚ] n. 報紙 Track 1436

例句 People need to stop reading the newspaper on the subway and accidentally hitting others with it.
人們不該在捷運上看報紙，還不小心用報紙打到別人。

搭配詞 read newspaper 看報紙

noise [nɔɪz] n. 喧鬧聲、噪音、聲音 Track 1437

例句 The workers upstairs are making too much noise for us to concentrate. 樓上的工人發出太大的噪音，我們都無法專心了。

搭配詞 make noise 製造噪音

noisy [ˋnɔɪzɪ] adj. 嘈雜的、喧鬧的、熙熙攘攘的 Track 1438

＊字尾-y有轉變為形容詞之意

例句 I can't hear you on the phone; it is too noisy here.
我聽不到你在電話中說什麼，這裡太吵了。

novel [ˋnɑvl̩] adj. 新穎的、新奇的 Track 1439

例句 His novel experience in the forest stunned us.
他在森林裡的新奇經歷讓我們目瞪口呆。

搭配詞 novel experience 新奇的經歷

nude [njud] n. 裸體、裸體畫 Track 1440

例句 The art students learn to draw nude in class.
藝術課學生們學習在課堂上畫裸體畫。

opera [ˋɑpərə] n. 歌劇 Track 1441

例句 "My Love from the Star" is a famous Korean soap opera.
「來自星星的你」是齣有名的韓劇。

搭配詞 soap opera 肥皂劇

orchestra [ˋɔrkɪstrə] n. 樂隊、樂團 Track 1442

例句 The chamber orchestra played a Mozart symphony.
那個樂隊表演了一首莫札特的交響樂。

搭配詞 chamber orchestra 室內管弦樂團

outfit [ˋaʊt͵fɪt] n. 裝備 ＊字首out-有「外」之意 Track 1443

例句 I need to buy a hunting outfit before I go to the forest.
在去森林前，我得買一套打獵裝備。

搭配詞 hunting outfit 打獵裝備

outlet [ˋaʊt͵lɛt] n. 逃離的出口、暢貨中心 Track 1444

＊字首out-有「外」之意

例句 We bought a lot of clothes at the outlet.
我們在暢貨中心買了很多衣服。

painting [ˋpentɪŋ] n. 繪畫 Track 1445

例句 We have a street painting in our neighborhood.
我們的鄰里有一幅街頭繪畫。

搭配詞 street painting 街頭繪畫

palace [ˋpælɪs] n. 宮殿 Track 1446

例句 All tourists were taking photos in front of the National Palace Museum. 遊客們都在故宮博物院前照相。

搭配詞 National Palace Museum 故宮博物院

paper [ˋpepɚ] n. 紙、報紙 Track 1447
例句 We're out of toilet paper. This is a crisis.
我們沒有廁所衛生紙了，這可是大危機。
搭配詞 toilet paper 廁所衛生紙

parade [pəˋred] n. 遊行 Track 1448
例句 We sat down and waited for the parade to come by.
我們坐下來等著遊行隊伍經過。

pastime [ˋpæs͵taɪm] n. 消遣 Track 1449
例句 Gardening is my favorite pastime.
種花種草是我最喜歡的消遣。
同義字 recreation

perform [pɚˋfɔrm] v. 執行、表演 Track 1450
例句 A robot can perform duties like a human being.
機器人可以如人類一般執行事務。
搭配詞 perform a duty 執行任務

performance [pɚˋʃɔrməns] n. 演出 Track 1451
＊字尾-ance有轉變為名詞之意
例句 Their brilliant performance last night was very impressive.
他們昨晚的精彩演出令人印象深刻。
搭配詞 brilliant performance 精彩的演出

photograph [ˋfotə͵græf] n. 照片 Track 1452
例句 I kept some old photographs of my mother.
我留著一些我媽媽的舊照片。
縮寫 photo

piano [pɪˋæno] n. 鋼琴 Track 1453
例句 The little girl was trying to teach the cat how to play the piano.
小女孩在試著教貓彈鋼琴。
搭配詞 play the piano 彈鋼琴

picture [ˋpɪktʃɚ] n. 圖片、相片 Track 1454
例句 Did you take a picture of the statue?
你有幫那個雕像照一張相片嗎？
搭配詞 take a picture 照相

picturesque [͵pɪktʃəˋrɛsk] adj. 如畫的 Track 1455
＊字尾-esque有「像」之意
例句 Next to the little village is a picturesque valley.
那個小村莊旁有風景如畫的山谷。
搭配詞 picturesque valley 風景如畫的山谷

play [ple] v. 遊戲、玩耍 Track 1456
例句 Little Tommy wanted to play with your son.
小湯米想和你的兒子一起玩。
搭配詞 play with 與……玩耍

playground [ˋpleˏgraʊnd] n. 運動場、遊戲場 Track 1457
例句 There are lots of children playing on the swings on the playground.
有許多小孩在遊戲場玩鞦韆。

plot [plɑt] n. 陰謀、情節 Track 1458
例句 The plot of the novel was very intriguing.
這本小說的情節很有意思。

poetry [ˋpoɪtrɪ] n. 詩、詩集 Track 1459
例句 I hate reading and memorizing poetry.
我討厭讀詩和背詩。

pop/popular [pɑp]/[ˋpɑpjələ˞] adj. 流行的 Track 1460
例句 Jay is a pop singer. 周杰倫是流行歌手。
搭配詞 pop singer 流行歌手

portrait [ˋportret] n. 肖像 Track 1461
例句 There is a portrait of our grandfather's lost love on the wall.
牆上有一幅爺爺舊愛的肖像。

poster [ˋpostə˞] n. 海報 Track 1462
例句 When Tom Cruise was in Taiwan, his movie posters were everywhere.
湯姆・克魯斯訪台時，他的電影海報到處都是。
搭配詞 movie poster 電影海報

print [prɪnt] n. 印跡、印刷字體、版 Track 1463
例句 This book is out of print. 這本書已經絕版了。
搭配詞 out of print 絕版

program [ˋprogræm] n. 節目、程式 Track 1464
例句 That's my favorite TV program. 那是我最喜歡的電視節目。
搭配詞 TV program 電視節目

puppet [ˋpʌpɪt] n. 木偶、傀儡 Track 1465
例句 We took our little son to see a puppet show on his birthday.
我們帶小兒子在他生日時去看木偶戲。
易混淆字 puppy 小狗

radio [ˋredɪˏo] n. 收音機 Track 1466
例句 The radio station is broadcasting the president's speech live.
收音機電台正在實況轉播總統的演說。
搭配詞 radio station 收音機電台

rehearsal [rɪˋhɝsḷ] n. 排演 ◀Track 1467

＊字首re-有「再次」之意

例句 We had a rehearsal hours before the play.

我們在演出前幾個小時排演了一次。

rehearse [rɪˋhɝs] v. 預演、排練 ◀Track 1468

＊字首re-有「再次」之意

例句 Can you rehearse the speech before formally going onstage?

你可以在正式上台前排練演講嗎？

搭配詞 rehearse a speech 排練演講

record [rɪˋkɔrd]/[ˋrɛkɚd] ◀Track 1469

v. 記錄、錄製 n. 紀錄、唱片 ＊字首re-有「再次」之意

例句 The singer prepares to make a new record.

這名歌手準備錄新唱片。

搭配詞 make a record 錄唱片

recreation [͵rɛkrɪˋeʃən] n. 娛樂 ◀Track 1470

＊字尾-tion有轉變為名詞的意思

例句 Fishing is my father's favorite recreation.

釣魚是我爸最喜歡的娛樂。

易混淆字 re-creation 再創

recreational [͵rɛkrɪˋeʃənḷ] adj. 娛樂的 ◀Track 1471

＊字尾-al有轉變為形容詞之意

例句 There is a new recreational center in the shopping mall.

購物中心裡有一個新的娛樂中心。

reel [ril] n./v. 捲軸、捲起 ◀Track 1472

例句 Look! He reeled in a big trout.

你看！他捲起了一隻很大的鱒魚。

relax [rɪˋlæks] v. 放鬆 ◀Track 1473

例句 He relaxed on the couch and fell asleep in half an hour.

他在沙發上放鬆，半個小時就睡著了。

resort [rɪˋzɔrt] n. 休閒勝地 ◀Track 1474

例句 We're going to a famous resort in Hawaii.

我們要去夏威夷的一個著名休閒勝地。

搭配詞 famous resort 著名休閒勝地

restrict [rɪˋstrɪkt] v. 限制 ◀Track 1475

例句 Their rules restricted non-members from dining in the club.

他們的規定限制非會員不得在俱樂部用餐。

搭配詞 restrict sb from doing sth 限制某人做某事

rhythmic [ˋrɪðəmɪk] adj. 有節奏的 ◀Track 1476

＊字尾-ic有轉變為形容詞之意

例句 I listened to the rhythmic beating of his heart.

我聽著他的心臟有節奏的跳動。

rhythm [ˋrɪðəm] n. 節奏、韻律 Track 1477

例句 The rhythm of this song makes me want to dance.
這首歌的節奏讓我很想跳舞。

riddle [ˋrɪdḷ] n. 謎語 Track 1478

例句 I still can't figure out the answer to the riddle she asked.
我還是搞不清楚她問的謎語的謎底。

易混淆字
middle 中間的

role [rol] n. 角色 Track 1479

例句 He played the leading role in the musical play.
他在音樂劇中扮演主角。

易混淆字
rule 規定

rot [rɑt] v. 腐敗 Track 1480

例句 Corruption will rot the government.
貪腐會讓政府變得腐敗。

同義字
decay

rumor [ˋrumɚ] n. 謠言 Track 1481

例句 Rumor has it that she is leaving the company.
有個謠言說她要離開公司了。

搭配詞
rumor has it 有謠言說

saloon [səˋlun] n. 酒店、酒吧 Track 1482

例句 He stayed in the saloon all night and got drunk.
他整晚在酒店，喝醉了。

scene [sin] n. 場景、風景 Track 1483

例句 I'll never forget the ocean scene in the movie when he confessed to her. 我永遠忘不了電影中他對她告白的海景。

搭配詞
ocean scene 海景

scenery [ˋsinərɪ] n. 風景、景色 Track 1484

例句 The scenery here is beyond description.
這裡的景色真是難以形容。

同義字
landscape

scenic [ˋsinɪk] adj. 舞臺的、風景秀麗的 Track 1485

＊字尾-ic有轉變為形容詞之意

例句 Which scenic spot is most higly-recommended around this city?
這個城市附近有哪個最被推崇的景點？

搭配詞
scenic spot 風景名勝

script [skrɪpt] n. 原稿、劇本 Track 1486

例句 The movie script can be found on the Internet.
這部電影劇本可以在網路上找到。

sculpture [ˋskʌlptʃɚ] n. 雕刻、雕塑、雕像 Track 1487

＊字尾-ure有轉變為名詞之意

例句 There is a sculpture garden in the center of the square.
在廣場中央有座雕像公園。

搭配詞
sculpture garden 雕塑公園

seesaw [ˋsiˏsɔ] n. 翹翹板 Track 1488

例句 There are many children in the park, waiting to play on the seesaw.
公園裡有許多小朋友，等著玩蹺蹺板。

sing [sɪŋ] v. 唱 Track 1489

例句 I'm terrible at singing. No kidding!
我很不會唱歌。沒騙你！

shore [ʃor] n. 岸、濱 Track 1490

例句 We like to walk along the shore on fine days.
天氣好的時候，我們喜歡沿著岸邊散步。

shrine [ʃraɪn] n. 廟、祠 Track 1491

例句 Every Sunday my mother goes to pray in the shrine.
每個星期天，我媽媽都到廟裡拜拜。

易混淆字
shine 閃亮

sightseeing [ˋsaɪtˏsiɪŋ] n. 觀光、遊覽 Track 1492

例句 We plan to do a lot of sightseeing today.
我們今天打算遊覽很多景點。

搭配詞
do sightseeing 觀光

sign [saɪn] n. 記號、標誌 Track 1493

例句 There is a road sign reminding drivers to slow down in this area.
這裡有個路標，提醒駕駛在這一區要放慢速度。

搭配詞
road sign 路標

sociable [ˋsoʃəbl] adj. 愛交際的、社交的 Track 1494

例句 I am not a sociable person; I prefer to be alone.
我不愛交際，我寧願一個人。

反義字
unsociable 不愛交際的

song [sɔŋ] n. 歌曲 Track 1495

例句 Which theme song do you want to play on your wedding?
你在婚禮上要放哪個主題歌？

搭配詞
theme song 主題曲

sound [saund] n. 聲音、聲響 Track 1496

例句 Did you make that weird sound?
那個奇怪的聲音是你發出的嗎？

souvenir [ˏsuvəˋnɪr] n. 紀念品、特產 Track 1497

例句 The tourists bought some postcards at the souvenirs shops.
觀光客在當地的紀念品店裡買了一些明信片。

搭配詞 souvenir shop 紀念品店

spectacle [ˋspɛktəkl̩] n. 奇觀 Track 1498

例句 Look! A car crash with ten cars involved! What a spectacle!
你看！波及十輛車的車禍耶！真是奇觀！

spectacular [spɛkˋtækjələ] adj. 壯觀的 Track 1499

例句 The movie last night was spectacular.
昨晚的電影真是壯觀。

spot [spɑt] n. 汙點、地點 Track 1500

例句 Let's find a shady spot where we can lay down and take a nap.
我們找個有陰影的地點躺下來睡覺吧。

statue [ˋstætʃu] n. 鑄像、雕像 Track 1501

例句 The Statue of Liberty was a gift given by France to America.
自由女神像是法國給美國的禮物。

搭配詞 the Statue of Liberty 自由女神像

stereo [ˋstɛrɪo] n. 立體音響 Track 1502

例句 Our van is equipped with a great car stereo.
我們的小貨車裝了一套很棒的立體音響。

搭配詞 car stereo 汽車音響

story [ˋstorɪ] n. 故事 Track 1503

例句 The children were fascinated by the story.
孩子們被故事給迷住了。

subscribe [səbˋskraɪb] v. 捐助、訂閱、預訂 Track 1504

例句 We subscribe to the TIME magazine. 我們訂閱了時代雜誌。

搭配詞 subscribe to 訂閱

subscription [səbˋskrɪpʃən] n. 訂閱、簽署、捐款 Track 1505

＊字尾-tion有轉變為名詞的意思

例句 The subscription fee of the magazine is $120 per month.
這份雜誌的每月訂閱費是120元。

搭配詞 subscription fee 訂閱費

symphony [ˋsɪmfənɪ] n. 交響樂、交響曲 Track 1506

例句 I love listening to symphonies.
我喜歡聽交響樂。

a b c d e f g h i j k l m n o p q r s t u v w x y z

tale [tel] n. 故事 Track 1507

例句 She looks like a princess from a fairy tale.
她看起來像是童話故事中的公主。

搭配詞
fairy tale 童話故事

talk [tɔk] v. 談話、聊天 Track 1508

例句 I need to talk to you about our new product.
我必須和你談談我們的新產品。

television/TV [ˋtɛlə͵vɪʒən] n. 電視 Track 1509

例句 My father watches daily news on cable television.
我爸在看電視上的每日新聞。

搭配詞
cable television 有線電視

theater [ˋθiətɚ] n. 戲院、劇場 Track 1510

例句 Let's go to the new theater. 我們去新戲院吧。

搭配詞
movie theater 電影院

thriller [ˋθrɪlɚ] Track 1511

n. 恐怖小說、恐怖電影、令人震顫的人事物 ＊字尾-er有轉變為名詞的意思

例句 I don't read thriller novels. They're too spooky.
我不喜歡恐怖小說，太讓人覺得毛骨聳然了。

搭配詞
thriller novel 恐怖小說

tone [ton] n. 風格、音調、色調 Track 1512

例句 The ring tone sounds very pleasant. 這個手機鈴聲很悅耳。

搭配詞
ring tone 手機鈴聲

toy [tɔɪ] n. 玩具 Track 1513

例句 He thinks the cat is his new toy.
他覺得那隻貓是他的新玩具。

tune [tjun] n./v. 調子、曲調、調音 Track 1514

例句 I like the tune but I don't like the lyrics.
我喜歡曲調，但我不喜歡歌詞。

易混淆字
turn 轉動

upload [ʌpˋlod] v. 上傳（檔案） Track 1515

＊字首up-有「上」之意

例句 What do you think about uploading these funny photos onto the Internet? 你要不要把這些好笑的照片上傳到網路上呢？

反義字
download 下載

video [ˋvɪdɪ͵o] n. 電視、錄影 Track 1516

例句 He has a video blog that shows funny clips.
他有個影音部落格，上面放了爆笑的影片。

搭配詞
video blog 影音部落格

videotape [ˋvɪdɪo͵tep] n. 錄影帶 Track 1517

例句 I have some old videotapes about wild life.
我有一些關於野生動物的舊錄影帶。

---

viewer [ˋvjuɚ] n. 觀看者、電視觀眾 Track 1518

＊字尾-er有「者」的意思

例句 A lot of viewers wrote letters to the show.
許多觀眾都寫信到節目去。

同義字 onlooker

---

violin [͵vaɪəˋlɪn] n. 小提琴 Track 1519

例句 He plays the violin in the orchestra. 他在交響樂團中拉小提琴。

搭配詞 play the violin 拉小提琴

---

visit [ˋvɪzɪt] v. 訪問、拜訪 Track 1520

例句 He visits his father frequently. 他經常拜訪他爸爸。

---

visitor [ˋvɪzɪtɚ] n. 訪客、觀光客 Track 1521

＊字尾-or有「者」的意思

例句 There are many frequent visitors in Vatican every year.
梵蒂岡每年都有很多固定的觀光客。

搭配詞 frequent visitor 常客

---

vogue [vog] n. 時尚、流行物 Track 1522

例句 Vegetarianism has obviously become a vogue.
素食主義明顯地蔚為流行。

搭配詞 in vogue 正在流行

NOTE

Test 06 關鍵英單總測驗第6回

以下測驗題皆出自書中第六回「**和樂有關的單字**」，快來檢視自己的學習成果吧！

一、選擇題

1. The Taroko National Park is a famous ____ spot in Taiwan.
   (A) parade
   (B) saloon
   (C) memory
   (D) scenic

2. He can play a lot of musical ____.
   (A) horn
   (B) harmonica
   (C) instruments
   (D) drum

3. He burst into ____ when he heard the joke.
   (A) laughter
   (B) imagination
   (C) group
   (D) fad

4. The Berlin Symphony ____ is going to Taipei next January.
   (A) Opera
   (B) Noise
   (C) Orchestra
   (D) Palace

5. Some children are playing dodge ball on the_____.
   (A) portrait
   (B) melody
   (C) playground
   (D) garden

6. She is a teacher with great ______.
   (A) gallery
   (B) enthusiasm
   (C) expressive
   (D) rehearsal

7. She is under a lot of pressure and needs to ____.
   (A) restrict
   (B) visit
   (C) display
   (D) relax

8. The singer _____ his concert due to the loss of his mother.
   (A) invited
   (B) plotted
   (C) cancelled
   (D) printed

9. She bought some _____ when she traveled in Korea.
   (A) souvenirs
   (B) rumors
   (C) sounds
   (D) vogue

10. The nanny hummed a ______ and rocked the baby to sleep.
    (A) lullaby
    (B) news
    (C) memory
    (D) pastime

二、克漏字測驗

The Flash, based on the DC Comics character Barry Allen, is an American superhero __1__ series.

The story is about Barry Allen, who witnessed his mother being murdered by a supernatural being. He then is taken in by Detective Joe West and his family. Barry grows up and becomes a crime scene __2__. After the city is bathed with a radiation during a thunderstorm, he discovers that he can move at a superhuman speed, and he uses his supernatural power to save people and tries to find out who killed his mother.

The special effects in the series are __3__, and the series have been watched by over 4.8 million __4__ in the US. Due to the excellent __5__ and great cast, the show now has fans all over the world.

1. (A) television
   (B) poetry
   (C) documentary
   (D) newspaper

2. (A) cinema
   (B) bingo
   (C) investigator
   (D) audience

3. (A) full
   (B) imagine
   (C) drama
   (D) spectacular

4. (A) puppets
   (B) viewers
   (C) novels
   (D) listeners

5. (A) rhythm
   (B) script
   (C) radio
   (D) scene

關鍵英單總測驗第6回
中譯與解答

一、選擇題

1. 太魯閣國家公園是台灣著名的景點。
   (A) 遊行
   (B) 酒吧
   (C) 回憶
   (D) 風景秀麗的

2. 他會彈奏很多種樂器。
   (A) 喇叭
   (B) 口琴
   (C) 樂器
   (D) 鼓

3. 他聽到這個笑話時大笑出聲。
   (A) 笑聲
   (B) 想像力
   (C) 群體
   (D) 一時的流行

4. 柏林交響樂團明年一月將來台北演出。
   (A) 歌劇
   (B) 噪音
   (C) 樂團
   (D) 皇宮

5. 有些小孩在操場玩躲避球。
   (A) 肖像
   (B) 旋律
   (C) 操場
   (D) 庭院

6. 她是很有熱忱的老師。
   (A) 畫廊
   (B) 熱忱
   (C) 表達的
   (D) 排演

7. 她的壓力很大，需要放鬆。
   (A) 限制
   (B) 拜訪
   (C) 展示
   (D) 放鬆

8. 這名歌手因母親過世而取消演唱會。
   (A) 邀請
   (B) 謀劃
   (C) 取消
   (D) 列印

9. 她到韓國旅遊時，買了一些紀念品。
   (A) 紀念品
   (B) 流言
   (C) 聲音
   (D) 時尚

10. 保姆哼著搖籃曲哄嬰兒入睡。
   (A) 搖籃曲
   (B) 新聞
   (C) 回憶
   (D) 消遣

二、克漏字測驗

《閃電俠》是一部美國超級英雄電視影集，它是根據DC漫畫的角色Barry Allen所改編拍攝而成。

Barry Allen小時候目睹母親被超自然物體謀殺，後來被Joe West警探一家人收留，長大後成為犯罪現場調查員。在一次城市被雷電籠罩並發生輻射外洩後，他發現自己能以超人的速度移動，並使用這個超能力拯救民眾，同時試圖尋找謀殺母親的兇手。

這部影集的特效十分精彩，在美國有超過480萬的觀眾。由於劇本和卡司陣容十分堅強，這部影集在世界各地都有粉絲。

1.
(A) 電視
(B) 詩集
(C) 紀錄片
(D) 報紙

2.
(A) 電影院
(B) 賓果
(C) 調查員
(D) 觀眾

3.
(A) 滿的
(B) 想像
(C) 戲劇
(D) 精彩的

4
(A) 木偶
(B) 觀眾
(C) 小説
(D) 聽眾

5.
(A) 韻律
(B) 劇本
(C) 收音機
(D) 場景

一、選擇題

1.(D) 2. (C) 3.(A) 4.(C) 5.(C)
6.(B) 7. (D) 8.(C) 9.(A) 10.(A)

二、克漏字測驗

1.(A) 2.(C) 3.(D)
4.(B) 5.(B)

Unit 07 和科技醫學有關的單字

多益測驗的命題強調生活化與實用性，學會這些與「科技醫學」有關的單字，不僅能讓你在多益考場上所向披靡，在日常生活上也可以靈活運用喔！

流行疾病可以這麼說

- **If we can't stop the virus from spreading, it will develop more and more variants.**
  如果我們無法阻止病毒持續傳播，病毒將會發展出越來越多變異株。
- **With the help of the vaccine, you will have enough antibodies to fight against the disease.**
  在疫苗的幫助下，你會有足夠的抗體來抵禦疾病。
- **Corona virus is a highly contagious virus that can travel through air after someone sneeze or cough.**
  冠狀病毒是一種具有高度傳染性的病毒，它可以在有人打噴嚏或咳嗽後透過空氣傳播。

過敏症狀可以這麼說

- **She is allergic to all kinds of nuts.**
  她對所有種類的堅果過敏。
- **Itchy eyes, swollen tongue and tighten chest are severe symptoms of allergy.**
  眼睛癢、舌頭腫脹和胸悶是嚴重過敏症狀。

受傷了可以這麼說

- **He was severely injured during the explosion.**
  他在那場爆炸中受了重傷。
- **He has multiple fractures in his arms and legs.**
  他的四肢皆有多處骨折。

描述美容產品可以這麼說

- **This lipstick shade complements all kinds of complexions.**
  這個唇膏顏色在任何膚色上都很好看。
- **This hair product can repair damaged hair and prevent hair loss from heat damage.**
  這項護髮產品可以修復受損髮，並預防高熱傷害髮質。

航太科技可以這麼說

- **This is the third artificial satellite they have launched this year.**
  這是他們今年發射的第三顆人造衛星。
- **We haven't had the ability to explore the galaxy out of solar system.**
  我們尚未有探索太陽系以外的銀河系的能力。

Unit 07 和科技醫學有關的單字

abdomen [ˋæbdəmən] n. 腹部 ◀Track 1523
例句 He felt great pain in the abdomen last night.
他昨晚半夜腹部劇痛。

同義字 belly

---

abortion [əˋbɔrʃən] n. 流產、墮胎 ◀Track 1524
＊字尾-tion有轉變為名詞的意思
例句 She regretted that she had an abortion. 她很後悔去墮胎。

---

ache [ek] n./v. 疼痛 ◀Track 1525
例句 After running a marathon, her legs ached for a week.
跑完馬拉松後，她的腿疼痛了一週。

同義字 pain

---

acknowledge [əkˋnɑlɪdʒ] v. 承認、供認 ◀Track 1526
例句 She acknowledged that the decision was a mistake.
她承認這個決定是錯的。

反義字 deny 否認

---

acne [ˋæknɪ] n. 粉刺、面皰 ◀Track 1527
例句 A healthy diet help get rid of acne.
健康飲食有助消除粉刺。

搭配詞 get rid of acne 消除粉刺

---

adolescence [ˏædḷˋɛsṇs] n. 青春期 ◀Track 1528
＊字尾-ence有轉變為名詞之意
例句 Most people have already found their own interests during adolescence. 許多人在青春期時就已經發現了自己的興趣。

搭配詞 during adolescence 處於青春期

---

adolescent [ˏædḷˋɛsṇt] adj. 青春期的、青少年的 ◀Track 1529
例句 His adolescent life was full of misery and pain.
他的青春期生活充滿不幸與悲傷。

同義字 teenaged

---

adulthood [əˋdʌltˏhud] n. 成年期 ◀Track 1530
例句 When you reach your adulthood, you may get your driver's license.
到了成年期時，你就可以去考駕照了。

---

affect [əˋfɛkt] v. 影響 Track 1531

例句 Global warming is affecting our eco-system more than ever before.
全球暖化越發衝擊我們的生態系統。

同義字 influence

agony [ˋægənɪ] n. 痛苦、折磨 Track 1532

例句 The wounded man was in terrible agony and called for help.
這個受傷的人非常痛苦，猛叫救命。

搭配詞 in agony 在痛苦中

artificial intelligence [ˏɑrtəˋfɪʃəl ɪnˋtɛlədʒəns] Track 1533
n. 人工智慧 ＊字尾-ence有轉變為名詞之意

例句 There will be a lot of AI robots to work for us in the future.
未來會有許多人工智慧的機器人替我們工作。

縮寫 AI

AIDS/acquired immune deficieny syndrome Track 1534
[edz]/[əˋkwaɪrd ɪˋmjun dɪˋfɪʃənsɪ ˋsɪnˏdrom] n. 愛滋病

例句 AIDS has become a chronic disease that can be managable.
愛滋病已成為可控制的慢性疾病。

alarm [əˋlɑrm] v./n. 驚恐、警報器 Track 1535

例句 He bought an alarm clock to wake him up in the morning.
他買了一個鬧鐘，以便早上叫醒他。

搭配詞 alarm clock 鬧鐘

alive [əˋlaɪv] adj. 活的 Track 1536

例句 He managed to stay alive without any food before any resue came.
在救難人員來到之前，他設法在沒食物的狀況下存活下來。

反義字 dead 死的

allergic [əˋlɝdʒɪk] adj. 過敏的、厭惡的 Track 1537

例句 Some people are allergic to propolis.
有些人對蜂膠會過敏。

搭配詞 allergic to sth 對某事過敏

allergy [ˋælədʒɪ] n. 反感、過敏 Track 1538

例句 If you have nose allergy, take off your nose ring.
如果你有鼻子過敏，就把鼻環拿下來吧。

aluminum [əˋlumɪnəm] n. 鋁 Track 1539

例句 A lot of cooking utensils are made of stainless steel instead of aluminum. 很多烹飪用具都是用不銹鋼來取代鋁做的。

ambulance [ˋæmbjələns] n. 救護車 Track 1540

例句 The pregnant woman's water just broke. We'd better call an ambulance. 那位孕婦的羊水剛破了，我們最好趕快叫救護車。

搭配詞 call an ambulance 叫救護車

animate [ˋænə͵met] v. 賦予……生命、製作成動畫 Track 1541
＊字尾-able有「使」的意思
例句 Kung Fu Panda is one of my favorite animated movies.
功夫熊貓是我最喜歡的動畫電影之一。
搭配詞 animated movie 動畫電影

ankle [ˋæŋkl̩] n. 腳踝 Track 1542
例句 He twisted his ankle while dancing in the competition.
他在跳舞比賽時扭到了腳踝。
搭配詞 twist sb's ankle 扭傷腳踝

antibiotic [͵æntɪbaɪˋɑtɪk] n. 抗生素、盤尼西林 Track 1543
＊字首anti-有「反」之意
例句 That antibiotics can be used against methicillin-resistant Staphylococcus aureus.
那種抗生素可以對付具有抗藥性的金黃色葡萄球菌。

antibody [ˋæntɪ͵bɑdɪ] n. 抗體 Track 1544
＊字首anti-有「反」之意
例句 Our bodies produce antibodies to fight against diseases.
我們的身體製造抗體以對付疾病。

arm [ɑrm] n. 手臂 Track 1545
例句 His arms are not strong enough to lift up the big stone.
他的手臂不夠強壯，無法舉起那個大石頭。

aspect [ˋæspɛkt] n. 方面、外貌、外觀 Track 1546
例句 If we look at things from different aspects, plan A is clearly a better choice. 若我們從各種方向看待這件事情，A計畫明顯地比較好。
搭配詞 from different aspects 從不同方面

aspirin [ˋæspərɪn] n. （藥）阿斯匹靈 Track 1547
例句 Aspirin can be used to alleviate pain and fever.
阿斯匹靈可以緩解疼痛和發燒。

assign [əˋsaɪn] v. 分派、指定 Track 1548
例句 We were assigned to finish the task. 我們被指派完成這項任務。
搭配詞 assign to 指定

asthma [ˋæzmə] n. 氣喘、哮喘 Track 1549
例句 It is reported that secondhand smoke is a major trigger of asthma attacks. 據報導，二手菸是引起氣喘的一大誘因。

asylum [əˋsaɪləm] n. 收容所、精神病院 Track 1550
例句 He began seeking political asylum after spreading the classified information on WikiLeak.
他在維基解密上散播機密資訊後，就開始尋求政治庇護。
搭配詞 political asylum 政治庇護

automatic teller machine [ˌɔtəˋmætɪk ˋtɛlɚ məˋʃin] n. 自動櫃員機 Track 1551

例句 Have you ever used an ATM to withdraw money?
你有用過自動櫃員機提錢嗎？

縮寫 ATM

---

atom [ˋætəm] n. 原子 Track 1552

例句 His research was about how to catch an atom.
他的研究是關於如何捕捉原子。

---

atomic [əˋtɑmɪk] adj. 原子的 Track 1553

＊字尾-ic有轉變為形容詞之意

例句 An atomic bomb can destroy a city completely.
一個原子彈可以完全毀滅一座城市。

搭配詞 atomic bomb 原子彈

---

automatic [ˌɔtəˋmætɪk] adj. 自動的 Track 1554

＊字尾-ic有轉變為形容詞之意

例句 A fully automatic washing machine is more expensive than a semiautomatic one. 一個全自動的洗衣機比半自動的洗衣機貴。

反義字 manual 手動的

---

barometer [bəˋrɑmətɚ] Track 1555

n. 氣壓計、晴雨錶、顯示變化的事物

例句 The barometer says it might rain soon.
從晴雨錶看來，可能快下雨了。

---

backbone [ˋbækˌbon] n. 脊骨、脊柱 Track 1556

例句 Semi-conductor Industry is the economic backbone of this country.
半導體業是這個國家的經濟支柱。

搭配詞 economic backbone 經濟支柱

---

bacteria [bækˋtɪrɪə] n. 細菌 Track 1557

例句 Lab assistants are able to multiply bacteria in the laboratory.
實驗室助手能在實驗室裡增生細菌。

---

bald [bɔld] adj. 禿頭的、禿的 Track 1558

例句 He's wearing a wig to cover his bald head.
他戴假髮以掩飾禿頭。

易混淆字 bold 大膽的

---

bandage [ˋbændɪdʒ] n. 繃帶 Track 1559

例句 He just had a car accident; that's why there's a bandage around his injured arm.
他剛出車禍，所以他受傷的手臂上才圍了一圈繃帶。

---

battery [ˋbætərɪ] n. 電池 Track 1560

例句 Your cell phone had gone dead. You need a battery charger.
你的手機沒電了，要用充電器充電。

搭配詞 battery charger 充電器

beep [bip] n. 嗶嗶聲 ◀ Track 1561

例句 Why is your watch making beeps?
你的手錶怎麼發出嗶嗶聲呢？

易混淆字
beef 牛肉

---

being [ˋbiɪŋ] n. 生命、存在 ◀ Track 1562

例句 I believe there are other sentient beings in the universe.
我相信宇宙中有其他具有感知的生物。

---

belly/stomach/tummy ◀ Track 1563

[ˋbɛlɪ]/[ˋstʌmək]/[ˋtʌmɪ] n. 腹、胃

例句 My stomach hurts really bad. 我的胃痛得好厲害。

同義字
abdomen

---

beneath [bɪˋniθ] adv./prep. 在……下面 ◀ Track 1564

例句 The carpet beneath your feet is very expensive.
在你腳下的地毯很貴。

---

bind [baɪnd] v. 綁、包紮 ◀ Track 1565

例句 Unfortunately, Paris Agreement is not legally-binding.
遺憾的是，「巴黎氣候協議」並不具有法律拘束力。

---

birth [bɝθ] n. 出生、血統 ◀ Track 1566

例句 Please fill in your date of birth in the form.
請在表格填入你的出生年月日。

---

bitter [ˋbɪtɚ] adj. 苦的 ◀ Track 1567

例句 The medicine tastes bitter. 那個藥吃起來很苦。

反義字
sweet 甜的

---

bleed [blid] v. 流血、放血 ◀ Track 1568

例句 The soldier bled to death after being shot.
這名士兵被槍射中，失血而死。

搭配詞
bleed to death 流血至死

---

blind [blaɪnd] adj. 瞎的 ◀ Track 1569

例句 I arranged a blind date for my sister. 我幫妹妹安排了相親。

搭配詞
blind date
盲目約會（相親）

---

blood [blʌd] n. 血液、血統 ◀ Track 1570

例句 There's not enough O RhD negative blood in the blood bank.
血庫的O型RH陰性血不夠了。

搭配詞
blood bank 血庫

a b c d e f g h i j k l m n o p q r s t u v w x y z

bloody [ˋblʌdɪ] adj. 血腥的 Track 1571

例句 It was a bloody battle, and many innocent civilians were killed.
那場戰爭很血腥，造成許多無辜民眾死亡。

body [ˋbɑdɪ] n. 身體 Track 1572

例句 Body language is useful, especially when you travel abroad.
肢體語言很有用，尤其是在出國旅行時。

搭配詞
body language 肢體語言

bomb [bɑm] n. 炸彈 Track 1573

例句 More than 100 people were killed in the suicide bomb attack.
超過100個民眾遭到自殺炸彈轟炸的攻擊而死亡。

bone [bon] n. 骨 Track 1574

例句 He was all skin and bones. 他只剩皮包骨了。

bony [ˋbonɪ] adj. 多骨的、骨瘦如柴的 Track 1575

＊字尾-y有轉變為形容詞之意

例句 She was an old, bony lady. 她是個老而骨瘦如柴的太太。

易混淆字
pony 小馬

bore [bor] v. 鑽孔、使厭煩 Track 1576

例句 In ancient times, people need to bore for water.
古時候人們必須鑽孔取水。

同義字
drill

born [bɔrn] adj. 天生的 Track 1577

例句 She was born with a silver spoon in her mouth.
她天生就含金湯匙出生。

bottom [ˋbɑtəm] n. 底部、臀部 Track 1578

例句 I thank him from the bottom of my heart. 我從心底謝謝他。

搭配詞
from the bottom of one's heart 打從心底

bowel [ˋbaʊəl] n. 腸子、惻隱之心 Track 1579

例句 He suffered form bowel cancer. 他受腸癌所苦。

brace [bres] n. 支架、矯正器 Track 1580

例句 I had braces when I was a little girl.
我還是個小女孩時有戴牙齒矯正器。

brain [bren] n. 腦、智力 Track 1581

例句 He racked his brain trying to hide the truth.
他絞盡腦汁隱藏真相。

搭配詞
rack one's brain 絞盡腦汁

breast [brɛst] n. 胸膛、胸部 Track 1582

例句 My mother prepared chicken breast salad for supper.
我媽媽準備了雞胸沙拉當晚餐。

搭配詞
chicken breast 雞胸肉

breath [brɛθ] n. 呼吸、氣息 Track 1583

例句 He held his breath to clean the dirty fish tank.
他屏住呼吸清理骯髒的魚缸。

搭配詞
hold breath 屏住呼吸

breathe [brið] v. 呼吸、生存 Track 1584

例句 Get off me! I can't breathe.
下去啦！我都不能呼吸了。

brick [brɪk] n. 磚塊 Track 1585

例句 She laid bricks to build a wall. 她砌磚頭建圍牆。

搭配詞
lay bricks 砌磚頭

bronze [brɑnz] n. 青銅 Track 1586

例句 Jack invited me to see the bronze exhibition next week.
傑克邀請我去看下個禮拜的青銅展。

brow(s) [braʊ(z)] n. 眉毛 Track 1587

例句 He's famous for his unibrow. 他因為他的一字眉而出名。

同義字
eyebrow

burn [bɝn] n./v. 燃燒 Track 1588

例句 You should pay attention, or you will burn the toast.
你應該注意一點，不然你會把吐司燒焦。

burst [bɝst] v. 破裂、爆炸 Track 1589

例句 She burst out into tears when her dog passed away.
她的狗狗死時，她的淚水潰堤了。

搭配詞
burst out into tears
淚水潰堤

cable [ˋkebl] n. 纜繩、電纜 Track 1590

例句 I would like a room with a cable TV.
我想要附有線電視的房間。

搭配詞
cable TV 有線電視

a b c d e f g h i j k l m n o p q r s t u v w x y z

caffeine [ˋkæfiɪn] n. 咖啡因 Track 1591

例句 I don't like to have coffee in the evening because too much caffeine keeps me awake.
我不喜歡晚上喝咖啡，因為太多咖啡因會讓我睡不著。

calcium [ˋkælsɪəm] n. 鈣 Track 1592

例句 Calcium is beneficial to our bones.
鈣對我們的骨頭很好。

camera [ˋkæmərə] n. 照相機 Track 1593

例句 I like to take pictures; therefore, I bought a digital camera.
我喜歡照相，所以我買了一台數位相機。

搭配詞 digital camera 數位相機

cancer [ˋkænsɚ] n. 癌 Track 1594

例句 There is a cure for blood cancer-Gleevec.
現在有治療血癌的藥，叫做基利克。

搭配詞 blood cancer 血癌

capsule [ˋkæpsl̩] n. 膠囊、太空艙 Track 1595

例句 For your health, you should take two capsules each day.
為了你的健康，你必須每天吃兩顆膠囊。

carbon [ˋkɑrbən] n. 碳、碳棒 Track 1596

例句 Too much carbon monoxide in the room can kill you.
房間裡太多一氧化碳會殺死你。

搭配詞 carbon monoxide 一氧化碳

care [kɛr] n./v. 小心、照料、憂慮 Track 1597

例句 She took good care of her grandchildren.
她照顧她的孫子孫女。

搭配詞 take care of 照顧

careful [ˋkɛrfəl] adj. 小心的、仔細的 Track 1598

＊字尾-ful有「充滿」的意思

例句 He is careful enough to find out all the mistakes in the paper.
他夠小心，能找出論文中所有的錯誤。

搭配詞 be careful 自己小心

casualty [ˋkæʒuəltɪ] Track 1599

n. 意外事故、（意外事件的）傷亡者

例句 It is reported that there were dozens of casualties in the train crash.
據報導，火車車禍中有許多傷亡者。

cause [kɔz] v. 引起 Track 1600

例句 There must be something causing the leak.
一定有什麼東西引起漏水。

cell [sɛl] n. 細胞 ◀Track 1601

例句 Can we see cells with a microscope?
我們可以用顯微鏡看到細胞嗎？

cell-phone/cellphone/mobile phone ◀Track 1602
[sɛl fon]/[sɛl fon]/[ˋmobɪl fon] n. 行動電話

例句 I just bought a new cell-phone for my mother as her birthday gift.
我剛替媽媽買了一支新的行動電話當生日禮物。

ceramic [səˋræmɪk] adj. 陶瓷的 ◀Track 1603

例句 The factory produces ceramic statues.
這個工廠製造陶瓷雕像。

搭配詞
ceramic statue 陶瓷雕像

cheek [tʃik] n. 臉頰 ◀Track 1604

例句 Sophia is a cute girl with rosy cheeks.
索菲雅是個有著紅潤臉頰的可愛女孩。

搭配詞
rosy cheeks 紅潤臉頰

chest [tʃɛst] n. 胸、箱子 ◀Track 1605

例句 He died from a chest wound during the war.
他在戰爭時期因胸口受傷而死。

chin [tʃin] n. 下巴 ◀Track 1606

例句 He got fat and had a double chin. 他變胖，有雙下巴了。

搭配詞
double chin 雙下巴

choke [tʃok] v. 使窒息、嗆 ◀Track 1607

例句 She choked on her food. 她被食物嗆到了。

反義字
breathe 呼吸

cholesterol [kəˋlɛstə͵rol] n. 膽固醇 ◀Track 1608

例句 You better stop eating too much cheese and meat. That will elevate the cholesterol in your body!
你別再吃乳酪和肉了，你身體裡的膽固醇會增加的。

chronic [ˋkrɑnɪk] adj. 長期的、持續的 ◀Track 1609

＊字尾-ic有轉變為形容詞之意

例句 Chronic Myeloid Leukemia is one of the chronic diseases that are manageable nowadays.
慢性骨髓性白血病是一種現今可以被控制的慢性病。

搭配詞
chronic disease 慢性病

chubby [ˋtʃʌbɪ] adj. 圓胖的、豐滿的 ◀Track 1610

例句 Miranda Kerr has chubby cheeks. 米蘭達寇兒有圓臉頰。

搭配詞
chubby cheeks 豐滿雙頰

circuit [ˋsɝkɪt] n. 電路、線路 Track 1611

例句 He's the only one who knows how to fix the circuits.
他是唯一一個知道怎麼修理電路的人。

clinic [ˋklɪnɪk] n. 診所 Track 1612

例句 He found that the clinic was closed by the time he arrived.
他抵達時，發現診所已經關門了。

clinical [ˋklɪnɪkl] adj. 門診的、臨床的、客觀的 Track 1613

例句 It seems that the new therapy hasn't passed the clinical trial yet.
看來新的療法還沒通過臨床試驗。

搭配詞 clinical trial 臨床試驗

clone [klon] n. 無性繁殖、複製品 Track 1614

例句 I don't know why this cell-phone is so popular; it's nothing but an iPhone clone. 我不知道這手機為什麼這麼受歡迎，它不過是個iPhone的複製品罷了。

coal [kol] n. 煤 Track 1615

例句 That old woman told me there are a great many coal mines in the central part of this town.
老太太告訴我在這座城市中心有許多煤礦場。

搭配詞 coal mine 煤礦場

comet [ˋkɑmɪt] n. 彗星 Track 1616

例句 Halley's Comet is the most famous comet in the Solar System.
哈雷彗星是太陽系中最著名的彗星。

搭配詞 Halley's Comet 哈雷彗星

compass [ˋkʌmpəs] n. 羅盤 Track 1617

例句 With a compass, you can find the place you want to go to easily.
有了羅盤，你就可以輕鬆地找到自己想去的地方。

complex [ˋkɑmplɛks] adj. 複雜的、合成的 Track 1618

＊字首com-有「共同」之意

例句 It's not necessary to write too many complex sentences.
不需要寫太多複雜的句子。

同義字 complicated

complexion [kəmˋplɛkʃən] n. 氣色、血色、膚色 Track 1619

＊字首com-有「共同」之意

例句 She has a nice complexion even without makeup.
她沒上妝氣色也很好。

搭配詞 a nice complexion 氣色很好

component [kəmˋponənt] n. 成分、零件 Track 1620

＊字首com-有「共同」之意

例句 A computer consists of thousands of components.
一台電腦由上千個零件組成。

comprise [kəm`praɪz] **v.** 由……構成、由……組成 *Track 1621*

＊字首com-有「共同」之意

例句 This medical team is comprised of 12 doctors and nurses.
這個醫療團隊由12名醫生與護士組成。

搭配詞 be comprised of 由……構成

---

computer [kəm`pjutɚ] **n.** 電腦 *Track 1622*

例句 I have to bring my laptop computer to work.
我得帶自己的筆記型電腦去上班。

搭配詞 laptop computer 筆記型電腦

---

computerize [kəm`pjutəˌraɪz] **v.** 用電腦處理 *Track 1623*

＊字尾-ize有「化」的意思

例句 We should work out a scheme to computerize the library service.
我們得想個計畫來用電腦處理圖書館服務。

---

consultant [kən`sʌltənt] **n.** 諮商師、顧問 *Track 1624*

例句 You should go see the consultant regularly once a week.
你得一週一次規律地去見諮商師。

---

contagious [kən`tedʒəs] **adj.** 接觸傳染性的 *Track 1625*

＊字尾-ious有轉變為形容詞之意

例句 SARS is a severe contagious disease and needs to be dealt with great caution. 嚴重急性呼吸道症候群是很嚴重的傳染病，必須非常小心處理它。

搭配詞 contagious disease 傳染病

---

copy [`kɑpɪ] **n.** 拷貝 *Track 1626*

例句 Please make a backup copy just in case.
請備份，以防萬一。

搭配詞 backup copy 備份

---

cord [kɔrd] **n.** 電線、韌帶、繩子 *Track 1627*

例句 Please tie up the package with heavy cords.
請用粗重的繩子把這個包裹綁好。

---

corpse [kɔrps] **n.** 屍體、屍首 *Track 1628*

例句 The police is trying to find out the identity of the unknown corpse.
警察正試圖找出無名屍的身分。

搭配詞 unknown corpse 無名屍

---

cough [kɔf] **v.** 咳出 *Track 1629*

例句 The cough syrup may not work for different types of cough.
這瓶咳嗽藥水對不同的咳嗽未必有效。

搭配詞 cough syrup 咳嗽藥水

---

cramp [kræmp] **n.** 抽筋、鉗子 *Track 1630*

例句 The tennis player always eats bananas to prevent cramps.
那個網球選手總是吃香蕉來預防抽筋。

搭配詞 leg cramp 小腿抽筋

a b c d e f g h i j k l m n o p q r s t u v w x y z

cripple [ˋkrɪp!] n. 瘸子、身障人士 Track 1631

例句 You should stop making fun of the cripple.
你不該嘲笑那個身障人士。

cure [kjʊr] n. 治療 Track 1632

例句 There is no rapid cure for a cold. 感冒沒有什麼快速的治療方法。

同義字
treatment

dead [dɛd] adj. 失靈的、壞了、死亡的 Track 1633

例句 The pen recorder suddenly went dead.
這支錄音筆突然壞了。

deadly [ˋdɛdlɪ] adj. 致命的 Track 1634

例句 If only the doctors could invent some new medicine to cure this deadly disease soon!
如果醫師們能快點發明一些新藥來治療這個致命疾病就好了！

搭配詞
deadly diseases 致命疾病

deaf [dɛf] adj. 耳聾 Track 1635

例句 He's tone deaf and sings terribly. 他音痴，唱歌很難聽。

搭配詞
tone deaf 音痴

death [dɛθ] n. 死、死亡 Track 1636

例句 Some people think that death penalty should not be abolished.
有些人認為不能廢除死刑。

搭配詞
death penalty 死刑

delicate [ˋdɛləkət] adj. 精細的、脆弱的 Track 1637

例句 She was a small and delicate old lady.
她是個小個子而脆弱的老太太。

反義字
rough 粗糙的

dental [ˋdɛnt!] adj. 牙齒的 Track 1638

例句 Dental records are often used to identify bodies.
辨認屍體時常會使用牙科紀錄。

搭配詞
dental record 牙科紀錄

dentist [ˋdɛntɪst] n. 牙醫、牙科醫生 Track 1639

例句 You should go to a dentist regularly.
你應該要規律地去看牙醫。

detect [dɪˋtɛkt] v. 查出、探出、發現 Track 1640

例句 The system detected an error in the message we sent to you.
在我們傳送給你的訊息中，系統偵測到錯誤。

搭配詞
detect an error 發現錯誤

develop [dɪˋvɛləp] **v.** 發展、開發 Track 1641

例句 They developed a plan for her surprise party.
他們為她的驚喜派對發展出了一個計畫。

development [dɪˋvɛləpmənt] **n.** 發展、開發 Track 1642

＊字尾-ment有轉變為名詞之意

例句 You should know that product development is the key to success.
你應該知道開發產品是成功的關鍵。

diabetes [ˏdaɪəˋbitiz] **n.** 糖尿病 Track 1643

例句 Her diabetes prevents her from eating a lot of things.
她的糖尿病讓她有很多東西不能吃。

易混淆字
diaper 尿布

diagnosis [ˏdaɪəgˋnosɪs] **n.** 診斷（複數） Track 1644

例句 I have to go to the hospital today because I need to know the doctor's diagnosis of my disease.
我今天得去醫院，因為我必須要知道醫師對我疾病的診斷。

diamond [ˋdaɪmənd] **n.** 鑽石 Track 1645

例句 The girl wishes for a big diamond ring.
那個女孩想要一個大鑽石戒指。

搭配詞
diamond ring 鑽石戒指

die [daɪ] **v.** 死 Track 1646

例句 His love for music would never die.
他對音樂的愛永遠不死。

反義字
live 活著

discovery [dɪˋskʌvərɪ] **n.** 發現 Track 1647

例句 The discovery caused a big sensation in the scientific world.
這個發現在科學界造成很大的轟動。

disease [dɪˋziz] **n.** 疾病、病症 Track 1648

例句 She had heart disease but it did not affect her daily life.
她有心臟病，但並不影響她的日常生活。

搭配詞
heart disease 心臟病

dose [dos] **n.** 一劑（藥）、藥量 Track 1649

例句 You need to take a daily dose of this medicine before going to bed.
你睡前必須要吃這個藥的每日劑量。

搭配詞
a dose of 一劑……的量

dream [drim] **v./n.** 夢 Track 1650

例句 I dreamed of being an actor when I was a child.
我從小夢想成為演員。

搭配詞
dream of 夢想

drug [drʌg] n. 毒品、藥物 Track 1651

例句 The reason he was put into prison was because he peddled drugs.
他被關進牢裡的理由是販賣毒品。

搭配詞 peddle drugs 販賣毒品

ear [ɪr] n. 耳朵 Track 1652

例句 In some societies, long earlobes are considered attractive.
在某些社會，長耳垂被視為具有吸引力。

搭配詞 earlobe 耳垂

ease [iz] v. 緩和、減輕、使舒適 Track 1653

例句 She eased his pain a little by holding his hand.
她握著他的手，稍微減輕了他的疼痛。

搭配詞 ease the pain of 減輕……的疼痛

elbow [`ɛl͵bo] n. 手肘 Track 1654

例句 Can you lick your elbow? 你舔得到自己的手肘嗎？

electron [ɪ`lɛktrɑn] n. 電子 Track 1655

例句 Have you ever used an electron microscope before?
你有用過電子顯微鏡嗎？

搭配詞 electron microscope 電子顯微鏡

electronic [ɪlɛk`trɑnɪk] adj. 電子的 Track 1656

例句 The zoo used electronic locks to open or close animals' enclosures.
這間動物園用電子鎖打開或關閉獸欄。

搭配詞 electronic lock 電子鎖

element [`ɛləmənt] n. 基本要素 Track 1657

例句 He's in his element when he swims. 他游泳時如魚得水。

搭配詞 in element 如魚得水

enable [ɪn`ebl̩] v. 使能夠 ＊字首en-有「使」之意 Track 1658

例句 The computer enabled us to do things a lot faster.
電腦讓我們能夠做事做得更快。

搭配詞 enable sb to do sth 使某人能夠做某事

epidemic [͵ɛpɪ`dɛmɪk] n. 傳染病 Track 1659

例句 A flu epidemic has raged through the school for weeks.
感冒傳染病已經在學校內肆虐好幾個星期了。

equipment [ɪ`kwɪpmənt] n. 裝備、設備 Track 1660

＊字尾-ment有轉變為名詞之意

例句 Do you have the right equipment to go hiking?
你有去登山的正確裝備嗎？

eruption [ɪˋrʌpʃən] n. 爆發 ◀Track 1661
＊字尾-tion有轉變為名詞的意思
例句 This is the 3rd time a volcanic eruption happened this year.
這是今年第三次火山爆發了。

搭配詞
volcanic eruption 火山爆發

existence [ɪgˋzɪstəns] n. 存在 ◀Track 1662
＊字尾-ence有轉變為名詞之意
例句 Do you know the oldest synagogue in existence?
你知道現存最古老的猶太教堂是那一間嗎？

搭配詞
in existence 現存的

experiment [ɪkˋspɛrəmənt] n. 實驗 ◀Track 1663
＊字尾-ment有轉變為名詞之意
例句 We did an experiment in science class. 我們在自然課做了實驗。

explode [ɪkˋsplod] v. 爆炸、推翻 ◀Track 1664
＊字首ex-有「外」的意思
例句 The police had to find the bomb immediately because it might explode any time. 警察必須立刻找到炸彈，因為它隨時可能爆炸。

explosion [ɪkˋsploʒən] n. 爆炸 ◀Track 1665
＊字首ex-有「外」的意思
例句 It's reported that more than 40 people were wounded in the explosion. 據報導，超過40個人在爆炸中受傷。

搭配詞
bomb explosion 炸彈爆炸

explosive [ɪkˋsplosɪv] n. 炸藥、爆炸物 ◀Track 1666
例句 Dynamite is a powerful explosive.
炸藥是個強力的爆炸物。

eye [aɪ] n. 眼睛 ◀Track 1667
例句 She put on some eye shadow to complete her look.
她刷了一些眼影，完成妝容。

搭配詞
eye shadow 眼影

eyelash/lash [ˋaɪ͵læʃ]/[læʃ] n. 睫毛 ◀Track 1668
例句 She has extraordinarily long and curly eyelashes.
她的睫毛異常地長又捲翹。

搭配詞
curly eyelashes 捲翹睫毛

eyelid [ˋaɪ͵lɪd] n. 眼皮 ◀Track 1669
例句 She had cute droopy eyelids. 她有著可愛的垂眼皮。

eyesight [ˋaɪ͵saɪt] n. 視力 ◀Track 1670
例句 The animal's good sense of smell compensates for its poor eyesight. 這個動物良好的嗅覺彌補了它不良的視力。

a b c d e f g h i j k l m n o p q r s t u v w x y z

face [fes] n. 臉、臉部 Track 1671

例句 Face-to-face communication can clear up misunderstandings.
面對面的溝通可以解決一些誤解。

搭配詞 face-to-face 面對面

factory [ˋfæktərɪ] n. 工廠 Track 1672

例句 My parents work in the same factory.
我父母在同一個工廠工作。

Fahrenheit [ˋfærən͵haɪt] n. 華氏、華氏溫度計 Track 1673

例句 Water freezes at 32 degrees Fahrenheit.
水在華氏32度結凍。

反義字 Celsius 攝氏

faint [fent] v. 昏厥 Track 1674

例句 The lady fainted in the heat.
那位女士因為高溫而昏厥了。

fat [fæt] n. 脂肪 Track 1675

例句 A fat-free diet cannot necessarily help you lose weight effectively.
不含脂肪的飲食不一定能有效幫助你減肥。

搭配詞 fat-free 不含脂肪的

fatigue [fəˋtig] n. 疲勞、勞累 Track 1676

例句 The team collapsed in fatigue.
整個隊伍都因疲勞而倒下了。

female [ˋfimel] adj. 女性的 Track 1677

例句 The female duck is less pretty than the male one.
母鴨比公鴨醜一些。

fever [ˋfivɚ] n. 發燒、熱、入迷 Track 1678

例句 I need some medicine because I have a slight fever.
我需要一些藥，因為我有點發燒。

搭配詞 have a fever 發燒

fiber [ˋfaɪbɚ] n. 纖維、纖維質 Track 1679

例句 The doctor recommended more high-fiber food in his diet.
醫生建議他多吃一點高纖食品。

搭配詞 high-fiber food 高纖食品

file [faɪl] n. 檔案 Track 1680

例句 He leaked out the classified files and was put to jail.
他因洩露機密檔案而入獄。

搭配詞 classified file 機密檔案

finger [ˋfɪŋɡɚ] **n.** 手指 Track 1681

例句 The system uses finger prints to identify people.
這套系統用指紋辨識人們的身分。

搭配詞 finger print 指紋

---

fire [faɪr] **n.** 火 Track 1682

例句 The hospital was on fire. 醫院失火了。

搭配詞 on fire 著火

---

flame [flem] **n.** 火焰 Track 1683

例句 The material is flame-retardant and inexpensive.
這個物質具防火效果，且不昂貴。

搭配詞 flame-retardant 阻燃的

---

flash [flæʃ] **n./v.** 閃亮 Track 1684

例句 The driver is flashing his lights at me.
那個司機正對我閃燈。

---

flashlight/flash [ˋflæʃ,laɪt]/[flæʃ] Track 1685

n. 手電筒、閃光

例句 I need to bring a flashlight with me, or I might get lost.
我得帶個手電筒，不然可能會迷路。

---

flesh [flɛʃ] **n.** 肉體、軀殼 Track 1686

例句 Her stockings are flesh-colored.
她的絲襪是肉色的。

---

flu [flu] **n.** 流行性感冒 Track 1687

例句 Don't pat the pigeon! You might get bird flu.
別跑去摸鴿子，你可能會得禽流感。

---

foot [fʊt] **n.** 腳 Track 1688

例句 There is a temple at the foot of that famous big mountain.
在那座有名的大山腳下有座寺廟。

搭配詞 on foot 用腳（行走）

---

foresee [forˋsi] **v.** 預知、看穿 Track 1689

例句 We can't foresee what will happen next.
我們無法預知接下來會發生什麼事。

同義字 predict

---

forehead [ˋfɔr,hɛd] **n.** 前額、額頭 Track 1690

例句 Let me feel your forehead so that I can tell whether you have a fever. 讓我摸一下你的額頭，我才知道你有沒有發燒。

forget [fɚˋgɛt] v. 忘記 Track 1691

例句 I forgot to bring my English dictionary. 我忘記帶英文字典了。

搭配詞 forget to do sth 忘記去做某事

forgetful [fɚˋgɛtfəl] adj. 健忘的、易忘的、忽略的 Track 1692

＊字尾-ful有「充滿」的意思

例句 My grandpa is very forgetful. 我爺爺非常健忘。

反義字 remindful 留心的

fracture [ˋfræktʃɚ] n. 破碎、骨折 Track 1693

例句 The fracture in his left leg is very serious.
他左腳的骨折很嚴重。

frail [frel] adj. 脆弱的、虛弱的 Track 1694

例句 She is is too frail to live by herself.
她太虛弱，無法一個人住。

同義字 weak

fuel [ˋfjuəl] n. 燃料 Track 1695

例句 We need to figure out how much diesel fuel the trucks need.
我們得搞清楚這些卡車到底需要多少柴油。

搭配詞 diesel fuel 柴油

fume [fjum] v. 發怒；生悶氣 Track 1696

例句 She was fuming to hear her father describing her as mentally unstable. 她聽到她爸爸形容她情緒不穩定，感到很生氣。

function [ˋfʌŋkʃən] n. 功能、作用 Track 1697

＊字尾-tion有轉變為名詞的意思

例句 The textbook explains clearly about the function of the veins in our bodies. 這本教科書清楚解釋我們身體裡的血管所扮演的功能。

fundamental [ˏfʌndəˋmɛntl] Track 1698

adj. 基礎的、根本的 ＊字尾-al有轉變為形容詞之意

例句 Learning grammar is fundamental if you want to master English.
若你要精通英文，學好文法是很根本的。

同義字 essential

galaxy [ˋgæləksɪ] n. 星雲、星系、一群出色的人物 Track 1699

例句 I've always been interested in looking at pictures of galaxies.
我一直對看星系的圖片很有興趣。

gasp [gæsp] n./v. 喘息、喘 Track 1700

例句 He was gasping hard after holding his breath for two minutes.
他憋氣兩分鐘後喘得很厲害。

gear [gɪr] n. 齒輪、排檔 Track 1701

例句 I don't know how to change gears. 我不知道怎麼換檔。

搭配詞 change gear 換檔

gender [ˋdʒɛndɚ] n. 性別 Track 1702

例句 He is gender neutral and colorblind.
他沒有性別歧視和種族偏見。

搭配詞 gender neutral 無性別歧視、性別中立

gene [dʒin] n. 基因、遺傳因子 Track 1703

例句 Kate has good genes from her parents.
凱特從父母那裡得到很好的基因。

generation [ˏdʒɛnəˋreʃən] n. 世代 Track 1704

＊字尾-tion有轉變為名詞的意思

例句 Pass on the fine tradition from generation to generation.
一個世代一個世代地把這個好傳統傳下去吧。

搭配詞 from generation to generation 世世代代

generator [ˋdʒɛnəˏretɚ] Track 1705

n. 創始者、產生者、發電機　＊字尾-or有「者」的意思

例句 Does anybody know how to use a generator?
這裡有人會用發電機嗎？

germ [dʒɝm] n. 細菌、微生物、病菌 Track 1706

例句 Some diseases are caused by germs.
有些疾病是細菌造成的。

ghost [gost] n. 鬼、靈魂 Track 1707

例句 I don't like ghost movies. They give me nightmares.
我不喜歡看鬼片，因為它們讓我做惡夢。

glasses [ˋglæsɪz] n. 眼鏡 Track 1708

例句 She wore her sunglasses to protect her eyes.
她戴太陽眼鏡保護眼睛。

搭配詞 wear glasses 戴眼鏡

groan [gron] n./v. 哼聲、呻吟 Track 1709

例句 The patient groaned all night. 那名病人呻吟了整晚。

易混淆字 grown 成熟的

gut(s) [gʌt(s)] n. 內臟、腸 Track 1710

例句 His guts were spilled all over the floor. How frightening!
滿地都是他的腸子，真是恐怖！

a b c d e f g h i j k l m n o p q r s t u v w x y z

habit [ˋhæbɪt] n. 習慣 Track 1711

例句 Why don't you get rid of this bad habit? It is not good for your health. 你為什麼不改掉這個壞習慣呢？對你的健康不好。

---

hacker [hækɚ] n. 駭客 ＊字尾-er有「者」的意思 Track 1712

例句 The hacker quickly found the password.
那名駭客很快地找到了密碼。

同義字 cracker

---

hair [hɛr] n. 頭髮 Track 1713

例句 The hair product tames curly hair effectively.
這個護髮產品能有效整理捲髮。

搭配詞 curly hair 捲髮

---

hand [hænd] n. 手 Track 1714

例句 This is a hand-made soap. 這是手工肥皂。

搭配詞 hand-made
手製的，手工的

---

harm [hɑrm] n. 損傷、損害 Track 1715

例句 Playing computer games all day long will do harm to your eyes.
整天玩電腦遊戲會對你的眼睛造成損害。

搭配詞 do harm 有害

---

harmful [ˋhɑrmfəl] adj. 引起傷害的、有害的 Track 1716
＊字尾-ful有「充滿」的意思

例句 Binge drinking is harmful to your liver. 酗酒對你的肝臟有害。

搭配詞 be harmful to 對……有害

---

heroin [ˋhɛroɪn] n. 海洛因 Track 1717

例句 He was arrested for selling heroin.
他因為販賣海洛因而被捕。

易混淆字 heroine 女英雄

---

head [hɛd] n. 頭、領袖 Track 1718

例句 The headquarters of Toys "R" Us is in New York.
玩具反斗城的總部在紐約。

搭配詞 headquarters 總部（一定要注意字尾加上s）

---

headphone(s) [ˋhɛd͵fon(z)] Track 1719
n. 頭戴式耳機、聽筒

例句 The sound quality of the headphones is excellent.
這個耳機的音質好極了。

---

heal [hil] v. 治癒、復原 Track 1720

例句 The cut should heal in no time.
割傷的地方很快就會復原了。

health [hɛlθ] n. 健康 Track 1721

例句 Tom has always been in good health. 湯姆一向都很健康。

healthful [ˋhɛlθfəl] adj. 有益健康的 Track 1722

＊字尾-ful有「充滿」的意思

例句 Successful people usually maintian a healthful diet.
成功的人通常都維持健康的飲食習慣。

搭配詞
healthful diet 營養餐

hear [hɪr] v. 聽到、聽說 Track 1723

例句 I've never heard of that. 我從來沒聽說這種事。

heart [hɑrt] n. 心、中心、核心 Track 1724

例句 This movie deeply touched my heart.
這部電影深深觸動了我的心。

搭配詞
touch one's heart 感觸人心

heat [hit] n. 熱、熱度 Track 1725

例句 Walking around in this heat isn't good for your health at all.
在這種熱度到處走路對你的健康一點都不好。

反義字
cold 寒冷

heaven [ˋhɛvən] n. 天堂 Track 1726

例句 I think Jack and Vicky are a match made in heaven.
我覺得傑克和維琪簡直就是天作之合。

同義字
paradise

hell [hɛl] n. 地獄、悲慘處境 Track 1727

例句 I told him to go to hell. 我叫他下地獄去吧。

hip [hɪp] n. 臀部、屁股 Track 1728

例句 Chris stands there with his hands on his hips.
克里斯站在那裡，雙手放在臀部上。

hormone [ˋhɔrmon] n. 荷爾蒙 Track 1729

例句 Emotional states can affect our hormone levels.
心情可能會影響我們的荷爾蒙。

補充
estrogen / testosterone
雌激素 / 睪酮素

hospital [ˋhɑspɪtl] n. 醫院 Track 1730

例句 Let's take the wounded dog to the animal hospital.
我們帶這隻受傷的狗狗到動物醫院吧。

搭配詞
animal hospital 動物醫院

human [`hjumən] n. 人 Track 1731

例句 Can you tell me how long humans existed on the Earth?
你可以告訴我人類在地球上存在多久了嗎？

搭配詞 human nature 人性

hunch [hʌntʃ] n. 瘤、直覺 Track 1732

例句 I have a hunch that he's the culprit.
我有個直覺，犯人是他。

搭配詞 have a hunch that 有……的直覺

hurt [hɝt] n./v. 傷害、傷痛 Track 1733

例句 Don't hurt yourself. You're not alone.
別做傷害自己的事，你不孤單。

搭配詞 hurt oneself 傷害自己

ill [ɪl] adj. 疾病、生病 Track 1734

例句 He is ill again. It's the third time this month.
他又生病了，是這個月的第三次。

同義字 sickness

industrial [ɪn`dʌstrɪəl] adj. 工業的 Track 1735

＊字尾-al有轉變為形容詞之意

例句 The Industrial Revolution has changed the way people live and work. 工業革命改變了人們生活和工作的型態。

搭配詞 Industrial Revolution 工業革命

infect [ɪn`fɛkt] v. 使感染 Track 1736

例句 He was infected with the flu so he took a day-off.
他被傳染感冒，請假一天。

搭配詞 infect with the flu 染上感冒

infection [ɪn`fɛkʃən] n. 感染、傳染病 Track 1737

＊字尾-tion有轉變為名詞的意思

例句 His feet were swollen from infection. 他的腳因感染而腫大。

inject [ɪn`dʒɛkt] v. 注入 ＊字首in-有「入」的意思 Track 1738

例句 Some diabetics need to inject insulin every day.
有些糖尿病患每天都要施打胰島素。

injection [ɪn`dʒɛkʃən] n. 注射、打針 Track 1739

＊字尾-tion有轉變為名詞的意思

例句 The baby is crying because the doctor is giving her an injection.
那個嬰兒正在哭，因為醫師正在幫她打針。

補充 vaccine 疫苗

injure [`ɪndʒɚ] v. 傷害、使受傷 Track 1740

例句 I've heard that he got injured in an accident.
我聽說他在一次意外中受傷。

搭配詞 get injured 受傷

injury [ˋɪndʒərɪ] n. 傷害、損害 ◀Track 1741

例句 His injuries seem quite serious. 他受的傷好像很嚴重。

同義字 wound

insight [ˋɪn͵saɪt] n. 洞察 ＊字首in-有「入」的意思 ◀Track 1742

例句 Her insight helps people better understand the severity of global warming. 她的洞見讓人們更了解全球暖化的嚴重性。

inspect [ɪnˋspɛkt] v. 調查、檢查 ◀Track 1743

＊字首in-有「入」的意思

例句 It takes me a lot of time to inspect these buildings in the city.
我花很多時間檢查城裡的建築。

Internet [ˋɪntɚ͵nɛt] n. 網際網路 ◀Track 1744

例句 Without Internet access, students are unable to cultivate information literacy. 沒有網路連線，學生無法培養資訊素養。

搭配詞 Internet access 連上網路

invent [ɪnˋvɛnt] v. 發明、創造 ◀Track 1745

例句 He invented a new type of equipment.
他發明了一種新設備。

invention [ɪnˋvɛnʃən] n. 發明、創造 ◀Track 1746

＊字尾-tion有轉變為名詞的意思

例句 The telephone is his greatest invention. 電話是他最棒的發明。

investigate [ɪnˋvɛstə͵get] v. 研究、調查 ◀Track 1747

例句 To investigate the crime, the police used a tracking device to identify the suspects.
為了調查這個刑事案，警方使用一種追蹤器來確認嫌疑犯。

搭配詞 investigate a crime 調查犯罪

investigator [ɪnˋvɛstə͵getɚ] n. 調查者、研究者 ◀Track 1748

＊字尾-or有「者」的意思

例句 He hired a private investigators to find out who murdered his child.
他僱了一名私家偵探協尋謀殺他小孩的犯人。

搭配詞 private investigator 私家偵探

iron [ˋaɪɚn] n. 鐵、熨斗 ◀Track 1749

例句 I have to go to my aunt's place and borrow an iron from her.
我要去我阿姨那裡跟她借個熨斗。

jaw [dʒɔ] n. 顎、下巴 ◀Track 1750

例句 My jaw dropped on hearing that Tom had broken up with his girlfriend.
我聽到湯姆和他女朋友分手，下巴都掉下來了。

joint [dʒɔɪnt] n. 接合處、關節 Track 1751

例句 He suffered from arthritis in his leg joints.
他的腿關節有風濕的毛病。

kidney [ˋkɪdnɪ] n. 腎臟 Track 1752

例句 Thanks to kidney dialysis treatments, he can survive and realize his dreams. 幸好透過洗腎治療，他能存活下來並實現夢想。

搭配詞 kidney dialysis 洗腎

knee [ni] n. 膝、膝蓋 Track 1753

例句 My sister fell over and hurt her knee.
我妹妹跌倒了，傷到了膝蓋。

lack [læk] n. 缺乏 Track 1754

例句 His lack of energy was caused by chronic fatigue syndromes.
他因長期性疲勞症候群而沒有元氣。

搭配詞 lack of energy 缺乏能量

lap [læp] n. 膝部 Track 1755

例句 The host asked her to sit with her hands on her lap.
主持人請她把手放在膝蓋上坐著。

易混淆字 lab 實驗室

laser [ˋlezɚ] n. 雷射 Track 1756

例句 I need a laser pointer for my presentation.
我在簡報時需要使用雷射筆。

搭配詞 laser pointer 雷射筆

launch [lɔntʃ] v. 發射 Track 1757

例句 This country has already launched a rocket successfully.
這個國家已經成功發射一艘火箭了。

搭配詞 launch a rocket 發射火箭

liquid crystal display Track 1758
[ˋlɪkwɪd ˋkrɪstḷ dɪˋsple] n. 液晶顯示器

例句 To increase efficiency, you'd better get a new LCD screen for your laptop. 要更有效率地工作，你得為你的筆電弄個更好的液晶顯示器螢幕。

縮寫 LCD

leg [lɛg] n. 腿 Track 1759

例句 Can you get a taxi for me? My legs hurt from walking.
你可以幫我叫計程車嗎？我走得腿好痛。

搭配詞 Break a leg. 祝你好運（尤其是在上臺演出之前）

life [laɪf] n. 生活、生命 Track 1760

例句 I've never seen something so strange in my entire life.
我一生還沒見過這麼奇怪的東西。

lip [lɪp] **n.** 嘴唇 ◀Track 1762

例句 He kissed her on the lips in front of her father.
他在她父親面前吻了她的嘴唇。

搭配詞 lip stick 唇膏

---

liquid [ˋlɪkwɪd] **n.** 液體 ◀Track 1763

例句 Milk is a kind of liquid. 牛奶是液體的一種。

---

listen [ˋlɪsn̩] **v.** 聽 ◀Track 1764

例句 I listened carefully to the lecture. 我很仔細聽那堂講課。

搭配詞 listen carefully 仔細聽

---

live [laɪv] **adj.** 有生命的、活的、直播的、帶電的 ◀Track 1765

例句 The show will have a live broadcast this coming Saturday.
那個節目將於週六現場直播。

搭配詞 live broadcast 現場直播

---

liver [ˋlɪvɚ] **n.** 肝臟 ◀Track 1766

例句 The doctor said there's something wrong with her liver.
醫生說她的肝有問題。

補充 cirrhosis 肝硬化

---

locomotive [͵lokəˋmotɪv] **n.** 火車頭 ◀Track 1767

例句 How many coaches can that locomotive pull?
那個火車頭能拉多少節車廂呢？

---

longevity [lɑnˋdʒɛvətɪ] **n.** 長壽 ◀Track 1768

例句 Proper rest and enough sleep contribute to longevity.
適當的休息與充足的睡眠都能幫助長壽。

---

look [lʊk] **n./v.** 看、樣子、臉色 ◀Track 1769

例句 Would you look after the baby for me?
你幫我照顧一下寶寶好嗎？

搭配詞 look after 照顧

---

lump [lʌmp] **n.** 塊、瘤 ◀Track 1770

例句 I had a lump in my throat when I heard he was bullied at school.
聽到他在學校被霸凌，我哽咽了。

搭配詞 have a lump in one's throat 喉嚨哽住，哽咽（因激動所致）

---

lung [lʌŋ] **n.** 肺臟 ◀Track 1771

例句 Smoking can lead to lung cancer. 抽菸可能導致肺癌。

搭配詞 lung cancer 肺癌

a b c d e f g h i j k l m n o p q r s t u v w x y z

machine [mə`ʃin] n. 機器、機械 Track 1772

例句 The company developed a smart washing machine that can be controlled using an app on your smart phone. 這家公司研發了智慧洗衣機，讓人們可以透過手機app控制洗衣。

搭配詞 washing machine 洗衣機

machinery [mə`ʃinərɪ] n. 機械 Track 1773

例句 New machinery costs a large sum of money.
新的機械需要很多錢。

mad [mæd] adj. 神經錯亂的、發瘋的、生氣的 Track 1774

例句 Your brother must have gone mad. 你哥哥大概氣壞了吧。

搭配詞 go mad 發瘋

magnet [`mægnɪt] n. 磁鐵 Track 1775

例句 She's a weirdo magnet. 她是個專門吸引怪咖的磁鐵。

make [mek] v. 做、製造 Track 1776

例句 My brother is a makeup artist. 我弟弟是化妝師。

搭配詞 makeup 化妝

malaria [mə`lɛrɪə] n. 瘧疾、瘴氣 Track 1777

例句 Malaria is prevalent in many tropical countries.
瘧疾在許多熱帶國家很猖獗。

male [mel] adj. 男性的 Track 1778

例句 Please send for a male nurse to take my temperature.
請找一個男護士來替我量體溫。

mankind/humankind Track 1779
[mæn`kaɪnd]/[`hjumən,kaɪnd] n. 人類

例句 Nikola Tesla was one of the greatest inventors known to mankind.
尼古拉特斯拉是人類所知最偉大的發明家之一。

同義字 human

marvel [`marvḷ] Track 1780
n./v. 令人驚奇的事物、奇蹟、感到驚奇

例句 We marveled at the magnificent castle.
我們對這座城堡感到驚嘆。

同義字 wonder

masculine [`mæskjəlɪn] n. 男性、陽性 Track 1781

例句 "Waiter" is the masculine noun for "waitress".
「waiter」是「waitress」的男性名詞說法。

反義字 feminine 女性

material [məˋtɪrɪəl] n. 物質、質料 Track 1782

例句 I would like to know the raw materials of this product.
我想知道這個產品的原料。

搭配詞
raw material 原料

measurable [ˋmɛʒərəbl̩] adj. 可測量的 Track 1783

＊字尾-able有「可以、能」的意思

例句 There has been a measurable improvement in Tom's work.
湯姆的表現有了可測量的進步。

measure [ˋmɛʒɚ] n. 措施 Track 1784

例句 It's time to take drastic measures to address global warming.
這時必須採取極端的措施，以解決全球暖化。

搭配詞
take measure to
採取措施以……

measurement [ˋmɛʒɚmənt] n. 測量、三圍 Track 1785

＊字尾-ment有轉變為名詞之意

例句 What are your measurements? 你的三圍多少？

mechanical [məˋkænɪkl̩] adj. 機械的 Track 1786

＊字尾-al有轉變為形容詞之意

例句 They were using a mechanical shovel to clear up the streets.
他們正使用機械剷子來清掃街道。

medical [ˋmɛdɪkl̩] adj. 醫學的 Track 1787

＊字尾-al有轉變為形容詞之意

例句 The fact that he survived from the terrible accident was a medical miracle. 他從這麼嚴重的意外存活下來，是個醫學奇蹟。

搭配詞
medical miracle 醫學奇蹟

medicine [ˋmɛdəsn̩] n. 醫學、藥物 Track 1788

例句 You should take medicine three times a day.
你應該每天要吃三次藥。

搭配詞
take medicine 服藥

metal [ˋmɛtl̩] n. 金屬 Track 1789

例句 Gold is a kind of precious metal. 黃金是貴金屬的一種。

搭配詞
precious metal 貴金屬

method [ˋmɛθəd] n. 方法 Track 1790

例句 You should use a simple and easy method to solve this problem.
你可以用個簡單直接的方法解決這個問題。

同義字
manner

microscope [ˋmaɪkrə͵skop] n. 顯微鏡 Track 1791

＊字首micro-有「微」之意

例句 The germs can only be seen with the aid of a microscope because they are too small. 這些細菌只能用顯微鏡來看，因為它們很小。

a b c d e f g h i j k l m n o p q r s t u v w x y z

mineral [ˋmɪnərəl] n. 礦物 Track 1792

例句 Please give me a bottle of mineral water, thanks.
請給我一瓶礦泉水，謝謝。

搭配詞 mineral water 礦泉水

miracle [ˋmɪrəkḷ] n. 奇蹟 Track 1793

例句 There's no miracle drug to cure the unknown disease.
這個不知名的疾病還沒有特效藥。

搭配詞 miracle drug 特效藥

mix [mɪks] v. 混合 Track 1794

例句 She can mix with a variety of people in her job.
她在職場上有辦法和各種人打交道。

搭配詞 mix with 與……打交道

mixture [ˋmɪkstʃɚ] n. 混合物 Track 1795

＊字尾-ure有轉變為名詞之意

例句 The juice is a mixture of apple juice and grape juice.
這果汁是蘋果汁和葡萄汁的混合物。

搭配詞 a mixture of sth and sth 某物與某物的混合物

monitor [ˋmɑnətɚ] n. 監視器 Track 1796

例句 Why don't you install a monitor in the conference room?
你為什麼不在會議室裝台監視器呢？

搭配詞 install a monitor 安裝監視器

moral [ˋmɔrəl] n./adj. 寓意、道德上的 Track 1797

例句 Do you really think what you did was moral?
你真的覺得你做的事合乎道德嗎？

搭配詞 morally sound 在道德上是對的

motor [ˋmotɚ] n. 馬達、發電機 Track 1798

例句 The salesman doesn't know which company produces this kind of electric motor. 那名售貨員不知道是哪個公司生產這種電動馬達。

mouth [maʊθ] n. 嘴、口腔 Track 1799

例句 Look at the mouth-watering cheesecake .
看這個令人垂涎三尺的起士蛋糕。

搭配詞 mouth-watering 令人垂涎三尺的

muscle [ˋmʌsḷ] n. 肌肉 Track 1800

例句 Jogging can not only develop your muscles but also helps you keep fit. 慢跑不但能鍛練你的肌肉，也能讓你保持健康。

搭配詞 develop one's muscle 鍛練肌肉

muscular [ˋmʌskjəlɚ] adj. 肌肉發達的、健壯的 Track 1801

例句 The basketball player is tall and muscular.
這名籃球選手又高又健壯。

搭配詞 muscular guy 肌肉發達的男子

mute [mjut] n./adj. 啞巴、沉默、沉默的 Track 1802

例句 He remained mute about his plans for the company's future.
他對於公司未來的規劃，保持沈默。

navel [ˋnevḷ] n. 中心點、肚臍 Track 1803

例句 He looked down at his own navel.
他低頭看自己的肚臍。

同義字
belly button

nail [nel] n. 指甲、釘子 Track 1804

例句 She applied purple nail polish on her nails.
她在指甲上擦紫色指甲油。

搭配詞
nail polish 指甲油

naked [ˋnekɪd] adj. 裸露的、赤裸的 Track 1805

例句 You can't walk on the street naked.
你不能赤裸地在大街上走。

同義字
bare

neck [nɛk] n. 頸、脖子 Track 1806

例句 Giraffes have long necks. 長頸鹿的脖子很長。

nerve [nɝv] n. 神經 Track 1807

例句 MI6 is the nerve center of the UK intelligence unit.
軍情六處是英國情報單位的神經中樞。

搭配詞
nerve centre
神經中樞、控制中心

nervous [ˋnɝvəs] adj. 神經質的、緊張的 Track 1808

＊字尾-ous有轉變為形容詞之意

例句 Even the most experienced dancers get nervous before performing on the stage.
就算是最有經驗的舞者，在上台表演前都還是會緊張。

同義字
tense

network [ˋnɛt͵wɝk] n. 網路 Track 1809

例句 Our team has developed a comprehensive marketing network.
我們的團隊發展了一個完善的銷售網絡。

搭配詞
marketing network
銷售網絡

nickel [ˋnɪkḷ] n. 鎳 Track 1810

例句 Please allow me to put in two nickels instead of a dime.
請允許我放入兩個五分鎳幣，而不是一個十分錢硬幣。

易混淆字
nickel 五分鎳幣

nightmare [ˋnaɪt͵mɛr] n. 惡夢、夢魘 Track 1811

例句 I had a nightmare last night. 我昨晚作了惡夢。

a b c d e f g h i j k l m n o p q r s t u v w x y z

nose [noz] n. 鼻子 Track 1812

例句 He had a running nose because of the flu.
他得流感，開始流鼻涕。

搭配詞
running nose 流鼻涕

nostril [ˋnɑstrəl] n. 鼻孔 Track 1813

例句 There was hair poking out of his nostrils.
他的鼻孔有毛跑出來。

nuclear [ˋnjuklɪɚ] adj. 核子的 Track 1814

例句 The nuclear power plant was decommissioned last year.
這座核電廠去年除役了。

搭配詞
nuclear power 核能

nucleus [ˋnjuklɪəs] n. 核心、中心、原子核 Track 1815

例句 Students learn about cell nucleus in biology class.
學生在生物課學習細胞核。

搭配詞
cell nucleus 細胞核

object [ˋɑbdʒɪkt] n. 物體 Track 1816

例句 Do you know the names of the objects in this lab?
你知道這個實驗室裡物體的名字嗎？

oil [ɔɪl] n. 油 Track 1817

例句 Don't add oil to the fire. 別火上加油了。

補充
olive oil 橄欖油

old [old] adj. 年老的、舊的 Track 1818

例句 You are never too old to learn. 學習永遠不嫌老。

反義字
young 年輕的

operate [ˋɑpə͵ret] v. 運轉、操作 Track 1819

例句 She died in the operating room about 10 minutes later.
她在手術室約十分鐘後死亡。

搭配詞
operating room 手術室

operation [͵ɑpəˋreʃən] n. 作用、操作、手術 Track 1820

＊字尾-tion有轉變為名詞的意思

例句 He is scheduled to have a minor operation on Friday.
他預計週五要動小手術。

搭配詞
minor operation 小型手術

orbit [ˋɔrbɪt] n. 軌道 Track 1821

例句 There are a number of satellites put into orbit in recent years.
近幾年有許多衛星被放在軌道上運行。

補充
earth orbit 地球軌道

organ [ˋɔrgən] n. 器官、機構 ◀Track 1822

例句 I have an organ donation card in my wallet.
我的錢包裡有一張器官捐贈卡。

搭配詞
organ donation 捐贈器官

organic [ɔrˋgænɪk] adj. 器官的、有機的 ◀Track 1823

*字尾-ic有轉變為形容詞之意

例句 Nowadays, organic food sometimes sells better than non-organic food. 現今，有機食物有時會賣得比非有機食物好。

搭配詞
organic food 有機食物

organism [ˋɔrgən͵ɪzəm] n. 有機體、生物體 ◀Track 1824

例句 How many single-celled organisms are there in the world?
這世界上有多少單細胞生物呢？

origin [ˋɔrədʒɪn] n. 起源 ◀Track 1825

例句 I'm taking classes on the origin of life.
我在上課學習生命的起源。

搭配詞
the origin of sth
某事物的起源

originality [ə͵rɪdʒəˋnælətɪ] n. 獨創力、創舉 ◀Track 1826

例句 Tom is distinguished for his originality. He has invented products that have revolutionized the way people live. 湯姆最特別的就是他的獨創力，他發明了許多產品，澈底顛覆人們的生活型態。

originate [əˋrɪdʒə͵net] v. 創造、發源 ◀Track 1827

例句 The style of architecture originated from the ancient Greeks.
這種建築風格是從古希臘人那裡發源的。

搭配詞
originate from 起源於

outbreak [ˋaut͵brek] n. 爆發、突然發生 ◀Track 1828

*字首out-有「外」之意

例句 The outbreak of the war will paralyze the traffic in the city.
戰爭爆發會造成城市內的交通癱瘓。

搭配詞
the outbreak of war
戰爭爆發

outer [ˋautɚ] adj. 外部的、外面的 ◀Track 1829

*字首out-有「外」之意

例句 I would like to learn more about the outer space.
我想學更多有關外太空的事。

搭配詞
outer space 外太空

pain [pen] n. 疼痛 ◀Track 1830

例句 He was in a lot of pain after the chemotherapy.
他化療後全身很痛苦。

同義字
ache

palm [pɑm] n. 手掌 ◀Track 1831

例句 She placed some money in his palm.
她在他的手掌中放入一些錢。

易混淆字
plum 梅子

panel [`pænḷ] n. 方格、平板 Track 1832

例句 Solar panels were installed on the roof to charge the battery.
太陽能電池板被安裝在屋頂，以充電到電池裡。

搭配詞 solar panel 太陽能電池板

paradise [`pærəˏdaɪs] n. 天堂 Track 1833

例句 Bhutan is a paradise on earth. 不丹是個人間天堂。

同義字 heaven

particle [`pɑrtɪkḷ] n. 微粒、極少量 Track 1834

例句 There wasn't a particle of truth in what he said.
他所說的話裡連極少的事實都沒有。

易混淆字 practical 實際的

password [`pæsˏwɝd] n. 口令、密碼 Track 1835

例句 You should enter your password to complete the login.
你得用密碼來登入系統。

搭配詞 enter password 輸入密碼

patient [`peʃənt] adj. 忍耐的、有耐心的 Track 1836

例句 The teacher is always patient with his students.
這位老師對學生總是很有耐心。

反義字 impatient 不耐煩的

paw [pɔ] n. 腳掌 Track 1837

例句 The cat batted at her owner with her paws.
那隻貓用腳掌打她的主人。

易混淆字 pawl 棘爪

petroleum [pə`trolɪəm] n. 石油 Track 1838

例句 There is a shortage of petroleum recently around the world.
最近在全世界有石油的短缺。

同義字 petrol

pharmacy [`fɑrməsɪ] n. 藥劑學、藥局 Track 1839

例句 Please get some painkillers from the pharmacy for me.
請從藥局幫我要一些止痛藥。

同義字 drugstore

physical [`fɪzɪkḷ] adj. 身體的 Track 1840

＊字尾-al有轉變為形容詞之意

例句 We had an physical examination before the classes start.
我們在課程開始前進行了身體檢查。

搭配詞 physical examination 身體檢查

pill [pɪl] n. 藥丸 Track 1841

例句 Jessica needs to take sleeping pills every night.
潔西卡每天晚上都需要吃安眠藥丸。

搭配詞 take a pill 服藥

pimple [ˋpɪmpl̩] n. 面皰、痘子、疙瘩 Track 1842

例句 Jane did not want to go on a date because she had a pimple on her face. 珍妮不想去約會，因為她臉上有青春痘。

同義字 acne

---

piss [pɪs] n. 尿液、小便 Track 1843

例句 He was pissed off that his wife was ungrateful for what he had done for her. 他太太對他的付出不感謝，讓他很火大。

搭配詞 piss off 火大（粗魯語）

---

plague [pleg] n. 瘟疫 Track 1844

例句 Kevin's been avoiding me like a plague since we quarrelled. 自從我們吵架後，凱文就一直像躲瘟疫一樣在躲我。

---

planet [ˋplænɪt] n. 行星 Track 1845

例句 The Earth is different from other planets in many aspects. 地球和其他行星有很多不同的地方。

---

plastic [ˋplæstɪk] adj. 塑膠的 Track 1846

例句 Lip augmentation is one type of plastic surgery. 豐唇是整型手術的一種。

搭配詞 plastic surgery 整型手術

---

pneumonia [njuˋmonjə] n. 肺炎 Track 1847

例句 Many people were infected with atypical pneumonia recently. 最近有許多人得了非典型肺炎。

搭配詞 atypical pneumonia 非典型肺炎

---

poison [ˋpɔɪzn̩] n. 毒藥 Track 1848

例句 It is said that the mushroom contained poison. 據說那香菇有毒。

---

pollutant [pəˋlutənt] n. 污染物 Track 1849

例句 We need to reduce air pollutants to protect public health. 我們須要降低空污物排放，以保障大眾健康。

搭配詞 air pollutant emissions 空污物排放

---

pollute [pəˋlut] v. 污染 Track 1850

例句 It is our duty to not pollute our environment. 我們的責任是不要污染環境。

搭配詞 pollute the environment 污染環境

---

posture [ˋpastʃɚ] n. 態度、姿勢 Track 1851

例句 Good posture is very important for health. 良好的姿勢對健康很重要。

a b c d e f g h i j k l m n o p q r s t u v w x y z

poverty [ˋpɑvətɪ] n. 貧窮 Track 1852

例句 Many people still live in abject poverty in this country.
這個國家許多人仍生活在赤貧之中。

搭配詞
abject poverty 赤貧

powerful [ˋpauəfəl] adj. 有力的 Track 1853

＊字尾-ful有「充滿」的意思

例句 The bomb is powerful enough to destroy this whole city.
炸彈夠有力，能夠毀掉整座城。

反義字
powerless 無力的

precision [prɪˋsɪʒən] n. 精準、精密 Track 1854

例句 It is necessary to make sure that all instruments are made with precision. 必須確認所有的器械都精密地製作完成。

同義字
niceness

prescribe [prɪˋskraɪb] v. 規定、開藥方 Track 1855

例句 She was prescribed medication for her blood pressure.
醫師開了藥方控制她的高血壓。

易混淆字
subscribe 訂閱

prescription [prɪˋskrɪpʃən] n. 指示、處方 Track 1856

＊字尾-tion有轉變為名詞的意思

例句 The pharmacist refused to dispense a prescription for abortion pills. 這位藥劑師拒絕依處方給墮胎藥。

搭配詞
dispense a prescription
依處方配藥

preventive [prɪˋvɛntɪv] n. 預防物、預防藥 Track 1857

＊字尾-ive有轉變為形容詞的意思

例句 We should prepare some preventives in advance.
我們必須先準備一些預防藥。

pregnancy [ˋprɛgnənsɪ] n. 懷孕 Track 1858

例句 She had pregnancy toxemia and nearly died.
她有妊娠毒血症，差一點就死了。

搭配詞
pregnancy toxemia
妊娠毒血症

pregnant [ˋprɛgnənt] adj. 懷孕的 Track 1859

例句 She is three months pregnant.
她已經懷孕三個月了。

prevent [prɪˋvɛnt] v. 預防、阻止 Track 1860

＊字首pre-有「先」之意

例句 To prevent the disaster from happening, we need to take preventive measures. 為了預防災害發生，我們應該採取預防措施。

搭配詞
prevent sth from happening
預防某事發生

prevention [prɪˋvɛnʃən] n. 預防 Track 1861

＊字首pre-有「先」之意

例句 Prevention is better than cure. 預防勝於治療。

printer [ˋprɪntɚ] n. 印刷工、印表機 Track 1862

＊字尾-er有轉變為名詞的意思

例句 I think we have to buy a new printer; this one is out of order.
我想我們得買個新的印表機了，這個壞了。

---

progress [ˋprɑgrɛs]/[prəˋgrɛs] n. 進展 v. 進步 Track 1863

例句 It took me a month to make some progress.
我花了一個月才有點進展。

搭配詞 make progress 有進展

---

prone [pron] adj. 俯臥的、易於……的 Track 1864

例句 Children of poor health are prone to catch colds in winter.
不健康的孩子在冬天就易於感冒。

搭配詞 prone to 易於……

---

protein [ˋprotiɪn] n. 蛋白質 Track 1865

例句 You should eat more food that's rich in protein.
你必須多吃一點蛋白質豐富的食物。

---

purify [ˋpjʊrəˏfaɪ] v. 淨化 Track 1866

＊字尾-ify有「化」的意思

例句 You can purify the water by distilling. 你可以用蒸餾來淨化水。

搭配詞 purify the water 淨化水質

---

pulse [pʌls] n. 脈搏 Track 1867

例句 She asked the doctor to take her pulse.
她請醫生量她的脈搏。

搭配詞 take one's pulse 量脈搏

---

pupil [ˋpjupḷ] n. 學生、瞳孔 Track 1868

例句 Her pupils are dilated. Something must be wrong with her.
她的瞳孔放大了，一定有什麼問題。

反義字 master 師傅

---

radiation [ˏredɪˋeʃən] n. 輻射、發光 Track 1869

＊字尾-tion有轉變為名詞的意思

例句 We don't know whether the apparatus will emit harmful radiation or not. 我們不知道這個儀器會不會發出有害的輻射。

---

radiator [ˋredɪˏetɚ] n. 發光體、散熱器 Track 1870

＊字尾-or有轉變為名詞的意思

例句 Please look over the radiator for me. 請幫我檢查這個散熱器。

---

radiate [ˋredɪˏet] v. 放射 Track 1871

例句 The sun in the sky radiates both light and heat every day.
天空上的太陽每天都放射出光線與熱能。

a b c d e f g h i j k l m n o p q r s t u v w x y z

radar [ˋredɑr] n. 雷達 Track 1872

例句 There are enemy aircrafts on the radar screen. What should we do now? 雷達螢幕上有敵機，現在我們該怎麼辦？

rare [rɛr] adj. 稀有的 Track 1873

例句 There are many rare animals in danger now.
現在有許多稀有動物面臨危機。

反義字
ordinary 普通的

rash [ræʃ] n. 疹子 Track 1874

例句 Karen has broken out in a rash.
凱倫起疹子了。

補充
hives 蕁麻疹

resistant [rɪˋzɪstənt] adj. 抵抗的 Track 1875

＊字尾-ant有轉變為形容詞之意

例句 He is resistant to change. 他很抗拒改變。

real [ˋrɪəl] adj. 真的、真實的 Track 1876

例句 I don't believe it's real. You must be kidding me.
我不相信這是真的。你一定在騙我。

reality [rɪˋælətɪ] n. 真實、現實 Track 1877

例句 In reality, I prefer Johnathan to be the project manager.
實際上，我比較希望強納生來做專案經理。

搭配詞
in reality 實際上

reason [ˋrizn̩] n. 理由 Track 1878

例句 She is absent for no reason today. 她今天無故缺席。

搭配詞
for no reason 沒有理由

recover [rɪˋkʌvɚ] v. 恢復、重新獲得 Track 1879

＊字首re-有「再次」之意

例句 He promised that as soon as he recovers from pneumonia, he will go home at once. 他答應一旦他的肺炎好了，就會馬上回家。

搭配詞
recover from 從……復元

recovery [rɪˋkʌvərɪ] n. 恢復 Track 1880

＊字首re-有「再次」之意

例句 He made a quick recovery from his illness.
他從他的疾病中快速地恢復了。

搭配詞
make a recovery 恢復

recycle [riˋsaɪkl̩] v. 循環利用、回收 Track 1881

＊字首re-有「再次」之意

例句 A lot of people are aware of the importance of recycling now.
許多人現在都知道回收的重要。

reduce [rɪˋdjus] v. 減輕、減少 ◀Track 1882
＊字首re-有「再次」之意
例句 He was unable to swallow and reduced to skin and bones.
他無法吞嚥，體重都減輕成皮包骨了。

反義字
increase 增加

repair [rɪˋpɛr] v. 修理、補救 ◀Track 1883
＊字首re-有「再次」之意
例句 The phone was so old that it wasn't worth repairing.
這個電話太老舊，不值得花錢修了。

同義字
fix

rib [rɪb] n. 肋骨 ◀Track 1884
例句 Do you know how many ribs a man has?
你知道一個人有幾根肋骨嗎？

robot [ˋrobət] n. 機器人 ◀Track 1885
例句 There will be a lot of AI robots being created in the future.
未來將會有很多人工智慧機器人問世。

搭配詞
AI robot 人工智慧機器人

rocket [ˋrɑkɪt] n. 火箭 ◀Track 1886
例句 An unmanned rocket is being sent into the orbit.
一台沒有搭載人員的火箭被送出去繞行地球軌道了。

搭配詞
unmanned rocket 無人火箭

sample [ˋsæmpl̩] n. 樣本 ◀Track 1887
例句 Please provide me with your product sample.
請提供我你的產品樣本。

搭配詞
blood sample 血液樣本

satellite [ˋsætl̩aɪt] n. 衛星 ◀Track 1888
例句 There are thirty-two known satellites in the solar system.
太陽系中有三十二個已知的衛星。

save [sev] v. 救、搭救、挽救、儲蓄 ◀Track 1889
例句 She has the habit of saving money every month.
她每個月都有存錢的習慣。

搭配詞
save money 存錢

science [ˋsaɪəns] n. 科學 ◀Track 1890
例句 I enjoy reading science fictions. 我喜歡看科幻小說。

搭配詞
science fiction 科幻小說

scientific [ˏsaɪənˋtɪfɪk] adj. 科學的、有關科學的 ◀Track 1891
例句 She dedicated all her life to scientific research.
她把一生都獻給了科學研究。

搭配詞
scientific research
科學研究

screen [skrin] n. 螢幕 Track 1892

例句 Wide-screen TVs are popular in recent years.
寬螢幕電視這幾年來很受歡迎。

搭配詞 wide-screen 寬螢幕的

shoulder [ˋʃoldɚ] n. 肩、肩膀 Track 1893

例句 You can come to me when you need a shoulder to cry on.
你受到委屈需要有人給你肩膀依靠時，可以來找我。

sick [sɪk] adj. 有病的、想吐的、厭倦的 Track 1894

例句 He had contagious conjunctivitis and took a sick leave.
他得了傳染性結膜炎，請病假休息。

搭配詞 sick leave 病假

sight [saɪt] n. 視力、情景、景象 Track 1895

例句 Her sight has started to fail after she turned 80.
她80歲後，視力就開始變差了。

搭配詞 short-sighted 近視的、目光短淺的

silicon [ˋsɪlɪkən] n. 矽 Track 1896

例句 The Silicon Valley has become a new economic model for its innovative science and technology.
矽谷已因它創新的科學與科技而成為新的經濟模範。

易混淆字 silicone 矽膠

silver [ˋsɪlvɚ] n. 銀 Track 1897

例句 Her false teeth were made of silver. 她的假牙是銀製的。

skeleton [ˋskɛlətn̩] n. 骨骼、骨架 Track 1898

例句 The poor old woman was reduced to a skeleton.
那位可憐的老太太瘦得只剩骨架了。

skin [skɪn] n. 皮、皮膚 Track 1899

例句 The skin care product is dermatologist-tested.
這款保養品經過皮膚科醫師測試。

搭配詞 skin care product 保養品

skull [skʌl] n. 頭蓋骨 Track 1900

例句 He had a skull fracture after he fell on the floor.
他在跌倒時頭骨骨折。

搭配詞 skull fracture 頭骨骨折

slash [slæʃ] n. 刀痕、裂縫 Track 1901

例句 The knife made a slash across his leg.
刀在他的腿上留下刀痕。

slight [slaɪt] adj. 輕微的 Track 1902

例句 He was born with a slight deformity which made him limp.
他天生有輕微的殘疾，使他走路跛腳。

smallpox [ˋsmɔl͵pɑks] n. 天花 Track 1903

例句 Smallpox has been brought under control by the use of vaccines.
天花已因使用疫苗而得到控制。

搭配詞 smallpox vaccine 天花疫苗

smell [smɛl] v. 嗅、聞到 Track 1904

例句 Do you smell something burning from the kitchen?
你有聞到廚房有東西燒焦嗎？

搭配詞 smell something burning 聞到某個東西燒焦

smog [smɑg] n. 煙霧、煙、霧霾 Track 1905

例句 Big cities usually have a problem with smog.
大城市常有霧霾的問題。

smother [ˋsmʌðɚ] v. 使窒息、掩飾 Track 1906

例句 Those children smothered the kitty with a plastic bag.
那群小孩用塑膠袋使小貓窒息。

sneeze [sniz] v. 打噴嚏 Track 1907

例句 Winnie caught a cold and sneezed a lot.
薇妮感冒了，而且打了很多噴嚏。

snore [snor] n./v. 鼾聲、打鼾 Track 1908

例句 Allen snores so loudly that his wife needs to take some sleeping pills before sleeping.
艾倫打鼾打得太大聲，他太太睡覺前都得吃安眠藥了。

sodium [ˋsodɪəm] n. 鈉 Track 1909

例句 People with high blood pressure should avoid food with high sodium. 高血壓的人必須避開高鈉含量的食物。

software [ˋsɔft͵wɛr] n. 軟體 Track 1910

例句 He knows where to download the software for free.
他知道要在哪裡免費下載這個軟體。

搭配詞 download a software 下載軟體

solar [ˋsolɚ] adj. 太陽的 Track 1911

例句 We will replace nuclear power with solar energy.
我們將以太陽能取代核能。

搭配詞 solar energy 太陽能

a b c d e f g h i j k l m n o p q r **s** t u v w x y z

solid [ˋsɑlɪd] adj. 固體的 Track 1912

例句 She could not eat solid food because she had a toothache.
她無法吃固體的食物，因為她牙痛。

反義字 liquid 液態的

sore [sor] adj. 疼痛的 Track 1913

例句 She had a sore throat because a fish bone was stuck in her throat.
一根魚骨頭卡在她的喉嚨裡，導致她喉嚨痛。

搭配詞 sore throat 喉嚨痛

soul [sol] n. 靈魂、心靈 Track 1914

例句 His wife is his soul mate. 他太太是他的靈魂伴侶。

搭配詞 soul mate 靈魂伴侶

space [spes] n. 空間、太空 Track 1915

例句 He threw a tantrum when he couldn't find a parking space.
他找不到停車位時，勃然大怒。

搭配詞 parking space 停車位

spacecraft [spesˏkræft] n. 太空船 Track 1916

例句 With the invention of the spacecraft, it is possible to travel to the moon. 因為有太空船的發明，就可以到月亮旅行了。

同義字 spaceship

special [ˋspɛʃəl] adj. 專門的、特別的 Track 1917

例句 He has quite a special accent. 他有個很特別的腔調。

spine [spaɪn] n. 脊柱、脊骨 Track 1918

例句 The ghost story is spine-chilling.
這個鬼故事令人聽了背脊都涼了。

搭配詞 spine-chilling 令人不寒而慄的（背脊都涼了）

sprain [spren] v. 扭傷 Track 1919

例句 No one knew how he sprained his ankle.
沒有人知道他怎麼扭傷他的腳踝。

搭配詞 sprain one's ankle 扭傷腳踝

sprawl [sprɔl] n./v. 伸開四肢的躺姿、任意伸展 Track 1920

例句 She sprawled on her bed with her laptop.
她帶著筆電伸開四肢躺在床上。

stage [stedʒ] n. 舞臺、階段 Track 1921

例句 Christine is dancing on the stage.
克麗絲汀在舞臺上跳舞。

搭配詞 on the stage 登臺演出

stammer [ˋstæmɚ] n. 結巴、口吃 Track 1922

例句 Tom is often taunted by his classmates because of his stammer.
湯姆常因口吃而被同學嘲笑。

stature [ˋstætʃɚ] n. 身高、身材 Track 1923

例句 I can easily recognize John by his red hair and short stature.
我很容易可以透過約翰的紅髮和矮小的身材而認出他。

搭配詞
short stature 身材短小

steam [stim] n. 蒸汽 Track 1924

例句 Who invented the steam engine? 是誰發明了蒸汽機的？

搭配詞
steam engine 蒸汽機

steel [stil] n. 鋼、鋼鐵 Track 1925

例句 Wendy is a person with a heart of steel.
溫蒂是個心如鋼鐵般堅定的人。

搭配詞
with a heart of steel
鋼鐵般的堅定

stereotype [ˋstɛrɪəˏtaɪp] n. 鉛版、刻板印象 Track 1926

例句 He doesn't conform to the usual stereotype of the city businessman.
他不符合一般城市生意人的刻板印象。

sting [stɪŋ] v. 刺、叮 Track 1927

例句 Linda was stung by bees in the forest.
琳達在樹林裡被蜜蜂叮了。

strangle [ˋstræŋgḷ] v. 勒死、絞死、（使）窒息 Track 1928

例句 She was strangled to death. 她被勒死了。

易混淆字
strange 奇怪的

stroke [strok] n. 打擊、中風 Track 1929

例句 I feel so sorry to hear that he had a stroke yesterday.
聽到他昨天中風，我很難過。

搭配詞
have a stroke 得到中風

strong [strɔŋ] adj. 強壯的、強健的 Track 1930

例句 Even though she was small, she was very strong.
雖然她身材矮小，但她很強壯。

反義字
weak 虛弱的

substitution [ˏsʌbstəˋtjuʃən] n. 代理、代替 Track 1931

＊字尾-tion有轉變為名詞的意思

例句 They are looking for a kind of medicine as its substitution.
他們在找一種可以代替的藥。

suffer [ˋsʌfɚ] v. 受苦、遭受 Track 1932

例句 Tom is suffering from smoking too much.
湯姆因抽太多菸而受苦。

搭配詞 suffer from 遭受⋯⋯

---

suffocate [ˋsʌfə͵ket] v. 使窒息 Track 1933

例句 It's suffocating here. Do you mind if I open the windows?
這裡快令人窒息了。你介意我開窗戶嗎？

同義字 smother

---

sulfur [ˋsʌlfɚ] n. 硫磺 Track 1934

例句 Sulfur has a pungent smell.
硫磺有種刺鼻味。

搭配詞 sulfuric acid 硫酸

---

supersonic [͵supɚˋsɑnɪk] Track 1935

adj. 超音波的、超音速的 ＊字首super-有「超」之意

例句 Developing the supersonic jet is quite an accomplishment.
發明超音速客機是個很棒的成就。

搭配詞 supersonic jet 超音速客機

---

surgery [ˋsɝdʒərɪ] n. 外科醫學、外科手術 Track 1936

例句 The doctor told me the laser surgery is scheduled within two weeks. 醫生告訴我雷射手術已訂在兩個禮拜內執行。

搭配詞 laser surgery 雷射手術

---

survey [ˋsɝve] n./v. 考察、測量、實地調查 Track 1937

例句 Sam went to England to conduct a field survey.
山姆去英國進行實地考查。

搭配詞 field survey
田野調查、實地考查

---

symptom [ˋsɪmptəm] n. 症狀、徵兆 Track 1938

例句 You have to tell me first when the symptom begins.
當有症狀開始的時候你必須第一個告訴我。

---

system [ˋsɪstəm] n. 系統 Track 1939

例句 His digestive system is very weak. 他的消化系統很弱。

搭配詞 digestive system 消化系統

---

tablet [ˋtæblɪt] n. 塊、片、碑、牌 Track 1940

例句 She brought her tablet computer with her everywhere.
她到哪裡都帶著她的平板電腦。

搭配詞 tablet computer 平板電腦

---

technical [ˋtɛknɪkl] adj. 技術上的、技能的 Track 1941

例句 The technical term sounds very abstract and hard to grasp.
這個術語聽起來很抽象，難以理解。

搭配詞 technical term 術語

technique [tɛk`nik] n. 技術、技巧 Track 1942

例句 In this course, students are required to learn modern management techniques. 在這堂課中，學生需要學習現代管理技術。

telegraph [`tɛlə͵græf] n. 電報 Track 1943

＊字首tele-有「遠的」之意

例句 She sent me a telegraph to tell me to come home.
她發了電報給我，要我回家。

telephone/phone [`tɛlə͵fon]/[fon] n. 電話 Track 1944

＊字首tele-有「遠的」之意

例句 Can I borrow your telephone? I need to talk to him right now.
我可以借你的電話嗎？我現在就需要和他講話。

telescope [`tɛlə͵skop] n. 望遠鏡 Track 1945

＊字首tele-有「遠的」之意

例句 Jeff looked through the telescope, observing the approaching ship.
傑夫透過望遠鏡觀察接近的船。

terrific [tə`rɪfɪk] adj. 驚人的 Track 1946

例句 He's a terrific teacher. He always has his student's interests at heart. 他是名傑出的老師，總是想著要為學生好。

反義字
moderate 中等的、適度的

texture [`tɛkstʃɚ] n. 質地、結構 Track 1947

＊字尾-ure有轉變為名詞之意

例句 Each variety of melon has its individual flavor and texture.
每種瓜都有自己的口味與質地。

theory [`θiərɪ] n. 理論、推論 Track 1948

例句 It seems good in theory, but it doesn't work in practice.
這理論上不錯，但實際上卻沒用。

搭配詞
in theory 理論上

therapy [`θɛrəpɪ] n. 療法、治療 Track 1949

例句 Gene therapy is the latest trend in medical research.
基因療法是醫學研究的最新趨勢。

搭配詞
gene therapy 基因療法

thermometer [θə`mɑmətɚ] n. 溫度計 Track 1950

例句 The nurse put the thermometer in the patient's mouth.
護士把溫度計放進病患的口中。

thigh [θaɪ] n. 大腿 Track 1951

例句 The water is already up to my thighs.
水已經淹到我的大腿了。

throat [θrot] **n.** 喉嚨 ◀ *Track 1952*

例句 The man grabbed the young man's throat suddenly.
那個男人突然抓住了年輕男子的喉嚨。

throb [θrɑb] **n.** 脈搏、抽痛 ◀ *Track 1953*

例句 He was my high school heartthrob.
他是我高中時期心儀的對象。

搭配詞 heartthrob 心儀的對象

thumb [θʌm] **n.** 拇指 ◀ *Track 1954*

例句 Some British people gave thumbs-up for Brexit.
有些英國人認同脫歐。

搭配詞 thumbs up 豎起大拇指，贊成某人／某事

tin [tɪn] **n.** 錫 ◀ *Track 1955*

例句 She bought a tin can to hold the flour.
她買了一個錫罐來裝麵粉。

搭配詞 tin can 錫罐

tiptoe [ˋtɪp͵to] **n.** 腳尖 ◀ *Track 1956*

例句 I need to stand on tiptoe to reach the shelf.
我必須踮腳尖才能碰到架子。

搭配詞 on tiptoe 踮腳尖的

tire [taɪr] **v.** 使疲倦 ◀ *Track 1957*

例句 I am tired of working for someone else, and that's why I started my own business.
替別人工作讓我太疲倦了，所以我開始了自己的事業。

搭配詞 be tired of 疲於

toe [to] **n.** 腳趾 ◀ *Track 1958*

例句 She loved the baby from head to toe.
她非常愛這個寶寶。

搭配詞 from head to toe 澈底的

tooth [tuθ] **n.** 牙齒、齒 ◀ *Track 1959*

例句 I have a sweet tooth for chocolate. 我愛吃巧克力。

搭配詞 sweet tooth 嗜吃甜食

touch [tʌtʃ] **n./v.** 接觸、碰、觸摸 ◀ *Track 1960*

例句 Don't touch the stray dog. It might have fleas.
別摸流浪狗，牠可能有跳蚤。

tongue [tʌŋ] **n.** 舌、舌頭 ◀ *Track 1961*

例句 She was tongue-tied when she found she was on TV.
她發現上了電視，緊張地說不出話來。

搭配詞 tongue-tied 說不出話的

toxic [ˋtɑksɪk] adj. 有毒的 Track 1962

例句 You need to be careful when you handle the toxic chemical.
你在處理有毒物質時必須要小心。

同義字 poisonous

tranquilizer [ˋtrænkwɪˏlaɪzɚ] n. 鎮靜劑 Track 1963

＊字尾-er有轉變為名詞的意思

例句 They had to use tranquilizer to stop him from thrashing about.
他們得用鎮靜劑阻止他到處翻來翻去。

transplant [ˋtrænsplænt]/[trænsˋplænt] Track 1964

n. 移植手術 ＊字首trans-有「穿越、轉變」之意

例句 The child was put on ECMO and waited for a heart transplant.
這個小孩被裝上葉克膜，等待心臟移植手術。

搭配詞 heart transplant 心臟移植手術

trauma [ˋtrɔmə] n. 外傷、創傷 Track 1965

例句 He hasn't recovered from the trauma. 他還沒從創傷中復元。

搭配詞 recover from the trauma 從創傷中復元

tuberculosis [tjuˏbɝkjəˋlosɪs] n. 肺結核、肺病 Track 1966

例句 His tuberculosis is too serious to be cured.
他的肺結核太嚴重，已經治不好了。

tumor [ˋtjumɚ] n. 腫瘤、瘤 Track 1967

例句 The doctor did an operation to remove his brain tumor.
醫師執行手術切除他的腦瘤。

搭配詞 brain tumor 腦瘤

typewriter [ˋtaɪpˏraɪtɚ] n. 打字機 Track 1968

＊字尾-er有轉變為名詞的意思

例句 Old typewriters are rare nowadays.
老舊的打字機現在已經很少看到了。

ulcer [ˋʌlsɚ] n. 潰瘍、弊病 Track 1969

例句 He has duodenal ulcers, so his digestion system is very weak.
他有十二指腸潰瘍，所以消化系統很弱。

搭配詞 duodenal ulcer 十二指腸潰瘍

uncover [ʌnˋkʌvɚ] v. 掀開、揭露 Track 1970

＊字首un-有「不、反」之意

例句 These two young reporters uncovered the whole plot.
這兩個年輕的記者揭露了整個陰謀。

反義字 cover 遮蓋

universe [ˋjunəˏvɝs] n. 宇宙、天地萬物 Track 1971

＊字首uni-有「單一的」之意

例句 You and I are just transient visitors in the universe.
你我都只是宇宙短暫的過客。

搭配詞 in the universe 宇宙間

upgrade [ˋʌp͵gred]/[͵ʌpˋgred] ◀Track 1972
n./v. 增加、向上、升級 ＊字首up-有「上」之意
例句 I need to upgrade my computer for better efficiency.
我得把我的電腦升級，才能更有效率。
反義字 downgrade 降級

upward(s) [ˋʌpwəd(z)] adv./adj. 向上的 ◀Track 1973
＊字首up-有「上」之意
例句 The balloon flew upward to the sky as soon as he loosened his grip. 他一放手，氣球就向上飛上天了。
反義字 downward 向下的

uranium [jʊˋrenɪəm] n. 鈾 ◀Track 1974
例句 It is illegal to trade uranium in our country.
在我們的國家，鈾交易是違法的。

urine [ˋjʊrɪn] n. 尿、小便 ◀Track 1975
例句 The doctor asked him for a urine sample.
醫生要求他提供尿液檢體。
搭配詞 urine sample 尿液檢體

utilize [ˋjutḷ͵aɪz] v. 利用、派上用場 ◀Track 1976
＊字尾-ize有「化」的意思
例句 Scientists are finding more efficient ways of utilizing solar energy.
科學家正在找出更多有效率利用太陽能的方式。
同義字 use

vaccine [ˋvæksin] n. 疫苗 ◀Track 1977
例句 Malaria vaccine was invented more than a century ago.
瘧疾疫苗在一百多年前被發明出來。
搭配詞 malaria vaccine 瘧疾疫苗

valiant [ˋvæljənt] adj. 勇敢的 ◀Track 1978
例句 The valiant knight saved the princess.
那個勇敢的騎士救了公主。

vary [ˋvɛrɪ] v. 使變化、改變 ◀Track 1979
例句 The results to the test may vary.
測驗的結果可能會有些變化。
同義字 change

vein [ven] n. 靜脈、特色 ◀Track 1980
例句 She has varicose veins due to standing for too long at work.
她因長期工作站立而患有靜脈曲張。
搭配詞 varicose veins 靜脈曲張

veteran [ˋvɛtərən] n. 老手、老練者 ◀Track 1981
例句 I suggest that you consult a veteran doctor about your illness, or it will get worse.
我建議你去找一個老練的醫師來諮詢，不然你的病情會加重的。
反義字 rookie 菜鳥

veterinarian [ˏvɛtərə`nɛrɪən] n. 獸醫 ◀Track 1982

例句 I take my cat to the veterinarian once a year.
我一年帶我的貓去獸醫一次。

縮寫
vet

visualize [`vɪʒuəˏlaɪz] v. 使可見、使具形象、想像 ◀Track 1983

＊字尾-ize有「化」的意思

例句 He looks much younger than I had visualized.
他的外表比我想像的年輕多了。

同義字
imagine

virus [`vaɪrəs] n. 病毒 ◀Track 1984

例句 I think we could definitely find ways to get rid of all the computer viruses soon. 我想我們絕對可以迅速找到方法摧毀所有的電腦病毒。

搭配詞
computer virus 電腦病毒

vomit [`vɑmɪt] n./v. 嘔吐物、嘔吐 ◀Track 1985

例句 The disgusting smell made him vomit on the bus.
那個噁心的味道讓他在公車上吐了。

搭配詞
vomit blood 吐血

ward [wɔrd] n. 行政區、守護、病房 ◀Track 1986

例句 Ben is put in an isolation ward becase his illness is so serious.
班被關進隔離病房，因為他的病太嚴重了。

易混淆字
word 字

warranty [`wɔrəntɪ] n. 依據、正當的理由、保固 ◀Track 1987

例句 The product warranty is valid only in the country where it is sold.
這個產品保固只限於它被銷售的國家。

搭配詞
product warranty 產品保固

waterproof [`wɔtə`pruf] adj. 防水的 ◀Track 1988

＊字尾-proof有「防」的意思

例句 I just bought a waterproof watch last week.
我上禮拜才買了一個防水的手錶。

weak [wik] adj. 無力的、虛弱的 ◀Track 1989

例句 She is too weak to work today. 她今天虛弱得無法工作。

反義字
strong 強壯的

weapon [`wɛpən] n. 武器、兵器 ◀Track 1990

例句 Anthrax can be used as a deadly weapon by terrorists.
炭疽病毒可能被恐怖份子用來當作致命武器。

搭配詞
deadly weapon 致命武器

weary [`wɪrɪ] adj. 疲倦的 ◀Track 1991

例句 You should sit on the bench and rest your weary limbs.
你應該坐在長凳上讓你疲倦的四肢休息一下。

同義字
tired

website [ˋwɛbˏsaɪt] n. 網站 Track 1992

例句 We can build a website for free and sell stuff online.
我們可以免費架設網站做網拍。

搭配詞
build a website 架設網站

weigh [we] v. 秤重 Track 1993

例句 How much do you weigh? 你（的體重）有多重?

weight [wet] n. 重、重量 Track 1994

例句 She is trying to lose weight and eats very little.
她在試著減重，所以吃得很少。

搭配詞
lose weight 減重

west [wɛst] n. 西方 Track 1995

例句 Which country lies to the west of Egypt?
哪個國家在埃及的西邊？

wholesome [ˋholsəm] adj. 有益健康的 Track 1996

例句 The wholesome food helped him recover from the illness quickly.
這些健康的食物幫助他很快從疾病恢復健康。

同義字
healthful

why [hwaɪ] adv. 為什麼 Track 1997

例句 Please let me know why he failed.
請告訴我他為什麼會失敗。

搭配詞
why not 為什麼不

withstand [wɪθˋstænd] v. 耐得住、經得起 Track 1998

例句 He proved that his theory could withstand the test of time.
他證明他的理論經得起時間考驗。

搭配詞
withstand the test of time
經得起時間考驗

woman [ˋwʊmən] n. 成年女人、婦女 Track 1999

例句 The woman has been crying all day long because she can't find her son. 那個女人哭了一整天，因為她找不到她的兒子。

worse [wɝs] adj. 更壞的、更差的 Track 2000

例句 I think he is getting worse. Let's send him to the hospital.
我覺得他的狀況好像更糟了，我們快送他去醫院吧。

反義字
better 更好的

wound [waʊnd] n. 傷口 Track 2001

例句 There is a bullet wound in his chest.
他的胸部有個子彈的傷口。

同義字
injury

wrinkle [ˋrɪŋkḷ] n. 皺紋 ◀Track 2002

例句 Everyone gets wrinkles when they're old.
每個人老了都會有皺紋。

易混淆字
twinkle 閃耀

wrist [rɪst] n. 腕關節、手腕 ◀Track 2003

例句 She grabbed her husband by the wrist and dragged him away.
她抓住她老公的手腕把他拖走了。

Xerox/xerox [ˋzirɑks] n. 全錄影印 ◀Track 2004

例句 Please xerox the document on the desk for me. I need it right this second. 請替我影印桌上的資料，我現在就要。

搭配詞
xerox machine 影印機

yawn [jɔn] n./v. 打呵欠 ◀Track 2005

例句 Please mind your manners and don't yawn in front of our guests.
請注意禮節，別在我們的客人面前打呵欠。

易混淆字
yarn 紗線

youthful [ˋjuθfəl] adj. 年輕的 ◀Track 2006

＊字尾-ful有「充滿」的意思

例句 No one can remain youthful forever. 沒有人可以永遠年輕。

搭配詞
youthful day 年輕歲月

Test 07 關鍵英單總測驗第7回

以下測驗題皆出自書中第七回「**和科技醫學有關的單字**」，快來檢視自己的學習成果吧！

一、選擇題

1. He _____ that the decision was wrong.
   (A) affected
   (B) caused
   (C) acknowledged
   (D) faced

2. The church is at the ____ of a hill.
   (A) hand
   (B) flash
   (C) foot
   (D) fuel

3. The wounded soldier _____ all night.
   (A) heard
   (B) injection
   (C) groaned
   (D) lacked

4. The ____ research provides a new treatment for cancer.
   (A) medical
   (B) radar
   (C) origin
   (D) preventive

5. Scientists are developing _______ medicine to provide better cancer care.
   (A) progress
   (B) recovery
   (C) precision
   (D) robot

6. The ___ doctor has rich experience in pediatric surgery.
   (A) ward
   (B) allergic
   (C) calcium
   (D) veteran

7. Global warming is caused by too much____ emission.
   (A) carbon
   (B) dose
   (C) explosion
   (D) cell

8. The man is too _____ to live alone.
   (A) liver
   (B) frail
   (C) navel
   (D) organic

9. The __________ of SARS caused worldwide panic in 2003.
   (A) parasite
   (B) pollutant
   (C) outbreak
   (D) particle

10. The little girl has ____ cheeks.
   (A) chubby
   (B) forgetful
   (C) infection
   (D) lump

二、克漏字測驗

There are many ___1___ throughout human history. One of the biggest is the ___2___. It has transformed the world into a global village.

When you have access to it, you have endless opportunities, information, and ___3___ social networks. With the new ___4___ on smart phones and WiFi, you can connect to the world no matter where you are.

To honor that memorable day when the first electronic message was ___5___ from one computer to another computer, people around the world celebrate The International Internet Day each year on October 29.

1. (A) solar
   (B) websites
   (C) mankind
   (D) inventions

2. (A) Internet
   (B) science
   (C) wrinkles
   (D) recycle

3. (A) frail
   (B) powerful
   (C) plastic
   (D) preventive

4. (A) technology
   (B) operation
   (C) plague
   (D) motor

5. (A) made
   (B) launched
   (C) transmitted
   (D) injured

關鍵英單總測驗第7回
中譯與解答

一、選擇題

1. 他承認決定是錯誤的。
   (A) 影響
   (B) 引起
   (C) 承認
   (D) 面對

2. 這座教堂在小山丘腳下。
   (A) 手
   (B) 肉體
   (C) 腳
   (D) 燃料

3. 受傷的士兵整夜痛苦呻吟。
   (A) 聽到
   (B) 注射
   (C) 痛苦呻吟
   (D) 缺乏

4. 這個醫療研究提供新的癌症治療方式。
   (A) 醫療的
   (B) 雷達
   (C) 起源
   (D) 預防的

5. 科學家正在研究精準治療，以提供更好的癌症醫療。
   (A) 進展
   (B) 復原
   (C) 精準
   (D) 機器人

6. 這名老練的醫師有豐富的小兒科手術經驗。
   (A) 病房
   (B) 過敏的
   (C) 鈣質
   (D) 老練的

7. 全球暖化是過量的碳排放造成的。
   (A) 碳
   (B) 劑量
   (C) 爆炸
   (D) 細胞

8. 這名男子太虛弱而法無獨居。
   (A) 肝臟
   (B) 虛弱
   (C) 肚臍
   (D) 有機的

9. 2003年SARS的爆發造成全球恐慌。
   (A) 寄生蟲
   (B) 污染物
   (C) 爆發
   (D) 微粒

10. 這個小女孩有圓滾滾的臉頰。
   (A) 圓滾滾
   (B) 健忘的
   (C) 感染
   (D) 腫包

二、克漏字測驗

人類歷史上有許多發明，其中最重大的莫過於網際網路，它將整個世界轉變為一個地球村。

當你有網路可以使用，你就有無限的機會、資訊，和強大的社群網絡。這個新科技運用在手機結合WiFi，你就可以在任何地方與世界連結。

為紀念電子訊息在電腦之間首次傳遞成功，人們每年都在10月29日這一天慶祝國際網際網路日。

1.
(A) 太陽的
(B) 網站
(C) 人類
(D) 發明

2.
(A) 網際網路
(B) 科學
(C) 皺紋
(D) 回收

3.
(A) 虛弱的
(B) 強大的
(C) 塑膠的
(D) 預防的

4
(A) 科技
(B) 手術
(C) 瘟疫
(D) 馬達

5.
(A) 製造
(B) 發射
(C) 傳送
(D) 傷害

一、選擇題

1.(C) 2.(C) 3.(C) 4.(A) 5.(C)
6.(D) 7.(A) 8.(B) 9.(C) 10.(A)

二、克漏字測驗

1.(D) 2.(A) 3.(B)
4.(A) 5.(C)

Unit 08 和運動有關的單字

多益測驗的命題強調生活化與實用性，學會這些與「運動」有關的單字，不僅能讓你在多益考場上所向披靡，在日常生活上也可以靈活運用喔！

冰上運動可以這麼說

- **The figure skater managed to land record-setting six quadruple jumps in his long program.**
  那名花滑選手破紀錄地在長曲項目中成功完成六個四周跳。
- **The judges spent more time than usual to check if the jump was fully rotated.**
  裁判們花了比平常更長的時間去確認那一跳是否有圈數不足的情形。
- **Becoming a professional hockey player has always been his dream.**
  成為一名職業冰球選手一直是他的夢想。

球類運動可以這麼說

- **Soccer is one of the most popular sports in the world.**
  足球是世界上最受歡迎的運動之一。
- **She started to play basketball since she was six.**
  她從六歲就開始打籃球。

田徑運動可以這麼說

- **The coach gives a pep talk to the team before the game.**
  教練在比賽前向隊伍說了些鼓舞士氣的話。

- **The camera captures the moment as she sprinting to the finish line.**
  鏡頭捕捉到了她全力衝刺到終點線的瞬間。

水上運動可以這麼說

- **He is the youngest athlete on the diving team.**
  他是跳水隊上最年輕的運動員。

- **Don't forget to stretch before you enter the swimming pool.**
  進入泳池前，別忘了先伸展。

運動場館可以這麼說

- **The capacity of the new stadium is 10,520.**
  新運動場的可容納人數是10,520人。

- **The Four Continents Figure Skating Championships will be held at Taipei Arena.**
  四大洲花式滑冰錦標賽將在台北小巨蛋舉行。

Unit 08 和運動有關的單字

ace [es] n. 傑出人才、王牌 Track 2007

例句 She's an ace tennis player.
她是一流的網球選手。

---

act [ækt] v. 行為、行動、法案 Track 2008

例句 He acted quite rashly. 他那個行動太魯莽了。

---

action [ˋækʃən] n. 行動、活動 Track 2009

例句 You'd better consult with your lawyer before taking any further action. 你最好先跟律師諮詢一下再採取更進一步的行動。

搭配詞
take action 採取行動

---

active [ˋæktɪv] adj. 活躍的 Track 2010

＊字尾-ive有轉變為形容詞之意

例句 You don't need to be experienced, but you'd better be an active participant. 你不需要有經驗，但你最好要是個活躍的參與者

反義字
inactive 不活躍的

---

activity [ækˋtɪvətɪ] n. 活動、活躍 Track 2011

例句 The most popular leisure activity is watching TV.
最受人們歡迎的休閒活動就是看電視。

搭配詞
leisure activity 休閒活動

---

alternate [ˋɔltɚ͵net]/[ˋɔltɚ͵nɪt] Track 2012

adj./v. 每隔……的輪流、交替

例句 We visit our grandparents in the countryside on alternate weekends. 我們每隔週末到鄉下探訪祖父母。

---

arena [əˋrinə] n. 競技場 Track 2013

例句 The UK has been an ally of the US in the international arena.
在國際場合上，英國一直是美國的盟友。

搭配詞
international arena
國際場合

---

athlete [ˋæθlit] n. 運動員 Track 2014

例句 The athlete's ambition is to win a gold medal in the Olympic Games. 這名運動員的志向是在奧運中奪得金牌。

---

athletic [æθ`lɛtɪk] adj. 運動的、強健的 Track 2015

＊字尾-ic有轉變為形容詞之意

例句 All employees are supposed to participate in the company's athletic meeting held in July. 所有員工都得參與七月辦的公司運動會。

搭配詞 athletic meeting 運動會

badminton [`bædmɪntən] n. 羽毛球 Track 2016

例句 This badminton racket is for the professional.
這支羽毛球拍是專業級的。

搭配詞 badminton racket 羽毛球拍

balance [`bæləns] n. 平衡 Track 2017

例句 Not every woman is able to keep balance between family and career. 不是每個女人都能在工作與家庭間取得平衡。

搭配詞 keep balance 維持平衡

ballet [bæ`le] n. 芭蕾 Track 2018

例句 She is a member of the contemporary ballet troupe.
她是當代芭蕾舞團的成員。

搭配詞 contemporary ballet 當代芭蕾

base [bes] n. 基底、壘、基地 Track 2019

例句 The movie is based on a true story.
這部電影是以一個真實故事為基礎所拍的。

baseball [`bes͵bɔl] n. 棒球 Track 2020

例句 He always wears a baseball cap whenever he goes.
他不論到哪老戴著棒球帽。

搭配詞 baseball cap 棒球帽

basket [`bæskɪt] n. 籃子、籃網、得分 Track 2021

例句 She bought a basket of eggs in the supermarket.
她在超市買了一籃子的雞蛋。

搭配詞 a basket of 一籃的

basketball [`bæskɪt͵bɔl] n. 籃球 Track 2022

例句 Jeremy Lin is an NBA basketball player. 林書豪是NBA籃球員。

搭配詞 basketball player 籃球員

bat [bæt] n. 蝙蝠、球棒 Track 2023

例句 She whacked the two men with a bat. 她用球棒打那兩個男人。

易混淆字 bet 打賭

bend [bɛnd] v. 使彎曲 Track 2024

例句 She bent over and picked up the pen. 她彎下腰撿起筆。

易混淆字 band 樂團

bet [bɛt] v. 下賭注 Track 2025

例句 "Dad, are you coming to school to see me play soccer?" "You bet!"
「老爸，你會來學校看我踢足球嗎?」「當然啦！」

搭配詞 you bet 當然

bounce [bauns] v. 彈、跳 Track 2026

例句 The ball bounced all the way into the ditch.
那顆球一路彈進了水溝。

bowling [ˋbolɪŋ] n. 保齡球 Track 2027

例句 He works part-time at the bowling alley after school.
他下課後去保齡球館兼差。

搭配詞 bowling alley 保齡球館

boxing [bɑksɪŋ] n. 拳擊 Track 2028

例句 He enjoys watching boxing games. 他喜歡看拳擊賽。

搭配詞 boxing game 拳擊比賽

break [brek] v./n. 休息、中斷、破裂 Track 2029

例句 The team took a short break after practicing for two hours.
練習了兩個小時後，球隊小小休息了一下。

搭配詞 take a break 休息一下

bury [ˋbɛrɪ] v. 埋 Track 2030

例句 He buried himself in work after his wife passed away.
他太太離世後，他就埋首於工作之中。

搭配詞 bury in 埋首於

camp [kæmp] n. 露營 Track 2031

例句 The children are going to a summer camp.
小朋友們即將前往夏令營。

搭配詞 summer camp 夏令營

canoe [kəˋnu] n. 獨木舟 Track 2032

例句 It is quite dangerous to go canoeing along the stream by yourself.
一個人滑獨木舟是很危險的。

搭配詞 go canoeing 划獨木舟

cast [kæst] v. 用力擲、選角 Track 2033

例句 The fisherman cast a net in the sea to catch fish.
漁民用力撒網到海裡捉魚。

challenge [ˋtʃælɪndʒ] n./v. 挑戰 Track 2034

例句 The company is ready to meet the challenges lying ahead of it.
這家公司已經準備好面對之後的挑戰了。

搭配詞 meet the challenge 接受挑戰

champion [ˋtʃæmpɪən] n. 冠軍 Track 2035

例句 He's very likely to be the swimming champion of the Olympic Games. 他很可能會是奧運游泳冠軍。

同義字 winner

championship [ˋtʃæmpɪənˏʃɪp] n. 冠軍賽 Track 2036

例句 It was Susan who won the spelling championship.
是蘇珊贏得了拼字冠軍賽。

搭配詞 win a championship 贏得冠軍

climb [klaɪm] v. 攀登、上升、爬 Track 2037

例句 He enjoys mountain climbing. 他喜歡爬山。

搭配詞 mountain climbing 爬山

coach [kotʃ] n. 教練、顧問 Track 2038

例句 The coach of the baseball team used to be a great pitcher.
這個棒球隊的教練曾是個很棒的投手。

易混淆字 couch 長沙發

compete [kəmˋpit] v. 競爭 Track 2039

例句 In order to compete with their products, we need to lower the market prices of our commodities.
為了要與他們的產品競爭，我們必須降低我們的產品價格。

搭配詞 compete with 與……競爭

competitor [kəmˋpɛtətɚ] n. 競爭者 Track 2040

＊字尾-or有「者」的意思

例句 Mike and Steve are business competitors in many areas.
麥克和史帝夫在許多部分都是商場競爭者。

搭配詞 business competitor 商場對手

contestant [kənˋtɛstənt] n. 競爭者、參賽者 Track 2041

例句 There are three contestants vying for the prize.
有三個參賽者在爭奪獎品。

dash [dæʃ] n. 快速跑步 Track 2042

例句 She dashed all the way to the store.
她一路快速跑到店裡。

defeat [dɪˋfit] v. 挫敗、擊敗 Track 2043

例句 Our basketball team was defeated by Belgium.
我們的籃球隊被比利時隊打敗了。

搭配詞 be defeated by 被……打敗

defend [dɪˋfɛnd] v. 保衛、防禦 Track 2044

例句 David Beckham tried a trick kick in the middle of the game, but the goalkeeper defended splendidly.
貝克漢在中場時踢變化球，但是對方守門員防禦得很漂亮。

defense [dɪˋfɛns] n. 防禦 Track 2045

例句 The woman shot the grizzly bear in self-defense.
那個女子出於自我防禦射殺了那隻大灰熊。

---

dive [daɪv] v. 跳水、潛心於 ＊過去式：dived/dove Track 2046

例句 He dived into the pool as if he were a fish.
他像魚一般跳進了池子裡。

搭配詞 dive into 跳入

---

dodge [dɑdʒ] v. 閃開、躲開 Track 2047

例句 The kids played dodge ball during the recess.
小朋友在下課時間玩躲避球。

搭配詞 dodge ball 躲避球

---

energetic [ˏɛnɚˋdʒɛtɪk] adj. 有精力的 Track 2048

例句 Although Mr. Yang is very old, he is still energetic.
雖然楊先生很老了，他還是很有精力。

同義字 vigorous

---

energy [ˋɛnɚdʒɪ] n. 能量、精力 Track 2049

例句 The little baby is still full of energy, while his mother is already exhausted. 那個小嬰兒還是很有精力，但他媽媽已經很疲累了。

搭配詞 full of energy 充滿活力

---

equal [ˋikwəl] adj. 同等的 Track 2050

例句 The two teams are equal in experience.
這兩支隊伍經驗都相同。

---

exercise [ˋɛksɚˏsaɪz] n./v. 運動 Track 2051

例句 Rita enjoys doing exercise, especially jogging.
麗塔喜歡做運動，尤其是慢跑。

搭配詞 do exercise 做運動

---

football [ˋfutˏbɔl] n. 足球、橄欖球 Track 2052

例句 There are some boys playing football on the playground.
有些男孩們在遊樂場踢足球。

搭配詞 play football 踢足球

---

golf [gɔlf] n. 高爾夫球 Track 2053

例句 His father is a manager of a golf course.
他的爸爸是一座高爾夫球場的經理。

搭配詞 golf course 高爾夫球場

---

gymnasium [dʒɪmˋnezɪəm] n. 體育館、健身房 Track 2054

例句 I prefer exercising outdoors to exercising in the gymnasium.
比起在體育館運動，我寧願在戶外運動。

縮寫 gym

healthy [ˋhɛlθɪ] adj. 健康的 Track 2055
＊字尾-y有轉變為形容詞之意
例句 Instant noodles are not healthy food. 泡麵不是健康的食物。

反義字
unhealthy 不健康的

hit [hɪt] v. 打、撞擊 Track 2056
例句 The old man was hit by a car when walking on the zebra-crossing yesterday. 那個老先生昨天在過斑馬線時被車撞了。

hockey [ˋhɑkɪ] n. 曲棍球 Track 2057
例句 My sister won a silver medal in the ice hockey competition.
我姊姊在冰上曲棍球比賽得到銀牌。

搭配詞
ice hockey 冰上曲棍球

hold [hold] v. 把握、控制、拿 Track 2058
例句 Hold on. Things will go your way.
堅持下去，會有海闊天空的一天。

搭配詞
hold on 堅持下去

holder [ˋholdɚ] n. 持有者、所有人 Track 2059
＊字尾-er有「者」的意思
例句 The runner used to be the 100 meters record holder.
這個跑者曾是百米紀錄保持人。

搭配詞
record holder 紀錄保持者

hop [hɑp] v. 跳過、單腳跳 Track 2060
例句 The rabbit hopped over to us.
那隻兔子朝我們跳過來。

hopeful [ˋhopfəl] adj. 有希望的 Track 2061
＊字尾-ful有「充滿」的意思
例句 We were hopeful that he would survive the earthquake.
我們都抱著希望，認為他會在地震中存活下來。

反義字
hopeless 沒有希望的

hound [haʊnd] n. 獵犬、有癮的人 Track 2062
例句 The hound followed his master everywhere.
那隻獵犬跟著主人到處去。

易混淆字
haunt 纏住（某人）

hug [hʌg] v. 抱、緊抱 Track 2063
例句 The mother gave her son a big hug as soon as she saw him.
那個媽媽一看到兒子，立刻大力擁抱他。

同義字
embrace

hunt [hʌnt] v. 獵取、狩獵 Track 2064
例句 He's constantly hunting for power.
他一直汲汲營營於獲取權力。

搭配詞
hunt for 獵取……

hurdle [ˋhɝdl] n. 障礙物、跨欄 Track 2065

例句 He won the championship in the hurdle race.
他贏得跨欄賽跑的冠軍。

搭配詞 hurdle race 跨欄賽跑

initial [ɪˋnɪʃəl] adj. 開始的 Track 2066

例句 Her initial reaction to his response was astonishment.
對於他的回應，她一開始的反應是很驚訝。

jog [dʒɑg] v. 慢跑 Track 2067

例句 He goes jogging every morning and practices tennis once in a while. 他每天清晨固定慢跑，偶爾練一下網球。

搭配詞 go jogging 去慢跑

jump [dʒʌmp] v. 跳躍、跳動 Track 2068

例句 She jumped up and down with joy when she learned she got admitted to Yale University.
她得知被耶魯大學錄取時，開心地跳來跳去。

kick [kɪk] v. 踢 Track 2069

例句 The game kicked off at 6 pm. 比賽在晚上6點已開始了。

搭配詞 kick off 開球、開始

kite [kaɪt] n. 風箏 Track 2070

例句 The park is a good place for flying kites.
公園是個放風箏的好地方。

搭配詞 fly a kite 放風箏

knock [nɑk] v. 敲、擊 Track 2071

例句 Please knock on the door before you come in.
請在進來前先敲門。

搭配詞 knock on the door 敲門

lift [lɪft] v. 舉起 Track 2072

例句 He gave her a lift after work. 他下班時載她一程。

搭配詞 give sb a lift 載某人一程

limit [ˋlɪmɪt] n. 限度、極限 Track 2073

例句 Be careful! You have exceeded the speed limit.
請小心！你超過速限了。

搭配詞 speed limit 速限

lose [luz] v. 遺失、失去 Track 2074

例句 She lost her face when she was humiliated by her husband in front of the public. 她在公眾場合被丈夫羞辱，感到很丟臉。

搭配詞 lose face 丟臉

loser [ˋluzɚ] n. 失敗者 ＊字尾-er有「者」的意思 Track 2075

例句 It's not shameful to be a loser in the contest.
成為比賽中的失敗者，也沒什麼好可恥的。

反義字
winner 贏家

loss [lɔs] n. 損失 Track 2076

例句 He was completely at a loss when he got the axe.
他失業時，完全不知所措。

搭配詞
be at a loss 不知所措

marathon [ˋmærə͵θɑn] n. 馬拉松 Track 2077

例句 Thousands of people take part in this marathon.
有上千個人參加這場馬拉松。

massage [məˋsɑʒ] n./v. 按摩 Track 2078

例句 She massaged her left leg to ease the cramping.
她按摩自己的左腳以減輕抽筋的情形。

易混淆字
message 信息

match [mætʃ] v. 與……相配 Track 2079

例句 Can you help me find a skirt to match this shirt?
你可以幫我找一條和這件衣服相配的裙子嗎？

medal [ˋmɛdḷ] n. 獎章 Track 2080

例句 He won the gold medal in the Olympic.
他在奧林匹克勇奪金牌。

搭配詞
gold medal 金牌

morale [məˋræl] n. 士氣 Track 2081

例句 The increase of salary has significantly boost the morale of the staff.
加薪讓工作人員的士氣大振。

搭配詞
boost morale 提振士氣

movable [ˋmuvəbḷ] adj. 可移動的 Track 2082
＊字尾-able有「可以、能」的意思

例句 He has a box of toy soldiers with movable arms and legs.
他有一箱手腳可以移動的玩具士兵。

move [muv] v. 移動、搬 Track 2083

例句 I haven't heard from him since he moved to another city.
自從他搬到另一座城市，我就沒有他的消息了。

反義字
stop 停止

movement [ˋmuvmənt] n. 運動、活動、移動 Track 2084
＊字尾-ment有轉變為名詞之意

例句 The environmental movement has successfully raised public awareness of global warming.
這個環保運動成功喚起大眾注意全球暖化的現象。

搭配詞
environmental movement
環保運動

pace [pes] n. 步伐 ◀Track 2085

例句 The patient recovered at a slow pace.
這個病患復原的步調很緩慢。

pat [pæt] v. 輕拍 ◀Track 2086

例句 He patted the dog on the head. 他輕拍狗的頭。

易混淆字
pet 寵物

pitch [pɪtʃ] v. 投擲 ◀Track 2087

例句 The teacher asked us to pitch the ball as far as possible.
老師請我們把球盡量投擲得遠一點。

反義字
catch 抓住

point [pɔɪnt] ◀Track 2088
n. 尖端、點、要點、（比賽中所得的）分數

例句 The main point of his speech was that he would put America's interests first. 他的演講要點就是美國利益至上。

搭配詞
main point 重點

punch [pʌntʃ] v. 以拳頭重擊 ◀Track 2089

例句 Justin punched the man on his face.
賈斯汀打了那個男人一拳。

race [res] n. 種族、比賽 ◀Track 2090

例句 Let's have a race and see who gets to school first.
我們來比賽看誰先到學校。

relay [ˋrɪle]/[rɪˋle] n. 接力（賽） ◀Track 2091

例句 All students will participate in the relay race except John.
所有學生都會參加接力賽，除了約翰以外。

regional [ˋridʒənl̩] adj. 區域性的 ◀Track 2092
＊字尾-al有轉變為形容詞之意

例句 I am glad to know that your team won the regional matches.
我很高興知道你們隊贏了區賽。

rest [rɛst] n. 休息 ◀Track 2093

例句 Why don't you take a rest while the baby is sleeping?
為什麼不趁寶寶睡覺時休息一下呢？

搭配詞
take a rest 休息

ride [raɪd] v. 騎、乘 ◀Track 2094

例句 I rode a scooter around Bali for several weeks.
我好幾個星期都騎機車繞著巴里島玩。

搭配詞
ride a scooter 騎機車

rotation [ro`teʃən] n. 旋轉 ◀Track 2095

＊字尾-tion有轉變為名詞的意思

例句 It is the earth's rotation that enables us to see the sun rise and set.
是因為地球旋轉，我們才能夠看到日升日落。

搭配詞 earth's rotation 地球自轉

rotate [ro`tet] v. 旋轉、輪流 ◀Track 2096

例句 We rotate positions when playing volleyball.
我們在打排球時會旋轉換位置。

搭配詞 merry-go-round 旋轉木馬

rock [rɑk] n./v. 搖動 ◀Track 2097

例句 He likes both rock music and classical music.
他喜歡搖滾樂和古典音樂。

搭配詞 rock music 搖滾樂

roll [rol] v. 滾動、捲 ◀Track 2098

例句 The money rolled in after the restaurant became famous.
那家餐廳出名後，生意就滾滾而來了。

搭配詞 roll in 大量湧進

rule [rul] n. 規則 ◀Track 2099

例句 The player broke the rule and got a red card from the referee.
這名球員違反規則，被裁判舉紅牌。

run [rʌn] v. 跑、運轉 ◀Track 2100

例句 He ran after the car, yelling and screaming.
他一邊大吼大叫、 一邊跑在那台車後面。

搭配詞 run after 跑在……後面

runner [`rʌnɚ] n. 跑者 ＊字尾-er有「者」的意思 ◀Track 2101

例句 The runner was exhausted after jogging for hours.
那名跑者跑了好幾個小時後，已經很累了。

shake [ʃek] v. 搖、發抖 ◀Track 2102

例句 The leaders shook hands when they first met at the summit.
兩位領袖在高峰會初次見面時，彼此握手致意。

搭配詞 shake hands 握手

shove [ʃʌv] v. 推 ◀Track 2103

例句 He shoved his friend into the lake as a joke.
他開玩笑把他朋友推進湖裡。

反義字 pull 拉

shun [ʃʌn] v. 避開、躲避 ◀Track 2104

例句 After the scandal, he was shunned by his wife and friends.
他爆發醜聞後，妻子和朋友都躲著他。

同義字 avoid

skate [sket] v. 溜冰、滑冰 Track 2105

例句 She enjoys ice skating very much. 她很喜歡溜冰。

搭配詞
ice skating 溜冰

ski [ski] v. 滑雪 Track 2106

例句 It doesn't snow here, so most people have never gone skiing in their lives. 這裡不下雪，所以大部分的人一輩子都沒滑雪過。

skinny [ˋskɪnɪ] adj. 皮包骨的 Track 2107

例句 I don't know why a skinny girl like her would still want to lose weight. 我不知道為什麼像她這樣皮包骨的女孩還會想減重。

slope [slop] n. 坡度、斜面 Track 2108

例句 There is an artificial ski slope in the village.
村內有一個人工的滑雪坡。

snare [snɛr] n. 陷阱、羅網 Track 2109

例句 I'm afraid that he has fallen into a snare laid by his enemy.
我擔心他掉入敵人設下的陷阱中了。

soar [sor] v. 上升、往上飛 Track 2110

例句 Although he was born with cerebral palsy, he soared higher than his parents had expected.
他雖然出生有腦性麻痺，但他的成就比他雙親預期得好很多。

易混淆字
sour 酸的

soccer [ˋsakɚ] n. 足球 Track 2111

例句 The coach is teaching a group of kids how to play soccer.
這名足球教練正在教一群小孩踢足球。

搭配詞
play soccer 踢足球

speak [spik] v. 說話、講話 Track 2112

例句 Don't speak ill of your former boss in a job interview.
在面試時別講你前任老闆的壞話。

搭配詞
speak ill of sb
講（某人）的壞話

speech [spitʃ] n. 言談、演講 Track 2113

例句 The candidate is giving a speech in the town square.
候選人正在市中心廣場演講。

搭配詞
give a speech 演講

sport [sport] n. 運動 Track 2114

例句 He likes all kinds of sports, especially baseball.
他喜歡各式各樣的運動，尤其是棒球。

a b c d e f g h i j k l m n o p q r s t u v w x y z

sportsmanship [ˋsportsmən͵ʃɪp] ◀Track 2115
n. 運動員精神
例句 The coach told them to take defeat with sportsmanship.
教練要他們以運動員精神接受失敗。

sprint [sprɪnt] v./n. 短距離賽跑、全力奔跑 ◀Track 2116
例句 You must sprint to the finish line. 你得全力奔跑到終點。

易混淆字
spirit 精神

stadium [ˋstedɪəm] n. 室外運動場 ◀Track 2117
例句 Tens of thousands of people crowded into the baseball stadium to see the game. 上萬人為了看比賽擠進了棒球場。

搭配詞
baseball stadium 棒球場

staff [stæf] n. 棒、竿子、全體人員 ◀Track 2118
例句 All the staff members are required to attend the meeting.
全體人員都必須出席這場會議。

搭配詞
staff member 員工

stand [stænd] v. 站起、立起 ◀Track 2119
例句 The audience stood up to applaud the performers.
觀眾們站起來為表演者鼓掌。

搭配詞
stand up 起立

strength [strɛŋθ] n. 力量、強度 ◀Track 2120
例句 It surprised everyone that our dainty little secretary had the strength to move the refrigerator.
我們弱小的秘書竟有力量移動冰箱，大家都嚇了一跳。

strengthen [ˋstrɛŋθən] v. 加強、增強 ◀Track 2121
＊字尾-en有「使」的意思
例句 You need to strengthen your skills if you want to be a professional.
你想成為職業專家的話，能力還需要增強。

反義字
weaken 削弱

stretch [strɛtʃ] v. 伸展、延伸 ◀Track 2122
例句 The frog stretched out its tongue to capture the insect.
那隻青蛙伸出舌頭要抓昆蟲。

strike [straɪk] v. 打擊 ◀Track 2123
例句 The thunder struck down the tree. 閃電把那棵樹打倒了。

搭配詞
strike down 擊倒

surf [sɝf] v. 衝浪、乘浪 ◀Track 2124
例句 My brother is good at swimming as well as surfing.
我哥哥不但擅長游泳，也很會衝浪。

sweat [swɛt] v. 流汗 ◀Track 2125

例句 He was sweating hard after the match.
比賽完後，他流汗得很厲害。

swim [swɪm] n./v. 游、游泳 ◀Track 2126

例句 It's really hot today. Let's go for a swim in the pool.
今天很熱，我們去泳池游泳吧。

搭配詞 go for a swim 去游泳

table tennis [ˋtebḷˋtɛnɪs] n. 乒乓球 ◀Track 2127

例句 The coach explained the rules of table tennis to us.
教練向我們解釋乒乓球的規則。

同義字 ping-pong

team [tim] n. 隊 ◀Track 2128

例句 The manager asked all his team members to respect each other.
經理要求他的團隊成員要互相尊重。

搭配詞 team member 隊員

tennis [ˋtɛnɪs] n. 網球 ◀Track 2129

例句 He's a professional tennis player. 他是職業網球選手。

搭配詞 tennis player 網球選手

tent [tɛnt] n. 帳篷 ◀Track 2130

例句 The campers pitched a tent near the lake.
這些露營的人在湖邊搭起了帳篷。

搭配詞 pitch a tent 搭帳篷

throw [θro] v. 投、擲、扔 ◀Track 2131

例句 He threw out the garbage on the street.
他在街道上扔掉垃圾。

搭配詞 throw out 扔掉

toss [tɔs] v. 投擲、搖盪、輾轉 ◀Track 2132

例句 Let's toss the coin to decide who will do the dishes.
我們來投擲錢幣，決定誰來洗碗。

同義字 throw

tournament [ˋtɜnəmənt] n. 競賽、比賽 ◀Track 2133

＊字尾-ment有轉變為名詞之意

例句 The tournament is not only open to the professionals but also the amateurs. 這場比賽不但開放給職業人士參加，也歡迎業餘人士。

triumphant [traɪˋʌmfənt] adj. 勝利的、成功的 ◀Track 2134

例句 Their triumphant smiles revealed their pride in their son.
他們勝利的笑容展現出他們對兒子的驕傲。

同義字 victorious

trophy [ˋtrofɪ] n. 戰利品、獎品、獎盃 Track 2135

例句 He won many trophies in his athletic career.
他在職業選手生涯中得過許多獎。

trot [trɑt] v. 小跑步 Track 2136

例句 The horse trotted over to his owner.
那匹馬小跑步到主人身邊。

tug-of-war [tʌg əv wɔr] n. 拔河 Track 2137

例句 The tug-of-war was the last and the best one of this series of sports competitions.
拔河是這一系列運動比賽的最後也最好玩的一個比賽。

turn [tɝn] n./v. 旋轉、轉動 Track 2138

例句 The neighbors take turns to clean the community center.
鄰居們輪流打掃社區中心。

搭配詞
take turns 輪流

underneath [ˏʌndɚˋniθ] adv. 在下面 Track 2139

＊字首under-有「下方的」之意

例句 There is a dog hiding underneath the car. 有隻狗藏在車子下。

unfold [ʌnˋfold] v. 攤開、打開 Track 2140

＊字首un-有「不、反」之意

例句 He unfolded the letter and read it for his mother.
他把信攤開，念給媽媽聽。

uphold [ʌpˋhold] v. 支持、支撐 Track 2141

＊字首up-有「上」之意

例句 We need to uphold these cultural customs in case they die out.
我們必須要支持著這些文化習俗，以免它們失傳了。

反義字
subvert 推翻

victorious [vɪkˋtorɪəs] adj. 得勝的、凱旋的 Track 2142

＊字尾-ous有轉變為形容詞之意

例句 Their victorious return was welcomed by the whole nation.
他們凱旋歸來，受到整個國家的歡迎。

搭配詞
victorious return 凱旋歸來

victor [ˋvɪktɚ] n. 勝利者、戰勝者 Track 2143

＊字尾-or有「者」的意思

例句 I bet my brother will be the victor in the contest.
我賭我弟弟會在比賽中成為勝利者。

victory [ˋvɪktərɪ] n. 勝利 Track 2144

例句 Let's hold a party to celebrate our victory.
我們來辦派對慶祝勝利吧。

volleyball [ˋvalɪ͵bɔl] n. 排球 Track 2145

例句 They played beach volleyball after the party.
派對結束後，他們玩起沙灘排球。

搭配詞
beach volleyball 沙灘排球

win [wɪn] v. 獲勝、贏 Track 2146

例句 If we work together, it will be a win-win situation.
如果我們合作的話，會是雙贏局面。

搭配詞
win-win situation 雙贏局面

winner [ˋwɪnɚ] n. 勝利者、優勝者 Track 2147

＊字尾-er有「者」的意思

例句 I think John will be the winner again. 我想約翰又會成為優勝者。

反義字
loser 輸家

wrestle [ˋrɛsl̩] v. 摔角、搏鬥 Track 2148

例句 He stayed up late to watch sumo-wrestling matches.
他熬夜看相撲比賽。

搭配詞
sumo-wrestling 相撲

yoga [ˋjogə] n. 瑜伽 Track 2149

例句 I never miss my yoga lesson, no matter how busy I am.
我從來不錯過瑜伽課，就算我再忙也一樣。

搭配詞
yoga lesson 瑜珈課

NOTE

Test 08 關鍵英單總測驗第8回

以下測驗題皆出自書中第八回「**和運動有關的單字**」，快來檢視自己的學習成果吧！

一、選擇題

1. The athlete started rigorous training 6 months before the ____ .
   (A) massage
   (B) sweat
   (C) runner
   (D) marathon

2. Although the team didn't win the champion in the World Cup, they showed great ____ and teamwork.
   (A) sportsmanship
   (B) hopeful
   (C) sprint
   (D) bet

3. Oliver Kahn,the sturdy German ____, is the first goalkeeper to win the Golden Ball award as the World Cup's best player.
   (A) defense (B) jog
   (C) challenge (D) defeat

4. The school children are playing ___ ball on the playground.
   (A) dodge
   (B) jump
   (C) punch
   (D) underneath

5. After hours of intensive training, he finally took a ____ and drink some water.
   (A) rest (B) lift
   (C) rotation (D) hunt

6. She learned how to ___ a horse when she was in high school.
   (A) run
   (B) hit
   (C) ride
   (D) trot

7. Trans fatty acids are not ____and can cause many heart diseases.
   (A) skinny
   (B) equal
   (C) victorious
   (D) healthy

8. Michelle Kwan won many______ throughout her figure skating career.
   (A) trophies
   (B) paces
   (C) limits
   (D) baskets

9. Ms. Wood is 70 years old but still very _____.
   (A) relay
   (B) energetic
   (C) yoga
   (D) competitor

10. He ____ over to pick up the ball.
    (A) throw
    (B) bent
    (C) hold
    (D) bat

二、克漏字測驗

Born in the County of Los Angeles, Jeremy Lin started playing __1__ at a young age. He became a top player at Palo Alto High School, where he was named the __2__ captain during his senior year.

However, life on the court wasn't always easy. Lin faced racism and disrespect because of his Asian origins, but he didn't let any hateful comments affect him. Lin proved that he was a force to be reckoned with after he got picked up by the New York Knicks. In 2012, he took the __3__ world by storm by helping the team secure a string of __4__ , and sparked a media sensation called "Linsanity."

Lin's story has inspired many across the globe. His willpower and __5__ show that it is possible to achieve a dream if one works hard and never gives up.

1. (A) arena
   (B) basketball
   (C) canoe
   (D) balance

2. (A) team
   (B) medal
   (C) hurdle
   (D) dodge

3. (A) coach
   (B) sports
   (C) stadium
   (D) energy

4. (A) losers
   (B) losses
   (C) morale
   (D) wins

5. (A) stretch
   (B) tug-of-war
   (C) spirit
   (D) relay

關鍵英單總測驗第8回
中譯與解答

一、選擇題

1. 這名運動員在馬拉松競賽前6個月就展開嚴格的訓練。
(A) 按摩
(B) 流汗
(C) 跑步者
(D) 馬拉松

2. 雖然這支隊伍並未贏得世界盃冠軍，他們仍展現絕佳的運動員精神和團隊合作默契。
(A) 運動員精神
(B) 有希望的
(C) 短跑競賽
(D) 打賭

3. 奧利佛卡恩的防守能力非常堅固，成為首位榮獲世界盃最佳球員的守門員。
(A) 防守員
(B) 慢跑
(C) 挑戰
(D) 挫敗

4. 學校學生正在操場上玩躲避球。
(A) 躲避
(B) 跳躍
(C) 重擊
(D) 在下方的

5. 他接受好幾小時的密集訓練後，終於休息一下並喝點水。
(A) 休息
(B) 舉起
(C) 旋轉
(D) 打獵

6. 她在高中時學會如何騎馬。
(A) 跑步
(B) 撞擊
(C) 騎乘
(D) 小跑步

7. 反式脂肪並不健康，並會帶來很多心臟病。
(A) 皮包骨的
(B) 平等的
(C) 勝利的
(D) 健康的

8. 關穎珊在花式溜冰的職業生涯中，獲得許多獎盃。
(A) 獎盃
(B) 步伐
(C) 極限
(D) 籃子

9. 伍德女士已70歲了，但仍精力充沛。
(A) 接力賽
(B) 有活力的
(C) 瑜伽
(D) 競爭者

10. 他彎下腰撿球。
(A) 扔掉
(B) 彎下
(C) 把握
(D) 擊球

二、克漏字測驗

林書豪出生於加州洛杉磯郡，從小就開始打籃球。他就讀帕羅奧圖高中時已成為該校頂尖的球員，在高三被推派為球隊隊長。

不過他在球場並非一帆風順，他曾因亞洲血統而遭遇種族歧視與輕蔑。他被尼克隊簽下後，開始證明他是不可忽視的球員。2012年，他幫助尼克隊奪得一連串的勝利，風靡了整個體壇，並引發媒體「林來瘋」的現象。

林書豪的故事激勵了世界各地的人，他的意志力和精神證明只要努力、永不放棄，夢想就可能成真。

1.
(A) 競技場
(B) 籃球
(C) 獨木舟
(D) 平衡

2.
(A) 隊伍
(B) 獎牌
(C) 障礙
(D) 躲避

3.
(A) 教練
(B) 運動
(C) 體育館
(D) 精力

4.
(A) 輸家
(B) 損失
(C) 士氣
(D) 獲勝

5.
(A) 伸展
(B) 拔河
(C) 精神
(D) 接力賽

一、選擇題

1.(D) 2.(A) 3.(A) 4.(A) 5.(A)
6.(C) 7.(D) 8.(A) 9.(B) 10.(B)

二、克漏字測驗

1.(B) 2.(A) 3.(B)
4.(D) 5.(C)

Unit 09 和動植物有關的單字

多益測驗的命題強調生活化與實用性，學會這些與「動植物」有關的單字，不僅能讓你在多益考場上所向披靡，在日常生活上也可以靈活運用喔！

水果可以這麼說

- **Mango shaved ice is my comfort food during summer.**
  芒果剉冰是在夏季最讓我感到療癒的食物。
- **Pineapple cakes are the best sellers in this bakery.**
  鳳梨酥是這家烘焙坊賣得最好的產品。
- **Strawberry is my favorite fruit.**
  草莓是我最喜歡的水果。

健康蔬食可以這麼說

- **She is a vegetarian. That's why she doesn't use any kind of animal product.**
  她是個素食者。這就是為什麼她不使用任何動物產品。
- **He insists on not using pesticide on his crops.**
  他堅持不在他的作物上用農藥。

去逛動物園可以這麼說

- **The chimpanzee is curious about what the zookeeper is doing.**
  那隻黑猩猩很好奇動物飼養員在做什麼。
- **The elephant use its trunk to grab food.**
  大象用牠的象鼻來抓取食物。

家養寵物可以這麼說

- **My pet parrot likes to imitate the sound of the door bell.**
  我的寵物鸚鵡喜歡模仿門鈴的聲音。
- **I adopted a puppy from the shelter yesterday.**
  我昨天從收容所領養了一隻小狗。

生態保育可以這麼說

- **We should protect this tropical forest, the habitat of various rare species.**
  我們應該保護這片作為多種稀有物種棲息地的熱帶雨林。
- **Wildlife rescue center is dedicated to raising orphaned and injured animals.**
  野生動物救援中心致力於養育失去親族照顧或受傷的動物。

Unit 09 和動植物有關的單字

alligator [ˋæləˏgetɚ] n. 短吻鱷 ◀ Track 2150

例句 The alligator population has declined dramatically in this swamp.
這個沼澤區的短吻鱷數量大幅度銳減。

---

almond [ˋɑmənd] n. 杏仁、杏樹 ◀ Track 2151

例句 For vegetarians, almond milk is a good alternative to cow's milk.
對於素食者來說，杏仁奶是取代牛乳的好選擇。

搭配詞 almond milk 杏仁茶

---

animal [ˋænəm!] n. 動物 ◀ Track 2152

例句 Owls are nocturnal animals. 貓頭鷹是夜行動物。

搭配詞 nocturnal animal 夜行動物

---

ant [ænt] n. 螞蟻 ◀ Track 2153

例句 The company developed an effective natural repellent for keeping ants away from the house.
這家公司研發有效的天然驅逐劑，讓螞蟻遠離屋內。

---

ape [ep] n. 猿 ◀ Track 2154

例句 The ape peered through the bars at us.
那隻猿猴從鐵桿間偷看我們。

---

apple [ˋæp!] n. 蘋果 ◀ Track 2155

例句 Let's make some apple pies for dessert.
我們來做蘋果派當甜點。

搭配詞 apple pie 蘋果派

---

ass [æs] n. 驢子、笨蛋、屁股 ◀ Track 2156

例句 The man is such a smart-ass. He always criticizes people without realizing his own problems.
那個男人很自以為是，總愛批評人，卻不知道自己有問題。

搭配詞 smart-ass 自以為是的人

---

bamboo [bæmˋbu] n. 竹子 ◀ Track 2157

例句 Bamboo shoots can be used in a variety of dishes.
竹筍可以被用在很多的料理。

搭配詞 bamboo shoot 竹筍

banana [bə`nænə] n. 香蕉 Track 2158

例句 Do you like bananas, pears, or apples?
你喜歡香蕉、梨子還是蘋果？

bark [bɑrk] v. （狗）吠叫 Track 2159

例句 The dog is barking at the drug trafficker.
那隻狗正在對一名走私毒品犯吠叫。

搭配詞 bark at 對……吠叫

beak [bik] n. 鳥嘴 Track 2160

例句 The owl pecked at me with its beak.
那隻貓頭鷹用牠的鳥嘴啄我。

易混淆字 beat 打、擊

bear [bɛr] n. 熊 Track 2161

例句 This teddy bear features moving limbs and a lovely smile.
這隻玩具熊的四肢可以轉動，而且笑容很可愛。

搭配詞 teddy bear 玩具熊

bee [bi] n. 蜜蜂 Track 2162

例句 My mother is as busy as a bee. 我媽媽和蜜蜂一樣忙碌。

搭配詞 busy as a bee 跟蜜蜂一樣忙碌

beetle [`bitl̩] n. 甲蟲 Track 2163

例句 A longhorn beetle has long antennae.
長角牛甲蟲有長長的觸角。

搭配詞 longhorn beetle 天牛；長角牛甲蟲

berry [`bɛrɪ] n. 漿果、莓 Track 2164

例句 She spread some berry jam on the toast.
她在吐司上塗了一些莓果醬。

搭配詞 berry jam 莓果醬

bird [bɝd] n. 鳥 Track 2165

例句 She is an early bird while her husband is a night owl.
她每天很早起，而她先生卻是個夜貓子。

搭配詞 early bird 早起的人

bite [baɪt] n. 咬、一口 Track 2166

例句 Let's grab a quick bite before the meeting.
我們在開會前先快點吃一口東西吧。

搭配詞 grab a bite 吃點東西

bloom [blum] v./n. 開花 Track 2167

例句 The flowers are all in bloom now. 這些花現在都開花了。

搭配詞 be in full bloom 開花
反義字 fade 凋謝

blossom [ˋblɑsəm] n. 開花、生長茂盛 Track 2168

例句 The cherry trees are in blossom. 櫻花樹正處於開花旺季。

搭配詞 in blossom 正在盛開

breed [brid] v. 生育、繁殖 Track 2169

例句 The Antarctic winter is the breeding season for emperor penguins. 南極冬天是國王企鵝的繁殖期。

搭配詞 breeding season 繁殖期

bud [bʌd] n. 芽、花蕾 Track 2170

例句 He has very sensitive taste buds. 他的味蕾很敏鋭。

搭配詞 taste bud 味蕾

buffalo [ˋbʌflo] n. 水牛、野牛 Track 2171

例句 There were lots of buffaloes in South Africa years ago. 多年前，南非有很多野牛。

易混淆字 baffle 阻礙

bug [bʌg] n. 小蟲、毛病、竊聽器、錯誤 Track 2172

例句 The software bug caused the fighter jet to miss its target. 這個軟體錯誤導致戰機無法瞄準目標。

搭配詞 software bug 軟體錯誤

bull [bul] n. 公牛 Track 2173

例句 The bull charged at the intruder. 那頭公牛朝著入侵者猛衝過去。

反義字 cow 母牛

bunch [bʌntʃ] n. 束、群、捆 Track 2174

例句 We need a bunch of carrots and some onions to make this special soup. 我們需要一捆紅蘿蔔和一些洋蔥來製作這道特別的湯。

易混淆字 brunch 早午餐

bush [buʃ] n. 灌木叢 Track 2175

例句 Please get to the point. Don't beat around the bush. 請說重點，不要拐彎抹角的説。

搭配詞 beat around the bush 拐彎抹角的説

butterfly [ˋbʌtɚ͵flaɪ] n. 蝴蝶 Track 2176

例句 The "butterfly effect" means small changes can have huge effects. 蝴蝶效應是指微小的改變可能造成巨大的後果。

搭配詞 butterfly effect 蝴蝶效應（「物物相關」的因果效應）

buzz [bʌz] n. 嗡嗡聲 Track 2177

例句 We can hear the bees buzzing from here. 我們可以從這裡聽到蜜蜂的嗡嗡聲。

cactus [ˋkæktəs] n. 仙人掌 Track 2178

例句 I water this cactus once a month.
我一個月替這棵仙人掌澆一次花。

calf [kæf] n. 小牛 Track 2179

例句 After the calf got stolen, the farmer suffered a loss of 3000 dollars.
小牛被偷後，農夫損失了3000元。

camel [ˋkæml̩] n. 駱駝 Track 2180

例句 When his girlfriend left him, it was the last straw on the camel's back. 他被女友甩了時，那是壓垮他的最後一根稻草。

易混淆字
caramel 焦糖

capture [ˋkæptʃɚ] v. 捉住、吸引 Track 2181

例句 The news captured everybody's attention.
這個消息吸引了大家的注意。

搭配詞
capture sb's attention
吸引某人的注意

carnation [kɑrˋneʃən] n. 康乃馨 Track 2182

例句 Carnations are used to express our love for our mothers.
康乃馨用來表達我們對母親的愛。

carp [kɑrp] n. 鯉魚 Track 2183

例句 Catching carp in the lake is easy for me.
在湖裡抓鯉魚對我來說很簡單。

cat [kæt] n. 貓、貓科動物 Track 2184

例句 The cat litter is made of silica. 這牌子的貓砂是由矽石做的。

搭配詞
cat litter 貓砂

catch [kætʃ] v. 捕捉、捕獲物 Track 2185

例句 He studied hard and finally caught up with the class.
他很用功唸書，最後終於趕上班上的進度了。

搭配詞
catch up 趕上

caterpillar [ˋkætɚ͵pɪlɚ] n. 毛毛蟲 Track 2186

例句 The toxic caterpillar can cause allergy and vomiting.
這種毒毛毛蟲可能會導致過敏和嘔吐。

搭配詞
toxic caterpillar 毒毛毛蟲

cattle [ˋkætl̩] n. 小牛 Track 2187

例句 The cattle have disappeared from the shed.
小牛們都從牛棚消失了。

補充
heifer 小乳牛

celery [ˋsɛlərɪ] n. 芹菜 ◀Track 2188
例句 He can't stand the taste of celery juice.
他受不了芹菜汁的味道。
搭配詞 celery juice 芹菜汁

cherry [ˋtʃɛrɪ] n. 櫻桃、櫻木 ◀Track 2189
例句 They went to Japan during the cherry blossom season.
他們在日本櫻花季期間去日本。
搭配詞 cherry blossom 櫻花

chick [tʃɪk] n. 小雞 ◀Track 2190
例句 Her chicks are running about the farm.
她的小雞繞著農場跑。

chicken [ˋtʃɪkɪn] n. 雞、雞肉 ◀Track 2191
例句 Would you care for some fried chicken? 你想來點炸雞嗎？
搭配詞 fried chicken 炸雞

chimpanzee [ˌtʃɪmpænˋzi] n. 黑猩猩 ◀Track 2192
例句 It is said that chimpanzees can develop social skills like human beings. 據說黑猩猩能像人類一樣發展社交技巧。

clam [klæm] n. 蛤蠣、蚌 ◀Track 2193
例句 The artwork was decorated with clam shells.
這件藝術品使用蚌殼來裝飾點綴。
搭配詞 clam shell 蚌殼

claw [klɔ] n. 爪 ◀Track 2194
例句 The cat sank her claws in my leg.
那隻貓把爪子插進我的腿了。
易混淆字 craw 動物的胃

clover [ˋklovɚ] n. 苜蓿、幸運草 ◀Track 2195
例句 I saw a four-leaf clover when hiking last week.
我上禮拜登山的時候看到一株四葉幸運草。

cock [kɑk] n. 公雞 ◀Track 2196
例句 He likes to imitate the cock crowing in the morning.
他喜歡一早學公雞叫。

cockroach [ˋkɑkˌrotʃ] n. 蟑螂 ◀Track 2197
例句 I hate to see cockroaches in my room.
我討厭在我房間裡看到蟑螂。
縮寫 roach

cocoon [kəˋkun] n. 繭 ◀ Track 2198

例句 Many cocoons can be found in the forest in this season.
在這個季節，森林裡可以找到不少繭。

---

coral [ˋkorəl] n. 珊瑚 ◀ Track 2199

例句 Coral reefs around the world are dying due to climate change.
全球珊瑚礁因為氣候變遷，存活下來的越來越少了。

搭配詞 coral reef 珊瑚礁

---

corn [kɔrn] n. 玉米 ◀ Track 2200

例句 We can use corn to feed our chicks.
我們可以用玉米來餵雞。

---

cow [kaʊ] n. 母牛、乳牛 ◀ Track 2201

例句 I feed these cows twice a day. 我一天餵這些牛兩次。

反義字 bull 公牛

---

crab [kræb] n. 蟹 ◀ Track 2202

例句 When a hermit crab grows too big, it will find a bigger shell and crawl into it.
當寄居蟹長太大時，牠會找個大一點的殼並爬進去住。

搭配詞 hermit crab 寄居蟹

---

creature [ˋkritʃɚ] n. 生物、動物 ◀ Track 2203

例句 What is that strange black-and-white creature over there?
那邊那個奇怪的黑白顏色的生物是什麼？

---

creep [krip] v. 爬、戰慄 ◀ Track 2204

例句 The tortoise crept along slowly.
那隻烏龜慢慢地爬。

---

cricket [ˋkrɪkɪt] n. 蟋蟀 ◀ Track 2205

例句 This kind of cricket can only be found in my hometown.
這種蟋蟀只有在我的家鄉才找得到。

---

crocodile [ˋkrɑkə͵daɪl] n. 鱷魚 ◀ Track 2206

例句 She shed crocodile tears when he was in trouble.
他陷入麻煩時，她假惺惺的掉了幾滴淚。

搭配詞 crocodile tears 假慈悲

---

crop [krɑp] n. 農作物 ◀ Track 2207

例句 They are too busy harvesting crops to talk to us.
他們忙著收成農作物，沒空跟我們聊天。

crow [kro] n. 烏鴉 ◀ Track 2208

例句 A crow kept cawing at me. 那隻烏鴉一直對我叫。

cultivate [ˋkʌltəˏvet] v. 耕種、培養 ◀ Track 2209

例句 He enjoys cultivating new hobbies.
他喜歡培養新的興趣。

daffodil [ˋdæfədɪl] n. 黃水仙 ◀ Track 2210

例句 She picked a daffodil from the hill.
她從山丘上摘了一株黃水仙。

damage [ˋdæmɪdʒ] n. 損害、損失 ◀ Track 2211

例句 The tsunami caused a lot of damage to the city.
那次海嘯對這座城市造成不少損失。

搭配詞 cause damage to 對……造成傷害

deer [dɪr] n. 鹿 ◀ Track 2212

例句 I nearly ran into a spotted deer yesterday.
我昨天差點遇見一隻梅花鹿。

搭配詞 spotted deer 梅花鹿

dinosaur [ˋdaɪnəˏsɔr] n. 恐龍 ◀ Track 2213

例句 The dinosaurs disappeared on the Earth in ancient times.
恐龍在古時候就從地球上消失了。

dog [dɔg] n. 狗 ◀ Track 2214

例句 The police dog was shot dead in a mission.
那隻警犬在執勤時中彈殉職。

搭配詞 police dog 警犬

dolphin [ˋdɑlfɪn] n. 海豚 ◀ Track 2215

例句 Visitors enjoy watching the dolphins. 訪客們都喜歡看海豚。

donkey [ˋdɑnkɪ] n. 驢子、傻瓜 ◀ Track 2216

例句 He is as stupid as a donkey. 他和隻驢子一樣笨。

dove [dʌv] n. 鴿子 ◀ Track 2217

例句 How many doves are there in the cage? 籠子裡有多少隻鴿子？

同義字 pigeon

dragon [ˋdrægən] n. 龍 Track 2218

例句 Dragon Boat Festival is a national holiday in Taiwan.
在台灣，端午節是國定假日。

搭配詞 dragon boat 龍舟

dragonfly [ˋdrægənˏflaɪ] n. 蜻蜓 Track 2219

例句 The dragonflies usually come out in the evenings.
蜻蜓總是在傍晚出現。

duck [dʌk] n. 鴨子 Track 2220

例句 How many ducks are there in the zoo in total?
動物園總共有幾隻鴨子？

duckling [ˋdʌklɪŋ] n. 小鴨子 Track 2221

例句 The supermodel was an ugly duckling when she was a little girl.
這個超模小時候是醜小鴨。

搭配詞 ugly duckling 醜小鴨

eagle [ˋigḷ] n. 鷹 Track 2222

例句 The sniper was eagle-eyed and never missed his target.
那位狙擊手目光銳利，射擊從不失誤。

搭配詞 eagle-eyed 目光銳利的

eel [il] n. 鰻魚 Track 2223

例句 Eels are slippery and hard to catch. 鰻魚滑滑的，很難抓。

elephant [ˋɛləfənt] n. 大象 Track 2224

例句 Elephant tourism is considered animal cruelty.
騎大象的觀光被視為是虐待動物的行為。

搭配詞 elephant tourism
騎大象的觀光

evergreen [ˋɛvɚˏgrin] n. 常青樹 Track 2225

例句 There are many evergreens on the side of the street.
路邊有許多常青樹。

extinct [ɪkˋstɪŋkt] adj. 滅絕的 Track 2226

例句 The extinct volcano is a tourist spot. 這座死火山是觀光景點。

搭配詞 extinct volcano 死火山

fertile [ˋfɝtḷ] adj. 肥沃的、豐富的 Track 2227

例句 The farmers like to work on fertile lands.
這些農夫喜歡在肥沃的土地上工作。

搭配詞 fertile land 肥沃的土地

fertilizer [ˋfɝtḷaɪzɚ] n. 肥料、化學肥料 Track 2228

＊字尾-er有「者」的意思

例句 The liquid fertilizer will accelerate the growth of these tomatoes.
這個液態肥料能加速這些蕃茄的生長。

搭配詞 liquid fertilizer 液態肥料

---

fish [fɪʃ] n. 魚、魚類 Track 2229

例句 Sometimes I wish I were a fish. 有時候我真希望自己是魚。

---

flea [fli] n. 跳蚤 Track 2230

例句 I like to go shopping in the flea market.
我喜歡去跳蚤市場買東西。

搭配詞 flea market 跳蚤市場

---

flip [flɪp] v. 跳動、拍打、翻 Track 2231

例句 The politician flip-flopped on the issue.
這名政客對這項議題的態度反反覆覆。

搭配詞 flip-flop 舉棋不定、反反覆覆

---

flower [ˋflauɚ] n. 花 Track 2232

例句 I need to buy some flowers to decorate my house.
我得去買些花來裝飾我的家。

---

fly [flaɪ] n./v. 蒼蠅、飛行 Track 2233

例句 If I see a fly in my room, I will kill it immediately.
如果我在我房間看到一隻蒼蠅，我會立刻殺了牠。

---

forest [ˋfɔrɪst] n. 森林 Track 2234

例句 This is one of the most beautiful forest parks in the world.
這是世界最美的森林公園之一。

搭配詞 forest park 森林公園

---

fowl [faul] n. 家禽（雞、鴨等） Track 2235

例句 How about having roast fowl for dinner?
晚餐吃烤家禽如何呢？

同義字 poultry

---

fox [fɑks] n. 狐狸、狡猾的人 Track 2236

例句 The hunter took a long time to find the fox and its cubs.
那個獵人花了很長的時間才找到那隻狐狸和牠的孩子。

搭配詞 fox fur 狐皮

---

fragrance [ˋfregrəns] n. 芬香、芬芳 Track 2237

例句 The fragrance of flowers makes me happy.
花的香味讓我很開心。

搭配詞 flower fragrance 花香

a b c d e f g h i j k l m n o p q r s t u v w x y z

fragrant [ˋfregrənt] adj. 芳香的、愉快的 Track 2238

例句 The air in the park is warm and fragrant in spring.
春天時公園裡的空氣溫暖又芳香。

反義字 stinky 臭的

frog [frɑg] n. 蛙 Track 2239

例句 The tree frog hopped over to the other side of the pond.
那隻樹蛙跳到池塘的另一邊去了。

搭配詞 tree frog 樹蛙

frost [frɔst] n. 霜、冷淡 Track 2240

例句 The frost damaged all the crops in the fields and plants by the road.
那次結霜對田地裡的作物與路邊的植物都造成了損傷。

fruit [frut] n. 水果 Track 2241

例句 I'd like to have dried fruits and vegetables in my salad.
我喜歡沙拉裡有果乾與蔬菜。

搭配詞 dried fruit 果乾

fur [fɝ] n. 毛皮、軟皮 Track 2242

例句 Who gave you this mink fur coat?
是誰給你這件貂皮大衣的？

搭配詞 mink fur coat 貂皮大衣

genuine [ˋdʒɛnjuɪn] adj. 真正的、非假冒的 Track 2243

例句 She is a genuinely nice person. 她是個真正的好人。

反義字 false 虛假的

ginger [ˋdʒɪndʒɚ] n./v. 薑、使……有活力 Track 2244

例句 I'd like a glass of ginger beer, please.
我要點一杯薑汁啤酒。

搭配詞 ginger beer 薑汁啤酒

giraffe [dʒəˋræf] n. 長頸鹿 Track 2245

例句 Giraffes have very long eyelashes.
長頸鹿有長長的睫毛。

glow [glo] n. 熾熱、發光 Track 2246

例句 The light sticks glow in the dark.
這些螢光棒在黑暗中發光。

goat [got] n. 山羊 Track 2247

例句 What's the difference between a goat and a sheep?
山羊跟綿羊之間差別在哪呢？

goose [gus] n. 鵝 ◀Track 2248

例句 I saw a flock of geese at the lake of the park.
我看到一群鵝在公園的湖邊。

搭配詞 goose feather 鵝毛

gorilla [gəˋrɪlə] n. 大猩猩 ◀Track 2249

例句 A gorilla is more powerful than a monkey.
大猩猩比猴子更有力。

grape [grep] n. 葡萄、葡萄樹 ◀Track 2250

例句 Please buy some grape wine and bring it to me.
請買一些葡萄酒，帶回來給我。

搭配詞 grape wine 葡萄酒

grapefruit [ˋgrep͵frut] n. 葡萄柚 ◀Track 2251

例句 Don't eat grapefruit after taking pills. 吃藥後別吃葡萄柚。

搭配詞 grapefruit juice 葡萄柚汁

grass [græs] n. 草 ◀Track 2252

例句 There are many little stones in the grass.
草中有很多小石頭。

grasshopper [ˋgræs͵hɑpɚ] n. 蝗蟲、蚱蜢 ◀Track 2253

＊字尾-er有「者」的意思

例句 He brought a giant grasshopper to school.
他帶了一隻巨大的蝗蟲到學校。

grassy [græsɪ] adj. 多草的 ◀Track 2254

＊字尾-y有轉變為形容詞之意

例句 Let's slide down this grassy hill. 我們從這個草坡上滑下去吧。

搭配詞 grassy hill 草坡

ground [graʊnd] n. 地面、土地 ◀Track 2255

例句 Her chair broke, so she sat on the ground instead.
她的椅子壞了，所以她就改坐在地上了。

grow [gro] v. 種植、生長 ◀Track 2256

例句 It's hard to predict what he will become after he grows up.
很難預測他長大後會變成什麼樣子。

搭配詞 grow up 長大

guava [ˋgwɑvə] n. 芭樂 ◀Track 2257

例句 I prefer guava juice to grapefruit juice.
比起葡萄柚汁，我比較喜歡芭樂汁。

habitat [ˋhæbə͵tæt] n. 棲息地 Track 2258

例句 The area is the natural habitat for giant pandas.
這地區是大貓熊的自然棲息地。

搭配詞 natural habitat 自然棲息地

harvest [ˋhɑrvɪst] n. 收穫 Track 2259

例句 The farmers gathered and celebrated after the harvest.
那些農夫在收穫後集合慶祝。

hatch [hætʃ] v. 計畫、孵化 Track 2260

例句 I would like to know when the eggs will hatch.
我想知道這些蛋什麼時候才會孵化。

hawk [hɔk] n. 鷹 Track 2261

例句 The hawk is circling the sky looking for prey.
那隻鷹正在天上盤旋找尋獵物。

hay [he] n. 乾草 Track 2262

例句 It's late. Let's hit the hay. 天色已晚，該睡覺了。

搭配詞 hit the hay 去睡覺

hedge [hɛdʒ] n. 樹籬、籬笆 Track 2263

例句 There is an opening in the hedge. 樹籬間有個開口。

hen [hɛn] n. 母雞 Track 2264

例句 Do you know how often the hen lays eggs?
你知道這隻母雞多久生一次蛋嗎？

搭配詞 hen house 雞舍

herb [ɝb] n. 草本植物 Track 2265

例句 The book shows you how to grow herbs indoors.
這本書教你如何在室內種植青草。

搭配詞 herbal tea 青草茶

herd [hɝd] n. 獸群、成群 Track 2266

例句 Elephants live in herds. 大象是群體生活的動物。

搭配詞 in herds 成群的

hippopotamus [͵hɪpəˋpɑtəməs] n. 河馬 Track 2267

例句 There are a lot of hippopotamuses in this river.
這條河中有很多河馬。

縮寫 hippo

honey [ˋhʌnɪ] n. 蜂蜜、花蜜 Track 2268

例句 We had pancake with butter and honey as breakfast.
我們早餐吃了煎餅搭配奶油和蜂蜜。

hoof [huf] n. 蹄 Track 2269

例句 Is there something wrong with the horse's hooves?
那匹馬的蹄有什麼問題嗎？

搭配詞 horse's hoof 馬蹄

horse [hɔrs] n. 馬 Track 2270

例句 She was a dark horse in the singing competition.
她是歌唱比賽的黑馬。

搭配詞 dark horse 黑馬

hum [hʌm] n. 嗡嗡聲 Track 2271

例句 I can hear the hum of bees as I walk out of my room.
我走出房間時可以聽到蜜蜂的嗡嗡聲。

易混淆字 ham 火腿

insect [ˋɪnsɛkt] n. 昆蟲 Track 2272

例句 You can use the ointment to treat the insect bites.
你可以用這個藥膏治療蟲咬傷口。

搭配詞 insect bite 蟲咬

ivory [ˋaɪvərɪ] n. 象牙 Track 2273

例句 The scholar lives in an ivory tower and lacks experience in the business. 這個學者住在象牙塔，缺乏業界實務經驗。

搭配詞 ivory tower 象牙塔

ivy [ˋaɪvɪ] n. 常春藤 Track 2274

例句 She graduated from one of the Ivy League schools.
她從常春藤盟校之一畢業。

搭配詞 Ivy League 常春藤聯盟

jasmine [ˋdʒæsmɪn] n. 茉莉 Track 2275

例句 The scent of this jasmine perfume is alluring.
這款茉莉香水的味道很誘人。

搭配詞 jasmine perfume 茉莉香水

jungle [ˋdʒʌŋg!] n. 叢林 Track 2276

例句 She came from humble beginnings but survived in the city jungle with her wits. 她的出身清寒，但靠著機智在都市叢林存活下來了。

搭配詞 city jungle 都市叢林

kangaroo [͵kæŋgəˋru] n. 袋鼠 Track 2277

例句 Have you ever seen a kangaroo in Australia?
你有在澳洲看到過袋鼠嗎？

kill [kɪl] v. 殺、獵物 Track 2278

例句 She finally managed to kill the cockroach.
她終於成功把蟑螂殺掉了。

kitten/kitty [ˋkɪtn̩]/[ˋkɪtɪ] n. 小貓 Track 2279

例句 We adopted the stray kitty after she was found in a garbage can.
這隻流浪小貓被人在垃圾堆中發現後，我們就收養了牠。

搭配詞
stray kitty 流浪小貓

koala [kəˋɑlə] n. 無尾熊 Track 2280

例句 The little girl clung to her father like a koala to a tree.
那個小女孩像無尾熊抱樹一般抱著她爸爸。

ladybug/ladybird [ˋledɪˌbʌg]/[ˋledɪˌbɝd] Track 2281
n. 瓢蟲

例句 Have you ever seen a ladybug? 你見過瓢蟲嗎？

同義字
ladybird

lamb [læm] n. 羔羊、小羊 Track 2282

例句 The little girl is as meek as a lamb.
那個小女孩和小羊一般溫順。

lawn [lɔn] n. 草地 Track 2283

例句 Lying on the lawn chair is more comfortable than sitting in the office.
躺在草皮躺椅上比坐在辦公室更好。

搭配詞
lawn chair 草皮躺椅

lay [le] v. 放置、產卵 Track 2284

例句 The tortoises lay their eggs in the sand.
這些烏龜在沙中產卵。

搭配詞
lay eggs 產卵

leaf [lif] n. 葉 Track 2285

例句 The fallen pine leaves look like a golden carpet on the ground.
這些松樹落葉看起來像是地上的金色地毯。

搭配詞
pine leaf 松樹葉

leap [lip] v. 使跳過、跳躍 Track 2286

例句 I saw a lot of fish leaping out of the water and landing on the shore.
我看到許多魚從水中跳出來，落在岸邊。

搭配詞
leap year 閏年

lemon [ˋlɛmən] n. 檸檬 Track 2287

例句 Which do you like better, lemons or oranges?
你比較喜歡哪一種，檸檬還是橘子？

leopard [ˋlɛpɚd] n. 豹 ◀ Track 2288

例句 The lady demanded that her husband buy her a leopard-print coat.
那個太太要求她的先生買一件豹紋大衣給她。

搭配詞 American leopard 美洲豹

lettuce [ˋlɛtɪs] n. 萵苣 ◀ Track 2289

例句 He was an expert in growing iceberg lettuce.
他是種捲心萵苣的專家。

搭配詞 iceberg lettuce 捲心萵苣

lily [ˋlɪlɪ] n. 百合花 ◀ Track 2290

例句 Amber is as beautiful as a lily. 安珀像百合花一樣漂亮。

limb [lɪm] n. 枝幹、四肢 ◀ Track 2291

例句 Her limbs were sore from too much lifting.
她因為搬太多東西而四肢痠痛。

lime [laɪm] n. 萊姆（樹）、石灰 ◀ Track 2292

例句 I like this lime-colored dress. 我喜歡這件萊姆色的洋裝。

lion [ˋlaɪən] n. 獅子 ◀ Track 2293

例句 He had the lion's share in the deal.
他在這筆交易中，獲得最大的利益。

搭配詞 lion's share 最大的份額

livestock [ˋlaɪv͵stɑk] n. 家畜 ◀ Track 2294

例句 Livestock husbandry is the economic backbone of this country.
這個國家的經濟支柱是畜牧業。

搭配詞 livestock husbandry 畜牧業

lizard [ˋlɪzɚd] n. 蜥蜴 ◀ Track 2295

例句 No matter what he does, somehow the lizard always gets into his room. 無論他怎麼做，那隻蜥蜴就是能跑進他房間裡。

易混淆字 wizard 巫師

locust [ˋlokəst] n. 蝗蟲 ◀ Track 2296

例句 Farmers are battling a plague of locusts in the area.
農民正在這個區域對抗蝗害。

搭配詞 a plague of locusts 蝗害

log [lɔg] n. 圓木 ◀ Track 2297

例句 There's a log blocking the way in the middle of the road.
路中央有塊圓木在擋路。

易混淆字 lot 很多

a b c d e f g h i j k l m n o p q r s t u v w x y z

lotus [ˋlotəs] n. 睡蓮、蓮花 Track 2298

例句 She made a dessert with lotus roots and mulberries.
她用蓮藕和桑椹做了一道甜點。

搭配詞 lotus root 蓮藕

lumber [ˋlʌmbɚ] n. 木材 Track 2299

例句 There are piles of lumber stacked in front of his house.
他家門口有一大堆木材。

同義字 timber

lush [lʌʃ] adj. 青翠的 Track 2300

例句 The pasture is filled with lush grass.
牧場滿滿都是青翠的草。

易混淆字 rush 衝

mammal [ˋmæml̩] n. 哺乳動物 Track 2301

例句 Whales are aquatic mammals that live in the sea.
鯨魚是住在海裡的哺乳動物。

搭配詞 aquatic mammal 水生哺乳動物

mango [ˋmæŋgo] n. 芒果 Track 2302

例句 People like eating mangos in summer.
人們喜歡在夏天吃芒果。

maple [ˋmepl̩] n. 楓樹、槭樹 Track 2303

例句 I had a waffle with maple syrup this morning.
我今天早上吃鬆餅配楓糖漿。

搭配詞 maple syrup 楓糖漿

meadow [ˋmɛdo] n. 草地 Track 2304

例句 There are many herds of cattle in the meadow.
草地上有許多牛群。

同義字 grassland

melon [ˋmɛlən] n. 甜瓜 Track 2305

例句 I just bought some winter melons from the market.
我剛從市場買了一些冬瓜。

搭配詞 winter melon 冬瓜

mermaid [ˋmɝˏmed] n. 美人魚 Track 2306

例句 The little girl wished she were a mermaid.
那個小女孩希望自己是美人魚。

migrant [ˋmaɪgrənt] n. 候鳥、移民 Track 2307

例句 The boss treats these migrant workers well and cares about their health. 這個老闆善待這些移工，並很關心他們的健康。

搭配詞 migrant worker 外來勞工；移工

mint [mɪnt] n. 薄荷 Track 2308

例句 He bought me a box of mints. 他買了一盒薄荷給我。

monkey [ˋmʌŋkɪ] n. 猴 Track 2309

例句 According to the studies, men and monkeys have many things in common. 根據研究，人與猴子有許多相似之處。

monster [ˋmɑnstɚ] n. 怪物 Track 2310

例句 She has a cute face, but inside she's a monster.
她有著可愛的臉龐，但內心卻是個怪物。

mosquito [məˋskito] n. 蚊子 Track 2311

例句 Mosquito nets can prevent millions of cases of malaria.
蚊帳能讓數百萬的人免於感染虐疾。

搭配詞
mosquito net 蚊帳

moss [mɔs] n. 苔蘚 Track 2312

例句 Moss is already growing in your bathroom. You have to clean it!
你的浴室都長苔蘚了，你也該清洗一下啊！

moth [mɔθ] n. 蛾、蛀蟲 Track 2313

例句 How do you tell a butterfly from a moth?
要如何分出蝴蝶和蛾？

易混淆字
mouth 嘴巴

mouse [maʊs] n. 老鼠 Track 2314

例句 When I lived in that old apartment, there was a mouse in the kitchen. 我以前住那個舊套房的時候，廚房裡有老鼠。

mow [mo] v. 收割 Track 2315

例句 Let me mow the lawn for you today.
今天讓我幫你割草坪吧。

搭配詞
mow the lawn 割草坪

mule [mjul] n. 騾 Track 2316

例句 Alice is stubborn as a mule. 艾莉絲跟騾一樣固執。

搭配詞
stubborn as a mule
跟騾一樣固執

mushroom [ˋmʌʃrum] n. 蘑菇 Track 2317

例句 I cannot tell edible mushrooms from poisonous ones.
我無法判斷哪些蘑菇可食，而哪些有毒。

a b c d e f g h i j k l m n o p q r s t u v w x y z

nest [nɛst] n. 鳥巢 Track 2318

例句 I found that there were several swallows living in the nest under the roof of our house.
我發現有幾隻燕子住在我們家屋頂下的鳥巢裡。

nut [nʌt] n. 堅果、螺帽 Track 2319

例句 Chewing betel nuts can cause oral cancer. You'd better quit the risky habit. 吃檳榔會導致口腔癌，你最好戒掉這個危險的習慣。

搭配詞 betel nut 檳榔

oak [ok] n. 橡樹、橡葉 Track 2320

例句 I don't know why oaks fall when reeds stand in the storm.
我真不懂為什麼橡樹在風暴中會倒下，蘆葦卻好好的。

octopus [ˋɑktəpəs] n. 章魚 Track 2321

例句 He brought an octopus home for dinner, but his children wanted to keep it as a pet.
他帶了一隻章魚回家當晚餐，但他的孩子們都想把牠當作寵物。

olive [ˋɑlɪv] n. 橄欖 Track 2322

例句 Extra virgin olive oil contains healthy fats.
特級初榨橄欖油含有健康的脂肪。

搭配詞 olive oil 橄欖油

onion [ˋʌnjən] n. 洋蔥 Track 2323

例句 The onion rings are crispy and delicious.
這些洋蔥圈很酥脆清甜。

搭配詞 onion ring 洋蔥圈

orange [ˋɔrɪndʒ] n. 柳丁、柑橘 Track 2324

例句 Do you like oranges or apples? 你喜歡橘子還是蘋果？

orchard [ˋɔrtʃɚd] n. 果園 Track 2325

例句 My family decided to expand the apple orchard next year.
我的家庭決定明年擴建蘋果園。

搭配詞 apple orchard 蘋果園

ostrich [ˋɔstrɪtʃ] n. 鴕鳥 Track 2326

例句 The ostrich can't fly, but it runs fast.
鴕鳥不會飛，但牠跑得真快。

owl [aul] n. 貓頭鷹 Track 2327

例句 My son is a night owl during summer vacation.
我兒子放暑假期間是夜貓子。

搭配詞 night owl 夜貓子

ox [ɑks] **n.** 公牛 Track 2328

例句 The Korean ox bone soup tastes delicious.
韓式牛骨湯很好喝。

---

oyster [ˋɔɪstɚ] **n.** 牡蠣、蠔 Track 2329

例句 I enjoy eating oyster omelets; they're really tasty.
我喜歡吃蚵仔煎，真是好吃。

搭配詞 oyster omelet 蚵仔煎

---

panda [ˋpændə] **n.** 貓熊 Track 2330

例句 We're going to the zoo to see the giant pandas.
我們要去動物園看貓熊。

搭配詞 giant panda 大貓熊

---

papaya [pəˋpaɪə] **n.** 木瓜 Track 2331

例句 There are many street vendors selling papaya milk in this country.
這個國家有很多街頭小販在賣木瓜牛乳。

搭配詞 papaya milk 木瓜牛乳

---

parrot [ˋpærət] **n.** 鸚鵡 Track 2332

例句 I don't know why the parrots like to repeat what people say.
我不知道為什麼鸚鵡喜歡重複人說的話。

---

peach [pitʃ] **n.** 桃子 Track 2333

例句 There are three big peaches on the table.
桌上有三顆大桃子。

---

peacock [ˋpiˏkɑk] **n.** 孔雀 Track 2334

例句 Peacocks show off their gorgeous tails in front of the visitors.
孔雀把牠們美麗的尾巴展現給訪客看。

---

peanut [ˋpiˏnʌt] **n.** 花生 Track 2335

例句 I spread some peanut butter on the toast.
我在吐司上抹了一些花生醬。

搭配詞 peanut butter 花生醬

---

pear [pɛr] **n.** 梨子 Track 2336

例句 We picked some pears from the trees this afternoon.
我們今天下午從樹上摘了一些梨子。

---

pearl [pɝl] **n.** 珍珠 Track 2337

例句 These necklaces are made of natural pearls.
這些項鍊是天然珍珠製成的。

搭配詞 pearl necklace 珍珠項鍊

peck [pɛk] n./v. 啄、啄痕、輕吻 Track 2338

例句 She gave a peck on his cheek when she was drunk.
她在喝醉時輕吻他的臉頰。

penguin [ˋpɛngwɪn] n. 企鵝 Track 2339

例句 Do you know why penguins can live in such a cold environment?
你知道為什麼企鵝可以住在這麼冷的環境嗎？

搭配詞 King Penguin 國王企鵝

pepper [ˋpɛpɚ] n. 胡椒 Track 2340

例句 Green pepper is one of the antioxidant-rich vegetables.
青椒是富含抗氧化物質的蔬菜之一。

搭配詞 green pepper 青椒

pesticide [ˋpɛstɪˏsaɪd] n. 農藥、殺蟲劑 Track 2341

例句 The farmers had no choice but to use pesticide.
這些農夫無可選擇，只能用農藥。

pet [pɛt] n. 寵物、令人愛慕之物 Track 2342

例句 I need to go to the pet shop to get some cat food.
我得去寵物店買一些貓食。

搭配詞 pet shop 寵物店

petal [ˋpɛtl̩] n. 花瓣 Track 2343

例句 To have a romantic dinner, you can decorate the table with rose petals. 要享用浪漫的晚餐，你可以用玫瑰花瓣裝飾桌子。

pig [pɪg] n. 豬 Track 2344

例句 My friend keeps a pig as a pet. 我朋友養一隻豬當寵物。

pigeon [ˋpɪdʒən] n. 鴿子 Track 2345

例句 Don't feed the pigeons in the park. 別餵公園的鴿子。

同義字 dove

pine [paɪn] n. 松樹 Track 2346

例句 There is a pine forest near my house. I like to take a walk there after dinner.
我家附近有座松樹林，我喜歡在吃完晚餐後在那裡散步。

pineapple [ˋpaɪnˏæpl̩] n. 鳳梨 Track 2347

例句 My mother likes to eat pineapples very much.
我媽媽很喜歡吃鳳梨。

plant [plænt] n. 植物、工廠 Track 2348

例句 How about growing some perennial plants?
要不要種一些常年生長的植物呢？

搭配詞
perennial plants
常年生長的植物

plantation [plænˋteʃən] n. 農場、種植園 Track 2349

＊字尾-tion有轉變為名詞的意思

例句 Hundreds of slaves are working in the plantation.
上百位奴隸在農場工作。

plentiful [ˋplɛntɪfəl] adj. 豐富的 Track 2350

＊字尾-ful有「充滿」的意思

例句 The weather has been very nice; the farmers therefore have a plentiful harvest this year.
天氣一直不錯，所以農夫們今年有個豐富的收成。

同義字
abundant

poisonous [ˋpɔɪznəs] adj. 有毒的 Track 2351

＊字尾-ous有轉變為形容詞之意

例句 I think he was bitten by a poisonous snake.
我想他是被毒蛇咬了。

同義字
toxic

pony [ˋponɪ] n. 小馬 Track 2352

例句 He played in Pony League Baseball when he was 13.
他13歲時在美國少棒聯盟打球。

搭配詞
Pony League 美國少棒聯盟

potato [pəˋteto] n. 馬鈴薯 Track 2353

例句 I would like to have roast chicken with mashed potato for dinner.
我想吃烤雞和馬鈴薯泥當晚餐。

搭配詞
mashed potato 馬鈴薯泥

poultry [ˋpoltrɪ] n. 家禽 Track 2354

例句 Don't you think poultry is rather cheap now?
你不覺得家禽現在很便宜嗎？

同義字
fowl

prairie [ˋprɛrɪ] n. 牧場、大草原 Track 2355

例句 The vast North American Prairie stretches west to the horizon.
北美大草原一路向西延伸到地平線。

搭配詞
North American Prairie
北美大草原

pumpkin [ˋpʌmpkɪn] n. 南瓜 Track 2356

例句 Would you care for some pumpkin pie later?
你待會想不想來點南瓜派？

搭配詞
pumpkin pie 南瓜派

puppy [ˋpʌpɪ] n. 小狗 Track 2357

例句 He's 70, but still remembers his puppy love.
他70歲了，仍對他的少年時期的戀愛念念不忘。

搭配詞
puppy love 少年時的戀愛

rabbit [ˋræbɪt] n. 兔子 Track 2358

例句 Rabbits can make long jumps. 兔子可以跳得很遠。

radish [ˋrædɪʃ] n. 蘿蔔 Track 2359

例句 My mother wants me to go to the supermarket and buy some radish cakes. 我媽媽要我去超市買一些蘿蔔糕。

搭配詞 radish cake 蘿蔔糕

rat [ræt] n. 老鼠 Track 2360

例句 Rats can carry diseases that may spread to humans. 老鼠可能帶有會傳染給人類的疾病。

reap [rip] v. 收割 Track 2361

例句 The peasants reap what they planted in spring. 農人們收割他們春天種的作物。

反義字 sow 播種

reptile [ˋrɛptaɪl] n. 爬蟲類 Track 2362

例句 I can't stand reptiles; they look creepy. 我受不了爬蟲類，他們看起來很恐怖。

rhinoceros/rhino [raɪˋnɑsərəs]/[ˋraɪno] Track 2363

n. 犀牛

例句 This is my first time seeing a rhinoceros in the zoo. 這是我第一次在動物園看到犀牛。

縮寫 rhino

roar [ror] v./n. 吼叫 Track 2364

例句 She was frightened by the roars of the tiger. 她被老虎的吼聲嚇到了。

robin [ˋrɑbɪn] n. 知更鳥 Track 2365

例句 You can tell that spring is coming soon once robins start appearing. 知更鳥開始出現，你就知道春天快來了。

rooster [ˋrustɚ] n. 公雞、好鬥者 Track 2366

例句 My grandmother keeps many hens but only one rooster. 我奶奶養很多隻母雞，但只有一隻公雞。

root [rut] n. 根源、根 Track 2367

例句 Radish is a kind of root vegetable. 蘿蔔是根莖類蔬菜的一種。

搭配詞 root vegetable 根莖類蔬菜

rose [roz] n. 玫瑰花、薔薇花 Track 2368

例句 I brought my girlfriend some roses.
我帶了一些玫瑰花給我的女友。

rude [rud] adj. 野蠻的、粗魯的 Track 2369

例句 You were rude to your parents; you should apologize.
你對你的父母太野蠻了，應該要道歉才對。

反義字 civilized 文明的

salmon [`sæmən] n. 鮭 Track 2370

例句 I would like some smoked salmon in my salad.
我想在沙拉中放一些燻鮭魚。

搭配詞 smoked salmon 燻鮭魚

scarecrow [`skɛr͵kro] n. 稻草人 Track 2371

例句 Farmers use scarecrows to scare away the birds.
農夫使用稻草人來嚇走鳥。

同義字 straw man

scatter [`skætɚ] v. 散佈 Track 2372

例句 Farmers start to scatter the seeds in the fields.
農人開始把種子散佈在田野中。

seagull [`sigʌl] n. 海鷗 Track 2373

例句 The sound of seagulls crying takes her back to her childhood days by the sea. 海鷗哭嚎的聲音讓她回憶起她在海邊的童年生活。

縮寫 gull

seal [sil] n./v. 海豹、印章、密封 Track 2374

例句 The letter is sealed off with wax. 這封信是用蠟密封的。

搭配詞 seal off 密封

seed [sid] n. 種子 Track 2375

例句 It's difficult for a plant to grow from a seed without enough water.
如果水不夠，種子就很難生長成植物。

shady [`ʃedɪ] adj. 多蔭的、成蔭的 Track 2376

例句 I like to go out for a walk on the shady avenue.
我喜歡在多蔭的街道上散步。

shark [`ʃɑrk] n. 鯊魚 Track 2377

例句 The loan shark forced the man to be homeless.
那個放高利貸的人迫使這個人無家可歸。

搭配詞 loan shark 高利貸者

sheep [ʃip] n. 羊、綿羊 ◀Track 2378

例句 He was considered the black sheep of his family.
他被視為是有辱門楣的人。

搭配詞 black sheep 害群之馬

shell [ʃɛl] n. 貝殼 ◀Track 2379

例句 She picked up shells to take home to her sister.
她撿起一些貝殼，要帶回家給妹妹。

同義字 crustacean 甲殼類動物

shrimp [ʃrɪmp] n. 蝦子 ◀Track 2380

例句 Shrimp is my favorite seafood. 蝦子是我最喜歡的海鮮。

shrub [ʃrʌb] n. 灌木 ◀Track 2381

例句 There are a lot of shrubs in the park. 公園裡有許多灌木。

silkworm [ˋsɪlkwɝm] n. 蠶 ◀Track 2382

例句 The skin care product contains silkworm cocoon ingredient.
這個護膚品含有蠶繭的成份。

搭配詞 silkworm cocoon 蠶繭

slaughter [ˋslɔtɚ] n. 屠宰 ◀Track 2383

例句 Their effort to stop mass slaughter in the country unfortunately failed.
他們企圖停止發生在這個國家的大屠殺，但很不幸地失敗了。

搭配詞 mass slaughter 大屠殺

slay [sle] v. 殺害、殺 ◀Track 2384

例句 It's illegal to slay cattle in India. 在印度要殺牛是不合法的。

同義字 kill

snail [snel] n. 蝸牛 ◀Track 2385

例句 He was very worried about the snail-paced progress of information literacy in the rural area.
他非常擔心鄉下地區民眾的資訊素養進步太過緩慢。

搭配詞 snail-paced 蝸牛一樣慢的

snake [snek] n. 蛇 ◀Track 2386

例句 He was taken to the hospital because he was bitten by a snake.
他因為被蛇咬，被帶去醫院了。

同義字 serpent

soil [sɔɪl] n. 土壤 ◀Track 2387

例句 The soil was no longer fertile so the farmers had to move away.
這裡的土壤不再肥沃了，所以農夫們只好搬走。

sow [so] v. 播、播種 Track 2388

例句 Farmers are starting to sow seeds now.
農夫們現在開始播種了。

反義字 reap 收割

soybean/soy [ˋsɔɪˋbin]/[sɔɪ] n. 大豆、黃豆 Track 2389

例句 Would you please buy a bottle of soy sauce in the shop for me?
你可以從店裡幫我買一罐醬油嗎？

搭配詞 soy sauce 醬油

sparrow [ˋspæro] n. 麻雀 Track 2390

例句 There is a worm in the sparrow's beak.
那隻麻雀的嘴裡咬著一隻蚯蚓。

spear [spɪr] n. 矛、魚叉 Track 2391

例句 How should we catch fish with a spear?
我們要怎麼用魚叉抓魚呢？

易混淆字 spare 騰出時間

spider [ˋspaɪdɚ] n. 蜘蛛 Track 2392

例句 Spider webs look pretty amazing. 蜘蛛網看起來很不可思議。

搭配詞 spider web 蜘蛛網

spinach [ˋspɪnɪtʃ] n. 菠菜 Track 2393

例句 I prefer cabbage to spinach. 比起菠菜，我比較喜歡甘藍菜。

squirrel [ˋskwɝəl] n. 松鼠 Track 2394

例句 I saw a lot of squirrels in the park. 我在公園看到許多松鼠。

stalk [stɔk] n. 軸、莖、柄狀物、（酒杯的）腳 Track 2395

例句 He cut the flower from its stalk. 他從莖部剪掉了那朵花。

stem [stɛm] n. 杆柄、莖幹 Track 2396

例句 The stem of the rose was broken. 那朵玫瑰的莖幹斷了。

易混淆字 stern 船尾

stingy [ˋstɪndʒɪ] adj. 有刺的、會刺的、小氣的 Track 2397

例句 He is a stingy man who doesn't like to part with his money.
他是個小氣的人，不喜歡與他的錢分開。

反義字 generous 慷慨的

straw [strɔ] n. 稻草 Track 2398

例句 Her harsh criticism was the last straw on a camel's back, and he never returned. 她的嚴詞批評是壓跨駱駝的最後一根稻草，他從此再也沒回來了。

搭配詞 the last straw on a camel's back 壓跨駱駝的最後一根稻草

strawberry [ˋstrɔ˴bɛrɪ] n. 草莓 Track 2399

例句 I like to have toast with strawberry jam as breakfast. 我喜歡吃吐司加草莓果醬當早餐。

stump [stʌmp] n. （樹的）殘株、樹樁、殘餘部分 Track 2400

例句 They used the tree stump as a table. 他們用樹樁當桌子。

substance [ˋsʌbstəns] n. 物質、物體、實質 Track 2401

例句 What substances are there in the soil? 泥土裡有什麼物質呢？

swallow [ˋswɑlo] n. 燕子 Track 2402

例句 The butler was required to wear a swallow-tailed coat when he worked. 這名管家被要求上班時要穿燕尾服。

搭配詞 swallow-tailed coat 燕尾服

swan [swɑn] n. 天鵝 Track 2403

例句 I can't tell black swans from black geese. 我分不清黑天鵝與黑鵝的差別。

搭配詞 black swan 黑天鵝

swarm [swɔrm] n. 群、群集 Track 2404

例句 I saw a swarm of bees behind our house. 我看到我們家後面有一群蜜蜂。

搭配詞 a swarm of 一群

tail [tel] n. 尾巴、尾部 Track 2405

例句 We are at the tail of the bus queue. 我們在等公車隊伍的尾巴處。

tangerine [ˋtændʒə˴rɪn] n. 柑、桔 Track 2406

例句 The tangerines I bought yesterday were very juicy. 我昨天買的柑橘非常多汁。

thrive [θraɪv] v. 繁茂、茁壯成長 Track 2407

例句 Few plants or animals can thrive in the desert. 很少有動植物可以在沙漠中茁壯成長。

易混淆字 strive 努力

throughout [θru`aut] prep. 遍佈、到處 Track 2408

例句 His accomplishment is renowned throughout the world.
他的成就舉世知名。

搭配詞 throughout the world 遍及全球

tiger [`taɪgɚ] n. 老虎 Track 2409

例句 A tiger in the zoo died. 動物園裡有一隻老虎死了。

timber [`tɪmbɚ] n. 木材、樹林 Track 2410

例句 Much timber was destroyed in the forest fire.
在森林大火中，許多木材都被燒毀了。

同義字 log

toad [tod] n. 癩蛤蟆 Track 2411

例句 The wizard cast a spell and turned the prince into a toad.
巫師施咒語把王子變成一隻蟾蜍。

tortoise [`tɔrtəs] n. 陸龜 Track 2412

例句 It is said that a tortoise is much bigger than a turtle.
據說陸龜比烏龜大多了。

trap [træp] n. 圈套、陷阱 Track 2413

例句 The police set a trap to catch the thief. 警察設下圈套要抓小偷。

搭配詞 set a trap 設下圈套

tree [tri] n. 樹 Track 2414

例句 People believe that tea tree oil is antibacterial.
人們相信茶樹精油能抗菌。

搭配詞 tea tree 茶樹

tropical [`trɑpɪkḷ] adj. 熱帶的 Track 2415

例句 There is luxuriant tropical vegetation in Singapore.
新加坡有很多熱帶的植物。

搭配詞 tropical vegetation 熱帶植物

trout [traut] n. 鱒魚 Track 2416

例句 I caught eight rainbow trouts in fifteen minutes.
我十五分鐘內就抓到了八條虹鱒魚。

搭配詞 rainbow trout 虹鱒魚

trunk [trʌŋk] n. 樹幹、大行李箱、象鼻 Track 2417

例句 Would you please help me open the trunk?
你可以幫我開行李箱嗎？

tub [tʌb] n. 桶、盆 Track 2418

例句 I like to relax in the bath tub. 我喜歡在澡盆裡放鬆。

易混淆字 tube 管子

tulip [ˋtjuləp] n. 鬱金香 Track 2419

例句 We took a lot of pictures in front of the tulip garden last week.
我們上禮拜在鬱金香園前照了許多相片。

搭配詞 tulip garden 鬱金香花園

tuna [ˋtunə] n. 鮪魚、金槍魚 Track 2420

例句 I want to buy some tuna sushi at the supermarket.
我想在超級市場買一些鮪魚壽司。

搭配詞 tuna sushi 鮪魚壽司

turtle [ˋtɝtl̩] n. 龜、海龜 Track 2421

例句 The turtle shell is full of moss. 這隻烏龜的龜殼佈滿青苔。

搭配詞 turtle shell 龜殼

twig [twɪg] n. 小枝、嫩枝 Track 2422

例句 Someone just snapped a twig right behind me.
有人剛在我後面弄斷了一根小樹枝。

vegetation [ˏvɛdʒəˋteʃən] n. 草木、植物 Track 2423
＊字尾-tion有轉變為名詞的意思

例句 The vegetation in the area is sparse. 那一區的植物很稀少。

同義字 plant

vine [vaɪn] n. 葡萄藤、藤蔓 Track 2424

例句 It takes a lot of time to pass through a jungle woven with vines.
要穿過充滿藤蔓的樹林很花時間。

補充 vineyard 葡萄園

violet [ˋvaɪəlɪt] n. 紫羅蘭、羞怯的人 Track 2425

例句 Shannon is no shrinking violet. 紗農不是個羞怯的人。

易混淆字 violent 兇暴的

walnut [ˋwɔlnət] n. 胡桃 Track 2426

例句 I used walnut to make a cake this afternoon.
我今天下午用胡桃做了一個蛋糕。

搭配詞 walnut cake 胡桃蛋糕

watermelon [ˋwɔtɚˏmɛlən] n. 西瓜 Track 2427

例句 I like to eat watermelons in the summer.
我在夏天很喜歡吃西瓜。

web [wɛb] n. 網、蜘蛛網、網路 Track 2428

例句 He used SKYPE and a webcam to chat with his familly.
他用SKYPE和網路攝影機和家人聯天。

搭配詞 webcam 網路攝影機

weed [wid] n. 野草、雜草 Track 2429

例句 Help me get rid of the weeds in the garden.
幫我把花園裡的雜草弄掉吧。

搭配詞 weed wiper 除草機

whale [wel] n. 鯨魚 Track 2430

例句 We took a ship to see whales. 我們坐上船去看鯨魚。

易混淆字 whole 全部的

wheat [hwit] n. 小麥、麥子 Track 2431

例句 The bread was made from wheat flour.
那個麵包是用小麥麵粉做的。

搭配詞 wheat flour 小麥麵粉

wild [waɪld] adj. 野生的、野性的 Track 2432

例句 I enjoy watching videos about wild animals.
我喜歡看野生動物的影片。

wildlife [ˋwaɪld͵laɪf] n. 野生生物 Track 2433

例句 We should try our best to protect wildlife and their habitats.
我們應該盡力保護野生生物與牠們生存的環境。

wing [wɪŋ] n. 翅膀、翼 Track 2434

例句 There is a wound on the wing of the bird.
那隻鳥的翅膀上有傷口。

wither [ˋwɪðɚ] v. 枯萎、凋謝 Track 2435

例句 The flower withered because there was no water.
因為沒有水，花就凋謝了。

補充 pine away 日漸憔悴

wolf [wʊlf] n. 狼 Track 2436

例句 The wolf dog let out a howl before disappearing into the woods.
那隻狼狗嚎叫一聲後就消失在樹林中了。

搭配詞 wolf dog 狼狗

wood(s) [wʊd(z)] n. 木材、樹林 Track 2437

例句 She's a babe in the woods. 她太過天真而易受騙。

搭配詞 a babe in the woods 沒有經驗的人；太過天真而易受騙的人

woodpecker [ˋwudˏpɛkɚ] n. 啄木鳥 Track 2438

＊字尾-er有「者」的意思

例句 Do you hear that pecking sound? It's a woodpecker.
你聽到那個啄東西的聲音了嗎？是啄木鳥。

worm [wɝm] n. 蚯蚓或其他類似的小蟲 Track 2439

例句 The naughty boy cut the worm in half.
那個頑皮的男孩把蚯蚓切成兩半了。

易混淆字
warm 溫暖的

yam/sweet potato [jæm]/[swit pəˋteto] Track 2440

n. 山藥、地瓜

例句 My grandparents grow yams, carrots, and potatoes in the yard of their hometown.
我的祖父母在他們家鄉的園子裡種植地瓜、蘿蔔和馬鈴薯。

zebra [ˋzibrə] n. 斑馬 Track 2441

例句 He hit the man who was walking on the zebra crossing.
他撞倒了那個走在斑馬線的男人。

搭配詞
zebra crossing 斑馬線

zoo [zu] n. 動物園 Track 2442

例句 My daughter aspires to be a zoo keeper when she grows up.
我女兒立志長大要當動物園管理員。

搭配詞
zoo keeper 動物園管理員

Test 09 關鍵英單總測驗第9回

以下測驗題皆出自書中第九回「**和動植物有關的單字**」，快來檢視自己的學習成果吧！

一、選擇題

1. My father is as busy as a ______ .
   (A) bee
   (B) shrimp
   (C) tortoise
   (D) bull

2. ____ are considered auspicious in Chinese culture.
   (A) Gorilla
   (B) Donkeys
   (C) Dragons
   (D) Fleas

3. I'd like to have a muffin with ____ syrup.
   (A) moss
   (B) meadow
   (C) cherry
   (D) maple

4. Some _________ are poisonous; therefore, they are not edible.
   (A) roar
   (B) parrots
   (C) scarecrows
   (D) mushrooms

5. She was bitten by a _______ in the desert.
   (A) tiger
   (B) snake
   (C) seal
   (D) soil

6. He keeps a lizard as a ______ .
   (A) nest
   (B) migrant
   (C) pet
   (D) monster

7. That's the last straw on a ______'s back.
   (A) camel
   (B) chimpanzee
   (C) crocodile
   (D) elephant

8. The typhoon caused great _____ to the city.
   (A) ground
   (B) damage
   (C) harvest
   (D) frost

9. The scholar lives in an _____ tower.
   (A) kangaroo
   (B) lemon
   (C) ivory
   (D) oak

10. She made a ____ pie for dessert.
    (A) tulip
    (B) hay
    (C) pumpkin
    (D) fertilizer

二、克漏字測驗

Plants are the primary __1__ for thousands of organisms. They also provide some of our energy needs. In some parts of the world, __2__ is the primary fuel used by people to cook their meals.

Because of their beauty, plants are important elements to our world. When we build houses and buildings, we usually plant some trees, __3__, and flowers to make what we have built much nicer.

However, due to over-logging and pollution, our planet is losing plants, __4__, and clean water at a dramatic rate. While government and society need to make a change, individuals can use less energy, save water, and eat less red meat to help save our planet and protect the __5__.

1. (A) shell
   (B) lawn
   (C) habitat
   (D) hedge

2. (A) herb
   (B) wood
   (C) ginger
   (D) fur

3. (A) shrubs
   (B) fragrance
   (C) crop
   (D) bud

4. (A) carps
   (B) daffodil
   (C) lions
   (D) animals

5. (A) mango
   (B) lotus
   (C) mint
   (D) wildlife

關鍵英單總測驗第9回
中譯與解答

一、選擇題

1. 我爸爸像蜜蜂一樣忙碌。
   (A) 蜜蜂
   (B) 蝦子
   (C) 陸龜
   (D) 公牛

2. 在中華文化中，龍是吉祥的象徵。
   (A) 大猩猩
   (B) 驢子
   (C) 龍
   (D) 跳蚤

3. 我想點一份楓糖漿馬芬蛋糕。
   (A) 青苔
   (B) 草地
   (C) 櫻花
   (D) 楓樹

4. 有些香菇是有毒的，因此不可食用。
   (A) 吼叫
   (B) 鸚鵡
   (C) 稻草人
   (D) 香菇

5. 她在沙漠中被一隻蛇咬傷。
   (A) 老虎
   (B) 蛇
   (C) 海豹
   (D) 土壤

6. 他養了一隻蜥蜴當寵物。
   (A) 巢
   (B) 候鳥
   (C) 寵物
   (D) 怪物

7. 這是壓跨駱駝的最後一根稻草。
   (A) 駱駝
   (B) 黑猩猩
   (C) 鱷魚
   (D) 大象

8. 颱風對這座城市造成重大損失。
   (A) 土地
   (B) 損失
   (C) 收成
   (D) 霜

9. 這名學者住在象牙塔裡。
   (A) 袋鼠
   (B) 檸檬
   (C) 象牙
   (D) 橡樹

10. 她做了一個南瓜派當甜點。
   (A) 鬱金香
   (B) 乾草
   (C) 南瓜
   (D) 肥料

二、克漏字測驗

植物提供數千種有機物體主要棲息地，也提供人類作為能源的用途。在世界某些國家，木頭是用以煮飯的主要燃料。

因為植物如此之美，它們成為讓世界繽紛的元素。我們蓋房子或建築總會在附近種些樹木、灌木、花朵來美化環境。

然而因為過度濫伐和污染，地球正以驚人的速度失去植物、動物和乾淨的水。政府和社會需要做出改變，個人也可以透過減少使用能源、節約用水、和少吃紅肉來拯救我們的地球，保護野生動物。

1.
(A) 貝殼
(B) 草地
(C) 棲息地
(D) 籬芭

2.
(A) 香草
(B) 木頭
(C) 薑
(D) 毛皮

3.
(A) 灌木
(B) 香水
(C) 殼物
(D) 花蕾

4
(A) 鯰魚
(B) 黃水仙
(C) 獅子
(D) 動物

5.
(A) 芒果
(B) 蓮花
(C) 薄荷
(D) 野生動物

一、選擇題

1.(A) 2.(C) 3.(D) 4.(D) 5.(B)
6.(C) 7.(A) 8.(B) 9.(C) 10.(C)

二、克漏字測驗

1.(C) 2.(B) 3.(A)
4.(D) 5.(D)

Unit 10 和時間有關的單字

多益測驗的命題強調生活化與實用性，學會這些與「時間」有關的單字，不僅能讓你在多益考場上所向披靡，在日常生活上也可以靈活運用喔！

值得紀念的事件可以這麼說

- **Mr. Smith ordered a custom cake for their wedding anniversary.**
  史密斯先生訂了一個客製蛋糕來慶祝他們的結婚紀念日。
- **Going to Antarctica could be a once-in-a-lifetime experience.**
  去南極洲很可能是一生一次的經歷。

描述事件的頻率可以這麼說

- **She goes to the piano class every Saturday.**
  她每星期六都去上鋼琴課。
- **They have extracurricular activity every semester.**
  他們每學期都有課外活動。
- **The Olympic Games are held every four years.**
  奧運會每四年舉辦一次。

歡度節慶可以這麼說

- **We celebrate Lunar New Year together every year.**
  我們每年都一起慶祝農曆新年。
- **We always receive a lot of pomelos on Mid Autumn Festival.**
  我們總是在中秋節收到很多柚子。

一天中的時辰可以這麼說

- **Good morning, class! How was your weekend?**
  同學們早安！週末過得如何啊？
- **He takes his daily dose of medicine every night.**
  他每天晚上都要吃當日份的藥。

強調先後順序可以這麼說

- **The little girl started crying soon after her mom left.**
  小女孩在她媽媽離開後不久就開始哭。
- **I prefer the latter idea than the former one.**
  跟前一個比起來，我比較喜歡後一個主意。

Unit 10 和時間有關的單字

a.m. [ˋeˋɛm] n. 上午 Track 2443

例句 I have a job interview at 10 a.m. tomorrow.
我明天上午十點有一場工作面試。

反義字
p.m. 下午

---

about [əˋbaut] prep. 大約 Track 2444

例句 Would you like to come to our party at about six o'clock tomorrow?
你願意來我們明天大約六點的派對嗎？

---

accidental [͵æksəˋdɛntḷ] adj. 偶然的、意外的 Track 2445

＊字尾-al有轉變為形容詞之意

例句 The accidental discovery of Penicillin saved the lives of countless people. 被意外發現的盤尼西林拯救無數人的生命。

---

adult [əˋdʌlt] adj. 成年的、成熟的 Track 2446

例句 He just turned 18, and now he has to buy adult train tickets.
他剛滿18歲，搭火車必須買成人票。

搭配詞
adult ticket 成人票

---

after [ˋæftɚ] adj. 以後的 Track 2447

例句 She accomplished the task after all.
她終究完成了這個工作。

搭配詞
after all 終究

---

afternoon [ˋæftɚ͵nun] n. 下午 Track 2448

例句 He usually takes a nap in the afternoon.
他通常在下午小睡一下。

搭配詞
in the afternoon 在下午

---

again [əˋgɛn] adv. 又、再 Track 2449

例句 The city is so beautiful! I definitely will visit it again.
這個城市很美，我一定會再來拜訪。

---

age [edʒ] n. 年齡 Track 2450

例句 The poor boy lost his family at the age of eight.
那個可憐的男孩才八歲的年齡就失去了家人。

搭配詞
at the age of 在……歲時

---

ago [ə`go] adv. 以前 Track 2451

例句 A long time ago, there lived a beautiful princess who had long blond hair. 很久以前，一位擁有金色長髮的美麗公主。

搭配詞 long time ago 很久以前

ahead [ə`hɛd] adj. 向前的、在……前面 Track 2452

例句 If you help me, I can finish it ahead of schedule.
如果你幫我，我可以在規劃的時間前完成。

搭配詞 ahead of schedule
規劃的時間前

already [ɔl`rɛdɪ] adv. 已經 Track 2453

例句 He had already left the office before I arrived.
他在我到的時候已經離開辦公室了。

anniversary [ˌænə`vɝsərɪ] n. 周年紀念日 Track 2454

例句 They are going to have a party to celebrate their 15th wedding anniversary.
他們要開一場派對慶祝他們的第15週年結婚紀念日。

搭配詞 wedding anniversary
結婚紀念日

annual [`ænjuəl] adj. 一年的、年度的 Track 2455

例句 I think it's time for me to write an annual report.
我想是時候該來寫年度報告了。

搭配詞 annual budget 年度預算

anytime [`ɛnɪˌtaɪm] adv. 任何時候 Track 2456

例句 You are welcome to visit us anytime.
你任何時候都可以來找我們。

appoint [ə`pɔɪnt] v. 指派 Track 2457

例句 Mr. Duke was appointed as the spokesman of the labor union.
杜克先生被指派為工會的發言人。

搭配詞 appoint sb as sth
指派某人某職務

appointment [ə`pɔɪntmənt] n. 指定、約定 Track 2458

＊字尾-ment有轉變為名詞之意

例句 I'm going to make an appointment with my dentist.
我要跟牙醫約時間。

搭配詞 make an appointment
約定時間

April [`eprəl] n. 四月 Track 2459

例句 They are expecting their first child in April.
他們的第一個孩子預計在四月出生。

縮寫 Apr.

August [`ɔgəst] n. 八月 Track 2460

例句 Jane is thinking about quitting in August.
珍妮在想在八月辭職。

縮寫 Aug.

autumn [ˋɔtəm] n. 秋季、秋天 Track 2461

例句 Autumn is my favorite season of the year.
秋天是我一年最喜歡的季節。

同義字 fall

---

awhile [əˋhwaɪl] adv. 暫時、片刻、一下 Track 2462

例句 Stay awhile and have a cup of tea, will you?
待一下，喝點茶，好不好？

反義字 forever 永遠

---

back [bæk] adj./adv. 後面的 Track 2463

例句 Step back, or you'll get hurt. 退後，否則你會受傷。

搭配詞 step back 退後

---

before [bɪˋfor] adv./prep. 以前 Track 2464

例句 I will leave for Germany before dawn.
黎明之前，我要前往德國。

搭配詞 before dawn 黎明之前

---

begin [bɪˋgɪn] v. 開始、著手 Track 2465

例句 What time does the meeting begin? 會議什麼時候開始?

同義字 start

---

behind [bɪˋhaɪnd] prep./adv. 在後 Track 2466

例句 The project fell behind schedule while the budget kept increasing.
這個計畫進度落後，預算又持續上升。

搭配詞 fall behind 落後

---

brief [brif] adj. 短暫的 Track 2467

例句 Let me make a brief summary about the movie.
我簡要地告訴你這部電影的故事內容。

搭配詞 brief summary 簡單摘要

---

calendar [ˋkæləndɚ] n. 日曆 Track 2468

例句 In the past, Chinese people used the lunar calendar instead of the western calendar. 過去，中國人使用陰曆而不是西曆。

搭配詞 lunar calendar 陰曆

---

carnival [ˋkɑrnəvl] n. 狂歡節慶 Track 2469

例句 People from all over the world crowded in the town for the carnival parade. 來自世界各地的人為了那場狂歡節慶聚集在這個城市。

搭配詞 carnival parade 狂歡遊行

---

casual [ˋkæʒuəl] adj. 偶然的、臨時的、輕便的 Track 2470

例句 Casual wear is not appropriate for such a formal meeting.
這麼正式的會議，便服是不適合的。

搭配詞 casual wear 便服

century [ˋsɛntʃərɪ] n. 世紀 Track 2471

例句 Yoyo Ma is regarded as one of the greatest cellists of the century.
馬友友被認為是這個世紀最棒的大提琴手之一。

childhood [ˋtʃaɪldˏhud] n. 童年時代 Track 2472

例句 The movie star had poor health in her childhood.
這名電影明星童年時代身體並不好。

搭配詞 in childhood 在童年時

Christmas [ˋkrɪsməs] n. 聖誕節 Track 2473

例句 We're going to spend our Christmas at my grandma's place this year. 我們今年聖誕節要在我奶奶那裡過。

縮寫 X'mas

clock [klɑk] n. 時鐘、計時器 Track 2474

例句 His biological clock was thrown completely out of kilter.
他的生理時鐘完全亂掉了。

搭配詞 biological clock 生理時鐘

current [ˋkɝənt] adj. 流通的、目前的 Track 2475

例句 As the editor-in-chief of the news agency, she is very familiar with current affairs. 她是報社總編，對時事很熟悉。

搭配詞 current affairs 時事

cycle [ˋsaɪkḷ] n. 週期、循環 Track 2476

例句 This is a vicious cycle. 這是個惡性循環。

搭配詞 vicious cycle 惡性循環

daily [ˋdelɪ] adj. 每日的 Track 2477

例句 He makes vacuuming the floor his daily routine.
他把用吸塵器吸地當作是每日必做的事。

搭配詞 daily routine 每日必做的事

date [det] n. 日期、約會 Track 2478

例句 Sorry, I have a date tomorrow. 抱歉，我明天有約會。

搭配詞 have a date 有約會

dawn [dɔn] n. 黎明、破曉 Track 2479

例句 They got up before dawn in order to enjoy the sunrise.
他們在黎明前起床以享受日出。

搭配詞 before dawn 在黎明前

day [de] n. 白天、日 Track 2480

例句 He worked day and night in order to earn more money.
他日以繼夜地工作，以賺更多錢。

搭配詞 day and night 日以繼夜地

daybreak [ˋdeˏbrek] n. 破曉、黎明 Track 2481

例句 By the time my father came back home, it was daybreak.
我爸回到家的時候，已經黎明了。

反義字
nightfall 黃昏

December [dɪˋsɛmbɚ] n. 十二月 Track 2482

例句 Christmas is on December 25th. 聖誕節在十二月25日。

縮寫
Dec.

---

dormitory [ˋdɔrməˏtorɪ] n. 宿舍 Track 2483

例句 It takes me half an hour to get to my dormitory from the library.
從圖書館到我的宿舍要半個小時。

縮寫
dorm

---

during [ˋdjʊrɪŋ] prep. 在……期間 Track 2484

例句 Would you help me look after Tim during my pregnancy?
你可以在我懷孕期間替我照顧提姆嗎？

搭配詞
during pregnancy
在懷孕期間

---

dusk [dʌsk] n. 黃昏、幽暗 Track 2485

例句 He practiced playing the piano from dawn till dusk.
他從凌晨到黃昏都在練習彈鋼琴。

---

early [ˋɝlɪ] adj. 早的、早期的、及早的 Track 2486

例句 He gets up early, so he's never late for work.
他總是很早起，所以上班從不遲到。

諺語
Early bird gets the worms.
早起的鳥兒有蟲吃。

---

era [ˋɪrə] n. 時代 Track 2487

例句 The death of the great emperor marked the end of an era.
那名偉大的皇帝死亡之時，也就是一個時代的終結之時。

---

eve [iv] n. 前夕 Track 2488

例句 It is our tradition to gather together for a big dinner on Christmas Eve. 我們的傳統是在聖誕節前夕團圓吃大餐。

搭配詞
New Year's Eve 新年前夕

---

evening [ˋivnɪŋ] n. 傍晚、晚上 Track 2489

例句 We had a great time this evening. Thank you for your hospitality.
我們今天晚上玩得很開心。謝謝你的熱情款待。

---

ever [ˋɛvɚ] adv. 曾經、永遠 Track 2490

例句 This is the best book that I have ever read.
這是我曾讀過最好的一本書。

exact [ɪgˋzækt] adj. 正確的、精確的 Track 2491

例句 When is the exact time and date of the meeting?
會議的精確時間與日期是什麼時候呢？

同義字 precise

fall [fɔl] n./v. 秋天、落下 Track 2492

例句 He fell down the stairs. 他從樓梯上摔下去了。

搭配詞 fall down 摔倒

February [ˋfɛbruˏɛrɪ] n. 二月 Track 2493

例句 Chinese New Year usually falls in February.
中國新年通常是在二月。

縮寫 Feb.

festival [ˋfɛstəvl̩] n. 節日 Track 2494

例句 We always have a barbecue party on the Moon Festival.
我們總是在中秋節開烤肉派對。

搭配詞 Moon Festival 中秋節

final [ˋfaɪnl̩] adj. 最後的、最終的 Track 2495

例句 You need to study harder in order to pass the final exam.
你要考過期末考，就得更認真讀書。

搭配詞 final exam 期末考

five [faɪv] n. 五 Track 2496

例句 I have been studying English for five years.
我已經讀英語五年了。

following [ˋfɑloɪŋ] adj. 下一個 Track 2497

例句 The following statement was issued by the White House.
以下聲明是由白宮發出。

搭配詞 following statement 以下聲明

forever [fɚˋɛvɚ] adj./adv. 永遠的、永遠地 Track 2498

例句 Nobody can stay alive forever. 沒有人可以永遠活著。

former [ˋfɔrmɚ] adj. 以前的、先前的 Track 2499

例句 It is inappropriate to speak ill of your former boss in job interviews.
在面試時講你先前的老闆的壞話是不適宜的。

反義字 later 之後的

forwards [ˋfɔrwɚdz] adv. 今後、將來、向前 Track 2500

例句 The man leaned forward(s) on the table with an evil smile.
那個男人向前靠著桌子，露出邪惡的笑容。

反義字 backwards 向後

Friday [ˋfraɪ͵de] n. 星期五 ◀ Track 2501

例句 Please submit your application form by Friday.
請在星期五前繳交報名表。

縮寫 Fri.

---

front [frʌnt] n. 前面 ◀ Track 2502

例句 I can't see anything if you stand in front of me.
如果你站在我前面，我就什麼都看不到了。

搭配詞 in front of 在前面

---

gradual [ˋgrædʒuəl] adj. 逐漸的、漸進的 ◀ Track 2503

例句 Don't worry. Your father is in gradual recovery.
別擔心，你父親已經逐漸在康復了。

搭配詞 gradual recovery 逐漸康復

---

happen [ˋhæpən] v. 發生、碰巧 ◀ Track 2504

例句 They happened to be seated next to each other in the movie theater. 他們在戲院碰巧坐在隔壁。

搭配詞 happen to 碰巧

---

hereafter [͵hɪrˋæftɚ] n. 來世、將來 ◀ Track 2505

例句 He is a man who doesn't believe in the hereafter.
他是個不相信有來世的人。

同義字 thereafter 其後、之後

---

holiday [ˋhɑlə͵de] n. 假期、假日 ◀ Track 2506

例句 Chinese New Year is a holiday season which lasts for more than a week. 農曆過年假期超過一個禮拜。

搭配詞 holiday season 假期

---

hour [aʊr] n. 小時、時刻 ◀ Track 2507

例句 Traffic jam usually occurs during the rush hour.
尖鋒時刻通常會塞車。

搭配詞 rush hour 尖鋒時刻

---

hourly [ˋaʊrlɪ] adj. 每小時的 ◀ Track 2508

例句 It is unbelievable that his hourly pay is less than NT$70.
很難想像，他每小時的薪水比70元台幣還少。

---

immediate [ɪˋmidɪət] adj. 直接的、立即的 ◀ Track 2509

例句 The drug has an immediate effect to alleviate abdominal pain.
那個藥對腹痛有立即的舒緩效果。

搭配詞 immediate effect
立即的影響

---

interval [ˋɪntɚvl̩] n. 間隔、休息時間 ◀ Track 2510

例句 She went to the ladies' room during the interval of the concert.
她在音樂會休息時間到女士洗手間去。

January [ˋdʒænjʊˌɛrɪ] n. 一月 ◀Track 2511
例句 It snows a lot here in January. 這裡一月經常下雪。
縮寫 Jan.

July [dʒuˋlaɪ] n. 七月 ◀Track 2512
例句 Summer vacation starts in July. 暑假在七月開始。
縮寫 Jul.

June [dʒun] n. 六月 ◀Track 2513
例句 George Michael's birthday was on June 25, 1963.
喬治麥克的生日是1963年6月24日。
縮寫 Jun.

junior [ˋdʒunjɚ] adj. 年少的 ◀Track 2514
例句 He is five years my junior. 他比我年輕五歲。
反義字 senior 年長的

lag [læg] n./v. 延緩 ◀Track 2515
例句 He got really bad jet lag after his flight to Africa.
他搭飛機抵達非洲後，飽受時差之苦。
搭配詞 jet lag 時差

last [læst] adj. 最後的、上一個 ◀Track 2516
例句 At last, he confessed that he had committed the crime.
他終於坦承犯罪。
搭配詞 at last 終於

late [let] adj. 遲的、晚的 ◀Track 2517
例句 The police will find him sooner or later. 警方遲早會找到他。
搭配詞 sooner or later 遲早

lately [ˋletlɪ] adv. 最近 ◀Track 2518
例句 I haven't seen him lately. 我最近都沒看到他。
同義字 recently

latest [ˋletɪst] adj. 最新的 ◀Track 2519
例句 I just bought Taylor Swift's latest album.
我剛買了泰勒絲的最新專輯。

latter [ˋlætɚ] adj. 後者的 ◀Track 2520
例句 Do you agree that the latter idea is better?
你也覺得後面那個主意比較好嗎？
易混淆字 letter 字

lengthen [ˋlɛŋθən] v. 加長 ◀Track 2521
＊字尾-en有「使」的意思
例句 It is said that saving time is lengthening life.
有人說省時間就是延長人生。

反義字
shorten 縮短

lifelong [ˋlaɪfˋlɔŋ] adj. 終身的 ◀Track 2522
例句 Cindy and the old lady became lifelong friends.
辛蒂和那位年長的女士成為終身的朋友。

搭配詞
lifelong friend 終身的朋友

lifetime [ˋlaɪf͵taɪm] n. 一生 ◀Track 2523
例句 This is a chance of a lifetime. You should grasp it!
這是一生一次的機會，你應該要把握住！

搭配詞
a chance of a lifetime
一生一次的機會

lunar [ˋlunɚ] adj. 月亮的、陰曆的 ◀Track 2524
例句 When is the Lunar New Year this year?
今年的陰曆新年是什麼時候？

搭配詞
lunar calendar 陰曆

March [mɑrtʃ] n. 三月 ◀Track 2525
例句 The monsoon season used to start in March.
雨季以前都是在三月開始。

縮寫
Mar.

maturity [məˋtjurətɪ] n. 成熟期、成熟 ◀Track 2526
例句 It is said that men truly reach maturity after they serve in the army.
有人說男人要當兵以後才會到達成熟期。

反義字
immaturity 未成熟

May [me] n. 五月 ◀Track 2527
例句 My parents celebrate their wedding anniversary in May.
我父母每年五月慶祝結婚紀念日。

meantime [ˋmin͵taɪm] n. 期間、同時 ◀Track 2528
例句 I'll look after your baby, and you can take a rest in the meantime.
我來照顧你的寶寶，與此同時你可以休息。

搭配詞
in the meantime 在此同時

meanwhile [ˋmin͵hwaɪl] adv. 同時 ◀Track 2529
例句 Gary cooked dinner; meanwhile, Sally set the table.
蓋瑞煮了晚餐，而莎莉同時在餐桌上擺碗筷。

同義字
meantime

medieval [͵mɪdɪˋivəl] adj. 中世紀的 ◀Track 2530
例句 The castle is a classic example of medieval architecture.
這個城堡是中世紀建築一個經典的例子。

搭配詞
medieval architecture
中世紀建築

Monday [ˋmʌnde] n. 星期一 Track 2531

例句 Our weekly meeting is held on every Monday morning.
我們每週的會議是在星期一早上開。

縮寫 Mon.

month [mʌnθ] n. 月 Track 2532

例句 He is tired of doing the same work for months.
他月復一月做一樣的工作，已經膩了。

搭配詞 for months 幾個月來

morning [ˋmɔrnɪŋ] n. 早上、上午 Track 2533

例句 The pregnant woman is suffering from morning sickness.
那個孕婦正飽受晨吐所苦。

搭配詞 morning sickness（孕婦的）晨吐

night [naɪt] n. 晚上 Track 2534

例句 It is dangerous to go out in the dark night by yourself.
黑夜一個人出去是很危險的。

noon [nun] n. 正午、中午 Track 2535

例句 We got 10 orders by noon.
到中午時，我們已收到10份訂單了。

反義字 midnight 半夜

November [noˋvɛmbɝ] n. 十一月 Track 2536

例句 Mr. Bullock will take his annual vacation in November.
卜洛克先生將在十一月放他的年度假期。

縮寫 Nov.

now [naʊ] adv. 如今、現在 Track 2537

例句 You're obviously overweight. You'd better start exercising from now on. 你很明顯就過重了，最好從現在開始運動。

搭配詞 from now on 從現在開始

nowadays [ˋnaʊəˏdez] adv. 當今、現在 Track 2538

例句 Traveling abroad is very common nowadays.
現在出國旅行很普遍了。

numerous [ˋnjumərəs] adj. 為數眾多的 Track 2539

＊字尾-ous有轉變為形容詞之意

例句 It is amazing to see numerous stars shining in the sky.
看到眾多的星星在空中閃耀，真是棒。

o'clock [əˋklɑk] adv. ……點鐘 Track 2540

例句 The secretary is asked to arrive in the office before 8 o'clock in the morning. 那名祕書被要求在早上八點前到達辦公室。

October [ɑk`tobɚ] n. 十月 ◀Track 2541

例句 We plan to take a trip in Europe in October.
我們計畫在十月到歐洲旅行。

縮寫
Oct.

often [`ɔfən] adv. 常常、經常 ◀Track 2542

例句 Amy goes to a swanky restaurant every so often.
愛咪偶爾會去高級餐廳用餐。

搭配詞
every so often 偶爾

order [`ɔrdɚ] n./v. 次序、順序、命令 ◀Track 2543

例句 She barked out orders at her children.
她大聲命令她的孩子。

p.m./P.M. [`pi`ɛm] n. 下午 ◀Track 2544

例句 I have an appointment with the dentist at 5 p.m..
我下午五點和牙醫有約。

反義字
a.m. 上午

past [pæst] n. 過去、從前 ◀Track 2545

例句 It was impossible to travel abroad by plane in the past.
過去不可能搭飛機出國旅行。

搭配詞
in the past 在過去

period [`pɪrɪəd] n. 期間、時代 ◀Track 2546

例句 You'd better not drink iced water during your menstrual period.
你在經期最好別喝冰水。

搭配詞
menstrual period 月經期

present [`prɛzn̩t] adj. 目前的 ◀Track 2547

例句 I cannot resign from my job at present.
我目前不能辭掉工作。

搭配詞
at present 目前

previous [`priviəs] adj. 先前的 ◀Track 2548

例句 I cannot attend the opening ceremony because of a previous engagement. 因為先前有約，所以我不能參加開幕典禮。

prospective [prə`spɛktɪv] adj. 將來的、未來的 ◀Track 2549

＊字尾-ive有轉變為形容詞的意思

例句 It is obvious that they are not likely to be our prospective clients.
他們明顯不太可能是我們未來的客戶。

punctual [`pʌŋktʃuəl] adj. 準時的 ◀Track 2550

例句 Everyone in the class is supposed to be punctual, including the teachers. 班上的每個人都該準時，包括老師。

反義字
unpunctual 不準時的

quarter [ˋkwɔrtɚ] n. 四分之一、一個季度 Track 2551

例句 It is a quarter after three.
現在是三點過四分之一小時（十五分）。

recent [risn̩t] adj. 最近的 Track 2552

例句 What have you been busy with in recent years?
你最近幾年都在忙什麼？

反義字
ancient 古代的

regular [ˋrɛgjəlɚ] adj. 平常的、定期的、規律的 Track 2553

例句 Mrs. Su has been a regular customer of our restaurant for many years. 蘇太太是定期來我們餐廳的顧客很多年了。

搭配詞
regular customer 常客

Saturday [ˋsætɚde] n. 星期六 Track 2554

例句 Few people work on Saturdays in this country.
這個國家很少有人在星期六工作。

縮寫
Sat.

schedule [ˋskɛdʒul] n. 時刻表 Track 2555

例句 We arrived at the airport on schedule.
我們準時抵達機場。

搭配詞
on schedule 準時

season [ˋsizn̩] n. 季節 Track 2556

例句 Autumn is my favorite season of the year.
秋天是我最喜歡的季節。

second [ˋsɛkənd] adj. 第二的 Track 2557

例句 She makes a living by selling second-hand cars.
她靠賣二手車維生。

搭配詞
second-hand 二手的

semester [səˋmɛstɚ] n. 半學年、一學期 Track 2558

例句 The new semester will begin in September.
學校新學期在九月開始。

senior [ˋsinjɚ] adj. 年長的 Track 2559

例句 He is ten years my senior. 他比我年長十年。

反義字
junior 年少的

September [sɛpˋtɛmbɚ] n. 九月 Track 2560

例句 Mary is going to job-hop to the computer company in September.
瑪麗在九月要跳槽到那家電腦公司。

縮寫
Sept.

sequence [ˋsɪkwəns] n. 順序、連續 Track 2561

例句 The teacher described the historical events in sequence.
那位老師照順序描述了歷史事件。

搭配詞 in sequence 按照順序

series [ˋsɪriz] n. 連續 Track 2562

例句 A series of deadly attacks occurred in India.
在印度發生了一連串的致命攻擊。

搭配詞 a series of 一連串

shortly [ˋʃɔrtlɪ] adv. 不久、馬上 Track 2563

例句 He resigned from his job shortly after he won a lottery.
他贏了樂透不久後，就辭職了。

同義字 soon

simultaneous [ˏsaɪmḷˋtenɪəs] Track 2564
adj. 同時發生的、同步的

例句 It is my ambition to be a simultaneous interpreter in the future.
我的志向是以後成為同步口譯員。

搭配詞 simultaneous interpreter 同步口譯員

someday [ˋsʌmˏde] adv. 將來有一天、來日 Track 2565

例句 You will meet your Mr. Right someday.
你將來有一天總會遇到你的真命天子。

同義字 sometime

sometime [ˋsʌmˏtaɪm] adv. 某些時候、來日 Track 2566

例句 Let's arrange a lunch together sometime next month.
我們下個月某個時候來安排一起吃午餐吧。

易混淆字 sometimes 有時候

soon [sun] adv. 很快地、不久 Track 2567

例句 She got pregnant soon after she was married.
她結婚後很快就懷孕了。

搭配詞 soon after 不久之後

span [spæn] n. 一段時間 Track 2568

例句 Biopharmaceutical medicine can effectively extend people's life span. 生醫能有效延長人類的壽命。

搭配詞 life span 壽命

spring [sprɪŋ] n./v. 春天、跳躍、彈回 Track 2569

例句 We will go to Spain during spring break.
我們在春假期間要去西班牙玩。

搭配詞 spring break 春假

start [stɑrt] v. 開始、起點 Track 2570

例句 The new school semester will start in the beginning of September.
新學期會在九月初開始。

a b c d e f g h i j k l m n o p q r s t u v w x y z

succession [sək`sɛʃən] n. 連續 Track 2571

例句 Larry has been named the best employee three years in succession. 賴瑞已經連續三年被認為是最佳員工了。

搭配詞 in succession 連續地

successive [sək`sɛsɪv] adj. 連續的、繼續的 Track 2572

＊字尾-ive有轉變為形容詞的意思

例句 It is frustrating that we have had three successive months of terrible business. 我們連續三個月生意都不好，真令人煩躁。

summer [`sʌmɚ] n. 夏天、夏季 Track 2573

例句 The weather in summer here is humid and hot.
這裡的夏天天氣濕熱。

搭配詞 summer vacation 暑假

Sunday [`sʌnde] n. 星期日 Track 2574

例句 No one wants to work on Sundays.
沒有人想在星期日工作。

縮寫 Sun.

temporary [`tɛmpə,rɛrɪ] adj. 暫時的 Track 2575

例句 He is only a temporary employee, not a regular one.
他只是個暫時的員工，不是正式的。

搭配詞 temporary employee 臨時員工

then [ðɛn] adv. 當時、那時、然後 Track 2576

例句 The Industrial Revolution began in the 18th century, and global temperature has been on the rise since then.
工業革命從18世紀展開，從那時起，全球氣溫一直在上升。

搭配詞 since then 從那時以來

thereafter [ðɛr`æftɚ] adv. 此後、以後 Track 2577

例句 He divorced his ex-wife and married another woman thereafter.
他和前妻離婚，此後又娶了另一個女人。

同義字 hereafter

third [θɝd] adj. 第三 Track 2578

例句 One-third of my income will go to investment.
我的三分之一收入都拿去投資了。

搭配詞 one-third 三分之一

Thursday [`θɝzde] n. 星期四 Track 2579

例句 I have an appointment on Thursday.
我在星期四有一場約。

縮寫 Thur.

time [taɪm] n. 時間、次數 Track 2580

例句 His dad made time to watch him play soccer.
他爸爸騰出時間去看他踢足球。

搭配詞 make time 騰出時間

today [tə`de] n. 今天 ◀Track 2581

例句 Don't put off till tomorrow what you can do today.
別把今天可以做的事留到明天做了。

tomorrow [tə`mɔro] n. 明天 ◀Track 2582

例句 The meeting will take place the day after tomorrow.
會議將在後天舉行。

搭配詞 the day after tomorrow 後天

tonight [tə`naɪt] n./adv. 今天晚上 ◀Track 2583

例句 We probably have to stay up late tonight.
我們今天晚上大概得很晚睡了。

Tuesday [`tjuzde] n. 星期二 ◀Track 2584

例句 I will visit Mr. Smith on Tuesday.
我會在星期二拜訪史密斯先生。

縮寫 Tue.

twilight [`twaɪ͵laɪt] n. 黎明、黃昏 ◀Track 2585

例句 The vampires come out at twilight.
黃昏時分，吸血鬼都出來了。

twist [twɪst] v. 扭曲 ◀Track 2586

例句 That's not what I meant. Please don't twist my words.
那不是我的意思，請別扭曲我所說的話。

搭配詞 twist sb's words 扭曲（某人的）話

usual [`juʒuəl] adj. 通常的、平常的 ◀Track 2587

例句 He doesn't feel well today, but he still goes to work as usual.
他今天感覺不太舒服，但他還是一如往常地去上班了。

搭配詞 as usual 一如往常

vacation [ve`keʃən] n. 假期 ◀Track 2588

例句 We plan to spend our summer vacation at the beach.
我們打算在海邊度過暑假。

Wednesday [`wɛnzde] n. 星期三 ◀Track 2589

例句 We are asked to accomplish the work by next Wednesday
我們被要求在下星期三前完成工作。

縮寫 Wed.

week [wik] n. 星期 ◀Track 2590

例句 She cleans her house once a week.
她每週大掃除一次。

搭配詞 once a week 每週一次

weekday [ˋwik͵de] n. 平日、工作日 Track 2591

例句 Business lunch is only provided during the weekdays.
商業午餐只在平日提供。

反義字
holiday 假日

weekend [ˋwik͵ɛnd] n. 週末（星期六和星期日） Track 2592

例句 How about going shopping with us this weekend?
這週末要不要跟我們去逛街呢？

weekly [ˋwiklɪ] adj. 每週的 Track 2593

例句 I have subscribed to the weekly magazine for years.
我已經訂閱這個每週出版品很多年了。

搭配詞
weekly magazine 週刊

when [wɛn] adv. 什麼時候、何時 Track 2594

例句 Don't make any decisions when you are angry.
生氣的時候不要下決定。

whenever [wɛnˋɛvɚ] adv. 無論何時 Track 2595

例句 You can call me whenever you need someone to talk to.
你無論什麼時候需要人陪你講話，都可以打給我。

while [waɪl] n. 一段時間 Track 2596

例句 I haven't heard from him for a while.
我有一段時間沒聽到他的消息了。

搭配詞
for a while 有一段時間

winter [ˋwɪntɚ] n. 冬季 Track 2597

例句 We eat sticky rice balls during winter solstice.
我們冬至都會吃湯圓。

搭配詞
winter solstice 冬至

year [jɪr] n. 年、年歲 Track 2598

例句 May you be abundantly blessed year after year.
祝你年年蒙受豐盛的祝福。

搭配詞
year after year 年復一年

yearly [ˋjɪrlɪ] adj. 每年的 Track 2599

例句 Mr. Louise will have his yearly medical examination in June.
路易斯先生會在六月進行他的年度健康檢查。

yesterday [ˋjɛstɚde] n. 昨天、昨日 Track 2600

例句 He came to New York the day before yesterday.
他前天有來紐約。

搭配詞
the day before yesterday
前天

Test 10 關鍵英單總測驗第10回

以下測驗題皆出自書中第十回「**和時間有關的單字**」，快來檢視自己的學習成果吧！

一、選擇題

1. They're going to celebrate their 30th wedding _____ .
   (A) era
   (B) calendar
   (C) daybreak
   (D) anniversary

2. When is the _____ departure time?
   (A) gradual
   (B) hereafter
   (C) exact
   (D) prospective

3. He exercises on a _____ basis.
   (A) regular
   (B) shortly
   (C) senior
   (D) twilight

4. She took five courses this _____ .
   (A) lifetime
   (B) semester
   (C) maturity
   (D) period

5. She got really bad jet _____ after a long flight.
   (A) order
   (B) schedule
   (C) lag
   (D) start

6. He quit his job after getting his _____-end bonuses.
   (A) year
   (B) week
   (C) yearly
   (D) past

7. Students are required to be _____ for the class.
   (A) often
   (B) meantime
   (C) late
   (D) punctual

8. The children spent their _____ in a summer camp.
   (A) vacation
   (B) autumn
   (C) age
   (D) century

9. She aspires to be a _____ interpreter.
   (A) second
   (B) simultaneous
   (C) following
   (D) medieval

10. She lives in the school _____ and has two roommates.
   (A) festival
   (B) sequence
   (C) dormitory
   (D) zone

二、克漏字測驗

According to a __1__ newspapers report, a __2__ capsule from 1914 was found near a construction site. Inside the capsule were a few pages of a New Orleans guidebook and a 1914 __3__.

The capsule would belong to the local museum and be displayed all __4__ around except every __5__, said the museum's general manager.

1.
(A) daily
(B) yearly
(C) tomorrow
(D) immediate

2.
(A) time
(B) interval
(C) present
(D) recent

3.
(A) season
(B) cycle
(C) calendar
(D) accidental

4.
(A) eve
(B) afternoon
(C) holiday
(D) year

5.
(A) Monday
(B) lunar
(C) schedule
(D) temporary

關鍵英單總測驗第10回 中譯與解答

一、選擇題

1. 他們將慶祝結婚30周年紀念日。
   (A) 時代
   (B) 日曆
   (C) 黎明
   (D) 周年紀念日

2. 出發的精確時間是何時?
   (A) 逐漸的
   (B) 來世
   (C) 精確的
   (D) 潛在的

3. 他規律運動。
   (A) 規律的
   (B) 不久的
   (C) 年長的
   (D) 黃昏

4. 她這學期修了5堂課。
   (A) 終身
   (B) 學期
   (C) 成熟期
   (D) 期間

5. 她在長途飛行後，深受時差之苦。
   (A) 秩序
   (B) 時刻表
   (C) 延遲
   (D) 開始

6. 他拿到年終獎金後就離職了。
   (A) 年
   (B) 週
   (C) 每年的
   (D) 過去

7. 學生被要求上課要準時。
   (A) 時常地
   (B) 同時地
   (C) 遲到的
   (D) 準時的

8. 這群孩子在夏令營度過假期。
   (A) 假期
   (B) 秋季
   (C) 年齡
   (D) 世紀

9. 她立志要當同步口譯員。
   (A) 第二的
   (B) 同步的
   (C) 下一個的
   (D) 中世紀的

10. 她住學校宿舍並有2名室友。
   (A) 節慶
   (B) 順序
   (C) 宿舍
   (D) 地區

二、克漏字測驗

根據一份每日發行的報紙報導，一個1914年的時空錦囊在一處工地附近被人發現。錦囊裡裝有幾頁的紐奧良指南和1914年的日曆。

錦囊將歸屬於當地博物館，該館館長表示，錦囊將全年展出，除了每週一例外。

1.
(A) 每日的
(B) 每年的
(C) 明天
(D) 立即的

2.
(A) 時間
(B) 休息時間
(C) 目前的
(D) 最近的

3.
(A) 季節
(B) 週期
(C) 日曆
(D) 意外的

4.
(A) 前夕
(B) 下午
(C) 假日
(D) 年

5.
(A) 星期一
(B) 陰曆的
(C) 時刻表
(D) 暫時的

一、選擇題

1.(D) 2.(C) 3.(A) 4.(B) 5.(C)
6.(A) 7.(D) 8.(A) 9.(B) 10.(C)

二、克漏字測驗

1.(A) 2.(A) 3.(C)
4.(D) 5.(A)

Unit 11 和正面情緒有關的單字

多益測驗的命題強調生活化與實用性，學會這些與「正面情緒」有關的單字，不僅能讓你在多益考場上所向披靡，在日常生活上也可以靈活運用喔！

開心愉快的氛圍可以這麼說

- **I'm glad to hear this delightful news.**
  我很高興聽到這個令人欣喜的消息。
- **Grandma was pleased that her reputation was rebuilt.**
  奶奶很高興她的名譽得到了回復。
- **Her perfect performance brings a smile on the coach's face.**
  她完美的表現讓教練笑容滿面。

形容人活潑有朝氣可以這麼說

- **Her dynamic energy led the team to their victory.**
  她的活力帶領團隊獲得勝利。
- **Working around a bunch of lively children can be tiresome.**
  在工作時有一群活力充沛的小孩在周圍是很累人的。

追求榮譽可以這麼說

- **Saving others from drowning is considered an heroic act.**
  拯救溺水的人被認為是英勇的行為。
- **The athlete had another glorious victory at the Grand Prix Finale.**
  這名運動選手在大獎賽決賽獲得又一次勝利。

莊嚴肅穆可以這麼說

- **I solemnly swear I will not cheat on test again.**
  我鄭重發誓，我不會再考試作弊了。
- **This majestic temple is a scared place for the believers.**
  這個雄偉的寺廟對信徒而言是神聖的場所。

有利於自己的狀況可以這麼說

- **I'm satisfied with the current situation.**
  我對現況感到滿足。
- **The previous offer is more favorable for us.**
  先前的提案對我們較為有利。

Unit 11 和正面情緒有關的單字

abundance [ə`bʌndəns] n. 充裕、富足 Track 2601

＊字尾-ance有轉變為名詞之意

例句 There are stars in abundance in the dark sky.
黑暗的天空充滿了星星。

反義字 shortage 匱乏

acknowledgment [ək`nɑlɪdʒmənt] Track 2602

n. 承認、坦白、確認　＊字尾-ment有轉變為名詞之意

例句 The teacher was given an award in acknowledgment of his dedication to education. 那位老師榮獲了感謝他對教育貢獻的獎。

acute [ə`kjut] adj. 敏銳的、激烈的 Track 2603

例句 She has an acute sixth sense.
她的第六感很敏銳。

adaptation [ˌædəp`teʃən] n. 適應、順應、改編 Track 2604

＊字尾-tion有轉變為名詞的意思

例句 This play is an adaptation of a best-selling novel.
這部劇是一本暢銷小說的改編。

同義字 adjustment

admirable [`ædmərəbḷ] adj. 令人欽佩的 Track 2605

＊字尾-able有「可以、能」的意思

例句 He is an admirable soldier. 他是位令人欽佩的軍人。

admire [əd`maɪr] v. 欽佩、讚賞 Track 2606

例句 We admire Mother Teresa's selfless devotion to the poor and sick.
我們很欽佩德蕾莎修女對於貧病人們所行的無私奉獻。

同義字 respect

adore [ə`dor] v. 崇拜、敬愛、喜愛 Track 2607

例句 I adore my grandfather a lot. He's the sweetest old man.
我很愛我爺爺，他是個超可愛的老人。

反義字 abhor 厭惡

advantage [əd`væntɪdʒ] n./v. 利益、優勢 Track 2608

例句 Falcon 9 rocket has the advantage of being reusable.
獵鷹9號火箭的優勢是可回收使用。

搭配詞 have the advantage of 佔優勢

agreeable [ə`griəbḷ] adj. 好說話的、令人愉快的 Track 2609
＊字尾-able有「可以、能」的意思
例句 Jenny is usually a very agreeable girl.
珍妮通常是很好說話的。

aloud [ə`laʊd] adv. 高聲地、大聲地 Track 2610
例句 Julia read the story aloud to the children.
茱麗雅大聲把故事念給孩子們聽。

amazement [ə`mezmənt] n. 吃驚、驚喜 Track 2611
＊字尾-ment有轉變為名詞之意
例句 To everyone's amazement, the tiny boy lifted up a truck.
讓大家吃驚的是，那個小男孩居然把卡車舉起來了。
搭配詞 to one's amazement 令人感到驚訝的是……

amiable [`emɪəbḷ] adj. 友善的、可親的 Track 2612
＊字尾-able有「可以、能」的意思
例句 My next-door neighbors are amiable people.
我的隔壁鄰居都是友善的人。
同義字 friendly

applicable [`æplɪkəbḷ] adj. 適用的、適當的 Track 2613
＊字尾-able有「可以、能」的意思
例句 The rules are not applicable here. 這些規定在這裡不適用。

approximate [ə`prɑksəmɪt] Track 2614
adj./v. 相近的、大概的
例句 Can you give me an approximate number?
可以給我一個大概的數字嗎？
搭配詞 the approximate number 概數

aptitude [`æptə͵tjud] n. 才能、資質 Track 2615
例句 The little girl has an aptitude for languages.
小女孩有語言方面的才能。
同義字 talent

articulate [ɑr`tɪkjə͵let] v. 清晰地發音 Track 2616
例句 Please articulate your thoughts carefully.
請小心點把你的想法說得清晰點。

artifact [`ɑrtɪ͵fækt] n. 加工品、手工藝品 Track 2617
例句 The ancient Egypt artifacts in the exhibition are amazing.
展覽中的古埃及手工藝品很棒。
搭配詞 ancient artifact 古老的手工藝品

attraction [ə`trækʃən] n. 魅力、吸引力 Track 2618
＊字尾-tion有轉變為名詞的意思
例句 The main attraction in this National Park is the waterfalls.
這個國家公園最主要的魅力就是它有瀑布。
反義字 repulsion 拒絕、嫌惡

beloved [bɪˋlʌvd] adj./n. 鍾愛的、心愛的、愛人 ◀Track 2619

例句 My beloved lady, why are you crying?
我心愛的女孩，妳哭什麼呢？

同義字 dear

beneficial [ˌbɛnəˋfɪʃəl] adj. 有益的、有利的 ◀Track 2620

＊字尾-ial有轉變為形容詞之意

例句 Exercising every morning is beneficial to us.
每天早上運動對我們有益。

best [bɛst] adj./n./adv. 最好的、最高程度地 ◀Track 2621

例句 Lord of the Rings trilogy was in the best-seller list in 1966.
魔戒三部曲在1966年曾在最暢銷的書單上榜。

搭配詞 best-seller 賣得最好的

better [ˋbɛtɚ] adj./adv./v./n. 較好的、更好的 ◀Track 2622

例句 This dish will taste better if you add some more pepper.
如果妳多加一點胡椒粉，這一道菜會更好吃。

blush [blʌʃ] v./n. 臉紅 ◀Track 2623

例句 Julia blushed at the mention of her lover's name.
一提到她愛人的名字，茱利亞就臉紅了。

brave [brev] adj./v. 勇敢的、冒（風險） ◀Track 2624

例句 The little girl was not brave enough to sleep alone.
小女孩不夠勇敢，不敢一個人睡。

calm [kɑm] n./v./adj. 寧靜、使平靜、平靜的 ◀Track 2625

例句 Calm down. Let's dial 911 for help. 冷靜，快打119求救。

搭配詞 calm down 平靜下來

carefree [ˋkɛrˏfri] adj. 無憂無慮的 ◀Track 2626

＊字尾-free有「不包含、沒有」之意

例句 She lives a carefree lifestyle and spends money whenever she wants. 她的人生無憂無慮，想花錢就花。

同義字 happy

carol [ˋkærəl] n./v. 頌歌、讚美詞 ◀Track 2627

例句 The children sang Christmas carols at St. Paul's Cathedral.
這群孩子在聖保羅大教堂唱起聖誕頌歌。

搭配詞 Christmas carol 聖誕頌歌

caution [ˋkɔʃən] n./v. 謹慎 ◀Track 2628

例句 You need to proceed with caution. 你必須謹慎前進。

a b c d e f g h i j k l m n o p q r s t u v w x y z

cautious [ˋkɔʃəs] adj. 謹慎的、小心的 Track 2629
＊字尾-ous有轉變為形容詞之意
例句 You'd better be cautious when approaching the lion.
靠近獅子時，最好要小心。

同義字 careful

certainty [ˋsɝtn̩tɪ] n. 肯定、有把握 Track 2630
＊字尾-ty有轉變為名詞之意
例句 How much is your certainty of success in this project?
你有多肯定這個計畫會成功？

character [ˋkærɪktɚ] n. 個性 Track 2631
例句 Harrison Ford is a character actor.
哈里遜福特是位性格演員。

搭配詞 a character actor 性格演員

charitable [ˋtʃærətəbl̩] Track 2632
adj. 溫和的、仁慈的、慈善事業的 ＊字尾-able有「可以、能」的意思
例句 She is a charitable old lady who gives generously to the poor.
她是個仁慈的老太太，總是慷慨地捐贈給窮人。

同義字 generous

charity [ˋtʃærətɪ] n. 慈悲、慈善、寬容 Track 2633
例句 Sam regularly donates money to charity.
山姆固定捐錢給慈善機構。

chat [tʃæt] v./n. 聊天、閒談 Track 2634
例句 I like to chat with her; she's hilarious.
我喜歡和她聊天，她超爆笑。

cheer [tʃɪr] n./v. 歡呼 Track 2635
例句 She cheered loudly when her favorite idol showed up.
她最喜歡的偶像出現時，她大聲歡呼。

cheerful [ˋtʃɪrfəl] adj. 愉快的、興高采烈的 Track 2636
＊字尾-ful有「充滿」的意思
例句 Kevin has become much more cheerful after he got himself a girlfriend. 凱文找了個女朋友以後，就變得愉快多了。

反義字 cheerless 不快樂的

cherish [ˋtʃɛrɪʃ] v. 珍愛、珍惜 Track 2637
例句 The woman cherished the gifts from her children.
這個女人很珍惜孩子們給她的禮物。

childish [ˋtʃaɪdɪʃ] adj. 孩子氣的 Track 2638
＊字尾-ish有「像、類似」的意思
例句 Don't be so childish! You're already thirty!
別這麼孩子氣，你都三十歲了！

反義字 adult 成年的

childlike [ˋtʃaɪldlaɪk] adj. 純真的、孩子般的 Track 2639

＊字尾-like有「像、類似」的意思

例句 She has a big, childlike eyes. 她有又大又純真的雙眼。

chuckle [ˋtʃʌkl̩] v./n. 輕輕地笑 Track 2640

例句 My parents were chuckling over the photographs taken when we were children. 我父母邊看著我們小時候的照片邊輕笑。

同義字 titter

civilize [ˋsɪvə͵laɪz] v. 啟發、使開化、使文明 Track 2641

＊字尾-ize有「使」的意思

例句 Can you at least try to be civilized to each other? 你們可不可以至少試著互相表現得像文明人一點？

clarity [ˋklærətɪ] n. 清澈透明 Track 2642

＊字尾-ity有轉變為名詞的意思

例句 The clarity of diction is vital for a public speaker. 公眾演講者一定要能清楚地講話。

cleanse [klɛnz] v. 清洗、使清潔 Track 2643

例句 The doctor cleansed the wound before stitching it. 醫師在把傷口縫起來前先清潔了傷口。

反義字 stain 沾汙

clearance [ˋklɪrəns] n. 清潔、解除、空隙 Track 2644

＊字尾-ance有轉變為名詞之意

例句 The store will hold a basement sale to make a clearance of the old stock. 那家店將辦清倉大拍賣以清空庫存。

搭配詞 make a clearance of 清理

close [klos]/[kloz] adj./adv. 靠近的、親近的 Track 2645

例句 Julia is my close friend. We have a lot in common. 茱利亞是我親近的好友。我們有很多共同點。

搭配詞 close friend 親近的好友

comfortable [ˋkʌmfətəbl̩] adj. 舒服的 Track 2646

＊字尾-able有「可以、能」的意思

例句 I just bought a comfortable and soft bed for my new house. 我剛為了我的新家買了一張舒服又柔軟的床。

common [ˋkɑmən] adj. 共同的、平常的、普通的 Track 2647

＊字首com-有「共同」之意

例句 Donald Trump and his daughter Ivanka Trump have a lot in common. 唐納川普和女兒伊凡卡有很多共同點。

搭配詞 in common (with) 與……有共同點

compassion [kəmˋpæʃən] n. 同情、憐憫 Track 2648

＊字首com-有「共同」之意

例句 The doctor showed no compassion for the patient. 醫師完全沒對他的病人表現出任何同情。

同義字 sympathy

a b c d e f g h i j k l m n o p q r s t u v w x y z

compassionate [kəmˋpæʃənɪt] Track 2649

adj. 憐憫的、慈悲的　＊字首com-有「共同」之意

例句 I think the compassionate judge will give him a light sentence.
我想那個慈悲的法官會判他輕刑。

compensate [ˋkɑmpənˏset] v. 抵銷、彌補 Track 2650

＊字首com-有「共同」之意

例句 Nothing can compensate for the loss of one's health.
沒有什麼能彌補失去的健康。

搭配詞 compensate for 補償、彌補

compensation [ˏkɑmpənˋseʃən] Track 2651

n. 報酬、賠償　＊字首com-有「共同」之意

例句 The current government promised to make compensation for victims persecuted by its former regime.
現任政府承諾針對受到前任政權迫害的受害者，將做出賠償。

搭配詞 make compensation for 賠償、補償

comprehensive [ˏkɑmprɪˋhɛnsɪv] Track 2652

adj. 全面的、廣泛的、包羅萬象的、綜合的、理解的
＊字尾-ive有轉變為形容詞之意

例句 They conducted a comprehensive review of the marketing strategies. 他們全面檢討行銷策略。

搭配詞 comprehensive ability 理解力

concede [kənˋsid] v. 承認 Track 2653

例句 You have no choice but to concede defeat in this matter.
你別無選擇，只能承認失敗了。

搭配詞 concede defeat 承認失敗

conception [kənˋsɛpʃən] Track 2654

n. 概念、計畫、懷孕、開始　＊字尾-tion有轉變為名詞的意思

例句 I have no conception of how to run a business.
我完全沒有概念如何經營一家公司。

反義字 misconception 錯誤的概念

concise [kənˋsaɪs] adj. 簡潔的、簡明的 Track 2655

例句 I need a clear and concise summary.
我需要一個清楚又簡潔的概要。

同義字 short

confidential [ˏkɑnfəˋdɛnʃəl] Track 2656

adj. 可信任的、機密的　＊字尾-ial有轉變為形容詞的意思

例句 She has confidential papers regarding the research and development of the rocket. 她持有關於火箭研發的機密文件。

搭配詞 confidential papers 機密文件

congratulate [kənˋgrætʃəˏlet] v. 恭喜 Track 2657

例句 We should congratulate him on his success.
我們應該祝賀他成功才對。

搭配詞 congratulate sb. on sth. 為某事向某人祝賀

conscience [ˋkɑnʃəns] n. 良心 Track 2658

例句 After killing the girl, his conscience bothered him every night.
殺了那個女孩後，他每晚都受到良心譴責。

consequence [ˋkɑnsə͵kwɛns] n. 結果、影響 Track 2659

例句 The company he worked for went bankrupt. In consequence, he lost his job. 他任職的公司倒閉了，結果他失業了。

搭配詞 in consequence 結果

consequent [ˋkɑnsə͵kwɛnt] Track 2660

adj. 必然的、隨之引起的 ＊字尾-ent有轉變為形容詞的意思

例句 Global warming and the consequent climate change will trigger disasters that cannot be reversed.
全球暖化及隨之引起的氣候變遷，將引發不可逆轉的災害。

反義字 inconsequent 矛盾的

considerate [kənˋsɪdərɪt] adj. 體貼的 Track 2661

例句 He is more considerate than anyone I have met.
他比任何我遇過的人都還體貼。

反義字 inconsiderate 不顧別人的

continual [kənˋtɪnjuəl] adj. 連續的 Track 2662

＊字尾-al有轉變為形容詞之意

例句 I am fed up with her continual nagging.
我受不了她連續的嘮叨。

同義字 continuous

convenient [kənˋvinjənt] adj. 適當的、方便的 Track 2663

例句 Is it convenient for you to speak of the issue now?
請問對你來說現在方便討論這個議題嗎？

同義詞 handy、easy to use

courage [ˋkɝɪdʒ] n. 勇氣 Track 2664

例句 Screw up your courage; it's time to fight.
鼓起勇氣吧，該戰鬥了。

搭配詞 screw up one's courage 鼓起勇氣

courteous [ˋkɝtjəs] adj. 有禮貌的 Track 2665

＊字尾-ous有轉變為形容詞之意

例句 It is not necessary to be so courteous to her.
不需要對她這麼禮貌。

同義字 polite

courtesy [ˋkɝtəsɪ] n. 禮貌 Track 2666

例句 Lack of courtesy is regarded as a disease of the modern society.
有人認為沒有禮貌是現代社會的通病。

credibility [͵krɛdəˋbɪlətɪ] n. 可信度、確實性 Track 2667

例句 Do you think what he said has any credibility?
你覺得他講的話有什麼可信度嗎？

credible [ˋkrɛdəbḷ] adj. 可信的、可靠的 Track 2668

＊字尾-ible有「可以、能」的意思

例句 Is your source credible? 你的消息來源是可靠的嗎？

反義字 incredible 難以置信的、極好的

criterion [kraɪˋtɪrɪən] n. 標準、基準 Track 2669

例句 What criterion do you use to judge the quality of a student's work?
你是用什麼標準來評量學生作品的品質呢？

同義字 measure

crucial [ˋkruʃəl] adj. 關係重大的 Track 2670

例句 These negotiations are crucial to the future of our firm.
這些協議對我們的公司未來關係重大。

同義字 important

curious [ˋkjʊrɪəs] adj. 求知的、好奇的 Track 2671

例句 He is very curious about my new boyfriend.
他對我的新男友很好奇。

反義字 incurious 無關心的

customary [ˋkʌstəmˏɛrɪ] adj. 慣例的、平常的 Track 2672

＊字尾-ary有轉變為形容詞之意

例句 It is customary to give others gifts on their birthdays.
在別人生日時給他們禮物是一種慣例。

同義字 accustomed

decent [ˋdisn̩t] adj. 端正的、合乎禮儀 Track 2673

例句 It's only decent to at least apologize when you're two hours late for a date. 約會遲到兩小時，至少也該道個歉才合乎禮儀吧。

反義字 indecent 下流的、粗鄙的

decisive [dɪˋsaɪsɪv] adj. 有決斷力的、決定性的 Track 2674

＊字尾-ive有轉變為形容詞之意

例句 Every team needs a decisive person to lead.
每個團隊都需要一個有決斷力的人來領導。

反義字 indecisive 無決斷力的

deliberate [dɪˋlɪbəret] v./adj. 仔細考慮 Track 2675

例句 We deliberated on what to do about the complaints carefully.
我們仔細考慮了對於抗議的事該如何處理。

反義字 hasty 輕率的

derive [dəˋraɪv] v. 引出、源自 Track 2676

例句 Many English words are derived from Latin.
許多英文字都出自拉丁文。

搭配詞 derive from 源自……

detach [dɪˋtætʃ] v. 派遣、分開 Track 2677

例句 I tried to detach the clip from the paper, but it won't come off.
我試著把夾子從紙上分開，但它都拔不下來。

反義字 attach 繫上

declaration [ˏdɛkləˋreʃən] n. 正式宣告 Track 2678

＊字尾-tion有轉變為名詞的意思

例句 The Declaration of Independence was written mostly by Thomas Jefferson. 美國獨立宣言大部分的內容是由傑佛遜撰擬的。

搭配詞 Declaration of Independence 美國獨立宣言

dedication [ˏdɛdəˋkeʃən] n. 奉獻、投入 Track 2679
＊字尾-tion有轉變為名詞的意思
例句 Her dedication is what led to her success.
她的投入是造就她成功的原因。

---

dedicate [ˋdɛdəˏket] v. 供奉、奉獻 Track 2680
例句 He dedicated his first book to his supportive wife.
他把他的第一本著作獻給一直在支持他的妻子。

搭配詞
dedicate to 將……獻給

---

deem [dim] v. 認為、視為 Track 2681
例句 Richard deemed it his duty to help others.
理查認為幫助他人是他的職責。

同義字
think

---

delight [dɪˋlaɪt] v./n. 欣喜、使高興 Track 2682
例句 The audience roared in delight when the performers came out.
表演者們一走出來，觀眾們就欣喜地大叫。

搭配詞
in delight 欣喜

---

delightful [dɪˋlaɪtfəl] adj. 令人欣喜的 Track 2683
＊字尾-ful有「充滿」的意思
例句 The taste of the macaroon was delightful.
馬卡龍吃起來真是令人欣喜。

反義字
sorrowful 悲傷的、傷心的

---

density [ˋdɛnsətɪ] n. 稠密、濃密 Track 2684
＊字尾-ity有轉變為名詞之意
例句 The density of the bushes made it impossible to see very far.
樹叢太濃密，讓人無法看得很遠。

同義字
denseness

---

dense [dɛns] adj. 密集的、稠密的 Track 2685
例句 There's a dense fog at the airport so we can't take off.
機場有濃密的霧，所以我們無法起飛。

同義字
compact

---

dependable [dɪˋpɛndəbl] adj. 可靠的 Track 2686
＊字尾-able有「可以、能」的意思
例句 He is a dependable and hard-working employee.
它是個可靠又努力的員工。

同義字
trustworthy

---

designate [ˋdɛzɪgˏnet] v./adj. 指出、指定的 Track 2687
例句 She is his designated successor.
她是他指定的繼任者。

---

destined [ˋdɛstɪnd] adj. 命運註定的 Track 2688
例句 It's a sad love story; they are destined never to see each other again. 這是個悲傷的愛情故事。他們命中註定再也不會見面。

deserve [dɪˋzɝv] v. 值得、應得 Track 2689

例句 He deserves the promotion; he's been working hard for this company. 他值得升遷，他一直很努力為公司工作。

desirable [dɪˋzaɪrəbḷ] adj. 值得的、稱心如意的 Track 2690

＊字尾-able有「可以、能」的意思

例句 This is a less than desirable outcome.
這是個不怎麼稱心如意的結果。

反義字 undesirable 令人不快的、討厭的

desire [dɪˋzaɪr] v./n. 渴望、期望 Track 2691

例句 The performance of the baseball player left a lot to be desired this season. 這名棒球員在這一季的表現仍有許多努力改善的空間。

搭配詞 leave a lot to be desired 有許多期望極須改進

desperate [ˋdɛspərɪt] adj. 絕望的 Track 2692

例句 The drowning man clawed desperately at the surface.
溺水的男人絕望地往水面亂抓。

反義字 hopeful 充滿希望的

despise [dɪˋspaɪz] v. 鄙視、輕視 Track 2693

＊字首des-有「否定、相反」之意

例句 You shouldn't despise a man because he is poor.
你不能因為一個人貧窮而鄙視他。

同義字 disdain

despite [dɪˋspaɪt] prep./n. 不管、不顧 Track 2694

＊字首des-有「否定、相反」之意

例句 Despite the fact that he's only 15, he's very precocious.
儘管他才15歲，他的心智非常早熟。

搭配詞 despite the fact that... 雖然……

determination [dɪ͵tɝməˋneʃən] n. 決心 Track 2695

＊字尾-tion有轉變為名詞的意思

例句 You need determination to overcome the adversity.
你需要決心才能克服這個逆境。

反義字 hesitation 猶豫

devote [dɪˋvot] v. 貢獻、奉獻 Track 2696

例句 He decides to devote himself to becoming a doctor.
他決定奉獻於成為醫生。

搭配詞 devote to 奉獻給……、致力於……

devotion [dɪˋvoʃən] n. 摯愛、熱愛、奉獻 Track 2697

＊字尾-tion有轉變為名詞的意思

例句 His devotion to his cause is admirable.
他對他目標的奉獻很令人讚賞。

同義字 fidelity

diverse [dɪˋvɝs] adj. 互異的、不同的、五花八門的 Track 2698

＊字首di-有「二」之意

例句 London is an ethnically diverse city. 倫敦是多元種族的城市。

反義字 same 同樣的

difficulty [ˋdɪfə͵kʌltɪ] n. 困難 ◀ Track 2699

＊字尾-ty有轉變為名詞之意

例句 Our engineer has difficulty finding a solution for this bug.
我們的工程師很難找到這項錯誤的解決方法。

diligent [ˋdɪlədʒənt] adj. 勤勉的、勤奮的 ◀ Track 2700

例句 Your little daughter is not only clever but also diligent.
你的小女兒不但聰明而且很勤奮。

同義字 persistent

disciplinary [ˋdɪsəplɪn͵ɛrɪ] adj. 紀律、訓育的 ◀ Track 2701

例句 It is wrong for you to take disciplinary measures under such a circumstance. 你在這樣的狀況下不應該用紀律規定來處理。

discreet [dɪˋskrit] adj. 謹慎的、慎重的 ◀ Track 2702

例句 Instead of being discreet, he blurted out the secret in front of everyone. 他完全沒謹慎，直接在大家面前把祕密講出來了。

反義字 indiscreet 不慎重的、輕率的

disposable [dɪˋspozəbl̩] ◀ Track 2703

adj. 可任意使用的、免洗的 ＊字首dis-有「分離」之意

例句 Due to mortgage, she doesn't have any disposable income to spend on luxury goods.
因為房貸，她沒有任何可支配所得可購買奢侈品。

搭配詞 disposable income 可支配所得

distinguished [dɪˋstɪŋgwɪʃt] adj. 卓越的 ◀ Track 2704

＊字首dis-有「分離」之意

例句 He is distinguished in many different spheres.
他在許多領域都很卓越。

divine [dəˋvaɪn] adj. 神的、神聖的 ◀ Track 2705

例句 Jesus is believed by Christians to be divine.
基督徒相信耶穌是神聖的。

due [dju] adj. 預定的、應給的 ◀ Track 2706

例句 Jason Wu became a famous designer due to his talent and hard work. 吳季剛由於天份和努力，而成為知名設計師。

搭配詞 due to 因為、由於

dynamic [daɪˋnæmɪk] ◀ Track 2707

adj./n. 動能的、動力的、活躍的、動力

例句 I enjoy working in a dynamic team.
我喜歡在有活力的團隊中工作。

反義字 static 靜的、靜態的、靜力的

ecstasy [ˋɛkstəsɪ] n. 狂喜、入迷 ◀ Track 2708

例句 He went into ecstasy after using drugs.
他嗑藥後整個陷入狂喜狀態。

同義字 rapture

elaborate [ɪˋlæbəˏrɪt]/[ɪˋlæbəˏret] Track 2709

adj./v. 精心的、詳細的、詳細說明

例句 Do you mind elaborating on the energy crisis and the solutions developed by your company?
你可以詳細說明能源危機和貴公司研發的解決方案嗎？

搭配詞
elaborate on 詳細說明

emotion [ɪˋmoʃən] n. 情感 Track 2710

例句 Sometimes I wonder if she has any emotions. She never even smiles. 有時我會好奇她到底有沒有情感。她甚至從來都不笑呢。

emotional [ɪˋmoʃənl] adj. 情感的 Track 2711

＊字尾-al有轉變為形容詞之意

例句 Linda is embarrassingly emotional in public.
琳達在眾人面前情感豐富到一種丟臉的程度。

enclosure [ɪnˋkloʒɚ] n. 圍住、附件 Track 2712

＊字尾-ure有轉變為名詞之意

例句 A woman jumped into a polar bear enclosure and was attacked by the bear. 一位女子跳入北極熊的圍欄裡，遭到熊的攻擊。

同義字
corral

encounter [ɪnˋkaʊntɚ] v./n. 意外的相遇、遭遇 Track 2713

例句 It was a strange encounter that brought us together.
我們會遇見是因為一次奇怪的遭遇。

encourage [ɪnˋkɝɪdʒ] v. 鼓勵 Track 2714

＊字首en-有「使」之意

例句 My best friend encouraged me to do it.
我最好的朋友鼓勵我去做。

反義字
discourage 使沮喪

encouragement [ɪnˋkɝɪdʒmənt] n. 鼓勵 Track 2715

＊字首en-有「使」之意

例句 The little boy was greatly inspired by words of encouragement from his hero Elon Musk. 那位小男孩因為他的英雄伊隆馬斯克一席鼓勵的話，獲得很大的啟發。

搭配詞
words of encouragement
鼓勵的話

endurance [ɪnˋdjʊrəns] n. 耐力 Track 2716

例句 She showed great endurance during the climb.
她在登山時展現了無比的耐力。

enhance [ɪnˋhæns] v. 提高、增強 Track 2717

例句 The knowledge will enhance your performance.
這些知識會增強你的表現。

同義字
improve

ensure/insure [ɪnˋʃʊr]/[ɪnˋʃʊr] v. 確保、保證 Track 2718

例句 I can ensure the quality of our product.
我可以保證我們的產品品質。

同義字
protect

enthusiastic [ɪn͵θjuzɪ`æstɪk] Track 2719

adj. 熱心的、熱衷的

例句 My brother is very enthusiastic about photography.
我哥哥對攝影很熱衷。

反義字 unenthusiastic 冷淡的

EQ/emotional quotient Track 2720

[i kju]/[ɪ`moʃən! `kwoʃənt] n. 情緒商數

例句 The supermodel has very high EQ.
這個超級名模的情商很高。

---

exceptional [ɪk`sɛpʃən!] adj. 優秀的 Track 2721

＊字尾-al有轉變為形容詞之意

例句 He is a man of exceptional talent.
他是個擁有優秀天賦的男人。

同義字 extraordinary

---

excitement [ɪk`saɪtmənt] n. 興奮、激動 Track 2722

＊字尾-ment有轉變為名詞之意

例句 Why the excitement? Sit down and tell me.
幹嘛這麼激動？坐下來告訴我。

---

exclusive [ɪk`sklusɪv] Track 2723

adj. 唯一的、排外的、獨家的 ＊字尾-ive有轉變為形容詞之意

例句 Some journalists are willing to get the exclusive news at any cost.
有些記者不惜任何代價要獲得獨家新聞。

---

execution [͵ɛksɪ`kjuʃən] n. 實行 Track 2724

＊字尾-tion有轉變為名詞的意思

例句 The idea is good, but the execution leaves much to be discussed.
主意是不錯，但要實行就得討論一下了。

---

exert [ɪg`zɝt] v. 運用、盡力 Track 2725

例句 He exerted all his influence to make them accept his plan.
他運用全部的影響力來讓他們接受他的計畫。

搭配詞 exert one's influence
運用（某人的）影響力

---

explicit [ɪk`splɪsɪt] adj. 明確的 Track 2726

例句 He avoids giving an explicit answer.
他避免給一個明確的答案。

同義字 clear

---

exploit [`ɛksplɔɪt]/[ɪk`splɔɪt] Track 2727

n./v. 功績、英勇的行為、利用

例句 His crazy exploits are still discussed many years after his death.
他的瘋狂事蹟一直到他死後多年還一直被討論著。

同義字 achievement

---

exploration [͵ɛksplə`reʃən] n. 探測 Track 2728

＊字尾-tion有轉變為名詞的意思

例句 The exploration of Mars is an important mission for SpaceX.
探測火星是SpaceX公司的重要任務。

搭配詞 exploration of Mars
探測火星

facilitate [fə`sɪlə,tet] v. 利於、使容易 Track 2729

例句 I think zip codes are used to facilitate mail service.
我想郵遞區號是用來讓寄信更容易。

同義字 help

familiarity [fə,mɪlɪ`ærətɪ] n. 熟悉、親密、精通 Track 2730

＊字尾-ty有轉變為名詞之意

例句 His familiarity with the local people surprises all of us.
他與當地人如此親密，讓我們都很驚訝。

搭配詞 Familiarity breeds contempt.
親不敬，熟生蔑。

fame [fem] n. 名聲、聲譽 Track 2731

例句 She lost most of her friends after her rise to fame.
她聲名大噪後，失去了大部分的朋友。

fan [fæn] n. 風扇、狂熱者 Track 2732

例句 Do you mind if I turn on the fan? It's so stuffy in the room.
你介意我開電扇嗎？房間裡好悶。

fanatic [fə`nætɪk] n. 狂熱者 Track 2733

例句 John is a sport fanatic. 約翰是個運動狂熱者。

同義字 zealot

favor [`fevɚ] n. 喜好 Track 2734

例句 She is very obedient in order to win the president's favor.
她非常聽話，以得到總統的喜愛。

搭配詞 win sb's favor 得某人歡心

favorable [`fevərəbḷ] adj. 有利的、討人喜歡的 Track 2735

＊字尾-able有「可以、能」的意思

例句 The company's prices are the most favorable.
這家公司的價格是最優惠的。

favorite [`fevɚrɪt] adj./n. 最喜歡的 Track 2736

例句 This is my favorite show.
這是我最喜歡的節目。

反義字 unpopular 不受歡迎的

feasible [`fizəbḷ] adj. 可實行的、可能的 Track 2737

＊字尾-ible有「可以、能」的意思

例句 I think this is a feasible scheme. 我覺得這個計畫是可行的。

同義字 possible

feedback [`fid,bæk] n. 回饋 Track 2738

例句 We need more feedback from our customers in order to improve our service. 我們需要多從消費者得到回饋，才能改善我們的服務。

feel [fil] v./n. 感覺、覺得 ◀Track 2739

例句 Please feel free to call me if you have any questions.
若你有任何問題，請別客氣打電話給我。

搭配詞 feel free 請便

feeling [ˋfilɪŋ] n. 感覺、感受 ◀Track 2740

例句 Her cruelty hurt my feelings. 她的冷酷，使我感覺難過。

搭配詞 hurt sb's feelings 使某人感覺難過

feelings [ˋfilɪŋz] n. 感情、敏感 ◀Track 2741

＊字尾-s有轉變為複數之意

例句 She tried to hide her true feelings for him.
她試著隱藏她對他真正的感情。

feminine [ˋfɛmənɪn] adj. 女性的、溫柔的 ◀Track 2742

＊字尾-ine有轉變為形容詞之意

例句 He always dresses in feminine clothes.
他總是穿著女性化的衣服。

fine [faɪn] adj. 美好的 ◀Track 2743

例句 It's a fine picture, but we have nowhere to hang it.
這畫是很美，但我們沒地方掛啊。

flourish [ˋflɝɪʃ] v./n. 繁榮、炫耀、活躍 ◀Track 2744

例句 The misunderstood child flourished in a loving environment.
被誤解的孩子在充滿愛的環境下就活躍了起來。

反義字 decline 衰退

fluency [ˋfluənsɪ] n. 流暢、流利 ◀Track 2745

例句 Fluency in foreign languages will be an advantage when looking for a job. 能流利地説外國語言會是找工作時的優勢。

fluent [ˋfluənt] adj. 流暢的、流利的 ◀Track 2746

例句 Sam can speak fluent English because he's been staying in the US for a long time.
山姆在美國住很久了，所以可以講很流暢的英文。

同義字 eloquent

fond [fɑnd] adj. 喜歡的 ◀Track 2747

例句 Sam is fond of playing guitar. 山姆很喜歡彈吉他。

搭配詞 be fond of 喜歡

fortunate [ˋfɔrtʃənɪt] adj. 幸運的、僥倖的 ◀Track 2748

例句 Julia is a fortunate girl. She won the lottery twice just last year!
茱利亞是個幸運的女孩。她去年就中了兩次樂透呢！

反義字 unfortunate
不幸的、倒霉的

a b c d e f g h i j k l m n o p q r s t u v w x y z

friendly [ˋfrɛndlɪ] adj. 友善的、親切的 Track 2749

例句 He's very friendly to animals and the environment.
他對動物和環境都很友善。

搭配詞
be friendly to 對某人友善

gay [ge] Track 2750

adj./n. 同性戀的、快樂的、快活的、同性戀者（多指男性）

例句 Andy told me that his cousin is gay.
安迪告訴我他的表哥是同性戀。

反義字
sad 令人悲痛的，可悲的

generous [ˋdʒɛnərəs] Track 2751

adj. 慷慨的、大方的、寬厚的

例句 It is rare for her to be so generous. 她很少這麼大方。

gentle [ˋdʒɛntl̩] adj. 溫和的、上流的 Track 2752

例句 My dog may be huge, but he's actually quite gentle.
我的狗可能是很大沒錯，但牠其實很溫和。

gentleman [ˋdʒɛntl̩mən] n. 紳士、家世好的男人 Track 2753

例句 Please bring this gentleman a glass of champagne.
請給這位紳士一杯香檳。

giggle [ˋgɪgl̩] v./n. 咯咯地笑 Track 2754

例句 Ellen burst into giggles when Tom told her she looked pretty today.
當湯姆告訴她她今天看起來很漂亮，艾倫便咯咯笑起來。

glad [glæd] adj. 高興的 Track 2755

例句 We are so glad to hear your good news.
我們很高興聽到你的好消息。

搭配詞
be glad to 樂於……

glance [glæns] v./n. 瞥視、看一下 Track 2756

例句 She glanced at the letter and recognized Tom's handwriting.
她瞥了信一眼，認出湯姆的字。

glorious [ˋglorɪəs] adj. 著名的、榮耀的 Track 2757

＊字尾-ous有轉變為形容詞之意

例句 The team had a glorious victory again.
這一隊又得到榮耀的勝利了。

反義字
inglorious 不名譽的、可恥的

good [gʊd] adj. 好的、優良的 Track 2758

例句 You should eat things that are good for you.
你該吃對你好的食物啊。

搭配詞
good for 有益於……

gossip [ˋgɑsəp] n./v. 閒聊、八卦 ◀Track 2759

例句 She considers reading gossip column a waste of time.
她認為看八卦專欄是浪費時間的事。

搭配詞
gossip column 八卦專欄

grace [gres] n. 優美、優雅 ◀Track 2760

例句 She took a bow and left the stage with grace.
她鞠躬，優雅地下台。

graceful [ˋgresfəl] adj. 優雅的、雅致的 ◀Track 2761

＊字尾-ful有「充滿」的意思

例句 She is a graceful dancer and we all adore her.
她是個優雅的舞者，我們都很喜歡她。

易混淆字
grateful 感激的

grand [grænd] adj. 宏偉的、大的、豪華的 ◀Track 2762

例句 I'll meet you at the entrance of the grand hall.
我會在大廳入口見你。

grateful [ˋgretfəl] adj. 感激的、感謝的 ◀Track 2763

＊字尾-ful有「充滿」的意思

例句 I am grateful for your help and the continued support.
我很感激你的幫助和持續的支持。

搭配詞
grateful for 為某事感激

gratitude [ˋgrætə͵tjud] n. 感激、感謝 ◀Track 2764

例句 She knelt down and cried tears of gratitude.
她跪下來落下感激的淚水。

同義字
thankfulness

great [gret] adj. 大量的、很好的、偉大的、重要的 ◀Track 2765

例句 Nikola Tesla was a great inventor.
尼古拉特斯拉是個偉大的發明家。

greeting(s) [ˋgritɪŋ(z)] n. 問候、問候語 ◀Track 2766

例句 He gave us a cheery greeting this morning.
他早上愉快地問候我們。

同義字
salutation

grin [grɪn] v./n. 露齒而笑 ◀Track 2767

例句 I really don't want to go to the blind date, but I guess I should just grin and bear it. 我實在不想去相親，不過我想我只能逆來順受。

搭配詞
grin and bear it 逆來順受

happy [ˋhæpɪ] adj. 快樂的、幸福的 ◀Track 2768

例句 You seem happy today. Any good news?
你今天看起來挺開心的。有什麼好消息嗎？

hearty [ˋhɑrtɪ] **adj.** 親切的、熱心的 ◀Track 2769

例句 Please accept my hearty congratulations on your wedding.
請接受我對你婚禮熱切的祝福。

heavy [ˋhɛvɪ] **adj./adv.** 重的、猛烈的、厚的 ◀Track 2770

例句 Please help me carry this heavy case to my bedroom.
請幫我把這個很重的箱子提到臥室。

heroic [hɪˋroɪk] **adj.** 英雄的、勇士的 ◀Track 2771

例句 The newspapers glorified his heroic deeds.
報紙把他的英雄事蹟放大了。

同義字 courageous

homesick [ˋhomˏsɪk] **adj.** 想家的、思鄉的 ◀Track 2772

例句 I feel homesick when I am far away from my hometown.
我離家鄉很遠的時候，都很想家。

honorary [ˋɑnəˏrɛrɪ] **adj.** 榮譽的 ◀Track 2773

例句 An honorary doctorate was conferred on him from Harvard University. 他獲頒哈佛大學榮譽博士學位。

搭配詞 honorary doctorate 榮譽博士

honesty [ˋɑnɪstɪ] **n.** 正直、誠實 ◀Track 2774

例句 He never treats us with honesty.
他從來不誠實地對待我們。

搭配詞 Honesty is the best policy. 誠實為上策。

honorable [ˋɑnərəbḷ] **adj.** 體面的、可敬的 ◀Track 2775

＊字尾-able有「可以、能」的意思

例句 Jack is an honorable man and will never do such a thing.
傑克是個可敬的人，絕不會做這種事。

同義字 respectful

hospitable [ˋhɑspɪtəbḷ] **adj.** 好客的 ◀Track 2776

＊字尾-able有「可以、能」的意思

例句 It is said that the Taiwanese are hospitable people.
有人說台灣人是很好客的。

hospitality [ˏhɑspɪˋtælətɪ] **n.** 款待、好客 ◀Track 2777

＊字尾-ity有轉變為名詞的意思

例句 Many thanks for the hospitality you showed me.
很感謝你對我的款待。

how [haʊ] **adv.** 怎樣、如何 ◀Track 2778

例句 How are you today? 你今天如何呢？

搭配詞 How come? 怎麼說？為什麼？

however [haʊˋɛvɚ] adv. 無論如何 Track 2779

例句 You won't be able to carry that rock however strong you are.
無論你多強壯，都不可能搬得動那塊大岩石。

ideal [aɪˋdiəl] adj./n. 理想的、完美的、理想 Track 2780

例句 Don't you think the weather today is ideal for a picnic?
你不覺得今天的天氣野餐很理想嗎？

同義字 perfect

immune [ɪˋmjun] adj. 免除的、免於……的 Track 2781

例句 The immune system of the old lady was weakened due to the poor living condition.
因為糟糕的居住環境，老婦人的免疫系統變得衰弱。

搭配詞 immunotherapy 免疫療法

implicit [ɪmˋplɪsɪt] adj. 含蓄的、不表明的 Track 2782

例句 Her silence gave implicit consent.
她不說話等於就是含蓄地同意了。

反義字 explicit 清楚的、明確的

indeed [ɪnˋdid] adv. 實在地、的確 Track 2783

例句 She is indeed a very good mechanic.
她的確是個很好的機械師。

搭配詞 A friend in need is a friend indeed. 患難見真情。

innocent [ˋɪnəsn̩t] adj. 無辜的、純潔的 Track 2784

例句 This hard evidence proves he is innocent.
這裡有確實的證據證明他是無辜的。

反義字 guilty 有罪的

innovative [ˋɪno͵vetɪv] adj. 創新的 Track 2785

例句 His innovative ideas were well-received by the CEO of the company. 他的創新思想獲得這間公司執行長的青睞。

搭配詞 innovative idea 創新思想

inquiry [ɪnˋkwaɪrɪ] n. 詢問、調查 Track 2786

例句 Please fill out this inquiry form for me.
請幫我填這份調查卷。

insistence [ɪnˋsɪstəns] n. 堅持 Track 2787

例句 The government's insistence on building a coal-fired power plant is making a lot of people mad.
政府堅持要蓋燃煤電廠，讓許多人很生氣。

intact [ɪnˋtækt] adj. 原封不動的、未受損傷的 Track 2788

例句 The design of the church was kept intact, except for the sanctuary which was reconstructed after World War II. 這間教堂除了避難室在二次大戰後被重建以外，其他設計是原封不動的。

搭配詞 keep (leave) intact 原封不動、保持原狀

intellectual [ˌɪntḷˋɛktʃuəl] adj. 智力的、聰明的 Track 2789

例句 He is highly intellectual and extremely modest.
他很聰明，而且極為謙卑。

反義字 ignorant 無知的

intelligence [ɪnˋtɛlədʒəns] n. 智力 Track 2790

例句 He is a man of very high intelligence.
他是個智力很高的人。

intelligent [ɪnˋtɛlədʒənt] adj. 有智慧（才智）的 Track 2791

＊字尾-ent有轉變為形容詞的意思

例句 Jack is an intelligent and modest person.
傑克是個有智慧又謙虛的人。

同義字 sensible

intend [ɪnˋtɛnd] v./n. 計畫、打算 Track 2792

例句 What do you intend to do next? 你接下來打算做什麼？

同義字 plan

intensity [ɪnˋtɛnsətɪ] n. 強度、強烈 Track 2793

＊字尾-ity有轉變為名詞的意思

例句 The poem showed great intensity of feeling.
這首詩表現了強烈的感情。

intensive [ɪnˋtɛnsɪv] adj. 強烈的、密集的 Track 2794

＊字尾-ive有轉變為形容詞的意思

例句 He had a heart attack and was sent to the ICU by paramedics.
他心臟病發，被急救人員送到加護病房。

搭配詞 intensive care unit (ICU) 加護病房

intention [ɪnˋtɛnʃən] n. 意向、意圖 Track 2795

＊字尾-tion有轉變為名詞的意思

例句 It was not my intention to fool you. 我並沒有意圖要騙你。

intimacy [ˋɪntəməsɪ] n. 親密 Track 2796

例句 The couple was not afraid of displaying their intimacy in public.
這對情侶不怕在公眾場合表現親密。

invaluable [ɪnˋvæljəbḷ] adj. 無價的、寶貴的 Track 2797

例句 A dictionary is an invaluable aid in learning a new language.
在學新語言時，字典是個寶貴的好幫手。

反義字 valueless

inventory [ˋɪnvənˌtorɪ] n. 庫存清單、庫存 Track 2798

例句 We'll conduct an inventory check once a month.
我們會一個月清點一次庫存。

同義字 stock

joy [dʒɔɪ] **n.** 歡樂、喜悅 Track 2799

例句 It is hard for me to describe my joy in words.
我很難用言語形容我的喜悅。

---

joyous [ˋdʒɔɪəs] **adj.** 歡喜的、高興的 Track 2800
＊字尾-ous有轉變為形容詞之意

例句 The family savored the joyous moment.
這一家人享受著歡喜的一刻。

同義字 joyful

---

just [dʒʌst] **adj.** 公正的、公平的 Track 2801

例句 He's a just man and will never make such a mistake.
他是個公正的人，才不會犯這種錯誤。

反義字 unjust 不公平的、不義的

---

keen [kin] **adj.** 熱心的、敏銳的 Track 2802

例句 She is very keen on music, and is planning to further her studies at the Hannover University of Music, Drama, and Media.
她很熱衷於音樂，正計畫到德國漢諾威音樂和戲劇學院深造。

搭配詞 keen on 熱衷於某事物、喜愛某事／某人

---

kind [kaɪnd] **adj.** 仁慈的、友善的 Track 2803

例句 It's so kind of you to invite us to dinner.
你邀我們吃晚餐，真是太友善了。

反義字 unkind 不仁慈的

---

kiss [kɪs] **v./n.** 吻 Track 2804

例句 Tom kissed her goodbye in front of her dad.
湯姆在她爸面前吻別她。

搭配詞 kiss goodbye 吻別

---

kneel [nil] **v.** 下跪 Track 2805

例句 I won't forgive you even if you kneel down before me.
就算你在我面前跪了，我也不會原諒你。

---

legendary [ˋlɛdʒəndˌɛrɪ] **adj.** 傳說的 Track 2806
＊字尾-ary有轉變為形容詞之意

例句 Robin Hood is a legendary hero. 羅賓漢是傳說的英雄。

搭配詞 legendary hero 傳說的英雄

---

leisurely [ˋliʒəlɪ] **adj./adv.** 悠閒的 Track 2807

例句 We took a leisurely walk through the park after dinner.
我們吃完晚飯後在公園裡悠閒地散步。

---

lessen [ˋlɛsn̩] **v.** 減少 ＊字尾-en有「使」之意 Track 2808

例句 I usually listen to some jazz to lessen my pressure.
我通常會聽爵士樂來減少壓力。

反義字 increase 增大、增加、增強

lest [lɛst] conj. 以免 Track 2809

例句 He ran away lest he should be seen.
他趕快跑走，以免被看見。

同義字
perchance

liable [ˋlaɪəbl] adj. 可能的、易……的 Track 2810

例句 People are liable to make mistakes when they're tired.
人們在累的時候比較可能犯錯。

搭配詞
be liable to 易……的

like [laɪk] v. 喜歡 Track 2811

例句 Like it or not, you should do your homework.
不管喜歡不喜歡，你都得做功課。

搭配詞
like it or not
不管喜歡不喜歡

likewise [ˋlaɪk͵waɪz] adv. 同樣地 Track 2812

＊字尾-wise有「而言」之意

例句 She was very good at cooking. Likewise, her daughter is also an excellent cook.
她很擅長料理。同樣地，她的女兒也是個很好的廚師。

同義字
similarly

likelihood [ˋlaɪklɪ͵hud] n. 可能性、可能的事物 Track 2813

例句 There is a strong likelihood that the party will be cancelled.
派對有很高的可能性被取消。

linger [ˋlɪŋgɚ] v. 留戀、徘徊 Track 2814

例句 Eric lingered outside the school after everybody else had gone home. 愛瑞克在大家都回家後，還在學校外面徘徊。

同義字
stay

lively [ˋlaɪvlɪ] adj. 有生氣的 Track 2815

例句 She has become more lively in the past year.
她在這一年來變得比較有生氣了。

lovely [ˋlʌvlɪ] adj. 美麗的、可愛的 Track 2816

例句 She's a lovely girl; I would like to take a picture with her.
她是個可愛的女孩，我真想和她合照。

lucky [ˋlʌkɪ] adj. 有好運的 Track 2817

＊字尾-y有轉變為形容詞之意

例句 How lucky you are to have won the big prize!
你贏得大獎，真好運啊！

maintenance [ˋmentənəns] n. 保持、維修 Track 2818

＊字尾-ance有轉變為名詞之意

例句 The machine requires monthly maintenance.
這台機器需要一個月維修一次。

反義字
abandonment 放棄

majestic [mə`dʒɛstɪk] **adj.** 莊嚴的、雄偉的 ◀Track 2819
＊字尾-ic有轉變為形容詞之意
例句 The building is majestic! 這座建築真是雄偉！

同義字 grand

---

mellow [`mɛlo] **adj./v.** 圓融 ◀Track 2820
例句 Age has mellowed her attitude.
年紀增長讓她的態度比較圓融了。

同義字 mature

---

memorable [`mɛmərəbl] **adj.** 值得紀念的 ◀Track 2821
＊字尾-able有「可以、能」的意思
例句 Graduation is a memorable event to me.
畢業對我來說是值得紀念的事情。

同義字 rememberable

---

memorial [mə`morɪəl] **adj./n.** 紀念的、紀念碑 ◀Track 2822
例句 They erected a memorial for the dead soldiers.
他們為死去的軍人們蓋了一座紀念碑。

搭配詞 memorial day 紀念日

---

mercy [`mɝsɪ] **n.** 慈悲 ◀Track 2823
例句 The boss sacked his employees without mercy.
這個老闆毫不留情地裁員了。

搭配詞 without mercy
毫不留情地、殘忍地

---

merit [`mɛrɪt] **n.** 價值、優點 ◀Track 2824
例句 This plan has as many merits as it has flaws.
這個計畫有多少優點，就有多少缺點。

---

metaphor [`mɛtəfɚ] **n.** 隱喻 ◀Track 2825
例句 The rose is often a metaphor for love in poetry.
玫瑰在詩中常用來隱喻愛情。

反義字 simile 明喻

---

miss [mɪs] **v./n.** 想念、懷念、錯過 ◀Track 2826
例句 I missed my train this morning; therefore, I was late for work.
我今天早上錯過火車，所以上班遲到了。

---

moderate [`mɑdərɪt] **adj.** 適度的、溫和的 ◀Track 2827
例句 The position requires moderate travel. Is that okay with you?
這個位置需要適度交通往返。你可以接受嗎？

反義字 immoderate 無節制的、過分的

---

modest [`mɑdɪst] **adj.** 謙虛的 ◀Track 2828
例句 Be more modest, or people won't like you.
請謙虛點，不然別人不會喜歡你。

反義字 immodest 不謙虛的、傲慢的

modesty [ˋmɑdəstɪ] n. 謙虛、有禮 Track 2829
＊字尾-ty有轉變為名詞之意
例句 His fake modesty is just annoying.
他假裝謙虛的態度真討厭。

mood [mud] n. 心情 Track 2830
例句 I am not in the mood to go out tonight.
我今天晚上不是想出門的心情。

搭配詞
in a ... mood 一時的情緒

muse [mjuz] v./n. 深思、靈感 Track 2831
例句 "What if we cast him for another character instead?" he mused.
「如果我們改讓他演另一個角色呢？」他深思著。

naive [nɑˋiv] adj. 天真的、幼稚的 Track 2832
例句 Stop being naive. You know how good a liar he is.
不要天真了，你也知道他說謊不眨眼。

同義字
innocent

naughty [ˋnɔtɪ] adj. 不服從的、淘氣的 Track 2833
例句 The little boy who lives next door is quite naughty.
住隔壁的小男孩很淘氣。

nice [naɪs] adj. 和藹的、善良的、好的 Track 2834
例句 Ben is a nice guy. He's always in your corner when you're down.
班是個好人，每次你很沮喪，他都陪在你旁邊。

搭配詞
nice guy 好人

nonviolent [nɑnˋvaɪələnt] adj. 非暴力的 Track 2835
＊字首non-有「不、反」之意
例句 Martin Luther King made many enemies in his nonviolent quest for equality at that time.
馬丁路德金在當時因他的非暴力請求平等，而造就不少敵人。

反義字
violent 暴力的

nothing [ˋnʌθɪŋ] Track 2836
n. 無關緊要的人、事、物；沒什麼事情
例句 The food was nothing special in that restaurant.
那間餐廳的食物沒什麼特別的。

搭配詞
nothing special
沒什麼特別的

noticeable [ˋnotɪsəbḷ] adj. 顯著的、顯眼的 Track 2837
＊字尾-able有「可以、能」的意思
例句 I've noticed that there was a noticeable change in the way she dresses. 我注意到她穿衣服的方式有顯著的改變。

notify [ˋnotə͵faɪ] v. 通知、報告 Track 2838
＊字尾-ify有「使」的意思
例句 We were notified of his decision that he wanted to study abroad.
我們收到通知，知道了他想要出國唸書的決定。

搭配詞
notify sb. of sth.
將某事通知某人

notion [ˋnoʃən] n. 觀念、意見、想法 Track 2839

例句 She has no notion of right or wrong. 她沒有對錯觀念。

搭配詞 have no notion of 不知道

novice [ˋnɑvɪs] n. 初學者 Track 2840

例句 I am a novice at playing the harp. 我是豎琴的初學者。

同義字 beginner

nowhere [ˋno͵hwɛr] adv./n. 無處地 Track 2841

例句 He came from nowhere to become a Hollywood actor.
他從默默無名到出人意料成為好萊塢演員。

搭配詞 from nowhere 從不知名處

oath [oθ] n. 誓約、盟誓 Track 2842

例句 He made an oath to give up gambling. 他發誓戒賭。

optimistic [͵ɑptəˋmɪstɪk] adj. 樂觀（主義）的 Track 2843

＊字尾-ic有轉變為形容詞的意思

例句 He is always optimistic about everything.
他總是對每件事都很樂觀。

反義字 pessimistic 悲觀的

outgoing [ˋaut͵goɪn] adj. 擅於社交的、外向的 Track 2844

例句 Karen is an outgoing person.
凱倫是個外向的人。

overeat [ˋovɚˋit] v. 吃得過多 Track 2845

＊字首over-有「越過、超過」之意

例句 Overeating will make you fat. 吃太多會讓你變胖。

overflow [͵ovɚˋflo] v. 滿溢 Track 2846

＊字首over-有「越過、超過」之意

例句 The bathtub is overflowing. 浴缸的水滿出來了。

同義字 spill

overhear [͵ovɚˋhɪr] v. 無意中聽到 Track 2847

＊字首over-有「越過、超過」之意

例句 I overheard someone crying in the room when I went upstairs last night. 我昨晚上樓時無意中聽到有人在房間裡哭。

oversleep [ˋovɚˋslip] v. 睡過頭 Track 2848

＊字首over-有「越過、超過」之意

例句 He overslept this morning and was late for work.
他今天早上睡過頭，上班遲到了。

pardon [ˋpɑrdn̩] n./v. 原諒 ◀ Track 2849

例句 I beg your pardon. I should have discussed it with you first.
請你原諒，我應該先跟你討論的。

搭配詞 beg sb's pardon 向某人賠不是、道歉

participant [pɑrˋtɪsəpənt] n./adj. 參與者 ◀ Track 2850

例句 The research participants were students of a psychology course who came because of their professor's demand. 研究參與者是心理學的學生，他們是被教授要求來參與的。

搭配詞 research participant 研究參與者

passion [ˋpæʃən] n. 熱情、戀情 ◀ Track 2851

例句 He has a passion for sudoku.
他對數獨遊戲有強烈的愛好。

搭配詞 have a passion for 熱愛

passionate [ˋpæʃənɪt] adj. 熱情的 ◀ Track 2852

例句 Sophie is passionate about her charity work.
蘇菲對她的慈善事業很熱情。

patience [ˋpeʃəns] n. 耐心 ◀ Track 2853

例句 The mother has no patience with her children.
這個媽媽對她的小孩沒有耐心。

搭配詞 have no patience with 對……沒耐心、不能容忍……

patron [ˋpetrən] n. 保護者、贊助人 ◀ Track 2854

例句 Modern artists have difficulty in finding patrons.
現代的藝術家很難找到贊助人。

搭配詞 patron saints 守護神

pause [pɔz] n./v. 暫停、中止 ◀ Track 2855

例句 After a brief pause, she answered my question.
暫停一下後，她回答了我的問題。

peek [pik] v./n. 偷看、一瞥 ◀ Track 2856

例句 She took a peek at the waiting list, and noticed that she wasn't there. 她偷看了候補名單，注意到她並沒有在上面。

同義字 glance

penetrate [ˋpɛnə͵tret] v. 刺入、穿透、滲透 ◀ Track 2857

例句 She has the kind of gaze that penetrates your soul.
她有那種可以穿透靈魂的眼神。

perceive [pɚˋsiv] v. 察覺 ◀ Track 2858

例句 I perceived that she didn't seem all there today.
我注意到她今天好像心不在焉。

同義字 sense

perfect [ˋpɝfɪkt] adj./v. 完美的 ◀Track 2859

例句 All I've ever wanted is to be the perfect son.
我就只想當個完美的兒子。

搭配詞
Practice makes perfect.
熟能生巧。

performer [pɚˋfɔrmɚ] n. 執行者、表演者 ◀Track 2860

＊字尾-er有「者」的意思

例句 She is a seasoned performer and sings beautifully.
她是個很有經驗的表演者，歌唱很動聽。

搭配詞
seasoned performer
有經驗的表演者

perseverance [͵pɝsəˋvɪrəns] ◀Track 2861

n. 堅忍、堅持、毅力　＊字尾-ance有轉變為名詞之意

例句 You can't complete the task if you lack perseverance.
如果妳沒有毅力，就無法完成任務。

同義字
application 專心致志

persevere [͵pɝsəˋvɪr] v. 堅持 ◀Track 2862

例句 In spite of failures, the scientist persevered in his experiments.
雖然失敗連連，這個科學家依然堅持做實驗。

搭配詞
persevere in 堅持

persist [pɚˋsɪst] v. 堅持、持續 ◀Track 2863

例句 The inquisitive child persisted in asking questions about the galaxy. 這個好奇的小孩持續問著銀河系的問題。

搭配詞
persist in 堅持

persistence [pɚˋsɪstəns] n. 固執、堅持 ◀Track 2864

例句 The old woman's persistence annoyed me.
老太太的固執讓我覺得很煩。

persistent [pɚˋsɪstənt] adj. 固執的、堅持不懈的 ◀Track 2865

＊字尾-ent有轉變為形容詞之意

例句 I don't understand his persistent complaining.
我不懂他幹嘛固執地一直抱怨。

pious [ˋpaɪəs] adj. 虔誠的 ◀Track 2866

＊字尾-ous有轉變為形容詞之意

例句 She is a pious follower of her god. 她對她心中的神很虔誠。

反義字
impious 不敬神的、不虔誠的、褻瀆的

piety [ˋpaɪətɪ] n. 虔敬　＊字尾-ty有轉變為名詞之意 ◀Track 2867

例句 Filial piety is considered an important virtue in Chinese society.
孝道在華人社會被視為重要的美德。

搭配詞
filial piety 孝心

plea [pli] n. 藉口、懇求 ◀Track 2868

例句 She left the party on the plea of a headache.
她以頭痛為藉口，離開派對。

搭配詞
on the plea 辯解、托詞、藉口

plead [plid] v. 懇求、為……辯護 Track 2869

例句 The boy pleaded his mother to buy him a new bike.
小男孩懇求他媽媽買一台新的腳踏車給他。

pleasant [ˋplɛzn̩t] adj. 愉快的 Track 2870

例句 The walk with him was very pleasant.
和他一起散步很愉快。

please [pliz] v. 請、使高興、取悅 Track 2871

例句 I am pleased to see our children get along so well.
我很高興看到我們的孩子們相處如此之好。

搭配詞
pleased 高興的

pleasure [ˋplɛʒɚ] n. 愉悅 Track 2872

＊字尾-ure有轉變為名詞之意

例句 Reading for pleasure can improve your literacy and mental health.
以閱讀作為消遣有助提升讀寫能力和心智健康。

搭配詞
for pleasure 為了消遣

pledge [plɛdʒ] n./v. 誓約 Track 2873

例句 You should take this ring as a pledge of our friendship.
你應該收下這個戒指當作我們友情的誓約。

pluck [plʌk] n. 勇氣 Track 2874

例句 She showed a lot of pluck in dealing with the intruders.
她在對付入侵者時表現出了很大的勇氣。

同義字
courage

polite [pəˋlaɪt] adj. 有禮貌的 Track 2875

例句 You should be polite to the elderly.
你應該要對年紀大的人有禮貌。

反義字
impolite 無禮的

ponder [ˋpɑndɚ] v. 仔細考慮 Track 2876

例句 She pondered all day before making a decision.
她仔細考慮了一整天才下決定。

搭配詞
ponder over 考慮、深思

praise [prez] n./v. 稱讚 Track 2877

例句 I don't like this guy because he praises his own work too much.
我不喜歡這個人，因為他老是稱讚自己的作品。

prediction [prɪˋdɪkʃən] n. 預言 Track 2878

＊字尾-tion有轉變為名詞的意思

例句 He was shocked when his own prediction actually came true.
他的預言真的成真時，他非常驚訝。

同義字
prophecy

preliminary [prɪˋlɪmə͵nɛrɪ] n./adj. 初步、預備的 Track 2879
*字首pre-有「先」之意
例句 The preliminary matches were already over. 預賽都打完了。

presume [prɪˋzum] v. 假設 Track 2880
*字首pre-有「先」之意
例句 I presume that you have not asked your manager about this.
我假設你還沒有問過主管這件事。

precaution [prɪˋkɔʃən] n. 警惕、預防 Track 2881
*字首pre-有「先」之意
例句 It is necessary to take precautions against theft.
應該要預防竊盜。
同義字 notification

precise [prɪˋsaɪs] adj. 明確的 Track 2882
例句 To be precise, the plane will take off at 6 a.m.
確切地說，飛機將在早上6點起飛。
搭配詞 to be precise 確切地說

preface [ˋprɛfɪs] n./v. 序言 Track 2883
*字首pre-有「先」之意
例句 You need to find someone to translate the preface from French to English. 你得找人把序言從法文翻成英文。
同義字 introduction

prefer [prɪˋfɝ] v. 偏愛、較喜歡 Track 2884
例句 Which do you prefer? Pizza or Steak?
你比較喜歡哪個？披薩還是牛排？
同義字 favor

preferable [ˋprɛfərəbl̩] adj. 較好的 Track 2885
*字尾-able有「可以、能」的意思
例句 I think the coffee in this restaurant is preferable to that of the convenience store. 我覺得這家餐廳的咖啡比便利商店的好。
搭配詞 preferable to 比……更好的

preference [ˋprɛfərəns] n. 偏好 Track 2886
例句 I have no preference, so go with whatever you like.
我沒有偏好，所以你喜歡哪個就哪個吧。
搭配詞 have a preference for 偏愛

pretty [ˋprɪtɪ] adj. 漂亮的、美好的 Track 2887
例句 She is pretty. I wonder if she has a boyfriend.
她很漂亮。我想知道她有沒有男朋友。
反義字 ugly 醜的、難看的

prevail [prɪˋvel] v. 戰勝、普及 Track 2888
例句 I believe that good will prevail against evil.
我相信正義會戰勝邪惡。

preview [ˋpriˏvju] n./v. 事先查閱、查看 Track 2889

＊字首pre-有「先」之意

例句 When can we see a preview of the new movie?
我們什麼時候可以看到新電影的預告片。

---

priceless [ˋpraɪslɪs] adj. 貴重的、無價的 Track 2890

＊字尾-less有「無」的意思

例句 The cultural heritage is priceless, and it attracts visitors from all over the world.
這個文化遺產是無價的，吸引了世界各地的觀光客前來。

同義字 valuable

---

pride [praɪd] n./v. 自豪 Track 2891

例句 She took pride in her son's achievements.
她以兒子的成就自豪。

搭配詞 take pride in 以……自豪

---

prior [ˋpraɪɚ] adj. 在前的、優先的 Track 2892

例句 She bought some cosmetics at the duty-free shop prior to her next flight to Boston. 她飛到波士頓前，在免稅商店買了一些化妝品。

搭配詞 prior to 在……之前

---

priority [praɪˋɔrətɪ] n. 優先權 Track 2893

＊字尾-ity有轉變為名詞的意思

例句 Your priority should be getting the injured to a safe place.
你優先該做的是把傷者帶到安全的地方。

---

profound [prəˋfaʊnd] adj. 極深的、深奧的 Track 2894

例句 That is a profound philosophical question.
那是個深奧的哲學問題。

反義字 shallow 淺的

---

progressive [prəˋgrɛsɪv] adj. 前進的、革新的 Track 2895

＊字尾-ive有轉變為形容詞的意思

例句 He is a progressive thinker. 他是個前衛的思想家。

---

procession [prəˋsɛʃən] n./v. 行進、行列、隊伍 Track 2896

例句 Thousands of people were joining the celebrity's funeral procession.
上千人加入了這位名人的喪禮隊伍。

---

profile [ˋprofaɪl] n. 側面 Track 2897

例句 Heiress to the family business, Mary keeps a low profile.
瑪麗是家族企業的繼承人，但她保持低調。

搭配詞 low profile 低調

---

prolong [prəˋlɔŋ] v. 延長 Track 2898

例句 The treatment will only prolong her agony.
治療只是延長她的痛苦。

搭配詞 prolong the agony 延長痛苦

promise [ˋprɑmɪs] n./v. 諾言 ◀Track 2899

例句 Can you promise me that you won't do it again?
你可以向我許諾你不會再做這種事了嗎？

promising [ˋprɑmɪsɪŋ] adj. 有可能的、有希望的 ◀Track 2900

＊字尾-ing有轉變為形容詞的意思

例句 He was voted as most promising singer in 2014.
他被票選為2014年最有潛力的歌手。

rational [ˋræʃənḷ] adj. 理性的 ◀Track 2901

例句 Let's be rational. We can't accommodate so many people in the house. 我們理性點吧，我們不能塞那麼多人到那棟房子裡啊。

反義字 absurd 不合理的、荒謬的

realization [ˏrɪələˋzeʃən] n. 現實、領悟 ◀Track 2902

＊字尾-tion有轉變為名詞的意思

例句 The realization came to me that I was ripped off.
我領悟到我被敲竹槓了。

renowned [rɪˋnaʊnd] adj. 著名的 ◀Track 2903

例句 My brother is a renowned movie director.
我哥哥是著名的電影導演。

recognize [ˋrɛkəgˏnaɪz] v. 認知、認得 ◀Track 2904

例句 No one recognized him because he wore a mask.
沒人認得他，因為他戴了面具。

同義字 acknowledge

recommend [ˏrɛkəˋmɛnd] v. 推薦、託付 ◀Track 2905

例句 Can you recommend a good restaurant?
你可以推薦一家好的餐廳嗎？

refresh [rɪˋfrɛʃ] v. 使恢復精神、重新整理 ◀Track 2906

＊字首re-有「再次」之意

例句 You need to refresh the page again.
你需要再重新整理網頁一次。

refreshment [rɪˋfrɛʃmənt] n. 清爽、茶點 ◀Track 2907

＊字首re-有「再次」之意

例句 Refreshments will be served at the meeting.
在會議上會提供茶點。

rejoice [rɪˋdʒɔɪs] v. 歡喜 ◀Track 2908

＊字首re-有「再次」之意

例句 We rejoiced when it was announced that there was no school today.
一宣布今天不上學，我們都很歡喜。

repay [rɪˋpe] v. 償還、報答 ◀Track 2909
＊字首re-有「再次」之意
例句 I will repay you the money you lent me last month.
我會把你上個月借我的錢還你。

同義字
requite

representation [ˌrɛprɪzɛnˋteʃən] ◀Track 2910
n. 代表、表示、表現　＊字首re-有「再次」之意
例句 He couldn't afford a legal representation and was helped by a lawyer who worked *pro bono*.
他付不出律師費，不過有獲得義務律師的幫忙。

reputation [ˌrɛpjəˋteʃən] n. 名譽、聲望 ◀Track 2911
＊字尾-tion有轉變為名詞的意思
例句 The restaurant has an excellent reputation for serving delicious food. 這家餐廳以賣美味的食物出名。

restoration [ˌrɛstəˋreʃən] n. 恢復 ◀Track 2912
＊字首re-有「再次」之意
例句 The restoration of the aircraft needed to be carried out soon.
飛機的修復需要盡快開始。

rescue [ˋrɛskju] v./n. 救援 ◀Track 2913
例句 The police doesn't know how to rescue the hostages yet.
警察還是不知道如何救出人質。

resolution [ˌrɛzəˋluʃən] n. 果斷、決心 ◀Track 2914
＊字尾-tion有轉變為名詞的意思
例句 My New Year's resolution is to give up smoking.
我的新年決心是要戒菸。

搭配詞
New Year's resolution
新年決心

respectable [rɪˋspɛktəbl̩] ◀Track 2915
adj. 可尊敬的、體面的　＊字尾-able有「可以、能」的意思
例句 My grandparents are very respectable people.
我的祖父母是很可敬的人。

反義字
contemptible 卑劣的、不屑一顧的

respectful [rɪˋspɛktfəl] adj. 恭敬的 ◀Track 2916
＊字尾-ful有「充滿」的意思
例句 It is necessary to listen in respectful silence.
必須要用恭敬的沈默來聆聽才行。

revive [rɪˋvaɪv] v. 復甦、復原 ◀Track 2917
＊字首re-有「再次」之意
例句 A little bit of whisky may revive him.
一點點威士忌可能就可以讓他復甦了。

同義字
restore

revolutionary [ˌrɛvəˋluʃənˌɛrɪ] adj. 革命的 ◀Track 2918
＊字尾-ary有轉變為形容詞之意
例句 I've found a revolutionary new way to grow wheat.
我找到了一種革命性的新種麥方法。

revolve [rɪˋvɑlv] v. 旋轉、循環 ◀Track 2919

＊字首re-有「再次」之意

例句 Their troubles revolve around money management.
他們的問題都圍繞著金錢管理打轉。

搭配詞
revolve around
旋轉、以……為中心

---

rigorous [ˋrɪgərəs] adj. 嚴格的、嚴密的 ◀Track 2920

＊字尾-ous有轉變為形容詞之意

例句 The scientists are making a rigorous study of the radiation problem in the area. 科學家們很嚴格地在研究著該地區的輻射問題。

同義字
strict

---

rigid [ˋrɪdʒɪd] adj. 嚴格的 ◀Track 2921

例句 The new recruits are not used to the rigid disciplines of the army.
這些新兵對軍隊的嚴格紀律還不習慣。

反義字
yielding 聽從的、柔順的

---

ripe [raɪp] adj. 成熟的 ◀Track 2922

例句 The time is ripe for her to run the family business.
她接手家族事業的時機成熟了。

搭配詞
the time is ripe for doing sth.（做）某事的時機成熟

---

robust [roˋbʌst] adj. 強健的 ◀Track 2923

例句 He is already 90, but still quite robust.
他已經九十歲了，但還是身體強健。

反義字
delicate 嬌貴的

---

romantic [roˋmæntɪk] adj. 浪漫的 ◀Track 2924

例句 Frenchmen are the most romantic people in the world.
法國人是世界上最浪漫的人。

---

sacred [ˋsekrɪd] adj. 神聖的 ◀Track 2925

例句 The shrine is a sacred place. 神殿是個神聖之地。

---

salute [səˋlut] v./n. 招呼、敬禮 ◀Track 2926

例句 We saluted the captain when he walked past.
我們在隊長經過時對他敬禮。

---

sane [sen] adj. 神智穩健的 ◀Track 2927

例句 I don't think anyone can talk to him and still remain sane.
我不覺得有誰可以跟他講完話還神智清楚的。

反義字
insane 精神病的、精神錯亂的、瘋狂的

---

satisfy [ˋsætɪsˏfaɪ] v. 使滿足 ◀Track 2928

例句 I am not satisfied with my job. 我對我的工作不滿足。

scent [sɛnt] n. 氣味、痕跡 Track 2929

例句 The scent of roses filled the air. 空氣中充滿了玫瑰的氣味。

scramble [ˋskræmbḷ] v./n. 攀爬、爭奪 Track 2930

例句 The kids scrambled over the rocks. 孩子們爬過了岩石。

sensation [sɛnˋseʃən] n. 感覺、知覺 Track 2931

＊字尾-tion有轉變為名詞的意思

例句 Did you feel that tingling sensation I felt just now?
我剛有一種震顫的感覺，你也有感覺到嗎？

同義字 sense

sense [sɛns] n. 感覺、意義 Track 2932

例句 His explanation doesn't make any sense to me.
他的解釋對我來說不具任何意義。

搭配詞 make sense 有意義

sensitive [ˋsɛnsətɪv] adj. 敏感的 Track 2933

例句 She's too sensitive and thinks that everyone is bullying her.
她太敏感了，總覺得每個人都在霸凌她。

搭配詞 be sensitive to 對……敏感、易受傷害

sensitivity [ˏsɛnsəˋtɪvətɪ] Track 2934

n. 敏感度、靈敏度、多愁善感

例句 Those who have sensitivity are able to create many beautiful stories. 有著善感個性的人能夠創造許多美麗的故事。

sentiment [ˋsɛntəmənt] n. 情緒、感情 Track 2935

＊字尾-ment有轉變為名詞之意

例句 I applaud your patriotic sentiments, but I don't quite agree with how you expressed them.
我激賞你的愛國情緒，但我不太同意你表現的方式。

sentimental [ˏsɛntəˋmɛntḷ] Track 2936

adj. 情感上的、多愁善感的 ＊字尾-al有轉變為形容詞之意

例句 Graduation season is a sentimental season.
畢業季是個很多愁善感的季節。

同義字 emotional

sexy [sɛksɪ] adj. 性感的 Track 2937

＊字尾-y有轉變為形容詞之意

例句 I think Jessica Alba is a sexy lady. 我覺得潔西卡艾芭很性感。

搭配詞 sexy lady 性感女子

sheer [ʃɪr] adj./adv. 垂直的、絕對的、澈底的、薄的 Track 2938

例句 He fainted from sheer horror. 他因澈底的驚嚇而昏倒了。

shout [ʃaʊt] v./n. 呼喊、喊叫 ◀Track 2939

例句 The child shouted at his brother to stop.
那個孩子叫他哥哥停下來。

shrewd [ʃrud] adj. 敏捷的、精明的 ◀Track 2940

例句 He is a shrewd businessman. 他是個精明的商人。

significant [sɪgˋnɪfəkənt] adj. 有意義的、明顯的 ◀Track 2941

例句 There has been a significant improvement since last month.
從上個月以來，已經有明顯的進步了。

反義字 insignificant 無足輕重的

silence [ˋsaɪləns] n./v. 沉默 ◀Track 2942

例句 Mary received the bad news in silence.
瑪麗沉默地接受了壞消息。

搭配詞 in silence 沉默地

sincere [sɪnˋsɪr] adj. 真實的、誠摯的 ◀Track 2943

例句 She offered a sincere apology for her behavior.
她為她的表現誠摯地道歉。

反義字 insincere 不誠實的、無誠意的

situation [ˏsɪtʃʊˋeʃən] n. 情勢 ◀Track 2944

＊字尾-tion有轉變為名詞的意思

例句 The situation is unfavorable for us; we should come up with a better solution. 情勢對我們不利；我們應該想個好一點的解決方式。

smack [smæk] v. 拍擊、甩打 ◀Track 2945

例句 She smacked her ex-boyfriend across the face.
她甩了前男友一巴掌。

smile [smaɪl] v./n. 微笑 ◀Track 2946

例句 No matter how busy you are, remember to smile.
無論你多忙，都要記得微笑。

sniff [snɪf] v./n. 吸氣、聞 ◀Track 2947

例句 He sniffed at the flowers by the street. 他聞了聞街邊的花。

搭配詞 sniff at 聞

solemn [ˋsɑləm] adj. 鄭重的、莊嚴的 ◀Track 2948

例句 He made a solemn promise to do better.
他鄭重地保證會做得更好。

反義字 frivolous 輕薄的、輕佻的

someone [ˋsʌm͵wʌn] pron. 一個人、某一個人 Track 2949

例句 Someone was looking for you a few minutes ago.
幾分鐘前有一個人在找你。

something [ˋsʌmθɪŋ] pron. 某物、某事 Track 2950

例句 Are you hiding something from me? 你有某事隱瞞我嗎？

搭配詞 something else 諸如此類的什麼

sometimes [ˋsʌm͵taɪmz] adv. 有時 Track 2951

例句 I go jogging in the neighborhood sometimes.
我有時會在社區中慢跑。

搭配詞 Homer sometimes nods. 智者千慮，必有一失。

soothe [suð] v. 安慰、撫慰 Track 2952

例句 You should try to soothe the crying child.
你應該試著安撫那個在哭的孩子。

反義字 enrage 激怒

sophisticated [səˋfɪstɪ͵ketɪd] Track 2953

adj. 世故的、有品味的

例句 She is actually a sophisticated woman. 她其實是個世故的女人。

反義字 unsophisticated 不世故的、純真的

spiritual [ˋspɪrɪtʃuəl] adj. 精神的、崇高的 Track 2954

例句 He is a very spiritual person. 他是個精神崇高的人。

搭配詞 spiritual home 樂土、心靈上的祖國

splendid [ˋsplɛndɪd] adj. 輝煌的、閃耀的 Track 2955

例句 They won another splendid victory.
他們又打了場輝煌的勝戰。

同義字 gorgeous

spontaneous [spɑnˋtenɪəs] Track 2956

adj. 自發的，不由自主的

例句 We burst into spontaneous laughter at his joke.
因為他講的笑話，我們不由自主大笑。

still [stɪl] adj. 無聲的、不動的 Track 2957

例句 Stay still, or he might see us. 別動，不然他會看到我們。

搭配詞 stand still 別動

stout [staut] adj. 強壯的、堅固的 Track 2958

例句 I bought a pair of stout boots last week.
我上禮拜買了一雙堅固的靴子。

反義字 feeble 虛弱的、無力的

straightforward [ˋstretˏfɔrwɚd] Track 2959

adj./adv. 直接的、正直的

例句 Can you give me a straightforward answer?
你可以給我一個直接的答案嗎？

同義字 frank

---

sturdy [ˋstɝdɪ] adj. 強健的、穩固的 Track 2960

例句 The chair is sturdy enough to hold a strong adult.
這椅子夠穩固，可以坐一個強壯的成人。

反義字 frail 身體虛弱的

---

subtle [ˋsʌtl̩] adj. 微妙的 Track 2961

例句 There's a subtle difference in his attitude.
他的態度有種微妙的不同。

反義字 simple 簡明的

---

such [sʌtʃ] adj. 這樣的、如此的 Track 2962

例句 She's such a good teacher that all the students like her.
她是如此好的一個老師，所有的學生都喜歡她。

搭配詞 such and such 如此這般的

---

super [ˋsupɚ] adj. 很棒的、超級的 Track 2963

例句 She did not want to become a super star.
她沒有想要成為超級巨星。

---

superb [sʊˋpɝb] adj. 極好的、超群的 Track 2964

例句 She is a superb actress. 她是個極好的演員。

---

superficial [ˋsupɚˋfɪʃəl] adj. 表面的、膚淺的 Track 2965

例句 She's really superficial and cares only about brands and money.
她非常膚淺，只關心品牌和錢。

反義字 radical 根本的

---

supreme [səˋprim] adj. 至高無上的 Track 2966

例句 He dreamed of becoming the supreme ruler of a vast empire.
他夢想成為一個廣大帝國至高無上的王者。

---

sure [ʃʊr] adj. 一定的、確信的 Track 2967

例句 Make sure he will come tomorrow. 要確定他明天會來。

搭配詞 make sure 確定

---

surprise [sɚˋpraɪz] n./v. 驚喜、詫異 Track 2968

例句 She was completely taken by surprise when she was announced the best leading actress at the Oscars.
奧斯卡獎宣布她榮獲最佳女主角時，她十分吃驚。

搭配詞 take by surprise 使吃驚

suspend [sə`spɛnd] v. 懸掛、暫停 Track 2969

例句 The lamp was suspended from the ceiling.
燈懸掛在天花板上。

sympathize [`sɪmpə͵θaɪz] v. 同情、有同感 Track 2970

例句 I can sympathize with you because I had a similar experience before. 我和你有同感，因為我也有過類似的經驗。

搭配詞 sympathize with 同情

sympathy [`sɪmpəθɪ] n. 同情 Track 2971

例句 He never had any sympathy for beggars.
他對乞丐從來沒有任何同情。

tame [tem] adj. 馴服的、單調的 Track 2972

例句 Cows are tame animals. 牛是溫馴的動物。

反義字 wild 野生的、未被人馴養的

temper [`tɛmpɚ] n. 脾氣 Track 2973

例句 Caroline has a hot temper and is difficult to get along with.
凱洛琳的脾氣不好，很難相處。

搭配詞 hot temper 發怒、發脾氣

temperament [`tɛmprəmənt] n. 氣質、性情 Track 2974

＊字尾-ment有轉變為名詞之意

例句 Allen has a romantic temperament. 艾倫有著浪漫的性情。

同義字 disposition

tender [`tɛndɚ] adj. 溫柔的、脆弱的、幼稚的 Track 2975

例句 He gave her a tender kiss before he left.
他在離開前給了她一個溫柔的吻。

tension [`tɛnʃən] n./v. 拉緊、緊張 Track 2976

例句 There was an air of tension at the meeting.
在會議上有種緊張感。

同義字 anxiety

thankful [`θæŋkfəl] adj. 欣慰的、感謝的 Track 2977

＊字尾-ful有「充滿」的意思

例句 I was thankful to him for his help. 我很感謝他的幫忙。

搭配詞 thankful to sb. for 為……感激

thoughtful [`θɔtfəl] adj. 深思的、思考的 Track 2978

＊字尾-ful有「充滿」的意思

例句 There's a thoughtful look on his face. 他臉上有種深思的表情。

tranquil [ˋtræŋkwɪl] adj. 安靜的、寧靜的 Track 2979

例句 I want to live a tranquil life in the countryside.
我想在鄉下過著寧靜的生活。

反義字
noisy 喧鬧的、嘈雜的

understandable [ˏʌndɚˋstændəbl̩] Track 2980

adj. 可理解的 ＊字尾-able有「可以、能」的意思

例句 Jack's reluctance to agree is understandable.
傑克不願同意是可以理解的。

undoubtedly [ʌnˋdaʊtɪdlɪ] adv. 無庸置疑地 Track 2981

＊字尾-ly有轉變為副詞之意

例句 That is undoubtedly true. 那無庸置疑地是真的。

upright [ˋʌpˏraɪt] adj./adv./n. 直立的姿勢 Track 2982

例句 Can cats stand upright? 貓可以直立站著嗎？

vapor [ˋvepɚ] n. 蒸氣 Track 2983

例句 A cloud is a mass of vapor. 雲就是一團蒸氣。

搭配詞
vapor bath 蒸氣浴

verbal [ˋvɝbl̩] adj. 言詞上的、口頭的 Track 2984

例句 Verbal agreements are unreliable; let's write it down.
口頭契約很不可靠，我們寫下來吧。

搭配詞
verbal (oral) agreement
口頭契約

versus [ˋvɝsəs] prep. ……對……（縮寫為vs.） Track 2985

例句 The big match tonight is France versus Spain. Do you wanna come over and watch together?
今晚的大賽是法國對西班牙，你要過來一起看嗎？

vigor [ˋvɪgɚ] n. 精力、活力 Track 2986

例句 Sam bounded into the room with vigor.
山姆充滿活力地跳進房間。

vigorous [ˋvɪgərəs] adj. 有活力的 Track 2987

＊字尾-ous有轉變為形容詞之意

例句 The children were vigorous. Their old nanny could not keep up.
孩子們很有活力。他們的老保姆根本追不上。

同義字
energetic

will [wɪl] n. 意志、意志力 Track 2988

例句 For the actress, acting is her passion, and she can cry at will.
對這名女演員來說，演戲是她熱愛的事，她能想哭就哭。

搭配詞
at will 任意

willing [ˋwɪlɪŋ] adj. 心甘情願的 ◀ Track 2989

例句 I am willing to listen if you want to talk.
你想講的話，我願意聽。

wink [wɪŋk] v./n. 眨眼、使眼色、閃爍 ◀ Track 2990

例句 The cat disappeared in a wink. 那隻貓咪一瞬間就消失了。

搭配詞
in a wink 一瞬間

witty [ˋwɪtɪ] adj. 機智的、詼諧的、風趣的 ◀ Track 2991

例句 The host in the show is very witty.
這個節目的主持人很風趣。

同義字
clever

worthwhile [ˋwɝθˋhwaɪl] adj. 值得的 ◀ Track 2992

例句 A ten-hour trip? Is it worthwhile?
十個小時的旅程喔？值得嗎？

worthy [ˋwɝðɪ] adj. 有價值的、值得的 ◀ Track 2993

＊字尾-y有轉變為形容詞之意

例句 I think this point is worthy of notice. 我覺得這一點值得注意。

搭配詞
worthy of 值得、適合、配得上

yearn [jɝn] v. 懷念、想念、渴望 ◀ Track 2994

例句 People yearn for success and wealth.
人們都渴望成功與富足。

搭配詞
yearn for 盼望、思念

yummy [ˋjʌmɪ] adj. 美味的 ◀ Track 2995

例句 What a yummy cake! 真是個美味的蛋糕啊！

zeal [zil] n. 熱誠、熱忱 ◀ Track 2996

例句 Her boss appreciates her zeal for work.
她的老闆很感謝她對工作的熱忱。

Test 11 關鍵英單總測驗第11回

以下測驗題皆出自書中第十一回「**和正面情緒有關的單字**」，快來檢視自己的學習成果吧！

一、選擇題

1. He is a _____ teacher who always put his students' interests first.
   (A) devoted
   (B) emotional
   (C) exceptional
   (D) feasible

2. The dress is _____ and exquisite.
   (A) hearty
   (B) intellectual
   (C) feminine
   (D) persistent

3. It is generally believed that good will _____ against evil.
   (A) recognize
   (B) prevail
   (C) scramble
   (D) promise

4. She always _____ when she sees Johnathon.
   (A) concedes
   (B) blushes
   (C) delightful
   (D) cherishes

5. He's a cruel man and never shows _____ for the handicapped.
   (A) tension
   (B) sympathy
   (C) abundance
   (D) attitude

6. He overcame the adversity with great courage and _____ .
   (A) disciplinary
   (B) metaphor
   (C) innocence
   (D) determination

7. He is a genius, but he's very _____ .
   (A) novice
   (B) modest
   (C) sheer
   (D) applicable

8. They handled the sensitive issue with _____ .
   (A) caution
   (B) density
   (C) fanatic
   (D) clearance

9. The idea is _____ . Let's do it.
   (A) immune
   (B) feasible
   (C) leisurely
   (D) favorite

10. We are cautiously _____ about the outcome.
   (A) optimistic
   (B) lively
   (C) intensive
   (D) naughty

二、克漏字測驗

We all know that life is not __1__. So how do we stay positive? Surround ourselves with positive people. How do we know if someone is positive? Positive people complain less, while negative ones always complain.

Doing __2__ work also helps you become a positive and __3__ person. According to a research, participants who chose to donate a portion of their income enjoyed activated __4__ centers in the brain. When your children see you donating money, they will also become more __5__ and compassionate.

1.
(A) acute
(B) cheer
(C) perfect
(D) decisive

2.
(A) charity
(B) amazement
(C) declaration
(D) courtesy

3.
(A) fluent
(B) desperate
(C) explicit
(D) happy

4.
(A) pleasure
(B) hospitality
(C) intention
(D) profile

5.
(A) majestic
(B) generous
(C) gossipy
(D) aggressive

關鍵英單總測驗第11回 中譯與解答

一、選擇題

1. 他是很有熱誠的老師，總是以學生的利益優先。
   (A) 奉獻的
   (B) 情緒化的
   (C) 傑出的
   (D) 可行的

2. 這件洋裝很女性化而且設計精緻。
   (A) 發自內心的
   (B) 聰明的
   (C) 女性化的
   (D) 堅持不懈的

3. 一般普遍相信邪不勝正。
   (A) 認同
   (B) 普及、勝過
   (C) 攀爬
   (D) 承諾

4. 她看到強納生總是會臉紅。
   (A) 承認
   (B) 臉紅
   (C) 愉悅的
   (D) 珍惜

5. 他是冷酷的男人，對有身心障礙的人士從沒有任何同情心。
   (A) 緊繃
   (B) 同情
   (C) 富庶
   (D) 態度

6. 他以堅韌的勇氣和決心克服了逆境。
   (A) 有紀律的
   (B) 隱喻
   (C) 無辜
   (D) 決心

7. 他是個天才，但仍很謙虛。
   (A) 初學者
   (B) 謙虛的
   (C) 純粹的
   (D) 可適用的

8. 他們審慎地處理這個敏感的議題。
   (A) 審慎
   (B) 稠密
   (C) 狂熱者
   (D) 清除

9. 這個想法是可行的，就這麼做吧。
   (A) 免疫的
   (B) 可行的
   (C) 悠閒的
   (D) 最愛的

10. 我們對結果抱以審慎樂觀的態度。
   (A) 樂觀的
   (B) 有朝氣的
   (C) 密集的
   (D) 淘氣的

二、克漏字測驗

我們都知道生命不完美，因此要如何維持正面呢？我們應讓自己被正面的人包圍。我們要如何知道哪些人是正面的呢？正面的人比較少抱怨，負面的人總是抱怨。

做慈善工作也能幫助我們成為正面、快樂的人。根據研究，選擇捐出部分收入的受試者，他們的大腦中樞會啟動愉悅感。當你的孩子看到你捐錢，他們也會成為比較慷慨、有同情心的人。

1.
(A) 激烈的
(B) 歡呼
(C) 完美的
(D) 有決斷力的

2.
(A) 慈善
(B) 驚喜
(C) 宣言
(D) 禮貌

3.
(A) 流暢的
(B) 絕望的
(C) 明確的
(D) 快樂的

4.
(A) 愉悅
(B) 好客
(C) 意圖
(D) 側面

5.
(A) 壯觀的
(B) 慷慨的
(C) 八卦的
(D) 侵略性的

一、選擇題

1.(A) 2.(C) 3.(B) 4.(B) 5.(B)
6.(D) 7.(B) 8.(A) 9.(B) 10.(A)

二、克漏字測驗

1.(C) 2.(A) 3.(D)
4.(A) 5.(B)

Unit 12 和負面情緒有關的單字

多益測驗的命題強調生活化與實用性，學會這些與「負面情緒」有關的單字，不僅能讓你在多益考場上所向披靡，在日常生活上也可以靈活運用喔！

討厭的事物可以這麼說

- **His persistence really irritates me.**
  他的固執讓我感到生氣。
- **He is reluctant to try eating durian.**
  他不願意嘗試吃榴槤。
- **The insensitive chose of words is considered offensive.**
  這樣缺乏敏感的用詞被認為是帶有冒犯性的。

揮之不去的壓力可以這麼說

- **I started to see a consultant after realizing that I couldn't handle the stress on my own.**
  在我明白自己無法處理壓力之後，我開始找諮商師尋求幫助。
- **I'm anxious about the possible outcome of my decision.**
  我對自己的選擇可能造成的結果感到擔心。

悲傷的情緒可以這麼說

- **It was with great sorrow that we announce the passing of our ace player, William Carter.**
  我們滿懷悲痛地公布我們的王牌球員威廉卡特的死訊。

- **Give him some time to grieve over his loss.**
  給他一些時間去悼念他逝去的親人。

恐懼的心情可以這麼說

- **Everything was in chaos after the earthquake hit.**
  地震過後，一切都陷於混亂中。
- **The little boy was terrified after seeing his friend murdered in front of him.**
  小男孩在目睹他的朋友被殺害之後恐懼萬分。

遇到詐騙可以這麼說

- **I might be biased, but that man is suspicious.**
  我或許帶有偏見，但那個男人確實很可疑。
- **He deceived that old lady into thinking he was her long lost child.**
  他欺騙那位老太太，讓老太太相信他是失散多年的兒子。

Unit 12 和負面情緒有關的單字

abuse [əˋbjuz] n./v. 濫用、虐待 Track 2997

例句 Child abuse issues are already under control in this country.
虐待兒童問題在這個國家已經得到控制了。

---

addiction [əˋdɪkʃən] n. 熱衷、上癮 Track 2998

＊字尾-tion有轉變為名詞的意思

例句 He is addicted to gambling. 他賭博成癮了。

搭配詞 be addicted to V-ing 上癮於……

---

afraid [əˋfred] adj. 害怕的、擔心的 Track 2999

例句 I am afraid of plane crashes. 我害怕墜機。

搭配詞 afraid of 害怕

---

anger [ˋæŋgɚ] n./v. 憤怒 Track 3000

例句 Kevn did something that he shouldn't have done out of anger.
凱文出於憤怒，做了不該做的事。

搭配詞 out of anger 出於憤怒

---

angry [ˋæŋgrɪ] adj. 生氣的 Track 3001

例句 She got angry with him for his rudeness.
他的無禮讓她很生氣。

搭配詞 get angry with sb 生（某人的）氣

---

annoyance [əˋnɔɪəns] n. 煩惱、困擾、煩悶 Track 3002

＊字尾-ance有轉變為名詞之意

例句 Much to her annoyance, he kept mocking at her.
她很氣惱他繼續嘲笑著她。

同義字 irritation

---

anxiety [æŋˋzaɪətɪ] n. 憂慮、不安、渴望 Track 3003

例句 The doctor specializes in treating patients with depression, anxiety, and panic attacks.
這名醫師擅長治療憂鬱症、焦慮症和恐慌症的病人。

同義字 uneasiness

---

anxious [ˋæŋkʃəs] adj. 憂心的、擔憂的 Track 3004

例句 I am anxious about the result of the exam.
我對考試結果很擔心。

搭配詞 be anxious about 擔憂

---

arrogant [ˋærəgənt] adj. 自大的、傲慢的 Track 3005

例句 The contestant is arrogant and overbearing.
這名競爭者很自大又霸道。

同義字 proud

---

assassinate [əˋsæsṇ͵et] v. 行刺 Track 3006

例句 The police have uncovered a plot to assassinate the president.
警察發現了一個暗殺總統的計畫。

同義字 murder

---

awful [ˋɔful] adj. 可怕的、嚇人的 Track 3007

例句 I still remember the awful earthquake even years afterwards.
就算過了很多年，我還是記得那次可怕的地震。

同義字 terrible

---

bad [bæd] adj./adv. 壞的 Track 3008

例句 It's too bad that he can't go camping with us.
他不能跟我們去露營，太遺憾了。

搭配詞 too bad 太遺憾了（用以表示同情）

---

bias [ˋbaɪəs] v./n. 偏心、偏袒 Track 3009

例句 Some parents have biases against girls.
有些父母對女孩有偏見。

同義字 prejudice

---

bizaare [bɪˋzɑr] adj. 古怪的、奇異的 Track 3010

例句 The way he thinks is quite bizaare. 他的思路很奇特。

---

blunder [ˋblʌndɚ] n. 大錯 Track 3011

例句 His blunder caused a serious problem to the company.
他犯的大錯帶給公司很嚴重的問題。

同義字 mistake

---

blunt [blʌnt] v. 使遲鈍 Track 3012

例句 The drugs blunted his senses. 藥品讓他的感覺變遲鈍了。

---

boil [bɔɪl] v./n. 沸騰、使發怒 Track 3013

例句 The girl was boiling in anger because her friends wouldn't listen.
女孩很生氣，因為她的朋友們都不聽她講話。

---

boycott [ˋbɔɪ͵kɑt] v./n. 杯葛、排斥 Track 3014

例句 The countries boycotted the event.
這些國家杯葛了那次的活動。

同義字 revolt

chaos [ˋkeɑs] n. 無秩序、大混亂 Track 3015

例句 The town was in chaos after the terrible tsunami.
在那次可怕的海嘯後，整座城鎮都在大混亂中。

反義字 order 有條理

clumsy [ˋklʌmzɪ] adj. 笨拙的 Track 3016

例句 She's very clumsy and often falls down the stairs.
她很笨拙，常從樓梯上摔下去。

同義字 awkward

collapse [kəˋlæps] v./n. 崩潰、倒塌 Track 3017

例句 The house collapsed during the earthquake.
地震時，那棟房子倒塌了。

同義字 crash

complain [kəmˋplen] v. 抱怨 Track 3018

例句 He kept complaining about work even when on a date.
他就連在約會的時候都在抱怨工作。

搭配詞 complain about 抱怨

conceit [kənˋsit] n. 自負、自大 Track 3019

例句 His conceit was intolerable to his colleagues.
他的同事無法忍受他的自負。

搭配詞 self-conceited 自負的

confusion [kənˋfjuʒən] n. 迷惑、混亂 Track 3020

例句 Your room is in a state of confusion. 你的房間一片混亂。

搭配詞 in confusion 混亂、雜亂

covet [ˋkʌvɪt] v. 垂涎、貪圖、渴望 Track 3021

例句 Tom finally won the prize that everyone coveted.
湯姆終於贏得所有人都垂涎的那項大獎。

同義字 desire

cowardly [ˋkauədlɪ] adj./adv. 怯懦的 Track 3022

例句 He was a cowardly boy, but grew up into a great leader.
他曾是個膽小的男孩，但卻長大成為一名偉大的領袖。

crazy [ˋkrezɪ] adj. 發狂的、瘋癲的 Track 3023

例句 The cow ran like crazy. 那頭牛發狂似地奔跑。

搭配詞 like crazy 發狂似地

cruel [ˋkruəl] adj. 殘忍的、無情的 Track 3024

例句 He is so cruel to his wife and children.
他對他的妻兒真殘忍。

cruelty [ˋkruəltɪ] n. 冷酷、殘忍 Track 3025

＊字尾-ty有轉變為名詞之意

例句 I can't stand his cruelty to animals anymore.
我再也受不了他對動物那麼殘忍了。

同義字 barbarity

cry [kraɪ] v./n. 叫聲、哭聲、大叫 Track 3026

例句 The little girl cried out for help when she fell down from the bicycle.
那個小女孩從腳踏車跌下來時，大叫求救。

搭配詞 cry out 大聲叫

decline [dɪˋklaɪn] v./n. 衰敗 Track 3027

＊字首de-有「反、去除」之意

例句 His health is on the decline. 他的健康正在衰退。

搭配詞 on the decline 在衰退

deceive [dɪˋsiv] v. 欺詐、詐騙 Track 3028

＊字首de-有「反、去除」之意

例句 She deceived the man into thinking she was trying to help him.
她矇騙那位男士誤以為她在幫助他。

defect [dɪˋfɛkt] n. 缺陷、缺點 Track 3029

＊字首de-有「反、去除」之意

例句 There's a defect in the merchandise we just received.
我們剛收到的產品有缺陷。

反義字 merit 長處、優點

deficiency [dɪˋfɪʃənsɪ] n. 匱乏、不足 Track 3030

＊字首de-有「反、去除」之意

例句 The bear cub was born with congenital deficiencies and was abandoned by its mother. 這隻熊寶寶有先天缺陷，而被熊媽媽遺棄。

搭配詞 congenital deficiency 先天缺陷

degrade [dɪˋgred] v. 降級、降等 Track 3031

＊字首de-有「反、去除」之意

例句 She was degraded from first class to business class because of a misunderstanding. 因為一場誤解，她被從頭等艙降等到商務艙了。

反義字 exalt 提升、提拔

denial [dɪˋnaɪəl] n. 否定、否認 Track 3032

＊字首de-有「反、去除」之意

例句 She was in denial and refused to believe that her pet chicken was cooked. 她一直否認事實，無法相信她的寵物雞被煮來吃了。

反義字 confirmation 確定、確證

deprive [dɪˋpraɪv] v. 剝奪、使……喪失 Track 3033

＊字首de-有「反、去除」之意

例句 The prisoner had been deprived of sleep for five months.
這名囚犯長達5個月被剝奪睡眠。

搭配詞 deprive... of 剝奪

detain [dɪˋten] v. 拘留 Track 3034

＊字首de-有「反、去除」之意

例句 We were detained at the airport for several hours.
我們在機場被拘留了好幾個小時。

deteriorate [dɪˋtɪrɪə͵ret] v. 惡化、降低 Track 3035
＊字首de-有「反、去除」之意
例句 His health deteriorated day after day. 他的健康每天都在惡化。

反義字
ameliorate 改善、改良

deter [dɪˋtɝ] v. 使停止做 Track 3036
＊字首de-有「反、去除」之意
例句 Low wages have been deterring many young people from having children. 低薪讓許多年輕人不敢生小孩。

反義字
recommend 建議

dilemma [dəˋlɛmə] n. 左右為難、窘境 Track 3037
＊字首di-有「兩、雙」之意
例句 Winnie is in a dilemma—should she get a job or go back to school? 溫妮遇到左右為難的狀況：她該去找工作還是回去唸書呢？

搭配詞
in a dilemma 進退兩難

disability [͵dɪsəˋbɪlətɪ] n. 無能、無力、殘缺 Track 3038
＊字首dis-有「不」之意
例句 Just because he has a disability doesn't mean you're better than he is. 他身體有一處殘缺，不代表你就比他好。

同義字
inability

disable [dɪsˋebl̩] v. 使無能力、使傷殘 Track 3039
＊字首dis-有「不」之意
例句 Pop-ups are disabled on my computer. 我的電腦上不會有彈出視窗。

同義字
cripple

disapprove [͵dɪsəˋpruv] v. 反對、不贊成 Track 3040
＊字首dis-有「不」之意
例句 My boss disapproved of the plan I proposed. 我老闆反對我提出的計畫。

搭配詞
disapprove of 不贊成、不同意

disastrous [dɪzˋæstrəs] adj. 災害的、悲慘的 Track 3041
例句 The results of the experiment were disastrous. 那場實驗的結果很慘。

同義字
catastrophic

discharge [dɪsˋtʃɑrdʒ] v./n. 排出、卸下 Track 3042
＊字首dis-有「不」之意
例句 There was discharge coming out of his ears. 他的耳朵中有排出物跑出來。

disclose [dɪsˋkloz] v. 暴露、露出 Track 3043
＊字首dis-有「不」之意
例句 This letter disclosed her identity. 這封信暴露了她的身分。

反義字
conceal 隱藏、隱瞞

discomfort [dɪsˋkʌmfɚt] n./v. 不安、使不自在 Track 3044
＊字首dis-有「不」之意
例句 I was discomforted by the hot weather when I traveled in Thailand. 當我抵達泰國時，被熱天氣搞得很不自在。

反義字
comfort 安逸、舒適

discrimination [dɪˏskrɪməˋneʃən] Track 3045

n. 辨別、歧視　＊字首dis-有「不」之意

例句 In American, racial discrimination used to be a serious problem.
在美國，種族歧視問題曾經很嚴重。

搭配詞 racial discrimination 種族歧視

disgrace [dɪsˋgres] n./v. 不名譽、恥辱 Track 3046

＊字首dis-有「不」之意

例句 You're a disgrace to our family. 你是我們家的恥辱。

dismay [dɪsˋme] n./v. 恐慌、沮喪 Track 3047

＊字首dis-有「不」之意

例句 To her dismay, her lover chose his wife over her.
讓她不開心的是，她的愛人選擇了他的太太，而不是她。

搭配詞 to one's dismay 使某人感到不開心

disregard [ˏdɪsrɪˋgɑrd] v./n. 不關心的、不注意的 Track 3048

＊字首dis-有「不」之意

例句 He disregarded everything we taught him.
他完全沒關心所有我們教他的事。

反義字 regard 注意、關心

distraction [dɪˋstrækʃən] Track 3049

n. 分心、精神渙散、心煩不安　＊字首dis-有「不」之意

例句 In the beginning, we thought he was just a distraction, but later, we realized he was a liability to our team. 我們剛開始以為他只是做些讓大家分心的事，後來我們了解到他是團隊的負擔。

搭配詞 a distraction 製造使人分心的事

distract [dɪˋstrækt] v. 分散、使分心 Track 3050

＊字首dis-有「不」之意

例句 The noise outside distracted her from her work.
外面的吵鬧讓她從工作分心了。

搭配詞 distract from 使從……分心

distrust [dɪsˋtrʌst] n./v. 不信任、不信 Track 3051

＊字首dis-有「不」之意

例句 She glared at the man with distrust.
她不信任地瞪著那個男人。

反義字 trust 信任、信賴

disadvantage [ˏdɪsədˋvæntɪdʒ] n. 缺點、不利 Track 3052

＊字首dis-有「不」之意

例句 I have a slight disadvantage to him in height, but I am much faster.
和他相比我的身高比較不利，但我的速度比較快。

disagree [ˏdɪsəˋgri] v. 不符合、不同意 Track 3053

＊字首dis-有「不」之意

例句 I disagree with what you said. 我不同意你說的話。

搭配詞 disagree with 與……意見不一

disappoint [ˏdɪsəˋpɔɪnt] v. 使失望 Track 3054

＊字首dis-有「不」之意

例句 I expected her to be here, but she disappointed me.
我期望她會來，但她讓我失望了。

反義字 encourage 鼓勵

disappointment [ˏdɪsəˋpɔɪntmənt] Track 3055
n. 令人失望的舉止 ＊字首dis-有「不」之意
例句 He sighed in disappointment when he realized that his date wasn't going to show up.
當他發現他約會的對象不會出現時，他失望地嘆氣。

disbelief [ˏdɪsbəˋlif] n. 不信、懷疑 Track 3056
＊字首dis-有「不」之意
例句 She stared in disbelief that she won the lottery.
她不敢相信她居然贏了樂透。

同義字
stare in disbelief 不敢相信

discourage [dɪsˋkɝɪdʒ] v. 阻止、妨礙 Track 3057
＊字首dis-有「不」之意
例句 This will discourage him from calling you again.
這應該會阻止他再打給你。

搭配詞
discourage ... from 勸阻

discouragement [dɪsˋkɝɪdʒmənt] Track 3058
n. 失望、氣餒 ＊字首dis-有「不」之意
例句 The failure was a great discouragement to him.
這次失敗對他來說是很大的打擊。

反義字
encouragement 鼓勵

disgust [dɪsˋgʌst] n./v. 厭惡、使噁心 Track 3059
＊字首dis-有「不」之意
例句 The smell of the fish disgusted me.
魚的氣味讓我覺得很噁心。

反義字
delight 高興

dislike [dɪsˋlaɪk] n./v. 討厭、不喜歡 Track 3060
＊字首dis-有「不」之意
例句 She is disliked by whoever knows her because she's a chronic liar.
她老是在騙人，認識她的人都不喜歡她。

dismiss [dɪsˋmɪs] v. 摒除、解散 Track 3061
＊字首dis-有「不」之意
例句 They dismissed the class early that day.
他們那天很早就解散下課了。

dispute [dɪˋspjut] n./v. 爭論 Track 3062
＊字首dis-有「不」之意
例句 Rebecca's honesty is beyond dispute.
雷貝卡的誠實是完全不需要爭論的。

搭配詞
beyond dispute 毫無爭議

distress [dɪˋstrɛs] n./v. 憂傷、苦惱 Track 3063
＊字首dis-有「不」之意
例句 Her death caused her family great distress.
她的死讓全家非常憂傷。

disturb [dɪˋstɝb] v. 使騷動、打擾 Track 3064
＊字首dis-有「不」之意
例句 I don't want to be disturbed after work. 下班後不要打擾我。

a b c d e f g h i j k l m n o p q r s t u v w x y z

doubtful [ˋdaʊtfəl] adj. 有疑問的、可疑的 Track 3065
＊字尾-ful有「充滿」的意思
例句 He was doubtful whether he could trust her.
他不知道是不是可以信任她。
同義字 distrustful

drastic [ˋdræstɪk] adj. 激烈的、猛烈的 Track 3066
例句 Drastic measures will be taken to save our friend.
我們得採取激烈手段來拯救我們的朋友。
同義字 extreme

drawback [ˋdrɔ͵bæk] n. 缺點、弊端 Track 3067
例句 Your idea has its drawbacks, as good as it is.
你的主意雖然很好，但還是有缺點。
同義字 disadvantage

dread [drɛd] n./v. 非常害怕 Track 3068
例句 Most people have a dread of snakes.
許多人都非常害怕蛇。

drowsy [ˋdraʊzɪ] adj. 沉寂的、懶洋洋的、睏的 Track 3069
＊字尾-y有轉變為形容詞之意
例句 I feel drowsy in the politics course. I need to get some coffee.
我上政治課都會覺得很睏，我得去買點咖啡。
反義字 awake 清醒的

dubious [ˋdjubɪəs] adj. 曖昧的、含糊的 Track 3070
＊字尾-ous有轉變為形容詞之意
例句 I was dubious about what he said. 我對他的話半信半疑。
搭配詞 be dubious about 懷疑、半信半疑

eccentric [ɪkˋsɛntrɪk] n. 古怪的人 Track 3071
例句 The old lady is an eccentric. I can't communicate with her.
那個老太太是個古怪的人，我無法和她溝通。

embarrass [ɪmˋbærəs] v. 使困窘 Track 3072
例句 Arthur was embarrassed by the question.
亞瑟因為這個問題而很困窘。
同義字 disconcert

embarrassment [ɪmˋbærəsmənt] Track 3073
n. 困窘、難為情　＊字尾-ment有轉變為名詞之意
例句 She blushed in embarrassment because the man kept looking at her. 因為那個男人一直看她，她難為情得臉紅了。
搭配詞 blush in embarrassment 難為情得臉紅

endanger [ɪnˋdendʒɚ] v. 使陷入危險 Track 3074
＊字首en-有「使」之意
例句 Air pollution containing PM2.5 is endangering public health.
空污中的細懸浮微粒PM2.5正在危害人們的健康。
同義字 risk

endure [ɪn`djʊr] v. 忍受 ◀Track 3075

例句 Mary couldn't endure her husband's physical and verbal violence any longer. 瑪麗再也忍受不了她老公的言行暴力了。

同義字 tolerate

envious [`ɛnvɪəs] adj. 羨慕的、嫉妒的 ◀Track 3076

＊字尾-ous有轉變為形容詞之意

例句 I am envious of Vivian's slim figure. 我很嫉妒薇薇安纖瘦的體態。

搭配詞 envious of 妒忌、羨慕

envy [`ɛnvɪ] n./v. 羨慕嫉妒 ◀Track 3077

例句 His colleagues were green with envy when he got a raise. 他加薪的時候，同事們嫉妒得臉都綠了。

exaggerate [ɪg`zædʒə͵ret] v. 誇大 ◀Track 3078

例句 Andy tends to exaggerate when telling stories. 安迪總是喜歡在說故事時誇大其詞。

同義字 overstate

exception [ɪk`sɛpʃən] n. 反對、例外 ◀Track 3079

＊字尾-tion有轉變為名詞的意思

例句 I work every day, with the exception of Sunday. 我天天工作，星期天例外。

excessive [ɪk`sɛsɪv] adj. 過度的 ◀Track 3080

例句 The movie is full of excessive violence and vulgar words. 這部電影內容充斥過度的暴力和髒話。

exclaim [ɪk`sklem] v. 驚叫 ◀Track 3081

例句 "How you've grown!" she exclaimed. 「你都長這麼大了！」她驚叫。

exclude [ɪk`sklud] v. 隔絕、不包含 ◀Track 3082

＊字首-ex有「外」的意思

例句 We didn't mean to exclude her from our group. 我們不是故意把她排除在我們的小團體外的。

反義字 include 包括、包含

exhaust [ɪg`zɔst] v. 耗盡 ◀Track 3083

＊字首-ex有「外」的意思

例句 We've exhausted all options. 我們已經用盡所有的方案了。

反義字 supply 供給

expel [ɪk`spɛl] v. 逐出、開除 ◀Track 3084

＊字首-ex有「外」的意思

例句 The headmaster decided to expel him from the school to make an example. 校長決定把他從學校開除，殺雞儆猴。

同義字 remove

expiration [͵ɛkspə`reʃən] n. 終結、過期 Track 3085

＊字尾-tion有轉變為名詞的意思

例句 Please let me know the expiration date of this credit card.
請告訴我這張信用卡的過期日。

搭配詞 expiration date 過期日期

expire [ɪk`spaɪr] v. 終止 Track 3086

例句 My landlord told me that my lease will expire on July 30th of this year. 我的房東告訴我說租約在今年7月30號會終止。

同義字 end

fascination [͵fæsə`neʃən] n. 迷惑、魅力、著迷 Track 3087

＊字尾-tion有轉變為名詞的意思

例句 Sarah has a fascination for polar bears. 莎拉對北極熊非常著迷。

fatal [`fetl̩] adj. 致命的、決定性的 Track 3088

例句 I have to warn you that even a very small mistake would be fatal to our plan. 我必須警告你，就連很小的錯誤都會對我們的計畫造成致命傷害。

同義字 deadly

fear [fɪr] n./v. 恐怖、害怕 Track 3089

例句 She cowered in fear from the giant bear.
她害怕地縮著身體遠離那隻大熊。

feeble [fibl̩] adj. 虛弱的、無力的 Track 3090

例句 She was old and feeble, but she was still lucid.
她年邁虛弱，但頭腦還是很清楚。

反義字 strong 強壯的、強健的

fierce [fɪrs] adj. 猛烈的、粗暴的、兇猛的 Track 3091

例句 The cheetah is a fierce animal. 獵豹是一種猛獸。

反義字 gentle 溫和的、和善的

fist [fɪst] n. 拳頭 Track 3092

例句 Johnson shook his fist at the intruder. 強森對入侵者揮舞拳頭。

flap [flæp] n./v. 慌亂（狀態）、鼓動 Track 3093

例句 The bird flapped its wings and flew away. 小鳥鼓動翅膀飛走了。

搭配詞 flap wings 振翅而飛

flatter [`flætɚ] v. 諂媚、奉承 Track 3094

例句 He was good at flattering people to get his way.
他擅長諂媚人，以達到自己的目的。

flutter [ˋflʌtɚ] v./n. 心亂、不安 Track 3095

例句 My heart is all of a flutter as I waited.
我一邊等，一邊緊張又興奮。

同義字 all of a flutter 緊張興奮

---

formidable [ˋfɔrmɪdəbl] Track 3096

adj. 令人敬畏的、難應付的 ＊字尾-able有「可以、能」的意思

例句 He is a formidable candidate in the election.
這是這場選舉中令人敬畏的候選人。

同義字 fierce

---

frantic [ˋfræntɪk] adj. 狂暴的、發狂的 Track 3097

例句 She ran into the room, looking frantic.
她衝進房間，看起來一臉狂暴。

同義字 excited

---

fret [frɛt] v./n. 煩躁、焦慮、弦樂器的品 Track 3098

例句 I wish Rebecca wouldn't fret about unimportant things.
我希望雷貝卡不要因為一些不重要的事焦慮。

搭配詞 fret about 憂愁、煩惱

---

fright [fraɪt] n. 驚駭、恐怖、驚嚇 Track 3099

例句 Jenny had stage fright and couldn't utter a sound on the stage.
珍妮害怕上台，在台上完全發不出聲。

搭配詞 stage fright 害怕上台

---

frighten [ˋfraɪtn̩] v. 震驚、使害怕 Track 3100

＊字尾-en有「使」的意思

例句 The giant dog frightened the little boy.
那隻大狗嚇到了小男孩。

---

frown [fraʊn] v./n. 皺眉、表示不滿 Track 3101

例句 The mother frowned at her son when he threw a tantrum.
那個母親對大發脾氣的兒子皺眉。

---

frustration [ˏfrʌsˋtreʃən] n. 挫折、失敗、煩 Track 3102

＊字尾-tion有轉變為名詞的意思

例句 Life is full of frustrations. 人生充滿了挫折。

---

furious [ˋfjʊrɪəs] adj. 狂怒的、狂鬧的 Track 3103

＊字尾-ous有轉變為形容詞之意

例句 Paul Walker, the leading actor of the Fast & Furious action franchise, died from a car accident.
玩命關頭系列電影的男主角保羅沃克在車禍喪生。

搭配詞 fast and furious 喧騰地、生動活潑的

---

fury [ˋfjʊrɪ] n. 憤怒、狂怒 Track 3104

例句 He was red with fury as he stomped into the room.
他跺腳走進房間時，憤怒得臉都紅了。

fuss [fʌs] n./v. 大驚小怪、忙亂 Track 3105

例句 Stop all this fuss and get back to your work.
別大驚小怪了，快回去工作。

grief [grif] n. 悲傷、感傷 Track 3106

例句 The poor woman sobbed in grief when she heard the news.
那個可憐的女人聽到消息時因悲傷而哭泣。

搭配詞 in grief 悲傷

grieve [griv] v. 悲傷、使悲傷 Track 3107

例句 She was grieving for the dead baby.
她為了死去的嬰兒而悲傷。

反義字 please 使高興

grim [grɪm] adj. 嚴厲的、糟糕的 Track 3108

例句 When she found her dad was a grim reaper in an organized crime, she was terrified.
她發現爸爸是組織型犯罪的冷酷殺手時，她嚇壞了。

搭配詞 grim reaper 死神

grumble [ˋgrʌmbl] v./n. 牢騷、不高興 Track 3109

例句 She never stops grumbling so I don't like to talk to her.
她總是滿腹牢騷，所以我不喜歡跟她講話。

同義字 complain

guilty [gɪlt] adj. 有罪的、內疚的 Track 3110

例句 She thought he was guilty but he was actually innocent.
她以為他有罪，但他其實是無辜的。

harass [həˋræs] v. 不斷地困擾 Track 3111

例句 The villagers have been harassed by the thieves recently.
這些村民最近被小偷給困擾著。

同義字 trouble

harassment [həˋræsmənt] n. 煩惱、騷擾 Track 3112

＊字尾-ment有轉變為名詞之意

例句 The Me Too movement denounces sexual harrassment.
「#Me Too」運動譴責性騷擾。

搭配詞 sexual harrassment 性騷擾

hardly [ˋhardlɪ] adv. 勉強地、僅僅、幾乎 Track 3113

例句 He could hardly see anything clearly in the dark.
他在黑暗中幾乎看不到任何東西。

搭配詞 hardly... when 一……就……

harsh [harʃ] adj. 粗魯的、嚴酷的 Track 3114

例句 They couldn't accept the harsh criticism.
他們無法接受這麼嚴酷的批評。

同義字 rough

hate [het] v./n. 憎恨、厭惡 Track 3115

例句 David is mean to me. I hate his guts.
大衛對我很刻薄，我對他恨之入骨。

搭配詞
hate sb's guts
對某人恨之入骨

---

hatred [ˋhetrɪd] n. 怨恨、憎惡 Track 3116

例句 The orphan's eyes are full of hatred.
那個孤兒的雙眼充滿怨恨。

同義字
enmity

---

hesitate [ˋhɛzə͵tet] v. 遲疑、躊躇 Track 3117

例句 Stop hesitating, or you'll lose your chance.
別再遲疑了，不然你要失去機會了。

反義字
determine 決定

---

hesitation [͵hɛzəˋteʃən] n. 遲疑、躊躇 Track 3118

*字尾-tion有轉變為名詞的意思

例句 After a brief hesitation, she finally said yes.
稍微遲疑了一下，她終於同意了。

---

hiss [hɪs] n./v. 噓聲 Track 3119

例句 The audience hissed at the unpopular actor.
觀眾們對那個不受歡迎的演員發出噓聲。

搭配詞
hiss at
（對某人）發出噓聲噓

---

horrible [ˋhɑrəbḷ] adj. 可怕的 Track 3120

例句 What a horrible story! I can't believe everyone died.
真是個糟糕的故事！我真難相信大家都死了。

同義字
frightful

---

horrify [ˋhɔrə͵faɪ] v. 使害怕、使恐怖 Track 3121

例句 We were horrified by what we saw.
我們被我們看到的東西給嚇到了。

---

hostile [ˋhɑstḷ] adj. 敵方的、不友善的 Track 3122

例句 I don't know why she is always so hostile to me.
我不懂她為什麼總是對我這麼不友善。

反義字
friendly 友好的、親切的

---

humiliate [hjuˋmɪlɪ͵et] v. 侮辱、羞辱 Track 3123

例句 She felt so humiliated that she left the room immediately.
她覺得太恥辱了，立刻離開房間。

同義字
embarrass

---

hypocrisy [hɪˋpɑkrəsɪ] n. 偽善、虛偽 Track 3124

例句 His hypocrisy makes me sick. 他虛偽的個性讓我都快吐了。

同義字
pretense

hypocrite [ˋhɪpəˏkrɪt] n. 偽君子 Track 3125

例句 The old lady pretends to be kind but is actually a hypocrite.
那個老太太假裝是個好人，但她其實是個偽君子。

同義字 pretender

---

hysterical [hɪsˋtɛrɪkḷ] adj. 歇斯底里的 Track 3126

例句 The victims' family members were all hysterical.
受害者的家屬都歇斯底里了。

同義字 uncontrollable

---

idiot [ˋɪdɪət] n. 傻瓜、笨蛋 Track 3127

例句 The manual is idiot proof.
這本說明手冊，連笨蛋也看得懂。

搭配詞 idiot proof 連笨蛋也懂的

---

idle [ˋaɪdḷ] adj./v. 閒置的、懶洋洋的 Track 3128

例句 I like to sit at home and idle away my time.
我喜歡坐在家，懶洋洋混時間。

搭配詞 idle away 閒混

---

ignore [ɪgˋnor] v. 忽視、不理睬 Track 3129

例句 I ignored everything Patty told me.
派蒂告訴我的事，我通通都忽視了。

同義字 disregard

---

indifference [ɪnˋdɪfərəns] n. 不關心、不在乎 Track 3130

＊字首in-有「不」、「無」的意思

例句 He has an indifference to politics. 他對政治完全不關心。

同義字 apathy

---

indifferent [ɪnˋdɪfərənt] Track 3131

adj. 無關緊要的、不關心的 ＊字首in-有「不」、「無」的意思

例句 She is indifferent to people's sufferings.
她對人們受的苦毫不關心。

搭配詞 be indifferent to
對……不關心

---

indignant [ɪnˋdɪgnənt] adj. 憤怒的 Track 3132

例句 She was startled by his indignant response.
他的憤慨回應，讓她很傻眼。

搭配詞 indignant response
憤慨的回答

---

indignation [ˏɪndɪgˋneʃən] n. 憤怒 Track 3133

＊字尾-tion有轉變為名詞的意思

例句 The news of child abuse aroused public indignation.
那個虐兒的新聞讓大眾一齊憤怒起來。

同義字 wrath

---

insult [ɪnˋsʌlt] v. 侮辱 Track 3134

例句 I never meant to insult you; please forgive me.
我不是故意要侮辱你的，請原諒我。

intense [ɪnˋtɛns] adj. 極度的、緊張的 ◀Track 3135

例句 She had an intense dislike for peanuts.
她對花生極度地厭惡。

同義字 drastic

---

intimidate [ɪnˋtɪmə͵det] v. 恐嚇 ◀Track 3136

例句 The small boy was intimidated by the eight-legged alien.
小男孩被八隻腳的外星人給嚇著了。

同義字 frighten

---

intrude [ɪnˋtrud] v. 侵入、打擾 ◀Track 3137

例句 Intruding in other people's conversations is not polite.
打擾其他人的對話很不禮貌。

反義字 extrude 逐出

---

intruder [ɪnˋtrudɚ] n. 侵入者、干擾者 ◀Track 3138

＊字尾-er有「者」的意思

例句 They chased out the intruders with guns.
他們用槍把侵入者趕走了。

---

invasion [ɪnˋveʒən] n. 侵犯、侵害 ◀Track 3139

例句 That sci-fi novel depicted an alien invasion.
那本科幻小說描寫了外星人入侵事件。

同義字 irruption

---

ironic [aɪˋrɑnɪk] adj. 諷刺的 ◀Track 3140

例句 Isn't it ironic that the girl you laughed at beat you at the game?
你嘲笑的女孩在比賽中打敗你，這不是很諷刺嗎？

---

irony [ˋaɪrənɪ] n. 諷刺、反諷 ◀Track 3141

例句 The greatest irony was that despite all his explanations, nobody believed him. 最諷刺的是他解釋了那麼多，卻沒人相信他。

同義字 satire

---

irritable [ˋɪrətəbl] adj. 暴躁的、易怒的 ◀Track 3142

＊字尾-able有「可以、能」的意思

例句 She is irritable today. I guess she had a fight with her husband again. 她今天很暴躁易怒，看來她又跟先生吵架了。

同義字 impatient

---

irritate [ˋɪrə͵tet] v. 使生氣 ◀Track 3143

例句 Jack's letter irritated me a little.
傑克寫的信讓我有點生氣。

反義字 appease 撫慰

---

irritation [͵ɪrəˋteʃən] n. 煩躁、惱怒、發炎 ◀Track 3144

＊字尾-tion有轉變為名詞的意思

例句 He could not hide his irritation and told the kids to leave the room.
他無法隱藏他的煩躁，叫孩子們離開房間。

jealous [ˋdʒɛləs] adj. 嫉妒的 ◀Track 3145

＊字尾-ous有轉變為形容詞之意

例句 She is jealous of her colleague's success.
她對她同事的成功很嫉妒。

搭配詞
jealous of 嫉妒……

jealousy [ˋdʒɛləsɪ] n. 嫉妒 ◀Track 3146

例句 A man driven by jealousy is capable of anything.
有嫉妒動機的人什麼都做得出來。

同義字
envy

jeer [dʒɪr] v./n. 戲弄、嘲笑 ◀Track 3147

例句 They jeered at their special needs classmate.
他們嘲笑他們智能障礙的同學。

反義字
respect 敬重、尊敬

jolly [ˋdʒɑlɪ] adj. 快樂的 ◀Track 3148

例句 Sophia is a plump, jolly lady.
蘇菲雅是個圓胖、快樂的女士。

lament [ləˋmɛnt] v./n. 悲痛、感嘆 ◀Track 3149

例句 She lamented that she never got a chance to see him.
她悲痛感嘆她都沒機會見他。

lame [lem] adj./v. 跛的、差的 ◀Track 3150

例句 Your dog ate your shoes? What a lame excuse.
你的狗把你的鞋子吃掉了？真是個爛藉口。

lengthy [ˋlɛŋθɪ] adj. 漫長的、冗長的 ◀Track 3151

＊字尾-y有轉變為形容詞之意

例句 It's a waste of time listening to such a lengthy and dreary speech.
聽這個又長又無趣的演講真是浪費時間。

搭配詞
lengthy speech 冗長的演講

limp [lɪmp] adj. 癱軟的、無力的 ◀Track 3152

例句 The little dog was too weak to lift its limp paws.
這隻小狗虛弱到無法舉起牠癱軟的腳掌。

load [lod] n./v. 負載 ◀Track 3153

例句 My work load is getting too heavy; I can't take it anymore.
我的工作負載太重了，我受不了了。

搭配詞
work load 工作負載

lone [lon] adj. 孤單的、孤獨的 ◀Track 3154

例句 He's a lone wolf. He doesn't trust any one.
他是獨來獨往的人，不相信任何人。

搭配詞
lone wolf 不與人來往的人

lonely [ˋlonlɪ] adj. 孤單的、寂寞的 ◀Track 3155

例句 He often feels rather lonely in this city.
他在這座城市中常覺得寂寞。

---

lonesome [ˋlonsəm] a. 孤獨的 ◀Track 3156

*字尾-some有「充滿」之意

例句 He felt lonesome at home last night.
他昨晚在家覺得很孤獨。

---

lousy [ˋlauzɪ] adj. 卑鄙的、很差的 ◀Track 3157

例句 He did a lousy job. He should work harder.
他的工作表現很差，應該勤快一點。

搭配詞 lousy job 做得不好的工作

---

lunatic [ˋlunə͵tɪk] n./adj. 瘋子 ◀Track 3158

例句 Are you a lunatic? Stop driving so fast!
你是瘋子嗎？不要開那麼快！

---

melancholy [ˋmɛlən͵kalɪ] n./adj. 悲傷、憂鬱 ◀Track 3159

例句 The old lady had melancholy eyes.
那個老太太有著憂鬱的雙眼。

反義字 pleasant 令人愉快的

---

menace [ˋmɛnɪs] n./v. 威脅 ◀Track 3160

例句 She spoke with menace in her voice.
她說話時帶著威脅的語氣。

同義字 threat

---

mischievous [ˋmɪstʃɪvəs] adj. 淘氣的、有害的 ◀Track 3161

*字尾-ous有轉變為形容詞之意

例句 There's a mischievous look on his face.
他的臉上有著淘氣的表情。

同義字 naughty

---

miser [ˋmaɪzɚ] n. 小氣鬼 *字尾-er有「者」之意 ◀Track 3162

例句 He is a miser; don't expect him to donate anything.
他是個小氣鬼，別期望他會捐任何東西。

同義字 moneygrubber

---

misery [ˋmɪzərɪ] n. 悲慘 ◀Track 3163

例句 They both flunked their physics exams and decided to go to the movie—misery loves company.
他們物理考試都不及格，決定一起去看電影，真是同病相憐。

搭配詞 Misery loves company.
同病相憐。

---

misunderstand [͵mɪsʌndɚˋstænd] v. 誤解 ◀Track 3164

*字首mis-有「誤」之意

例句 You misunderstood what I said. Let me explain it again.
你誤解我的話了，讓我再解釋一次。

反義字 understand 理解

a b c d e f g h i j k l m n o p q r s t u v w x y z

moan [mon] n./v. 呻吟（聲）、悲嘆 Track 3165

例句 The patient moaned loudly in bed.
那個病人在床上大聲呻吟。

同義字 wail

mock [mɑk] v./n. 嘲弄、笑柄 Track 3166

例句 John mocked his classmate for being the slowest runner in class.
約翰嘲弄他同學是全班跑得最慢的。

mournful [ˋmornfəl] adj. 悲痛的 Track 3167

＊字尾-ful有「充滿」的意思

例句 She was mournful all day because of the death of her pet hamster.
因為她的寵物黃金鼠死了，她一整天都很悲痛。

反義字 happy 歡悅的、幸福的

mutter [ˋmʌtɚ] v./n. 抱怨、低聲嘀咕 Track 3168

例句 We heard a mutter of discontent.
我們聽到有人不滿地低聲嘀咕。

同義字 mumble

nag [næg] v. 嘮叨 Track 3169

例句 She never stops nagging, so I just block her out.
她總是嘮叨不停，所以我就左耳進右耳出。

nasty [ˋnæstɪ] adj. 汙穢的、惡意的 Track 3170

例句 What a nasty smell! Did you forget to take out the trash?
真是個污穢的味道！你忘記倒垃圾了嗎？

negative [ˋnɛgətɪv] adj./n. 否定的、消極的、底片 Track 3171

＊字尾-ive有轉變為形容詞的意思

例句 Stop being so negative all the time. 不要老是這麼消極。

notorious [noˋtorɪəs] adj. 聲名狼藉的 Track 3172

＊字尾-ous有轉變為形容詞之意

例句 She is notorious for taking advantage of her colleague.
她因愛佔同事便宜而聲名狼籍。

反義字 famous 著名的、出名的

nonsense [ˋnɑnsɛns] n. 廢話、無意義的話 Track 3173

＊字首non-有「無」之意

例句 She is full of stuff and nonsense all the time.
她這個人老是胡說八道。

搭配詞 stuff and nonsense
胡說八道

nuisance [ˋnjusn̩s] n. 討厭的人、麻煩事 Track 3174

例句 Andy always makes a nuisance of himself.
安迪老做一些令人討厭的事。

搭配詞 make a nuisance of oneself
令人討厭

oblige [ə`blaɪdʒ] v. 使不得不、強迫 Track 3175

例句 He was obliged to abandon that plan.
他不得不放棄那個計畫。

obscure [əb`skjʊr] Track 3176

v./adj. 使陰暗、使模糊、使難以理解

例句 The clouds obscured the moon. 雲讓月亮變得模糊。

反義字 clear 使明亮

obstinate [`ɑbstənɪt] adj. 執拗的、頑固的 Track 3177

例句 The old man is as obstinate as a mule.
這個老人非常頑固。

搭配詞 as obstinate as a mule
非常頑固的

offend [ə`fɛnd] v. 使不愉快、使憤怒、冒犯 Track 3178

例句 He didn't like to offend people, so he stayed out of arguments.
他不喜歡冒犯人，所以他都不吵架的。

反義字 appease 撫慰

offense [ə`fɛns] n. 冒犯、進攻 Track 3179

例句 The offense on his team is weaker than the defence.
他們隊上的進攻能力比防守能力差。

offensive [ə`fɛnsɪv] adj. 令人不快的、冒犯的 Track 3180

例句 It's rude to use such offensive language.
用這種冒犯的字眼是很不禮貌的。

反義字 inoffensive 不觸犯人的

oppose [ə`poz] v. 和……起衝突、反對 Track 3181

例句 As opposed to watching TV after work, she took courses to enhance her professionalism.
她下班後不是看電視，而是去上課增強專業。

搭配詞 as opposed to
與……對照、與……對比

opposition [͵ɑpə`zɪʃən] n. 反對的態度 Track 3182

＊字尾-tion有轉變為名詞的意思

例句 His views stand in opposition to those who say AI will not destroy humanity.
相較那些說人工智慧不會毀滅人類的人，他抱持相反的意見。

搭配詞 in opposition to
與……的意見相反

overdo [͵ovɚ`du] v. 做得過火 Track 3183

＊字首over-有「越過、超過」之意

例句 You should work hard, but don't overdo it.
你應該要努力工作，但不要做得過火。

搭配詞 overdo things 過分努力

overwhelm [͵ovɚ`wɛlm] v. 淹沒、征服、壓倒、使……難以承受 Track 3184

＊字首over-有「越過、超過」之意

例句 She was overwhelmed by the terrible news.
她難以承受這糟糕的消息。

同義字 crush

a b c d e f g h i j k l m n o p q r s t u v w x y z

painful [ˋpenfəl] adj. 痛苦的 Track 3185
＊字尾-ful有「充滿」的意思
例句 She was so terrible in acting that it was almost painful to watch her movie.
她對演戲實在太不在行了，光看她的電影都覺得有點慘不忍睹。

同義字
achy

panic [ˋpænɪk] n./v. 驚恐、使恐慌 Track 3186
例句 The fire alarm caused a lot of panic.
火警警報造成了許多人的驚恐。

passive [ˋpæsɪv] adj. 被動的、消極的 Track 3187
例句 Teachers don't like passive students.
老師們不喜歡被動的學生。

反義字
active 積極的

pathetic [pæˋθɛtɪk] adj. 悲慘的 Track 3188
例句 This is the worst performance I've ever seen. How pathetic!
這是我見過最差的表演。真慘啊！

同義字
pitiful

peril [ˋpɛrəl] n. 危險 Track 3189
例句 Our planet is in peril if we don't take action.
我們再不採行動，地球就危險了。

搭配詞
in peril 危險

perish [ˋpɛrɪʃ] v. 滅亡 Track 3190
例句 It's reported that a hundred people perished in the fire last night.
據報導指出，一百個人在昨晚的大火中喪生。

pessimistic [ˌpɛsəˋmɪstɪk] adj. 悲觀的 Track 3191
例句 She's a pessimistic person, so talking to her will only make you feel miserable. 她人很悲觀，跟她聊只會讓你覺得更悲情而已。

反義字
optimistic 樂觀的

playful [ˋplefəl] adj. 愛玩的 Track 3192
＊字尾-ful有「充滿」的意思
例句 She motioned him to come over with a playful gesture.
她用一種打趣般的手勢把他叫過來。

反義字
serious 嚴肅的

plunge [plʌndʒ] v./n. 陷入、急降 Track 3193
例句 The stocks are plunging at the moment. 現在股市正在大跌。

prejudice [ˋprɛdʒədɪs] n./v. 偏見 Track 3194
例句 You should listen to her without prejudice.
你應該不帶偏見，聽她的說法。

搭配詞
without prejudice
無偏見地、無損權利地

prick [prɪk] v./n. 刺痛 ◀ Track 3195

例句 Tom felt a prick of conscience after being unfaithful to his wife.
湯姆對妻子不忠以後，受到良心的譴責。

搭配詞
prick(s) of conscience
良心的譴責

---

proud [praʊd] adj. 驕傲的 ◀ Track 3196

例句 Your mom should be proud of you.
你媽應該要為你感到驕傲。

搭配詞
proud of 為……而驕傲

---

quarrel [ˋkwɔrəl] n./v. 爭吵 ◀ Track 3197

例句 I just had a quarrel with my boyfriend.
我剛跟男朋友爭吵了。

搭配詞
quarrel with 與……爭吵

---

quarrelsome [ˋkwɔrəlsəm] adj. 愛爭吵的 ◀ Track 3198

例句 His brothers are very greedy and quarrelsome.
他的兄弟們都很貪心又愛爭吵。

同義字
argumentative

---

rage [redʒ] n./v. 狂怒 ◀ Track 3199

例句 He was in a rage when he received the letter.
他收到那封信時勃然大怒。

搭配詞
in a rage 勃然大怒

---

refund [rɪˋfʌnd]/[ˋrɪfʌnd] v./n. 償還、退還 ◀ Track 3200

例句 You can ask for a refund from the store with your receipt.
你可以持發票向商家要求退錢。

搭配詞
ask for a refund 要求退錢

---

regardless [rɪˋgɑrdlɪs] adj. 不關心的、不注意的 ◀ Track 3201

＊字尾-less有「無」的意思

例句 Regardless of what he said, the rule is still coming into effect tomorrow. 不管他剛說什麼，明天這個規定依然會開始執行。

搭配詞
regardless of 儘管、不論

---

reckless [ˋrɛklɪs] adj. 不關心的、不注意的 ◀ Track 3202

＊字尾-less有「無」的意思

例句 Most of the motorcyclists are very reckless.
大部分的摩托車騎士都很不小心。

同義字
foolhardy

---

refusal [rɪˋfjuzḷ] n. 拒絕 ◀ Track 3203

例句 Sam shook his head in refusal. 山姆拒絕地搖頭。

---

refute [rɪˋfjut] v. 反駁 ◀ Track 3204

例句 Silence is one of the hardest arguments to refute.
沉默是最難反駁的一種論點之一。

同義字
argue

regret [rɪ`grɛt] v./n. 後悔、遺憾 Track 3205

例句 He told her with regret that she didn't get the job.
他很遺憾地告訴她，她沒得到這份工作。

搭配詞
with regret 遺憾地

reluctant [rɪ`lʌktənt] adj. 不情願的 Track 3206

例句 It's quite obvious that Michelle is reluctant to do this.
很明顯地，蜜雪兒不願意做這件事。

反義字
willing 願意的、樂意的

resent [rɪ`zɛnt] v. 憤恨 Track 3207

例句 I resent having to get his permission for everything I do.
我做什麼都要得到他同意，這讓我很憤恨。

反義字
submit 甘受

resentment [rɪ`zɛntmənt] n. 憤慨 Track 3208

例句 He showed his resentment at the government.
他對於政府表現出憤慨。

同義字
displeasure

resist [rɪ`zɪst] v. 抵抗 Track 3209

例句 Nobody could resist her charm once they see her beauty.
一看到她的美貌，就沒人能抵抗她的魅力。

反義字
obey 服從

restrain [rɪ`stren] v. 抑制 Track 3210

例句 The child was unable to restrain herself from yelling at her uncle.
那個孩子無法抑制自己，對她舅舅大吼。

反義字
impel 推動

retort [rɪ`tɔrt] v./n. 反駁 Track 3211

例句 "You're no better yourself," she retorted.
「你自己也沒比較好啊，」她反駁道。

同義字
rebut

revolt [rɪ`volt] v./n. 叛亂、反叛 Track 3212

例句 The people in this city broke out in revolt.
這座城市裡的人開始叛亂。

反義字
obey 服從

ridicule [`rɪdɪkjul] n./v. 嘲笑 Track 3213

例句 Saying something this stupid is like inviting ridicule.
講這麼蠢的話，就像是在邀人家來嘲笑你一樣。

ridiculous [rɪ`dɪkjələs] adj. 荒謬的 Track 3214

＊字尾-ous有轉變為形容詞之意

例句 Don't you think it is a ridiculous suggestion?
你不覺得這個建議很荒謬嗎？

risk [rɪsk] **n.** 危險、風險 ◀Track 3215

例句 Jack is ready to take a risk.
傑克已經準備好要承擔風險了。

搭配詞
take a risk 有危險、冒風險

roughly [ˋrʌflɪ] **adv.** 粗暴地、粗略地、大致地 ◀Track 3216

＊字尾-ly有轉變為副詞之意

例句 Roughly speaking, your essay is pretty good.
大致上來說，你的論文寫得不錯。

搭配詞
roughly speaking
大致上來說

sacrifice [ˋsækrəˏfaɪs] **n./v.** 犧牲 ◀Track 3217

例句 He sacrificed a great deal for his children.
他為了他的孩子犧牲不少。

sad [sæd] **adj.** 令人難過的、悲傷的 ◀Track 3218

例句 The Lake House is a very sad movie.
《觸不到的戀人》是一部很悲傷的電影。

搭配詞
sad movie 傷心的電影

scandal [ˋskændl̩] **n.** 醜聞、恥辱 ◀Track 3219

例句 I am not interested in the sex scandal at all.
我對這個性醜聞一點興趣也沒有。

搭配詞
sex scandal 性醜聞

scar [skɑr] **n.** 傷痕、疤痕 ◀Track 3220

例句 Will this leave a scar on my face?
這會在我臉上留疤嗎？

同義字
blemish

scare [skɛr] **n./v.** 驚嚇、使害怕 ◀Track 3221

例句 My cat gets scared easily. 我的貓常常受驚。

scary [ˋskɛrɪ] **adj.** 駭人的 ◀Track 3222

例句 I don't want to hear this scary story at night.
我晚上不想聽這個恐怖故事。

同義字
frightening

scheme [skim] **n./v.** 計畫、陰謀 ◀Track 3223

例句 Why don't you ask about the outcome of his scheme directly?
為什麼你不直接問他計畫的結果呢？

scorn [skɔrn] **n./v.** 輕蔑、蔑視 ◀Track 3224

例句 They all look at the boy with scorn at school.
他們在學校總是用輕蔑的眼神看那個男孩。

scream [skrim] v./n. 大聲尖叫、發出尖叫聲 Track 3225

例句 She screamed and yelled at her daughter very often that the girl left home and paddled her own canoe.
她對女兒常常大吼大叫，結果女兒離家出走，自力更生。

selfish [ˋsɛlfɪʃ] adj. 自私的、不顧別人的 Track 3226

例句 No one likes to make friends with selfish people.
沒人喜歡和自私的人做朋友。

反義字 selfless 無私的

separation [ˏsɛpəˋreʃən] n. 分離、隔離 Track 3227

例句 Separation from friends always makes me sad.
和朋友分離總讓我傷心。

同義字 division

severe [səˋvɪr] adj. 嚴厲的、嚴重的 Track 3228

例句 The punishment to animal cruelty has become more severe in order to deter people from abusing animals.
虐待動物的懲罰變得更嚴厲，以遏止類此事件的發生。

反義字 lenient 寬大的、仁慈的

shabby [ˋʃæbɪ] adj. 衣衫襤褸的 Track 3229

例句 An old man in shabby clothes came to knock on my door.
一個衣衫襤褸的老人來敲我的門。

反義字 decent 正派的、合乎禮儀的

shameful [ˋʃemfəl] adj. 恥辱的、可恥的 Track 3230

＊字尾-ful有「充滿」的意思

例句 There's nothing to feel shameful about. 沒什麼好覺得可恥的。

同義字 disgraceful

shiver [ˋʃɪvɚ] n./v. 顫抖 Track 3231

例句 The gruesome details of the murder gave me the shivers.
這段對謀殺案寫實的描述令我戰慄。

搭配詞 give sb. the shivers 使戰慄

shortsighted [ˋʃɔrtˋsaɪtɪd] Track 3232

adj. 近視的、短視近利的

例句 I was shortsighted, so I didn't recognize him.
我近視，所以沒認出他。

shy [ʃaɪ] adj. 害羞的、靦腆的 Track 3233

例句 She is too shy to speak in front of the whole class.
她太害羞了，無法在全班面前說話。

sigh [saɪ] v./n. 嘆息、嘆氣 Track 3234

例句 She sighs all day and looks sad.
她整天嘆氣、看起來很難過。

silly [ˋsɪlɪ] adj. 傻的、愚蠢的 ◀Track 3235

例句 You look silly wearing that small hat.
你戴那個小帽子看起來真傻。

skeptical [ˋskɛptɪkḷ] adj. 懷疑的 ◀Track 3236

例句 Many people were skeptical about what he said.
許多人懷疑他說的話。

搭配詞
skeptical about 對……懷疑

sloppy [ˋslɑpɪ] adj. 邋遢的、懶散的 ◀Track 3237

例句 Her sloppy handwriting made her teacher mad.
她邋遢的字讓她老師不高興。

同義字
slipshod

sly [slaɪ] adj. 狡猾的、陰險的 ◀Track 3238

例句 The sly girl tried to steal her friend's boyfriend.
那個狡猾的女孩試著搶走她朋友的男友。

smash [smæʃ] n./v. 激烈的碰撞 ◀Track 3239

例句 The two cars smashed into each other.
那兩台車激烈地互相碰撞。

sneak [snik] v. 潛行、偷偷地走 ◀Track 3240

例句 Jack managed to sneak in through the back door of the classroom.
傑克從教室後門偷偷溜進去了。

搭配詞
sneak in 偷偷潛入

sneaky [ˋsnikɪ] adj. 鬼鬼祟祟的 ◀Track 3241

例句 This sneaky girl was disliked by the rest of the class.
這個鬼鬼祟祟的女孩受到全班的討厭。

sneer [snɪr] v./n. 冷笑 ◀Track 3242

例句 "You think you can beat me?" he sneered.
「你以為你能打敗我喔？」他冷笑道。

同義字
mock

sob [sɑb] v./n. 哭訴、啜泣 ◀Track 3243

例句 The poor little boy sobbed himself to sleep.
那個可憐的小男孩哭著睡著。

sorrow [ˋsɑro] n./v. 悲傷 ◀Track 3244

例句 The sorrow of losing her son left lines on her face.
失去兒子的悲傷使得她臉上留下了線條。

sorrowful [ˋsɑrəfəl] adj. 哀痛的、悲傷的 Track 3245
＊字尾-ful有「充滿」的意思
例句 You look sorrowful. What's the problem?
你看起來很悲傷。是什麼問題呢？
同義字 sad

sorry [ˋsɔrɪ] adj. 難過的、惋惜的、抱歉的 Track 3246
例句 I feel sorry for what happened to you.
我聽到你發生的事，感到很難過。
搭配詞 feel sorry for 為……感到可惜、對……表同情

startle [ˋstɑrtḷ] v. 使驚嚇 Track 3247
例句 We were startled by something in the bushes.
我們被樹叢裡不知道是什麼的東西給嚇了一跳。

strain [stren] n. 緊張、沈重的壓力 Track 3248
例句 You will be working under a lot of strains if you take this job.
如果接下這個工作，你會有很大的壓力。

strange [strendʒ] adj. 陌生的、奇怪的、不熟悉的 Track 3249
例句 Strange to say, I think I fall in love with you.
說來奇怪，我想我愛上你了。
搭配詞 strange to say 說來奇怪

stress [strɛs] n. 壓力 Track 3250
例句 How do you handle your stress?
你都怎麼對付壓力呢？

strict [strɪkt] adj. 嚴格的 Track 3251
例句 My father was very strict with us when we were young.
我們還小時，爸爸對我們很嚴格。
搭配詞 be strict with 對……要求嚴格

stumble [ˋstʌmbḷ] v. 絆倒、失足、錯誤 Track 3252
例句 She stumbled across the typos in his essay.
她偶然發現他的論文裡的打字錯誤。
搭配詞 stumble across 偶然發現

stun [stʌn] v. 嚇呆、震驚 Track 3253
例句 She was stunned to see what a beauty her sister has become.
她看到她妹妹變得這麼漂亮，都嚇呆了。
同義字 shock

stutter [ˋstʌtɚ] v. 結巴 Track 3254
例句 His brother stutters. 他弟弟講話結巴。
同義字 stammer

suicide [ˋsuə͵saɪd] n. 自殺、自滅 ◀Track 3255

例句 The number of suicides has increased these years.
這幾年來自殺人數增加了。

反義字
homicide 殺人

superstition [͵supɚˋstɪʃən] n. 迷信 ◀Track 3256

＊字尾-tion有轉變為名詞的意思

例句 Winnie is that kind of girl who believes in superstitions.
溫妮是會相信迷信的那種女生。

同義字
folklore

superstitious [͵supɚˋstɪʃəs] adj. 迷信的 ◀Track 3257

＊字尾-ous有轉變為形容詞之意

例句 I always put my right shoe on first; I am quite superstitious.
我穿鞋總是先穿右腳，我很迷信。

suppress [səˋprɛs] v. 壓抑、制止 ◀Track 3258

例句 He couldn't suppress his anger when he learned that his wife was unfaithful. 當他得知妻子不忠時，他無法壓抑自己的憤怒。

同義字
restrain

suspicious [səˋspɪʃəs] adj. 可疑的 ◀Track 3259

＊字尾-ous有轉變為形容詞之意

例句 I am suspicious of the company's intentions.
我很懷疑那個公司的意圖。

搭配詞
be suspicious of 覺得可疑

tangle [ˋtæŋgl̩] v./n. 混亂、糾結 ◀Track 3260

例句 My headphone wires are tangled.
我的耳機線都糾結在一起了。

tedious [ˋtidɪəs] adj. 沉悶的 ◀Track 3261

＊字尾-ous有轉變為形容詞之意

例句 Her story is so tedious. I hope she never tells it again.
她的故事好沉悶，我希望她永遠別再講了。

反義字
exciting 令人興奮的

tear [tɪr]/[tɛr] n./v. 眼淚、撕開 ◀Track 3262

例句 That girl told her sad story in tears.
那個女孩流著淚陳述她的悲傷的故事。

搭配詞
in tears 流著淚地

tease [tiz] v./n. 嘲弄、揶揄 ◀Track 3263

例句 She hates to be teased about her figure.
她討厭人家嘲弄她的身材。

同義字
annoy

tempt [tɛmpt] v. 誘惑、慫恿 ◀Track 3264

例句 She was very tempted to press the button just to see what would happen. 她受到誘惑，很想按下按鈕，看會發生什麼事。

temptation [tɛmp`teʃən] n. 誘惑 ◀Track 3265
＊字尾-tion有轉變為名詞的意思
例句 Johnny couldn't resist the temptation of drugs.
強尼無法抗拒毒品的誘惑。

搭配詞
resist temptation 抗拒誘惑

---

tense [tɛns] v./adj. 緊張 ◀Track 3266
例句 I am all tensed up when I have to speak in public.
我要在公眾場合演講時，總覺得緊張。

搭配詞
be tensed up 緊張

---

terrible [`tɛrəbl̩] adj. 可怕的、駭人的 ◀Track 3267
例句 The documentary showed some terrible scenes.
那個紀錄片中有些很可怕的畫面。

同義字
dreadful

---

terrify [`tɛrə͵faɪ] v. 使恐懼、使驚嚇 ◀Track 3268
例句 The little girl was terrified of thunder and lightning.
這個小女孩非常害怕雷電。

搭配詞
be terrified of
非常害怕的

---

terror [`tɛrɚ] n. 恐懼、恐怖 ◀Track 3269
例句 He fled in terror when he saw the murder happen.
他看到謀殺發生時，恐懼地逃離現場。

搭配詞
in terror 恐懼地

---

thrill [θrɪl] v./n. 戰慄、刺激 ◀Track 3270
例句 He felt a thrill when he stepped on stage.
他一踏上台，就感到很刺激。

---

timid [`tɪmɪd] adj. 羞怯的、膽小的 ◀Track 3271
例句 Sam is too timid to speak to the bigger boy.
山姆太膽小，不敢和那個大男孩講話。

反義字
bold 大膽的

---

tiresome [`taɪrsəm] adj. 無聊的、可厭的 ◀Track 3272
例句 Her endless complaints are getting tiresome.
她抱怨不停實在很討厭。

---

torment [`tɔr͵mɛnt] n./v. 苦惱、折磨 ◀Track 3273
例句 The kidnapper tormented the girl in all sorts of ways.
綁架犯用各種方式折磨那個女孩。

同義字
afflict

---

torture [`tɔrtʃɚ] n./v. 折磨、拷打 ◀Track 3274
例句 They used water torture on the American prisoners.
他們對美國囚犯動用水刑。

搭配詞
water torture 水刑

tremble ['trɛmbl] v./n. 顫抖、發抖 Track 3275

例句 There was a tremble in his voice. 他的聲音帶點顫抖。

trivial [ˋtrɪvɪəl] adj. 平凡的、淺薄的、微小的 Track 3276

例句 She's always angry over such trivial matters.
她總是為了微小的事而生氣。

trouble [ˋtrʌbl] n./v. 憂慮、麻煩 Track 3277

例句 The boy was in big trouble because he lost his mom's diamond.
那個男孩因為把媽媽的鑽石弄丟，麻煩大了。

搭配詞
in trouble 處困難中

troublesome [ˋtrʌbl̩səm] adj. 麻煩的、困難的 Track 3278

例句 The troublesome news caused an uproar in the school.
那個麻煩的消息讓整所學校一片混亂。

同義字
vexatious

upset [ʌpˋsɛt] v./adj. 顛覆、使心煩 Track 3279

例句 He upset the applecart by telling our rival what we're going to do next. 他告訴我們的對手我們下一步要怎麼做，而打亂我們的計劃。

搭配詞
upset the applecart
打亂計劃或安排

vacuum [ˋvækjuəm] n. 真空、空虛 Track 3280

例句 His wife's death left a vacuum in his life.
他太太的死在他的生命中留下一片空虛。

vague [veg] adj. 不明確的、模糊的 Track 3281

例句 He was quite vague about what just happened.
有關剛發生的事，他講得很模糊。

反義字
clear 清楚的、清晰的

vanity [ˋvænətɪ] n. 虛榮心、自負 Track 3282

例句 Many young girls buy things out of vanity.
許多小女孩因為虛榮心而買東西。

vulnerable [ˋvʌlnərəbl̩] adj. 易受傷害的、脆弱的 Track 3283

＊字尾-able有「可以、能」的意思

例句 Babies are vulnerable to cold temperature.
寶寶處於低溫之中，是很脆弱的。

搭配詞
vulnerable to
容易受……的傷害

wail [wel] v./n. 嚎哭 Track 3284

例句 The little boy burst into loud wails because he got lost at the park.
小男孩因為在公園迷路而大聲嚎哭。

同義字
cry

weep [wip] v./n. 哭泣 ◀Track 3285

例句 She wept all night out of worry. 她擔心得哭了整晚。

wicked [ˋwɪkɪd] adj. 邪惡的、壞的 ◀Track 3286

例句 People thought him to be dangerous and wicked.
人們都覺得他又危險又邪惡。

搭配詞
There's no peace for the wicked. 惡人永無寧日

woe [wo] n. 悲哀、悲痛 ◀Track 3287

例句 Her life was full of woe. 她的生命充滿了悲痛。

worry [ˋwɝɪ] v./n. 憂慮、擔心 ◀Track 3288

例句 He is worried about his debts, so he takes a lot of part-time jobs.
他對他的債務很擔心，所以他就打很多工。

搭配詞
worry about 焦慮

yucky [ˋjʌkɪ] adj. 令人厭惡的、噁心的 ◀Track 3289

例句 The food in the company's dining hall is yucky. I want to eat out today.
公司餐廳的食物很噁心，我今天想出去吃。

Test 12 關鍵英單總測驗第12回

以下測驗題皆出自書中第十二回「**和負面情緒有關的單字**」，快來檢視自己的學習成果吧！

一、選擇題

1. Punishments on animal _____ will become more severe.
   (A) abuse
   (B) disability
   (C) boycott
   (D) anger

2. She was in a _____ whether she should continue her study or work.
   (A) discrimination
   (B) harsh
   (C) dilemma
   (D) indifference

3. The boy was _____ by a school yard bully.
   (A) refunded
   (B) intimidated
   (C) sobbed
   (D) reluctant

4. She was ______ to see her half-sister become the Duchess of Sussex.
   (A) terrible (B) startled
   (C) drowsy (D) wicked

5. He was _______ to learn that he flunked the physics exam.
   (A) arrogant
   (B) discouraged
   (C) disbelief
   (D) envious

6. My credit card will _____ in January 2022.
   (A) intrude
   (B) expire
   (C) frown
   (D) expel

7. He went through a lot of ________ before landing his first job.
   (A) frustrations
   (B) negative
   (C) guilty
   (D) sorrowful

8. She is ______ for her lack of work ethic.
   (A) defect
   (B) excessive
   (C) grim
   (D) notorious

9. He felt so _____ by Jane's message that he blocked her on Skype and Facebook.
   (A) humiliated
   (B) perish
   (C) jolly
   (D) torment

10. The boy was _____ by the giant dog.
    (A) frightened
    (B) ironic
    (C) misery
    (D) hatred

二、克漏字測驗

Betty's husband is very __1__ and moody. He is extremely opinionated and never seems to be happy about anything. After years of marriage, Betty feels __2__. She has been prescribed an anti-depressant to handle the negativity that she is exposed to on a daily basis.

Their children also can't take this anymore and want to get out of the __3__. They encourage their dad to seek professional help. They understand their dad won't become Mr. Sunshine overnight. All they want is that their dad won't live a __4__ life and will someday stop __5__ the entire family.

1.
(A) negative
(B) menace
(C) lament
(D) resent

2.
(A) selfish
(B) exhausted
(C) shabby
(D) sneaky

3.
(A) lonesome
(B) hypocrisy
(C) irritation
(D) misery

4.
(A) confusion
(B) idle
(C) pessimistic
(D) distress

5.
(A) hesitating
(B) fretting
(C) tormenting
(D) coveting

關鍵英單總測驗第12回
中譯與解答

一、選擇題

1. 虐待動物的懲罰會變得更嚴重。
   (A) 虐待
   (B) 殘缺
   (C) 杯葛
   (D) 生氣

2. 她遇到左右為難的況狀，不知道到底該繼續唸書或去工作。
   (A) 歧視
   (B) 粗魯的
   (C) 兩難
   (D) 不在乎

3. 這名男孩遭到學校惡霸恐嚇。
   (A) 退錢
   (B) 恐嚇
   (C) 啜泣
   (D) 不情願的

4. 她看到同父異母的妹妹成為薩塞克斯公爵夫人，感到吃驚。
   (A) 可怕的
   (B) 吃驚
   (C) 睏的
   (D) 邪惡的

5. 他知道自己物理考試不及格之後，感到很沮喪。
   (A) 高傲的
   (B) 沮喪的
   (C) 不相信
   (D) 嫉妒的

6. 我的信用卡將在2022年1月到期。
   (A) 侵入
   (B) 終止、過期
   (C) 皺眉
   (D) 開除

7. 他找到第一份工作之前，經歷很多挫折。
   (A) 挫折
   (B) 負面的
   (C) 罪惡感
   (D) 悲傷的

8. 她因為缺乏職業道德，而聲名狼藉。
   (A) 缺陷
   (B) 過度的
   (C) 嚴厲的
   (D) 聲名狼藉的

9. 他覺得被珍的留言羞辱，而把她在Skype和臉書上都封鎖掉了。
   (A) 羞辱
   (B) 滅亡
   (C) 快樂的
   (D) 折磨

10. 小男孩被大狗嚇到了。
   (A) 驚嚇
   (B) 諷刺的
   (C) 悲慘
   (D) 仇恨

二、克漏字測驗

貝蒂的先生很負面又情緒化，他非常固執而且對任何事都感到不滿意。經過多年的婚姻生活，貝蒂感到很疲憊，醫生開給她抗憂鬱藥物，以應付每天暴露在負情能量的生活。

他們的小孩再也無法忍受這種生活，想要從這個悲慘中解脫出來，所以鼓勵父親尋求專業協助。他們明白父親不會在一夕之間變成陽光先生，但他們只求父親不要一直過著悲觀的生活，並有一天能停止折磨全家人。

1.
(A) 負面的
(B) 威脅
(C) 感嘆
(D) 憤恨的

2.
(A) 自私的
(B) 精疲力盡的
(C) 衣衫襤褸的
(D) 鬼鬼祟祟的

3.
(A) 寂寞的
(B) 偽善
(C) 生氣
(D) 悲慘

4.
(A) 迷惑
(B) 懶洋洋的
(C) 悲觀的
(D) 憂傷

5.
(A) 遲疑
(B) 煩惱
(C) 折磨
(D) 垂涎

一、選擇題

1.(A) 2.(C) 3.(B) 4.(B) 5.(B)
6.(B) 7.(A) 8.(D) 9.(A) 10.(A)

二、克漏字測驗

1.(A) 2.(B) 3.(D)
4.(C) 5.(C)

Unit 13 和職業有關的單字

多益測驗的命題強調生活化與實用性，學會這些與「職業」有關的單字，不僅能讓你在多益考場上所向披靡，在日常生活上也可以靈活運用喔！

演藝人員可以這麼說

- **The singer hired a group of extraordinary dancers for her concert.**
  那名歌手為演唱會聘請了一群優秀的舞者。
- **Although Robert is the leading actor of this movie, he was absent from the premiere.**
  雖然羅伯是這部電影的男主角，但是他沒有出席首映會。
- **Wolfgang Amadeus Mozart was one of the greatest composers in history.**
  沃夫岡・阿瑪迪斯・莫札特是歷史上最傑出的作曲家之一。

軍警公職可以這麼說

- **The policeman is checking her driving license.**
  警察正在查看她的駕照。
- **He was in the Marine Corps back in 2009, and was assigned to a special squad for a rescue mission.**
  他在2009年時是海軍陸戰隊隊員。並且因為一次營救任務被分派到一個特殊隊伍。

服務業從業人員可以這麼說

- **Jenny's assistant is running errands for her.**
  珍妮的助理正在幫她跑腿。

- **She used to be a waitress at Martin's restaurant.**
  她曾經是馬丁餐廳裡的服務生。

求職可以這麼說

- **In order to work in this company, he applied to several jobs.**
  為了在這間公司工作，他申請了多項不同職位。
- **She lists all her license and qualifications on her resume.**
  她把所有執照與證書列在她的履歷上。

描述自己的專業可以這麼說

- **I specialize in human behavior.**
  我專攻人類行為。
- **He is the best surgeon in this hospital who has performed successful operations on many difficult cases.**
  他是這家醫院最優秀的外科醫生，成功執行了許多困難的手術。

Unit 13 和職業有關的單字

ability [ə`bɪlətɪ] n. 能力 Track 3290

例句 I will help you to the best of my ability.
我會就自己能力所來幫助你。

搭配詞 to the best of one's ability 就自己能力所及

---

absence [`æbsn̩s] n. 缺席 Track 3291

例句 He was an absent-minded student but later became an accomplished poet.
他在學生時期常常心不在焉，但後來成為很有成就的詩人。

搭配詞 absent-minded 心不在焉、發呆的

---

absent [`æbsn̩t] adj. 缺席的 Track 3292

例句 I wonder why he is absent from this important meeting.
我好奇這麼重要的會議他怎麼缺席。

搭配詞 be absent from 不在、缺曠

---

absurd [əb`sɝd] adj. 不合理的、荒謬的 Track 3293

例句 What an absurd excuse! A bear stole your cell phone?
真是個荒謬的藉口！一隻熊偷走了你的手機?

反義字 reasonable 通情達理的、講道理的

---

accept [ək`sɛpt] v. 接受 Track 3294

例句 Sharon didn't accept my suggestion. She said it was absolutely ridiculous. 莎朗沒有接受我的建議，她說實在太蠢了。

反義字 refuse 拒絕

---

accomplish [ə`kɑmplɪʃ] v. 達成、完成 Track 3295

例句 I'm afraid that it's too difficult for me to accomplish the task alone.
恐怕我沒辦法一個人完成這個工作。

搭配詞 to accomplished sth 達成（某事）

---

accomplishment [ə`kɑmplɪmənt] Track 3296

n. 達成、成就 ＊字尾-ment有轉變為名詞之意

例句 After finishing the job, Kate felt a great sense of accomplishment.
完成工作時，凱特感覺到強烈的成就感。

同義字 attainment

---

accountant [ə`kaʊntənt] n. 會計師 Track 3297

例句 Would you please help me find a good accountant?
可以請你幫我找個好的會計師嗎？

同義字 bookkeeper

---

accustom [əˋkʌstəm] v. 使習慣於 Track 3298

例句 Josh quickly became accustomed to his new life in Canada.
喬許很快就習慣了在加拿大的新生活。

搭配詞 become accustomed to 對……變得習以為常

achieve [əˋtʃiv] v. 實現、完成 Track 3299

例句 Finally, Jade achieved her dream as a famous singer.
潔德終於實現了成為知名歌手的夢想。

反義字 fail 失敗

actor [ˋæktɚ] n. 男演員 Track 3300

＊字尾-or有「者」的意思

例句 It takes practice to become an excellent actor.
要成為好演員需要練習。

actress [ˋæktrɪs] n. 女演員 Track 3301

＊字尾-ess有「女性」的意思

例句 Natalie Portman won the Best Leading Actress award at the Oscars for her role in Black Swan.
娜塔莉波曼因主演黑天鵝，而獲得奧斯卡最佳女主角。

搭配詞 best leading actress 最佳女主角

adjustment [əˋdʒʌstmənt] n. 調整、調節 Track 3302

＊字尾-ment有轉變為名詞之意

例句 The company finally made an adjustment to the budget.
公司終於調整了預算。

administer/administrate Track 3303

[ədˋmɪnəstɚ]/[ədˋmɪnə͵stret] v. 管理、照料

例句 It takes brains to administer a school. 管理一所學校需要腦筋。

administration [əd͵mɪnəˋstreʃən] Track 3304

n. 經營、管理、施行 ＊字尾-tion有轉變為名詞的意思

例句 Her work involved administration of first aid to the wounded.
她的工作和對傷者施行緊急復甦有關。

administrative [ədˋmɪnə͵stretɪv] Track 3305

adj. 行政上的、管理上的

例句 He studied the administrative law carefully.
他很謹慎地研究行政法。

搭配詞 administrative law 行政法

administrator [ədˋmɪnə͵stretɚ] n. 管理者 Track 3306

＊字尾-or有「者」的意思

例句 Only the administrator can access the information.
只有管理者有權使用這些資訊。

同義字 manager

admiral [ˋædmərəl] n. 海軍上將 Track 3307

例句 Lucy's son wants to be an admiral when he grows up.
露西的兒子長大後想成為海軍上將。

搭配詞 fleet admiral 海軍元帥

advertiser [ˋædvɚˏtaɪzɚ] n. 廣告商 ◀Track 3308

＊字尾-er有「者」的意思

例句 Will you tell me how the advertisers plan to promote our product?
你可以告訴我廣告商打算怎麼推銷我們的產品嗎？

同義字 adman

adviser/advisor [ədˋvaɪzɚ] n. 顧問 ◀Track 3309

＊字尾-er有「者」的意思

例句 Anyone who is good at marketing can be our advisor.
任何擅長行銷的人都可以當我們的顧問。

同義字 counsellor

advocate [ˋædvəkɪt]/[ˋædvəˏket] ◀Track 3310

n./v. 提倡者、提倡

例句 He always plays devil's advocate in the meeting.
他開會時總是故意唱反調。

搭配詞 devil's advocate 提倡反面論點的人

agency [ˋedʒənsɪ] n. 代理商、經紀公司 ◀Track 3311

例句 Helen likes planning her own trips instead of consulting a travel agency. 海倫喜歡計畫自己的旅行，而不是找旅行社。

搭配詞 travel agency 旅行社

agenda [əˋdʒɛndə] n. 議程、待辦事項 ◀Track 3312

例句 Let's work out the agendas for the next two meetings.
我們來把之後兩次會議的議程先擬出來吧。

agent [ˋedʒənt] n. 代理人、探員 ◀Track 3313

例句 Ethan Hunt is a secret agent who handles extremely dangerous and difficult missions.
伊森韓特是情報探員，處理極度危險、困難的任務。

搭配詞 secret agent 情報探員

alter [ˋɔltɚ] v. 更改、改變 ◀Track 3314

例句 This plan should be altered. It is too hard to carry out.
這個計畫應該要更改，太難實行了。

反義字 preserve 維持

amateur [ˋæməˏtʃur] adj./n. 業餘的 ◀Track 3315

例句 Kelly is only an amateur photographer, but she takes fabulous pictures. 凱莉只是個業餘攝影師，但她能拍很好的照片。

反義字 professional 職業的

analysis [əˋnæləsɪs] n. 分析 ◀Track 3316

例句 His analysis of the problem shows great insight.
他對這個問題的分析展現出很精闢的見解。

analyze [ˋænḷˏaɪz] v. 分析、解析 ◀Track 3317

例句 Would you analyze this data for me?
可以幫我分析這個數據嗎？

反義字 synthesize 綜合

applicant [ˋæpləkənt] n. 申請人、應徵者 Track 3318

例句 There were few applicants for the job because the wages were too low. 這個工作的應徵者很少，因為薪水太少了。

同義字 candidate

apprentice [əˋprɛntɪs] n. 學徒 Track 3319

例句 Everyone knows that the painting was actually finished by his apprentice. 大家都知道這幅畫其實是他的學徒完成的。

同義字 learner

architect [ˋɑrkəˌtɛkt] n. 建築師 Track 3320

例句 Who is the architect that designed this building?
設計這棟建築的建築師是誰？

同義字 designer

arrange [əˋrendʒ] v. 安排、籌備 Track 3321

例句 Would you like to arrange a personal interview?
你想要安排一場個人面試嗎？

artist [ˋɑrtɪst] n. 藝術家、大師 Track 3322

例句 Marc Chagall is a great artist whose paintings are full of love and hope. 夏卡爾是個很棒的藝術家，他的畫總是充滿愛與希望。

同義字 master

assignment [əˋsaɪnmənt] n. 分派的作業、任命 Track 3323

＊字尾-ment有轉變為名詞之意

例句 The professor gives us lots of assignments since we have a long spring break. 因為我們的春假很長，教授給了我們很多功課。

搭配詞 homework assignment 回家作業

assistant [əˋsɪstənt] n. 助手、助理 Track 3324

＊字尾-ant有「者」之意

例句 Jenny is an assistant professor at Princeton University.
珍妮是普林斯頓大學的助理教授。

搭配詞 assistant professor 助理教授

astronaut [ˋæstrəˌnɔt] n. 太空人 Track 3325

例句 There are only four astronauts in the spacecraft.
這架太空梭中只有四個太空人。

astronomer [əˋstrɑnəmɚ] n. 天文學家 Track 3326

＊字尾-er有「者」的意思

例句 I wish I could be a great astronomer like him one day.
我真希望某天可以跟他一樣成為一個很棒的天文學家。

attend [əˋtɛnd] v. 出席 Track 3327

例句 It doesn't matter whether he will attend the meeting or not.
他有沒有出席會議都沒關係。

attendant [ə`tɛndənt] n. 侍者、服務生 ◀Track 3328
＊字尾-ant有「者」之意
例句 Being a flight attendant is one of Evita's dreams since she was a little girl. 成為空中小姐是愛薇塔從小以來的一個夢想。

搭配詞
flight attendant
空中小姐、空少

author [`ɔθɚ] n. 作家、作者 ◀Track 3329
＊字尾-or有「者」的意思
例句 He is my favorite author. I have read all his novels.
他是我最喜歡的作者。我已經讀過他全部的小說了。

反義字
reader 讀者

baby-sitter [`bebɪsɪtɚ] n. 保姆 ◀Track 3330
＊字尾-er有「者」的意思
例句 Jamie hired a babysitter to look after her son.
潔米雇了一個保姆來照顧她的兒子。

bandit [`bændɪt] n. 強盜、劫匪 ◀Track 3331
例句 There are two bandits waiting to pounce outside the gate.
大門外有兩個劫匪等著要襲擊。

banker [`bæŋkɚ] n. 銀行家 ◀Track 3332
＊字尾-er有「者」的意思
例句 There are some rumors about that famous banker.
有一些關於那個知名銀行家的流言。

barber [`bɑrbɚ] n. 男士髮廊的理髮師 ◀Track 3333
＊字尾-er有「者」的意思
例句 Jason is the only barber who can do my hair right.
傑森是唯一一個可以把我的頭髮弄好的理髮師。

barbershop [`bɑrbɚ,ʃɑp] n. 男士髮廊 ◀Track 3334
例句 This is a famous barbershop. You should give it a try some day.
這是家有名的男士髮廊。你應該找一天試試看。

bass [bes] n. 低音樂器、男低音歌手 ◀Track 3335
例句 Gerry was a fine bass in the choir when he was in senior high.
傑瑞在高中的時候是優秀的合唱團男低音歌手。

beggar [`bɛgɚ] n. 乞丐 ＊字尾-ar有「者」的意思 ◀Track 3336
例句 What do you think about the story of that beggar's misfortunes?
你對那個乞丐悲慘的故事有什麼感想呢？

成語
Beggars can't be choosers.
要飯的無法挑肥揀瘦。

believable [bɪ`livəbl] adj. 可信任的 ◀Track 3337
＊字尾-able有「可以、能」的意思
例句 I don't think what he said is believable.
我不覺得他講的是可信的。

反義字
unbelievable 難以置信的

blacksmith [ˋblækˏsmɪθ] n. 鐵匠、鍛工 Track 3338

例句 A blacksmith's job is not an easy one.
鐵匠的工作很困難。

bonus [ˋbonəs] n. 分紅、紅利、附贈 Track 3339

例句 My husband is expecting a large end-of-the-year bonus.
我老公預期會得到高額的年底分紅。

boom [bum] n./v. 隆隆聲、繁榮 Track 3340

例句 Business has been booming since we reopened.
我們重新開業以後生意很興隆。

反義字
slump 衰退

boss [bɔs] n. 老闆、主人 Track 3341

例句 My boss is a perfectionist.
我老闆是個完美主義者。

反義字
follower 部下

boxer [ˋbɑksɚ] n. 拳擊手 Track 3342

＊字尾-er有「者」的意思

例句 The boxer has fought with many opponents, and he won every battle. 這名拳擊手與許多對手對打過，每一場都贏。

branch [bræntʃ] n. 枝狀物、分店、分公司 Track 3343

例句 The bank has many branches in this area.
這家銀行在這一區有很多分行。

brand [brænd] n. 品牌 Track 3344

例句 Brand name drugs are more expensive than their generic equivalents.
原廠藥比學名藥貴多了。

搭配詞
brand name 品牌名稱、商標

budget [ˋbʌdʒɪt] n. 預算 Track 3345

例句 Tim lives on a tight budget. 提姆的生活預算很吃緊。

搭配詞
on a budget 預算拮据

business [ˋbɪznɪs] n. 商業、買賣 Track 3346

＊字尾-ness有轉變為名詞之意

例句 Does the recession influence your business these days?
經濟不景氣這一陣子有影響你的生意嗎？

busy [ˋbɪzɪ] adj. 忙的、繁忙的 Track 3347

例句 My mother is as busy as a bee all day.
我媽整天都忙得像隻蜜蜂一樣。

butcher [ˋbutʃɚ] **n.** 屠夫、劊子手 ◀Track 3348
＊字尾-er有「者」的意思
例句 The butcher gave the dog some meat.
那個屠夫給了那隻狗一些肉。

capitalist [ˋkæpətḷɪst] **n.** 資本家 ◀Track 3349
＊字尾-ist有「主義者」的意思
例句 There is no such thing as a kind capitalist.
沒有什麼慈善資本家這種東西。

同義字 financier

captain [ˋkæptɪn] **n.** 船長、艦長、隊長 ◀Track 3350
例句 I don't want to be the captain of the team.
我不想當這個團隊的隊長。

諺語 I'm the captain of my soul.
我是自己命運的主宰。

career [kəˋrɪr] **n.** （終身的）職業、生涯 ◀Track 3351
例句 Cloud computing skills can enhance your career prospects.
雲端運算技能可以助長你的職業前景。

同義字 vocation

carpenter [ˋkɑrpəntɚ] **n.** 木匠 ◀Track 3352
＊字尾-er有「者」的意思
例句 How long have you been a carpenter in this place?
你在這裡當木匠多久了呢？

carrier [ˋkærɪɚ] **n.** 運送者 ◀Track 3353
＊字尾-er有「者」的意思
例句 Being a mail carrier is not as easy as you think.
當信件運送者沒你想得這麼簡單。

cashier [kæˋʃɪr] **n.** 出納員 ◀Track 3354
例句 Kim found a job as a cashier right after graduation.
琴恩一畢業就找到了出納員的工作。

chef [ʃɛf] **n.** 廚師、主廚 ◀Track 3355
例句 Would you like to try our chef's salad? It's a perfect entree for lunch. 你要嚐嚐我們的主廚沙拉嗎？它是搭配午餐的絕佳前菜。

搭配詞 chef's salad 主廚沙拉

chemist [ˋkɛmɪst] **n.** 化學家、藥商 ◀Track 3356
＊字尾-ist有「者」的意思
例句 You can get this kind of medicine at the chemist's shop.
這種藥在藥房可以買到。

clerk [klɝk] **n.** 職員 ◀Track 3357
例句 There are only four clerks in our company.
我們的公司只有四個職員。

client [ˋklaɪənt] n. 委託人、客戶 Track 3358

例句 Vicky introduced some clients to me.
薇琪介紹了一些客戶給我。

同義字 customer

colleague [ˋkɑlig] n. 同僚、同事 Track 3359

例句 The new colleague is friendly and easy-going.
那個新同事很友善又好相處。

同義字 ally

colonel [ˋkɝnḷ] n. 陸軍上校 Track 3360

例句 Colonel Sanders was the founder of the Kentucky Fried Chicken.
桑德斯上校是肯德基炸雞的創辦人。

搭配詞 Colonel Sanders 桑德斯上校（肯德基爺爺）

columnist [ˋkɑləmɪst] n. 專欄作家 Track 3361

＊字尾-ist有「者」的意思

例句 The popular columnist comments on current affairs.
那個受歡迎的專欄作家在評論時事。

同義字 editorialist

comedian [kəˋmidɪən] n. 喜劇演員 Track 3362

例句 The comedian's performance is very amusing.
那個喜劇演員的表演很有趣。

command [kəˋmænd] v./n. 命令、指揮 Track 3363

例句 He commanded his team to take out their weapons.
他命令他的團隊把武器都拿出來。

成語 Your wish is my command.
你的願望就是我必須完成的使命。（阿拉丁神燈）

commander [kəˋmændɚ] n. 指揮官 Track 3364

＊字尾-er有「者」的意思

例句 As the commander-in-chief, I will make American great again.
身為一國最高統帥，我將使美國再度強大。

搭配詞 commander-in-chief 最高統帥

commentator [ˋkɑmənˏtetɚ] n. 時事評論家 Track 3365

＊字尾-or有「者」的意思

例句 I think they will invite him to be the sports commentator for Fox Sports. 我想他們會邀請他當福斯體育台的體育評論家。

搭配詞 sports commentator 體育評論家

commerce [ˋkɑmɝs] n. 商業、貿易 Track 3366

例句 Could you tell me how to maximize the benefits of electronic commerce? 你可以告訴我怎麼讓電子貿易的優勢達到最大嗎？

同義字 trade

commercial [kəˋmɝʃəl] adj./n. 商業的、廣告 Track 3367

例句 All the commercials on this channel are boring.
這一台的廣告都很無聊。

補充 business school 商學院、商業學校

committee [kəˋmɪtɪ] n. 委員會、會議 Track 3368

例句 What do you think of the committee's decision?
你覺得委員會的決定如何？

---

commodity [kəˋmɑdətɪ] n. 商品、物產 Track 3369

例句 The prices of commodities are stable this year, but the wages are relatively low. 今年的商品價格還算穩定，但薪水相較起來較低。

同義字 product

---

compact [ˋkɑmpækt]/[kəmˋpækt] Track 3370

n./adj. 契約、緊湊的

例句 The two countries made a compact. 那兩個國家訂了契約。

同義字 agreement

---

companion [kəmˋpænjən] n. 同伴 Track 3371

例句 She is my boon companion. 她是我的閨密。

搭配詞 boon companion 密友

---

company [ˋkʌmpənɪ] n. 公司、同伴 Track 3372

例句 Their company closed down last week.
他們公司上禮拜關門了。

同義字 association

---

competition [ˏkɑmpəˋtɪʃən] n. 競爭、競爭者 Track 3373

＊字尾-tion有轉變為名詞的意思

例句 Because there is so much unemployment, the competition for jobs is fierce. 因為失業情形這麼嚴重，所以找工作的競爭也很激烈。

---

competitive [kəmˋpɛtətɪv] adj. 競爭的 Track 3374

＊字尾-ive有轉變為形容詞之意

例句 He is a naturally competitive and aggressive person.
他天生是個愛競爭又愛攻擊人的人。

同義字 rival

---

complaint [kəmˋplent] n. 抱怨、訴苦 Track 3375

例句 The customer made a complaint about a beauty advisor at a makeup counter. 有位顧客投訴美妝專櫃的櫃姐。

搭配詞 make a complaint 投訴

---

complete [kəmˋplit] adj. 完整的 Track 3376

例句 Would you please give me a complete report?
你可以給我完整的報告嗎？

反義字 incomplete 不完全的、不完整的

---

compose [kəmˋpoz] v. 組成、作曲 Track 3377

例句 I don't know how to compose music on the computer.
我不知道怎麼用電腦作曲。

composer [kəm`pozɚ] n. 作曲家、設計者 Track 3378

＊字尾-er有「者」的意思

例句 He is not only a composer but also a conductor.
他不但是作曲家，也是指揮家。

同義字 creator

conductor [kən`dʌktɚ] n. 指揮、指導者、售票員 Track 3379

＊字尾-or有「者」的意思

例句 My dream is to be a symphony orchestra conductor.
我的夢想是成為交響樂團的指揮家。

同義字 leader

contend [kən`tɛnd] v. 抗爭、奮鬥 Track 3380

例句 The company is too small to contend against large companies.
這個公司太小了，無法與大公司競爭。

同義字 fight

control [kən`trol] v./n. 管理、控制 Track 3381

例句 Don't worry. Everything is under control.
別擔心，一切都在掌控之中。

搭配詞 under control 在控制之下

corporation [ˏkɔrpə`reʃən] n. 公司、企業 Track 3382

＊字尾-tion有轉變為名詞的意思

例句 He works for a corporation as a business advisor.
他在大企業擔任商業顧問。

同義字 industry

correspondent [ˏkɔrə`spandənt] n. 通信者、通訊記者 Track 3383

例句 There are many correspondents from The New York Times residing in many countries. 紐約時報有很多通訊記者住在不同的國家。

同義字 communicator

council [`kaʊnsḷ] n. 議會、會議 Track 3384

例句 The forum will be held in the council chamber tomorrow morning.
論壇將在明早於會議廳舉行。

搭配詞 council chamber （尤指官方用途的）會議廳

counsel [`kaʊnsḷ] n. 忠告、法律顧問 Track 3385

例句 Listen to the counsel of your elders, or you will regret later on.
聽長者的忠告，不然你以後會後悔。

counselor [`kaʊnsḷɚ] n. 顧問、參事 Track 3386

＊字尾-or有「者」的意思

例句 I think you'd better go to the counselor.
我覺得你還是去找顧問吧。

courageous [kə`redʒəs] adj. 勇敢的 Track 3387

＊字尾-ous有轉變為形容詞之意

例句 It was courageous of him to stand up to his boss.
他敢與他的老闆抗爭，真是勇敢。

同義字 brave

cowboy [ˋkaʊˏbɔɪ] n. 牛仔 ◀Track 3388

例句 Tom dressed up as a cowboy for the party.
湯姆為了派對打扮成牛仔的樣子。

同義字 buckaroo

---

critic [ˋkrɪtɪk] n. 批評家、評論家 ◀Track 3389

例句 People don't regard him as a good critic.
人們不覺得他是個好的評論家。

同義字 commentator

---

critical [ˋkrɪtɪkḷ] adj. 批判的 ◀Track 3390

例句 The teacher tried to foster her students' critical thinking skills by teaching them the art of debate.
老師教她的學生辯論的技巧，以訓練他們批判思考的能力。

搭配詞 critical thinking 批判性思考

---

cunning [ˋkʌnɪŋ] adj./n. 精明的、狡猾的 ◀Track 3391

例句 The salesman is too cunning. 這名銷售員太狡詐了。

反義字 honest 誠實的、正直的

---

customer [ˋkʌstəmɚ] n. 顧客、客戶 ◀Track 3392

＊字尾-er有「者」的意思

例句 Lily is working in the customer service center at the City Hall.
莉莉在市政府的顧客服務中心工作。

---

dancer [ˋdænsɚ] n. 舞者 ＊字尾-er有「者」的意思 ◀Track 3393

例句 Her dream to be a ballet dancer was shattered by her knee injury.
她成為芭蕾舞者的夢想被膝蓋的傷給毀滅了。

搭配詞 ballet dancer 芭蕾舞者

---

deal [dil] n./v. 買賣、交易 ◀Track 3394

例句 It's a deal! I'll get the poster for you, and you'll get the mug for me.
那就決定交易了！我幫你買海報，你幫我買馬克杯。

---

dealer [ˋdilɚ] n. 商人 ＊字尾-er有「者」的意思 ◀Track 3395

例句 Never have I expected that he would become a drug dealer.
我從沒想過他會成為毒梟。

搭配詞 drug dealer 毒品販賣商

---

deputy [ˋdɛpjətɪ] n. 代表、代理人 ◀Track 3396

例句 Would you like to be my deputy while I am away?
我不在時，你可以當我的代理人嗎？

---

designer [dɪˋzaɪnɚ] n. 設計師 ◀Track 3397

＊字尾-er有「者」的意思

例句 My dream was to be an interior designer, but I had no talent.
我想當室內設計師，但我沒有天分。

同義字 creator

detective [dɪˋtɛktɪv] n. 偵探、探員 Track 3398

例句 The detective found out the culprit to the murder.
那名偵探找出了謀殺的兇手。

同義字 investigator

diplomat [ˋdɪpləmæt] n. 外交官 Track 3399

例句 Her parents are career diplomats so she lived abroad when young.
她的父母是職業外交官，所以她小時候住在國外。

搭配詞 career diplomat 職業外交官

director [dəˋrɛktɚ] n. 指揮者、導演 Track 3400

＊字尾-or有「者」的意思

例句 The director asked us to do the last scene again.
導演請我們再演一次上一個鏡頭。

doctor/doc/Dr. [ˋdɑktɚ] n. 醫生 Track 3401

＊字尾-or有「者」的意思

例句 The doctor examined her ears and throat.
那名醫生檢查了她的耳朵和喉嚨。

drawer [ˋdrɔɚ] n. 抽屜、製圖員 Track 3402

＊字尾-er有「者」的意思

例句 The files are in the second drawer. 文件都在第二個抽屜。

drawing [ˋdrɔɪŋ] n. 繪圖 Track 3403

例句 The new marketing strategy doesn't work. Now let's go back to the drawing board.
新的市場行銷策略不管用，我們現在要重新開始規畫了。

搭配詞 back to the drawing board 回到原點，重新開始

driver [ˋdraɪvɚ] n. 駕駛員、司機 Track 3404

＊字尾-er有「者」的意思

例句 Stop being a back-seat driver. I know exactly what to do.
別多管閒事，我知道該怎麼做。

搭配詞 back-seat driver 在後座對司機指手畫腳的人

economist [ɪˋkɑnəmɪst] n. 經濟學家 Track 3405

＊字尾-ist有「主義者」的意思

例句 My boss wants to invite the famous economist to give us a speech.
我老闆想邀請那位有名的經濟學家來給我們演講。

edit [ˋɛdɪt] v. 編輯 Track 3406

例句 He edited this book very quickly so that it can be published soon.
他很快地編輯了這本書，讓它可以快點出版。

editor [ˋɛdɪtɚ] n. 編輯者 Track 3407

＊字尾-or有「者」的意思

例句 She is the editor-in chief of the famous fashion magazine.
她是知名時尚雜誌的總編輯。

同義字 reviser

efficiency [ə`fɪʃənsɪ] n. 效率 ◀ Track 3408

例句 She's looking for an efficiency apartment near her office.
她正在找離辦公室近、附有小廚房及浴室的小公寓。

搭配詞
efficiency apartment 附有小廚房及浴室的小公寓

efficient [ɪ`fɪʃənt] adj. 有效率的 ◀ Track 3409

例句 Peggy is an efficient secretary.
佩姬是個有效率的秘書。

electrician [ˌɪlɛk`trɪʃən] n. 電機工程師 ◀ Track 3410

例句 I need an electrician to fix my electric meter.
我需要一個電機工程師來修我的電表。

embark [ɪm`bɑrk] v. 從事、搭乘 ◀ Track 3411

例句 I heard that he was about to embark on a new business venture.
我聽說他要從事新的創業投資了。

搭配詞
embark on 著手、開始

employ [ɪm`plɔɪ] v./n. 從事、雇用 ◀ Track 3412

例句 She was employed at the dentists.
她受雇於一家牙醫。

employee [ˌɛmplɔɪ`i] n. 從業人員、職員 ◀ Track 3413

＊字尾-ee有「被……者」的意思

例句 The employees were disappointed with their salary.
那些職員對他們的薪水很失望。

反義字
employer 雇主、僱用者

employer [ɪm`plɔɪɚ] n. 老闆、雇主 ◀ Track 3414

＊字尾-er有「者」的意思

例句 What do you think of our new employer?
你覺得我們的新老闆如何？

同義字
boss

engineer [ˌɛndʒə`nɪr] n. 工程師 ◀ Track 3415

＊字尾-er有「者」的意思

例句 I want to be an engineer like my father.
我想和我爸一樣當個工程師。

同義字
guide

enterprise [`ɛntɚˌpraɪz] n. 企業 ◀ Track 3416

例句 The enterprise will go bankrupt sooner or later.
那個企業遲早要破產的。

同義字
business

errand [`ɛrənd] n. 任務、跑腿 ◀ Track 3417

例句 Ryan enjoys running errands for his friends.
萊恩喜歡替他的朋友們跑腿。

搭配詞
run an errand 跑腿

expand [ɪk`spænd] v. 擴大、延長 Track 3418
＊字首ex-有「外」的意思
例句 We want to expand our business to India.
我們想擴大業務到印度。

expansion [ɪk`spænʃən] n. 擴張 Track 3419
＊字首ex-有「外」的意思
例句 It's time for the company to consolidate after several years of rapid expansion. 快速擴張好幾年後，這公司也該穩定下來了。
反義字 contraction 收縮、縮短

experience [ɪk`spɪrɪəns] n./v. 經驗 Track 3420
例句 We value working experience in our candidates.
我們很重視應徵人選的工作經驗。

expert [`ɛkspɝt] n. 專家 Track 3421
例句 He is an expert with computers. 他是電腦專家。
反義字 amateur 業餘從事者

farmer [`fɑrmɚ] n. 農夫 Track 3422
＊字尾-er有「者」的意思
例句 There are still a great many poor farmers in India.
印度還有很多貧窮的農夫。
同義字 granger

fireman/firewoman [`faɪrmən]/[`faɪrwumən] Track 3423
n. 男消防員／女消防員
例句 The firemen were unable to put out the fire.
這些消防員無法把火撲滅。
同義字 fire fighter

fisherman [`fɪʃɚmən] n. 漁夫 Track 3424
例句 The fishermen had a lot to say about water pollution.
對於水污染話題，漁夫們有很多話要說。
同義字 fisher

fishery [`fɪʃərɪ] n. 漁業、水產業、養魚場 Track 3425
例句 We went to the fishery to look for fish for our restaurant.
我們到養魚場去找我們餐廳可以用的魚。

fit [fɪt] adj./v./n. 適合的、適合 Track 3426
例句 He tried to fit in at his new school, but it was difficult.
他嘗試要試應新學校，但有困難。
搭配詞 fit in 適合

fulfillment [fulˋfɪlmənt] n. 實現、成就感 Track 3427
＊字尾-ment有轉變為名詞之意
例句 I think work can give you a sense of fulfillment.
我覺得工作可以給你帶來成就感。
搭配詞 a sense of fulfillment 成就感

future [ˋfjutʃɚ] n./adj. 未來、將來的 ◀Track 3428

例句 The boy wants to be an astronaut in the future because he wants to travel in space.
那個男孩未來想成為太空人，因為他想在太空中旅行。

搭配詞
in the future 今後

---

gardener [ˋgɑrdṇɚ] n. 園丁、花匠 ◀Track 3429

＊字尾-er有「者」的意思

例句 The gardener is trimming up the trees in the garden now.
那個園丁正在花園裡修剪樹。

---

general [ˋdʒɛnərəl] n. 將領、將軍 ◀Track 3430

例句 He was a general when he was in the army.
他以前在軍隊中是當將軍的。

---

guard [gɑrd] n./v. 警衛 ◀Track 3431

例句 The guard would not let us in.
那個警衛不讓我們進去。

---

guideline [ˋgaɪd͵laɪn] n. 指導方針、指標 ◀Track 3432

例句 Follow his guidelines and you'll be fine.
跟著他的方針做，就不會有問題。

---

hairdresser [ˋhɛr͵drɛsɚ] n. 理髮師 ◀Track 3433

＊字尾-er有「者」的意思

例句 Ask the hairdresser to trim your beard.
請理髮師幫你修剪鬍鬚吧。

同義字
barber

---

headquarters [ˋhɛd͵kwɔrtɚz] n. 總部、大本營 ◀Track 3434

＊字尾-s有轉變為複數之意

例句 The company wants to move its headquarters to a bigger building.
那個公司想把總部搬到一棟比較大的大樓。

同義字
base

---

hire [haɪr] v./n. 雇用、租用 ◀Track 3435

例句 Let's hire a guide to take us on a tour of the city.
我們來雇用一個導遊帶我們去參觀城市吧。

---

historian [hɪsˋtorɪən] n. 歷史學家 ◀Track 3436

例句 Evans is not only a writer but also a historian.
伊凡斯不但是個作家，也是歷史學家。

---

host [host] n. 主人、主持人、一大群 ◀Track 3437

例句 I think he will be the host for tonight's show.
我想他應該會是今晚節目的主持人。

housekeeper [ˋhaus͵kipɚ] n. 主婦、管家 Track 3438
＊字尾-er有「者」的意思
例句 The housekeeper accidentally dumped all her letters into the trash.
那個管家不小心把她的信件都倒到垃圾桶了。
同義字 homemaker

hunter [ˋhʌntɚ] n. 獵人 ＊字尾-er有「者」的意思 Track 3439
例句 The hunters gathered around the area with their guns.
獵人們帶著槍在這一區集合。

indicate [ˋɪndə͵ket] v. 指出、指示 Track 3440
例句 Will you please indicate your expected salary in your resume?
你可以在履歷表裡面指出期望多少薪水嗎？
同義字 show

industrialize [ɪnˋdʌstrɪəl͵aɪz] v. （使）工業化 Track 3441
＊字尾-ize有「使」的意思
例句 Many towns in the coastal area are industrialized.
沿岸許多城市已經工業化了。

industry [ˋɪndəstrɪ] n. 工業 Track 3442
例句 I really love working in the hotel industry.
我很喜歡在旅館業工作。

inspector [ɪnˋspɛktɚ] n. 視察員、檢查者 Track 3443
＊字尾-or有「者」的意思
例句 The inspector asked for details of the missing cars.
那名視察員詢問關於失竊車輛的細節。

instructor [ɪnˋstrʌktɚ] n. 教練、指導者、講師 Track 3444
＊字尾-or有「者」的意思
例句 The English instructor is very patient and professional.
這名英語講師很有耐心，也很專業。

interpreter [ɪnˋtɝprɪtɚ] n. 解釋者、翻譯員 Track 3445
＊字尾-er有「者」的意思
例句 Please arrange for an interpreter at the meeting.
請在會場現場安排一名翻譯員。
同義字 exponent

interview [ˋɪntɚ͵vju] n./v. 面談、接見 Track 3446
例句 She was late for the interview and left a bad impression.
她面試遲到了，給對方留下不好的印象。
同義字 question

introduction [͵ɪntrəˋdʌkʃən] n. 引進、介紹 Track 3447
＊字尾-tion有轉變為名詞的意思
例句 The students were given an introductory course on how to use the smart library and its information commons. 這群學生上介紹課程，以了解如何使用這座智慧圖書館及其中的資訊共享空間。
搭配詞 introductory course 介紹課程

inventor [ɪnˋvɛntɚ] **n.** 發明家 ◀Track 3448

＊字尾-or有「者」的意思

例句 A lot of inventors were thought to be crazy at first.
很多發明家一開始都被當作是瘋子。

同義字 creator

---

invest [ɪnˋvɛst] **v.** 投資 ◀Track 3449

例句 He invested a lot of time in helping children.
他投資許多時間在幫助兒童上。

反義字 divest 剝奪

---

investment [ɪnˋvɛstmənt] **n.** 投資額、投資 ◀Track 3450

＊字尾-ment有轉變為名詞之意

例句 She was cautious and didn't like to make highly risky investments.
她人很小心，不喜歡做高風險的投資。

搭配詞 make investments 投資理財

---

janitor [ˋdʒænɪtɚ] **n.** 管門者、看門者 ◀Track 3451

＊字尾-or有「者」的意思

例句 The school janitor knows all the ins and outs of the big school building. 管理員知道學校大樓的所有出入口。

搭配詞 school janitor 學校管理員

---

job [dʒɑb] **n.** 工作 ◀Track 3452

例句 Because of the financial crisis, it's hard for people to find a job.
因為經濟危機，人們難以找到工作。

---

journalist [ˋdʒɝnḷɪst] **n.** 新聞工作者 ◀Track 3453

＊字尾-ist有「者」的意思

例句 He is a journalist and therefore travels a lot.
他是個新聞工作者，經常在旅行。

同義字 newspaperman

---

judge [dʒʌdʒ] **n.** 法官、裁判 ◀Track 3454

例句 The judge sentenced the murderer to death.
法官判了兇手死刑。

---

knight [naɪt] **n.** 騎士、武士 ◀Track 3455

例句 The handsome knight saved the life of a beautiful princess.
那名英俊的騎士救了美麗的公主一命。

---

labor [ˋlebɚ] **n./v.** 勞工、勞動 ◀Track 3456

例句 She labored for five years on that book.
她為了這本書努力工作了五年。

---

landlady [ˋlændˌledɪ] **n.** 女房東 ◀Track 3457

例句 My landlady wouldn't allow us to keep pets.
我的房東太太不讓我們養寵物。

反義字 landlord 房東

a b c d e f g h i j k l m n o p q r s t u v w x y z

landlord [ˋlændˏlɔrd] n. 房東、主人、老闆 Track 3458

例句 The landlord forgot to collect rent last month.
房東上個月忘記收房租了。

同義字 proprietor

lawyer [ˋlɔjɚ] n. 律師 ＊字尾-er有「者」的意思 Track 3459

例句 She is a famous international human rights lawyer.
她是知名的國際人權律師。

同義字 attorney

layman [ˋlemən] n. 普通信徒、外行人 Track 3460

例句 The terms are difficult for a layman to understand.
這些專有名詞對外行人來説很難理解。

反義字 priest 牧師、神父

lecturer [ˋlɛktʃərɚ] n. 講師 Track 3461

＊字尾-er有「者」的意思

例句 Will you tell me what the assistant lecturer is talking about?
你可以告訴我助理講師到底在説什麼嗎？

搭配詞 assistant lecturer 助理講師

librarian [laɪˋbrɛrɪən] n. 圖書館員 Track 3462

例句 My father is a university librarian at Oxford.
我爸爸是牛津大學的圖書館館長。

搭配詞 university librarian 大學圖書館長（librarian是館員，美國大學的university librarian是館長）

license [ˋlaɪsn̩s] n. 執照 Track 3463

例句 The suspect's car did not have a license plate.
嫌犯的車子並沒有汽車牌照。

搭配詞 license plate 執照號碼牌、汽車牌照

lifeguard [ˋlaɪfˏgɑrd] n. 救生員 Track 3464

例句 You should swim only in places where there is a lifeguard.
你只能在有救生員的地方游泳。

linguist [ˋlɪŋgwɪst] n. 語言學家、通曉數國語言的人 Track 3465

＊字尾-ist有「主義者」的意思

例句 I'm not a linguist, so I wouldn't know about phonetics.
我不是語言學家，所以我對語音學可不瞭解。

magician [məˋdʒɪʃən] n. 魔術師 Track 3466

例句 A good magician knows how to grab the audience's attention.
優秀的魔術師都知道怎麼吸引觀眾的目光。

同義字 conjurer

maid [med] n. 女僕、少女 Track 3467

例句 She was a hotel maid and later was promoted to management.
她原本是飯店女僕，後來被升遷到管理部門。

manage [ˋmænɪdʒ] v. 管理、處理 ◀Track 3468

例句 I believe that he can manage this by himself this time.
我相信他這次可以自己處理。

manageable [ˋmænɪdʒəbḷ] ◀Track 3469

adj. 可管理的、易處理的 ＊字尾-able有「可以、能」的意思

例句 Thanks to the development of new drugs, some cancers are becoming manageable diseases.
由於新藥的開發，有些癌症逐漸變成可被處理治療的疾病了。

management [ˋmænɪdʒmənt] n. 處理、管理 ◀Track 3470

＊字尾-ment有轉變為名詞之意

例句 My major was management engineering.
我大學主修管理工程學。

搭配詞
management engineering
管理工程學

manager [ˋmænɪdʒɚ] n. 經理 ◀Track 3471

＊字尾-er有「者」的意思

例句 Have you talked to the new manager?
你和新來的經理聊過了嗎？

補充
fugleman 示範兵

manufacture [͵mænjəˋfæktʃɚ] ◀Track 3472

n./v. 製造業；製造

例句 Their company manufactures light bulbs.
他們的公司製造燈泡。

manufacturer [͵mænjəˋfæktʃərɚ] n. 製造者 ◀Track 3473

＊字尾-er有「者」的意思

例句 The New York-based toy manufacturer filed for bankruptcy protection in September. 總部設在紐約的玩具製造商在9月申請破產保護。

搭配詞
toy manufacturer
玩具製造商

marine [məˋrin] n. 海軍陸戰隊隊員 ◀Track 3474

例句 He is a U.S. marine and is rarely at home.
他是美國海軍陸戰隊隊員，所以不常在家。

marshall [ˋmɑrʃəl] n. 元帥、司儀 ◀Track 3475

例句 He was appointed marshall last month.
他上個月被任命為元帥。

master [ˋmæstɚ] n. 主人、大師 ◀Track 3476

＊字尾-er有「者」的意思

例句 That artist is really a master of his time.
那名藝術家真是他那個年代的大師。

mastery [ˋmæstərɪ] n. 優勢、精通、掌握 ◀Track 3477

例句 All the teachers were impressed with Tom's mastery of economic theories. 所有老師都對湯姆精準掌握經濟學說感到印象深刻。

同義字
rule

mechanic [mə`kænɪk] n. 機械工 Track 3478

例句 Every mechanic has met such problems before.
每個機械工都遇過這種問題。

同義字 machinist

meeting [`mitɪŋ] n. 會議 Track 3479

例句 The two leaders held a closed-door meeting in Switzerland.
兩國領袖在瑞士舉辦閉門會議。

搭配詞 a closed-door meeting 閉門會議

mention [`mɛnʃən] v./n. 提起 Track 3480

例句 She doesn't mind at all if we mention this matter at the meeting.
她完全不介意我們在開會時提起這件事。

merchandise [`mɝtʃən͵daɪz] n. 商品 Track 3481

例句 The defected merchandise is already sent back.
有損壞的商品已經送回去了。

同義字 goods

merchant [`mɝtʃənt] n./adj. 商人 Track 3482

例句 The merchant is annoyed to see his goods stolen.
那名商人發現他的商品被偷，非常不悅。

merge [mɝdʒ] v. 合併 Track 3483

例句 It is his idea to merge the two firms.
合併兩個公司是他的主意。

messenger [`mɛsn̩dʒɚ] n. 使者、信差 Track 3484

＊字尾-er有「者」的意思

例句 He earns some pocket money after school as a messenger boy.
他放學後兼當送信男孩來賺點零用錢。

同義字 courier

mill [mɪl] n. 磨坊、工廠 Track 3485

例句 May and her sisters all work at the mill.
梅依和她的姊妹們都在這個磨坊工作。

搭配詞 The mills of God grind slowly, yet they grind exceeding small.
天網恢恢，疏而不漏。

miller [`mɪlɚ] n. 磨坊主人 Track 3486

＊字尾-er有「者」的意思

例句 The miller makes flour. 這個磨坊主人專門製作麵粉。

millionaire [͵mɪljən`ɛr] n. 百萬富翁 Track 3487

例句 How would you spend your money if you were a millionaire?
如果你是百萬富翁，會怎麼花你的錢呢？

miner [ˋmaɪnɚ] n. 礦工 ＊字尾-er有「者」的意思 ◀Track 3488

例句 Ted is too old to work as a coal miner.
泰德太老了，不能當個礦工。

補充
hard hat 工地安全帽

minister [ˋmɪnɪstɚ] n. 神職人員、部長、大臣 ◀Track 3489
＊字尾-er有「者」的意思

例句 The prime minister resigned after being found driving under the influence. 首相被發現酒駕後辭去職務。

搭配詞
prime minister 首相

ministry [ˋmɪnɪstrɪ] n. 牧師、部長、部 ◀Track 3490

例句 None of us knows that this senior high school isn't under the direct control of the Ministry of Education.
我們都不知道這家高中沒有直接由教育部控管。

mission [ˋmɪʃən] n. 任務 ◀Track 3491

例句 Sara went to Russia on a mission.
莎拉去俄國出任務。

同義字
errand

missionary [ˋmɪʃən͵ɛrɪ] n. 傳教士 ◀Track 3492

例句 As a missionary, Henry naturally asks his children to have faith in god. 亨利是傳教士，自然會要求孩子們信上帝。

mobile [ˋmobɪl] adj. 可動的 ◀Track 3493

例句 May I use your mobile phone? Mine is out of battery.
我可以用你的行動電話嗎？我的沒電了。

搭配詞
mobile phone 行動電話

monk [mʌŋk] n. 僧侶、修道士 ◀Track 3494

例句 The monks copied the Bible by hand.
修道士們用手抄寫聖經。

反義字
nun 修女、尼姑

mouthpiece/spokesperson ◀Track 3495
[ˋmaʊθ͵pis]/[ˋspoks͵pɝsn̩] n. 發言人、代言人、喉舌

例句 Because Sam is out of office this week, his assistant has to be the mouthpiece.
因為山姆這個禮拜不進辦公室，他的助理就得當代言人。

musician [mjuˋzɪʃən] n. 音樂家 ◀Track 3496

例句 Hank is a talented musician.
漢克是個有天分的音樂家。

同義字
performer

nanny [ˋnænɪ] n. 奶媽、保姆 ◀Track 3497

例句 They can't afford a nanny to take care of their children.
他們沒錢雇用保姆來照顧小孩。

negotiation [nɪ͵goʃɪ`eʃən] n. 協商、協議 Track 3498

＊字尾-tion有轉變為名詞的意思

例句 The doors of the meeting room are still closed, so no one knows how the negotiation is going.
會議室的門還關著，所以沒人知道協商進行得如何了。

negotiate [nɪ`goʃɪ͵et] v. 商議、談判 Track 3499

例句 Jenny is able to successfully negotiate with this big firm.
珍妮能夠成功和這家大公司談判。

newscaster [`nuzkæstɚ] n. 新聞播報員 Track 3500

＊字尾-er有「者」的意思

例句 This newscaster is well known for her perfect pronunciation.
那名新聞播報員因完美的發音廣為人知。

novelist [`nɑvḷɪst] n. 小說家 Track 3501

＊字尾-ist有「者」的意思

例句 Annie has dreamed of becoming a novelist since she was little.
安妮從小就夢想當小說家。

nun [nʌn] n. 修女、尼姑 Track 3502

例句 As a nun, she lives in a convent.
身為修女，她住在修道院。

反義字
monk 修道士、僧侶

nurse [nɝs] n. 護士 Track 3503

例句 A compassionate nurse, Florence Nightingale devoted her entire life to the treatment for the poor and the suffering. 南丁格爾是深具同情心的護士，畢生奉獻於治療貧窮、困苦的人們。

observer [əb`zɝvɚ] n. 觀察者、觀察員 Track 3504

＊字尾-er有「者」的意思

例句 These reports are from different observers, they therefore vary a lot. 這些報導是不同的觀察者寫的，所以有滿大的差別。

同義字
spectator

obvious [`ɑbvɪəs] adj. 顯然的、明顯的 Track 3505

＊字尾-ous有轉變為形容詞之意

例句 It's obvious that they are in love. 他們顯然在戀愛中。

同義字
apparent

occupation [͵ɑkjə`peʃən] n. 職業 Track 3506

＊字尾-tion有轉變為名詞的意思

例句 Do not give strangers your personal information, such as your name, age and occupation.
別給陌生人你的個人資料，像你的名字、年齡與職業。

office [`ɔfɪs] n. 辦公室 Track 3507

例句 I'm an office worker, and my sister is a makeup artist.
我是上班族，妹妹是化妝師。

搭配詞
office workers 上班族

operator [ˋɑpəˏretɚ] n. 操作者 ◀Track 3508
*字尾-or有「者」的意思
例句 It is necessary for our company to hire some computer operators.
我們公司得雇一些電腦操作員。

opposite [ˋɑpəsɪt] adj. 相對的、對立的 ◀Track 3509
例句 She sits in the opposite seat. 她坐在對面的位置。

organization [ˏɔrgənəˋzeʃən] n. 組織、機構 ◀Track 3510
*字尾-tion有轉變為名詞的意思
例句 Red Cross is a nonprofit organization. 紅十字會非營利機構。

搭配詞
nonprofit organization
非營利機構

organize [ˋɔrgənˏaɪz] v. 組織、系統化 ◀Track 3511
*字尾-ize有「使」的意思
例句 We want to organize the project in a more manageable way.
我們想用更能有效管理的方式組織這次計畫。

反義字
disorganize 擾亂、瓦解

organizer [ˋɔrgənˏaɪzɚ] n. 組織者 ◀Track 3512
*字尾-er有「者」的意思
例句 Angie is the event organizer of this annual meeting.
安琪是這場年會的活動組織人。

搭配詞
event organizer 活動組織人

overwork [ˋovɚˋwɝk] v. 過度工作 ◀Track 3513
*字首over-有「越過、超過」之意
例句 More and more people die of overworking.
越來越多人因過度工作而過世。

painter [ˋpentɚ] n. 畫家 ◀Track 3514
*字尾-er有「者」的意思
例句 Vincent van Gogh is my favorite painter.
梵谷是我最喜歡的畫家。

partner [ˋpartnɚ] n./v. 伙伴；合伙 ◀Track 3515
*字尾-er有「者」的意思
例句 They were business partners back in 1990.
他們在1990年當時還是生意伙伴。

pay/salary/wage [pe]/[ˋsælərɪ]/[wedʒ] ◀Track 3516
n. 薪水
例句 My boss never gives me my pay on time.
我老闆總是不準時給我薪水。

peasant [ˋpɛzn̩t] n. 佃農、農夫 ◀Track 3517
例句 The proud rich man looks down on peasants.
那個驕傲的富翁看不起佃農。

同義字
farmer

peddler [ˋpɛdlɚ] n. 小販 Track 3518

＊字尾-er有「者」的意思

例句 Josh enjoys bargaining with the peddlers at the night market.
喬許喜歡在夜市和小販討價還價。

permanent [ˋpɝmənənt] adj. 永久的 Track 3519

例句 If a child's primary teeth are healthy, it will help the development of better permanent teeth.
小孩的乳牙如果很健康，未來的恆齒也會長得比較好。

搭配詞
permanent tooth 恆齒

personnel [ˏpɝsnˋɛl] n. 人員、人事部門 Track 3520

例句 No one knows how to contact the related personnel.
沒人知道怎麼聯絡相關人員。

pharmacist [ˋfɑrməsɪst] n. 藥劑師 Track 3521

＊字尾-ist有「者」的意思

例句 After obtaining a pharmacist license, he started to sell over-the-counter drugs. 他取得藥劑師執照後，開始賣成藥。

搭配詞
pharmacist license
藥劑師執照

philosopher [fəˋlɑsəfɚ] n. 哲學家 Track 3522

＊字尾-er有「者」的意思

例句 Aristotle is not only a good philosopher, but also an outstanding teacher. 亞里斯多德不但是個好的哲學家，也是個好老師。

photographer [fəˋtɑgrəfɚ] n. 攝影師 Track 3523

＊字尾-er有「者」的意思

例句 As an amateur photographer, Jamie's photography skills are truly impressive.
傑米是個業餘攝影師，但是他的攝影技術令人印象深刻。

搭配詞
amateur photographer
業餘攝影師

physician [fəˋzɪʃən] n. （內科）醫師 Track 3524

例句 She grabbed the physician and asked him about her husband's condition. 她抓住內科醫師，問他她先生的狀況。

反義字
surgeon 外科醫生

physicist [ˋfɪzɪsɪst] n. 物理學家 Track 3525

＊字尾-ist有「者」的意思

例句 Albert Einstein is one of the greatest physicists in the world.
愛因斯坦是世界上最棒的物理學家之一。

pianist [pɪˋænɪst] n. 鋼琴師 Track 3526

＊字尾-ist有「者」的意思

例句 She is a gifted pianist. 她是個很有天分的鋼琴師。

pickpocket [ˋpɪkˏpɑkɪt] n. 扒手 Track 3527

例句 Caught red handed, the pickpocket was arrested by the police.
那名扒手被當場逮住，被警察逮捕了。

pilot [ˋpaɪlət] n. 飛行員、領航員 Track 3528

例句 The airline is recruiting pilots and ground crew. Why don't you give it a try? 那個航空公司在徵求飛行員與地勤。你何不去試試看呢？

pirate [ˋpaɪrət] n. 海盜 Track 3529

例句 The pirates attack other ships and steal from them.
那些海盜攻擊其他的船隻，並偷走船上的東西。

pitcher [ˋpɪtʃɚ] n. 投手 ＊字尾-er有「者」的意思 Track 3530

例句 The coach tried to calm the angry pitcher down.
教練試著要生氣的投手冷靜下來。

片語
pitcher mound 投手丘

player [ˋpleɚ] n. 運動員、演奏者、玩家 Track 3531
＊字尾-er有「者」的意思

例句 The basketball player was greeted with cheers from his fans.
那名籃球員被他粉絲的歡呼迎接。

playwright [ˋpleˏraɪt] n. 劇作家 Track 3532

例句 The playwright often comes up with strange new ideas.
那名劇作家常想出奇怪的新點子。

plumber [ˋplʌmɚ] n. 水管工 Track 3533
＊字尾-er有「者」的意思

例句 He caught his wife making out with the plumber.
他逮到他太太與水管工親熱。

poacher [ˋpotʃɚ] n. 偷獵者 Track 3534
＊字尾-er有「者」的意思

例句 The government decided to punish the poachers who illegally hunt animals. 政府決定處罰違法盜獵動物的偷獵者。

poet [ˋpoɪt] n. 詩人 Track 3535

例句 Emily Dickinson is a famous American poet who was usually clothed in white. 愛蜜莉迪金森是個有名的美國詩人，總是穿著白色。

police [pəˋlis] n. 員警 Track 3536

例句 If you get lost, you can ask for help at the police station.
如果你迷路了，可以去警察局求助。

搭配詞
police station
警察局、派出所

policeman/cop [pəˋlismən]/[kɑp] n. 員警 Track 3537

例句 The policeman was criticized for excessive enforcement of the law.
這名員警被批評執法過當。

politician [ˏpɑləˋtɪʃən] n. 政治家 Track 3538

例句 In my opinion, only one of the presidential candidates is a politician; the others are clowns.
在我看來，總統候選人中只有一個是政治家，其他的都是小丑。

porter [ˋportɚ] n. 搬運工 Track 3539

＊字尾-er有「者」的意思

例句 He nearly forgot to tip the porter. 他差點忘記給搬運工小費。

pose [poz] n./v. 姿勢、擺出 Track 3540

例句 Julia is striking a pose for photographers in Cannes.
茱莉雅參加坎城影展，在攝影師前擺姿勢。

搭配詞 strike a pose 擺姿勢

position [pəˋzɪʃən] n. 位置、工作職位、形勢 Track 3541

＊字尾-tion有轉變為名詞的意思

例句 He climbed to the position he is in now because of his hard work.
他能夠攀到現在的職位，是因為他努力地工作。

practical [ˋpræktɪk!] adj. 實用的 Track 3542

例句 Patricia is useless to our team. She never comes up with practical proposals.
派翠西亞對我們的團隊來說沒什麼用，她從來不提出實用的建議。

pressure [ˋprɛʃɚ] n. 壓力 Track 3543

例句 In my opinion, your child is under too much pressure.
在我看來，你的孩子壓力太多了。

搭配詞 under pressure 高壓

priest [prist] n. 神父 Track 3544

例句 People confess to the priests what they have done wrong.
人們對神父懺悔他們做錯的事。

搭配詞 high priest 高僧、祭司長

productivity [ˏprodʌkˋtɪvətɪ] n. 生產力 Track 3545

例句 We must not overestimate our agricultural productivity.
我們不能高估我們的農業生產力。

搭配詞 agricultural productivity 農業生產力

produce [prəˋdjus]/[ˋprɑdjus] v./n. 生產、農產品 Track 3546

例句 This factory is big enough to produce lots of products.
這家工廠夠大，能夠生產許多產品。

反義字 consume 消耗、花費、耗盡

producer [prəˋdjusɚ] n. 製造者 Track 3547

＊字尾-er有「者」的意思

例句 One of the reasons why this company is the best producer of air-conditioners is their great emphasis on quality management.
這家公司之所以是最佳冷氣製造商的其中一個原因，就是他們很強調品質管理。

反義字 consumer 消費者

product [ˋprɑdəkt] n. 產品 ◀Track 3548

例句 Their products are always copied by other companies.
他們的產品總是被其他公司抄襲。

補充 production 生產

profession [prəˋfɛʃən] n. 專業、職業 ◀Track 3549

例句 Both of my parents are elementary school teachers by profession.
我的雙親都以小學教師為職業。

搭配詞 by profession 作為職業

professional [prəˋfɛʃənl̩] n. 專業的 ◀Track 3550

＊字尾-al有轉變為形容詞之意

例句 We often ask experts for professional advice.
我們常請專家提供專業意見。

搭配詞 professional advice 專業意見

professor [prəˋfɛsɚ] n. 教授 ◀Track 3551

＊字尾-or有「者」的意思

例句 Although Ann is the youngest professor in this university, she teaches very well. 雖然安妮是這所大學最年輕的教授，但她教得很好。

同義字 pedagogue

profit [ˋprɑfɪt] n. 利潤、利益 ◀Track 3552

例句 There is no profit in selling books or magazines here.
在這裡賣書或雜誌不會有利潤的。

project [ˋprɑdʒɛkt]/[prəˋdʒɛkt] n./v. 計畫、預計 ◀Track 3553

例句 Just project yourself into this awkward situation.
設想一下你處於這麼尷尬的情境。

搭配詞 project oneself into 設想自己處身於

propaganda [ˏprɑpəˋgændə] n. 宣傳活動 ◀Track 3554

例句 There has been a lot of anti-corporal punishment propaganda in recent years. 最近幾年有許多反體罰的宣傳活動。

同義字 advertisement

psychologist [saɪˋkɑlədʒɪst] n. 心理學家 ◀Track 3555

＊字尾-ist有「者」的意思

例句 Sigmund Freud was thought by some to be an outstanding psychologist. 有些人認為佛洛伊德是個優秀的心理學家。

qualification(s) [ˏkwɑləfəˋkeʃən(z)] ◀Track 3556

n. 資格、證照

例句 What qualifications do you have for the job?
你有什麼這個工作需要的資格嗎？

反義字 disqualification 取消資格、無資格

quality [ˋkwɑlətɪ] n. 品質 ◀Track 3557

例句 The seamless care service provided by the hospital has improved the quality of patients' lives in leaps and bounds.
這家醫院的無縫式照護服務大幅改善了病人的生活品質。

a b c d e f g h i j k l m n o p q r s t u v w x y z

quit [kwɪt] v. 離去、解除 Track 3558

例句 He is sick of his job and is considering quitting.
他受不了他的工作了，在考慮要離開。

rate [ret] n. 比率、速率 Track 3559

例句 At this rate, we'll never finish the project.
用這個速率，我們永遠也完成不了這個計畫。

搭配詞 at all rates 無論如何

recruit [rɪˋkrut] v. 聘用、募兵 Track 3560

例句 Some of the professors in this university are recruited from America.
這所大學的一些教授是從美國聘過來的。

同義字 enlist

retrieve [rɪˋtriv] v./n. 取回、挽救 Track 3561

＊字首re-有「再次」之意

例句 The manager told me to retrieve some files for him.
主管要我幫他去取回一些文件。

同義字 recover

recorder [rɪˋkɔrdɚ] n. 紀錄員、錄音機 Track 3562

＊字首re-有「再次」之意

例句 In my childhood, my parents used a tape recorder to record my singing. 小時候，我父母用卡帶錄音機把我唱歌的聲音錄下來。

搭配詞 tape recorder 錄音機

replacement [rɪˋplesmənt] n. 取代 Track 3563

＊字尾-ment有轉變為名詞之意

例句 We think Mindy is the perfect replacement for the cook who left.
我們認為敏蒂是離開的廚師最好的取代者。

reporter [rɪˋportɚ] n. 記者 Track 3564

＊字尾-er有「者」的意思

例句 Sonia refused to tell her experience to the reporters.
索尼雅不願把她的經驗告訴記者。

同義字 journalist

represent [ˏrɛprɪˋzɛnt] v. 代表、象徵 Track 3565

例句 I represent my company. If you have any problems, please contact me. 我是公司的代表。如果有問題，請和我聯絡。

representative [rɛprɪˋzɛntətɪv] adj./n. 典型的、代表的、代表 Track 3566

例句 He is the representative of the delegation.
他是這個訪團的代表。

搭配詞 be a representative of 代表……的

researcher [riˋsɝtʃɚ] n. 研究員 Track 3567

＊字尾-er有「者」的意思

例句 As a researcher, he always stays up late or sleeps in his lab.
身為研究員，他總是熬夜或直接在實驗室裡睡。

resign [rɪˋzaɪn] v. 辭職、使順從 ◀ Track 3568

例句 She resigned from her job after two months.
兩個月後，她辭職了。

resignation [ˏrɛzɪgˋneʃən] n. 辭職、讓位 ◀ Track 3569

＊字尾-tion有轉變為名詞的意思

例句 He just tendered his resignation. 他剛提出辭呈。

搭配詞
tender one's resignation
提出辭呈

resource [rɪˋsors] n. 資源 ◀ Track 3570

例句 The country has a vast land with limited natural resources.
這個國家領土很大，但天然資源有限。

搭配詞
limited resource 資源有限

resume [ˋrɛzəˏme]/[rɪˋzjum] n. 摘要、履歷表 ◀ Track 3571

例句 If you want me to write a recommendation letter for you, give me your resume.
如果你要我為你寫一封推薦信，就把你的履歷表給我。

retire [rɪˋtaɪr] v. 隱退、退休 ◀ Track 3572

例句 Andy really has to retire and enjoy his life.
安迪真的應該退休享受生活了。

retirement [rɪˋtaɪrmənt] n. 退休 ◀ Track 3573

＊字尾-ment有轉變為名詞之意

例句 Ted finally has time to pursue his interests after retirement.
退休後，泰德終於有時間去發展他的興趣了。

rivalry [ˋraɪvəlrɪ] n. 競爭 ◀ Track 3574

例句 Rivalry among business firms is intense now. We must be innovative.
商業公司之間的競爭現在很激烈，我們得更創新。

同義字
competition

routine [ruˋtin] n. 慣例 ◀ Track 3575

例句 Mike has been in this office for two months, but he still hasn't gotten used to the routine.
麥克已經在這個辦公室兩個月了，但還沒習慣這裡的慣例。

同義字
habit

safeguard [ˋsefˏgɑrd] n./v. 保護者、警衛、保護 ◀ Track 3576

例句 This new law should safeguard us against identity thieves.
這個新的法規應該會保護我們不被盜用個資者影響。

sailor [ˋselɚ] n. 船員、海員 ◀ Track 3577

＊字尾-or有「者」的意思

例句 My dad is a sailor so I don't see him often.
我爸是個船員，所以我不常見到他。

salary [ˋsælərɪ] n. 薪水、薪俸 Track 3578

例句 All I want is a job with good salary.
我就只想要個有不錯薪水的工作罷了。

同義字 pay

salesperson [ˋselzˏpɝsn̩] n. 售貨員、推銷員 Track 3579

例句 The salesperson enthusiastically showed us this new air-conditioner.
這名推銷員興奮地向我們展示這台新的冷氣。

satisfaction [ˏsætɪsˋfækʃən] n. 滿足 Track 3580

＊字尾-tion有轉變為名詞的意思

例句 It brings me great satisfaction to see that they conceded defeat.
看到他們認輸，我很滿足。

搭配詞 bring sb satisfaction 使滿意

scholar [ˋskɑlɚ] n. 有學問的人、學者 Track 3581

＊字尾-ar有「者」的意思

例句 His grandfather is a scholar who specializes in Chinese history.
他的爺爺是個專精於中國歷史的學者。

同義字 savant

scientist [ˋsaɪəntɪst] n. 科學家 Track 3582

＊字尾-ist有「者」的意思

例句 He had solid scientific training during his undergraduate years.
他讀大學時有受過紮實的科學訓練。

搭配詞 scientific training 科學訓練

sculptor [ˋskʌlptɚ] n. 雕刻家、雕刻師 Track 3583

＊字尾-or有「者」的意思

例句 Rodin is my favorite sculptor. 羅丹是我最喜歡的雕刻家。

同義字 carver

secretary [ˋsɛkrəˏtɛrɪ] n. 秘書 Track 3584

例句 Julia is the current Secretary-General to the president.
茱莉雅是現任總統府祕書長。

搭配詞 Secretary-General 祕書長

servant [ˋsɝvənt] n. 僕人、傭人 Track 3585

例句 The public servant was charged with embezzlement.
這名公務員因貪瀆而被起訴。

搭配詞 public servant
公僕、公務員

serve [sɝv] v. 服務、招待 Track 3586

例句 We have enough people to serve the dishes, so you don't need to help. 我們有足夠的人可以服務上菜，所以你不用幫忙。

server [ˋsɝvɚ] n. 伺服器 ＊字尾-er有「者」的意思 Track 3587

例句 The server is down due to a DDOS (distributed denial-of-service) attack. 由於遭到阻斷服務攻擊，伺服器癱瘓了。

service [ˋsɝvɪs] n./v. 服務 ◀Track 3588

例句 This restaurant is highly recommended for its great service.
這個餐廳因為極佳的服務非常受到推薦。

shaver [ˋʃevɚ] n. 理髮師、電動刮鬍刀 ◀Track 3589

＊字尾-er有「者」的意思

例句 He likes to use an electric shaver while taking a bath.
他喜歡在洗澡時使用電動刮鬍刀。

搭配詞
electric shaver 電動刮鬍刀

shepherd [ˋʃɛpɚd] n./v. 牧羊人、牧羊 ◀Track 3590

例句 The farmer raised many shepherd dogs to take care of the sheep.
農場主人養了許多牧羊犬來管理羊群。

搭配詞
shepherd dog 牧羊犬

sheriff [ˋʃɛrɪf] n. 警長 ◀Track 3591

例句 The sheriff is notorious for being impolite.
那個警長因無禮而惡名昭彰。

singer [ˋsɪŋɚ] n. 歌唱家、歌手、唱歌的人 ◀Track 3592

＊字尾-er有「者」的意思

例句 Lady Gaga is my favorite singer. She just starred in the movie called A Star Is Born. 女神卡卡是我最喜歡的歌手。她最近主演了《一個巨星的誕生》這部片。

同義字
vocalist

soldier [ˋsoldʒɚ] n. 軍人 ＊字尾-er有「者」的意思 ◀Track 3593

例句 I don't know how long my brother has been a soldier.
我不知道我哥哥當軍人已經多久了。

speaker [ˋspikɚ] n. 演說者 ◀Track 3594

＊字尾-er有「者」的意思

例句 Professor Lin is our speaker tonight. 今晚的講者是林教授。

相關詞
hearer 聽者

specialist [ˋspɛʃəlɪst] n. 專家 ◀Track 3595

＊字尾-ist有「者」的意思

例句 Both Mr. and Mrs. Keller are specialists in physics.
凱勒先生與太太都是物理專家。

同義字
expert

specialize [ˋspɛʃəˏlaɪz] v. 專長於、專攻 ◀Track 3596

例句 She specializes in medicine. 她專攻藥學。

搭配詞
specialize in 專攻

spokesperson [ˋspoksˏpɝsn̩] n. 發言人 ◀Track 3597

例句 The spokesperson denied the accusation furiously.
發言人生氣地否認這項指控。

sponsor [ˋspɑnsɚ] n. 贊助者 Track 3598

例句 We are not able to get enough sponsors.
我們沒能找到足夠的贊助者。

同義字 supporter

sportsman [ˋsportsmən] n. 運動員 Track 3599

例句 Fiona is not only a sportswoman, but also an enthusiastic sports fan. 費歐娜不但是個女運動員，也是個熱情的運動迷。

相關詞 sportswoman 女運動員

standard [ˋstændɚd] n./adj. 標準、標準的 Track 3600

例句 Not all the products meet the standard, and we have to send back some of them.
不是全部的產品都符合標準，所以我們得送一些回去。

搭配詞 meet the standard 合乎標準

statesman [ˋstetsmən] n. 政治家 Track 3601

例句 Martin Luther King is not only an excellent statesman, but also a landmark of human right.
馬丁路德金不但是個優秀的政治家，更是個人權方面的重要人物。

status [ˋstetəs] n. 地位、身分 Track 3602

例句 People with high social-economic status tend to have healthier diet.
高社經地位的人多半飲食習慣較健康。

搭配詞 social-economic status 社會經濟地位

stern [stɝn] adj. 嚴格的 Track 3603

例句 Patricia received a stern rebuke from her superior.
派翠西亞被主管嚴格地責罵。

同義字 strict

steward [ˋstjuwɚd] n. 服務生、空服員 Track 3604

例句 Don't press the buzzer, or the steward will come running immediately.
別按鈴，不然服務生馬上就會跑來了。

相關詞 stewardess 女空服員

strategy [ˋstrætədʒɪ] n. 戰略、策略 Track 3605

例句 They don't want to change their marketing strategy.
他們不願改變銷售策略。

同義字 planning

studio [ˋstjudɪˏo] n. 工作室、播音室 Track 3606

例句 Emma designed a superb studio for her partners.
愛瑪為她的伙伴們設計了一間很棒的工作室。

style [staɪl] n. 風格、時尚 Track 3607

例句 Culottes are in style again. 褲裙又再度成為時尚。

搭配詞 in style 盛大、時髦

submit [səb`mɪt] v. 屈服、提交 Track 3608

例句 We have no choice but to submit to the new rules.
我們別無選擇，不得不屈服於新規定。

搭配詞
submit to 屈服於

succeed [sək`sid] v. 成功 Track 3609

例句 He didn't succeed because he didn't try hard enough.
他沒有成功，因為他不夠努力。

success [sək`sɛs] n. 成功 Track 3610

例句 The performance was a tremendous success.
這場表演獲得了很大的成功。

successful [sək`sɛsfəl] adj. 成功的 Track 3611

＊字尾-ful有「充滿」的意思

例句 The operation was successful. 手術很成功。

反義字
unsuccessful 不成功的、失敗的

suggestion [səg`dʒɛstʃən] n. 建議 Track 3612

＊字尾-tion有轉變為名詞的意思

例句 Ellie often comes up with interesting suggestions.
愛莉常想出有趣的建議。

summon [`sʌmən] v. 召集 Track 3613

例句 We summoned several specialists to aid us.
我們召集了許多專家來幫助我們。

supervise [`supɚvaɪz] v. 監督、管理 Track 3614

例句 When he was supervising the workers in the mine, he fell and got hurt. 他在監督礦場的工人時跌倒受傷了。

同義字
direct

supervision [ˏsupɚ`vɪʒən] n. 監督、管理 Track 3615

例句 He works for a project under the supervision of Prof. Joseph Nye.
他在約瑟夫奈爾教授的指導下，做這項計畫。

搭配詞
under supervision 在監督下

supervisor [ˏsupɚ`vaɪzɚ] n. 監督者、管理人 Track 3616

＊字尾-or有「者」的意思

例句 Rita is a good supervisor. She never scolds us.
麗塔是個好主管，她從來不會罵我們。

surgeon [`sɝdʒən] n. 外科醫生 Track 3617

例句 The hospital is short of doctors, so there is only one surgeon in the emergency room.
這家醫院的醫生人力短缺，所以急診室只有一個外科醫生。

相關詞
physician 內科醫生

tailor [ˋtelɚ] n./v. 裁縫師、裁縫 Track 3618
＊字尾-or有「者」的意思
例句 He is so fat that he needs to find a tailor to customize his clothes.
他太胖了，得找一個裁縫師幫他特別訂製衣服。

搭配詞
The tailor makes the man.
佛要金裝，人要衣裝。

target [ˋtɑrgɪt] n. 目標、靶子 Track 3619
例句 Our target audience are 20~30 years old.
我們的目標讀者群是20～30歲的人。

搭配詞
target audience 目標讀者群

task [tæsk] n. 任務 Track 3620
例句 We think Jay is the best person to perform this task.
我們認為小傑是最適合完成這個任務的人。

teacher [ˋtitʃɚ] n. 教師、老師 Track 3621
＊字尾-er有「者」的意思
例句 You can't be a good teacher if you're not enthusiastic.
沒有熱情，你就不能當個好老師。

technician [tɛkˋnɪʃən] n. 技師、技術員 Track 3622
例句 We will send technicians to fix the errors.
我們會派一些技術員去處理這些問題。

therapist [ˋθɛrəpɪst] n. 治療學家、物理治療師 Track 3623
＊字尾-ist有「者」的意思
例句 After the traumatic experience, he should see a therapist.
他經歷創傷經驗，應該去看諮商師。

搭配詞
see a therapist 去諮商

toil [tɔɪl] n. 辛勞、苦工 Track 3624
例句 He felt tired after the long toil.
他在長時間做苦工後非常疲累。

反義字
rest 休息

trademark [ˋtred͵mɑrk] n. 標記、商標 Track 3625
例句 The actress has her trademark smile on her face.
那個女演員臉上掛著她的招牌笑容。

同義字
brand

trader [ˋtredɚ] n. 商人 ＊字尾-er有「者」的意思 Track 3626
例句 I am not a very experienced trader.
我不是個很有經驗的商人。

transcript [ˋtræn͵skrɪpt] n. 抄本、副本 Track 3627
＊字首trans-有「穿越、轉變」之意
例句 Can you provide a transcript of your grades?
可以提供你的成績單影本嗎？

transaction [trænˋsækʃən] n. 處理、辦理、交易 Track 3628
＊字首trans-有「穿越、轉變」之意
例句 The transaction is already complete. You can take back your credit card now. 交易已完成，你可以收回信用卡了。
同義字 deal

translator [trænsˋletɚ] n. 翻譯者、翻譯家 Track 3629
＊字首trans-有「穿越、轉變」之意
例句 Angie dreams of being an excellent translator.
安琪夢想成為一個優秀的翻譯。

tutor [ˋtjutɚ] n. 家庭教師、導師 Track 3630
＊字尾-or有「者」的意思
例句 My tutor often brings me to cafes to study.
我的家教常帶我到咖啡店唸書。

typist [ˋtaɪpɪst] n. 打字員 Track 3631
＊字尾-ist有「者」的意思
例句 The typist quit her job after she hurt her fingers.
那名打字員在手指受傷後就辭掉工作了。

undertake [ˏʌndɚˋtek] v. 承擔、擔保、試圖 Track 3632
例句 I don't want to undertake this mission.
我不想承擔這個任務。
同義字 try

usher [ˋʌʃɚ] n. 引導員、帶位者 Track 3633
＊字尾-er有「者」的意思
例句 The usher handed us our popcorn. 帶位者拿了爆米花給我們。
同義字 escort

vendor [ˋvɛndɚ] n. 攤販、小販 Track 3634
＊字尾-or有「者」的意思
例句 I bought this tie from a street vendor.
我從路邊攤販買了這個領帶。
同義字 seller

vend [vɛnd] v. 叫賣、販賣 Track 3635
例句 We can buy a lot of things from vending machines.
我們可以從販賣機買到很多東西。
搭配詞 vending machine 自動販賣機

verge [vɝdʒ] n. 邊際、邊 Track 3636
例句 She is on the verge of a nervous breakdown.
她已經在崩潰邊緣了。
同義字 margin

violinist [ˏvaɪəˋlɪnɪst] n. 小提琴手 Track 3637
＊字尾-ist有「者」的意思
例句 Her daughter is a professional violinist.
她女兒是職業小提琴家。
類似單字 celloist 大提琴手

vocational [vo`keʃənḷ] adj. 職業上的、業務的 Track 3638

＊字尾-al有轉變為形容詞之意

例句 The vocational training provided by this company doesn't help me do my job better. 這家公司提供的職業訓練並不會讓我工作做得更好。

搭配詞 vocational training 職業培訓

waiter/waitress [`wetɚ]/[`wetrɪs] Track 3639

n. 服務生／女服務生　＊字尾-ess有「女性」的意思

例句 I earned pocket money by working as a waiter during summer vacation. 我在暑假擔任服務生賺取零用錢。

同義字 steward

ware [wɛr] n. 製品、貨品 Track 3640

例句 I am not familiar with porcelain ware.
我對瓷製品不是很瞭解。

搭配詞 porcelain ware 瓷製品

witch/wizard [wɪtʃ]/[`wɪzɚd] Track 3641

n. 女巫師／男巫師

例句 In some societies, people go to see a witch doctor when they get sick. 有些地方，人們生病了就去看巫醫。

搭配詞 witch doctor 巫醫

worker [`wɝkɚ] n. 工作者、工人 Track 3642

＊字尾-er有「者」的意思

例句 They have enough skilled workers to finish this project.
他們有足夠有能力的工人可以完成這個計畫。

workshop [`wɝk͵ʃɑp] n. 小工廠、研討會 Track 3643

例句 Would you like to join our workshop?
你想加入我們的研討會嗎？

同義字 workroom

writer [`raɪtɚ] n. 作者、作家 Track 3644

＊字尾-er有「者」的意思

例句 He is my favorite writer. I read all of his books last summer.
他是我最喜歡的作家。我去年夏天把他全部的作品都讀完了。

Test 13 關鍵英單總測驗第13回

以下測驗題皆出自書中第十三回「**和職業有關的單字**」，快來檢視自己的學習成果吧！

一、選擇題

1. He's a renowned Michelin _____ at a five-star hotel.
(A) engineer
(B) chef
(C) miller
(D) colonel

2. Steven Hawking was a _____ in physics.
(A) specialist
(B) judge
(C) electrician
(D) statesman

3. Two _____ from our Major Crimes Bureau arrested a murderer hiding in the Orange County.
(A) farmers
(B) detectives
(C) janitors
(D) editors

4. She is a senior _____ for Children's Services at a public library.
(A) nun (B) peasant
(C) librarian (D) sculptor

5. Neil Armstrong was a famous ______, who inspired a generation to explore the outer space.
(A) astronaut
(B) composer
(C) banker
(D) designer

6. She was an ________ of Foxconn Technology Group.
(A) employee
(B) journalist
(C) gardener
(D) merchant

7. The _____ was caught red handed.
(A) propaganda
(B) routine
(C) strategy
(D) pickpocket

8. The _______ tried his best to save the patient's life in the emergency room.
(A) surgeon
(B) historian
(C) instructor
(D) driver

9. He works at the _____ service center at a department store.
(A) blacksmith
(B) applicant
(C) customer
(D) correspondent

10. The company's _____ is located in Berlin.
(A) mouthpiece
(B) poacher
(C) headquarters
(D) shepherd

二、克漏字測驗

The 2018 Nobel Prize winner in medicine, James Allison, is a prominent __1__ at the MD Anderson Cancer Center. His discoveries have led to new cancer treatments for the deadliest cancers.

When he was young, Allison was inspired by a math __2__ to pursue a career in science. After getting his Ph. D. degree, he worked as an assistant __3__ at the MD Anderson. He later moved to New York to become the __4__ of the Ludwig Center for Cancer. His research focuses on understanding the mechanisms that govern T-cell responses. His wife is a __5__ he met at the MD Anderson.

1.
(A) historian
(B) scholar
(C) fireman
(D) engineer

2.
(A) miner
(B) interpreter
(C) teacher
(D) magician

3.
(A) professor
(B) nanny
(C) musician
(D) monk

4.
(A) salesperson
(B) permanent
(C) novelist
(D) director

5.
(A) singer
(B) vendor
(C) playwright
(D) colleague

關鍵英單總測驗第13回 中譯與解答

一、選擇題

1. 他是一家五星飯店的知名米其林主廚。
   (A) 工程師
   (B) 主廚
   (C) 磨坊主人
   (D) 陸軍上校

2. 史蒂芬霍金是物理學的專家。
   (A) 專家
   (B) 法官
   (C) 電工
   (D) 政治家

3. 重大刑案局的兩位探員在橙郡逮捕了一個殺人犯。
   (A) 農民
   (B) 探員
   (C) 管門員
   (D) 編輯

4. 她在公共圖書館的兒童服務區擔任資深館員。
   (A) 尼姑、修女
   (B) 農民
   (C) 圖書館館員
   (D) 雕刻家

5. 尼爾阿姆斯壯是知名的太空人，啟發了一個世代的人們探索外太空。
   (A) 太空人
   (B) 作曲家
   (C) 銀行家
   (D) 設計師

6. 她是富士康科技集團的員工。
   (A) 員工
   (B) 記者
   (C) 園丁
   (D) 商人

7. 這個扒手當場被逮住。
   (A) 宣傳文宣
   (B) 慣例
   (C) 策略
   (D) 扒手

8. 那位外科醫師在急診室全力搶救他的病人。
   (A) 外科醫師
   (B) 歷史學家
   (C) 視察員
   (D) 駕駛

9. 他在百貨公司的客服中心工作。
   (A) 鐵匠
   (B) 應徵者
   (C) 客戶
   (D) 通訊記者

10. 這家公司的總部位在柏林。
   (A) 代言人
   (B) 盜獵者
   (C) 總部
   (D) 牧羊人

二、克漏字測驗

2018年諾貝爾醫學獎得主James Allison是安德森癌症中心的傑出學者，他的研究發現為許多致命的癌症帶來新的治療方式。

Allison小時候受到數學老師啟發，決定長大要投入科學領域。他取得博士後，在安德森癌症中心擔任助理教授，隨後搬到紐約，成為Ludwig Center for Center的主任。他的研究著重在了解主導T細胞反應的機制，而他的妻子是他在安德森癌症中心的同事。

1.
(A) 歷史學家
(B) 學者
(C) 消防員
(D) 工程師

2.
(A) 礦工
(B) 口譯員
(C) 老師
(D) 魔術師

3.
(A) 教授
(B) 保姆
(C) 音樂家
(D) 和尚

4.
(A) 銷售員
(B) 永久的
(C) 小說家
(D) 主任

5.
(A) 歌手
(B) 攤販
(C) 劇作家
(D) 同事

一、選擇題

1.(B) 2.(A) 3.(B) 4.(C) 5.(A)
6.(A) 7.(D) 8.(A) 9.(C) 10.(C)

二、克漏字測驗

1.(B) 2.(C) 3.(A)
4.(D) 5.(D)

Unit 14 和自然氣候有關的單字

多益測驗的命題強調生活化與實用性，學會這些與「自然氣候」有關的單字，不僅能讓你在多益考場上所向披靡，在日常生活上也可以靈活運用喔！

舒適宜人的天氣可以這麼說

- **I like to go for a walk on sunny days.**
  我喜歡在晴朗的日子出去散步。
- **I like the cool breeze during autumn.**
  我喜歡秋天涼爽的微風。

惡劣的天氣可以這麼說

- **It's raining cats and dogs outside.**
  外面正下著滂沱大雨。
- **Today is too foggy. We are not able to get a good view of Mount Fuji.**
  今天太多霧了。我們會沒有辦法清楚看到富士山。
- **It's not safe to go out on typhoon days. You might get hit by fallen objects.**
  颱風天出門不安全。你有可能會被掉落的物體打中。

氣象災害可以這麼說

- **Five people were reported missing after the sudden flood.**
  有五個人在那場突如其來的水災中失蹤。
- **The earthquake strikes shortly after the alarm sounded.**
  地震警報響起後，地震就緊接著到來。

氣候變遷可以這麼說

- **People become more aware of the extreme weather caused by climate change.**
  人們對氣候變遷造成的極端氣象有了更多覺察。
- **Climate change is caused by greenhouse gas emission.**
  氣候變遷是由溫室氣體排放所造成。

氣象預報可以這麼說

- **Don't forget to check the weather forecast for your destination before you go.**
  出發前別忘了查看目的地的氣象預報。
- **The weather experts are analyzing the satellite cloud image.**
  氣象專家們正在分析衛星雲圖。

Unit 14 和自然氣候有關的單字

abnormal [æb`nɔrml̩] adj. 反常的 Track 3645
＊字首ab-有「偏離」 之意
例句 The FBI agent specializes in abnormal psychology.
這位FBI探員專精變態心理學。

搭配詞
abnormal psychology 變態心理學

---

abound [ə`baund] v. 充滿 Track 3646
例句 Performances, exhibitions, and other activities abound in the city in spring. 春天時，城市裡充滿表演、展覽和其他活動。

搭配詞
abound in 富於

---

accommodation [ə͵kɑmə`deʃən] Track 3647
n. 適應、住處　＊字尾-tion有轉變為名詞的意思
例句 We need to find accommodation before the storm comes.
我們得在暴風雨來之前找到住處。

---

according [ə`kɔrdɪŋ] adj. 根據…… Track 3648
例句 According to the weather forecast, it will rain tomorrow.
根據氣象預報，明天會下雨。

搭配詞
according to 根據、按照

---

accordingly [ə`kɔrdɪŋlɪ] Track 3649
adv. 因此、於是、相應地　＊字尾-ly有轉變為副詞之意
例句 If terrorists launch an attack, our counter-terrorism and special operations unit will react accordingly. 若恐怖份子發動攻擊，我們的反恐特種部隊將據此做出相應的反應。

搭配詞
react accordingly 據此做出相應的反應

---

adapt [ə`dæpt] v. 使適應 Track 3650
例句 I'm still trying to adapt to the dry weather here.
我還在試著適應這裡的乾燥天氣。

搭配詞
adapt to 適應於

---

air [ɛr] n. 空氣、氣氛 Track 3651
例句 She put on airs after becoming an Internet celebrity.
她成了網紅以後，就裝腔作勢了。

搭配詞
put on airs 裝腔作勢

---

air-conditioner [`ɛr͵kən`dɪʃənɚ] n. 空調 Track 3652
＊字尾-er有轉變為名詞的意思
例句 We normally keep the air-conditioner on in summer.
我們在夏天通常會開空調。

---

analyst [ˋænəlɪst] n. 分解者、分析者 ◀Track 3653

例句 He is a highly-trained and seasoned financial analyst.
他是個經過訓練、經驗老到的財經分析師。

搭配詞 financial analyst 財經分析家

atmosphere [ˋætməsˏfɪr] n. 大氣、氣氛 ◀Track 3654

例句 The pollution that people produce can affect the atmosphere of the Earth. 人們製造的污染可能會影響到地球的大氣。

同義字 aerosphere

awake [əˋwek] v. 喚醒、提醒 ◀Track 3655

例句 The sudden noise from the street awoke me.
街上突然傳來的聲音把我喚醒了。

aware [əˋwɛr] adj. 注意到的、覺察的 ◀Track 3656

例句 He is well aware of having done something wrong.
他充分意識到自己做錯事了。

搭配詞 well aware of 充分瞭解或意識到

badly [ˋbædlɪ] adv. 非常地、惡劣地 ◀Track 3657

＊字尾-ly有轉變為副詞之意

例句 I need some food badly. 我非常需要食物。

bait [bet] n. 誘餌 ◀Track 3658

例句 Our company manufactures artificial fish bait that fish simply can't resist. 我們的公司製造人工魚餌，讓魚兒無法抵擋誘惑。

搭配詞 fish bait 魚餌

barefoot [ˋbɛrˏfut] adj./adv. 赤足的 ◀Track 3659

例句 It feels good to walk barefoot in the stream.
在小溪中赤腳走路很舒服。

搭配詞 to walk barefoot 打赤腳

barren [ˋbærən] ◀Track 3660

adj. 不毛的、土地貧瘠的、不孕的

例句 It's difficult to live in barren lands. 住在不毛之地很困難。

反義字 fertile 多產的、繁殖力強的

beforehand [bɪˋforˏhænd] adv./adj. 事先、預先 ◀Track 3661

例句 We should prepare for the hurricane beforehand.
我們該先為颶風做準備。

blizzard [ˋblɪzəd] n. 暴風雪 ◀Track 3662

例句 It is very dangerous to drive during a blizzard.
暴風雪時開車很危險。

同義字 snowstorm

blur [blɝ] n./v. 模糊、朦朧 Track 3663

例句 The road is a blur because of the heavy rain.
因為雨下得太大，道路一片朦朧。

breeze [briz] n. 微風 Track 3664

例句 We enjoy walking in the breeze in the evening.
我很享受在晚上微風中散步。

搭配詞 in the breeze 在微風中

bright [braɪt] adj./adv. 明亮的、開朗的 Track 3665

例句 It's a bright new day. 今天又是明亮的、新的一天。

brisk [brɪsk] adj./v. 活潑的、輕快的 Track 3666

例句 My little sister is a brisk walker. 我的妹妹走路很輕快。

反義字 inactive 無生氣的

brutal [ˋbrutl̩] adj. 野蠻的、殘暴的 Track 3667

例句 It was very brutal of the man to abuse his child.
那個男人虐待自己的孩子，真是殘暴。

同義字 cruel

cease [sis] v./n. 停息 Track 3668

例句 The storm finally ceased after three days.
三天後，風雨終於停息了。

補充 ceaselessly 不停地

chill [tʃɪl] v. 使變冷 Track 3669

例句 I'd like to chill my lemonade so it tastes better.
我想把我的檸檬汁變冷，才會更好喝。

chunk [tʃʌŋk] n. 厚塊、相當大部份 Track 3670

例句 He shoveled out a big chunk of snow.
他剷出了一大塊的雪。

同義字 lump

clear [klɪr] adj./adv. 清楚的、明確的、澄清的 Track 3671

例句 The skies are clear; it should be a good day for flying.
天空很澄清，今天應該很適合飛行。

climate [ˋklaɪmɪt] n. 氣候 Track 3672

例句 You'd better not change your job in the current economic climate.
目前的經濟形勢下，你最好不要換工作。

搭配詞 economic climate 經濟情勢

a b c d e f g h i j k l m n o p q r s t u v w x y z

cloud [klaud] n. 雲 Track 3673

例句 There are many grey clouds in the sky. It will probably rain soon.
天上有很多烏雲。應該快下雨了。

---

cloudy [ˋklaudɪ] adj. 烏雲密佈的、多雲的 Track 3674
＊字尾-y有轉變為形容詞之意

例句 It's too cloudy for us go to the beach today.
今天太多雲了，我們不能去海邊。

反義字 bright 明亮的

---

clue [klu] n. 線索 Track 3675

例句 They had no clues why their classmate went on a shooting spree at school.
針對同班同學在校園進行恐怖槍擊的原因，他們毫無線索。

搭配詞 have no clues 一無所知、不知如何是好、缺乏能力

---

coast [kost] n. 海岸、沿岸 Track 3676

例句 They had a lovely apartment by the coast.
他們在海岸邊有個美麗的套房。

補充 The coast is clear.
危險已過。

---

cold [kold] adj. 冷的 Track 3677

例句 She gave me a cold shoulder when I asked her for help.
我向她求助時，她顯得很冷漠。

搭配詞 give sb a cold shoulder
（對某人）冷漠的、無情的

---

collection [kəˋlɛkʃən] n. 聚集、收集 Track 3678
＊字尾-tion有轉變為名詞的意思

例句 He has a collection of different seeds. 他收集了各種種子。

同義字 accumulation

---

compatible [kəmˋpætəbḷ] Track 3679
adj. 一致的、和諧的、能共處的 ＊字尾-ible有「可以、能」的意思

例句 My device was not compatible with the computer.
我的裝置和電腦不相容。

搭配詞 compatible with
與……相容的

---

conquer [ˏkɑŋkɚ] v. 征服 Track 3680

例句 The king demanded his army to conquer the island.
國王命令他的軍隊征服這座島。

反義字 submit

---

conserve [kənˋsɝv] v. 保存、保護 Track 3681

例句 It's best to conserve water in a state of emergency.
在緊急狀況時最好要保存水。

同義字 preserve

---

contaminate [kənˋtæməˏnet] v. 污染 Track 3682

例句 The chemical can contaminate the food.
這個化學物質可能污染食物。

同義字 pollute

continental [ˌkɑntəˋnɛntḷ] adj. 大陸的、洲的 Track 3683

＊字尾-al有轉變為形容詞之意

例句 If you stay in that hotel overnight, you can enjoy a free continental breakfast. 若你在那間旅館過夜，第二天可享有免費歐陸式早餐。

搭配詞 continental breakfast 歐陸式早餐

convert [kənˋvɝt] v. 變換、轉換 Track 3684

例句 The bank will convert your dollars into pounds.
銀行會把你的美金轉換成英鎊。

cool [kul] adj. 涼的、涼快的、酷的 Track 3685

例句 The cool breeze blew against his face.
涼快的微風吹過他的臉。

cozy [ˋkozɪ] adj. 溫暖而舒適的 Track 3686

例句 I'd love to put a cozy sofa in the living room.
我想放一張溫暖舒適的沙發在客廳。

同義字 comfortable

creek [krik] n. 小灣、小溪、麻煩 Track 3687

例句 The kids enjoy playing down at the creek.
孩子們喜歡在小溪那裡玩。

crunch [krʌntʃ] n./v. 嘎吱的聲音、危機、關鍵時刻 Track 3688

例句 The goalkeeper performs quite well at crunch time.
這名守門員在球局很危急時，仍表現很好。

搭配詞 at crunch time 面對艱難時

crystal [ˋkrɪstḷ] n./adj. 結晶、水晶 Track 3689

例句 Crystal is often used to make fancy wine glasses.
水晶常被拿來做成高級的酒杯。

搭配詞 crystal ball 水晶球

damp [dæmp] adj. 潮濕的 Track 3690

例句 Mom put damp clothes into the tumble dryer.
媽媽把潮濕的衣服放進烘衣機。

dark [dɑrk] adj./n. 黑暗、暗處 Track 3691

例句 He is a dark horse in the competition.
他是這場賽事的黑馬。

搭配詞 dark horse 黑馬

descent [dɪˋsɛnt] n. 下降 Track 3692

＊字首de -有「下」之意

例句 The plane disappeared during the descent.
那架飛機在下降時消失了。

反義字 ascent 上升

deadline [ˋdɛd.laɪn] n. 期限 Track 3693

例句 You'd better get your income taxes done before the deadline.
你最好在繳稅期限之前，成完申報所得稅。

搭配詞
before the deadline
在期限之前

decay [dɪˋke] v./n. 腐朽、腐爛 Track 3694

例句 Experts are trying to stop the decay of the ancient building.
專家正試著阻止那棟古老的建築腐朽。

同義字
rot

deny [dɪˋnaɪ] v. 否認、拒絕 Track 3695

例句 You can't deny that their work is better than ours.
你不能否認他們的作品就是比我們好。

depth [dɛpθ] n. 深度、深淵 Track 3696

例句 He reported the crime scene in depth.
他深度報導犯案現場。

搭配詞
in depth 完全而澈底的

dew [dju] n. 露水、露 Track 3697

例句 You can see morning dew on the grass and the leaves.
你可以在草與葉子上看到晨露。

搭配詞
morning dew 晨露

dim [dɪm] adj. 微暗的 Track 3698

例句 It is hard to read since the light in the room is too dim.
房間裡的燈太暗了，很難讀書。

dirt [dɝt] n. 泥土、塵埃 Track 3699

例句 He threw dirt at his best friend. 他中傷自己的好友。

搭配詞
throw dirt at 中傷

disaster [dɪzˋæstɚ] n. 天災、災害 Track 3700

例句 My hair is a disaster today.
我的頭髮今天真是一場災難。

downward [ˋdaʊnwɚd] Track 3701
adj./adv. 下降地、向下地

例句 His life went downward spiral after his wife divorced him.
他的妻子和他離婚後，他的生活就向下沉淪了。

搭配詞
downward spiral 向下沉淪

downwards [ˋdaʊnwɚdz] Track 3702
adv. 下降地、向下地

例句 Is that car coming downwards? 那台車正在往下開過來嗎？

反義字
upwards 向上地

dreadful [ˋdrɛdfəl] **adj.** 可怕的、恐怖的 ◀Track 3703

＊字尾-ful有「充滿」的意思

例句 The weather was dreadful this winter.
今年冬天的天氣很糟。

同義字 terrible

---

dreary [ˋdrɪərɪ] **adj.** 陰鬱的、淒涼的、枯燥的 ◀Track 3704

例句 We had a long and dreary journey on the train.
我們在火車上度過漫長、枯燥的旅程。

同義字 gloomy

---

drip [drɪp] **v./n.** 滴下 ◀Track 3705

例句 Blood dripped from his nose after he bumped his head.
他撞到頭之後，血從他的鼻子滴下。

---

drizzle [ˋdrɪzḷ] **n./v.** 細雨、毛毛雨、滴灑 ◀Track 3706

例句 There's a drizzle outside, but we can still go for a walk.
外面下著毛毛雨，但我們還是可以去散步。

同義字 sprinkle

---

drought [draʊt] **n.** 乾旱、久旱 ◀Track 3707

例句 How long do you think the drought will last this year?
你覺得今年乾旱會持續多久？

同義字 aridity

---

drown [draʊn] **v.** 淹沒、淹死 ◀Track 3708

例句 He drowned his sorrows after his child passed away.
他的小孩過世後，他就開始藉酒澆愁。

搭配詞 drown one's sorrows 藉酒澆愁

---

dry [draɪ] **adj.** 乾的、枯燥無味的 ◀Track 3709

例句 The paint on the bench is not dry yet.
長椅上的油漆還沒有乾。

---

duration [djʊˋreʃən] **n.** 持久、持續 ◀Track 3710

＊字尾-tion有轉變為名詞的意思

例句 I don't think that the duration of their business relationship will last very long. 我覺得他們的生意關係不會持續很久。

---

dusty [ˋdʌstɪ] **adj.** 覆著灰塵的 ◀Track 3711

＊字尾-y有轉變為形容詞之意

例句 "How have you been?" "Not so dusty."
「你最近好嗎？」「還不錯。」

搭配詞 not so dusty 還好、還不錯

---

dwarf [dwɔrf] **adj.** 矮子的、矮種的 ◀Track 3712

例句 There is a dwarf lemon tree in our garden.
我們的園子裡有一顆矮種檸檬樹。

反義字 giant 巨人般的、巨大的

earthquake [ˋɝθ͵kwek] n. 地震 Track 3713

例句 Some people have never experienced earthquakes before.
有些人從來沒有經歷過地震。

ebb [ɛb] n./v. 退潮、衰退 Track 3714

例句 The election brought his credibility to the lowest ebb.
這次的選舉把他的信任度壓到了最低點。

eclipse [ɪˋklɪps] n./v. 蝕（月蝕等） Track 3715

例句 Have you ever seen a lunar eclipse? 你看過月蝕嗎？

搭配詞 lunar eclipse 月蝕

eligible [ˋɛlɪdʒəbl] adj. 適當的、能夠的 Track 3716

＊字尾-ible有「可以、能」的意思

例句 Prince Harry used to be one of the most eligible bachelors in the world. But now he's already spoken for.
哈利王子曾是全球最黃金的單身漢之一，不過現在他死會了。

搭配詞 eligible bachelor 黃金單身漢

emerge [ɪˋmɝdʒ] v. 浮現 Track 3717

例句 The sea lion emerged from the water.
那隻海獅從水中浮現。

反義字 submerge 淹沒

erode [ɪˋrod] v. 蝕 Track 3718

例句 We can see that the sea has eroded the cliff over the years.
我們可以看到多年來海洋侵蝕了山丘。

同義字 corrode

eternal [ɪˋtɝnl] adj. 永恆的 Track 3719

例句 People believe that a wedding ring is a symbol of eternal love.
人們相信結婚戒指是永恆的愛的象徵。

搭配詞 (the) eternal love 永恆的愛

eternity [ɪˋtɝnətɪ] n. 永遠、永恆 Track 3720

例句 Libraries are places to store human knowledge for eternity.
圖書館將人類知識永恆的存留下來。

搭配詞 for eternity 維持到永遠

evil [ˋivl] adj./n. 邪惡的、罪惡 Track 3721

例句 Sometimes I think my cat is actually evil.
有時我覺得我的貓其實是很邪惡的。

evolution [͵ɛvəˋluʃən] n. 發展、進化、演化 Track 3722

＊字尾-tion有轉變為名詞的意思

例句 The teacher is telling us about the evolution of human race.
老師在跟我們講人類演化的事。

反義字 devolution 退化

evolve [ɪ`vɑlv] v. 演化、發展 Track 3723

例句 Google has evolved and changed the way people live.
Google不斷的演化，並改變人們的生活習慣。

同義字 develop

factor [`fæktɚ] n. 因素、要素 Track 3724

例句 Many factors will influence the outcome of the experiment.
許多因素都會影響實驗的結果。

fade [fed] v. 凋謝、變淡、變暗 Track 3725

例句 The light is already fading outside.
外面的光線已經開始變暗了。

fairly [`fɛrlɪ] adv. 相當地、公平地 Track 3726

＊字尾-ly有轉變為副詞之意

例句 It's a fairly good book; why don't you read it?
這是本相當不錯的書。你為什麼不讀讀看呢？

反義字 unjustly 不公平地

falter [`fɔltɚ] v. 猶豫、結巴地說 Track 3727

例句 He faltered for a while, but was still unable to make a firm decision.
他結巴了一陣子，但還是沒辦法下決定。

同義字 hesitate

fascinate [`fæsn̩,et] v. 迷惑、吸引 Track 3728

例句 The students were fascinated by his ideas.
學生們都被他的點子給吸引了。

同義字 captivate

flake [flek] n. 雪花、薄片 Track 3729

例句 The little girl ran around trying to catch snow flakes.
小女孩跑來跑去，試著要抓住片片雪花。

搭配詞 snow flake 雪花

flare [flɛr] n./v. 閃光、燃燒 Track 3730

例句 She flared up at his criticism.
她聽到他的批評時，勃然大怒。

搭配詞 flare up 突然爆發、勃然大怒

flicker [`flɪkɚ] v./n. 閃耀 Track 3731

例句 There was a flicker of light there just now.
剛剛那裡有光閃耀了一下。

同義字 flicker

float [flot] v. 使漂浮 Track 3732

例句 The body was found floating in the river.
那個屍體被發現漂浮在河上。

a b c d e f g h i j k l m n o p q r s t u v w x y z

flood [flʌd] n. 洪水、水災 ◀Track 3733

例句 This must be the most terrible flood in this century.
這應該是這個世紀最糟糕的一次水災。

---

flow [flo] v./n. 流出、流動 ◀Track 3734

例句 Most rivers on the earth eventually flow into the sea.
地球上大部分的河都會流入海中。

---

fluid [ˋfluɪd] adj./n. 流體 ◀Track 3735

例句 I have no idea what the fluid I was forced to drink was.
我不知道剛我被逼著喝下的流體到底是什麼。

反義字
solid 固體

---

flush [flʌʃ] v. 沖水、使興奮 ◀Track 3736

例句 He always forgets to flush the toilet.
他每次都忘記沖馬桶。

---

foam [fom] n./v. 泡沫 ◀Track 3737

例句 The movie adapted from Mark Twain's novel had critics foaming at the mouth.
改編自馬克吐溫的小說所拍成的電影讓影評人士非常生氣。

搭配詞
be foaming at the mouth 非常生氣

---

fog [fɑg] n. 霧 ◀Track 3738

例句 He's in a fog as to what he should do next.
他很困惑，不知道下一步該怎麼做。

搭配詞
in a fog 困惑、迷惑

---

foggy [ˋfɑgɪ] adj. 多霧的、朦朧的 ◀Track 3739

例句 It's very foggy today; would you please drive as slowly as possible?
今天很多霧，可以請你盡量開慢一點嗎？

---

forecast [ˋforˏkæst] v./n. 預測、預報 ◀Track 3740

例句 No one is able to forecast how long the ceasefire will last.
沒有人可以預測停戰會停多久。

同義字
prediction

---

fossil [ˋfɑsḷ] n. 化石、舊事物 ◀Track 3741

例句 I'm always interested in dinosaur fossils.
我對恐龍化石總是很有興趣。

---

freeze [friz] v./n. 凍結 ◀Track 3742

例句 If you don't come in, you'll freeze to death soon.
你如果不趕快進來，很快會凍死的。

搭配詞
freeze to death 凍死

frequent [ˋfrikwənt] adj. 常有的、頻繁的 Track 3743

例句 She is a frequent traveler to the United Kingdom.
她經常去英國旅遊。

---

fresh [frɛʃ] adj. 新鮮的、無經驗的、淡（水）的 Track 3744

例句 The water is fresh here and safe to drink.
這裡的水很新鮮，可以放心喝。

---

glacier [ˋgleʃɚ] n. 冰河 Track 3745

例句 A glacier is a moving mass of snow and ice. Have you seen one before? 冰河是一大片移動的雪和冰。你見過嗎？

補充 iceberg 冰山

---

glare [glɛr] v./n. 怒視、瞪眼 Track 3746

例句 She glared at her ex-boyfriend when she saw him in the restaurant kissing another girl.
她看到前男友和另一個女孩在餐廳親吻時，一直瞪著他。

搭配詞 glare at 怒目而視

---

gleam [glim] n. 一絲光線 Track 3747

例句 With you here, we have a gleam of hope.
有你在，我們就有一絲希望。

---

glide [glaɪd] v./n. 滑行、稍稍地、消逝 Track 3748

例句 I've always wanted to try a hang glider.
我一直很想試試看滑翔翼。

同義字 cruise

---

glimpse [glɪmps] n./v. 瞥見、隱約看見 Track 3749

例句 I caught a glimpse of a deer behind the trees.
我在樹後面瞥見一頭鹿。

搭配詞 catch a glimpse of 一眼瞥見

---

glisten [ˋglɪsn̩] v./n. 閃耀、閃爍 Track 3750

例句 Her eyes are glistening with tears. What's going on?
她的眼睛閃爍著淚光。到底怎麼了？

同義字 sparkle

---

gloomy [ˋglumɪ] adj. 幽暗的、暗淡的 Track 3751

＊字尾-y有轉變為形容詞之意

例句 The skies are especially gloomy today. Remember to bring an umbrella. 天空今天特別幽暗，要記得帶傘。

反義字 delightful 令人愉快的

---

gravity [ˋgrævətɪ] n. 重力、嚴重性 Track 3752

例句 Nobody could mess with the law of gravity.
沒有人能勝過萬有引力定律。

搭配詞 the law of gravity 萬有引力定律

graze [grez] v./n. 吃草、畜牧 Track 3753

例句 The cattle graze happily in the fields.
牛兒們快樂地在原野上吃草。

同義字 feed

greenhouse [ˋgrin͵haus] n. 溫室 Track 3754

例句 He didn't listen carefully in class when the teacher talked about the greenhouse effect.
老師在上課提到溫室效應時，他沒有認真聽。

搭配詞 greenhouse effect 溫室效應

guess [gɛs] v./n. 猜測、猜想 Track 3755

例句 I guess it might be raining soon.
我猜快要下雨了。

gust [gʌst] n. 狂風 Track 3756

例句 A gust of wind blew the door shut.
一陣狂風把門吹得自己關上了。

同義字 blast

hail [hel] n./v. 歡呼、冰雹 Track 3757

例句 It has hailed the whole night, and then it stopped in the morning.
整夜都下冰雹，到了早上就停了。

heavenly [ˋhɛvənlɪ] adj. 天空的、天堂的 Track 3758

例句 The moon is one of the heavenly bodies in the universe.
月亮是宇宙中的天體之一。

搭配詞 heavenly bodies 天體

honk [hɔŋk] v. 雁鳴、按汽車喇叭 Track 3759

例句 We honked at the driver in front of us.
我們對前面司機按喇叭。

同義字 toot

horizon [həˋraɪzn̩] n. 地平線、水準線 Track 3760

例句 The sun is rising above the horizon.
太陽從地平線上緩緩升起。

hot [hɑt] adj. 熱的、熱情的、辣的 Track 3761

例句 Some people like to wash their faces with hot water.
有些人喜歡用熱水洗臉。

howl [haul] v./n. 吠聲、怒號 Track 3762

例句 The poor Shiba Inu howled when he discovered that he was being taken to the vet.
那隻可憐的柴犬一發現他要被帶去看獸醫了，就大聲怒號。

humid [ˋhjumɪd] adj. 潮濕的 ◀ Track 3763

例句 The weather is always very humid during summer in Taiwan.
台灣的夏天天氣總是很潮濕。

反義字
dry 乾燥的

---

hurricane [ˋhɝɪ͵ken] n. 颶風 ◀ Track 3764

例句 There was nothing left after the hurricane.
颶風過後，什麼都不剩了。

---

hydrogen [ˋhaɪdrədʒən] n. 氫、氫氣 ◀ Track 3765

例句 We learned in science class that water is made up of oxygen and hydrogen. 我們在自然課學到水是由氧和氫組成的。

---

ice [aɪs] n./v. 冰 ◀ Track 3766

例句 The ice is slippery. Please don't stand on it.
冰很滑，請不要站在上面。

搭配詞
iced tea 冰茶

---

iceberg [ˋaɪs͵bɝg] n. 冰山 ◀ Track 3767

例句 The case of child abuse is only the tip of the iceberg.
這件虐童案只是冰山的一角。

搭配詞
the tip of the iceberg
冰山一角

---

if [ɪf] conj. 如果、是否 ◀ Track 3768

例句 If only I could be your girlfriend.
要是我是你的女朋友就好了。

搭配詞
if only 倘若

---

immense [ɪˋmɛns] adj. 巨大的、極大的 ◀ Track 3769

例句 There's an immense improvement in his grades.
他的成績有巨大的成長。

同義字
huge

---

impact [ˋɪmpækt] v./n. 衝擊、影響 ◀ Track 3770

例句 Climate change will have a huge impact on our planet.
氣候變遷會對地球造成重大影響。

搭配詞
have an impact on 對（某人／事）具有影響力

---

incense [ˋɪnsɛns] n. 香味、香 ◀ Track 3771

例句 Do you mind if I light some candles and incense in the room?
你介意我在房間裡點蠟燭和點香嗎？

---

keep [kip] v./n. 保持、維持、生活費 ◀ Track 3772

例句 He kept on saying the same thing.
他繼續說著同樣的事。

搭配詞
keep on 繼續

latitude [ˋlætə͵tjud] n. 緯度 Track 3773

例句 The two cities are at the same latitude.
這兩個城市是位於同一個緯度。

相關詞 longitude 經度

lightning [ˋlaɪtnɪŋ] n./adj. 閃電；閃電似的 Track 3774

例句 He rushed to the airport with lightning speed.
他很快就趕到機場了。

搭配詞 with lightning speed 很快

long [lɔŋ] adj./adv. 長（久）的 Track 3775

例句 It's a long shot, but you can give it a try.
雖然希望不大，你還是可以試試看。

搭配詞 long shot 希望不大的嘗試

longitude [ˋlɑndʒə͵tjud] n. 經度 Track 3776

例句 We had to memorize the longitude of our city.
我們得記得我們城市所在的經度。

相關詞 latitude 緯度

luck [lʌk] n. 幸運 Track 3777

例句 Lady Luck is a fickle lover.
幸運女神令人捉摸不定。

搭配詞 Lady Luck 幸運女神

may [me] aux. 可以、可能 Track 3778

例句 It's clear now, but it may rain in the afternoon.
現在天氣晴朗，但下午可能會下雨。

maybe [ˋmebɪ] adv. 或許、大概 Track 3779

例句 You always say "maybe." Why don't you just give me a straight answer? 你每次都說「大概吧」。為什麼不直接回答我呢？

同義字 possibly

mist [mɪst] n. 霧 Track 3780

例句 It is dangerous for people to walk in the heavy mist.
在大霧中行走很危險。

搭配詞 in a mist 在迷霧中

moist [mɔɪst] adj. 潮濕的 Track 3781

例句 It has been a year but she still can't get used to the moist climate here. 已經過一年了，她還是無法習慣這裡潮濕的環境。

反義字 dry 乾燥的

moisture [ˋmɔɪstʃɚ] n. 溼氣、水分 Track 3782

＊字尾-ure有轉變為名詞之意

例句 She applied some moisture cream on her face.
她在臉上擦了一些潤濕霜。

搭配詞 moisturizer 保濕霜

moon [mun] n. 月亮 ◀Track 3783

例句 When I was accepted by Princeton, I was over the moon.
當我被普林斯頓大學錄取時，我高興至極。

搭配詞
over the moon 高興至極

more [mor] adj. 更多的、更大的 ◀Track 3784

例句 Why does he have more money than I do?
為什麼他比我更有錢？

mud [mʌd] n. 爛泥、稀泥 ◀Track 3785

例句 It's too difficult for us to walk in the mud with this kind of shoes.
我們穿這種鞋子，太難在爛泥裡走路了。

muddy [ˋmʌdɪ] adj. 泥濘的 ◀Track 3786

例句 She took off her muddy shoes before going into the house.
她在進入房子前，先把泥濘的鞋子脫掉。

同義字
miry

nature [ˋnetʃɚ] n. 自然界、大自然 ◀Track 3787

例句 My parents want me to get close to nature.
我父母要我親近大自然。

nearly [ˋnɪrlɪ] adv. 幾乎 ◀Track 3788

*字尾-ly有轉變為副詞之意

例句 It nearly snows every day in winter here.
這裡冬天幾乎天天下雪。

necessary [ˋnɛsə͵sɛrɪ] ◀Track 3789

adj. 必要的、不可缺少的

例句 It's not necessary to bring an umbrella on a sunny day.
大晴天沒有必要帶雨傘。

neither [ˋniðɚ] adj. 兩者都不 ◀Track 3790

例句 Neither of us had money for bus tickets, so we walked home.
我們兩個都沒有錢買公車票，所以我們就用走的回家。

反義字
either（兩者之中）任一的

nobody [ˋno͵bɑdɪ] pron. 無人 ◀Track 3791

例句 He's quiet, but he's nobody's fool.
他很安靜，但為人精明，不易上當。

搭配詞
be nobody's fool 為人精明，不易上當

none [nʌn] pron. 沒有人 ◀Track 3792

例句 None of us wanted to go picnicking today.
今天我們沒有人想去野餐。

notice [ˋnotɪs] n./v. 公告、注意 Track 3793

例句 How do I make my crush notice me?
我要怎麼讓我暗戀的人注意到我呢？

occur [əˋkɝ] v. 發生、存在、出現 Track 3794

例句 It occurred to me that I forgot to bring my umbrella.
我剛想到忘了帶雨傘。

搭配詞 occur to 被想起、被想到

occurrence [əˋkɝəns] n. 出現、發生的事件 Track 3795

＊字尾-ence有轉變為名詞之意

例句 There was a strange occurrence in the village today.
今天在那個村莊發生了一件奇怪的事。

omit [oˋmɪt] v. 遺漏、省略、忽略 Track 3796

例句 You have to tell me what happened without omitting anything.
你必須要毫無省略地告訴我發生了什麼事。

反義字 neglect

ordinary [ˋɔrdṇ͵ɛrɪ] adj./n. 普通的 Track 3797

例句 When people in New York saw two airplanes crash into the Twin Towers, they realized it was not an ordinary day. 當紐約人看到兩架飛機衝撞雙子星大樓時，他們意識到那不是尋常的一天。

搭配詞 ordinary day 普通的一天

oxygen [ˋɑksədʒən] n. 氧 Track 3798

例句 All the passengers wore their oxygen masks wrong during an emergency landing.
飛機緊急迫降時，所有乘客戴氧氣面罩的方式都不正確。

搭配詞 oxygen mask 氧氣面罩

ozone [ˋozon] n. 臭氧 Track 3799

例句 The pollution has damaged the ozone layer.
污染造成了臭氧層的傷害。

搭配詞 ozone layer 臭氧層

phase [fez] n. 階段 Track 3800

例句 This was a key phase of history when many important events happened. 這是個歷史的重要階段，許多重大事件都在這時發生。

搭配詞 a key phase 重要階段

phenomenon [fəˋnɑmə͵nɑn] n. 現象 Track 3801

例句 It's a natural phenomenon; there's nothing to worry about.
那是個自然現象，沒什麼好擔心的。

同義字 event

plain [plen] adj./n. 明白的、平原 Track 3802

例句 Cheetahs ran on the plain as fast as they could.
獵豹以最快的速度在平原上奔跑。

plenty [ˋplɛntɪ] Track 3803
n./adj./adv. 豐富的、很多的、充分地
例句 There is no need to rush because we still have plenty of time.
不用趕，我們還有很多時間。

搭配詞
plenty of 大量的

---

poetic [poˋɛtɪk] adj. 詩意的 Track 3804
例句 The scenery here is poetic. 這裡的景色充滿詩意。

反義字
prosaic 散文的、散文體的

---

portion [ˋporʃən] n. 部分 Track 3805
例句 This rich man is willing to give a major portion of his money to charities. 這名有錢人願意把他大部分的錢給慈善機構。

同義字
part

---

predict [prɪˋdɪkt] v. 預測 Track 3806
＊字首pre-有「先」之意
例句 The weather forecast predicted that a storm was coming towards the island. 天氣預報預測暴風雨要來到島上了。

同義字
foresee

---

preservation [ˏprɛzɚˋveʃən] n. 保存 Track 3807
＊字尾-tion有轉變為名詞的意思
例句 This painting is in an excellent state of preservation.
這幅畫保存得很好。

---

preserve [prɪˋzɝv] v. 保存、維護 Track 3808
例句 It's important to preserve our natural resources.
維護自然資源是很重要的。

反義字
abandon 丟棄、拋棄

---

primitive [ˋprɪmətɪv] adj. 原始的 Track 3809
例句 The modern society is far more advanced than the primitive society. 現代社會比原始社會進步太多了。

同義字
ancient

---

principal [ˋprɪnsəpḷ] adj. 首要的 Track 3810
例句 Our principal problem is that we lack materials.
我們首要的問題是我們缺乏材料。

同義字
main

---

quack [kwæk] n./v. 嘎嘎的叫聲 Track 3811
例句 We heard wild ducks quacking in the lake.
我們聽到野鴨在湖裡嘎嘎叫。

---

quake [kwek] v./n. 搖動、地震 Track 3812
例句 The quake that happened in Japan killed nearly 10,000 people.
在日本發生的那場地震造成幾乎一萬人死亡。

同義字
shake

queer [kwɪr] adj. 違背常理的、奇怪的 Track 3813

例句 Aaron is a queer fish. 艾倫是個怪咖。

搭配詞 queer fish 古怪的人、難以理解的人

quest [kwɛst] n./v. 探索、探求 Track 3814

例句 Man will suffer many setbacks in his quest for truth, but eventually he will find it. 我們在探索真相的過程中會遇到很多問題，但最後我們終究會找到真相。

quiet [ˋkwaɪət] adj./n./v. 安靜的 Track 3815

例句 Please keep quiet in the library. 在圖書館請保持安靜。

搭配詞 keep quiet 保持安靜

quiver [ˋkwɪvɚ] v./n. 顫抖 Track 3816

例句 The children quivered in the cold. 孩子們在寒冷中顫抖。

同義字 shake

rain [ren] n./v. 雨、雨水 Track 3817

例句 We have a lot of rain in winter. 我們冬天很多雨。

rainbow [ˋren͵bo] n. 彩虹 Track 3818

例句 Can you stop chasing rainbows and be more realistic? 你可以不要老做不著邊際的夢，實際一點嗎？

搭配詞 chase rainbows 做不著邊際的夢

rainfall [ˋren͵fɔl] n. 降雨量 Track 3819

例句 The annual rainfall in this area is way below average. 這一區的年降雨量遠低於平均。

搭配詞 annual rainfall 年降雨量

rainy [ˋrenɪ] adj. 多雨的 Track 3820

＊字尾-y有轉變為形容詞之意

例句 You should save money for a rainy day. 你應該存點錢，有備無患。

搭配詞 save money for a rainy day 未雨綢繆

rather [ˋræðɚ] adv. 寧願 Track 3821

例句 I would rather play than work. 我寧可玩也不要工作。

搭配詞 rather than 寧願

raw [rɔ] adj. 生的、原始的 Track 3822

例句 You can't eat raw meat. It has to be cooked. 你不能吃生肉。要先煮過才行。

ray [re] n. 光線 Track 3823

例句 The rays of the sun could not penetrate my heavy curtains.
太陽強烈的光線無法穿透我厚重的窗簾。

搭配詞
sunlight ray 太陽光線

---

repress [rɪˋprɛs] v. 壓制 Track 3824

例句 The government repressed the protesters with tear gas.
政府用催淚瓦斯壓制抗議者。

反義字
incite 激勵、激起

---

restraint [rɪˋstrent] n. 抑制 Track 3825

例句 Her anger was beyond restraint.
她的憤怒已經無法抑制了。

搭配詞
beyond restraint 無法限制地

---

ready [ˋrɛdɪ] adj. 做好準備的 Track 3826

例句 I'm ready to take the new challenge.
我做好準備接受新的挑戰了。

---

rear [rɪr] n./adj. 後面；後面的 Track 3827

例句 You can see the car behind you from the rear mirror.
你可以用後照鏡看到你後面的車。

搭配詞
rear mirror 後照鏡

---

regulate [ˋrɛgjəˌlet] v. 調節、管理 Track 3828

例句 The thermometer equipment helps to regulate the temperature of the fridge. 溫度計儀器幫助調節冰箱內的溫度。

同義字
manage

---

ripple [ˋrɪpḷ] n. 波動、潺潺聲 Track 3829

例句 He threw the pebble into the lake and made ripples on the surface.
他把石頭丟進湖裡，造成水面上的波動。

搭配詞
make a ripple 造成波動

---

river [ˋrɪvɚ] n. 江、河 Track 3830

例句 They pitched a tent by the river. 他們在河邊搭帳篷。

搭配詞
by the river 在河邊

---

roam [rom] v./n. 漫步、流浪 Track 3831

例句 The tourist spent the day roaming around in the city.
那名觀光客一整天都在城市內漫步。

---

safe [sef] adj. 安全的 Track 3832

例句 He came back safe and sound from the war zone.
他從戰區平安無事的回來了。

搭配詞
safe and sound 平安無事的

salvation [sælˋveʃən] n. 救助、拯救 Track 3833

＊字尾-tion有轉變為名詞的意思

例句 The rain became the farmer's salvation after the drought.
雨成為農夫在乾旱後的救星。

---

sand [sænd] n. 沙、沙子 Track 3834

例句 Children are playing in the sand. 孩子們在沙裡玩。

---

sea [si] n. 海 Track 3835

例句 The sea is rough today. 今天海上很不穩。

---

seldom [ˋsɛldəm] adj./adv. 不常地、很少地 Track 3836

例句 It seldom snows in the subtropical zone.
在亞熱帶地區很少難得下雪。

---

sensible [ˋsɛnsəbl] adj. 可感覺的、理性的 Track 3837

＊字尾-ible有「可以、能」的意思

例句 She is a sensible old lady. 她是位很理性的老太太。

反義字
absurd 不合理的

---

serene [səˋrin] adj. 寧靜的、安詳的 Track 3838

例句 She is always serene and calm, like nothing can surprise her.
她總是安詳又平靜，好像什麼都無法讓她驚訝。

反義字
furious 狂怒的、狂暴的

---

shine [ʃaɪn] v./n. 照耀、發光、發亮 Track 3839

例句 Rain or shine, I'll be there for you.
不論發生什麼事，我都會陪著你。

搭配詞
rain or shine 不論晴雨、不論發生什麼事

---

shiny [ˋʃaɪnɪ] adj. 發亮的、晴朗的 Track 3840

例句 We polished the car so it looks shiny again.
我們擦過了那台車，讓它再度變得發亮。

同義字
lustrous

---

shorten [ˋʃɔrtn̩] v. 縮短、使變短 Track 3841

＊字尾-en有「使」的意思

例句 The new highway shortens the distance between the two cities.
新的高速公路使得兩個城市之間的距離縮短了。

---

shower [ˋʃauɚ] n./v. 陣雨、淋浴 Track 3842

例句 I take a shower every morning before going to work.
我每天早上去工作前都會淋浴。

搭配詞
take a shower 淋浴

simmer [ˋsɪmɚ] n./v. 沸騰的狀態 ◀Track 3843

例句 The soup is simmering on the stove.
湯在爐子上沸騰著。

since [sɪns] adv./prep./conj. 從……以來 ◀Track 3844

例句 He never came back since then.
從那時起，他再也沒回來了。

搭配詞 since then 從那時以來

sky [skaɪ] n. 天、天空 ◀Track 3845

例句 There are thousands of stars twinkling in the night sky in summer.
夏天時夜晚天上有幾千顆星星閃耀著。

slam [slæm] n./v. 砰然聲、砰地關上 ◀Track 3846

例句 He slammed the door angrily. 他生氣地砰地關上門。

sleepy [ˋslipɪ] adj. 想睡的、睏的 ◀Track 3847

＊字尾-y有轉變為形容詞之意

例句 I'm a bit sleepy, so I'll go take a nap.
我有點睏，所以我去小睡一下。

反義字 wakeful 不眠的、失眠的

slow [slo] adj./adv. 慢的、緩慢的 ◀Track 3848

例句 Her car is very slow. 她的車很慢。

smoke [smok] n. 煙、煙塵、吸菸 ◀Track 3849

例句 The government has been promoting a smoke-free environment these years. 政府近年來在推行無菸環境。

搭配詞 No smoking. 不准吸菸。

snow [sno] n./v. 雪 ◀Track 3850

例句 The weather report says that there will be snow next week.
氣象報告說下禮拜會下雪。

snowy [snoɪ] adj. 多雪的、積雪的 ◀Track 3851

＊字尾-y有轉變為形容詞之意

例句 The snowy weather makes it inconvenient for drivers.
多雪的天氣對駕駛來說很不方便。

so [so] adv. 這樣、如此地、所以 ◀Track 3852

例句 He goes to the pub once in a while—so what?
他偶爾會去酒吧喝幾杯，所以又怎麼樣呢？

搭配詞 So what? 所以又怎樣？

somebody [ˋsʌm͵bɑdɪ] pron. 某人、有人 Track 3853

例句 Somebody paid the politician back in his own coin through mockery and mimicry.
有人用嘲諷和模仿那位政客的方式，以其人之道還治其人之身。

搭配詞 Pay somebody back in his own coin. 以其人之道還治其人之身。

somewhere [ˋsʌm͵wɛr] adv. 在某處 Track 3854

例句 We should go somewhere fun tonight.
我們今天晚上去某處好玩的地方吧。

spread [sprɛd] v. 展開、蔓延 Track 3855

例句 The flames spread quickly. 烈焰蔓延得很快。

spring [sprɪŋ] v. 彈開、突然提出、突然出現 Track 3856

例句 We are about to spring a surprise attack on the enemies.
我們將要突襲敵人。

star [stɑr] n. 星、恆星 Track 3857

例句 You can see stars in the sky on a clear night.
晴朗的夜晚可以看到天上的星星。

stop [stɑp] v./n. 停止 Track 3858

例句 We hope that the heavy rain will stop soon.
我們希望大雨可以快點停。

storm [stɔrm] n. 風暴 Track 3859

例句 He's making a storm in a teacup again.
他又在小題大作了。

搭配詞 a storm in a teacup 小題大作（英式英語）

stormy [ˋstɔrmɪ] adj. 暴風雨的、多風暴的 Track 3860

＊字尾-y有轉變為形容詞之意

例句 The fishermen returned safely from the stormy seas.
漁民們在暴風雨中的驚濤駭浪中平安歸來。

搭配詞 stormy seas 暴風雨中的驚濤駭浪

sudden [ˋsʌdn̩] adj. 突然的 Track 3861

例句 All of a sudden, John was screaming and rolling on the ground.
約翰突然地在地上滾、大吼大叫。

搭配詞 all of a sudden 突然地

sun [sʌn] n. 太陽、日 Track 3862

例句 When will the sun come up? 太陽什麼時候出來？

sunny [ˋsʌnɪ] **adj.** 充滿陽光的 ◀Track 3863
＊字尾-y有轉變為形容詞之意
例句 It's such a sunny day. Let's go out for a walk.
真是個充滿陽光的日子啊！我們出去散步吧。

反義字
unsunned 不見於陽光的

---

surge [sɝdʒ] **n.** 大浪 ◀Track 3864
例句 The surge swept the boat away. 大浪把船捲走了。

同義字
wave

---

survive [sɚˋvaɪv] **v.** 倖存、殘存 ◀Track 3865
例句 Unfortunately, no one survived the plane crash.
很不幸地，這場空難沒有倖存者。

---

swamp [swɑmp] **n.** 沼澤 ◀Track 3866
例句 The heavy rain nearly turned the park into a swamp.
大雨幾乎把公園變成沼澤。

---

swell [swɛl] **v./n.** 膨脹 ◀Track 3867
例句 He has a swollen head after the acquisition of the company.
他收購這家公司後，變得很自負。

搭配詞
have a swollen head 自負

---

swift [swɪft] **adj./adv.** 迅速的 ◀Track 3868
例句 They swiftly found a solution to the problem.
他們迅速地找到了解決問題的方法。

反義字
slow 慢的

---

temperature [ˋtɛmprətʃɚ] **n.** 溫度、氣溫 ◀Track 3869
例句 The temperature suddenly dropped to 0 degrees.
溫度一下就掉到零度了。

---

tempest [ˋtɛmpɪst] **n.** 大風暴、暴風雨 ◀Track 3870
例句 She made a tempest in a teapot over the incident.
她對這起事件的發生，反應很大驚小怪。

搭配詞
a tempest in a teapot
大驚小怪（美式英語）

---

thunder [ˋθʌndɚ] **n./v.** 雷、打雷 ◀Track 3871
例句 I was awoken by the sound of the thunder last night.
我昨晚被雷聲吵醒。

---

tornado [tɔrˋnedo] **n.** 龍捲風 ◀Track 3872
例句 The tornado destroyed the entire village.
龍捲風毀滅了整座村莊。

同義字
whirlwind

a b c d e f g h i j k l m n o p q r s t u v w x y z

torrent [ˋtɔrənt] n. 洪流、急流 Track 3873

例句 A torrent of water swept the log away.
一陣急流把木頭沖走了。

同義字 flood

---

transparent [trænsˋpɛrənt] adj. 透明的 Track 3874

＊字首trans-有「穿越、轉變」之意

例句 We kept the cricket in a transparent jar.
我們把蟋蟀放進一個透明的罐子裡。

反義字 opaque 不透明的、不透光的

---

trick [trɪk] n. 詭計、訣竅 Track 3875

例句 The trick to doing this right is to calculate the timing right.
要正確達成這件事的訣竅，就是要把時機算好。

---

twinkle [ˋtwɪŋkḷ] v./n. 閃爍、發光 Track 3876

例句 Thousands of stars are twinkling in the sky.
上千的星星在空中閃爍。

---

type [taɪp] n. 類型 Track 3877

例句 I don't like this type of movie.
我不喜歡這個類型的電影。

---

typhoon [taɪˋfun] n. 颱風 Track 3878

例句 The disastrous typhoon caused a lot of casualties.
這個可怕的颱風造成了許多傷亡。

同義字 storm

---

umbrella [ʌmˋbrɛlə] n. 雨傘 Track 3879

例句 Let's bring an umbrella in case it rains.
我們帶把傘吧，以免下雨。

同義字 parasol

---

unanimous [juˋnænəməs] adj. 一致的、和諧的 Track 3880

＊字首un-有「不、反」之意

例句 The society hasn't achieved unanimous agreement on the legalization of euthanasia.
社會對於安樂死立法，還未取得一致的同意。

搭配詞 unanimous agreement 一致的同意

---

undergo [ˏʌndɚˋgo] v. 度過、經歷 Track 3881

＊字首under-有「下方的」之意

例句 His life underwent great changes after he got divorced.
他的生活在離婚後經歷了極大的改變。

同義字 experience

---

until/till [ənˋtɪl]/[tɪl] prep./conj. 直到……為止 Track 3882

例句 I couldn't sleep until midnight last night.
我昨天直到半夜為止都睡不著。

up [ʌp] adv./prep./adj. 向上地 ◀ Track 3883

例句 The elevator is going up. Please wait for another one.
電梯正在向上，請等另一台來。

vanish [ˋvænɪʃ] v. 消失、消逝 ◀ Track 3884

例句 Many species have vanished from the Earth.
許多物種都從地球上消失了。

variable [ˋvɛrɪəbḷ] adj. 不定的、易變的 ◀ Track 3885

＊字尾-able有「可以、能」的意思

例句 The weather here can be variable. 這裡的天氣可能很易變。

variation [͵vɛrɪˋeʃən] n. 變動 ◀ Track 3886

＊字尾-tion有轉變為名詞的意思

例句 There are variations in prices for vegetables from season to season.
這裡的蔬菜價錢一季一季都有變動。

very [ˋvɛrɪ] adv. 很、非常 ◀ Track 3887

例句 It is very cool here during the autumn.
這裡秋天都很涼爽。

want [wɑnt] v./n. 想要、要；需要 ◀ Track 3888

例句 She was covered in sweat and in want of a shower.
她流很多汗且想要淋浴。

搭配詞
in want of 需要

water [ˋwɔtɚ] n. 水 ◀ Track 3889

例句 Water is indispensable for people to survive.
水對人們的生存來說是不可或缺的。

wave [wev] n. 浪、波 ◀ Track 3890

例句 He made waves again in the office.
他又在辦公室興風作浪了。

搭配詞
make waves 興風作浪

weather [ˋwɛðɚ] n. 天氣 ◀ Track 3891

例句 Do you know what today's weather will be like?
你知道今天的天氣會怎樣嗎？

wind [wɪnd] n. 風 ◀ Track 3892

例句 The strong wind might blow the tent away.
強風可能會把帳棚吹走。

windy [ˋwɪndɪ] adj. 多風的 ◀Track 3893

＊字尾-y有轉變為形容詞之意

例句 It's probably too windy to have a picnic today.
今天風太大了，大概不能野餐。

wonder [ˋwʌndɚ] v./n. 奇蹟、驚奇 ◀Track 3894

例句 He's a violent man. No wonder his wife left him.
他有暴力傾向，難怪太太離開他。

搭配詞
no wonder 意料之中

wonderful [ˋwʌndɚfəl] adj. 令人驚奇的、很好的 ◀Track 3895

＊字尾-ful有「充滿」的意思

例句 What a wonderful chance! 真是個好機會！

反義字
ordinary 平常的

worst [wɝst] adj. 最壞的、最差的 ◀Track 3896

例句 I think we need to prepare for the worst.
我想我們得為最糟的情況做準備。

Test 14 關鍵英單總測驗第14回

以下測驗題皆出自書中第十四回「**和自然氣候有關的單字**」，快來檢視自己的學習成果吧！

一、選擇題

1. It's very _____ in the polar region.
(A) hot
(B) downward
(C) cold
(D) flood

2. The little mermaid chose to become _____ of the sea because she didn't want to kill the prince.
(A) foams
(B) glaciers
(C) fossils
(D) icebergs

3. He took off his _______ shirt and washed it clean.
(A) rainy
(B) swamp
(C) muddy
(D) swift

4. We all should cut carbon emissions to reduce _____ effect.
(A) greenhouse
(B) heavenly
(C) gloomy
(D) rainfall

5. He's making a ______ in a teapot again.
(A) sun
(B) storm
(C) flake
(D) cloud

6. It's difficult to grow anything on the _____ land.
(A) barren (B) cozy
(C) moist (D) fresh

7. _____ Katrina is one of the most catastrophic natural disasters in the U.S. history.
(A) Blizzard
(B) Horizontal
(C) Continental
(D) Hurricane

8. It was too _____ to drive yesterday. So they parked their car on the side of the road.
(A) humid
(B) foggy
(C) lightening
(D) ordinary

9. We can't survive without _____ .
(A) smoke
(B) tempests
(C) oxygen
(D) tornados

10. They used to be enemies. But it's all _____ under the bridge.
(A) water
(B) stars
(C) moon
(D) sun

二、克漏字測驗

In August 2005, Hurricane Katrina hit the western __1__ of the United States, causing catastrophic damage from central Florida to eastern Texas. At least 1,836 people died in the natural disaster and the subsequent __2__. It was one of the deadliest hurricanes in the US history since 1928.

The storm dropped heavy __3__ and damaged about 100 homes. Its strong __4__ downed a lot of trees and powerlines. Patients who were not evacuated at the local hospitals were left without fresh __5__ for five days after the hurricane's landfall.

1.
(A) coast
(B) horizon
(C) glimpse
(D) chunk

2.
(A) creek
(B) breeze
(C) blizzard
(D) floods

3.
(A) quake
(B) rainfall
(C) ozone
(D) mud

4.
(A) serene
(B) ripples
(C) winds
(D) rainbow

5.
(A) water
(B) umbrellas
(C) waves
(D) sun

關鍵英單總測驗第14回 中譯與解答

一、選擇題

1. 極地地區很冷。
   (A) 炎熱的
   (B) 向下地
   (C) 冷的
   (D) 洪水

2. 小美人魚選擇變成海裡的泡泡，因為她不想殺害王子。
   (A) 泡泡
   (B) 冰河
   (C) 化石
   (D) 冰山

3. 他把泥濘的襯衫脫掉並把它洗乾淨。
   (A) 下雨的
   (B) 沼澤
   (C) 泥巴的
   (D) 迅速的

4. 我們都應減少碳排放量以減緩溫室效應。
   (A) 溫室
   (B) 天堂的
   (C) 幽暗的
   (D) 降雨量

5. 他又在小題大作了。
   (A) 太陽
   (B) 暴風雨
   (C) 雪花
   (D) 雲

6. 在這塊貧瘠的土地要種任何東西都很困難。
   (A) 貧瘠的
   (B) 溫暖舒適的
   (C) 濕潤的
   (D) 新鮮的

7. 卡崔娜颶風是美國有史以來最具毀滅性的天災之一。
   (A) 暴風雪
   (B) 地平線的
   (C) 大陸的
   (D) 颶風

8. 昨天路面霧太大，不能開車，所以他們把車停在路邊。
   (A) 潮濕的
   (B) 朦朧的、霧茫茫的
   (C) 閃電
   (D) 尋常的

9. 我們沒有氧氣就無法存活。
   (A) 煙
   (B) 暴風雨
   (C) 氧氣
   (D) 龍捲風

10. 他們曾經是敵人，不過現在已事過境遷了。
   (A) 水
   (B) 星星
   (C) 月亮
   (D) 太陽

二、克漏字測驗

2005年8月，卡崔娜颶風重創美國西岸，向佛羅里達州中部到德州東部帶來重大災害，至少有1,836個人死於那場天災和隨之而來的洪水，是美國自1928年以來最致命的颶風之一。

這場暴風雨帶來巨大的降雨量，摧毀了約100戶房屋，強風也吹倒許多樹木和電線，而在當地醫院沒被撤離的病患，在颶風過境後，有長達5天沒有乾淨的水可用。

1.
(A) 海岸
(B) 地平線
(C) 瞥見
(D) 大厚塊

2.
(A) 小溪
(B) 微風
(C) 暴風雪
(D) 洪水

3.
(A) 地震
(B) 降雨量
(C) 臭氧層
(D) 泥巴

4
(A) 平靜的
(B) 漣漪
(C) 風
(D) 彩虹

5.
(A) 水
(B) 雨傘
(C) 波浪
(D) 太陽

一、選擇題

1.(C) 2.(A) 3.(C) 4.(A) 5.(B)
6.(A) 7.(D) 8.(B) 9.(C) 10.(A)

二、克漏字測驗

1.(A) 2.(D) 3.(B)
4.(C) 5.(A)

Unit 15 和顏色形狀有關的單字

多益測驗的命題強調生活化與實用性，學會這些與「顏色形狀」有關的單字，不僅能讓你在多益考場上所向披靡，在日常生活上也可以靈活運用喔！

描述幾何圖形可以這麼說

- **Parthenon is a great example of using bilateral symmetry in architecture.**
  帕德嫩神廟是在建築中運用軸對稱的極佳範例。
- **There are two pairs of parallel straight lines in a rectangle.**
  一個長方形當中，有兩對相互平行的直線。

形容物體顏色可以這麼說

- **The actress wore black eye shadow to symbolize the dark side of the character.**
  那名女演員畫了黑色的眼影，來象徵這個角色的黑暗面。
- **That bright pink dress with a bulky bow on the front is the tackiest dress I have ever seen.**
  那件前面有個巨大蝴蝶結的亮粉色裙子，是我見過最俗氣的裙子。
- **Combine red and blue together makes purple.**
  將紅色和藍色混和在一起，會得到紫色。

服飾的花色可以這麼說

- **The model is wearing a lovely polka dot mini skirt.**
  模特身穿一件可愛的圓點迷你裙。

- He is wearing a monochromatic blue suit with white snickers.
  他穿著一套藍色系的西裝搭配白色帆布鞋。

逛展覽可以這麼說

- The publisher put a gigantic banner at the hallway to advertize their new book.
  出版社在走廊放了一幅巨大的橫幅來為新書打廣告。
- The exhibit will be held at Talpei World Trade Center.
  展覽將在台北世貿中心舉辦。

手工藝品可以這麼說

- This gorgeous headpiece was made of crystal beads and wire.
  這件華麗的頭飾是用水晶珠與鐵絲做成的。
- The calligrapher sells her handwriting Spring Festival couplets at the market.
  那名書法家在市場販賣她的手寫春聯。

Unit 15 和顏色形狀有關的單字

abstract [ˋæbstrækt] adj. 抽象的 ◀Track 3897

例句 Picasso's paintings are very abstract.
畢卡索的畫很抽象的。

搭配詞
abstract painting 抽象畫

abstraction [æbˋstrækʃən] n. 抽象、空泛 ◀Track 3898

＊字尾-tion有轉變為名詞的意思

例句 John always talks in abstractions. 約翰說話總是很空泛。

易混淆字
subtraction 減法

accuracy [ˋækjərəsɪ] n. 正確、精密 ◀Track 3899

例句 The computer can calculate the trajectory of the missle with accuracy. 這部電腦能精確地計算出飛彈的彈道。

搭配詞
with accuracy 精確地

adjust [əˋdʒʌst] v. 調節、對準 ◀Track 3900

例句 She adjusted herself well to the new working environment.
她成功地調適自己，適應了新的工作環境。

搭配詞
adjust oneself to 自我調適

analogy [əˋnælədʒɪ] n. 類似 ◀Track 3901

例句 She made an analogy between dancing ballet and flying.
她把跳芭蕾比喻成飛翔。

搭配詞
make an analogy between
使用類似譬喻

appear [əˋpɪr] v. 出現、顯得 ◀Track 3902

例句 Her name appeared on the victim list of the air crash.
她的名字出現在空難罹難者的名單。

反義字
disappear 消失

artificial [ˏɑrtəˋfɪʃəl] adj. 人工的 ◀Track 3903

例句 I don't like those artificial flowers on the table.
我不喜歡桌上的人造花。

搭配詞
artificial intelligence
人工智慧

attachment [əˋtætʃmənt] n. 連接、附著 ◀Track 3904

＊字尾-ment有轉變為名詞之意

例句 Enclosed please find an e-mail attachment.
請見本電郵併附的附加檔案。

搭配詞
e-mail attachment
電子郵件附加檔案

attempt [ə`tɛmpt] v. 嘗試、企圖 Track 3905

例句 He attempted to make a comeback but failed.
他嘗試東山再起，卻失敗了。

搭配詞 attempt to 試著

attract [ə`trækt] v. 吸引 Track 3906

例句 The polar bear cub attracts many people to the zoo.
這隻北極熊寶寶吸引很多人到動物園看牠。

搭配詞 Opposites attract. 異性相吸

attractive [ə`træktɪv] adj. 吸引人的、動人的 Track 3907

＊字尾-ive有轉變為形容詞之意

例句 As an attractive teenage girl, she was signed by a modeling agency in New York.
她在青少女時期就出落得很動人，被紐約模特兒經紀公司簽下。

awkward [`ɔkwəd] Track 3908

adj. 笨拙的、不熟練的、尷尬的

例句 There was an awkward silence when he walked into the room.
他一進入房間，原本大家熱烈的交談瞬間陷入尷尬的寂靜。

搭配詞 awkward silence 尷尬的寂靜

badge [bædʒ] n. 徽章 Track 3909

例句 He was given a badge of honor for his heroic service in the military.
他因在軍中英勇表現而被授予榮耀徽章。

搭配詞 badge of honor 榮耀徽章

banner [`bænə] n. 旗幟、橫幅 Track 3910

例句 He spent US$2,000 to buy a web banner for advertisement.
他花了2千美元買了一個網頁橫幅廣告。

搭配詞 web banner 網站頁面頂上的橫幅

beautify [`bjutə,faɪ] v. 美化 Track 3911

＊字尾-ify有「使」的意思

例句 She put on some makeup to beautify herself.
她化了點妝，打扮自己。

big [bɪg] adj. 大的 Track 3912

例句 He was a big bully and was expelled by school.
他是個大惡霸，被學校開除了。

搭配詞 a big bully 大惡霸

black [blæk] adj. 黑色的 Track 3913

例句 During the Black History Month, festivities and events are held to commemorate the achievements made by African Americans.
每年的美國黑人歷史月，有舉辦許多活動來紀念非裔美籍人士所做出的貢獻。

搭配詞 Black History Month 美國黑人歷史月

blue [blu] adj./n. 藍色的、藍色 Track 3914

例句 Who wears blue to weddings?
誰會穿藍色衣服去參加婚禮啊？

breadth [brɛdθ] n. 寬度、幅度 Track 3915

例句 His teacher was surprised by his breadth of knowledge in ancient Greek history. 他的老師對他在古希臘歷史的淵博知識，深感驚訝。

易混淆字 breath 呼吸

brink [brɪŋk] n. 邊緣 Track 3916

例句 The company was almost on the brink of bankruptcy due to mismanagement. 因為管理不當，這家公司幾乎瀕臨倒閉。

搭配詞 brink of bankruptcy 瀕臨倒閉

broaden [ˋbrɔdn̩] v. 加寬 Track 3917

＊字尾-en有「使」的意思

例句 I want to study abroad to broaden my horizons. 我想出國唸書，擴大我的視野。

搭配詞 broaden one's horizons 擴大自己的視野

brown [braʊn] adj. 褐色的、棕色的 Track 3918

例句 A brown bear entered his house and ate the food in the fridge. 一隻棕熊闖進他家，並吃了冰箱的食物。

搭配詞 brown bear 棕熊

browse [braʊz] v. 瀏覽 Track 3919

例句 He browseed through the novel in the bookstore. 他在書店瀏覽了一本小說。

搭配詞 browse through 瀏覽

bulky [ˋbʌlkɪ] adj. 龐大的 Track 3920

＊字尾-y有轉變為形容詞之意

例句 He got hurt when moving the bulky equipment. 他搬運笨重的機器時，不小心受傷了。

calligraphy [kəˋlɪgrəfɪ] n. 筆跡、書法 Track 3921

例句 My grandpa practices Chinese calligraphy every day. 我祖父每天都要練書法。

cardboard [ˋkɑrd͵bɔrd] n. 卡紙、硬紙板 Track 3922

例句 The mall provides free cardboard boxes for customers when they go shopping there to reduce the use of plastic bags. 這間購物中心提供免費紙箱給前來消費的顧客，以減少塑膠袋的使用。

搭配詞 cardboard box 紙箱

characteristic [͵kærɪktəˋrɪstɪk] n. 特徵 Track 3923

例句 The ability to use a computer and the Internet is one of the defining characteristics of information literacy. 會使用電腦及網路是資訊素養的界定特徵之一。

搭配詞 defining characteristic 界定特徵

characterize [ˋkærɪktə͵raɪz] Track 3924

v. 描述……的性質、具有……特徵 ＊字尾-ize有「化」的意思

例句 What characterizes her is her lively personality. 她擁有的特徵就是她活潑的個性。

circle [ˋsɝkḷ] n. 圓形 Track 3925

例句 Thanks to circle lenses, you can have a pair of mesmerizing green eyes.
由於圓形瞳孔放大片的問世，你也可以擁有一雙迷人的綠色眼珠。

搭配詞 circle lenses 圓形瞳孔放大片

circular [ˋsɝkjələ] adj. 圓形的 Track 3926

例句 The new policy encompasses several areas, from Industry 4.0 to the circular economy. 新政策包含許多領域，從工業4.0到循環經濟。

搭配詞 circular economy 循環經濟

coherent [koˋhɪrənt] adj. 連貫的、有條理的 Track 3927

例句 The police asked her more questions to establish if she was coherent. 警方問她更多的問題，以確認她的說法是否連貫。

反義字 incoherent 無條理的、不呼應的

color [ˋkʌlə] n. 顏色 Track 3928

例句 He's upset that he's colorblind.
他對於自己是色盲感到沮喪。

搭配詞 colorblind 色盲

colorful [ˋkʌləfəl] adj. 富有色彩的 Track 3929

＊字尾-ful有「充滿」的意思

例句 The Christmas tree was covered with colorful decorations.
聖誕樹上佈滿色彩豐富的裝飾。

搭配詞 colorful decorations 色彩豐富的裝飾

column [ˋkɑləm] n. 圓柱、專欄、欄 Track 3930

例句 Ann Landers had had a personal-advice column in America for 47 years. 47年來，藍德斯一直在美國撰寫一個提供建議的專欄。

搭配詞 personal-advice column 提供個人建議的專欄

combine [kəmˋbaɪn] v. 聯合、結合 Track 3931

例句 Many women strive to combine family life with their career.
很多婦女努力兼顧家庭與事業。

conceive [kənˋsiv] v. 構想、構思 Track 3932

例句 The science fair was conceived by the school principal.
這個科學展是由學校校長構思的。

concentrate [ˋkɑnsṇˏtret] v. 集中 Track 3933

例句 It is hard for me to concentrate on my work in a noisy environment.
我在吵鬧的環境很難集中精神。

搭配詞 concentrate on 把精神集中在某事上

concentration [ˏkɑnsṇˋtreʃən] n. 集中、專心 Track 3934

＊字尾-tion有轉變為名詞的意思

例句 She found that listening to classical music could improve her concentration. 她發現聽古典音樂有助提升她的專注力。

concept [ˋkɑnsɛpt] n. 概念 Track 3935

例句 The abstract concept of physics is hard for me to comprehend.
這個抽象的物理概念對我來說，很難理解。

cone [kon] n. 圓錐 Track 3936

例句 The recipe shows you how to make ice cream cones at home.
這個食譜教你怎麼在家做冰淇淋圓錐筒。

搭配詞
ice cream cone
裝冰淇淋的圓錐筒（甜筒）

consist [kənˋsɪst] v. 組成、構成 Track 3937

例句 The team consists of five financial experts and three stock brokers.
這個團隊由五位財經專家和三位證券經紀人組成。

搭配詞
consist of 由……組成

constitute [ˋkɑnstəˏtjut] v. 構成、制定 Track 3938

例句 Children constitute only 30% of the city's population.
孩童僅佔這座城市人口的30%。

搭配詞
consitute of 由……組成

constructive [kənˋstrʌktɪv] adj. 建設性的 Track 3939

＊字尾-ive有轉變為形容詞之意

例句 We appreciate your constructive feedback and send you our best wishes. 我們感謝您建設性的回饋，並祝萬事如意。

搭配詞
constructive feedback
建設性的回饋

contain [kənˋten] v. 包含、含有 Track 3940

例句 The online game contains acts of violence and hatred to colored people. 這個線上遊戲內容含有暴力行為及對有色人種的仇恨。

continue [kənˋtɪnjʊ] v. 繼續、連續 Track 3941

例句 The soap opera is to be continued.
這部肥皂劇還未完待續。

搭配詞
to be continued 未完待續

continuous [kənˋtɪnjʊəs] n./adj. 不斷的、連續的 Track 3942

＊字尾-ous有轉變為形容詞之意

例句 The boss highly values the importance of continuous education for his employees. 這位老闆非常重視員工的繼續教育。

搭配詞
continuous education
繼續教育

contrary [ˋkɑntrɛrɪ] adj. 矛盾、反面 Track 3943

例句 I thought he would give me a hand. On the contrary, he just pretended he didn't know me.
我以為他會幫我忙，結果相反，他假裝不認識我。

搭配詞
on the contrary 相反地

contrast [ˋkɑnˏtræst] n. 對比 Track 3944

例句 The poverty of the refugees is in stark contrast to the wealth of the local people. 難民貧窮的情形與當地富裕的人民形成強烈的對比。

搭配詞
in contrast 相反地

cover [ˋkʌvɚ] n. 封面、表面 Track 3945

例句 The software allows you to design your book cover, and it's incredibly easy. 這個軟體讓你能夠設計自己的書封，而且操作起來不可思議的簡單。

搭配詞 book cover 書封

craft [kræft] n. 手工藝 Track 3946

例句 The exhibit featured aboriginal crafts.
這個展覽展示原住民手工藝品。

同義字 handicraft

crooked [ˋkrukɪd] adj. 彎曲的、歪曲的、狡詐的 Track 3947

例句 The crooked politician was found guilty of embazzlement.
那位狡詐的政客被發現犯貪瀆罪。

cross [krɔs] n. 十字形、交叉 Track 3948

例句 Her necklace was in the shape of a cross.
她的項鍊是個十字的形狀。

搭配詞 Cross my heart and hope to die. 我所說屬實（否則不得好死）

crude [krud] adj. 天然的、未加工的、粗野的 Track 3949

例句 The price of crude oil has fluctuated over the past few months.
過去幾個月來，原油價格波動不斷。

搭配詞 crude oil 原油

cube [kjub] n. 立方體、正六面體 Track 3950

例句 He can solve the Rubik's cube in one minute.
他可以在一分鐘之內解開魔術方塊。

搭配詞 rubiks cube 魔術方塊

curve [kɝv] n. 曲線 Track 3951

例句 Janet practices yoga everyday to perfect her body curves.
珍妮每天都練瑜伽，讓身體曲線變得完美。

搭配詞 body curve 身體曲線

deep [dip] adj. 深的 Track 3952

例句 How deep is your love? I really want to know.
你對我的愛有多深？我真的很想知道。

deepen [ˋdipən] v. 加深、變深 Track 3953

＊字尾-en有「使」的意思

例句 The exchange has deepened the mutual understanding beween the two nations. 這兩國之間的交流，強化了雙方的互相瞭解。

definite [ˋdɛfənɪt] adj. 確定的 Track 3954

例句 They are very definite about how many children they want to adopt.
他們很確定想要領養幾個孩子。

demand [dɪˋmænd] v./n. 要求 ◀Track 3955

例句 The hijackers demanded US$20 millions of ransom.
劫機犯要求20萬美元的贖金。

demonstration [ˏdɛmənˋstreʃən] ◀Track 3956

n. 證明、示範 ＊字尾-tion有轉變為名詞的意思

例句 Would you please give me a demonstration of how to operate the machine? 你可以示範如何操作這台機器嗎？

device [dɪˋvaɪs] n. 裝置、設計 ◀Track 3957

例句 He used a special device to track the double agent.
他用特殊裝置，追蹤那位雙面間諜。

devise [dɪˋvaɪz] v. 設計、想出 ◀Track 3958

例句 Mickey Mouse is a cartoon character devised by Walt Disney.
米老鼠是由華德迪士尼想出來的卡通角色。

differ [ˋdɪfɚ] v. 不同、相異 ◀Track 3959

例句 Though some people say AI robots can be controlled, I choose to differ. 有些人說人工智慧機器人是可以受控制的，我卻持有不同的意見。

搭配詞 choose to differ 持有不同的意見

different [ˋdɪfərənt] adj. 不同的 ◀Track 3960

例句 His leading style is very different from his predecessors.
他的領導風格和他的前輩迥然不同。

搭配詞 different from 和……不同

difficult [ˋdɪfəˏkʌlt] adj. 困難的 ◀Track 3961

例句 It is difficult to impose carbon fees in every country.
要每個國家都課徵排碳費是有困難的。

搭配詞 difficult to 做……很困難

direct [dəˋrɛkt] adj. 筆直的、直接的 ◀Track 3962

例句 Michelle is direct and straightforward; never mind.
蜜雪兒講話很直接，別在意。

disguise [dɪsˋgaɪz] v. 掩飾 ◀Track 3963

＊字首dis-有「不」之意

例句 She lost her job, but it turned out that it was a blessing in disguise.
她失業了，結果發現這個際遇是祝福的偽裝。

搭配詞 in disguise 偽裝的

dot [dɑt] n. 圓點 ◀Track 3964

例句 She looked charming in the vintage polka dot dress.
她穿這件經典款圓點洋裝很迷人。

搭配詞 polka dot 圓點花樣

a b c d e f g h i j k l m n o p q r s t u v w x y z

easy [ˋizɪ] adj. 容易的、不費力的 Track 3965

例句 It's not easy to stop cyber bullying.
要遏止網路霸凌並非容易的事。

edge [ɛdʒ] n. 邊、邊緣 Track 3966

例句 He was a bit on edge before the interview.
他面試前有些緊張不安。

搭配詞 on edge 緊張

else [ɛls] adj. 其他、另外 Track 3967

例句 If you could be someone else, who would you want to be?
如果你可以變成其他人，你想成為誰？

搭配詞 someone else 其他人

emphasis [ˋɛmfəsɪs] n. 重點、強調 Track 3968

例句 Our parents put a lot of emphasis on our education.
我們的雙親很重視我們的教育。

搭配詞 put emphasis on 強調某事

emphasize [ˋɛmfə͵saɪz] v. 強調 Track 3969

＊字尾-ize有「化」的意思

例句 Our teacher emphasized the importance of being on time.
我們老師很強調準時的重要性。

emphatic [ɪmˋfætɪk] adj. 強調的、有力的 Track 3970

例句 He issued an emphatic statement, which some disagreed was true.
他發表一篇有力的聲明，但有些人不能認同其真實性。

end [ɛnd] v. 結束 Track 3971

例句 He established his own company but ended up losing everything he had. 他創業發展結果卻慘賠結束。

搭配詞 end up 以……結束

ending [ˋɛndɪŋ] n. 結局、結束 Track 3972

例句 The marriage of a prince and a princess is not always a happy ending. 王子與公主的婚姻不全然永遠是快樂的結局。

搭配詞 happy ending 快樂的結局

enlarge [ɪnˋlɑrdʒ] v. 擴大、詳述 Track 3973

＊字首en-有「使」之意

例句 They enlarged the garden and grew a lemon tree there.
他們擴建庭院並種了一顆檸檬樹。

enormous [ɪˋnɔrməs] adj. 巨大的 Track 3974

例句 His hard work finally paid off, and he began getting enormous success. 他努力地工作終於得回報，開始獲得巨大的成功。

同義字 huge

enough [ə`nʌf] adj. 充足的、足夠的 Track 3975

例句 He had enough money to buy a decent house.
他有足夠的錢購買間像樣的房子。

essence [`ɛsn̩s] n. 本質 Track 3976

例句 His statement, in essence, implied that the law was too lenient to child abusers. 他的聲明本質上暗指法律對虐童者太過寬鬆。

搭配詞
in essence 本質上來說

evident [`ɛvədənt] adj. 明顯的 Track 3977

例句 We are not sure if the truths are self-evident enough.
我們不確定這些事實是否足以採信。

搭配詞
self-evident 不證自明的

exaggeration [ɪg͵zædʒə`reʃən] n. 誇張、誇大 Track 3978

＊字尾-tion有轉變為名詞的意思

例句 He said the movie was the best he had seen, but I think that's an exaggeration.
他說這部電影是他看過最好看的，但我覺得他誇大了。

excellent [`ɛksl̩ənt] adj. 極好的、優異的 Track 3979

例句 The house is in excellent condition.
這間房子狀況非常良好。

同義字
outstanding

exhibit [ɪg`zɪbɪt] n./v. 展示 Track 3980

＊字首ex-有「外」的意思

例句 The exhibit will be held at the Dr. Sun Yat-sen Memorial Hall.
展覽將在國父紀念館舉行。

exotic [ɛg`zɑtɪk] adj. 外來的、異國情調的 Track 3981

例句 There are many exotic restaurants in this city.
這個城市有很多異國情調的餐廳。

搭配詞
exotic restaurants
異國情調的餐廳

extend [ɪk`stɛnd] v. 延長 Track 3982

＊字首ex-有「外」的意思

例句 He needs to extend his visa. 他的簽證需要延展。

extent [ɪk`stɛnt] n. 範圍、程度 Track 3983

＊字首ex-有「外」的意思

例句 He lagged behind to some extent.
某種程度來說，他的進度是落後的。

搭配詞
to some extent
某種程度來說

extraordinary [ɪk`strɔrdn̩͵ɛrɪ] Track 3984

adj. 特別的、卓越的 ＊字首extra-有「超」的意思

例句 He's an extraordinary diplomat. 他是卓越的外交官。

extreme [ɪk`strim] adj. 極度的、極端的 Track 3985
＊字首ex-有「外」的意思
例句 He has been bullied quite a lot at school; no wonder he has gone to extremes. 他在校常被霸凌，難怪走上極端。

搭配詞
go to extremes 走極端

fantastic [fæn`tæstɪk] Track 3986
adj. 想像中的、奇異古怪的
例句 Your idea is fantastic. 你的點子好極了。

fantasy [`fæntəsɪ] n. 空想、異想、幻想 Track 3987
例句 Lord of the Rings is a fantasy novel. 魔戒是奇幻小說。

搭配詞
fantasy novel 奇幻小說

feature [`fitʃɚ] n. 特徵、特色 Track 3988
例句 Her doll face is her best feature.
她如同洋娃娃的臉蛋是最引人注目的特色。

finish [`fɪnɪʃ] v. 完成、結束 Track 3989
例句 We finished our homework at 10 pm.
我們在晚上十點完成功課。

focus [`fokəs] n. 焦點、焦距 Track 3990
例句 He has been the focus of the media since he was a child.
他從小就是媒體的焦點。

follow [`fɑlo] v. 跟隨、遵循、聽得懂 Track 3991
例句 My little sister follows me around whenever I go.
不論我去哪裡，我的小妹妹到處跟著我。

搭配詞
follow around 跟著到處去

formal [`fɔrml̩] adj. 正式的、有禮的 Track 3992
例句 A state banquet is formal. Please dress in suits.
國宴是正式的場合，請穿著西裝來。

format [`fɔrmæt] n. 格式、版式 Track 3993
例句 It's the same magazine, but in a new format.
是同一本雜誌，只是格式不同。

foster [`fɔstɚ] v. 養育、收養、培養 Track 3994
例句 She lived in a foster home when she was a teenager.
她青春期住在寄養家庭。

搭配詞
foster home 寄養家庭

fragile [ˋfrædʒəl] adj. 脆的、易碎的 Track 3995

例句 The little girl is sensitive and fragile.
這女孩個性很敏感脆弱。

fragment [ˋfrægmənt] n. 破片、碎片 Track 3996

＊字尾-ment有轉變為名詞之意

例句 They had a fight last night, and I saw lots of fragments at the front door in the morning. Coincidence? I think not. 他們昨晚大打一架，今天早上我在門口看到一堆碎片。是巧合嗎？我看不是喔。

frame [frem] v. 構築、框架、為……裝框 Track 3997

例句 Will you frame the picture for me? It was painted by my eight-year-old daughter.
你可以幫我把這張畫框起來嗎？是我八歲的女兒畫的。

搭配詞 window frame 窗框

fraud [frɔd] n. 欺騙、詐欺 Track 3998

例句 It was a phone fraud! Hang up the phone.
那是電話詐騙！掛斷電話。

搭配詞 phone fraud 電話詐騙

freak [frik] n. 怪胎、異想天開 Track 3999

例句 He was a freak at school but later became a billionaire.
他學生時期是怪胎，不過後來變成億萬富翁。

free [fri] adj. 自由的、免費的 Track 4000

例句 The organizer offered free entry to the exhibit.
主辦單位提供大眾免費入場觀賞展覽。

搭配詞 free entry 免費入場

general [ˋdʒɛnərəl] adj. 大體的、一般的 Track 4001

例句 In general, students in this school enjoy science classes more than liberal arts.
大體來説，這所學校的學生喜歡理科課程勝過文科課程。

搭配詞 in general 大體來説

gesture [ˋdʒɛstʃɚ] n. 手勢、姿勢 Track 4002

例句 He made a rude gesture and irritated his friends.
他比了一個粗魯的手勢，惹火了他的朋友。

搭配詞 rude gesture 粗魯的手勢

gift [gɪft] n. 禮物、天賦 Track 4003

例句 He got a Tesla Model 3 for his birthday gift.
他的生日禮物是特斯拉Model 3的電動車。

搭配詞 birthday gift 生日禮物

gigantic [dʒaɪˋgæntɪk] adj. 巨人般的、巨大的 Track 4004

例句 The building is gigantic and attention-grabbing.
這棟建築很巨大、醒目。

同義字 enormous

glee [gli] n. 喜悅、高興 Track 4005

例句 He clapped his hands with glee. 他高興地拍手。

gold [gold] n./adj. 黃金、金的 Track 4006

例句 Mother Teresa had a heart of gold.
德蕾莎修女有顆慈悲心。

搭配詞 have a heart of gold 心地善良

golden [goldn̩] adj. 金色的、黃金的 Track 4007

例句 Silence is golden. 沉默是金。

搭配詞 golden rule 重要的準則

gorgeous [ˋgɔrdʒəs] adj. 華麗的、極好的 Track 4008

＊字尾-ous有轉變為形容詞之意

例句 You look gorgeous in the dress! 你穿這件洋裝好美！

反義字 simple 樸實的

gray/grey [gre]/[gre] n./adj. 灰色 Track 4009

例句 My grandfather's hair is turning white from grey.
我奶奶的頭髮從灰色漸漸變白了。

green [grin] n./adj. 綠色的 Track 4010

例句 Her best friend married a billionaire, and she was green with envy.
她最好的朋友嫁了億萬富翁，她嫉妒得臉都綠了。

handful [ˋhændˏful] n. 一些、一把 Track 4011

例句 Only a handful of his classmates attended his birthday party.
只有一些同學參加他的生日派對。

同義字 fistful

handwriting [ˋhændˏraɪtɪŋ] n. 手寫、筆跡 Track 4012

例句 His handwriting is too small to be legible.
他的筆跡太小，讓人很難讀得懂。

同義字 penmanship

hard [hɑrd] adj. 硬的、難的 Track 4013

例句 It's hard for him to read because he has dyslexia.
對他來說，閱讀是很困難的，因為他有閱讀障礙。

harden [ˋhɑrdn̩] v. 使硬化、變硬、變堅強 Track 4014

＊字尾-en有「使」的意思

例句 The severe training hardened the soldiers.
艱苦的訓練把士兵鍛鍊得更加堅強。

harmony [ˋhɑrmənɪ] **n.** 一致、和諧　Track 4015
例句 His view is in harmony with mine. 他的觀點和我一致。

搭配詞
in harmony with
與……協調一致

---

hemisphere [ˋhɛməs͵fɪr] **n.** 半球體、半球　Track 4016
例句 We need to protect animals living in the Northern hemisphere.
我們要保護住在北半球的動物。

搭配詞
the Northern Hemisphere
北半球

---

high [haɪ] **adj.** 高的　Track 4017
例句 He has high blood pressure and needs to take medicine everyday.
他有高血壓，每天都要吃藥控制。

---

hollow [ˋhɑlo] **adj.** 中空的　Track 4018
例句 The man who had hollow cheeks was terribly sick.
這個雙頰凹陷的男人病得很重。

同義字
empty

---

huge [hjudʒ] **adj.** 龐大的、巨大的　Track 4019
例句 The project is a huge undertaking for a newcomer.
這個專案對新進人員是個巨大的工程。

反義字
diminutive 小的、微小的

---

imaginable [ɪˋmædʒɪnəbl̩] **adj.** 可想像的　Track 4020
＊字尾-able有「可以、能」的意思
例句 This is the most beautiful song imaginable.
這是可想像最美的一首歌。

反義字
unimaginable 難以想像的

---

imaginary [ɪˋmædʒə͵nɛrɪ] **adj.** 想像的、虛構的　Track 4021
例句 The little girl had a lot of imaginary friends.
那個小女孩有很多虛構的朋友。

同義字
fanciful

---

imaginative [ɪˋmædʒə͵netɪv]　Track 4022
adj. 有想像力的、富於想像的　＊字尾-ive有轉變為形容詞的意思
例句 The company developed an imaginative new approach to tackle the problems.
這間公司發展出具有想像力的方法，來解決這些問題。

反義字
unimaginative
沒有想像力的

---

imitate [ˋɪmə͵tet] **v.** 仿效、模仿　Track 4023
例句 The boy likes to imitate the way his father walks.
這男孩喜歡模仿爸爸走路的樣子。

反義字
create 創造、創作

---

imitation [͵ɪməˋteʃən] **n.** 模仿、仿造品　Track 4024
＊字尾-tion有轉變為名詞的意思
例句 The painting is just an imitation of a famous work.
這幅畫只是一幅名作的仿造品。

搭配詞
in imitation of 為了仿效

a b c d e f g h i j k l m n o p q r s t u v w x y z

inner [ˋɪnɚ] adj. 內部的、心靈的 Track 4025

例句 I think she has both inner and outer beauty.
我覺得她內在、外在皆美麗。

搭配詞
inner beauty 內在美

key [ki] adj. 主要的、關鍵的 Track 4026

例句 Once you forget the key word, you can't log in anymore.
你一忘記關鍵字，就不能登入了。

搭配詞
key word 關鍵字、密語

large [lɑrdʒ] adj. 大的、大量的 Track 4027

例句 He is a larger than life character. 他是令人印象很深刻的人。

搭配詞
larger than life 更活躍的（而可能更受人注目）

layer [ˋleɚ] n. 層 Track 4028

例句 She sprinkled some sugar on each layer of the apple pie.
她在蘋果派的每一層都灑上糖粉。

同義字
level

lean [lin] v./n. 傾斜、倚靠 Track 4029

例句 She leaned on me because she couldn't walk.
因為她走不動，所以靠在我的身上。

let [lɛt] v. 讓 Track 4030

例句 Let us go shopping online.
讓我們線上購物吧。

lighten [ˋlaɪtn̩] v. 變亮、減輕 Track 4031

＊字尾-en有「使」的意思

例句 He tried to lighten the mood by telling a joke.
他試著講笑話來讓減輕凝重的氣氛。

反義字
darken 使變暗

likely [ˋlaɪklɪ] adj./adv. 可能的 Track 4032

例句 John is most likely to win the competition.
約翰很可能會贏得這場比賽。

搭配詞
most likely 很可能

limitation [ˏlɪməˋteʃən] n. 限制 Track 4033

＊字尾-tion有轉變為名詞的意思

例句 There is a word limitation for each submission.
每篇投稿都有字數限制。

line [laɪn] n. 線、線條 Track 4034

例句 I drew a line on the ground.
我在地上畫了一條線。

list [lɪst] n. 清單、目錄、列表 Track 4035

例句 We are on the waiting list. They'll call us when it's our turn.
我們在在候補名單上，輪到我們時他們會打給我們。

搭配詞 on the waiting list 在候補名單

logo [ˋlɔgo] n. 商標、標誌 Track 4036

例句 He designed the logo for their company.
他為他們公司設計了商標。

搭配詞 company logo 公司商標

lower [ˋloɚ] v. 降低 Track 4037

例句 Can you lower the price a little?
你可以把價格降低一點點嗎？

magnify [ˋmægnə͵faɪ] v. 擴大、放大 Track 4038

＊字尾-ify有「使」的意思

例句 We will magnify the words for my grandmother to read.
我們會把文字放大，以讓我奶奶好讀。

makeup [ˋmek͵ʌp] n. 結構、化妝 Track 4039

例句 The actress wore heavy makeup for her role.
那位女演員為了這個角色，化了很濃的妝。

搭配詞 heavy makeup 濃妝

margin [ˋmɑrdʒɪn] n. 邊緣 Track 4040

例句 You can write your notes in the margin of the page.
你可以在書頁邊緣做筆記。

同義字 border

masterpiece [ˋmæstɚ͵pis] n. 傑作、名著 Track 4041

例句 This whole series of books is a masterpiece that you cannot miss.
這整個系列的書都是個你決不能錯過的傑作。

同義字 masterwork

maximum [ˋmæksəməm] adj./n. 最大的、最高的 Track 4042

例句 The maximum speed on the highway is 100 km; don't exceed it.
高速公路上最高的速度是100公里，別超過了。

反義字 minimum 最小量、最小的

midst [mɪdst] n. 中央、中間 Track 4043

例句 Tina should be somewhere in the midst of the crowd.
蒂娜應該在那一群人中間某個地方。

搭配詞 in the midst of 在……之中

mimic [ˋmɪmɪk] v./n. 模仿者；模仿 Track 4044

例句 His parrot is good at mimicking human's talking.
他的鸚鵡擅長模仿人類說話。

同義字 ape

miniature [ˋmɪnɪətʃɚ] n. 縮圖、縮影 Track 4045

例句 The model is just like Audrey Hepburn in miniature.
那個模特兒就像是縮小版的奧黛麗赫本。

搭配詞
in miniature
小型的、在小規模上

minimal [ˋmɪnɪm!] adj. 最小的 Track 4046

例句 We were careful to make only minimal damage to the goods.
我們很小心，貨品只受了最小的損傷。

反義字
maximal 最大的

minimize [ˋmɪnə͵maɪz] v. 減到最小 Track 4047

＊字尾-ize有「化」的意思

例句 We tried hard to minimize the loss in this accident.
我們努力試著把意外中的損失減到最小。

反義字
maximize 增加到最大

miraculous [məˋrækjələs] adj. 奇蹟的 Track 4048

＊字尾-ous有轉變為形容詞之意

例句 It was miraculous that she was still alive.
她還活著真是奇蹟。

同義字
marvelous

missing [ˋmɪsɪŋ] adj. 失蹤的、缺少的 Track 4049

例句 The child went missing, and his parents were devastated.
這名小孩失蹤，他的父母方寸大亂。

搭配詞
go missing 失蹤

mode [mod] n. 款式、模式 Track 4050

例句 We set the game to easy mode.
我們把遊戲調到簡單模式。

modernization [͵mɑdɚnəˋzeʃən] n. 現代化 Track 4051

＊字尾-tion有轉變為名詞的意思

例句 The local people oppose the modernization in their town.
當地人反對他們城市的現代化。

modernize [ˋmɑdɚn͵aɪz] v. 現代化 Track 4052

＊字尾-ize有「化」的意思

例句 They must modernize the equipment in this hospital.
他們必須把這家醫院的器具現代化。

mold [mold] n. 模型 Track 4053

例句 The children in the family seem to be cast in the same mold.
這家的小孩好像都是一個模子印出來的。

搭配詞
be cast in the same mold
屬於同一個類型、有同樣性格

monotonous [məˋnɑtənəs] adj. 單調的 Track 4054

例句 His monotonous tone made me fall asleep.
他單調的聲調讓我睡著了。

反義字
various 形形色色的

monotony [mə`nɑtənɪ] n. 單調 ◀Track 4055

例句 The monotony of his work makes Phil want to quit.
單調的工作讓菲爾想辭職不幹。

反義字 variety 多樣化

monstrous [`mɑnstrəs] adj. 奇怪的、巨大的 ◀Track 4056

＊字尾-ous有轉變為形容詞之意

例句 I dreamt about a monstrous creature last night; it was so scary!
我昨晚夢到一個巨大的怪物，真是可怕啊！

同義字 grotesque

must [mʌst] aux. 必須、必定 ◀Track 4057

例句 You must follow the school rules before you graduate.
你在畢業前必須要遵守校規。

搭配詞 You must be kidding. 你一定是在開玩笑

near [nɪr] ◀Track 4058

adj./adv. 近的、接近的、近親的、親密的

例句 Your house is near his. 你的房子離他的很近。

need [nid] n./v./aux. 需要、必要 ◀Track 4059

例句 We all need friends in our life. 我們生活中都需要朋友。

never [`nɛvɚ] adv. 從來沒有、決不、永不 ◀Track 4060

例句 Never judge a book by its cover. 永遠不要以貌取人。

new [nju] adj. 新的 ◀Track 4061

例句 He likes to try new food. 他喜歡嘗試新食物。

next [nɛkst] adj. 其次的、下一個 ◀Track 4062

例句 We'll have a field trip next week. 我們下禮拜有戶外教學。

搭配詞 next week 下星期

no/nope [no]/[nop] adj./adv./n. 沒有、不、無 ◀Track 4063

例句 I have trouble saying no. 我很難說不。

搭配詞 No kidding. 不騙你。

nod [nɑd] v./n. 點、彎曲 ◀Track 4064

例句 He nodded at me, but I don't think I know who he is.
他對我點頭，但我不覺得我知道他是誰。

oblong [ˋɑblɔŋ] n./adj. 長方形 Track 4065

例句 She wants a round table instead of an oblong one.
她想要一張圓桌而不是一張長方形的桌子。

on [ɑn] Track 4066

prep. （表示地點）在……上、在……的時候、在……狀態中

例句 The view on the top of the mountain is very nice.
山頂上的景觀很好。

搭配詞 put on 穿上

other [ˋʌðɚ] adj. 其他的、另外的 Track 4067

例句 If you have any other requests, please don't hesitate to let us know. 你有什麼其他的要求的話，請不要猶豫，讓我們知道。

搭配詞 each other 互相

outline [ˋaut͵laɪn] n. 外形、輪廓 Track 4068

＊字首out-有「外」之意

例句 It is hard for people to see the outline of these buildings clearly at night time. 晚上人們很難清楚看到這些建築的輪廓。

oval [ˋovl̩] adj./n. 橢圓形的 Track 4069

例句 It seems highly likely that Caviezel will reach the Oval Office.
看來卡維佐入主白宮的機會很高。

搭配詞 Oval Office 橢圓辦公室（白宮裡美國總統的私人辦公室）

over [ˋovɚ] prep. 在……上方、遍及、超過 Track 4070

例句 The pilot flew a small airplane over the Atlantic Ocean.
飛行員駕駛小飛機橫越大西洋。

搭配詞 Over my dead body.
只要我還有一口氣在，就不准那樣做。

overhead [ˋovɚ͵hɛd] Track 4071

adj./adv. 頭頂上的、位於上方的　＊字首over-有「越過、超過」之意

例句 Would you please help me put it in the overhead cabinet?
你可以幫我放到上方的櫥櫃裡嗎？

pale [pel] adj. 蒼白的 Track 4072

例句 Her face was deadly pale because she's sick.
她的臉非常蒼白，因為她生病了。

parallel [ˋpærə͵lɛl] n./adj. 平行線、平行的 Track 4073

例句 These two roads are parallel.
這兩條路是平行線。

part [pɑrt] n. 部分 Track 4074

例句 We'll do our part to maintain regional peace and stability.
我們將盡一份力維持區域和平與穩定。

搭配詞 do one's part 盡本分

particular [pəˋtɪkjələ] adj. 特別的 ◀Track 4075

例句 What in particular do you like about me?
你喜歡我哪一點呢？

搭配詞 in particular 尤其是

pattern [ˋpætən] n. 模型、圖樣 ◀Track 4076

例句 I like flowery patterns for my curtains.
我喜歡我的窗簾有花的圖樣。

同義字 design

peculiar [pɪˋkjuljə] adj. 獨特的、奇怪的 ◀Track 4077

例句 He has his own peculiar way of painting.
他有自己獨特的繪畫方式。

peer [pɪr] v. 偷看 ◀Track 4078

例句 She peered out from behind the curtains.
她從布簾後面偷看出來。

同義字 look

perfection [pəˋfɛkʃən] n. 完美 ◀Track 4079

＊字尾-tion有轉變為名詞的意思

例句 The performance tonight is perfection. 今晚的演出真是完美。

perhaps [pəˋhæps] adv. 也許、可能 ◀Track 4080

例句 Have you looked under the bed? Perhaps it's down there.
你看過床下了嗎？可能在下面呢。

同義字 maybe

perspective [pəˋspɛktɪv] n. 透視、觀點 ◀Track 4081

例句 He gave some feedback from an artistic perspective.
他從一個藝術的觀點提供了意見。

persuasion [pəˋsweʒən] n. 說服 ◀Track 4082

例句 She did not listen to his persuasion. 她沒有被他說服。

反義字 dissuasion 勸阻、規勸

persuasive [pəˋswesɪv] adj. 有說服力的 ◀Track 4083

＊字尾-ive有轉變為形容詞之意

例句 This is a very persuasive speech. Don't you think so?
這是場很有說服力的演講，你不覺得嗎？

pink [pɪŋk] n./adj. 粉紅色、粉紅的 ◀Track 4084

例句 Would you like this pink dress? I think it looks great on you.
妳要不要這件粉紅色的洋裝呢？我覺得在妳身上很好看。

plan [plæn] n./v. 計畫、安排 Track 4085

例句 He has planned the whole event in advance.
他已經先把整個活動計畫好了。

polish [ˋpɑlɪʃ] v./n. 擦亮、潤飾 Track 4086

例句 Ann spent a long time polishing her article before sending it to her professor. 安妮花了很長一段時間潤飾自己的文章，才繳交給教授。

搭配詞 nail polish 指甲油

poor [pur] adj. 貧窮的、可憐的、差的、壞的 Track 4087

例句 Let's bring this poor doggie home and give him some warm milk.
我們把這隻可憐的狗狗帶回家，給牠一點溫牛奶吧。

搭配詞 poor fellow 可憐蟲

popularity [͵pɑpjəˋlærətɪ] n. 名望、流行 Track 4088

例句 He has had a high popularity since his first movie.
自從他的第一部電影以來，他就很有名望。

反義字 unpopularity 不受歡迎

portray [porˋtre] v. 描繪、表現 Track 4089

例句 He portrays a king in his new stage performance.
他在他新的舞台表演中飾演一個國王。

同義字 represent

possible [ˋpɑsəbḷ] adj. 可能的 Track 4090

例句 Please tell me the result as soon as possible.
請盡可能快速告訴我結果。

搭配詞 if possible 如有可能

proper [ˋprɑpɚ] adj. 適當的、合乎禮節的 Track 4091

例句 She is always prim and proper. 她總是拘謹又有禮。

prove [pruv] v. 證明、證實 Track 4092

例句 The evidence you have is enough to prove that he is the criminal.
你持有的證據已經足夠證實他是犯人了。

purity [ˋpjurətɪ] n. 純粹 Track 4093

例句 The writer depicts her as a girl of purity and kindness in the story.
這名作家將她描繪成一個純粹又和善的女孩。

反義字 impurity 不純、不潔

publish [ˋpʌblɪʃ] v. 出版 Track 4094

例句 I believe that this book will be a hit once it is published.
我相信這本書一旦出版，一定會大賣。

publisher [ˋpʌblɪʃɚ] n. 出版者、出版社 Track 4095
＊字尾-er有「者」的意思
例句 He asked the publisher to print his book for him.
他請那個出版社替他印書。

---

pure [pjʊr] adj. 純粹的 Track 4096
例句 The wall is pure white and the ceiling is water blue.
牆壁是純白色的，而天花板是水藍色。

---

purple [ˋpɝpḷ] n./adj. 紫色、紫色的 Track 4097
例句 He was born to the purple, and was a great philanthropist.
他出生於皇室，並且是個偉大的慈善家。

搭配詞
born to the purple
生於王室或顯貴的家庭

---

purpose [ˋpɝpəs] n./v. 目的、意圖 Track 4098
例句 Why did you do this on purpose? 你為什麼故意這麼做？

搭配詞
on purpose 故意地

---

pyramid [ˋpɪrəmɪd] n. 金字塔、角錐 Track 4099
例句 She took several pictures of the pyramid.
她照了許多張金字塔的照片。

---

quite [kwaɪt] adv. 完全地、相當、頗 Track 4100
例句 He learned quite a bit about human anatomy from his father, who was a medical expert.
他從身為醫學專家的父親身上，學到相當多的人類解剖學。

搭配詞
quite a bit 相當多

---

recur [rɪˋkɝ] v. 重現 ＊字首re-有「再次」之意 Track 4101
例句 Jane feels sad when those memories recurred to her.
當這些回憶再度重現，珍妮覺得很傷心。

搭配詞
recur to 再現、重新想起

---

redundant [rɪˋdʌndənt] adj. 過剩的、冗長的 Track 4102
＊字首re-有「再次」之意
例句 He was made redundant after his boss decided to streamline the company's structure. 他的老闆決定精簡公司結構，把他解僱了。

搭配詞
be made redundant
被解僱的、失業的

---

refine [rɪˋfaɪn] v. 精煉、陶冶、完善 Track 4103
＊字首re-有「再次」之意
例句 These jewels are lovely and refined.
這些珠寶很漂亮、很精煉。

同義字
purify

---

reflective [rɪˋflɛktɪv] adj. 反射的、反映的 Track 4104
＊字尾-ive有轉變為形容詞之意
例句 These teenagers' behavior is reflective of their education at home.
這些青少年的表現反映了他們在家受的教育。

resemblance [rɪˋzɛmbləns] n. 類似 Track 4105
例句 I bear a striking resemblance to my dad.
我和爸爸長得很像。

搭配詞
bear resemblance to
與……相像

reasonable [ˋriznəbl̩] adj. 合理的 Track 4106
*字尾-able有「可以、能」的意思
例句 That is a reasonable choice for him to make.
他做那個選擇是很合理的。

反義字
unreasonable 不合理的

rectangle [ˋrɛktæŋgl̩] n. 長方形 Track 4107
例句 Her bag is rectangle-shaped.
她的包包是長方形的。

red [rɛd] n./adj. 紅色、紅的 Track 4108
例句 He was as red as beetroot when he saw her.
他見到她時，滿臉通紅。

搭配詞
as red as beetroot
滿臉通紅

reveal [rɪˋvil] v./n. 揭露、表明 Track 4109
例句 He was revealed to be the criminal.
他被揭露是罪犯。

reverse [rɪˋvɝs] adj./v./n. 顛倒 Track 4110
例句 The book looks at biblical history in reverse.
這本書採倒序法來看聖經的歷史。

搭配詞
in reverse 順序相反、顛倒方向

rim [rɪm] n. 邊緣 Track 4111
例句 There is a pink ribbon on the rim of the girl's hat.
那個女孩的帽緣上有個粉紅色的蝴蝶結。

rip [rɪp] n. 裂口 Track 4112
例句 He doesn't know how to sew up the rip in his sleeve.
他不知道怎麼縫上他袖子的裂口。

round [raʊnd] adj. 圓的、球形的 Track 4113
例句 The chubby boy has some freckles on his round face.
那個胖呼呼的男孩圓臉上有些雀斑。

搭配詞
round face 圓臉

row [ro] n. 排、行、列 Track 4114
例句 There are eleven tables in a row.
一排有十一張桌子。

same [sem] adj./adv. 同樣的 ◀ Track 4115

例句 Nobody likes wars, At the same time, terrorism is spreading to many countries.
沒人喜歡戰爭，於此同時，恐怖主義正持續蔓延至更多國家。

搭配詞 at the same time 同時

---

satisfactory [ˌsætɪsˋfæktərɪ] adj. 令人滿意的 ◀ Track 4116

例句 The result was perfectly satisfactory to the company's CEO.
對公司總經理來説，這個結果很令人滿意。

反義字 unsatisfactory 令人不滿的

---

sector [ˋsɛktɚ] n. 區 ◀ Track 4117

例句 Several sectors in this disk are destroyed.
磁碟裡許多區都損壞了。

---

seem [sim] v. 似乎 ◀ Track 4118

例句 He seems unhappy. What happened?
他似乎不太開心。發生了什麼事？

---

shadow [ˋʃædo] n. 陰暗之處、影子 ◀ Track 4119

例句 The child sat in the shadow, looking scared.
那個小孩坐在陰暗處，看起來很害怕。

搭配詞 in the shadow
在暗處、無臉見人

---

shallow [ˋʃælo] adj. 淺的、膚淺的 ◀ Track 4120

例句 The water is shallow here. 這裡的水很淺。

反義字 deep 深的

---

short [ʃɔrt] adj. 短的、不足的 ◀ Track 4121

例句 The dress is too short. I can see your underwear!
這洋裝太短了。我看得到妳的內褲耶！

---

shrink [ʃrɪŋk] v./n. 收縮、退縮 ◀ Track 4122

例句 Don't put this T-shirt into the drier because it will shrink.
別把這件T恤放進乾衣機，因為會收縮。

---

side [saɪd] n. 邊、旁邊、側面 ◀ Track 4123

例句 He stood by my side in my darkest time.
他在我人生最黑暗時，支持著我。

搭配詞 stand by sb's side
支持某人

---

similar [ˋsɪmələ] adj. 相似的、類似的 ◀ Track 4124

例句 Would you please give us a reply using a similar format?
可以請你用相似的格式回復我們的信嗎？

搭配詞 be similar to 和……相似

similarity [ˌsɪmə`lærətɪ] n. 類似、相似 Track 4125

例句 There are a few similarities between the twins.
這對雙胞胎之間有一些類似的地方。

反義字
difference 差別、差異

simply [`sɪmplɪ] adv. 簡單地、樸實地 Track 4126

例句 To put it simply, we are running out of time.
簡單地說，我們沒時間了。

同義字
easily

sketch [skɛtʃ] n./v. 素描、草圖、概略 Track 4127

例句 He did a quick sketch of the tree.
他快速地素描了這棵樹。

搭配詞
sketch book 寫生簿

slender [`slɛndɚ] adj. 苗條的 Track 4128

例句 She was slender and had beautiful long hair.
她很苗條，有著美麗的長髮。

反義字
fat 肥胖的

slide [slaɪd] v. 滑動 Track 4129

例句 She slid the files over to her colleague.
她把文件滑過去給她的同事。

slim [slɪm] adj. 苗條的 Track 4130

例句 My mother is slim and beautiful.
我的母親又苗條又美麗。

同義字
slender

smooth [smuð] adj./adv. 平滑的 Track 4131

例句 Her skin is silk-smooth and milk-white.
她的皮膚既絲滑又如牛奶般白。

搭配詞
Smooth water runs deep.
深慮之士寡言笑

soft [sɔft] adj. 軟的、柔和的 Track 4132

例句 The once soft touch became a formidable leader.
這個容易說話的人，最後變成了一位可敬的領袖。

搭配詞
soft touch 容易説服的人、容易襲擊的對手

some [sʌm] adj./pron. 某一些的、若干的 Track 4133

例句 I hope we'll meet some day to rekindle our friendship.
希望我們未來某一天有機會再見面，重拾友誼。

搭配詞
some day 某一天

somewhat [`sʌmˌwɑt] adv./pron. 多少、幾分 Track 4134

例句 I think his report is somewhat exaggerated.
我覺得他的報告多少有點誇大了。

sort [sɔrt] n. 種類、樣子 ◀Track 4135

例句 He's not the right sort of guy for you.
他對妳來說不是適合的那種男人。

搭配詞
a sort of 某種的、像……的東西

---

sphere [sfɪr] n. 球、天體 ◀Track 4136

例句 There are nine spheres in the solar system.
太陽系有九個天體。

同義字
ball

---

spiral [ˋspaɪrəl] n./adj. 螺旋、螺旋形之物 ◀Track 4137

例句 The spiral staircase leads to the top.
這些螺旋梯通到頂上。

---

spire [spaɪr] n. 尖塔、尖頂 ◀Track 4138

例句 We can see the spire of that building in the distance.
我們可以看到遠處那棟建築的尖頂。

---

square [skwɛr] ◀Track 4139

adj./n. 公正的、方正的、正方形、廣場

例句 She won the tennis game fair and squre.
她光明正大贏了網球賽。

搭配詞
fair and squre 光明正大

---

straight [stret] adj./adv. 筆直的、正直的 ◀Track 4140

例句 She hated it when people touched her long straight hair.
她討厭人家摸她的長直髮。

---

streak [strik] n. 條紋 ◀Track 4141

例句 There are purple streaks in her hair.
她的頭髮有紫色的條紋。

---

stripe [straɪp] n. 斑紋、條紋 ◀Track 4142

例句 Do you want stripes on your tie?
你想要領帶上有條紋嗎？

搭配詞
wear the stripes 入獄

---

structural [ˋstrʌktʃərəl] adj. 構造的、結構上的 ◀Track 4143

＊字尾-al有轉變為形容詞之意

例句 The earthquake should cause no structural damage.
這次地震應該不會造成結構上的傷害。

---

superiority [səˏpɪrɪˋɔrətɪ] n. 優越、卓越 ◀Track 4144

＊字尾-ity有轉變為名詞的意思

例句 She enjoys rubbing her superiority in others' faces.
她喜歡在他人面前展現出優越。

反義字
inferiority 劣勢、劣等

surface [ˋsɝfɪs] n./adj. 表面、粗淺的 Track 4145

例句 So far, we've only scratched the surface of the possibilities of immunotherapy.
我們對於運用免疫療法的可能性，仍在很粗淺的階段。

搭配詞 scratch the surface 略懂皮毛

symbol [ˋsɪmbḷ] n. 象徵、標誌 Track 4146

例句 What's the chemical symbol for lithium?
鋰的化學符號是什麼？

搭配詞 chemical symbol 化學符號

symbolize [ˋsɪmbḷ͵aɪz] v. 象徵 Track 4147

＊字尾-ize有「化」的意思

例句 Not everyone knows what the Oscar awards symbolize.
不是每個人都知道奧斯卡獎象徵著什麼。

同義字 represent

symmetry [ˋsɪmɪtrɪ] n. 對稱、相稱 Track 4148

例句 Order and symmetry were important elements of beauty.
秩序與對稱是美觀的重要元素。

反義字 assymetry 不對稱

take [tek] v. 抓住、拾起、量出、帶 Track 4149

例句 He took off his raincoat before entering the office.
他進辦公室前把雨衣脱掉了。

搭配詞 take off 脫去

tall [tɔl] adj. 高的 Track 4150

例句 Not every girl is tall enough to become a model.
不是每個女孩都夠高，可以當模特兒。

tan [tæn] n. 日曬後的顏色、棕褐色 Track 4151

例句 She got a lovely tan during the summer.
她在夏天時曬成好看的棕褐色。

搭配詞 get a tan 曬成棕褐色

than [ðæn] conj./prep. 比 Track 4152

例句 Nobody can sign the document other than youself.
沒人能替你簽這張文件，除了你自己。

搭配詞 other than 除了

thing [θɪŋ] n. 東西、物體 Track 4153

例句 All their things were destroyed in the tsunami.
他們所有的東西全被海嘯摧毀了。

tiny [ˋtaɪnɪ] adj. 極小的 Track 4154

例句 There is a tiny mole on his left cheek.
他的左頰有個極小的痣。

反義字 large 大的

together [tə`gɛðɚ] adv. 在一起、緊密地 ◀Track 4155

例句 The boy put together a model plane without reading the instructions.
那個小男孩沒看說明書就組合好一架模型飛機。

搭配詞
put together 組合

too [tu] adv. 也、太 ◀Track 4156

例句 I think it's too early for you to get married.
我覺得你要結婚太早了。

top [tɑp] adj./n. 頂端的、頂部 ◀Track 4157

例句 There are 26 floors in that building, and he lives on the top floor.
這棟大樓有26層樓，他住在頂樓。

total [`totḷ] adj. 全部的、完全的 ◀Track 4158

例句 His experiment ended in total failure.
他的實驗完全失敗了。

toward(s) [tə`wɔrd(z)] ◀Track 4159
prep. 對……、向……、對於……

例句 He strided proudly towards his family.
他驕傲地邁開大步走向他的家人。

trace [tres] v. 追溯、描繪 ◀Track 4160

例句 Our children enjoy tracing pictures.
我們的孩子們喜歡描圖。

transform [træns`fɔrm] v. 改變 ◀Track 4161
＊字首trans-有「穿越、轉變」之意

例句 How about transforming the basement into a guest room?
要不要把地下室改變成客房呢？

triangle [`traɪ,æŋgḷ] n. 三角形 ◀Track 4162
＊字首tri-有「三」之意

例句 Little Janet just learn how to draw triangles and circles.
小珍妮剛學會如何畫三角形和圓形。

try [traɪ] v. 試驗、嘗試 ◀Track 4163

例句 She tried out for Romeo and Juliet held by the drama club.
她參加話劇社辦的羅密歐與茱麗葉選角。

搭配詞
try out 試用、參加選拔

under [`ʌndɚ] prep. 小於、下面 ◀Track 4164

例句 Let's lie down under the tree and take a rest.
我們躺在樹下休息吧。

underline [ˌʌndɚˋlaɪn] v. 畫底線 ◀Track 4165
＊字首under-有「下方的」之意
例句 Please underline the key points in the article.
請在文章中的重點下面畫底線。

upon [əˋpɑn] prep. 在……上面 ◀Track 4166
例句 She put a crown upon the latest Miss Universe.
她把皇冠戴在最新出爐的環球小姐頭上。

upper [ˋʌpɚ] adj. 在上位 ◀Track 4167
例句 Being a member of an upper class family, she married the entrepreneur who was older than her father.
她來自上流社會家庭，嫁給一位比她父親年紀大的企業家。
搭配詞 upper classes 上流社會

utter [ˋʌtɚ] adj. 完全的、極度的 ◀Track 4168
例句 She was in utter surprise when her boyfriend proposed.
她的男友求婚時，她感到十分驚訝。

vacancy [ˋvekənsɪ] n. 空缺、空白 ◀Track 4169
例句 He is the best candidate to fill this vacancy.
他是填補這個空缺的最佳人選。
同義字 emptiness

visual [ˋvɪʒuəl] adj. 視覺的 ◀Track 4170
例句 The program provides comprehensive courses for people considering a career in visual art.
這個計畫提供完整課程，提供想從事視覺藝術的人進修。

white [waɪt] adj./n. 白色的 ◀Track 4171
例句 The chemicals are very effective to control white ants.
這些化學物質對於控制白蟻非常有效。
搭配詞 white ant 白蟻

wreath [riθ] n. 花環、花圈、圈狀物 ◀Track 4172
例句 She laid a wreath at her mother's tomb.
她在母親的墳前放了一個花圈。
同義字 garland

wrong [rɔŋ] adj. 壞的、錯的 ◀Track 4173
例句 Something's wrong with the computer. It seems to have viruses.
電腦好像有什麼地方壞了，好像中毒了。

yellow [ˋjɛlo] adj./n. 黃色的、黃色 ◀Track 4174
例句 I hate to say this, but you have a yellow streak.
我實在很不想說，但你太懦弱了。
搭配詞 a yellow streak 生性怯懦

Test

15 關鍵英單總測驗第15回

以下測驗題皆出自書中第十五回「**和顏色形狀有關的單字**」，快來檢視自己的學習成果吧！

一、選擇題

1. It's difficult to _____ when you're studying near a construction site.
(A) deepen
(B) imitate
(C) concentrate
(D) disguise

2. Please close the _____ compartment and fasten your seat belt before the airplane takes off.
(A) overhead
(B) round
(C) similar
(D) spiral

3. He wants to study overseas to ___ his horizons.
(A) broaden
(B) conceive
(C) focus
(D) browse

4. The purpose of the meeting is to _________ mutual understanding between the two nations.
(A) harden (B) peer
(C) foster (D) recur

5. All the faculty members were made _____ when the school was closed down.
(A) shadow (B) redundant
(C) short (D) coherent

6. The new app can measure blood sugar with _____ .
(A) accuracy
(B) emphatic
(C) characteristic
(D) exaggeration

7. He lives a _____ life without movies, party, or fun.
(A) pale (B) tiny
(C) pink (D) monotonous

8. You can use your mobile _____ to connect to the Internet.
(A) margins
(B) devices
(C) outlines
(D) formats

9. The firefighters showed ________ courage when performing rescue operations on September 11, 2011.
(A) enormous
(B) imaginable
(C) minimal
(D) reflective

10. My family _____ of 5 people—my parents, two elder sisters, and me.
(A) contains
(B) refines
(C) underlines
(D) consists

二、克漏字測驗

Neuschwanstein Castle is one of the most popular tourist destinations in the world. It is an __1__ of a medieval castle. The beautiful __2__ of the architecture instills peace in visitors and viewers alike.

__3__ by the wonderful exterior design and finely-crafted furnishings, the castle was originally a home for the king. Today, it has become a __4__ of Romanticism due to its lavish rooms and __5__ paintings.

1.
(A) imaginary
(B) imitation
(C) inner
(D) miniature

2.
(A) oval
(B) popularity
(C) logo
(D) symmetry

3.
(A) Characterized
(B) Lighten
(C) Revealed
(D) Seemed

4.
(A) frame
(B) symbol
(C) layer
(D) exhibit

5.
(A) beautify
(B) evident
(C) gorgeous
(D) bulky

關鍵英單總測驗第15回
中譯與解答

一、選擇題

1. 在工地附近唸書，是很難集中注意力的。
   (A) 加深
   (B) 模仿
   (C) 集中注意力
   (D) 偽裝

2. 飛機起飛前，請關好上方行李置物櫃並繫好你的安全帶。
   (A) 上方的
   (B) 圓形的
   (C) 相似的
   (D) 螺旋的

3. 他想出國唸書，擴展自己的視野。
   (A) 擴展
   (B) 構想
   (C) 專注
   (D) 瀏覽

4. 這場會議的目的在於培養兩國之間的互相瞭解。
   (A) 硬化
   (B) 偷看
   (C) 培養
   (D) 復發

5. 學校被迫關閉時，所有教職員都失業了。
   (A) 影子
   (B) 多餘的
   (C) 不足的
   (D) 連貫的

6. 這款新的app能精確地測量血糖量。
   (A) 精確
   (B) 強調的
   (C) 特徵
   (D) 誇大

7. 他不看電影、不參加宴會或享樂，過著很單調的生活。
   (A) 蒼白的
   (B) 微小的
   (C) 粉紅色的
   (D) 單調的

8. 你可以使用行動裝置來連接網路。
   (A) 邊緣
   (B) 裝置
   (C) 輪廓
   (D) 格式

9. 消防員在2011年9月11日執行救援行動時，展現無比巨大的勇氣。
   (A) 巨大的
   (B) 可想像的
   (C) 最小的
   (D) 反射的

10. 我家由5個人組成：我父母、2個姊姊和我。
   (A) 包含
   (B) 精煉
   (C) 強調、劃底線
   (D) 由……組成

二、克漏字測驗

新天鵝堡是全球最受觀迎的觀光聖地之一，它是模仿中古世紀城堡的建築，美麗的對稱感為訪客和觀賞者注入一股祥和的氛圍。

這座城堡以絕佳的外觀設計和精緻的家飾著稱，原本是國王的居所。如今因它內部豪華的房間和美麗的藝術畫，而成為浪漫主義的象徵。

1.
(A) 想像的
(B) 模仿
(C) 內部的
(D) 縮影

2.
(A) 橢圓形的
(B) 名望
(C) 商標
(D) 對稱

3.
(A) 以……著稱
(B) 減緩
(C) 顯露
(D) 看起來

4.
(A) 框架
(B) 象徵
(C) 層
(D) 展覽

5.
(A) 美化
(B) 明顯的
(C) 華麗的
(D) 龐大的

一、選擇題

1.(C) 2.(A) 3.(A) 4.(C) 5.(B)
6.(A) 7.(D) 8.(B) 9.(A) 10.(D)

二、克漏字測驗

1.(B) 2.(D) 3.(A)
4.(B) 5.(C)

Unit 16 和工具有關的單字

多益測驗的命題強調生活化與實用性，學會這些與「工具」有關的單字，不僅能讓你在多益考場上所向披靡，在日常生活上也可以靈活運用喔！

去逛五金行可以這麼說

- **That old apartment has a lot of things to be fixed.**
  那棟老舊公寓有很多東西待修理。
- **We need to go buying some hardware first.**
  我們得先去買五金用品。
- **Do they sell door knobs?**
  他們有賣圓形門把手嗎？

裝修房子可以這麼說

- **In the end, we decided to modify the whole apartment.**
  最後，我們決定修改整間公寓。
- **First, we need to renew the old electric wiring.**
  首先，我們要翻新老舊的電線線路。

運動用品可以這麼說

- **The blade of a figure skate has two edges, the outer edge and the inner edge.**
  花式滑冰用的冰刀有兩個刀刃，外側刀刃與內側刀刃。
- **The arrow didn't even touch the archery target.**
  那支箭連箭靶都沒碰到。

生活中的裝飾品可以這麼說

- **She used some colorful wrapping paper to decorate the cabinet.**
  她用鮮豔的包裝紙來裝飾廚櫃。
- **She drilled a hole on the wall to hang the poster.**
  她在牆上鑽了一個洞來掛海報。

安裝軟體可以這麼說

- **This new filter makes you look like someone else.**
  這個新濾鏡讓你看起來不像自己了。
- **You can install this App on your cell phone.**
  你可以在你的手機上安裝這個應用程式。

Unit 16 和工具有關的單字

accelerate [æk`sɛlə͵ret] v. 促進、加速進行 Track 4175

例句 She accelerated hard to catch up with the car she was following.
她用力加速以追上她正在尾隨的那台車。

反義字 decelerate 使減速

---

acceleration [æk͵sɛlə`reʃən] n. 加速、促進 Track 4176

＊字尾-tion有轉變為名詞的意思

例句 The teacher taught us how to calculate the acceleration of gravity.
老師教我們如何計算重力加速度。

搭配詞 acceleration of gravity 重力加速度

---

accessory [æk`sɛsərɪ] n. 附件、零件 Track 4177

例句 Would you please ask her to buy some accessories for me?
你可以請她幫我買一些零件嗎？

同義字 addition

---

advertisement [͵ædvɚ`taɪzmənt] n. 廣告 Track 4178

＊字尾-ment有轉變為名詞之意

例句 Do you like the new advertisement on television?
你喜歡電視上的新廣告嗎？

同義字 announcement

---

amplify [`æmplə͵faɪ] v. 擴大、放大、詳述 Track 4179

＊字尾-ify有「化」的意思

例句 This machine can be used to amplify sound.
這個機器可以用來擴大聲音。

同義字 increase

---

antenna [æn`tɛnə] n. 觸角、觸鬚、天線 Track 4180

例句 There is an antenna on the back of the car.
車子後面有一根天線。

---

arrow [`æro] n. 箭 Track 4181

例句 Do you know how to shoot an arrow?
你知道怎麼射箭嗎？

搭配詞 shoot an arrow 射箭

---

available [ə`veləbḷ] Track 4182

adj. 可利用的、可取得的、有空的 ＊字尾-able有「可以、能」的意思

例句 My boss is not available this week.
我老闆這週沒有空。

反義字 unavailable 無法利用的、得不到的

ax/axe [æks] n. 斧 Track 4183

例句 George got the axe for negligence of duty.
喬治因怠忽職守，而被解雇。

搭配詞 get the axe 被解雇、被開除

backpack [ˋbæk͵pæk] n. 背包 Track 4184

例句 He always goes to school with a backpack and lunch box.
他總是帶著背包和餐盒去上學。

bang [bæŋ] v./n. 重擊 Track 4185

例句 I heard a bang against the window and saw a sparrow lying on the ground. 我聽到窗戶有重擊聲，後來看到有隻麻雀躺在地上。

搭配詞 bang against 猛擊

bar [bɑr] n. 條、棒、橫木、酒吧 Track 4186

例句 The serial killer was finally put behind the bars.
那個罪犯最後終於坐牢了。

搭配詞 behind bars 坐牢

barrel [ˋbærəl] n. 大桶 Track 4187

例句 Johnny is a barrel of laughs.
強尼是個開心果。

搭配詞 a barrel of laughs 開心果

basin [ˋbesn̩] n. 盆、水盆 Track 4188

例句 She filled the basin with water so she could wash her underwear.
她在盆裡裝滿水，用來洗內褲。

同義字 tub

batter [ˋbætɚ] v. 連擊、重擊 Track 4189

例句 The plane was battered after the storm.
這台飛機在暴風雨中被連擊得很殘破。

bazaar [bəˋzɑr] n. 市場、義賣會 Track 4190

例句 There are many flavors of cheese for sale at the bazaar.
在市場可以買到很多不同口味的乳酪。

binoculars [baɪˋnɑkjələz] n. 雙筒望遠鏡 Track 4191

＊字尾-s有轉變為複數之意

例句 He bought a pair of binoculars for his son as his birthday present.
他買了一副雙筒望遠鏡給兒子當生日禮物。

blade [bled] n. 刀鋒、刀身 Track 4192

例句 She used the blade to cut herself.
她用刀鋒割自己。

blend [blɛnd] v./n. 使混合、使交融、混合物 Track 4193

例句 The family just moved to this community and tried to blend in with their neighbors.
這家人剛搬進這個社區，並試著融入他們鄰居的生活。

搭配詞 blend in 融入（某團體）

brass [bræs] n. 黃銅、銅器 Track 4194

例句 There was a brass statue at the door.
門口有一座黃銅雕像。

breakdown [ˋbrekˏdaʊn] n. 故障、崩潰 Track 4195

例句 He had a mental breakdown after the traumatic experience.
他經歷創痛的經驗後，精神崩潰了。

同義字 collapse

breakthrough [ˋbrekˏθru] n. 突破 Track 4196

例句 I hope scientists will have a major breakthrough in the treatment of cancer. 我希望科學家在癌症的治療上，會有重大的突破。

搭配詞 have a breakthrough 有所突破

bruise [bruz] n./v. 青腫、瘀傷 Track 4197

例句 I have a few cuts and bruises after I came back from the bicycle trip. 我從腳踏車之旅回來後，有幾處割傷與瘀傷。

同義字 wound

brush [brʌʃ] n. 刷子 Track 4198

例句 Tom is a nice guy, but he's as daft as a brush.
湯姆是個好人，就是太蠢了。

搭配詞 be (as) daft as a brush 非常愚蠢

bucket [ˋbʌkɪt] n. 水桶、提桶 Track 4199

例句 The drug lord kicked the bucket last night for unknown reason.
那個毒梟昨晚翹辮子了，原因不明。

搭配詞 kick the bucket 翹辮子

bulb [bʌlb] n. 電燈泡 Track 4200

例句 The light bulb just burned out; we need to buy a new one.
這燈泡燒壞了，我們得去買一個新的。

搭配詞 light bulb 燈泡

bulge [bʌldʒ] n./v. 腫脹、突出 Track 4201

例句 Her impeccable look helps her get the bulge in the modeling industry. 她無瑕的外貌，讓她在模特兒界佔盡優勢。

搭配詞 get the bulge on 佔優勢、佔上風

bully [ˋbʊlɪ] n. 暴徒、霸凌 Track 4202

例句 The schoolyard bully came from a problem family.
這個學校的霸凌者，來自一個問題家庭。

搭配詞 schoolyard bully 學校霸凌者

calculator [ˋkælkjə͵letɚ] n. 計算機 Track 4203
＊字尾-or有「者」的意思
例句 Would she want a calculator as a birthday gift?
她會想要計算機當生日禮物嗎？

can [kæn] v./n. 裝罐、罐頭、桶 Track 4204
例句 The trash can is full to the brim.
垃圾桶已經滿出來了。
搭配詞 trash can 垃圾桶

cane [ken] n. 手杖、棒 Track 4205
例句 Sarah tried to sell sugar canes from door to door to raise money for the sick old man.
莎拉挨家挨戶賣枴杖糖，幫忙募款給那位年邁生病的老人。
搭配詞 sugar cane 枴杖糖

cap [kæp] n. 帽子、蓋子 Track 4206
例句 He wore his cap backwards to look cool.
他把帽子反著戴，以看起來很酷。

capability [͵kepəˋbɪlətɪ] n. 能力 Track 4207
例句 He doesn't have the capability to run a company.
他沒有開公司的能力。
同義字 ability

certain [ˋsɝtən] adj. 一定的、特定的 Track 4208
例句 He couldn't tell for certain if he could finish the task before the deadline. 他無法確定是否可以在期限前完成這項工作。
搭配詞 for certain 無疑的

chain [tʃen] n. 鏈子 Track 4209
例句 You shouldn't use a chain to tie up your dog.
你不應該用鏈子來綁狗。

charcoal [ˋtʃɑr͵kol] n. 炭、木炭 Track 4210
例句 Would you please help me take out the charcoal from the trunk?
你可以幫我從後車廂把木炭拿出來嗎？

check [tʃɛk] n./v. 檢查、支票 Track 4211
例句 You might need to check out your oven.
你可能要檢查一下你的烤箱。
搭配詞 check out 檢查

chop [tʃɑp] v./n. 砍、劈 Track 4212
例句 The firefighter chopped the branches off the tree nearby a window to rescue people trapped inside the house.
消防員把靠窗的樹枝砍掉，以便救出被困在屋內的人。
搭配詞 chop off 砍掉

clamp [klæmp] n. 夾子、鉗子 ◀Track 4213

例句 You will need a clamp and a hammer.
你會需要夾子和鎚子。

同義字 clasp

---

clarify [ˋklærə͵faɪ] v. 澄清、變得明晰 ◀Track 4214

＊字尾-ify有「化」的意思

例句 I hope I did clarify the president's statement at the press conference.
我希望我在記者會中有把總統的聲明稿澄清地很明晰。

同義字 explain

---

clench [klɛntʃ] v./n. 緊握 ◀Track 4215

例句 I clenched my fists in anger.
我氣得緊握拳頭。

搭配詞 clench one's fists 緊握拳頭

---

clip [klɪp] n./v. 夾子、紙夾、修剪 ◀Track 4216

例句 Please keep these forms together with a paper clip.
請用夾子把這些文件夾在一起。

---

clutch [klʌtʃ] v./n. 抓握 ◀Track 4217

例句 She clutched the ticket to the zoo in her hand.
她在手中抓著動物園的門票。

---

collector [kəˋlɛktɚ] n. 收集的器具、收藏家 ◀Track 4218

＊字尾-or有「者」的意思

例句 The pop star launched a collection's edition perfume named Déjà Vu. 那位流行歌星推出了一款收藏版的香水，名為「似曾相識」。

搭配詞 collector's edition 收藏家的版本

---

collide [kəˋlaɪd] v. 相撞 ◀Track 4219

例句 It is reported that the bus collided with a bicycle when rounding the corner. 據報導，那台公車在轉彎時和腳踏車相撞了。

同義字 conflict

---

collision [kəˋlɪʒən] n. 相撞、碰撞、撞擊 ◀Track 4220

例句 The measure comes into collision with public interests.
這項措施和公眾利益起了衝突。

搭配詞 come into collision with 和……衝突

---

consult [kənˋsʌlt] v. 請教、諮詢 ◀Track 4221

例句 It would be good if you consult him first.
如果你先找他諮詢會比較好。

---

consumer [kənˋsumɚ] n. 消費者 ◀Track 4222

＊字尾-er有「者」的意思

例句 He spent a lot of time conducting consumer research.
他花很多時間做消費者調查。

搭配詞 consumer research 市場調查

container [kən`tenɚ] n. 容器 Track 4223
＊字尾-er有「者」的意思
例句 Plastic containers are light and convenient but environmentally unfriendly. 塑膠容器很輕便，但對環境不友善。
搭配詞 plastic container 塑膠容器

contribute [kən`trɪbjut] v. 貢獻 Track 4224
例句 Inventor of the World Wide Web, Sir Tim Berners-Lee, has contributed to innovating information technology and communications. 提姆・柏納-李爵士發明了網際網路，對資通訊科技做出創新的貢獻。
搭配詞 contribute to 捐助、幫助

cooperate [ko`ɑpə͵ret] v. 協力、合作 Track 4225
例句 We need to cooperate to ensure the success of this project. 我們要合作才能確保這個計畫能成功。
同義字 collaborate

cooperation [ko͵ɑpə`reʃən] n. 合作、協力 Track 4226
＊字尾-tion有轉變為名詞的意思
例句 In cooperation with a science research center, students are able to experience the differences of temperatures between a smart window and a regular one. 我們和科學研究中心合作，讓學生能體驗智能窗戶和一般窗戶溫控的不同。
搭配詞 in cooperation with 和……合作

cope [kop] v. 處理、對付 Track 4227
例句 I don't know how to cope with the news of my sister's death. 我不知道如何應對我妹妹過世的新聞。
搭配詞 cope with 處理

cork [kɔrk] n. 軟木塞 Track 4228
例句 The cork flew off with a pop. 軟木塞啪的一聲飛出去了。
同義字 plug

correspond [͵kɔrə`spɑnd] v. 符合、相當 Track 4229
例句 The suspect's story didn't correspond with his wife's version. 嫌犯的陳述和他太太所說的不相符。
搭配詞 correspond with 相符

counter [`kaʊntɚ] n. 櫃檯、計算機 Track 4230
例句 They bought the prescription drugs under the counter. 他們非法買進處方藥。
搭配詞 under the counter 祕密地、非法地

crack [kræk] n. 裂縫、瑕疵 Track 4231
例句 The earthquake made some cracks in the wall. 地震讓牆上出現一些裂縫。

crane [kren] n. 起重機 Track 4232
例句 We need a crane to fix this house. 我們需要起重機來修理這棟房子。

creak [krik] n. 輾軋聲 Track 4233

例句 Why are the stairs always creaking?
樓梯怎麼老是發出輾軋聲呢？

crouch [krautʃ] v./n. 蹲伏、屈膝姿勢 Track 4234

例句 She crouched down on the floor, looking for the cat.
她蹲在地上找貓。

同義字 squat

crush [krʌʃ] v./n. 毀壞、壓榨 Track 4235

例句 She crushed the lemon to get lemon juice.
她壓榨檸檬以得到檸檬汁。

crutch [krʌtʃ] n. 支架、枴杖 Track 4236

例句 My brother broke his leg, so he needs a pair of crutches.
我哥哥腿摔斷了，所以他需要一副枴杖。

搭配詞 Good news goes on crutches; ill news flies apace. 好事不出門，壞事傳千里。

curb [kɝb] n. 抑制器、抑制 Track 4237

例句 They placed a curb on expenditures because they didn't have enough funds. 他們抑制花費，因為沒有足夠的資金。

cut [kʌt] v. 切、割、剪、砍、削、刪 Track 4238

例句 If you cut the electricity, people will be complaining.
如果你切斷電源，大家都會抗議的。

dart [dɑrt] n./v. 鏢、鏢槍、猛衝 Track 4239

例句 My dog darted to the door suddenly because he saw my mom.
我的狗突然猛衝到門口，因為牠看到了我的媽媽。

同義字 dash

destroy [dɪ`strɔɪ] v. 損毀、毀壞 Track 4240

例句 The typhoon destroyed his new tree house.
颱風把他的新樹屋毀壞了。

destruction [dɪ`strʌkʃən] n. 破壞、毀滅 Track 4241

＊字尾-tion有轉變為名詞的意思

例句 His wild ambition will lead him to his destruction one day.
他瘋狂的企圖心會讓他哪天面臨毀滅。

同義字 demolition

diagnose [`daɪəgnoz] v. 診斷 Track 4242

例句 He is diagnosed with a rare disease.
他被診斷出罕見疾病。

同義字 analyze

diversity [də`vɝsətɪ] n. 差異處、不同點、多樣性 Track 4243
＊字首di-有「二」之意
例句 New York is a city full of cultural diversity.
紐約是個多元文化的都市。
搭配詞 cultural diversity 多元文化

diversion [də`vɝʒən] Track 4244
n. 脫離、轉向、令人分心的事物 ＊字首di-有「二」之意
例句 I will make a diversion so that you can escape.
我會製造讓他們分心的事，好讓你可以逃跑。
同義字 deflection

divert [də`vɝt] v. 使轉向、轉移 Track 4245
＊字首di-有「二」之意
例句 How about using these toys to divert the children's attention?
用這些玩具來轉移孩子們的注意力如何呢？

dial [`daɪəl] n. 刻度盤 Track 4246
例句 He checked the speed dial.
他看了一下速度刻度盤。

diary [`daɪərɪ] n. 日誌、日記本 Track 4247
例句 She kept a diary for many years.
她寫了許多年的日記。
搭配詞 keep a diary 寫日記

dictionary [`dɪkʃən,ɛrɪ] n. 字典、詞典 Track 4248
例句 If you have any questions about vocabulary, ask Elon. He's a walking dictionary.
如果你有任何字彙的問題，問伊隆吧，他是活字典。
搭配詞 walking dictionary 活字典

dig [dɪg] v. 挖、挖掘 Track 4249
例句 The dog dug out a time capsule from the ground.
我家狗狗挖出一個時空膠囊。
搭配詞 dig out 發掘出、挖掘

digest [daɪ`dʒɛst]/[`daɪdʒɛst] v./n. 瞭解、消化、摘要 Track 4250
例句 We need some time to digest the knowledge we learned.
我們需要一些時間消化學到的知識。
同義字 absorb

digestion [də`dʒɛstʃən] n. 領會、領悟、消化 Track 4251
＊字尾-tion有轉變為名詞的意思
例句 I heard that this kind of tea acts as an aid to digestion.
我聽說這種茶對消化有幫助。
反義字 indigestion 消化不良

dip [dɪp] v./n. 浸、沾 Track 4252
例句 Don't try to dip your finger into unknown liquids.
別把你的手指浸到未知的液體中。

dismantle [dɪsˋmæntḷ] **v.** 拆開、分解、扯下 Track 4253
＊字首dis-有「不」之意
例句 Please help me dismantle the faulty machine.
請幫我拆開壞掉的機器吧。

同義字 disassemble

dispensable [dɪˋspɛnsəbḷ] **adj.** 非必要的 Track 4254
＊字首dis-有「不」之意
例句 She doesn't have too much dispensable income to spend on luxury goods. 她沒有太多可支配所得，來買奢侈品。

反義字 indispensable 必要的

disperse [dɪˋspɝs] **v.** 使散開、驅散 Track 4255
＊字首dis-有「不」之意
例句 The police used tear gas to disperse the mob.
警察用催淚瓦斯來驅散滋事民眾。

反義字 collect 使集合

disposal [dɪˋspozḷ] **n.** 分佈、配置 Track 4256
＊字首dis-有「不」之意
例句 The real estate tycoon has five butlers at his disposal.
這個房地產大亨有5個管家隨時伺候他。

搭配詞 at sb's disposal 供任意使用

dissolve [dɪˋzɑlv] **v.** 使溶解 Track 4257
＊字首dis-有「不」之意
例句 You have to dissolve the tablet in warm water first.
你得先把那片藥用熱水溶解。

同義字 melt

distort [dɪsˋtɔrt] **v.** 曲解、扭曲 Track 4258
＊字首dis-有「不」之意
例句 His face was distorted with rage when he learned the truth.
他得知事實時，臉都因憤怒而扭曲了。

同義字 twist

dispense [dɪˋspɛns] **v.** 分送、處理掉、免除 Track 4259
＊字首dis-有「不」之意
例句 I'm afraid that we'll have to dispense with our house.
我們恐怕得把房子處理掉了。

搭配詞 dispense with 用不著、擺脫、處理掉

dispose [dɪˋspoz] **v.** 佈置、處理 Track 4260
＊字首dis-有「不」之意
例句 He doesn't know how to dispose of his old apartment.
他不知道怎麼處理他的舊套房。

搭配詞 dispose of 去除（或處理、捨棄）某人／某物

distinction [dɪˋstɪŋkʃən] **n.** 區別、辨別 Track 4261
＊字尾-tion有轉變為名詞的意思
例句 You should treat your children without distinction.
你必須無區別地對待你的孩子。

distinctive [dɪˋstɪŋktɪv] **adj.** 與眾不同的 Track 4262
＊字尾-ive有轉變為形容詞之意
例句 The designer has a very distinctive style.
這個設計師有個與眾不同的風格。

同義字 individual

drill [drɪl] n./v. 鑽、錐 Track 4263

例句 No names, no pack drill, but some high-ranking managers have used company profits to fund personal trips.
姑隱其名，但有些高階經理人動用公司獲利，支付個人旅遊費。

搭配詞 no names, no pack drill 姑隱其名

dumb [dʌm] adj. 啞的、笨的 Track 4264

例句 A dumb show is performed in pantomime.
默劇是用無聲的方式演出。

搭配詞 dumb show 默劇、做手勢

dump [dʌmp] v. 拋棄、放棄、捨棄 Track 4265

例句 He shirked all his responsibilities and dumped the problem in the newcomer's lap.
他把責任推得一乾二淨，把問題推給了新進人員。

搭配詞 dump sth in sb's lap 將某事推給他人負責

earnest [ˋɝnɪst] adj. 認真的 Track 4266

例句 He sent me a present and a handmade card to express his earnest apology. 他給了我一個禮物和一張手工卡片以表示他認真的道歉。

equip [ɪˋkwɪp] v. 裝備 Track 4267

例句 The gym is equipped with treadmills, dumb-bells, and punching bags. 這間健身中心配備齊全，有跑步機、啞鈴、沙包。

搭配詞 equip with 給……配備、給……裝備

excuse [ɪkˋskjuz] n. 藉口 Track 4268

例句 It's easy to make excuses when you don't want to do something.
不想做某件事時，找藉口很容易。

execute [ˋɛksɪ͵kjut] v. 實行 Track 4269

例句 They met some difficulties when executing the new policy.
他們在實行新規範時遇到了一些困難。

同義字 do

exist [ɪgˋzɪst] v. 存在 Track 4270

例句 I don't know if aliens exist or not.
我不知道外星人到底存不存在。

同義字 live

experimental [ɪk͵spɛrəˋmɛntḷ] adj. 實驗性的 Track 4271

＊字尾-al有轉變為形容詞之意

例句 Two patients received an experimental treatment during the outbreak of the epidemic. 這個傳染病爆發時，有兩位病患接受實驗性治療。

同義字 exploratory

explore [ɪkˋsplor] v. 探查、探險、探究 Track 4272

＊字首ex-有「外」的意思

例句 His dream is to explore the world. 他的夢想是到全世界探險。

同義字 search

expose [ɪk`spoz] v. 暴露、揭發 ◀Track 4273
＊字首ex-有「外」的意思
例句 She did not like to expose herself to the sun.
她不喜歡暴露在陽光下。
搭配詞 expose to 暴露於、使遭受

exposure [ɪk`spoʒɚ] n. 顯露、暴露 ◀Track 4274
＊字首ex-有「外」的意思
例句 The exposure of the body under chemical substances can be harmful. 身體暴露在化學物質之下，可能是有害的。
同義字 disclosure

extra [`ɛkstrə] adj./adv. 額外的 ◀Track 4275
＊字首ex-有「外」的意思
例句 Would you like to have extra whipped cream?
你要不要額外的鮮奶油呢？
同義字 additional

facility [fə`sɪlətɪ] n. 容易、靈巧、能力 ◀Track 4276
例句 She learned six languages with facility.
她輕而易舉學會6種語言。
搭配詞 with facility 輕而易舉

fair [fɛr] adj./adv. 公平的、合理的 ◀Track 4277
例句 Dad wants us to study hard, which is fair enough, but can we relax during the weekend? 老爸要我們用功唸書，這很合理，但是我們週末時可以放鬆一下嗎?
搭配詞 fair enough 有道理

filter [`fɪltɚ] n. 過濾器 ◀Track 4278
例句 Can we buy a new air filter? The old one is not working.
我們可以買個新的空氣過濾器嗎？舊的壞了。
搭配詞 air filter 空氣過濾器

fireproof [`faɪr͵pruf] adj. 耐火的、防火的 ◀Track 4279
＊字尾-proof有「防」的意思
例句 There is nothing that can make the house completely fireproof.
沒有什麼能讓房子完全防火。

fix [fɪks] v. 使穩固、修理 ◀Track 4280
例句 Dad will fix up the tree house before spring.
老爸會在春天來臨前把樹屋修好。
搭配詞 fix up 修理好、修補

flaw [flɔ] n. 瑕疵、缺陷 ◀Track 4281
例句 There is a flaw in this painting.
這幅畫有瑕疵。
同義字 defect

flick [flɪk] n./v. 輕打聲、彈開 ◀Track 4282
例句 The girl flicked the dust off her clothes with her fingers.
那個女孩用手指彈開衣服上的灰塵。
搭配詞 flick off 彈掉、抖掉

fling [flɪŋ] v. 扔投、猛衝 Track 4283

例句 He flung his backpack on his bed.
他把背包扔到床上。

foil [fɔɪl] n. 箔片、鋁箔紙、襯托、陪襯物 Track 4284

例句 Let's put the chicken in foil and send it into the oven.
我們把雞包到鋁箔紙裡，放進烤箱吧。

formulate [ˋfɔrmjə͵let] Track 4285
v. 明確地陳述、用公式表示

例句 He formulated his idea clearly so that his boss would approve.
他明確地陳述自己的主意，好讓老闆同意。

同義字
define

forsake [fəˋsek] v. 拋棄、放棄、捨棄 Track 4286

例句 He forsook his wife and children.
他拋棄了太太和孩子。

反義字
protect 保護

foul [faʊl] v. 使污穢、弄髒、使堵塞 Track 4287

例句 Grease has fouled this drain.
這個排水口被油污堵塞了。

foundation [faʊnˋdeʃən] n. 基礎、根基 Track 4288
＊字尾-tion有轉變為名詞的意思

例句 The sudden death of her husband shook the foundations of her belief. 她的丈夫驟逝，使她原本的信仰動搖了。

搭配詞
shake the foundations of (sth) 使人原本的信念動搖

friction [ˋfrɪkʃən] n. 摩擦、衝突 Track 4289
＊字尾-tion有轉變為名詞的意思

例句 The constant friction wore out the handles of my bag.
長期摩擦把我包包的提把給損壞了。

fulfill [fʊlˋfɪl] v. 實踐、實現、履行 Track 4290

例句 She fulfilled herself as an actress.
身為女演員，她充分發揮了自己的天份。

搭配詞
fulfil oneself 完全實現自己的抱負、充分發揮自己的才能

functional [ˋfʌŋkʃənl̩] adj. 作用的、機能的 Track 4291
＊字尾-al有轉變為形容詞之意

例句 These replacement machines are not functional either.
這些替代的機器也沒有作用。

fuse [fjuz] n. 保險絲、熔線 Track 4292

例句 She knows how to mend a fuse.
她知道怎麼修理保險絲。

glue [glu] n. 膠水、黏膠 Track 4293

例句 Would you please buy a bottle of glue for me in the stationery shop?
你可以在文具店幫我買一瓶膠水嗎？

同義字 paste

grind [graɪnd] v./n. 研磨、碾 Track 4294

例句 Some people grind their teeth during sleep.
有些人睡覺會磨牙。

搭配詞 grind one's teeth 咬牙切齒

grip [grɪp] v./n. 緊握、抓住、掌握 Track 4295

例句 He lost his grip when he found that his girlfriend left him for good.
他發現女友永遠離開他，而失控了。

搭配詞 lose one's grip 失勢、失控

hack [hæk] v. 割、劈、砍 Track 4296

例句 They hacked away at the bushes that are blocking the road.
他們著手劈開擋路的樹叢。

hammer [ˋhæmɚ] n. 鐵鎚 Track 4297

例句 You can find some nails and a hammer in the second drawer.
你可以在第二個抽屜找到一些釘子和一個鎚子。

handicap [ˋhændɪˏkæp] Track 4298

v./n. 使不利；障礙、吃虧、殘疾

例句 He was handicapped due to congenital disease.
他因為天生疾病，而成為殘疾人士。

handicraft [ˋhændɪˏkræft] n. 手工藝品 Track 4299

例句 He has been deeply interested in handicrafts recently.
他最近對手工藝品很有興趣。

handle [ˋhændl̩] n. 把手 Track 4300

例句 Our boss flew off the handle this morning when he learned that the company's profits have dropped significantly.
我們的老闆早上得知公司獲利大減，而發飆了。

搭配詞 fly off the handle 勃然大怒

hardship [ˋhɑrdʃɪp] n. 艱難、辛苦 Track 4301

例句 It is obvious that your grandmother suffered too many hardships in the past. 明顯地你的奶奶在過去歷經很多艱難的事。

同義字 trouble

hardware [ˋhɑrdˏwɛr] n. 五金用品 Track 4302

例句 They have shown a strong interest in your hardware.
他們對你的五金用品表現出明顯的興趣。

同義字 metalware

harness [ˋhɑrnɪs] n. 馬具 Track 4303

例句 Right after a business trip, he was back in harness.
他出差一回來，又立刻上工了。

搭配詞
in harness 在工作中

haul [hɔl] v./n. 用力拖拉、一次獲得的量 Track 4304

例句 A truck hauled my car away.
一台卡車把我的車拖走了。

heater [ˋhitɚ] n. 電熱器 Track 4305

＊字尾-er有「者」的意思

例句 The house is equipped with a heater, hot water, and a little kitchen.
這個房子有電熱器、熱水和一個小廚房。

反義字
cooler 冷卻器

hole [hol] n. 孔、洞 Track 4306

例句 After losing all his money in the stock market, he found himself in a hole. 他在股市中賠掉所有的錢以後，陷入了困境。

搭配詞
in a hole 處於困境

hood [hud] n. 罩、蓋、連衣帽 Track 4307

例句 Take off your hood and wash your face.
把連衣帽拿下來，去洗臉吧。

同義字
cover

hose [hoz] n. 水管 Track 4308

例句 The firemen need to make sure they have enough fire hoses to put out the big fire.
消防員們必須確定他們有足夠的水管以滅掉大火。

同義字
pipe

hover [ˋhʌvɚ] v./n. 徘徊、翱翔 Track 4309

例句 The helicopter hovered around the area.
那台直昇機在那一區徘徊。

同義字
flit

hurl [hɝl] v./n. 投 Track 4310

例句 He hurled the ball at his friend.
他把球投向他的朋友。

illuminate [ɪˋluməˏnet] v. 照明、點亮、啟發 Track 4311

例句 A lovely smile illuminated her face.
一個可愛的笑容照亮了她的臉。

同義字
light

inform [ɪnˋfɔrm] v. 通知、報告 Track 4312

例句 Do you mind if I inform him of the good news now?
你介意我現在通知他好消息嗎？

搭配詞
inform sb of sth
把某事通知某人

ink [ɪŋk] n. 墨水、墨汁 Track 4313

例句 Will you please correct the mistakes in the article with red ink?
你可以用紅色墨水字來標示並矯正文章裡的錯誤嗎？

input [ˋɪn͵put] n. 輸入 ＊字首in-有「裡」的意思 Track 4314

例句 Our input system is different from yours.
我們的輸入法系統和你們的不同。

insert [ɪnˋsɝt] v. 插入 ＊字首in-有「裡」的意思 Track 4315

例句 They had to insert another chapter into the book.
他們得插入另一章到書裡。

同義字
introduce

install [ɪnˋstɔl] v. 安裝、裝置 Track 4316
＊字首in-有「裡」的意思

例句 My father is going to install a new air-conditioner in our room.
我爸打算要在我們的房間裡安裝一台新的冷氣。

installation [͵ɪnstəˋleʃən] n. 就任、裝置 Track 4317
＊字尾-tion有轉變為名詞的意思

例句 The installation of the telephone in our room will take less than an hour. 在我們房間裡裝置電話只需要花不到一個小時。

instinct [ˋɪnstɪŋkt] n. 本能、直覺 Track 4318
＊字首in-有「裡」的意思

例句 You should always trust your instinct and do what you think is right.
你應該總是相信自己的直覺，做自己覺得對的事。

integrate [ˋɪntə͵gret] v. 整合 Track 4319
＊字首in-有「裡」的意思

例句 I want to integrate his ideas into our plan.
我想把他的主意融合到我們的計畫中。

搭配詞
integrate into 融合

interact [͵ɪntəˋrækt] v. 交互作用、互動 Track 4320
＊字首inter-有「互相」的意思

例句 My teacher always encourages us to interact in class in English.
我老師總是鼓勵我們上課時用英語互動。

interaction [͵ɪntəˋækʃən] n. 交互影響、互動 Track 4321
＊字尾-tion有轉變為名詞的意思

例句 Their interaction is awkward. 他們互動得很尷尬。

interfere [͵ɪntəˋfɪr] v. 妨礙 Track 4322
＊字首inter-有「互相」的意思

例句 It would be better if he didn't interfere with my plan.
他不妨礙我的計畫會比較好。

搭配詞
interfere with 妨礙

intermediate [ˌɪntəˋmidɪət] adj. 中間的、中級的 Track 4323
例句 Not every student in our class passed the intermediate level exam held by the language center.
班上不是每個學生都通過語言中心舉辦的中級測驗。
同義字 middle

interruption [ˌɪntəˋrʌpʃən] Track 4324
n. 中斷、妨礙 ＊字尾-tion有轉變為名詞的意思
例句 Stop making interruptions in class. 別打斷大家上課。

intonation [ˌɪntoˋneʃən] n. 語調、吟詠 Track 4325
＊字尾-tion有轉變為名詞的意思
例句 He spends much time perfecting his pronunciation and intonation.
他花很多時間讓他的發音與語調完美。

investigation [ɪnˌvɛstəˋgeʃən] n. 調查 Track 4326
＊字尾-tion有轉變為名詞的意思
例句 Would you please take over my investigation?
你可以接手我的調查嗎？
同義字 inspection

involve [ɪnˋvɑlv] v. 牽涉、包括 Track 4327
例句 He was somehow involved in the crime.
他不知為何地牽涉到這項犯罪。
搭配詞 be involved in 關心、熱心、涉及、加入、參加、被牽連

involvement [ɪnˋvɑlvmənt] n. 涉入、連累 Track 4328
＊字尾-ment有轉變為名詞之意
例句 He is convinced that his parents' involvement will ruin their relationship. 他很確定他父母一涉入，就會毀了這段感情。

isolate [ˋaɪsḷˌet] v. 孤立、隔離 Track 4329
例句 He felt very isolated from his peers.
他覺得被同儕孤立了。
同義字 separate

isolation [ˌaɪsḷˋeʃən] n. 分離、孤獨 Track 4330
＊字尾-tion有轉變為名詞的意思
例句 It is impossible for any country to develop in isolation.
任何國家都不可能獨自發展。
搭配詞 in isolation 單獨地、獨自地、個別地

itch [ɪtʃ] v./n. 癢；渴望 Track 4331
例句 The pregnant woman had an itch for some ice cream.
這位孕婦渴望吃冰淇淋。
搭配詞 have an itch for 渴望得到

jar [dʒɑr] n. 刺耳的聲音、廣口瓶 Track 4332
例句 I need you to help me loosen the lid of this jar.
我需要你幫我把這個廣口瓶的瓶蓋弄鬆。

keyboard [ˋkiˏbord] n. 鍵盤、電子琴 Track 4333

例句 What's the matter with your keyboard? It is not working at all.
你的鍵盤怎麼了？完全沒用呢。

---

kit [kɪt] n. 工具箱 Track 4334

例句 You don't need to bring your kit here. I have one.
你不用帶工具箱，我自己有。

同義字 equipment

---

knife [naɪf] n. 刀 Track 4335

例句 She twisted the knife by mocking at him.
她在傷口上灑鹽，模仿取笑他。

搭配詞 twist the knife 在傷口上灑鹽

---

knob [nɑb] n. 圓形把手、球塊 Track 4336

例句 You should replace the old knobs on the doors.
你應該要把門上的把手換過。

---

knot [nɑt] n. 結 Track 4337

例句 The thought of delivering a speech in front of his class tied him in knots. 想到要在全班面前演說，他就緊張了。

搭配詞 tie sb in knots 使某人緊張

---

knuckle [ˋnʌkḷ] n./v. 指關節、開始認真工作 Track 4338

例句 He cracked his knuckles and got down to work.
他折折指關節，開始工作。

---

label [ˋlebḷ] n. 標籤 Track 4339

例句 I don't like putting labels on people.
我不喜歡給人貼上標籤。

同義字 tag

---

lid [lɪd] n. 蓋子 Track 4340

例句 The news blew the lid off the family's secret.
這個新聞揭發了這家族的秘密。

搭配詞 blow the lid off 揭發事實、暴露

---

loosen [ˋlusṇ] v. 鬆開、放鬆 Track 4341

＊字尾-en有「使」的意思

例句 The athlete always spends 30 minutes loosening up before his regular training.
這個運動員總是先花30分鐘熱身，接著展開平日的訓練。

搭配詞 loosen up 熱身

---

loudspeaker [ˋlaudˋspikɚ] n. 擴音器 Track 4342

例句 Don't scream over the loudspeaker. You'll make the whole school deaf! 別用擴音器大叫，全校都要聾了！

同義字 speaker

a b c d e f g h i j k l m n o p q r s t u v w x y z

magnitude [ˋmægnəˏtjud] n. 重大 Track 4343

例句 She never realized the magnitude of her achievement.
她一直沒發現自己的成就多麼重大。

manipulate [məˋnɪpjəˏlet] v. 巧妙操縱 Track 4344

例句 He said he was manipulated by someone.
他說他是被別人操縱了。

同義字 handle

mingle [ˋmɪŋg!] v. 混合、社交往來 Track 4345

例句 I like to mingle with people at parties.
我喜歡在派對和人們社交。

同義字 mix 混合

mirror [ˋmɪrɚ] n. 鏡子 Track 4346

例句 Check yourself in the mirror before going out.
出門前先照照鏡子。

modify [ˋmɑdəˏfaɪ] v. 修改 Track 4347

＊字尾-ify有「化」的意思

例句 It's time for you to modify the article you are going to send tomorrow. 現在你該修改你明天要送出去的文章了。

同義字 change

mold [mold] v. 鑄模、塑造 Track 4348

例句 The sea waves mold the costal profile through the passage of time.
在時間的流逝之下，海浪塑造出了海岸線的輪廓。

同義字 shape

momentum [moˋmɛntəm] n. 動量、氣勢 Track 4349

例句 His campaign finally gained momentum.
他的宣傳活動終於有了氣勢。

同義字 force

mouthpiece [ˋmaʊθˏpis] n. 樂器吹口 Track 4350

例句 You must clean the mouthpiece of the flute daily.
你必須每天清理長笛的吹口。

navigate [ˋnævəˏget] v. 控制航向、航行 Track 4351

例句 Who was the first to navigate the Atlantic Ocean?
誰是第一個航行大西洋的人？

同義字 sail

neglect [nɪˋglɛkt] v./n. 疏忽、不顧 Track 4352

例句 You shouldn't neglect your children.
你不該疏忽你的孩子。

反義字 endeavor 努力、力圖

net [nɛt] n. 網 ◀ Track 4353

例句 You need to mend this net or you won't catch any fish with it.
你得修補這張網，不然你是抓不到魚的。

搭配詞
mend the net 補網

nevertheless [͵nɛvəðə`lɛs] ◀ Track 4354

adv. 儘管如此、然而

例句 Nevertheless, I still went with him anyway.
儘管如此，我還是跟他去了。

同義字
however

norm [nɔrm] n. 基準、規範、正常 ◀ Track 4355

例句 It never stops raining here. Is this the norm?
這裡都下雨下不停的，這樣是正常的嗎？

oar [or] n. 槳、櫓 ◀ Track 4356

例句 She accidentally dropped an oar into the lake.
她不小心把一把槳弄掉進湖裡了。

obstacle [`ɑbstəkl̩] n. 障礙物、妨礙 ◀ Track 4357

例句 His parents are the only obstacle in their marriage.
他父母是他們婚姻中唯一的障礙。

同義字
hurdle

open [`opən] adj. 開的、公開的 ◀ Track 4358

例句 He made the business deal with his eyes open.
他明知有問題，但還是完成這筆生意了。

搭配詞
with your eyes open
明知有危險、問題

operational [͵ɑpə`reʃənl̩] adj. 操作的 ◀ Track 4359

＊字尾-al有轉變為形容詞之意

例句 Do you mind telling me what the operational hours of the central air conditioning system are? 你介意告訴我中央空調的操作時間嗎？

oral [`orəl] adj. 口述的 ◀ Track 4360

例句 She gave an oral instruction as to the disposal of her real estates.
她口頭指示如何處理她的房產。

搭配詞
oral instruction 口授

paddle [`pædl̩] n./v. 槳、用槳划 ◀ Track 4361

例句 She left her hometown to paddle her own canoe.
她離開家鄉，自力更生了。

搭配詞
paddle one's own canoe
自力更生、獨立自主

pail [pel] n. 桶子 ◀ Track 4362

例句 I noticed that there was an axe inside his pail.
我注意到他的桶子裡放了一把斧頭。

同義字
bucket

participation [pɑrˏtɪsə`peʃən] n. 參加 Track 4363
＊字尾-tion有轉變為名詞的意思
例句 Thank you for your active participation in this event.
謝謝你積極參與這次活動。

搭配詞
active participation
積極參與

partnership [`partnɚˏʃɪp] n. 合夥 Track 4364
例句 The company will enter into partnership with the corporation.
這家公司將與這家集團合夥做生意。

搭配詞
enter into partnership with
與……合夥、與……合做生意

paste [pest] n. 漿糊 Track 4365
例句 I used some paste to glue the cards together.
我用了一些漿糊把卡黏在一起。

pierce [pɪrs] v. 刺穿 Track 4366
例句 She pierced the balloon with a needle.
她用針刺破了氣球。

pipe [paɪp] n. 管子 Track 4367
例句 He prepared to smoke the pipe of peace with his colleague in the meeting. 他準備要在會議向同事表示和好。

搭配詞
smoke the pipe of peace
表示和好

pipeline [`paɪpˏlaɪn] n. 管線 Track 4368
例句 The production of the new vehicle is in the pipeline.
新車的生產正在籌備中。

搭配詞
in the pipeline
在處理或運送中

pit [pɪt] n. 坑洞 Track 4369
例句 My grandfather had spent all his life in a mine pit.
我爺爺一生都在礦坑中度過。

plow [plau] n./v. 犁 Track 4370
例句 Do what you want, but don't put the plow before the oxen.
想做什麼就做吧，但別本末倒置了。

搭配詞
put the plow before the oxen 把犁放在牛前面（本末倒置）

plug [plʌg] n./v. 插頭、插 Track 4371
例句 Please plug my laptop in. It's running out of battery.
請把我的筆電插電吧，快沒電了。

poke [pok] v./n. 戳、捅、干涉、撥弄 Track 4372
例句 It's not proper to poke your nose into people's business.
探聽別人的事不太好。

搭配詞
poke your nose into
探聽、干涉

portable [ˋportəbl̩] adj. 可攜帶的 ◀Track 4373
＊字尾-able有「可以、能」的意思
例句 Why don't you buy a portable computer? I think it's more convenient.
為什麼你不買一台可攜帶的電腦呢？我覺得比較方便。

反義字
stationary 不動的

prehistoric [ˏprihɪsˋtɔrɪk] adj. 史前的 ◀Track 4374
例句 Dinosaurs were one of the most notable prehistoric reptiles.
恐龍是史前時代最著名的爬蟲類動物之一。

搭配詞
prehistoric animal
史前時代的動物

presentation [ˏprɛzn̩ˋteʃən] ◀Track 4375
n. 贈送、呈現、報告 ＊字尾-tion有轉變為名詞的意思
例句 He gave a wonderful presentation in front of his colleagues.
他在同事面前做了很棒的報告。

搭配詞
give a presentation
做簡報、報告

press [prɛs] n./v. 印刷機、新聞界、按 ◀Track 4376
例句 Press the red button and the recording will start.
請按下紅色按鈕，錄音就會開始了。

prize [praɪz] n. 獎品 ◀Track 4377
例句 He hurt his foot and didn't get the first prize in this competition.
他腳受傷，沒有在這場比賽中得到一獎。

proficiency [prəˋfɪʃənsɪ] n. 熟練、精通 ◀Track 4378
例句 His clients were surprised at his language proficiency in German.
他的客戶很驚訝他的德文如此精通。

搭配詞
language proficiency
語言精通程度

prohibit [prəˋhɪbɪt] v. 禁止、使不可能 ◀Track 4379
例句 Food and drink are prohibited in the library.
圖書館裡禁止飲食。

provoke [prəˋvok] v. 激起、激起 ◀Track 4380
例句 Don't provoke me with those dirty words!
別用這些髒字挑釁我！

反義字
appease 平息、撫慰

procedure [prəˋsidʒɚ] n. 手續、程式 ◀Track 4381
例句 These are just standard procedures; nothing to worry about.
這些都只是標準的手續，沒什麼好擔心的。

同義字
process

proceed [prəˋsid] v. 進行 ◀Track 4382
例句 Now that we're alone, we may proceed with the plan.
現在只有我們，可以開始進行計畫了。

production [prəˋdʌkʃən] n. 製造、生產 Track 4383
＊字尾-tion有轉變為名詞的意思
例句 The new fragrance is in production. 新開發的香水正在生產中。
搭配詞 in production 在生產中

productive [prəˋdʌktɪv] Track 4384
adj. 生產的、多產的、有成效的 ＊字尾-ive有轉變為形容詞之意
例句 We had a very productive dialogue with our clients.
我們與客戶的對話很有成效。

profitable [ˋprɑfɪtəbḷ] adj. 有利的 Track 4385
＊字尾-able有「可以、能」的意思
例句 He noticed that it is not profitable to all of the partners.
他注意到這並沒有對每個合夥伙伴都有利。
反義字 profitless 無利的

prominent [ˋprɑmənənt] Track 4386
adj. 突出的、顯眼的
例句 He has a very prominent chin. 他的下巴很突出。
反義字 common 普通的

promotion [prəˋmoʃən] n. 增進、促銷、升遷 Track 4387
＊字尾-tion有轉變為名詞的意思
例句 I am so glad to hear that you got a promotion in only three months.
我很高興聽到你在三個月內就升遷了。
反義字 demotion 降級

prop [prɑp] v. 支撐 Track 4388
例句 She propped herself up with pillows to alleviate the shortness of breath. 她用枕頭把自己支撐起來，以緩解呼吸急促的不適。
搭配詞 prop up 支撐……

prophet [ˋprɑfɪt] n. 先知 Track 4389
例句 He claimed himself a prophet who could predict disasters.
他宣稱自己是個先知，能預測災難。

provide [prəˋvaɪd] v. 提供 Track 4390
例句 People in the community provided the police with valuable information about the suspects.
關於嫌犯，社區居民提供警方很有用的訊息。
搭配詞 provide with
供給、為……裝備上

publication [ˌpʌblɪˋkeʃən] n. 發表、出版 Track 4391
＊字尾-tion有轉變為名詞的意思
例句 His family has been working in the publication industry for a long time ago. 他的家庭從很久以前就在出版界工作。
同義字 publishing

publicity [pʌbˋlɪsətɪ] n. 宣傳、關注 Track 4392
例句 This controversial advertisement got a lot of publicity at that time.
這個有爭議性的廣告當時很受到關注。
搭配詞 get publicity 引起宣傳效果

puff [pʌf] v. 噴煙、吹 ◀ Track 4393

例句 The little boy huffed and puffed about the new rule, but started to quiet down after his older sister had a talk with him. 小男孩大聲抱怨新規矩，不過姊姊和他談了一下，他就安靜下來了。

搭配詞 huff and puff 大聲抱怨

pull [pul] v./n. 拉、拖 ◀ Track 4394

例句 I don't have enough strength to pull these nails out.
我沒有力氣把這些釘子拉出來。

pursuit [pɚˋsut] n. 追求 ◀ Track 4395

例句 The police was in hot pursuit of the robbers.
警方對於搶劫犯窮追不捨。

搭配詞 in hot pursuit 窮追不捨

push [puʃ] v./n. 推、推動 ◀ Track 4396

例句 She pushed the door open easily.
她輕鬆地把門推開了。

put [put] v. 放置 ◀ Track 4397

例句 It's getting cold. Put on your sweater.
天氣變冷了，穿上你的毛衣。

搭配詞 put on 穿上

quotation [kwoˋteʃən] n. 引用、報價 ◀ Track 4398

＊字尾-tion有轉變為名詞的意思

例句 Please bring the quotation and the statistics to the office.
請把報價和數據帶到辦公室來。

rack [ræk] n. 架子、折磨 ◀ Track 4399

例句 He was on the rack when his wife was in a coma.
他的太太陷入昏迷時，他的內心感到很痛苦。

搭配詞 on the rack 十分痛苦

raise [rez] v. 舉起、抬起、提高、養育 ◀ Track 4400

例句 Could you raise your arms and legs? Do they hurt?
你舉得起你的手和腳嗎？會痛嗎？

rattle [ˋrætl̩] n. 嘎嘎聲 ◀ Track 4401

例句 The rattle of the windows gave me the creeps.
窗戶的嘎嘎聲讓我有點害怕。

同義字 clatter

reach [ritʃ] v. 伸手拿東西、到達 ◀ Track 4402

例句 As a child, he was inspired by Elon Musk to reach for the stars.
他從小就受到伊隆馬斯克的啟發，要努力達成夢想。

搭配詞 reach for the stars
心比天高

realistic [rɪə`lɪstɪk] adj. 現實的 Track 4403

例句 Let's be realistic; it's not going to work.
我們實際點吧，不會成功的。

反義字
unrealistic 不切實際的

recognition [ˏrɛkəg`nɪʃən] n. 認知、認可 Track 4404

＊字尾-tion有轉變為名詞的意思

例句 In recognition of his achievements, the institution offered him a research grant. 為了肯定他的成就，這所機構提供他研究獎助金。

搭配詞
in recognition of
褒獎、肯定

reference [`rɛfərəns] n. 參考 Track 4405

例句 If you turn to the last page, you can see the references.
如果你翻到最後一頁，就可以看到參考資料。

reflect [rɪ`flɛkt] v. 反射、考慮 Track 4406

例句 The company is suspected of tax evasion, and it does not reflect well on its reputation.
這家公司有逃稅的嫌疑，給人對公司名聲不好的印象。

搭配詞
reflect on sb/sth
給人（尤指不好的）印象

reflection [rɪ`flɛkʃən] n. 反射、反映 Track 4407

＊字尾-tion有轉變為名詞的意思

例句 A person's appearance is a reflection of his personality.
一個人的外表反映了他的個性。

reform [rɪ`fɔrm] v./n. 改進 Track 4408

＊字首re-有「再次」之意

例句 All these ridiculous rules must be reformed as soon as possible.
這些很扯的規則應該要盡快改進。

regarding [rɪ`gɑrdɪŋ] prep. 關於 Track 4409

例句 With regard to your suggestion, we will put it into consideration.
關於你的建議，我們將納入考慮。

搭配詞
with regard to 關於、至於

regulation [ˏrɛgjə`leʃən] n. 調整、法規 Track 4410

＊字尾-tion有轉變為名詞的意思

例句 Once you immigrate to Australia, you must figure out the country's rules and regulations.
你移民到澳洲後，就一定要瞭解這個國家的各種規定。

搭配詞
rules and regulations
規章制度

rein [ren] n. 箝制、韁繩 Track 4411

例句 The rider fell off from the horse before he could take the reins.
那個騎士還沒抓住韁繩就摔下馬了。

reject [rɪ`dʒɛkt] v. 拒絕 Track 4412

例句 She rejected the big company's offer and took the job near where she lives. 她拒絕了那家大公司，而選擇了她家附近的工作。

反義字
accept 接受

relaxation [ˌrilæksˋeʃən] n. 放鬆 ◀Track 4413
＊字尾-tion有轉變為名詞的意思
例句 A little relaxation is acceptable during the work days.
工作日放鬆一下下是可以接受的。

同義字
rest

relieve [rɪˋliv] v. 減緩 ◀Track 4414
例句 A porter relieved me of my luggage.
行李員幫我推行李。

搭配詞
relieve sb of 幫（某人）拿

remedy [ˋrɛmədɪ] n./v. 療法、治療、補救 ◀Track 4415
例句 The herbal remedy is very effective without upsetting your stomach.
這個草本藥方非常有療效，又不會引起胃不舒服。

諺語
The remedy is worse than the evil. 飲鴆止渴

repeat [rɪˋpit] v./n. 重複 ＊字首re-有「再次」之意 ◀Track 4416
例句 Would you repeat what you said again?
你可以把你講的話再重複一次嗎？

reproduce [ˌriprəˋdjus] v. 複製、再生 ◀Track 4417
＊字首re-有「再次」之意
例句 Is it okay to reproduce the company logo here?
把公司商標複製到這裡用沒關係嗎？

同義字
copy

research [ˋrisɝtʃ] n./v. 調查、研究 ◀Track 4418
例句 She's a research fellow in the institution.
她是這間機構的研究員。

搭配詞
research fellow 研究員

retain [rɪˋten] v. 保持 ＊字首re-有「再次」之意 ◀Track 4419
例句 You should add a little bit of water to retain its moisture.
你應該要再加一點點水讓它保濕。

反義字
abandon 放棄

revise [rɪˋvaɪz] v./n. 修正、校訂 ◀Track 4420
＊字首re-有「再次」之意
例句 Always revise your article before you send it.
把文章送出前要先校訂一下。

同義字
correct

revision [rɪˋvɪʒən] n. 修訂 ◀Track 4421
＊字首re-有「再次」之意
例句 The school rules are in need of revision. 校規需要修訂了。

同義字
correction

rod [rɑd] n. 竿、棒、教鞭 ◀Track 4422
例句 His rod broke when he was fishing.
他在釣魚的時候，竿子壞了。

rope [rop] n. 繩、索 Track 4423

例句 He's broke, and his wife left him. He's at the end of his rope.
他破產了，老婆離他而去，他感到山窮水盡。

搭配詞 be at the end of one's rope 精疲力盡、束手無策

rub [rʌb] v./n. 摩擦 Track 4424

例句 My dog and cat rub along pretty well.
我的狗狗和貓咪相處和睦。

搭配詞 rub along 相處和睦

rubber [ˋrʌbɚ] n. 橡膠、橡皮 Track 4425

例句 She made herself a jump rope with many rubber bands.
她用很多橡皮筋替自己做了一條跳繩。

搭配詞 rubber band 橡皮筋

rumble [ˋrʌmbḷ] n. 隆隆聲 Track 4426

例句 We heard the occasional rumble of a passing truck because we live next to the main road.
因為我們就住在大路旁，所以不時會聽到卡車開過的隆隆聲。

rustle [ˋrʌsḷ] n. 沙沙響 Track 4427

例句 Did you hear a rustling sound coming from the cabinet?
你有聽到櫥子裡沙沙響的聲音嗎？

saddle [ˋsædḷ] n. 鞍 Track 4428

例句 He bought a saddle and bridle for his horse riding class.
他為了他騎馬的課程買了馬鞍和馬具。

saw [sɔ] v./n. 鋸 Track 4429

例句 He used a saw to cut down the tree.
他用鋸子把樹砍下來。

scan [skæn] v./n. 掃描 Track 4430

例句 The scan function of this machine is broken.
這台機器的掃描功能壞了。

同義字 examine

scissors [ˋsɪzɚz] n. 剪刀 Track 4431

＊字尾-s有轉變為複數之意

例句 One can easily tell that the news article is a scissors-and-paste job.
這篇新聞很明顯是剪貼出來的作品。

搭配詞 scissors and paste 剪貼工作、編輯工作

scoop [skup] n. 舀取的器具、一勺的量 Track 4432

例句 Please give me two scoops of vanilla ice cream.
請給我兩球香草冰淇淋。

scrape [skrep] v./n. 磨擦聲、擦掉、擦傷 Track 4433

例句 I fell down a little hill and scraped on my knee.
我從一個小山坡滾下來，擦傷了膝蓋。

scratch [skrætʃ] v. 抓、刮 Track 4434

例句 My cat loves to scratch the paint on the wall.
我的貓喜歡抓牆上的漆。

screw [skru] n. 螺絲 Track 4435

例句 You will need several screws and a hammer.
你會需要一些螺絲和一個鎚子。

screwdriver [ˋskruˏdraɪvɚ] n. 螺絲起子 Track 4436

＊字尾-er有「者」的意思

例句 Will you buy me a screwdriver?
你可以幫我買一個螺絲起子嗎？

shape [ʃep] v./n. 使成形、形狀 Track 4437

例句 The band took shape when they finally found their lead singer.
這支樂團找到主唱後，終於成形了。

搭配詞 take shape 形成、使成形

sharp [ʃɑrp] adj. 鋒利的、刺耳的、尖銳的、嚴厲的 Track 4438

例句 I cut my fingers with that sharp knife.
我用那把鋒利的刀割到手指了。

sharpen [ˋʃɑrpn̩] v. 使銳利、使尖銳 Track 4439

＊字尾-en有「使」的意思

例句 My mother sharpens her kitchen knife every month.
我媽媽每個月都磨刀使它更尖銳。

同義字 point

shatter [ˋʃætɚ] v./n. 粉碎、砸破 Track 4440

例句 No one can shatter the old man's faith.
沒有人能粉碎那個老人的信仰。

同義字 destroy

shift [ʃɪft] v./n. 變換 Track 4441

例句 He shifted his position a little.
他變換了一下姿勢。

shortage [ˋʃɔrtɪdʒ] n. 不足、短缺 Track 4442

例句 The drought led to severe food shortage.
這場乾旱引起了嚴重的食物短缺。

同義字 lack

shovel [ˋʃʌvl̩] v. 剷除 Track 4443

例句 It is not easy for a lady to shovel all the coal into the truck.
要一名女士把這些煤都剷到卡車裡，真是太難了。

shut [ʃʌt] v. 關上、閉上 Track 4444

例句 Please shut the door gently. 請輕輕關上門。

shuttle [ˋʃʌtl̩] v./n. 往返、接駁 Track 4445

例句 You can take the shuttle bus to the train station.
你可以搭接駁車到火車站。

搭配詞
space shuttle 太空梭

signature [ˋsɪgnətʃɚ] n. 簽名 Track 4446

＊字尾-ure有轉變為名詞之意

例句 I wonder how he faked my signature to get money from my bank account. 我好奇他如何偽造我的簽名，從我的銀行帳戶拿到錢。

significance [sɪgˋnɪfəkəns] n. 重要性 Track 4447

＊字尾-ance有轉變為名詞之意

例句 He did not get the significance of the hint.
他不理解這個提示的重要性。

同義字
importance

site [saɪt] v./n. 設置、位址 Track 4448

例句 They have chosen the site for the museum.
他們決定了博物館的位址。

同義字
place

skilled [skɪld] adj. 熟練的、能力好的 Track 4449

例句 She is a skilled surgeon with considerable experience in pediatric surgery. 她是醫術熟練的外科醫師，在小兒科手術方面有很豐富的經驗。

反義字
unskilled 不熟練的、拙劣的

skim [skɪm] v. 瀏覽、去除 Track 4450

例句 I only skimmed through the newspapers.
我只是粗略看了一點報紙。

搭配詞
skim through 粗略地瀏覽

skip [skɪp] v./n. 略過、跳過 Track 4451

例句 It doesn't matter if you skip some details in this movie.
你略過這部電影裡的一些細節也沒關係。

slap [slæp] v./n. 掌擊 Track 4452

例句 The news hit him like a cold slap in the face.
這個消息對他來說有如臉上被冷冷打了一掌。

sledge/sled [slɛdʒ]/[slɛd] n. 雪橇 Track 4453

例句 I was totally nervous the first time I sat on the sledge.
我第一次坐雪橇時非常緊張。

slip [slɪp] v./n. 滑倒 Track 4454

例句 I slipped on the floor because it was wet.
我在地上滑倒，因為地上濕濕的。

slogan [ˋslogən] n. 標語、口號 Track 4455

例句 Our new slogan is popular among young people.
我們的口號在年輕人之中很受歡迎。

slump [slʌmp] v./n. 下跌、衰退、倒下 Track 4456

例句 The man slumped forward in his chair.
那個男人坐在椅子上往前倒下。

snap [snæp] v./n. 折斷、迅速抓住 Track 4457

例句 The twig snapped as soon as the boy stepped on it.
那個男孩一踩到樹枝，它就折斷了。

socket [ˋsɑkɪt] n. 凹處、插座 Track 4458

例句 He felt an aching around his eye sockets.
他感到眼窩痛痛的。

搭配詞
eye socket 眼睛凹處

solution [səˋluʃən] n. 溶解、解決、解釋 Track 4459

＊字尾-tion有轉變為名詞的意思

例句 I think the solution to this problem is to do nothing.
我覺得這個問題的解決方式就是什麼都不做。

solve [sɑlv] v. 解決 Track 4460

例句 Would you please help us find a way to solve the problem?
你可以幫我們想一個方法解決這個問題嗎？

同義字
answer

spade [sped] n. 鏟子 Track 4461

例句 David calls a spade a spade, even he knows it might irritate people.
大衛講話很直，即使他知道會得罪人。

搭配詞
call a spade a spade
直言不諱

spark [spɑrk] n. 火花、火星 Track 4462

例句 Her eyes had a wild spark that attracted many boys.
她的眼裡有種野性的火花，吸引了許多男孩。

a b c d e f g h i j k l m n o p q r s t u v w x y z

sparkle [ˋspɑrkḷ] v./n. 閃爍 Track 4463

例句 People always mention the sparkle of his eyes and his charming smile. 人們總是提到他閃爍的雙眼和迷人的笑容。

同義字 shine

spike [spaɪk] n. 長釘、釘尖 Track 4464

例句 There were many sharp spikes on the chairs in the park. 在那所公園的椅子上有很多尖釘。

split [splɪt] n./v. 裂口、分開、份額 Track 4465

例句 He feels that he has a split personality. 他覺得自己人格分裂。

搭配詞 split personality 人格分裂

sponge [spʌndʒ] n. 海綿 Track 4466

例句 Using a clean sponge to wipe the surface will help. 用乾淨的海綿擦表面會有幫助的。

spray [spre] n. 噴霧器 Track 4467

例句 My children like the smell of the organic bug spray. 我的小孩喜歡這款有機防蟲液的味道。

搭配詞 bug spray 防蟲液

stack [stæk] v./n. 堆、堆疊 Track 4468

例句 It took him an hour to find his homework in a stack of newspapers. 他花了一個小時從一堆報紙中找到他的作業。

stagger [ˋstægɚ] v./n. 搖晃、蹣跚 Track 4469

例句 He staggered into the room drunk. 他醉醺醺地搖晃著走進房間。

stain [sten] v. 弄髒、汙染 Track 4470

例句 I am afraid that you have stained your tie with sauce. 你的領帶恐怕被醬料弄髒了。

反義字 cleanse 使清潔

stake [stek] n. 樁 Track 4471

例句 A wooden stake is what we use to kill vampires. 我們都用木樁來殺吸血鬼。

stall [stɔl] n. 商品陳列台、攤位 Track 4472

例句 He ran a fruit stall in the market. 他在市場有個水果攤。

搭配詞 fruit stall 水果攤

staple [ˋstepl̩] n. 釘書針、主要產物 Track 4473

例句 He sealed the box with carton staples.
他用封箱針把箱子封起來。

stapler [ˋsteplɚ] n. 釘書機 Track 4474

例句 Would you please lend me your stapler? I can't find mine.
你可以借我你的釘書機嗎？我找不到我的。

stick [stɪk] n. 棍、棒 Track 4475

例句 Sticks and stones may break my bones, but they will never crush my spirit.
棍棒和石頭或許會打斷我的骨頭, 但它們永遠無法使我退縮。

stimulate [ˋstɪmjəˏlet] v. 刺激、激勵 Track 4476

例句 We're brainstorming for ideas that will stimulate business.
我們正在腦力激盪找方法來刺激生意。

反義字 deaden 緩和

stimulation [ˏstɪmjəˋleʃən] n. 刺激、興奮、激勵 Track 4477

＊字尾-tion有轉變為名詞的意思

例句 These youngsters need some stimulation to gain confidence.
這些年輕人需要一點激勵才會有信心。

stock [stɑk] n. 庫存 Track 4478

例句 The company has over 10,000 bags in stock.
這家公司還有1萬個包包的庫存。

搭配詞 in stock 有存貨

stone [ston] n. 石、石頭 Track 4479

例句 We can kill two birds with one stone if we go to the fast food restaurant together to get what you need as I pick up my son there.
我們一起去那家速食店，你可以買餐點，我順便在那裡接兒子，可謂一石二鳥。

搭配詞 kill two birds with one stone 一石二鳥

stove [stov] n. 火爐、爐子 Track 4480

例句 The living room is as hot as a stove.
客廳熱得跟火爐一樣。

同義字 oven

straighten [ˋstretn̩] v. 弄直、整頓 Track 4481

＊字尾-en有「使」的意思

例句 My bedroom is in a mess. Let's straighten it up.
我的房間超亂的，我們整頓一下吧。

string [strɪŋ] n. 弦、繩子、一串 Track 4482

例句 She tied a string to the stick and used it to fish.
她在棍子上綁了一條繩子，用來釣魚。

a b c d e f g h i j k l m n o p q r s t u v w x y z

stuff [stʌf] n. 東西、材料 Track 4483

例句 Don't believe any of the crazy stuff he told you.
別相信他跟你講的那些瘋瘋癲癲的東西。

stunt [stʌnt] n. 特技、表演、驚人之舉 Track 4484

例句 The stunt man was seriously injured in the accident.
這個特技替身演員發生意外，身受重傷。

搭配詞 stunt man 特技替身演員

sustain [səˋsten] v. 支持、支撐 Track 4485

例句 It is hard for us to sustain our development without funds.
沒有資金，我們很難支撐住發展。

同義字 support

swap [swɑp] v./n. 交換 Track 4486

例句 Do you want to swap your stickers with me?
你想跟我交換貼紙嗎？

sway [swe] v./n. 搖擺、支配 Track 4487

例句 The scientist has a considerable amount of sway in the academic community. 這個科學家在學術界擁有很大的影響力。

搭配詞 have a considerable amount of sway 很有影響力

sword [sord] n. 劍、刀 Track 4488

例句 He used two swords, one in each hand.
他用兩把劍，一手一把。

tack [tæk] n. 大頭釘、方針 Track 4489

例句 Don't leave tacks lying around on the ground. It's dangerous!
別在地上放一堆大頭釘，很危險！

tackle [ˋtækḷ] v. 著手處理、捉住 Track 4490

例句 Can you tell us how to tackle this problem?
你可以告訴我們如何著手處理這個問題嗎？

tank [tæŋk] n. 水槽、水缸、坦克 Track 4491

例句 He considered the fish tank part of an interior design.
他認為魚缸是室內設計的一部分。

搭配詞 fish tank 魚缸

tap [tæp] n. 輕拍聲 Track 4492

例句 He specializes in tap dance.
他是踢踏舞專家。

搭配詞 tap dance 踢踏舞

tape [tep] **n.** 膠帶、捲尺、磁帶 *Track 4493*

例句 Would you lend me your tape?
你可以借我膠帶嗎？

tighten [ˈtaɪtn] **v.** 勒緊、使堅固 *Track 4494*

＊字尾-en有「使」的意思

例句 Would you like to help me tighten my tie?
你可以幫我繫好我的領帶嗎？

tool [tul] **n.** 工具、用具 *Track 4495*

例句 Some bosses consider their employees as merely tools.
有些老闆認為他們的員工只是工具。

同義字 implement

torch [tɔrtʃ] **n.** 火炬、手電筒 *Track 4496*

例句 Please light the torch. I can't see the path.
請點起火炬吧，我看不到路了。

tough [tʌf] **adj.** 困難的 *Track 4497*

例句 He's a tough nut to crack.
他這個人很難說服。

搭配詞 a tough nut 棘手的問題、難相處的人

transfer [trænsˋfɝ] **v.** 轉移 *Track 4498*

例句 He will transfer all his property to his daughter.
他會把他的財產都轉移給女兒。

treat [trit] **v.** 處理、對待 *Track 4499*

例句 Please treat this little puppy gently.
請溫柔地對待這隻小狗。

treatment [tritmənt] **n.** 款待、處理 *Track 4500*

＊字尾-ment有轉變為名詞之意

例句 She is usually given preferential treatment because her dad is an influential politician.
她爸爸是很有影響力的政治人物，所以她常常得到別人的優待。

搭配詞 give sb. preferential treatment 偏向某人、得到優待

trigger [ˋtrɪgɚ] **n.** 扳機 *Track 4501*

例句 He pulled the trigger but missed the target.
他扣了扳機，卻沒有射中。

tube [tjub] **n.** 管、管子 *Track 4502*

例句 Let's cool down the glass tube before we start our experiment.
我們在開始實驗前，先把玻璃管放涼吧。

同義字 pipe

tug [tʌg] v./n. 用力拉 Track 4503

例句 We need to practice tug of war after school.
我們下課要練拔河。

搭配詞
tug of war 拔河比賽、兩派間的激烈鬥爭

use [juz] v./n. 使用、消耗 Track 4504

例句 Do you know how to use this machine?
你知道怎麼使用這台機器嗎？

user [ˋjuzɚ] n. 使用者 ＊字尾-er有「者」的意思 Track 4505

例句 To log into the website, you need a user name and a password.
上這個網站需要建立使用者名稱和密碼。

搭配詞
user name 使用者名稱

utensil [juˋtɛnsl̩] n. 用具、器皿 Track 4506

例句 Let's buy new cooking utensils for our new kitchen.
我們來為新廚房買新的廚具吧。

同義字
implement

waste [west] v./n. 浪費、濫用 Track 4507

例句 He wasted too much time looking for a job.
他浪費太多時間找工作了。

watch [watʃ] v./n. 注視、觀看、注意 Track 4508

例句 There are many people watching football on TV tonight.
有許多人今天晚上在看電視上的足球轉播。

welcome [ˋwɛlkəm] v./n./adj./int. 歡迎 Track 4509

例句 We warmly welcome you to the amusement park.
我們熱誠歡迎您來這所遊樂園。

搭配詞
welcome to 歡迎來到……

what [wat] pron./adj./int. 什麼 Track 4510

例句 What about David? Should we tell him the bad news?
大衛怎麼辦？我們該告訴他這個壞消息嗎？

搭配詞
what about ～怎麼辦

whether [ˋwɛðɚ] conj. 是否、無論如何 Track 4511

例句 Let's go to my father and ask whether he would like to help us.
我們去找我爸，問他是否願意幫我們。

which [wɪtʃ] pron./adj. 哪一個 Track 4512

例句 He waited to see which way the cat jumps before making a long-term strategy. 他在規畫長期策略前，先觀望情勢。

搭配詞
to see which way the cat jumps 觀望情勢

whip [hwɪp] n. 鞭子 ◀Track 4513

例句 The teacher cracked the whip to push his students to study harder.
老師發威督促學生用功唸書。

搭配詞
crack the whip 施威、督促

whistle [ˋwɪsl̩] n. 口哨、汽笛、哨子 ◀Track 4514

例句 He blew the whistle on the CTO's embezzlement and put himself in a dilemma. 他揭發技術總監的貪瀆，讓自己陷入兩難。

搭配詞
blow the whistle on
中止、告密、揭發

wire [waɪr] n. 金屬絲、電線 ◀Track 4515

例句 A wire is stronger than a rope.
金屬絲比繩子更堅固。

with [wɪð] prep. 具有、帶有、和……一起、用 ◀Track 4516

例句 The Duchess of Sussex is with child.
薩塞克斯公爵夫人梅根有身孕了。

搭配詞
with child 懷孕

wooden [ˋwudn̩] adj. 木製的 ◀Track 4517

例句 Why not put those letters in that wooden box?
怎麼不把這些信放到那個木製箱子裡呢？

work [wɝk] v./n. 工作、勞動 ◀Track 4518

例句 He works so hard for his family.
他為了他的家庭非常努力工作。

wrap [ræp] v./n. 包裝 ◀Track 4519

例句 I bought some pretty wrapping paper to wrap the gifts.
我買了一些漂亮的包裝紙來包裝禮物。

wring [rɪŋ] v./n. 絞、絞扭、擰 ◀Track 4520

例句 Give those clothes a wring before hanging them.
先擰一下那些衣服再掛起來。

yield [jild] v./n. 產出、讓出 ◀Track 4521

例句 They have no choice but to yield to his oppression.
他們別無選擇，只能屈服來自於他的壓迫。

搭配詞
yield to 屈服

zoom [zum] v./n. 調整焦距使物體放大或縮小 ◀Track 4522

例句 Do you know how to use the zoom in function of the copy machine?
你知道怎麼用影印機的放大功能嗎？

NOTE

Test 16 關鍵英單總測驗第16回

以下測驗題皆出自書中第十六回「**和工具有關的單字**」，快來檢視自己的學習成果吧！

一、選擇題

1. He _____ US$1 million to support people who were displaced by the civil war.
(A) dip
(B) input
(C) dumped
(D) contributed

2. The new app has a graphic _____, which is very user-friendly.
(A) loudspeaker
(B) quotation
(C) interface
(D) rod

3. My hairdresser cut my _____ ends and then gave my hair a trim.
(A) split (B) foil
(C) tap (D) chain

4. The website has its _____ style with features to enhance user experience.
(A) dumb
(B) instinct
(C) distinctive
(D) portable

5. A child of Lebanese immigrants, his English _____ is the highest at school.
(A) intonation
(B) proficiency
(C) calculator
(D) staple

6. The candidate's campaign _____ is "Do the right things; do things right."
(A) slogan (B) revision
(C) site (D) pursuit

7. His lack of social connection is an _____ in his career path.
(A) pipeline
(B) paddle
(C) obstacle
(D) dictionary

8. The _____ scholar is renowned for his discovery in tyrosine kinases, which lead to the development of target therapy.
(A) exposure
(B) dispensable
(C) available
(D) prominent

9. We need more renewable energy to _____ the transition to a sustainable economy.
(A) batter
(B) accelerate
(C) distort
(D) amplify

10. How are we going to take the engine apart? We need a _____.
(A) torch
(B) wring
(C) screwdriver
(D) pipeline

二、克漏字測驗

A technology entrepreneur and engineer, Elon Musk, is the founder of SpaceX and co-founder of Tesla Motor. When he was young, he was considered a nerd and got __1__ a lot. He got beaten so badly that he had to be hospitalized. Nevertheless, he didn't let those kids __2__ his spirit.

In 2002, he founded SpaceX and the company made a major __3__ in 2015—they made reusable rockets possible and space __4__ a reality. Now, he's finding a __5__ to ship people to live on Mars.

1.
(A) skipped
(B) poked
(C) bullied
(D) integrated

2.
(A) interact
(B) crush
(C) handle
(D) forsake

3.
(A) friction
(B) disposal
(C) breakthrough
(D) cooperation

4.
(A) exploration
(B) antenna
(C) relaxation
(D) shuttle

5.
(A) shift
(B) reflection
(C) participation
(D) solution

關鍵英單總測驗第16回 中譯與解答

一、選擇題

1. 他奉獻了一百萬美元協助因內戰而流離失所的人們。
(A) 沾、浸
(B) 輸入
(C) 丟掉
(D) 奉獻

2. 這款新的應用程式有圖像式介面，是對使用者友善的設計。
(A) 擴音器
(B) 報價
(C) 介面
(D) 竹竿

3. 我的美髮師先把我的分岔剪掉，接著修剪我的頭髮。
(A) 分岔
(B) 鋁箔片
(C) 輕拍聲
(D) 鍊子

4. 這個網站有獨特的設計，並附有能提升使用者經驗的功能。
(A) 笨拙的
(B) 本能、直覺
(C) 獨特的
(D) 可攜式的

5. 他是黎巴嫩移民的小孩，英文的精通度卻是全校最頂尖的。
(A) 語調
(B) 精通程度
(C) 計算機
(D) 訂書針

6. 這名候選人的競選口號是「做對的事；把事做對」。
(A) 口號
(B) 修訂
(C) 位址
(D) 追求

7. 缺乏人脈是他事業發展的障礙。
(A) 管線
(B) 槳
(C) 障礙
(D) 字典

8. 這名傑出的學者因發現酪氨酸激酶而享有盛名，他的發現促進了標靶治療的發展。
(A) 暴露
(B) 非必要的
(C) 有空的
(D) 傑出的

9. 我們需要更多再生能源，以加速轉型成為永續經濟。
(A) 重擊
(B) 加速
(C) 扭曲
(D) 放大

10. 我我們要怎麼把引擎拆掉呢?我們需要一個螺絲起子。
(A) 火把
(B) 擰扭
(C) 螺絲起子
(D) 管線

二、克漏字測驗

身為科技創業家和工程師，伊隆馬斯克是SpaceX的創辦人和特斯拉電動車的共同創辦人。他小時候被大家認為是書呆子，經常被霸凌，還曾被打到住院，但他並沒有讓那些霸凌他的小孩摧毀他的志氣。

2002年他創辦SpaceX，該公司在2015年取得重大突破：他們創造出可回收火箭，使太空探險能夠成真。如今他正在尋找解決方法，把人類送到火星居住。

1.
(A) 跳過
(B) 戳
(C) 霸凌
(D) 整合

2.
(A) 互動
(B) 壓碎
(C) 處理
(D) 拋棄

3.
(A) 磨擦
(B) 配置
(C) 突破
(D) 合作

4.
(A) 探索
(B) 天線
(C) 放鬆
(D) 接駁

5.
(A) 轉換
(B) 反射
(C) 參加
(D) 解決方法

一、選擇題

1.(D) 2.(C) 3.(A) 4.(C) 5.(B)
6.(A) 7.(C) 8.(D) 9.(B) 10.(C)

二、克漏字測驗

1.(C) 2.(B) 3.(C)
4.(A) 5.(D)

Unit 17 和家庭社會有關的單字

多益測驗的命題強調生活化與實用性，學會這些與「家庭社會」有關的單字，不僅能讓你在多益考場上所向披靡，在日常生活上也可以靈活運用喔！

婚禮可以這麼說

- **We made a prenuptial agreement after we got engaged.**
  我們在訂婚後達成了婚前協議。
- **The wedding ceremony will start at 10 a.m.**
  婚禮儀式將在早上十點開始。

小家庭中的成員可以這麼說

- **I have two elder sisters, Emma and Jenny.**
  我有兩位姐姐，艾瑪跟珍妮。
- **My mom used to do all the housework when I was little.**
  在我小的時候，我媽媽一人包攬所有家事。
- **My brother broke up with his girl friend last week.**
  我哥上禮拜跟他的女朋友分手了。

家族中的親戚可以這麼說

- **How do you tell the identical twins apart?**
  你是如何分辨這兩位同卵雙胞胎的？
- **Auntie Gok always gives the best fashion advice.**
  郭阿姨總是給出最佳的時尚建議。

家庭活動可以這麼說

- **He blamed himself for not trying hard enough to catch the ball.**
  他對於不夠努力接住球感到自責。

- **The kids donated their toys to the orphanage.**
  孩子們將他們的玩具捐給了孤兒院。

爸媽對孩子的關愛可以這麼說

- **Parents usually have high expectation on their children.**
  家長通常對自己的小孩抱有很高的期望。

- **The result of the game is nothing compared to your health. Your wellbeing values the most.**
  比賽的結果跟你的健康比起來一點都不重要。你的幸福最重要。

Unit 17 和家庭社會有關的單字

abide [əˋbaɪd] v. 容忍、忍耐 Track 4523
例句 We should abide by the law. 我們應該遵守法律。

搭配詞
abide by 遵從、遵守

---

accessible [ækˋsɛsəbl̩] Track 4524
adj. 可親的、容易接近的、能進入的 ＊字尾-ible有「可以、能」的意思
例句 I'm afraid that this database is only accessible to certain members.
恐怕只有某些特定成員才能進入這個資料庫。

反義字
inaccessible 達不到的、難進入的

---

acquaintance [əˋkwentəns] n. 認識的人 Track 4525
＊字尾-ance有轉變為名詞之意
例句 He's just an acquaintance; we're not really friends.
他只是認識的人而已，我們不是真的是朋友。

搭配詞
make sb's acquaintance 結識某人

---

admit [ədˋmɪt] v. 容許……進入、承認 Track 4526
例句 I admit that I'm in the wrong.
我承認是我錯了。

---

adopt [əˋdɑpt] v. 收養 Track 4527
例句 Why don't you adopt a dog if you are so fond of little animals?
既然你那麼喜歡小動物，那為什麼不收養一隻狗呢？

反義字
discard 拋棄

---

advice [ədˋvaɪs] n. 忠告、建議 Track 4528
例句 Would you mind if I ask the nurses in the clinic for advice?
你介意我問診所的護士有什麼建議嗎？

搭配詞
ask sb for advice 詢問某人的建議

---

advise [ədˋvaɪz] v. 勸告 Track 4529
例句 It was the second time that she advised me to quit my job.
這是她第二次勸告我辭職。

同義字
counsel

---

affection [əˋfɛkʃən] n. 親情、情愛、愛慕 Track 4530
＊字尾-tion有轉變為名詞的意思
例句 I have a deep affection for my old friend.
我對我的老朋友充滿深深的感情。

a b c d e f g h i j k l m n o p q r s t u v w x y z

affectionate [əˋfɛkʃənɪt] adj. 摯愛的 Track 4531

例句 The dog nuzzled his owner in an affectionate manner.
那隻狗充滿愛意地拱牠的主人。

同義字 loving

affirm [əˋfɝm] v. 斷言、證實 Track 4532

例句 I can affirm that the girl did quite a bit of research.
我可以證實這個女孩做了一些研究。

反義字 deny 否定、否認

afford [əˋford] v. 能負擔 Track 4533

例句 Can you really afford to buy a motorcycle at the moment?
你現在真的負擔得起買一台機車的錢嗎？

搭配詞 can afford to 能負擔

afterward(s) [ˋæftəwəd(z)] adv. 以後 Track 4534

例句 He quickly finished his food and went out soon afterwards.
他很快地吃完了食物，之後很快就出去了。

反義字 beforehand 事先

against [əˋgɛnst] prep. 反對、不同意 Track 4535

例句 He did what his boss told him to do, even though it went against the grain of his nature.
他照老闆的吩咐去做，即使這有違他的本性。

搭配詞 go against the grain of one's nature 違背某人本性

agree [əˋgri] v. 同意、贊成 Track 4536

例句 I couldn't agree with you more.
我再同意你不過了。（我完全同意你。）

搭配詞 agree with 吻合、同意

agreement [əˋgrimənt] n. 同意、一致、協議 Track 4537

＊字尾-ment有轉變為名詞之意

例句 The children were all in agreement that the wicked stepfather should not stay. 孩子們都同意邪惡的繼父不能留下來。

alike [əˋlaɪk] adj./adv. 相似的、相同的 Track 4538

例句 He's a Marlon Brando look-alike.
他和馬龍白蘭度長得很像。

搭配詞 look-alike 長得很像

allow [əˋlaʊ] v. 允許、准許 Track 4539

例句 She doesn't allow her kids to go out.
她不允許她的孩子出門。

although [ɔlˋðo] conj. 雖然、縱然 Track 4540

例句 Although I got there on time, the bus had left already.
雖然我準時到了，但公車已經先跑了。

同義字 though

ancestor [ˋænsɛstɚ] n. 祖先、祖宗 ◀Track 4541

例句 Our ancestors passed down some pretty strange traditions.
我們的祖先傳下了一些有點奇怪的傳統。

反義字
descendant 子孫、後裔

annoy [əˋnɔɪ] v. 煩擾、使惱怒 ◀Track 4542

例句 That chatty passenger annoyed us so much.
那個多話的乘客惹惱了我們。

anonymous [əˋnɑnəməs] adj. 匿名的 ◀Track 4543

例句 Who kept sending me anonymous letters?
是誰一直寄匿名信給我？

同義字
nameless

anybody/anyone [ˋɛnɪˏbɑdɪ]/[ˋɛnɪˏwʌn] ◀Track 4544

pron. 任何人

例句 It's anybody's guess who will win the game.
誰會贏這場比賽，是任何人都說不準的事。

搭配詞
anybody's guess
任何人都說不準的事

anyhow [ˋɛnɪˏhaʊ] adv. 隨便、無論如何 ◀Track 4545

例句 Anyhow, I don't think it concerns us.
隨便啦，我想反正跟我們也無關。

同義字
anyway

anyway [ˋɛnɪˏwe] adv. 無論如何、反正 ◀Track 4546

例句 It's fine. I won't be here anyway.
沒關係，反正我到時候也不會來。

同義字
anyhow

apologize [əˋpɑləˏdʒaɪz] v. 道歉、認錯 ◀Track 4547

例句 We apologize to you for any inconveniences caused by our oversight. 因我們的疏失造成你的不便，在此深表歉意。

搭配詞
apologize to sb for
因……向某人道歉

apology [əˋpɑlədʒɪ] n. 謝罪、道歉 ◀Track 4548

例句 I owe you an apology for what I did at the party; I hope you can forgive me.
對於我在派對上做的事，我欠你一個道歉。我希望你可以原諒我。

application [ˏæpləˋkeʃən] n. 應用、申請 ◀Track 4549

＊字尾-tion有轉變為名詞的意思

例句 She just sent in an application for that position.
她剛送進那個職位的申請。

appreciation [əˏpriʃɪˋeʃən] ◀Track 4550

n. 賞識、鑑識、感激 ＊字尾-tion有轉變為名詞的意思

例句 He expressed his sincere appreciation to her for her timely help.
對於她的及時幫助，他向她表達誠摯感激。

搭配詞
express one's appreciation to sb for sth 表達感激

approval [ə`pruvḷ] n. 承認、同意 Track 4551

例句 I hope the arrangements will meet with your approval.
我希望這些安排會得到你的贊同。

arise [ə`raɪz] v. 出現、發生 Track 4552

例句 Please call me if any problems arise.
如果出現什麼問題請打給我。

assist [ə`sɪst] v. 援助、協助 Track 4553

例句 She assisted them in designing the new apartment.
她協助他們設計新套房。

反義字 resist 反抗

aunt/auntie/aunty [ænt]/[`ænti]/[`æntɪ] Track 4554

n. 伯母、姑、嬸、姨

例句 How long will you stay at your aunt's home in the summer time?
你夏天要在阿姨家待多久？

award [ə`wɔrd] n./v. 獎品、獎賞 Track 4555

例句 My father was awarded the best employee of the year.
我爸爸得了年度最佳員工的獎賞。

同義字 reward

baby [`bebɪ] n./adj. 嬰兒的 Track 4556

例句 She has such a baby face that we can't tell how old she is.
她的娃娃臉，讓我們很難猜出她的真實年齡。

搭配詞 baby face 娃娃臉

baby-sit [`bebɪ.sɪt] v. （臨時）照顧嬰孩 Track 4557

例句 Zoe's godmother will come to babysit her baby for three months.
柔伊的教母會來幫她照顧嬰兒三個月。

bankrupt [`bæŋkrʌpt] adj. 破產的 Track 4558

例句 His business in the shoe market was a total failure and he went bankrupt. 他在製鞋業的生意澈底失敗，宣告破產了。

搭配詞 go bankrupt 宣告破產

belong [bə`lɔŋ] v. 屬於 Track 4559

例句 This set of tea pots belongs to Joanna.
這一組茶壺屬於喬安娜。

搭配詞 belong to 屬於

belongings [bə`lɔŋɪŋz] n. 所有物、財產 Track 4560

＊字尾-s有轉變為複數之意

例句 We should remember to bring our personal belongings when we get off the bus. 我們下公車時要記得帶我們的私人所有物。

同義字 property

benefit [ˋbɛnəfɪt] n./v. 益處、利益 Track 4561

例句 Regular exercise will benefit you in many ways.
規律運動在各方面都對你有益處。

bid [bɪd] n./v. 投標、投標價 Track 4562

例句 Our company finally won the bid.
我們公司終於贏得投標。

blame [blem] v./n. 責備 Track 4563

例句 He took the blame for the mistake his colleague made.
他把同事犯的錯承擔下來接受指責。

搭配詞 take the blame 承擔指責

bless [blɛs] v. 祝福 Track 4564

例句 God bless you! What a huge sneeze!
上帝祝福你！你剛那個噴嚏也太大聲了吧！

bodily [ˋbɑdɪlɪ] adj. 身體上的、物質上的 Track 4565

例句 He was arrested for causing bodily harm to his classmate.
他因為對同學造成身體上的傷害而被捕。

反義字 mental 精神的、心理的

bosom [ˋbʊzəm] adj. 知心的、親密的 Track 4566

例句 She is my bosom friend. 她是我的知心好友。

搭配詞 bosom friend 知心朋友

boy [bɔɪ] n. 男孩 Track 4567

例句 Is the baby a girl or a boy?
那個嬰兒是個女孩還是男孩？

boyhood [ˋbɔɪhʊd] n. 男孩時代、童年 Track 4568

例句 He was very naughty in his boyhood.
他在男孩時代很頑皮。

反義字 adulthood 成年時期

breakup [ˋbrekˏʌp] n. 分散、分手、瓦解 Track 4569

例句 Did you hear about Joe and Julia's breakup?
你聽說了喬伊和茱麗雅分手的事嗎？

bride [braɪd] n. 新娘 Track 4570

例句 Let's toast to the bride and groom!
我們敬新娘與新郎一杯！

反義字 bridegroom 新郎

a b c d e f g h i j k l m n o p q r s t u v w x y z

bridegroom/groom [ˋbraɪdˏgrʊm]/[grʊm] Track 4571
n. 新郎
例句 Prince Harry, the bridegroom, was dressed in the uniform of the Blues and Royals. 新郎哈利王子穿著英國皇家騎兵團的深藍色軍服。

相關詞 bride 新娘

bring [brɪŋ] v. 帶來 Track 4572
例句 He brings out the best in me.
他把我本性中最好的一面帶出來了。

搭配詞 bring out 拿出、帶出

brother [ˋbrʌðɚ] n. 兄弟 Track 4573
例句 Once you see my brother, you will know how tall he is.
你一看到我哥哥，就會知道他有多高了。

brotherhood [ˋbrʌðɚˏhʊd] Track 4574
n. 兄弟關係、手足之情、兄弟會
例句 The brotherhood operated in secret.
這個兄弟會組織行事很神祕。

burden [ˋbɝdn̩] n. 負荷、負擔 Track 4575
例句 As a teenager, he carried the burden of feeding his whole family.
他在青少年時就扛著養活一家人的負擔。

caress [kəˋrɛs] v./n. 愛撫、擁抱、撫摸 Track 4576
例句 The man caressed his young son.
那個男人撫摸著他年幼的兒子。

同義字 pet

case [kes] n. 情形、情況、箱、案例 Track 4577
例句 May I know how to contact you? Just in case.
可以知道你的聯絡方式嗎？以防萬一。

搭配詞 in case 假如、以防萬一

ceremony [ˋsɛrəˏmonɪ] n. 典禮、儀式 Track 4578
例句 Please help yourself. We don't stand on ceremony.
要吃什麼自己夾，我們家不拘束。

搭配詞 stand on ceremony 拘束、拘禮

certificate [sɚˋtɪfəkɪt] n. 證書、憑證 Track 4579
例句 We will get a certificate after three months of training.
我們在訓練三個月後會拿到一張證書。

chase [tʃes] v./n. 追求、追逐 Track 4580
例句 The dog was chasing butterflies.
那隻小狗在追逐蝴蝶。

chatter [ˋtʃætɚ] v. 喋喋不休、講個不停 Track 4581

例句 The teachers asked the children to stop chattering in class.
老師們請孩子們不要在上課時講個不停。

同義字 babble

chief [tʃif] adj. 主要的、首席的 Track 4582

例句 Our chief executive officer will quit for another company.
我們的首席執行長要跳槽了。

搭配詞 chief executive officer 首席執行長

child [tʃaɪld] n. 小孩 Track 4583

例句 They had their first child in their early twenties.
他們在二十歲出頭時有了第一個小孩。

communicate [kəˋmjunə͵ket] v. 溝通、交流 Track 4584

例句 It is important for parents to communicate with their teenage children. 父母和青少年小孩做好溝通是很重要的。

搭配詞 communicate with 與……溝通

comparison [kəmˋpærəsn̩] n. 對照、比較 Track 4585

＊字首com-有「共同」之意

例句 I can't make comparison between these two artworks.
我無法比較這兩件藝術作品。

concern [kənˋsɝn] v. 關心、涉及 Track 4586

例句 You should at least call your parents once a week. They are concerned about you.
你至少一個禮拜得打一次電話給你父母。他們關心你。

concerning [kənˋsɝnɪŋ] prep. 關於 Track 4587

例句 Recently I am reading some documents concerning the history of handmade crafts. 最近我在讀一些關於手工藝歷史的文件。

同義字 regarding

conclude [kənˋklud] v. 締結、結束、得到結論 Track 4588

例句 They concluded that their president is a hopeless bigot.
他們得到結論，認為他們的總統是無藥可救的偏執狂。

conclusion [kənˋkluʒən] n. 結論、終了 Track 4589

例句 In conclusion, he gave us some constructive advice.
最後，他給我們一些建設性的意見。

搭配詞 in conclusion 最後

condition [kənˋdɪʃən] n. 條件、情況 Track 4590

＊字尾-tion有轉變為名詞的意思

例句 He kept his car in good condition. 他把他的車況維持得很好。

搭配詞 in condition 健康

a b c d e f g h i j k l m n o p q r s t u v w x y z

conduct [ˋkɑndʌkt]/[kənˋdʌkt] Track 4591
n./v. 行為、舉止、施行
例句 The teacher punished him for his terrible conduct.
老師因他不好的行為而處罰了他。

同義字
behavior

confident [ˋkɑnfədənt] adj. 有信心的 Track 4592
例句 I am quite confident of his ability to solve the problem.
我對他的能力很有信心，認為他能解決這道難題的。

搭配詞
be confident of
對……有信心、確信

confuse [kənˋfjuz] v. 使迷惑 Track 4593
例句 Their strange pronunciation confused me a lot.
他們奇怪的發音讓我很迷惑。

connect [kəˋnɛkt] v. 連接、連結 Track 4594
例句 Would you please connect me to the accounting department?
你可以幫我接到會計部嗎？

connection [kəˋnɛkʃən] n. 連接、連結 Track 4595
＊字尾-tion有轉變為名詞的意思
例句 The internet connection is very bad here.
這裡的網路連結很差。

conscious [ˋkɑnʃəs] adj. 意識到的 Track 4596
例句 He was conscious of some presence other than himself in the room.
他意識到房間裡除了他還有別的生物存在。

搭配詞
conscious of 意識到

considerable [kənˋsɪdərəbl̩] Track 4597
adj. 應考慮的、相當多的 ＊字尾-able有「可以、能」的意思
例句 He holds a considerable amount of sway in this deal.
這筆交易中，他有相當大的影響力。

搭配詞
a considerable amount of
大量的

consideration [kənˏsɪdəˋreʃən] n. 考慮 Track 4598
＊字尾-tion有轉變為名詞的意思
例句 We should take his family's situation into consideration.
我們應該考慮到他家人的處境。

搭配詞
take sth into consideration
考慮到

constant [ˋkɑnstənt] adj. 不變的、不斷的 Track 4599
例句 The world is in constant change.
世界不斷地在改變。

反義字
inconstant 易變的、無常的

conversation [kɑnvəˋseʃən] n. 交談、談話 Track 4600
＊字尾-tion有轉變為名詞的意思
例句 I had a decent conversation with that senator.
我和那個參議員有不錯的談話。

cost [kɔst] n./v. 代價、價值、費用 ◀Track 4601

例句 He's determined to accomplish the task at all costs.
他不惜任何代價，都要完成這項任務。

搭配詞
at all costs 無論如何、不惜任何代價

couple [ˋkʌpḷ] n. 配偶、一對 ◀Track 4602

例句 We have a couple of months to prepare for the project.
我們還有幾個月的時間，準備這項計畫。

搭配詞
a couple of 一些、少數

cousin [ˋkʌzn̩] n. 堂（表）兄弟姊妹 ◀Track 4603

例句 How many cousins do you have?
你有幾個堂（表）兄弟姊妹？

cradle [ˋkredḷ] n. 搖籃 ◀Track 4604

例句 Rock the cradle gently, or you'll wake the baby.
輕輕搖搖籃就好，不然你會把寶寶吵醒。

cub [kʌb] n. 幼獸、年輕人 ◀Track 4605

例句 The bear cub was orphaned after his mother was killed by a hunter.
這隻幼熊在媽媽被獵人殺了以後，變成孤兒。

搭配詞
bear cub 熊的幼仔

curiosity [ˏkjʊrɪˋɑsətɪ] n. 好奇心 ◀Track 4606

例句 To satisfy his curiosity, he tried cat food to see what it tasted like.
為了滿足自己的好奇心，他試吃了貓食，看看味道如何。

搭配詞
Curiosity killed the cat.
好奇心惹禍

curse [kɝs] v. 詛咒、罵 ◀Track 4607

例句 She cursed under her breath.
她小聲罵了一句。

cute [kjut] adj. 可愛的、聰明伶俐的 ◀Track 4608

例句 We are taking photos of this cute baby.
我們在替這個可愛的小寶寶照相。

同義字
adorable

daddy/dad [ˋdædɪ]/[dæd] n. 爸爸 ◀Track 4609

例句 My dad is in his fifties.
我爸現在五十幾歲。

反義字
mom 媽媽

danger [ˋdendʒɚ] n. 危險 ◀Track 4610

例句 She is in danger of losing her job.
她有失去工作的危險。

搭配詞
in danger 有危險

darling [ˋdɑrlɪŋ] n. 親愛的人 Track 4611

例句 They will hold a birthday party for their darling baby girl.
他們將為他們親愛的寶貝女兒辦一場生日派對。

同義字 beloved

daughter [ˋdɔtɚ] n. 女兒 Track 4612

例句 The couple has three daughters.
那對夫婦有三個女兒。

dear [dɪr] adj. 昂貴的、親愛的 Track 4613

例句 Dear Grandma, how have you been?
親愛的奶奶，近來如何？

decide [dɪˋsaɪd] v. 決定 Track 4614

例句 She decided to stay in London.
她決定要留在倫敦。

depend [dɪˋpɛnd] v. 依賴、依靠 Track 4615

例句 His mother has no one to depend on except him.
他媽媽除了他以外，沒有人可以依靠了。

搭配詞 depend on 確信、堅信、信賴、取決於

detail [ˋditel] n. 細節、條款 Track 4616

例句 He explained what happened in detail.
他把事發經過詳細說明。

搭配詞 in detail 詳細說明

determine [dɪˋtɝmɪn] v. 決定 Track 4617

例句 Your appearance doesn't determine who you are.
你的外表無法決定你是誰。

同義字 decide

dialogue [ˋdaɪəˏlɔg] n. 對話 Track 4618

例句 All the dialogues in the script sound unnatural.
這個劇本裡所有的對話感覺都很不自然。

同義字 conversation

diaper [ˋdaɪpɚ] n. 尿布 Track 4619

例句 Do you know how to change the diapers?
你知道怎麼換尿布嗎？

搭配詞 change a diaper 換尿布

dignity [ˋdɪgnətɪ] n. 威嚴、尊嚴 Track 4620

例句 Please at least leave him some dignity.
請留給他一點尊嚴吧。

diligence [ˋdɪlədʒəns] n. 勤勉、勤奮 ◀Track 4621

例句 Diligence redeems stupidity. 勤能補拙。

反義字 idleness 懶惰

---

dissuade [dɪˋswed] v. 勸阻、勸止 ◀Track 4622

＊字首dis-有「不」之意

例句 My mom dissuaded me from moving abroad.
我媽勸阻我不要搬到國外。

反義字 persuade 說服

---

disciple [dɪˋsaɪpl̩] n. 信徒、門徒 ◀Track 4623

例句 The scripture recorded that he had twelve disciples.
宗教經典記載他有12名門徒。

---

discriminate [dɪˋskrɪmə͵net] ◀Track 4624

v. 辨別、差別對待 ＊字首dis-有「不」之意

例句 No one has taught him to discriminate between right and wrong.
沒有人教過他辨別對錯。

---

distinct [dɪˋstɪŋkt] adj. 明顯的、獨特的 ◀Track 4625

＊字首dis-有「不」之意

例句 There is a distinct difference between the two.
這兩者之間有很明顯的差別。

反義字 indistinct 分不開的

---

distinguish [dɪˋstɪŋgwɪʃ] ◀Track 4626

v. 辨別、分辨、區分 ＊字首dis-有「不」之意

例句 I can't distinguish between these two colors.
我區分不出這兩種顏色有什麼差。

---

divorce [dəˋvors] n./v. 離婚、解除婚約 ◀Track 4627

例句 They have been thinking about divorce for years.
他們已經考慮要離婚好幾年了。

反義字 marriage 結婚

---

donation [ˋdoneʃən] n. 捐贈物、捐款 ◀Track 4628

＊字尾-tion有轉變為名詞的意思

例句 He made a donation to the orphanage.
他捐款給孤兒院。

---

donate [ˋdonet] v. 贈與、捐贈 ◀Track 4629

例句 They donated money to the earthquake victims.
他們捐錢給地震受災者。

---

donor [ˋdonɚ] n. 寄贈者、捐贈人 ◀Track 4630

＊字尾-or有「者」的意思

例句 The man is a sperm donor; as a result, he has 50 children.
這名男子是精子捐贈人，結果有50個孩子。

搭配詞 sperm donor 精子捐贈人

doom [dum] n. 命運、末日 Track 4631

例句 The small insect was lured to its doom.
那隻小蟲被引誘過去，面臨死亡。

eager [ˋigɚ] adj. 渴望的、熱心的 Track 4632

例句 She is eager to try out the new dish.
她熱切地想試吃新菜。

earnings [ˋɝnɪŋz] n. 收入 Track 4633

＊字尾-s有轉變為複數之意

例句 It's very rude of you to ask people about their earnings.
問別人的收入是很不禮貌的。

同義字 wages

effect [əˋfɛkt] n. 影響、效果 Track 4634

例句 The regulation will take effect next year.
這個規定將於明年生效。

搭配詞 take effect 生效

ego [ˋigo] n. 自我 Track 4635

例句 He has a huge ego.
他的自我意識超強。

elder [ˋɛldɚ] adj. 年長的 Track 4636

例句 Come here and meet my elder sister.
來這裡見我年長的姊姊吧。

同義字 older

embrace [ɪmˋbres] v./n. 包圍、擁抱 Track 4637

例句 The couple embraced each other for a long time.
這對情侶擁抱了很長一段時間。

同義字 hug

endeavor [ɪnˋdɛvɚ] v./n. 努力 Track 4638

例句 She endeavors to improve the quality of children's education.
她致力改善孩子們的教育品質。

engage [ɪnˋgedʒ] v. 僱用、允諾、訂婚、從事 Track 4639

例句 They announced that they are engaged.
他們宣布要訂婚了。

engagement [ɪnˋgedʒmənt] n. 預約、訂婚 Track 4640

＊字尾-ment有轉變為名詞之意

例句 She received a shiny engagement ring yesterday.
她昨天得到了閃亮亮的訂婚戒。

反義字 disengagement 解除婚約

enlargement [ɪn`lɑrdʒmənt] n. 擴張、放大 Track 4641

＊字尾-ment有轉變為名詞之意

例句 My mother asks us to send her an enlargement of our baby's photo.
我媽媽請我們送她一張我們寶寶的放大照片。

---

estate [ə`stet] n. 財產 Track 4642

例句 His business is about real estate.
他的工作和不動產有關。

搭配詞 real estate 不動產

---

esteem [əs`tim] v./n. 尊重 Track 4643

例句 We all have great esteem for the unsung hero.
我們都對這位無名英雄十分敬重。

---

exchange [ɪks`tʃendʒ] v./n. 交換 Track 4644

例句 The terrorists demanded a ransom in exchange for the hostages.
恐怖份子要求贖金來交換人質。

搭配詞 in exchange for 交換

---

excite [ɪk`saɪt] v. 刺激、使興奮、鼓舞 Track 4645

例句 We are all very excited about the good news.
我們對於這個喜訊，都感到很興奮。

搭配詞 be excited about 對……是興奮的

---

expect [ɪk`spɛkt] v. 期望 Track 4646

例句 Is this the parcel you are expecting?
這是你期望拿到的包裹嗎？

---

expectation [͵ɛkspɛk`teʃən] n. 期望 Track 4647

例句 My mom has a great expectation of our success.
我媽媽對我們的成功期望很高。

---

expense [ɪk`spɛns] n. 費用 Track 4648

例句 You need to take records of your expenses, or you will become broke soon. 你應該要記錄你的花費，不然你很快就會破產了。

---

faithful [`feθfəl] adj. 忠實的、耿直的、可靠的 Track 4649

＊字尾-ful有「充滿」的意思

例句 Our old dog has been very faithful to my family.
我們的老狗對我們的家庭很忠實。

同義字 loyal

---

familiar [fə`mɪljɚ] adj. 熟悉的、親密的 Track 4650

例句 I am not so familiar with my neighborhood.
我對我的社區不太熟悉。

搭配詞 be familiar with 熟悉、精通

family [ˋfæməlɪ] n. 家庭 Track 4651

例句 My family name is Norman.
我的姓氏是諾曼。

搭配詞
family name 姓氏

fate [fet] n. 命運、宿命 Track 4652

例句 She believes that they met because of fate.
她相信他們遇見是宿命。

father [ˋfɑðɚ] n. 父親 Track 4653

例句 My father was very strict when we were young.
我們小時候，我爸爸很嚴格。

搭配詞
Like father, like son.
有其父必有其子。

fiancé/fiancee [ˏfiənˋse] n. 未婚夫／未婚妻 Track 4654

例句 My fiancé is a funny and honest man with brown hair.
我的未婚夫是個好笑、誠實、有著棕髮的男人。

finance [faɪˋnæns] n. 財務 Track 4655

例句 He works in the finance department of a large corporation.
他在一間大企業的財務部門上班。

forgive [fɚˋgɪv] v. 原諒、寬恕 Track 4656

例句 After living in bitterness for years, he finally decided to forgive and forget about the incident.
他活在痛苦回憶裡多年以後，終於決定放下那段舊惡。

搭配詞
forgive and forget 不念舊惡

found [faʊnd] v. 建立、打基礎 Track 4657

例句 They founded the school ten years ago.
他們在十年前建立這所學校。

friend [frɛnd] n. 朋友 Track 4658

例句 After the incident, I realize that they're only fair-weather friends.
發生事情後，我了解了他們只是酒肉朋友。

搭配詞
a fair-weather friend
酒肉朋友

friendship [ˋfrɛndʃɪp] n. 友誼、友情 Track 4659

例句 She cherished their friendship, but he did not.
她珍惜他們之間的友情，但他並不珍惜。

同義字
amity

frustrate [ˋfrʌstret] v. 使受挫、擊敗 Track 4660

例句 She was frustrated because her parents wouldn't listen.
她的父母就是不聽，讓她很受挫。

反義字
fulfil 實現、滿足

fund [fʌnd] **n.** 資金、財源 ◀Track 4661

例句 We are raising funds for the street dogs.
我們在為流浪狗募資金。

gathering [ˋgæðərɪŋ] **n.** 集會、聚集 ◀Track 4662

例句 We don't mind you inviting him to our small social gathering.
我們不介意你邀請他來我們的小集會。

generosity [ˏdʒɛnəˋrɑsətɪ] **n.** 慷慨、寬宏大量 ◀Track 4663

例句 She showed a lot of generosity towards the orphans.
她對孤兒們表現得很慷慨。

girl [gɝl] **n.** 女孩 ◀Track 4664

例句 The little girl had a pretty pink dress on.
那個小女孩穿著一件漂亮的粉紅色洋裝。

give [gɪv] **v.** 給、提供、捐助 ◀Track 4665

例句 She gave her toys to her little sister.
她把玩具都給妹妹了。

glory [ˋglorɪ] **n.** 榮耀、光榮 ◀Track 4666

例句 She brought glory to her family by winning the game.
她因為贏得比賽而為她家帶來了光榮。

grandchild [ˋgrændˏtʃaɪld] ◀Track 4667
n. （外）孫子、（外）孫女

例句 My grandfather is proud of his 10 grandchildren.
我爺爺為他的十個孫子孫女感到驕傲。

granddaughter [ˋgrændˏdɔtə] ◀Track 4668
n. 孫女、外孫女

例句 His granddaughter broke his precious china but he didn't get mad.
他的孫女打碎了他珍貴的瓷器，但他沒有生氣。

相關詞 grandson 孫子、外孫子

grandfather/grandpa ◀Track 4669
[ˋgrændˏfɑðə]/[ˋgrændpɑ] **n.** 祖父、外祖父

例句 My grandfather just had surgery on his knees yesterday.
我祖父昨天才動了膝蓋的手術。

grandmother/grandma ◀Track 4670
[ˋgrændˏmʌðə]/[ˋgrændˏmʌ] **n.** 祖母、外祖母

例句 My grandmother is surely the most stylish grandmother in the world.
我奶奶一定是全世界最時髦的奶奶。

grandson [ˋgrændˏsʌn] n. 孫子、外孫 Track 4671
例句 I am the oldest grandson of my grandfather.
我是我爺爺年紀最大的孫子。

相關詞
granddaughter
孫女、外孫女

---

grave [grev] n. 墓穴、墳墓 Track 4672
例句 Swearing at your boss is like digging your own grave.
對著你老闆罵髒話，簡直就是自掘墳墓。

搭配詞
dig one's own grave
自掘墳墓

---

grope [grop] v./n. 摸索 Track 4673
例句 She was groping for her glasses in the darkness.
她在黑暗中摸索著找她的眼鏡。

---

guarantee [ˏgærənˋti] v./n. 擔保、作保 Track 4674
例句 Our products come with a two-year guarantee.
我們的產品保固期是2年。

---

guest [gɛst] n. 客人 Track 4675
例句 If you want to drive my car, be my guest.
如果你想開我的車，別客氣。

搭配詞
be my guest 請便、別客氣

---

guidance [ˋgaɪdn̩s] n. 引導、指導 Track 4676
＊字尾-ance有轉變為名詞之意
例句 I need my parents' guidance. 我需要父母的指引。

搭配詞
need guidance 需要指引

---

gulf [gʌlf] n. 灣、海灣、鴻溝 Track 4677
例句 I always hope that there will be no gulf between my kids and me.
我總是希望我與孩子們之間不會有鴻溝。

---

he [hi] pron. 他 Track 4678
例句 He is a hardworking man with grey hair.
他是個有著灰髮、努力工作的男人。

---

heir [ɛr] n. 繼承人 Track 4679
例句 I heard that she is the only legal heir of the rich family.
我聽說她是這個富有的家族唯一一個法定繼承人。

---

hello [həˋlo] Track 4680
int./n. 哈囉（問候語）、喂（電話應答語）
例句 How about saying hello to our new teacher?
要不要和我們的新老師說聲哈囉呢？

搭配詞
say hello to 向某人打招呼

her [hɝ] pron. 她的 Track 4681

例句 Let's visit her at her new apartment.
我們到她的新公寓拜訪她吧。

heritage [ˋhɛrətɪdʒ] n. 遺產 Track 4682

例句 I did not know that these ancient buildings are also part of the national heritage.
我不知道這些古老的大樓也是國家遺產的一部分。

搭配詞
national heritage 國家遺產

hers [hɝz] pron. 她的、她的東西 Track 4683

例句 I know your address and telephone number, but not hers.
我知道你的地址和電話，但不知道她的。

him [hɪm] pron. 他 Track 4684

例句 It is very sweet of him to pack all the boxes for you.
他幫你收這些箱子真是太好了。

his [hɪz] pron. 他的、他的東西 Track 4685

例句 Don't you know that his wife is my cousin?
你不知道他的太太是我表姊嗎？

home [hom] n. 家、家鄉 Track 4686

例句 I go home once a week to see my parents.
我每個禮拜回家一次看父母。

搭配詞
go home 回家

honeymoon [ˋhʌnɪ͵mun] n./v. 蜜月、度蜜月 Track 4687

例句 Where did you go on your honeymoon trip? Did you have fun?
你蜜月旅行去哪？好玩嗎？

hope [hop] v./n. 希望、期望 Track 4688

例句 He hopes that he can find a job at the end of the month.
他希望可以在月底前找到工作。

host/hostess [host]/[ˋhostɪs] n. 主人、女主人 Track 4689

例句 The hostess of this party is a friend of mine.
這個派對的女主人是我的朋友。

household [ˋhaus͵hold] adj. 家庭的 Track 4690

例句 Ivanka Trump has been a household name since she became the first daughter of the United States.
伊凡卡川普自從貴為美國第一千金，成為家喻戶曉的名人。

搭配詞
household name
家喻戶曉的名人

housewife [ˋhausˏwaɪf] n. 家庭主婦 Track 4691

例句 She's a great housewife who knows how to cook and bake.
她是個厲害的家庭主婦，懂得如何煮菜與烘焙。

housework [ˋhausˏwɝk] n. 家事 Track 4692

例句 My husband knows how to do housework well.
我丈夫很清楚怎麼做家事。

humanity [hjuˋmænətɪ] n. 人類、人道 Track 4693

例句 This is a weapon strong enough to wipe out all humanity.
這個武器夠強，能夠將全人類給殺光。

husband [ˋhʌzbənd] n. 丈夫 Track 4694

例句 It is hard to find an ideal husband.
要找個理想的丈夫真是太困難了。

hush [hʌʃ] v. 使寂靜 Track 4695

例句 She told her kids to hush.
她要她的孩子們安靜。

I [aɪ] pron. 我 Track 4696

例句 I am interested in studying astrophysics.
我對學習天體物理學很有興趣。

identical [aɪˋdɛntɪkḷ] adj. 相同的 Track 4697

例句 They look just the same because they're identical twins.
他們長得一模一樣，因為他們是同卵雙胞胎。

搭配詞
identical twins 同卵雙胞胎

identification [aɪˏdɛntəfəˋkeʃən] Track 4698

n. 身分證、識別 ＊字尾-tion有轉變為名詞的意思

例句 To apply for the membership, we need your identification document.
我們需要你的身分文件，才能幫你幫會員。

identity [aɪˋdɛntətɪ] n. 身分 Track 4699

例句 Please show me your identity card before entering.
入內之前請先給我看你的身分證。

important [ɪmˋpɔrtṇt] adj. 重要的 Track 4700

例句 It is important to find your own calling in life.
找到自己人生中該做的事是很重要的。

indulge [ɪn`dʌldʒ] v. 沉溺、放縱、遷就 Track 4701

例句 He indulged himself in alcohol after divorce.
他離婚後，就沉溺在酒精裡。

搭配詞 indulge in 沉溺於

inherit [ɪn`hɛrɪt] v. 繼承、接受 Track 4702

例句 He inherited a fortune from his parents.
他從他父母那裡繼承到了許多錢。

同義字 receive

inspiration [ɪnspə`reʃən] n. 鼓舞、激勵、靈感 Track 4703

＊字尾-tion有轉變為名詞的意思

例句 Jack is a huge inspiration in every aspect of her paintings.
傑克在各方面都是她繪畫的靈感泉源。

同義字 stimulation

inspire [ɪn`spaɪr] v. 啟發、鼓舞、激起 Track 4704

例句 I am inspired by Nikola Tesla's autobiography.
我從尼古拉特斯拉的自傳獲得啟發。

同義字 encourage

instead [ɪn`stɛd] adv. 替代 Track 4705

例句 He took the bus to school today instead of riding a bike.
他今天搭公車到學校，替代騎腳踏車。

搭配詞 instead of 代替、與其

insurance [ɪn`ʃurəns] n. 保險 Track 4706

＊字尾-ance有轉變為名詞之意

例句 I have 5 insurance policies. 我有5張保險單。

搭配詞 insurance policy 保險單

intimate [`ɪntəmɪt] n./adj. 知己、親近的 Track 4707

例句 He is not only my colleague but also my intimate friend.
他不只是我的同事，也是我的親密好友。

it [ɪt] pron. 它 Track 4708

例句 I can't see it anywhere.
我到處都沒看到它。

its [ɪts] n. 它的 Track 4709

例句 Not so many people know its true value.
沒有很多人知道它的真正價值。

juvenile [`dʒuvən!] Track 4710

n./adj. 青少年、孩子、青少年的

例句 Proper counseling and guidance can effectively prevent juvenile delinquency. 適當的諮商和指引能有效避免青少年犯罪。

搭配詞 juvenile delinquency 青少年犯罪

keeper [ˋkipɚ] n. 看守人、主人 ◀Track 4711

＊字尾-er有「者」的意思

例句 The shop keeper sells a lot of exotic goods.
這個店主人賣很多異國產品。

kid [kɪd] n. 小孩 ◀Track 4712

例句 How many kids do you have?
你有幾個孩子？

kin [kɪn] n. 親族、親戚 ◀Track 4713

例句 She wrote Kevin's name as her next of kin.
她在親屬欄填了凱文的名字。

lady [ˋledɪ] n. 女士、淑女 ◀Track 4714

例句 Do you know that young lady?
你認識那個年輕淑女嗎？

leisure [ˋliʒɚ] n. 空閒 ◀Track 4715

例句 Marry in haste, and repent at leisure.
倉促結婚後悔多。

搭配詞 at leisure 有空、清閒

lie [laɪ] n./v. 謊言 ◀Track 4716

例句 There are lots of lies on TV.
電視上有很多謊言。

loan [lon] n./v. 借貸 ◀Track 4717

例句 He loaned us his car.
他把他的車借給我們。

love [lʌv] n./v. 愛 ◀Track 4718

例句 John and Olivia are in love.
約翰和奧莉薇雅在戀愛中。

搭配詞 Love is blind.
愛情是盲目的。

lover [ˋlʌvɚ] n. 愛人 ＊字尾-er有「者」的意思 ◀Track 4719

例句 Have you seen her lover? What does he look like?
你看過她的愛人嗎？他長什麼樣子？

lure [lur] n./v. 誘餌、誘惑 ◀Track 4720

例句 The boy was lured into gang life when he was only eight years old.
那名男孩8歲時就被引誘進幫派的生活。

同義字 decoy

luxurious [lʌgˋʒurɪəs] adj. 奢侈的、奢華的 Track 4721

＊字尾-ous有轉變為形容詞之意

例句 Look at these luxurious furniture! I can't believe my eyes.
快看這些奢華的家具！我真不敢相信我的眼睛。

反義字 economical 節約的

luxury [ˋlʌkʃərɪ] n. 奢侈品、奢侈 Track 4722

例句 He lives in the lap of luxury and doesn't know what suffering is.
他在優裕的環境中生活，不知人間疾苦。

搭配詞 in the lap of luxury 在優裕的環境中

madam [ˋmædəm] n. 夫人、女士 Track 4723

例句 Would you like to see some other jewelries, madam?
妳想再看看一些其他珠寶嗎，女士？

同義字 madame

man [mæn] n. 成年男人 Track 4724

例句 There are lots of men but only a few women in our department.
我們的部門有許多男人，但只有幾個女人。

marriage [ˋmærɪdʒ] n. 婚姻 Track 4725

例句 We all need to learn how to manage a happy marriage.
我們都必須學著經營一段快樂的婚姻。

marry [ˋmærɪ] v. 使結為夫妻、結婚 Track 4726

例句 The couple got married at St George's Chapel in London.
這對佳人在倫敦聖喬治禮拜堂結婚。

mate [met] n. 配偶 Track 4727

例句 Deep in my heart, I know he is my ideal mate.
在我心深處，我知道他是我理想的配偶。

mature [məˋtjur] adj. 成熟的 Track 4728

例句 He is not mature enough to take care of his mom.
他不夠成熟，無法照顧自己的母親。

反義字 immature 未成熟的

me [mi] n. 我 Track 4729

例句 Excuse me. Can you tell me how long I can keep these tools?
不好意思，你可以告訴我我能留著這些工具多久嗎？

搭配詞 excuse me 請問，不好意思

merry [ˋmɛrɪ] adj. 快樂的 Track 4730

例句 My grandfather had merry, twinkling eyes.
我爺爺有著快樂的、發亮的眼睛。

mild [maɪld] adj. 溫和的 Track 4731

例句 John has a mild manner and never raises his voice.
約翰的舉止溫和，從不大聲說話。

mislead [mɪsˋlid] v. 誤導 Track 4732

＊字首out-有「誤」之意

例句 The guidebook misled us. 導覽書誤導了我們。

Miss/miss [mɪs] n. 小姐 Track 4733

例句 You left your purse, miss!
妳錢包沒拿，小姐！

mistress [ˋmɪstrɪs] n. 情婦 Track 4734

例句 She is a mistress of the rich businessman.
她是這個富人的情婦。

mommy/mom [ˋmɑmɪ]/[mɑm] n. 媽咪 Track 4735

例句 What did your mom look like when she was a teenager?
你媽媽在十幾歲時長得怎樣呢？

mother [ˋmʌðɚ] n. 母親、媽媽 Track 4736

例句 She is a mother of two boys and one girl.
她是兩男一女的母親。

motherhood [ˋmʌðɚhud] n. 母性、母親的身份 Track 4737

例句 My friend told me how she enjoys every moment of motherhood.
我朋友告訴我，她享受身為母親的每一刻。

Mr./Mister [ˋmɪstɚ] n. 對男士的稱呼、先生 Track 4738

例句 When she got married, she wasn't sure if her husband was her Mr. Right. 她結婚時並不確定先生是不是她的真命天子。

搭配詞
Mr. Right 真命天子

Mrs. [ˋmɪsɪz] n. 夫人 Track 4739

例句 What does Mrs. White look like?
白夫人長得怎樣呢？

Ms. [mɪz] n. 女士 Track 4740

例句 Ms. Breton, would you like a glass of water?
布雷頓女士，妳要來一杯水嗎？

mutual [ˋmjutʃʊəl] adj. 相互的、共同的 Track 4741

例句 We have a lot of mutual interests.
我們有很多共同興趣。

my [maɪ] pron. 我的 Track 4742

例句 My Goodness. You just bumped into Angelina Jolie on the street?
我的天哪，你剛剛在路上巧遇安潔莉娜裘莉？

搭配詞 my goodness 我的天哪

name [nem] n. 名字、姓名、名稱、名義 Track 4743

例句 Her name is Julianne Moore.
她的名字是茱莉安摩爾。

nap [næp] n./v. 小睡、打盹 Track 4744

例句 I need to take a nap at noon. What about you?
我中午要小睡一下。你呢？

necessity [nəˋsɛsətɪ] n. 必需品、必要性 Track 4745

例句 She felt the necessity of answering the call.
她覺得接這通電話有其必要性。

needy [ˋnidɪ] adj. 貧窮的、貧困的 Track 4746

＊字尾-y有轉變為形容詞之意

例句 There are many needy families in our country.
我國有許多貧困的家庭。

nephew [ˋnɛfju] n. 姪子、外甥 Track 4747

例句 My nephew is a member of the baseball team.
我姪子是棒球隊的隊員。

反義字 niece 姪女、外甥女

newly-wed [ˋnjulɪˏwɛd] n. 新婚夫婦 Track 4748

例句 How are the newly-weds getting on with each other?
這對新婚夫婦過得如何呢？

nickname [ˋnɪkˏnem] n. 綽號 Track 4749

例句 I enjoy coming up with nicknames for everyone.
我喜歡為大家想綽號。

同義字 moniker

niece [nis] n. 姪女、外甥女 Track 4750

例句 My niece will come to live with us for several months.
我姪女會來和我們住幾個月。

反義字 nephew 姪子、外甥

nominate [ˋnɑmə͵net] v. 提名、指定 Track 4751

例句 She is nominated the best singer of the year.
她被提名為年度最佳歌手。

nonetheless [͵nʌnðəˋlɛs] adv./conj. 儘管如此、然而 Track 4752

例句 She is young, but I respect her nonetheless.
她很年輕，然而我還是尊敬她。

notable [ˋnotəbl̩] n. 名人、出眾的人 Track 4753

＊字尾-able有「可以、能」的意思

例句 There are many notables attending the ceremony.
有許多名人參加那場典禮。

nurture [ˋnɝtʃɚ] v. 養育、培育 Track 4754

例句 They nurtured their son to become an artist.
他們把兒子培育成了藝術家。

同義字 rear

occasion [əˋkeʒən] n. 事件、場合 Track 4755

例句 Tomorrow will be your parents' wedding anniversary. Why don't you take this occasion to thank them?
明天是你父母的結婚紀念日。何不利用這個場合來謝謝他們呢？

offspring [ˋɔfsprɪŋ] n. 子孫、後裔 Track 4756

例句 Their offspring are intelligent and charming.
他們的子孫都很聰明、迷人。

同義字 descendant

oppress [əˋprɛs] v. 壓迫、威迫 Track 4757

例句 It is obvious that a tyrannical president who oppresses people will be overthrown one day.
一個壓迫人民的暴君總統明顯地總有一天會被推翻。

同義字 burden

oppression [əˋprɛʃən] n. 壓迫、壓制 Track 4758

例句 Some Rohingyas could no longer stand the oppression and chose to flee to other countries.
有些羅興亞人再也無法忍受壓迫，選擇逃離到別的國家。

同義字 persecution

option [ˋɑpʃən] n. 選擇、取捨 Track 4759

例句 Could you tell me how many options do we have?
你可以告訴我我們有幾種選擇嗎？

optional [ˋɑpʃənl̩] adj. 非強制性的、可選擇的 Track 4760

＊字尾-al有轉變為形容詞之意

例句 Would you please tell me if the optional course is as boring as everybody says?
你可以告訴我選修課是不是和大家說的一樣無聊嗎？

同義字 voluntary

orphan [ˋɔrfən] **n.** 孤兒 ◀ Track 4761

例句 This orphan will stay at our home for several months.
這名孤兒會在我們家待幾個月。

---

orphanage [ˋɔrfənɪdʒ] **n.** 孤兒院 ◀ Track 4762

例句 We will find someone to run the orphanage.
我們會找人來管理孤兒院。

---

our(s) [ˋaʊr(z)] **pron.** 我們的（東西） ◀ Track 4763

例句 How long will it take to get to our office?
去我們的辦公室要多久？

---

outsider [ˌautˋsaɪdɚ] **n.** 局外人 ◀ Track 4764

＊字尾-er有「者」的意思

例句 It is not easy for an outsider to understand why this could happen.
對局外人來說很難瞭解為什麼會發生這種事。

諺語 The outsider sees the best of the game. 旁觀者清。

---

own [on] **pro./adj.** 自己的 ◀ Track 4765

例句 After he turned 18, he was pretty much on his own.
他18歲以後就幾乎靠自己了。

搭配詞 on one's own 憑自己、獨立地

---

papa/pop [ˋpɑpə]/[pɑp] **n.** 爸爸 ◀ Track 4766

例句 I look like my papa.
我看起來很像我爸爸。

反義字 mama 媽媽

---

parent(s) [ˋpɛrənt(s)] **n.** 雙親、家長 ◀ Track 4767

例句 We still live with our parents.
我們還跟雙親住在一起。

---

payment [ˋpemənt] **n.** 支付、付款 ◀ Track 4768

＊字尾-ment有轉變為名詞之意

例句 They demanded payment immediately.
他們要求馬上付款。

同義字 remuneration

---

pension [ˋpɛnʃən] **n.** 退休金 ◀ Track 4769

例句 He lived quite happily on pension.
他領退休金就過得很愉快。

---

plight [plaɪt] **n.** 誓約、婚約、困境、苦境 ◀ Track 4770

例句 The man was in a sad plight.
那個男人在悲傷的困境中。

搭配詞 in a plight 在困境中

possession [pə`zɛʃən] n. 擁有物、財產 Track 4771

例句 His possessions could fit in one backpack.
他的所有財產一個背包就裝得下。

postponement [post`ponmənt] n. 延後 Track 4772

＊字尾-ment有轉變為名詞之意

例句 She was not happy with the postponement of the meeting.
對於會議延後，她不是很高興。

potential [pə`tɛnʃəl] n./adj. 潛力 Track 4773

例句 She had a lot of potential in dancing.
她很有跳舞的潛力。

搭配詞 have potential 有潛力

preach [pritʃ] v./n. 傳教、說教、鼓吹 Track 4774

例句 The man devoted all his life to preaching.
這個男人一生都投入於傳教。

precious [`prɛʃəs] adj. 珍貴的 Track 4775

例句 You have to make good use of every precious minute.
每個珍貴的一分一秒都不能浪費。

predecessor [͵prɛdɪ`sɛsɚ] Track 4776

n. 祖先、前輩、原有的事物　＊字尾-or有「者」的意思

例句 We don't think the new employee is better than his predecessor.
我們不覺得這個新員工有比他的前任前輩來得好。

反義字 successor 後繼者

price [praɪs] n. 價格、代價 Track 4777

例句 I got this laptop at a low price.
我用很低的價格買到這台筆電。

primary [`praɪ͵mɛrɪ] adj. 主要的 Track 4778

例句 Tom's primary virtue is his honesty.
湯姆主要的優點是他的誠實。

privacy [`praɪvəsɪ] n. 隱私 Track 4779

例句 Can you give us some privacy?
可以給我們一些隱私嗎？

private [`praɪvɪt] adj./n. 私密的；私下 Track 4780

例句 Let's discuss this issue in private.
我們私下討論這件事吧。

搭配詞 in private 私下地

privilege [ˋprɪvḷɪdʒ] n. 特權 ◀Track 4781

例句 We envy him for having such a privilege.
我們羨慕他有這樣的特權。

同義字 advantage

probable [ˋprɑbəbḷ] adj. 可能的 ◀Track 4782

＊字尾-able有「可以、能」的意思

例句 The probable cause of his death is kidney failure.
他的死因很可能是腎衰竭。

同義字 likely

process [ˋprɑsɛs] n. 過程 ◀Track 4783

例句 How much weight did you lose in the process?
在這個過程中，你的體重減輕多少？

搭配詞 in the process 在進行過程中

proof [pruf] n. 證據 ◀Track 4784

例句 They claim that they have enough proof to win the case.
他們堅稱他們有足夠的證據來支持這個案件。

propose [prəˋpoz] v. 提議、求婚 ◀Track 4785

例句 My brother is going to propose to his girlfriend this weekend.
我哥哥這週末要和他女友求婚。

搭配詞 propose to 向……求婚

protection [prəˋtɛkʃən] n. 保護 ◀Track 4786

＊字尾-tion有轉變為名詞的意思

例句 You must wear a hard hat as a protection when working at construction sites.
你在建築工地工作時，一定要戴工地安全帽保護自己。

protective [prəˋtɛktɪv] adj. 保護的 ◀Track 4787

＊字尾-ive有轉變為形容詞之意

例句 It is normal for a mother to feel protective towards her children.
母親對孩子覺得很保護是正常的。

recipient [rɪˋsɪpɪənt] n. 接受者 ◀Track 4788

例句 If the recipient is not found, the mail will be returned to the post office. 如果找不到收件人，信件就會退回到郵局。

reliance [rɪˋlaɪəns] n. 信賴、依賴 ◀Track 4789

例句 My suggestion is to not place too much reliance on what he said, or you will regret it.
我建議你不要太信賴他講的話，不然你會後悔。

retail [ˋritel] n./adj./adv./v. 零售 ◀Track 4790

例句 My job title is a retail seller.
我的工作職稱是零售商。

revival [rɪˋvaɪvl̩] n. 復甦 Track 4791

例句 There is a visible sign of a revival in the economy.
經濟明顯看得出有復甦跡象。

react [rɪˋækt] v. 反應 ＊字首re-有「再次」之意 Track 4792

例句 She reacted violently when he touched her.
他一摸她，她就有很激烈的反應。

reaction [rɪˋækʃən] n. 反應 Track 4793

＊字尾-tion有轉變為名詞的意思

例句 His reaction to her words was dramatic.
他聽了她說的話，做出戲劇化的反應。

反義字 action

reconcile [ˋrɛkənˏsaɪl] v. 調停、和解 Track 4794

＊字首re-有「再次」之意

例句 The girls finally reconciled after the fight.
女孩們終於在吵架後和好了。

同義字 settle

receipt [rɪˋsit] n. 收據 Track 4795

例句 Would you please give me a receipt?
你可以給我一張收據嗎？

receiver [rɪˋsivɚ] n. 收受者 Track 4796

＊字尾-er有「者」的意思

例句 Why don't you write down the receiver's name on the envelope?
為什麼不把收件人的名字寫在信封上呢？

反義字 sender 寄件人

refuge/sanctuary [ˋrɛfjudʒ]/[ˋsæŋktʃuˏɛrɪ] Track 4797

n. 避難（所）

例句 Residents took refuge from the cyclone in a gym.
居民因為颶風，而到體育館避難。

搭配詞 take refuge from 尋求庇護

relate [rɪˋlet] v. 敘述、有關係 Track 4798

例句 She is related to the boss.
她和老闆有親戚關係。

搭配詞 relate to 與……有關

relation [rɪˋleʃən] n. 關係 Track 4799

＊字尾-tion有轉變為名詞的意思

例句 There is no relation between the two people.
這兩個人之間沒有關係。

relationship [rɪˋleʃənˏʃɪp] n. 關係、感情關係 Track 4800

例句 Is there any relationship between them? It is confusing.
他們之間到底有沒有關係？很難懂耶。

release [rɪˋlis] v./n. 解放、釋放 Track 4801

例句 The kidnapper released the little girl.
綁架犯釋放了小女孩。

反義字
capture 捕獲

reliable [rɪˋlaɪəbḷ] adj. 可靠的 Track 4802

＊字尾-able有「可以、能」的意思

例句 I don't think this detergent is reliable.
我不覺得這牌的清潔劑是可靠的。

反義字
unreliable 不可靠的

relief [rɪˋlif] n. 放鬆、減輕 Track 4803

例句 He breathed a sigh of relief on hearing the news that his daughter was back from the war zone.
他聽到女兒從戰區回來了，便鬆了一口氣。

rely [rɪˋlaɪ] v. 依賴 Track 4804

例句 You should learn not to rely on your parents so much.
你應該學著不要這麼依賴你父母。

搭配詞
rely on 依靠、信賴

remain [rɪˋmen] v. 殘留、仍然、繼續 Track 4805

例句 A few apples remain on the stand.
有幾顆蘋果留在台子上。

remind [rɪˋmaɪnd] v. 提醒、使想起 Track 4806

例句 The picture reminds us of the good old days.
這張照片讓我們回想起過去那段美好的時光。

搭配詞
remind of 使回想起

replace [rɪˋples] v. 代替 Track 4807

例句 The CEO tried to replace the factory's workers with AI robots.
這位執行長試圖以人工智慧機器人取代工廠的勞工。

搭配詞
replace with 以……取代

reply [rɪˋplaɪ] v./n. 回答、答覆 Track 4808

例句 Please reply to me as soon as possible because I am leaving soon.
請盡快回答我，因為我快離開了。

request [rɪˋkwɛst] n./v. 要求 Track 4809

例句 Would you please allow me to make a small request?
你可以讓我提一個小小的要求嗎？

resemble [rɪˋzɛmbḷ] v. 類似 Track 4810

例句 She did not resemble her father.
她和她爸爸長得不相似。

反義字
differ 相異

reserve [rɪˋzɝv] v./n. 保留 Track 4811

例句 Let's reserve the energy for later.
我們把體力保留到待會用吧。

respond [rɪˋspɑnd] v. 回答 Track 4812

例句 She didn't respond to his question.
她沒有回答他的問題。

搭配詞 respond to 對……作出反應、對……作出回答

response [rɪˋspɑns] n. 回應、答覆 Track 4813

例句 In response to your inquiry, we provide the following information that might be of help.
為答覆你的詢問，我們提供以下資訊希望對你有幫助。

搭配詞 in response to 作為對……的答覆

responsibility [rɪˏspɑnsəˋbɪlətɪ] n. 責任 Track 4814

例句 These kids are too young to have a sense of responsibility.
這些孩子太小了，還沒什麼責任感。

reunion [riˋjunjən] n. 重聚、團圓 Track 4815

＊字首re-有「再次」之意

例句 How often do you have a class reunion?
你們多久辦一次班級聚會？

同義字 gathering

revenue [ˋrɛvəˏnju] n. 收入 Track 4816

例句 The hotel is trying to increase its revenue.
這家飯店正試著增加收入。

reward [rɪˋwɔrd] n. 報酬、獎賞 Track 4817

例句 He got a reward for finding the criminal.
他因為找到了犯人而得到報酬。

romance [roˋmæns] n. 羅曼史、浪漫 Track 4818

例句 Everyone enjoys a little bit of romance in their lives.
大家都喜歡生活中有一點浪漫。

saving(s) [ˋsevɪŋ(z)] n. 拯救、救助、存款 Track 4819

例句 Is it safer to put all your savings into an account?
把全部的存款都放到一個帳戶中，安全嗎？

搭配詞 savings account 存款帳戶

scold [skold] v./n. 責備 Track 4820

例句 He was scolded roundly for his mistakes.
他因為犯錯而被痛罵。

搭配詞 scold roundly 痛罵

secure [sɪˋkjʊr] v./adj. 保護、安全的 ◀Track 4821

例句 Sleeping in his arms makes me feel secure.
在他懷中睡著讓我覺得很安全。

---

seduce [sɪˋdjus] v. 引誘、慫恿 ◀Track 4822

例句 I was seduced by the cakes laid out in the fridge and decided to buy one to cheer myself up.
我被冰箱裡陳設的蛋糕引誘，決定買一個回家犒賞自己。

同義字 tempt

---

self [sɛlf] n. 自己、自我 ◀Track 4823

例句 The supermarket offers self-help check out service.
這家超市提供自助式付費服務。

---

sermon [ˋsɝmən] n. 佈道、講道 ◀Track 4824

例句 We listened to a sermon at the church.
我們在教堂聽了一場佈道。

---

setting [ˋsɛtɪŋ] n. 安置、背景、環境 ◀Track 4825

例句 I think that this is an ideal setting for picnic.
我覺得這是適合野餐的一個地點環境。

同義字 background

---

sex [sɛks] n. 性、性別 ◀Track 4826

例句 What sex is your dog?
你家小狗是公的還是母的？

---

sexual [sɛkʃuəl] adj. 性的 ◀Track 4827

例句 Everyone knows that AIDS can be transmitted by sexual activities.
大家都知道愛滋病可以透過性行為傳染。

搭配詞 sexual harassment 性騷擾

---

share [ʃɛr] n./v. 份、分享 ◀Track 4828

例句 She shared the cake with her brother.
她和弟弟分享她的蛋糕。

---

she [ʃi] pron. 她 ◀Track 4829

例句 She looks great in that blue dress.
她穿那件藍色洋裝看起來真棒。

---

shrug [ʃrʌg] v./n. 聳肩 ◀Track 4830

例句 He just shrugged off and said nothing.
他只是不理會，什麼也沒說。

搭配詞 shrug off 不理、擺脫

silent [ˋsaɪlənt] adj. 沉默的 Track 4831

例句 Would you please be silent? The students are taking a quiz.
你可以安靜嗎？學生們在考試。

sincerity [sɪnˋsɛrətɪ] n. 誠懇、真摯 Track 4832

例句 Her sincerity about everything is endearing.
她凡事都很誠懇對待的態度非常討喜。

sir [sɝ] n. 先生 Track 4833

例句 Would you like some pears, sir?
你想來點梨子嗎，先生？

sister [ˋsɪstɚ] n. 姐妹、姐、妹 Track 4834

例句 She has a half-sister who is jealous of her.
她有個同父異母的姊姊很嫉妒她。

搭配詞 half-sister 同父異母或同母異父之姊妹

snarl [snɑrl] v./n. 漫罵、咆哮 Track 4835

例句 The cat snarled when he saw the dog.
那隻貓看到那隻狗時，咆哮一聲。

snort [snɔrt] v./n. 鼻息、哼氣 Track 4836

例句 The girl snorted a laugh.
那個女孩哼氣地笑了出來。

sober [ˋsobɚ] v. 使清醒 Track 4837

例句 I'm sure a basin of cold water can sober you up.
我想用一缸冷水就能讓你清醒了。

搭配詞 sober up （使某人）醒酒或清醒

soften [ˋsɔftən] v. 使柔軟 Track 4838

＊字尾-en有「使」的意思

例句 Her face softened when she saw the baby.
她看到那個小寶寶，表情立刻柔軟下來。

solitary [ˋsɑlə͵tɛrɪ] adj. 隱居的、獨自的 Track 4839

例句 She enjoyed solitary life. 她享受獨自一人生活。

solo [ˋsolo] n./adj./adv./v. 獨唱、獨奏、單獨表演 Track 4840

例句 She had a solo live at the club last night.
她昨晚在俱樂部有獨唱現場表演。

搭配詞 solo live 獨唱現場表演

son [sʌn] n. 兒子 Track 4841

例句 My son loves to go picnicking. 我兒子喜歡去野餐。

specimen [ˋspɛsəmən] n. 樣本、樣品 Track 4842

例句 This is the specimen of the new product.
這是新產品的樣本。

同義字 sample

spectator [ˋspɛktetɚ] n. 觀眾、旁觀者 Track 4843

＊字尾-or有「者」的意思

例句 The Super Bowl drew thousands of spectators.
超級盃吸引了上千的觀眾。

同義字 viewer

spend [spɛnd] v. 花費、付錢 Track 4844

例句 Where did you spend all your salary?
你把薪水都花到哪去了？

搭配詞 spend oneself 消耗掉、變弱

splendor [ˋsplɛndɚ] n. 燦爛、光輝 Track 4845

例句 We marveled at the splendor of the waterfall.
我們對瀑布燦爛的模樣大為讚嘆。

同義字 brilliance

spouse [spauz] n. 配偶、夫妻 Track 4846

例句 It's not fair of you to compare your spouse with other people's.
拿你的配偶和其他人的比較就太不公平了。

同義字 mate

squash [skwɑʃ] n./v. 擠壓的聲音、壓扁 Track 4847

例句 She squashed the cake when she sat on it.
她坐在蛋糕上，把它壓扁了。

squat [skwɑt] n./v. 蹲下的姿勢、蹲 Track 4848

例句 We squatted down under the tree.
我們蹲在樹下。

同義字 crouch

stare [stɛr] v./n. 盯、凝視 Track 4849

例句 Why are you staring at me? 你幹嘛盯著我看？

搭配詞 stare at 盯著看

steer [stɪr] v. 駕駛、引導 Track 4850

例句 He steered us away from the terrible scene.
他引導我們離開那個可怕的場景。

stepchild [ˋstɛp͵tʃɪld] n. 前夫（妻）所生的孩子 Track 4851

例句 It's hard for a parent to treat a stepchild as his or her own.
要一個父母對待前夫（妻）的孩子如己出，實在很困難。

stepfather [ˋstɛp͵fɑðɚ] n. 繼父、後父 Track 4852

例句 Her stepfather was kind to her and sent her to an elite school.
她的繼父對她很慈祥，送她去唸菁英學校。

stepmother [ˋstɛp͵mʌðɚ] n. 繼母、後母 Track 4853

例句 Have you seen her stepmother?
你有看到她的後母嗎？

stock [stɑk] n. 存貨、紫羅蘭、股票 Track 4854

例句 The books are currently out of stock.
這本書目前缺貨了。

搭配詞 out of stock 缺貨

storage [ˋstorɪdʒ] n. 儲存、倉庫 Track 4855

例句 Don't you think that the meat should be kept in cold storage?
你不覺得這肉應該冷凍儲存嗎？

stranger [ˋstrendʒɚ] n. 陌生人 Track 4856

＊字尾-er有「者」的意思

例句 Is it normal to feel nervous among so many strangers?
在這麼多陌生人中覺得緊張是正常的嗎？

stray [stre] n. 漂泊者、流浪者 Track 4857

例句 They picked up a stray cat from the street.
他們從街上撿到一隻流浪狗。

搭配詞 stray cat 流浪貓

stride [straɪd] v./n. 跨步、大步 Track 4858

例句 She took the problem in her stride.
她很輕易地就解決了這個問題。

搭配詞 take sth. in one's stride 輕易解決、從容應付

stubborn [ˋstʌbɚn] adj. 頑固的 Track 4859

例句 My grandfather is so stubborn that we don't know how to communicate with him.
我爺爺太頑固了，以致我們不知道怎麼跟他溝通。

successor [səkˋsɛsɚ] n. 後繼者、繼承人 Track 4860

＊字尾-or有「者」的意思

例句 His daughter is his only successor. 他女兒是他唯一的繼承人。

反義字 predecessor 前輩、祖先

suggest [sə`dʒɛst] v. 提議、建議 ◀Track 4861

例句 It is wise of you to suggest that he should stay in his hometown.
你建議他留在家鄉，是明智的。

同義字
hint

suspense [sə`spɛns] n. 懸而未決、擔心 ◀Track 4862

例句 The suspense is killing me.
這種懸疑的心情快讓我緊張死了。

sympathetic [ˌsɪmpə`θɛtɪk] ◀Track 4863

adj. 表示同情的、有同情心的

例句 We all know that he is a very sympathetic person.
我們都知道他是個很有同情心的人。

反義字
unsympathetic 不同情的、冷漠的

talkative [`tɔkətɪv] adj. 健談的 ◀Track 4864

例句 She is too talkative to keep your secret.
她太健談了，無法替你保守祕密。

反義字
taciturn 沉默寡言的

taunt [tɔnt] n./v. 辱罵、奚落 ◀Track 4865

例句 Some boys taunted him because he had red hair.
有些男孩因為他的紅髮而辱罵他。

teenager [`tinˌedʒɚ] n. 青少年 ◀Track 4866

＊字尾-er有「者」的意思

例句 Time flies! My daughter is already a teenager.
時光飛逝啊！我女兒現在已經是青少女了。

同義字
teen

tenant [`tɛnənt] n. 承租人 ◀Track 4867

例句 The tenants of the building all signed the contract.
這棟大樓的承租人都簽了這份合約。

搭配詞
tenant farmer 佃農

thank [θæŋk] v./n. 感謝、謝謝 ◀Track 4868

例句 Thank you so much for your help.
非常謝謝你的幫忙。

搭配詞
thank you 謝謝你

thorn [θɔrn] n. 刺、荊棘 ◀Track 4869

例句 There is a thorn in my foot.
我的腳上被荊棘刺到了。

thrift [θrɪft] n. 節約、節儉 ◀Track 4870

例句 Thrift is different from being stingy.
節約和小氣是不同的。

反義字
waste 浪費

a b c d e f g h i j k l m n o p q r s t u v w x y z

thrifty [θrɪftɪ] adj. 節儉的 Track 4871

例句 Both of my parents are the thrifty kind.
我父母都是節儉的那種人。

反義字
wasteful 浪費的

tolerable [ˋtɑlərəbḷ] adj. 可容忍的、可忍受的 Track 4872

＊字尾-able有「可以、能」的意思

例句 The pain is tolerable. 這種痛還算可忍受。

反義字
intolerable 不能忍受的、無法容忍的

tolerance [ˋtɑlərəns] n. 容忍 Track 4873

例句 She had no tolerance for noisy people.
她無法容忍吵鬧的人。

反義字
intolerance 無法忍受

tolerant [ˋtɑlərənt] adj. 忍耐的、容忍的 Track 4874

例句 Why are you tolerant of such violence?
你怎麼能忍受這種暴力呢？

搭配詞
be tolerant of 對……忍耐、對……寬容

tolerate [ˋtɑlə͵ret] v. 寬容、容忍 Track 4875

例句 Terrorism cannot be tolerated and should be roundly condemned.
恐怖主義不能被容忍，必須受到嚴厲的譴責。

同義字
endure

tomb [tum] n. 墳墓、塚 Track 4876

例句 Can you see what is written on the tomb stone?
你看得到墓碑上寫的是什麼字嗎？

同義字
grave

true [tru] adj. 真的、對的 Track 4877

例句 Her dream came true when she married her prince charming.
她嫁給她的白馬王子，夢想成真。

搭配詞
come true 成事實、實現

trust [trʌst] v./n. 信任 Track 4878

例句 People won't trust you if you don't trust them first.
你不先信任別人，別人就不會信任你。

twin [twɪn] n./adj. 雙胞胎、成對的 Track 4879

例句 The twin brothers look exactly the same.
這對雙胞胎兄弟長得一模一樣。

uncle [ˋʌŋkḷ] n. 叔叔、伯伯、舅舅、姑父、姨父 Track 4880

例句 Tell them you're Richard Branson's business partner, and Bob's your uncle, they'll invite you to the club. 告訴他們你是理查．布蘭森的事業夥伴，然後就會一切如意，他們就會邀請你加入俱樂部。

搭配詞
Bob's your uncle. 一切如意

us [ʌs] pron. 我們 ◀Track 4881

例句 The boss asked us to accomplish the task by bext Monday.
老闆要我們在下週一前完成這項工作。

搭配詞
let's say 比如、建議

value [ˋvælju] n. 價值 ◀Track 4882

例句 You can't take his words at face value.
你不能相信他字面上的話。

搭配詞
face value 字面意義、表面價值

violence [ˋvaɪələns] n. 暴力 ◀Track 4883

例句 Violence and drugs are things you shouldn't try.
你不應該嘗試暴力或吸毒。

we [wi] pron. 我們 ◀Track 4884

例句 We have known each other for ten years.
我們已經認識十年了。

wed [wɛd] v. 嫁、娶、結婚 ◀Track 4885

例句 I am going to wed my old friend's sister this weekend.
我這週末要和我老朋友的妹妹結婚。

wedding [ˋwɛdɪŋ] n. 婚禮、結婚 ◀Track 4886

例句 Did I show you my wedding ring?
我有給你看過我的結婚戒指嗎？

widow/widower [ˋwɪdo]/[ˋwɪdəwɚ] ◀Track 4887
n. 寡婦／鰥夫

例句 She became a widow at the age of thirty-seven.
她在37歲時成為寡婦。

wife [waɪf] n. 妻子 ◀Track 4888

例句 I met my wife at a baseball game.
我在一場棒球賽遇見我的妻子。

wish [wɪʃ] v./n. 希望、願望 ◀Track 4889

例句 I wish I could travel the world before I turn thirty.
我希望可以在三十歲前到世界各地旅行。

woo [wu] v. 求婚、求愛、爭取……的支持 ◀Track 4890

例句 I was surprised to learn that he was trying to woo my best friend.
我驚訝地發現他試著要追求我最好的朋友。

同義字
pursue

young [jʌŋ] adj. 年輕的、年幼的 Track 4891

例句 There are many young people fooling around in the square.
有許多年輕人在廣場玩鬧。

youth [juθ] n. 青年 Track 4892

例句 I stayed at a youth hostel when I traveled in London.
我在倫敦旅遊時住在青年旅館。

搭配詞
youth hostel 青年旅館

Test 17 關鍵英單總測驗第17回

以下測驗題皆出自書中第十七回「**和家庭社會有關的單字**」，快來檢視自己的學習成果吧！

一、選擇題

1. Please don't leave your personal _____ unattended, or, you can put them in the locker.
(A) belongings
(B) input
(C) dumped
(D) contributions

2. The _____ mother bear is protective of her cubs.
(A) accessible
(B) identical
(C) affectionate
(D) needy

3. The young rhino became an _____ after his mother was killed for her ivory.
(A) predecessor
(B) juvenile
(C) orphan
(D) oppression

4. My arm was cut by a _____.
(A) thorn (B) tomb
(C) share (D) propose

5. He has spent three years in helping the world better understand the _____ of the refugees from Myanmar.
(A) household
(B) merry
(C) gulf
(D) plight

6. Ms. Chen Shu-chu donates most of her fortune and shows extraordinary _____ to the needy.
(A) gathering
(B) exchange
(C) curiosity
(D) generosity

7. The chairman _____ the meeting with a closing speech.
(A) brought
(B) apologized
(C) concluded
(D) shared

8. He _____ his shoulders as if it had nothing to do with him.
(A) shrugged
(B) affirmed
(C) arise
(D) tolerated

9. She _____ the opportunity to be an actress and went to Hollywood.
(A) indulged (B) embraced
(C) lured (D) founded

10. The doctor emphasized the _____ of eating fresh vegetables and fruit.
(A) occasion
(B) possession
(C) necessity
(D) price

二、克漏字測驗

Jim Caviezel is an American actor. One of his most successful TV series is Person of Interest, in which he played a former CIA agent working in secret to prevent __1__ crimes before they actually happen.

Jim __2__ a high school English teacher in 1996, and they adopted three children from China who had cancer. He and his wife never think that adopting sick children is a __3__. Instead, they feel __4__ to have them. Together they live as one happy __5__.

1.
(A) violent
(B) mild
(C) grave
(D) notable

2.
(A) inherited
(B) nurture
(C) married
(D) preach

3.
(A) privilege
(B) burden
(C) reaction
(D) stock

4.
(A) solitary
(B) stubborn
(C) tolerant
(D) blessed

5.
(A) gathering
(B) inspiration
(C) heritage
(D) family

關鍵英單總測驗第17回
中譯與解答

一、選擇題

1. 請留意隨身物品，或存放於置物櫃裡。
   (A) 隨身物品
   (B) 輸入
   (C) 丟掉
   (D) 奉獻

2. 熊媽媽對她的熊寶寶充滿愛意，並很保護牠們。
   (A) 可近用的
   (B) 相同的
   (C) 充滿愛意的
   (D) 貧窮的

3. 有人為了犀牛媽媽的犀牛角而殺害她，讓小犀牛變成孤兒了。
   (A) 前輩
   (B) 青少年
   (C) 孤兒
   (D) 壓迫

4. 我的手臂被荊棘刺傷了。
   (A) 荊棘
   (B) 墳墓
   (C) 分量
   (D) 求婚

5. 他花了3年時間，幫助世人更加了解緬甸難民的困境。
   (A) 家庭的
   (B) 快樂的
   (C) 海灣
   (D) 困境

6. 陳樹菊女士幾乎把所有財產都捐出來了，對貧困的人相當慷慨大方。
   (A) 集會
   (B) 交換
   (C) 好奇的
   (D) 慷慨

7. 主席演說閉幕詞，來結束會議。
   (A) 帶來
   (B) 道歉
   (C) 結束
   (D) 分享

8. 他聳了聳肩，好像這件事與他完全無關。
   (A) 聳（肩）
   (B) 斷言
   (C) 發生
   (D) 忍受

9. 她欣然接受這個成為女演員的機會，去好萊塢發展了。
   (A) 放縱
   (B) 欣然接受
   (C) 誘惑
   (D) 建立

10. 醫師強調攝取新鮮蔬果的必要。
   (A) 場合
   (B) 擁有物
   (C) 必要
   (D) 代價

二、克漏字測驗

吉姆卡維佐是美國演員，最成功的電視作品之一是《疑犯追蹤》，他在其中扮演一位中情局前探員，任務是祕密地在暴力犯罪發生前，就防患於未然。

吉姆在1996年與一位高中英文老師結婚，他們收養了三名罹患癌症的中國小孩。他和妻子從不認為收養病童是個負擔，反而覺得很幸福，而且全家過著和樂融融的生活。

1.
(A) 暴力的
(B) 溫和的
(C) 墳墓
(D) 知名的

2.
(A) 繼承
(B) 栽培
(C) 結婚
(D) 傳教

3.
(A) 特權
(B) 負擔
(C) 反應
(D) 存貨

4.
(A) 獨自的
(B) 頑固的
(C) 忍耐的
(D) 蒙福

5.
(A) 集會
(B) 鼓舞
(C) 遺產
(D) 家庭

一、選擇題

1.(A) 2.(C) 3.(C) 4.(A) 5.(D)
6.(D) 7.(C) 8.(A) 9.(B) 10.(C)

二、克漏字測驗

1.(A) 2.(C) 3.(B)
4.(D) 5.(D)

150個 新制多益必備關鍵慣用語

150個 新制多益必備關鍵慣用語

❶ **a blessing in disguise** 因禍得福
❷ **a drop in the ocean** 滄海一粟
❸ **a hot potato** 燙手山芋
❹ **a party pooper** 掃興的人
❺ **a perfect storm** 完美風暴，糟到不能再糟的局面
❻ **a piece of cake** 簡單，不費吹灰之力
❼ **a rule of thumb** 經驗之談，經驗法則
❽ **a sight for sore eyes** 見到你真好
❾ **against the clock** 搶時間，分秒必爭地
❿ **A miss is as good as a mile.** 失之毫釐，差之千里。
⓫ **Actions speak louder than words.** 坐而言不如起而行。
⓬ **add insult to injury** 在傷口上灑鹽
⓭ **as happy as a clam** 快樂地像蛤蜊一樣，開心得不得了
⓮ **back to the drawing board** 重新開始
⓯ **be fixed in one's ways** 老古板，故步自封，不願改變
⓰ **be flying blind** 盲目行事
⓱ **be the spitting image of sb** 長得一模一樣
⓲ **be caught in the crossfire** 夾在交叉火力中間，受到兩面夾擊
⓳ **be stuck / caught between a rock and a hard place** 進退兩難
⓴ **bend over backwards** 竭盡所能
㉑ **beyond a doubt** 毫無疑問地
㉒ **bite the bullet** 忍受痛苦，咬緊牙關，硬著頭皮

㉓ **bite the hand that feeds you** 忘恩負義

㉔ **bite one's tongue** 保持沉默

㉕ **blow hot and cold** 反覆無常，不斷改變主意

㉖ **bone up on sth** 刻苦用功學習

㉗ **bread and butter** 生計、主要收入來源

㉘ **break a leg** 祝好運

㉙ **breathe down sb's neck** 緊盯某人、監視

㉚ **bump into** 巧遇

㉛ **burn the candle at both ends** 蠟燭兩頭燒

㉜ **by the book** 循規蹈矩，照章辦事

㉝ **can't make heads or tails of sth** 頭尾分不清，完全搞不懂

㉞ **carry the day** 得勝

㉟ **cash cow** 搖錢樹

㊱ **come down on sb like a ton of bricks** 嚴懲某人

㊲ **come to one's senses** 恢復理性、醒悟過來

㊳ **come out in the wash** 某事最終會得到圓滿的解決

㊴ **cost sb an arm and a leg** 非常昂貴的事物，代價太大

㊵ **cozy up on sb** 巴結、討好別人

㊶ **cram for sth** 臨時抱佛腳

㊷ **cut to the chase** 開門見山，直接切入重點

㊸ **drift along / muddle along** 得過且過

㊹ **drive sb up the wall** 快把（某人）逼瘋了

㊺ **echo chamber** 同溫層

㊻ **eat like a horse** 食量大如牛

㊼ **earn / get / score brownie points** 得到讚許

48 **Every cloud has a silver lining.**
每朵雲都鑲著一條銀邊；總有撥雲見日的一天。

49 **feel under the weather** 身體不舒服

50 **find your feet** 站穩腳步，適應新環境

51 **fits and starts** 時斷時續

52 **fix sb's wagon** 設法報復某人

53 **flat on one's back** 臥病在床

54 **flip one's lid** 失控大怒

55 **flog a dead horse** 鞭打死馬，白費力氣

56 **fly off the handle** 勃然大怒

57 **food for thought** 引人深思的事

58 **for a song** 非常便宜地

59 **from the ground up** 澈底從頭開始，重起爐灶

60 **get over sth** 克服、將……忘掉

61 **get stood up** 被放鴿子、爽約

62 **got up on the wrong side of the bed** （某人當天）諸事不順

63 **give sb a piece of one's mind** 嚴斥、教訓（某人）

64 **give sb the cold shoulder** 冷落（某人）

65 **go into orbit** 迅速增長；成功、順利

66 **go the extra mile** 加倍付出努力

67 **have a chip on one's shoulder** （因委屈或不如人而）耿耿於懷

68 **have a field day** 大顯身手

69 **have a foot in both camps** 腳踏兩隻船

70 **have ants in one's pants** 坐立不安

71 **hit below the belt** 用不正當、卑劣的手段攻擊別人

72 **hit the ceiling (= hit the roof)** 勃然大怒

73 **hit the nail on the head** 指出要害，十分中肯

74 **Hold your horses.** 別著急，且慢。

75 **icing on the cake** 錦上添花

76 **If it's not one thing, it's another.** 問題層出不斷。

77 **in the heat of the moment** 盛怒之下

78 **It takes two to tango.** 兩人才能跳探戈，雙方都有責任。

79 **judge a book by its cover** 以貌取人

80 **jump on the bandwagon** 趕流行

81 **jump the gun** （思慮欠周）過早行動

82 **keep an eye on sb** 注意，留心

83 **keep your chin up** 別灰心、振作

84 **keep a straight face** 板著臉，忍住不笑

85 **kick the bucket** 翹辮子，死翹翹

86 **kill two birds with one stone** 一箭雙鵰，一舉兩得

87 **leave no stone unturned** 竭盡全力，不遺餘力

88 **let the cat out of the bag** 說漏嘴

89 **let sleeping dogs lie** 避免衝突，過去的事就讓它隨風而逝

90 **like a bull in a china shop** 公牛進了瓷器店，即魯莽闖禍的人

91 **like riding a bicycle** 永遠不會忘記怎麼做的事

92 **like two peas in a pod** 非常相像

93 **look like a million dollars** 看來很迷人、漂亮

94 **love me, love my dog** 愛屋及烏

95 **make a fuss** 大驚小怪

96 **make no bones about sth** 直言不諱

97 **make one's jaw drop** （讓某人）跌破眼鏡

98 **on cloud nine** 樂不可支

99 **once in a blue moon** 非常罕見

100 **over the moon** 欣喜若狂

101 **over the top** 太超過，太過分
102 **paddle your own canoe** 自力更生
103 **paint oneself into a corner** 讓自己陷入困境
104 **pick up the slack** 收拾爛攤子
105 **Practice makes perfect.** 熟能生巧。
106 **pull strings** 透過重要人物，在幕後操盤、牽線
107 **put all your eggs in one basket** 孤注一擲
108 **put one's best foot forward** 全力以赴
109 **put one's finger on sth** 確切指出（不對勁之處）
110 **put the cart before the horse** 本末倒置
111 **pull one's leg** 開（某人）玩笑
112 **put sb on the spot** 讓（某人）難堪
113 **rack one's brains** 絞盡腦汁
114 **ring a bell** 對某事有印象，聽起來很熟悉
115 **rock bottom** 最低點
116 **rule of thumb** 經驗法則
117 **sit on the fence** 維持中立，觀望而不表態
118 **shape up or ship out** 好好做，不然就走人
119 **string someone along** 長期哄騙某人，以達到自己的私利
120 **under the table** 暗地裡、私下
121 **under the weather** 身體不舒服
122 **until / till the cows come home** 等到牛回家，很久、長時間地
123 **see eye to eye with sb** 與某人觀點一致
124 **shoot the breeze** 閒聊
125 **slip of the tongue** 講錯話
126 **smell a rat** 感覺不對勁
127 **speak of the devil** 說曹操，曹操就到

⑫⑧ **speak the same language** 有類似的想法

⑫⑨ **spill the beans** 洩露秘密

⑬⓪ **take a rain check** 改天吧

⑬① **take it from me** 聽我的，我説的不會錯

⑬② **talk a mile a minute** 説話連珠似炮

⑬③ **talk sb into sth** 説服（某人）做某事

⑬④ **talk sb out of sth** 勸退（某人）做某事

⑬⑤ **the apple of sb's eye** （某人的）心肝寶貝

⑬⑥ **the ball's in sb's court** 輪到（某人）決定了

⑬⑦ **the coast is clear** 危險已過

⑬⑧ **throw sb a bone** 給某人的東西，但不符他的期望

⑬⑨ **to see red** 大怒

⑭⓪ **trump card** 王牌、絕招

⑭① **tongue in cheek** 説著玩地

⑭② **talk the talk ... walk the walk** 説一套，做一套

⑭③ **water under the bridge** 事過境遷

⑭④ **when pigs fly** 絕不可能發生的事

⑭⑤ **Well begun is half done.** 好的開始是成功的一半。

⑭⑥ **We'll cross that bridge when we come to it.** 船到橋頭自然直。

⑭⑦ **When it rains, it pours.** 屋漏偏逢連夜雨。

⑭⑧ **You are what you eat.** 人如其食。

⑭⑨ **You asked for it.** 你活該。

⑮⓪ **You can say that again.** 你説的沒錯。

英語學習 系列019

全方面破解英文多益單字：高分單字╳關鍵搭配詞╳萬用例句的必勝三「步」曲

有效累積單字儲備量，輕鬆掌握新制多益高分祕訣

作　　者　張慈庭英語教學團隊◎著
顧　　問　曾文旭
社　　長　王毓芳
編輯統籌　耿文國、黃璽宇
主　　編　吳靜宜
英文編輯　姸君
執行主編　潘妍潔
執行編輯　吳芸蓁、吳欣容
美術編輯　王桂芳、張嘉容
法律顧問　北辰著作權事務所　蕭雄淋律師、幸秋妙律師

初　　版　2022年05月
出　　版　捷徑文化出版事業有限公司──資料夾文化出版
電　　話　（02）2752-5618
傳　　真　（02）2752-5619

定　　價　新台幣500元／港幣167元
產品內容　1書

總 經 銷　知遠文化事業有限公司
地　　址　222新北市深坑區北深路3段155巷25號5樓
電　　話　（02）2664-8800
傳　　真　（02）2664-8801

港澳地區總經銷　和平圖書有限公司
地　　址　香港柴灣嘉業街12號百樂門大廈17樓
電　　話　（852）2804-6687
傳　　真　（852）2804-6409

▲本書圖片由 Shutterstock、123RF提供。

國家圖書館出版品預行編目資料

全方面破解英文多益單字：高分單字╳關鍵搭配詞╳萬用例句的必勝三「步」曲／張慈庭英語教學團隊著. -- 初版. -- 臺北市：資料夾文化, 2022.05
面；　公分（英語學習：019）
ISBN 978-626-7116-01-2(平裝)
1. CST: 多益測驗　2. CST: 詞彙
805.1895　　111002196